The Princes
of Ireland

ALSO BY EDWARD RUTHERFURD

Sarum

Russka

London

The Forest

DOUBLEDAY

New York   London   Toronto

Sydney   Auckland

The Princes of Ireland

❈ THE DUBLIN SAGA ❧

EDWARD
RUTHERFURD

PUBLISHED BY DOUBLEDAY
a division of Random House, Inc.

DOUBLEDAY and the portrayal of an anchor with a dolphin are
registered trademarks of Random House, Inc.

Book design by Caroline Cunningham

Library of Congress Cataloging-in-Publication Data
Rutherfurd, Edward.
The princes of Ireland : the Dublin saga / Edward Rutherfurd.— 1st ed.
p. cm.
1. Ireland—History—To 1172—Fiction. 2. Mythology, Celtic—
Fiction. 3. Dublin (Ireland)—Fiction. 4. Princes—Fiction. I. Title.

PR6068.U88P75 2004
823'.914—dc22
2003070005
ISBN 0-7394-6814-6

PRINTED IN THE UNITED STATES OF AMERICA

[March 2004]

First Edition

1   3   5   7   9   10   8   6   4   2

For Susan,
Edward and Elizabeth

CONTENTS

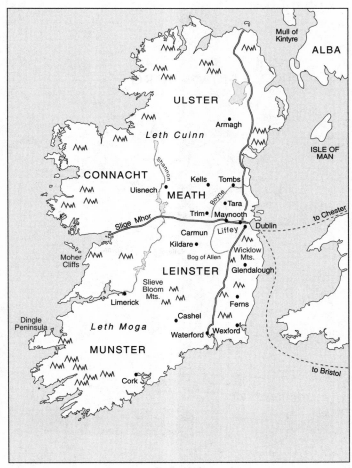

IRELAND

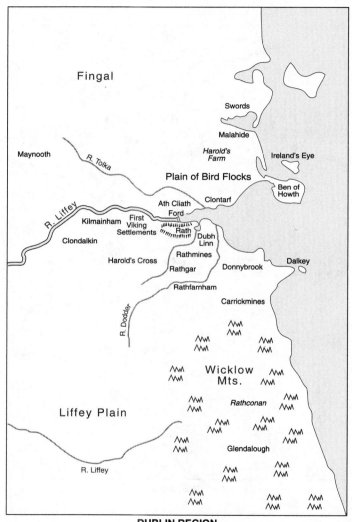

DUBLIN REGION

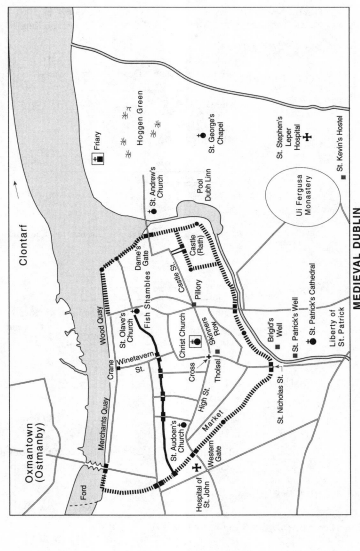

Clontarf

Oxmantown
(Ostmanby)

Ford

Merchants Quay

Crane

Winetavern
St.

Wood Quay

St. Olave's
Church

Fish Shambles

Christ Church

Cross

Tholsel

High St.

St. Audoen's
Church

Market

Western
Gate

Hospital of
St. John

Dame's
Gate

St. Andrew's
Church

Friary

Hoggen Green

St. George's
Chapel

St. Stephen's
Leper
Hospital

St. Kevin's Hostel

Pool
Dubh Linn

Castle
(Rath)

Castle St.

Pillory

Skinner's
Row

Uí Fergusa
Monastery

Brigid's
Well

St. Patrick's Well

St. Patrick's Cathedral

Liberty of
St. Patrick

St. Nicholas St.

MEDIEVAL DUBLIN

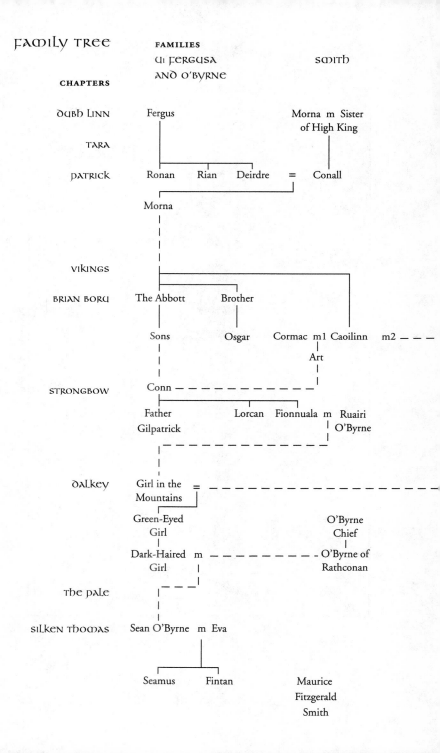

FAMILY TREE

Uí FERGUSA
AND O'BYRNE

SMITH

CHAPTERS

ÒUBh LINN

Fergus   Morna m Sister
                                of High King

TARA

PATRICK   Ronan   Rian   Deirdre   =   Conall

Morna

VIKINGS

BRIAN BORU   The Abbott   Brother

               Sons   Osgar   Cormac m1 Caoilinn   m2 — — —
                                                 Art

STRONGBOW   Conn — — — — — — — — —

               Father   Lorcan   Fionnuala m Ruairi
               Gilpatrick   O'Byrne

ÒALKEY   Girl in the = — — — — — — — — — — — — —
               Mountains

               Green-Eyed   O'Byrne
               Girl   Chief

               Dark-Haired m — — — — — — — — O'Byrne of
               Girl | Rathconan

ThE PALE

SILKEN ThOMAS Sean O'Byrne m Eva

               Seamus   Fintan   Maurice
                                       Fitzgerald
                                       Smith

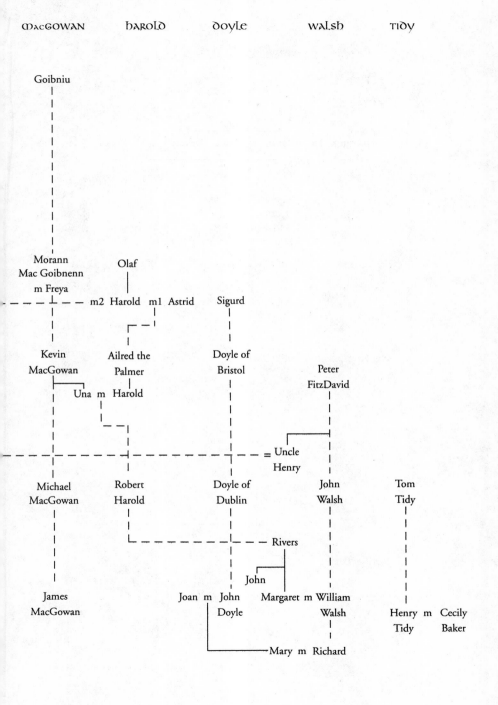

PREFACE

T HIS BOOK IS, first and foremost, a novel. All the characters whose family fortunes the novel follows down the generations are fictitious; but in telling their stories, I have set them amongst people and events that either did exist, or might have done. The historical context, wherever it is known, is given accurately, and where questions of interpretation arise, I have sought either to reflect, or give a balanced view of the opinions of today's best scholars. From time to time it has been necessary to make small adjustments to complex events in order to aid the narrative; but these adjustments are few and none does any violence to history.

In recent decades, Ireland in general and Dublin in particular, have been very fortunate in the quality of the historical attention they have received. During the extensive research required to write this book, I have been privileged to work with some of Ireland's most distinguished scholars, who have generously shared their knowledge with me and corrected my texts. Their kind contributions are mentioned in the Acknowledgements. Thanks to the scholarly work of the last quarter century, there has been a reevaluation of certain aspects of Ireland's history; and as a result, the story that follows may contain a number of surprises for many readers. I have provided a few additional notes in the Afterword at the end of this volume for those curious to know more.

Irish personal names, place names, and technical terms appear throughout in their most simple and familiar forms. Modern books published in Ireland use an accent mark, the fada, to indicate when a vowel is long and certain other forms of spelling to indicate correct pronunciation. To many readers outside Ireland, however, these forms might be confusing, and so they have not been used in the text of this novel. But I have provided a pronunciation guide with the Afterword, and readers uncertain about any word should find it there.

The Princes
of Ireland

EMERALD SUN

LONG AGO. Long before Saint Patrick came. Before the coming of the Celtic tribes. Before the Gaelic language was spoken. At the time of Irish gods who have not even left their names.

So little can be said with certainty; yet facts can be established. In and upon the earth, evidence of their presence remains. And, as people have done since tales were told, we may imagine.

In those ancient times, on a certain winter's morning, a small event occurred. This we know. It must have happened many times: year after year, we may suppose; century after century.

✥

Dawn. The midwinter sky was already a clear, pale azure. Very soon, the sun would arise from the sea. Already, seen from the island's eastern coast, there was a golden shimmering along the horizon.

It was the winter solstice, the shortest day of the year. If, in that ancient time on the island, the year was designated by a date, the system of designation is not known.

The island was actually one of a pair that lay just off the Atlantic edge of the European mainland. Once, thousands of years before, when both were locked in the great white stasis of the last Ice Age, they had been joined to each other by a stone causeway that ran from the north-eastern corner of the smaller, western island across to the upper part of its neighbour which, in turn, was joined in the south by a chalky land bridge to the continental mainland. At the ending of the Ice Age, however, when the waters from the melting Arctic came flooding down the world, they covered over the stone causeway, then smashed through the chalk bridge, thus creating two islands in the sea.

The separations were quite narrow. The drowned causeway from the western island that would one day be called Ireland to the promontory of Britain known as the Mull of Kintyre was only a dozen miles across; the gap between the white cliffs of south-east England and the European continent was just over twenty.

It might have been expected, therefore, that the two islands would be very similar. And in a way they were. But there were subtle differences. For when the floodwaters cut them off, they were, as yet, only slowly warming up from their Arctic condition. Plants and animals were still returning to them from the warmer south. And when the stony causeway was flooded, it seems that some species that had reached the southern part of the larger, eastern island had not yet had time to cross to the western. So while the oak, hazel, and ash were abundant on both islands, the mistletoe that grows upon British oaks had not found its way onto Irish trees. And for the same reason—singular blessing—while the British have been plagued with snakes, including the venomous adder, there were never any snakes in Ireland.

The western island upon which the sun was about to rise was mostly covered with thick forest, interspersed with areas of bog. Here and there, handsome mountain ranges arose. The land had many rivers rich in salmon and other fish; and the greatest of these flowed out into the Atlantic in the west after meandering through a complex series of lakes and waterways through the island's central interior. But to those who first came there, two other features of the natural landscape would in particular have been remarked upon.

The first was mineral. Here and there, in clearings in the dense forest or upon the open mountainsides, outcrops of rock appeared, forced up from the bowels of the earth, which contained a magical glint of quartz. And in some of these glittering rocks there were deeper veins of gold. As a result, in the several parts of the island where these outcrops were to be found, the streams literally ran with the dust and nodules of gleaming gold.

The second was universal. Whether it was the dampness of the wind sweeping in from the Atlantic, or the gentle warmth of the Gulf Stream, or the way the light fell at that latitude, or some confluence of these and other factors, there was in the island's vegetation an extraordinary emerald green found nowhere else. And perhaps it was this ancient combination of emerald green and flowing gold that gave the western island its reputation as a place where magical spirits dwelt.

And what men dwelt upon the emerald island? Before the Celtic tribes of later times, the names of the people who had arrived there belong only to legend: the descendants of Cessair, Partholon, Nemed; the Fir Bolg and the Tuatha De Danaan. But whether these were actual men or the names of their ancient gods, or both, it is hard to say. There were hunters in Ireland, after the Ice Age. Then farmers. That much is certain. No doubt people came there from various places. And, as in other parts of Europe, the people of the island knew how to build with stone and make weapons of bronze and fashion handsome pottery. They traded, too, with merchants who came from even such faraway places as Greece.

Above all, they made ornaments from the island's plenteous gold. Ornaments for the neck, bracelets of golden twist, earrings, sun discs of hammered gold—the Irish goldsmiths surpassed most others in Europe. Craftsmen-magicians they might be called.

❖

At any moment the sun would appear over the horizon, blazing its great, golden path across the sea.

At a point approximately halfway up the island's eastern coast there lay a broad and pleasant bay between two headlands. From the southern headland, the view down the coast was of a range of hills, including two little volcanic mountains rising by the sea so elegantly that a visitor might have supposed himself transported to the warmer climes of southern Italy. Above the other headland, a broad plain stretched northwards towards the more distant mountains that lay below the vanished causeway to the second island. In the middle of the bay spread the wide marshes and sands of a river estuary.

Now the sun was breaking over the horizon, sending a burning, golden flash across the sea. And as the sun's rays hurtled over the bay's northern headland and across the plain beyond, it encountered an answering flash, as though, upon the ground, there lay a great, cosmic reflector. The flash was indeed of singular interest. For it emanated from a large and remarkable object that was made by the hand of Man.

About twenty-five miles to the north of the bay, and flowing west to east, there lay another fine river. It ran through a valley whose lush green land contained some of the richest soil on Earth. And it was on the gently sloping ridge on the northern bank of this river that the people of the island had built several large and impressive structures, the chief of which had just sent the dazzling flash into the sky.

They were huge, circular, grassy mounds. But they were by no means clumsy earthworks. Their sheer, cylindrical sides and broad, convex roofs suggested a most careful internal construction. Their bases were set with monumental stones whose surfaces were incised with designs—circles, zigzags, and strange, hallucinatory spirals. But most striking of all was that the whole surface towards the rising sun was faced with white quartz; and it was this huge, curving, crystalline wall which now, catching the sunrise, sparkled, gleamed, and flashed a reflected solar fire back into the sky on that clear midwinter dawning.

Who built these monuments above the quiet, swan-glided waters of the river? We cannot be sure. And for what had they constructed them? As resting places for their princes: that is known. But what princes lay within and whether their spirits were benign or threatening can only be guessed. There they lay, however, ancient ancestors of the island's people, spirits in waiting.

As well as tombs, however, these great mounds were also sanctuaries which, at certain times, were to receive the divine and mysterious forces of the universe which brought cosmic life to the land. And it was for this reason, during the night which had just ended, that the door to the sanctuary had been opened.

For in the centre of the flashing quartz façade there was a narrow entrance, flanked by monumental stones, behind which a thin, somewhat uneven but straight passageway, lined with standing stones, led into the heart of the great mound, ending in a trefoil inner chamber. Within the passage and chamber, as outside, many of the stones were inscribed with patterns, including the strange set of three swirling spirals. And the narrow passage was oriented so that precisely on the dawn of the winter solstice, the face of the rising sun as it broke over the horizon would penetrate directly through the top of the doorway and send its warm rays along the dark passage into the centre.

Up in the sky now, the sunbeams flashed—over the bay, over the island's coastline, across the winter forests and little clearings which, as the sunbeams passed, were suddenly bathed in the gleam of the sun's face as it emerged from the watery horizon. Over the river valley the sunbeams flew, towards the mound whose flashing quartz, picking up a reflected light from the green landscape all around, seemed itself to be on fire, shining like an emerald sun.

Was there something cold and fearful in that greenish glare, as the sun's rays burst through the portals into the dark passage of the mound? Perhaps.

But now a wonderful thing occurred. For such was the cunning construction of the passage that, as the sun gradually rose, the sun's beams, as though abandoning their wonted speed entirely, slowly and softly stole along the passage, no faster than a creeping child, foot by foot, bringing a gentle glow to the stones as they went, until they reached the triple chamber of the heart. And there, gathering speed once more, they flashed off the stones, dancing this way and that, bringing light and warmth and life to the midwinter tomb.

ONE

Ðubh Linn

≈ AD 430 ≈

I

LUGHNASA. High summer. It would be harvest season soon.
Deirdre stood by the rail and surveyed the scene. It should
have been a cheerful day, but it brought only anguish to her. For the
father she loved and the one-eyed man were going to sell her. And
there was nothing she could do.

She did not see Conall at first.

The custom at the races was that the men rode naked. The tradition
was ancient. Centuries ago, the Romans had remarked on how the
Celtic warriors despised the protection of breastplates and liked to
strip naked for battle. A tattooed warrior, his muscles bulging, his
hair raised in great spikes, and his face distorted in war frenzy was a
frightening sight, even to trained Roman legionaries. Sometimes
these fierce Celtic warriors in their chariots would choose to wear a
short cloak that streamed behind them; and in some parts of the
Roman Empire, the Celtic horsemen would wear breeches. But here

on the western island, the tradition of nakedness had been carried into the ceremonial races, and young Conall was wearing nothing but a small protective loincloth.

The great festival of Lughnasa was held at Carmun once every three years. The site of Carmun was eerie. In a land of wild forest and bog, it was an open grassy space that stretched, green and empty, halfway to the horizon. Lying some distance west of the point where, if you were following it upstream, the Liffey's course began to retreat eastwards on the way to its source in the Wicklow Mountains, the place was absolutely flat, except for some mounds in which ancestral chiefs were buried. The festival lasted a week. There were areas reserved for food and livestock markets, and another where fine clothes were sold; but the most important quarter was where a large racetrack was laid out on the bare turf.

The track was a magnificent sight. People were encamped all around, in tents or temporary huts, whole clans together. Men and women both were dressed in their brilliant cloaks of scarlet, blue, or green. The men wore the splendid gold torcs—like thick amulets—round their necks; the women sported all kinds of ornament and bracelet. Some men were tattooed, some had long flowing hair and moustaches, others had their hair caked with clay and raised into terrifying warlike spikes. Here and there stood a splendid war chariot. The horses were in pens. There were campfires where the bards would tell tales. A group of jugglers and acrobats was just arriving. Throughout the camp, the sound of a harp, a bone whistle, or a bagpipe could be heard in the summer air, and the scent of roasting meat and honey cakes seemed to mingle in the light smoke that drifted across the scene. And on a ceremonial mound by the racetrack, presiding over the whole proceedings, was the King of Leinster.

There were four parts of the island. To the north lay the territories of the ancient tribes of Ulaid, the province of warriors. To the west lay a lovely province of magical lakes and wild coasts—the land of the druids, they called it. To the south, the province of Muma, renowned for its music. It was there, according to legend, that the Sons of Mil had first met the goddess Eriu. And fourthly, in the east lay the rich pastures and fields of the tribes of Lagin. The provinces had been recognised since time out of mind, and as Ulster, Connacht, Munster, and Leinster they would remain the geographical divisions of the island for all times to come.

But life was never static on the island. In recent generations there had been important changes among the ancient tribes. In the northern half of the island—Leth Cuinn, the half of the head, as they liked to call it—powerful clans had arisen to assert their dominance over the southern half, Leth Moga. And a new central province known as Mide, or Meath, had also come into being, so that now people spoke of the island's five parts rather than four.

Over all the great clan chiefs in each of the five parts, the most powerful usually ruled as a king, and sometimes the greatest of these would proclaim himself High King and demand that others recognise him and pay him tribute.

✤

Finbarr looked at his friend and shook his head. It was midafternoon and Conall was about to race.

"You could at least smile," Finbarr remarked. "You're such a sad fellow, Conall."

"I'm sorry," the other replied. "I don't mean to be."

That was the trouble with being too highly born, Finbarr considered. The gods paid too much attention to you. It was ever thus in the Celtic world. Ravens would fly over the house to announce the death of a clan chief, swans would desert the lake. A king's bad judgement could affect the weather. And if you were a prince, the druids made prophesies about you from before the day you were born; and after that, there was no escape.

Conall: slim, dark, aquiline, handsome—a perfect prince. And a prince he was. Conall, son of Morna. His father had been a matchless warrior. Hadn't he been buried standing up, in a hero's mound, facing towards the enemies of his tribe? It was the finest compliment you could pay to a dead man in the Celtic world.

In the family of Conall's father, it was unlucky for any man to wear red. But that was only the beginning of Conall's troubles. He had been born three months after his father's death. That alone made him special. His mother was the sister of the High King, who became his foster father. That meant the whole island would be watching him. And then the druids had had their say. The first had shown the baby a selection of twigs from various trees and the infant had stretched out a tiny hand towards the hazel. "He will be a poet, a man of learning," the druid declared. A second had made a darker prediction. "He will cause the death of a fine warrior." But so long as this was in battle, the family took it as a good omen. It was the third druid, however, who pronounced the three geissi which were to follow Conall all his life.

The geissi—the prohibitions. When a prince or a great warrior lived under geissi he had better be careful. The geissi were terrible, because they always came to pass. But since, like so many priestly pronouncements, they sounded like a riddle, you couldn't always be certain what they meant. They were like traps. Finbarr was glad no one had bothered to lay any geissi on him. The geissi on Conall, as everyone at the High King's court knew, were as follows:

Conall shall not die until:
   First: He has laid his own clothes in the earth.
   Second: He has crossed the sea at sunrise.
   Third: He has come to Tara through a black mist.

The first made no sense; the second he must take care never to do. The third seemed impossible. There were often mists at the High King's royal seat at Tara, but there had never been a black one.

Conall was a careful fellow. He respected family tradition. Finbarr had never seen him wear anything red. Indeed Conall even avoided touching anything of that colour. "So it seems to me,"

Finbarr had once told him, "that if you can just stay away from the sea, you'll live forever."

They had been friends since the day, in childhood, when a hunting party that included young Conall had stopped at Finbarr's family's modest farm to rest. The two boys had met and played, and before long had a wrestling match and then played the game with stick and ball which the islanders call hurling, while the men looked on. A little while later Conall had asked if he might seek out his new acquaintance again; within a month they were fast friends. And when, soon afterwards, Conall had asked if Finbarr might join the royal household and train to become a warrior, this had been granted. Finbarr's family had been overjoyed at such an opportunity for him. The friendship of the two boys had never wavered. If Conall loved Finbarr's good nature and high spirits, Finbarr admired the young aristocrat's quiet, deeper thoughtfulness.

Not that Conall was always reserved. Though not the brawniest of the young champions, he was probably the finest athlete. He could run like a deer. Only Finbarr could keep up with him when they raced their light, two-wheeled war chariots. When Conall threw a spear, it seemed to fly like a bird, and with deadly accuracy. He could whirl his shield round so fast that you could scarcely see it. And when he struck with his favourite shining sword, it was said that others may give harder blows, but take care—Conall's blade is always swifter. The two boys were also musical. Finbarr liked to sing, Conall to play the harp, which he did well; and as boys they would sometimes entertain the company at the High King's feasts. These were happy times when, good-humouredly, the High King would pay them as though they were hired musicians. The warriors all liked and respected Conall. Those who remembered Morna agreed: the son had the makings of a similar leader.

And yet—this was the strange thing to Finbarr—it was as if Conall wasn't really interested.

Conall had been only six the first time he disappeared; and his mother had already been searching all afternoon when, just before sundown, he appeared with an old druid who quietly told her, "The boy's been with me."

"I found him in the woods," Conall had explained, as if his absence was the most natural thing in the world.

"What did you do with the druid all day?" his mother asked after the old man had left.

"Oh, we talked."

"What about?" his astonished mother asked.

"Everything," he said happily.

It had been the same ever since his childhood. He would play games with the other boys, but then he'd disappear. Sometimes he'd take Finbarr with him, and they would wander in the woods or along the streams. Finbarr could imitate bird calls. Conall liked that. And there was hardly a plant on the island that the young prince couldn't name. But even on these walks sometimes Finbarr would sense that, much as his friend loved him, he wished to be alone; and then he would leave him, and Conall would wander away for half a day.

He always insisted to Finbarr that he was happy. Yet when he was deep in thought, his face would take on a look of melancholy; or sometimes when he was playing the harp, the tune would become strangely sad. "Here comes the man whom sorrow makes his friend," Finbarr would say affectionately when Conall returned from his lonely wanderings; but the young prince would only laugh, or punch him playfully and break into a run.

It was hardly surprising that by the time he reached the age of manhood at seventeen, the other young men should refer to Conall, not without awe, as the Druid.

There were three classes of learned men on the island. The humblest were the bards, the storytellers who would entertain the company at a feast; of a higher class entirely were the filidh, guardians of the genealogies, makers of poetry, and even sometimes of prophesy; but above them both, and more fearsome, were the druids.

It was said that long ago, before the Romans had come there, the most learned and skilful druids had lived on the neighbouring island of Britain. In those days, the druids used to sacrifice not only animals but men and women, too. That was long ago, however. The druids were in the western island now, and nobody could remember the last human sacrifice.

The training of a druid could take twenty years. He would often know most of what the bards and filidh knew; but beyond that, he was a priest, with the secret knowledge of the sacred spells and numbers and of how to speak with the gods. The druids performed the sacrifices and ceremonies at midwinter and the other great festivals of the year. The druids directed upon which days to sow the crops and slaughter the animals. Few kings would dare start any enterprise without consulting the druids. Quarrel with them and their words could be so sharp, it was said, that they raised blisters. A druid's curse could last for seventeen generations. Wise advisers, respected judges, learned teachers, feared enemies: the druids were all these things.

But beyond this lay something more mysterious. Some druids, like shamans, could go into trances and enter the otherworld. They could even change their own shape into that of a bird or an animal. Was there something of this mystical quality, Finbarr sometimes wondered, in his friend Conall?

Certainly he had always spent a lot of time with the druids, ever since that childhood encounter. By the time he was twenty, it was said, he knew more than most of the young men training for the priesthood. Such an interest was not thought strange. Many of the druids came from noble families; some of the greatest warriors had studied with druids or filidh in the past. But Conall's degree of interest was unusual, as was his expertise. His memory was phenomenal.

Whatever Conall said, it seemed to Finbarr he was sometimes lonely.

To seal their friendship, some years earlier, the prince had given him a puppy. Finbarr had taken the little fellow everywhere. He called him Cuchulainn, after the hero of legend. Only gradually, as the puppy grew, had Finbarr come to realise the nature of the gift. For Cuchulainn turned out to be a magnificent hunting hound, of the kind for which merchants came to the western island from far across the sea, and for which they would pay with ingots of silver or Roman coins. The hound was probably priceless. It never left his side.

"If ever something happens to me," Conall once told him, "your hound Cuchulainn will be there to remind you of me and of our friendship."

"You'll be my friend as long as I live," Finbarr assured him. "I expect it's I who will die first." And if he couldn't give the prince a present of similar value in return, he could at least, he thought, make sure that his own friendship was as constant and loyal as the hound Cuchulainn was to him.

Conall also had another talent. He could read.

The people of the island were not strangers to the written word. The merchants from Britain and Gaul who came to the ports could often read. The Roman coins they used had Latin letters on them. Finbarr knew several amongst the bards and druids who could read. A few generations ago, the learned men of the island, using vowel and consonant sounds from Latin, had even invented a simple writing of their own for carving memorials in Celtic upon standing posts or stones. But though from time to time one would come upon a standing stone with these strange ogham scratch marks, like notches on a tally stick, down its edge, this early Celtic writing system had never become widely used. Nor, Finbarr knew, was it used for recording the island's sacred heritage.

"It is not hard to tell why," Conall had explained to him. "Firstly, the knowledge of the druids is secret. You wouldn't want some unworthy person reading it. That would anger the gods."

"And the priests would lose their secret power as well," Finbarr remarked.

"That is perhaps true. But there is a further reason. The great possession of our learned men, bards, filidh, and druids is their feat of memory. This makes the mind very strong. If we wrote down all our knowledge so that we didn't have to remember it, our minds would grow weak."

"So why have you learned to read?" Finbarr had asked.

"I am curious," Conall had said, as if this were natural. "Besides," he had smiled, "I am not a druid."

How often had those words echoed in Finbarr's mind. Of course his friend was not a druid. He was going to be a warrior. And yet . . . Sometimes when Conall sang and closed his eyes, or when he returned from one of his solitary wanderings with a far-away, melancholy look, as though he were in a dream, Finbarr couldn't help wondering if his friend had not entered . . . He did not know what. A borderland of some kind.

And so he had not really been surprised when, towards the end of spring, Conall had confessed: "I want to take the druid's tonsure."

The druids shaved straight up from their ears over the top of the head. The effect of this tonsure was to give a high, rounded forehead; unless of course the druid was already going bald at the front, in which case the tonsure hardly showed. In Conall's case, since his hair was thick, the tonsure would leave a dark, V-shaped shaved area over his brow.

There had certainly been princely druids before. Indeed, many people on the island considered the druid caste to be higher than even kings. Finbarr had looked at his friend thoughtfully.

"What will the High King say?" he had asked.

"It is hard to say. It is a pity that my mother was his sister."

Finbarr knew all about Conall's mother: her devotion to his father's memory, her determination that her son should follow in his father's footsteps as a warrior. When she had died two years ago, she had begged the High King—her brother—to make sure that her husband's line should be continued.

"Druids marry," Finbarr pointed out. Indeed, the druid's position was often transferred from father to son. "You could have children who would be warriors."

"That is true," said Conall. "But the High King may think otherwise."

"Could he forbid you, if the druids want you to join them?"

"I think," Conall replied, "that if the druids know the High King does not wish it, they will not ask."

"What will you do?"

"Wait. Perhaps I can persuade them."

It had been a month later that the High King had summoned Finbarr.

"Finbarr," he had begun, "I know you are my nephew Conall's closest friend. You know of his wish to become a druid?" Finbarr had nodded. "It would be a good thing if he changed his mind," the High King said. That was all. But from the High King, it was enough.

⁘

She hadn't wanted to come. There were two reasons. The first, Deirdre knew, was selfish. She didn't like leaving home.

It was a strange place to live, but she loved it. In the middle of the island's eastern coast, a river, having descended from the wild Wicklow Mountains just to the south and made a sweeping inland curve, came out through an estuary into a broad bay with two headlands—as if, Deirdre thought, the Earth goddess Eriu, the island's mother, was stretching her arms to embrace the sea. Inland, the river formed a broad flood basin known as the Liffey Plain. It was a river of changing moods, subject to sudden rages. When it was angry, its swollen waters would hurtle down from the mountains in violent flash floods which carried all before them. But these fits of rage were only occasional. Most of the time, its waters were tranquil and its voice was soft, whispering, and melodic. With its wide tidal waters, wooded marshes, and low mudflats fringed with grasses, the estuary was usually a place of silence, but for the cries of the distant gulls and the piping curlews and the heron gliding over the shell-strewn shoreline strands.

It was almost deserted, except for the few scattered farmsteads under her father's rule. Two small features there were, however, each of which had already given the place a name. One, just before the river opened out into its mile-wide marshy estuary, was man-made: a wooden trackway across the marshland, which crossed the river at its shallowest point on hurdles and continued until it reached firmer ground on the northern bank. Ath Cliath this was called in the island's Celtic tongue—the Ford of Hurdles—which was pronounced roughly as "Aw Cleeya."

The second feature was natural. For the spot where Deirdre was standing lay at the eastern end of a low ridge that ran along the southern bank overlooking the ford. Below her, a stream came from the south to join the river, and just before it did so, encountering the end of the little ridge, it made a small bend, in whose angle there had developed a deep, dark pool. Blackpool, they called it: Dubh Linn. To the ear it sounded "Doov Lin."

But though it had two names, hardly anybody lived there. Up on the slopes of the Wicklow Mountains there had been settlements since time out of mind. There were fishing villages and even small harbours along the coast both north and south of the river's mouth. Down by the river marshes, however, though Deirdre loved their quiet beauty, there was not much reason to settle.

For Dubh Linn was a borderland, a no-man's-land. The territories of powerful chiefs lay to the north, south, and west of the estuary, but even if one or the other claimed a sovereignty from time to time, they had little interest in the area; and so her father, Fergus, had remained undisturbed as the chieftain of the place.

Deserted as it might be, Fergus's territory was not without significance, for it lay at one of the island's important crossroads. Ancient tracks, often hewn through the island's thick forests and known as slige, came from north and south to cross at the ford. The old Slige Mhor, the Great Road, ran west. As well as being the guardian of the crossing, Fergus also offered the island's customary hospitality to travellers at his house.

Once, the place had been busier. For centuries, the open sea beyond the bay had been more like a great lake between the two islands where the many tribes of her people dwelt, and across which they had traded, and settled, and married back and forth for many generations. When the mighty Roman Empire had taken over the eastern island—Britain, they had called it—Roman merchants had come to the western island and set up little trading posts along the coast, including the bay, and would sometimes come into the estuary. Once, she knew, Roman troops had even landed and set up a walled camp from which the disciplined Roman legionaries with their bright armour had threatened to take over the western isle as well. But they had not succeeded. They had gone away, and the magical western island had been left in peace. She was proud of that. Proud of the land and people of Eriu who had kept to the ancient ways and never submitted.

And now the mighty Roman Empire was in retreat. Barbarian tribes had breached her borders; the imperial city of Rome itself had been sacked; the legions had left Britain; and the Roman trading posts were deserted.

Some of the more adventurous chieftains on the western island had done well out of these changing times. There had been huge raids on the now defenceless Britain. Gold, silver, slaves—all kinds of goods had come across to enrich the bright halls of Eriu. But these expeditions went out from harbours farther up the coast. Though merchants still ventured from time to time into the Liffey estuary, the place was hardly busy.

The house of Fergus, son of Fergus, consisted of a collection of huts and stores—some thatched, some roofed with turf—in a circular enclosure on the rise above the pool, surrounded by an earth wall and fence. This ring fort, to give the little earthwork its technical name, was one of a number starting to appear on the island. In the local Celtic tongue it was called a rath. In essentials, the rath of Fergus was a larger version of the simple farmstead—a dwelling house and four animal sheds—to be found all over the more fertile parts of the island. There was a small piggery, a cattle pen, a grain store, a handsome hall, and a smaller secondary dwelling house. Most of these were circular, with strong wattle walls. Into these various accommodations could easily be fitted Fergus, his family, the cattleman and his family, the shepherd, two other families, three British slaves, the bard—for the chief, mindful of his status, kept his own bard, whose father and grandfather had held the position before him—and, of course, the livestock. In practice, these numerous souls were seldom all there at the same time. But they could still be accommodated for the simple reason that people were accustomed to sleeping communally. Set on the modest rise overlooking the ford, this was the rath of Fergus, son of Fergus. Below it, a small water mill by the stream and a landing place by the river completed the settlement.

The second reason why Deirdre hadn't wanted to come concerned her father. She was afraid he was going to be killed.

Fergus, son of Fergus. The ancient society of the western island was a strict hierarchy, with many classes. Each class, from king or druid to slave, had its derbfine, its blood price to be paid in case of death or injury. Every man knew his status and that of his ancestors. And Fergus was a chief.

He was respected by the people of the scattered farmsteads that he called his tribe as a chief of kindly but sometimes uncertain temper. At a first meeting the tall chieftain might seem silent and aloof—but not for long. If he caught sight of one of the farmers who owed him obedience, or one of his cattlemen, it could mean a long and expansive conversation. Above all, he loved to meet new people, for the guardian of the isolated Ford of Hurdles was deeply curious. A traveller at Ath Cliath would always be splendidly fed and entertained, but he could abandon any hope of going about his business until Fergus was satisfied that he had yielded every scrap of information, personal and general, that he possessed and then listened to the chief talk, and talk some more, and yet some more again.

If a visitor were especially favoured, Fergus would offer wine and then, going over to a table on which his prize possessions were kept, return with a pale object cupped reverently in his hands. It was a human skull. It had been carefully worked, however. The crown of the skull had been cut neatly off and the circular hole had been rimmed with gold. It was quite light. The pale bone felt smooth, delicate, almost like an egg. The empty eye sockets stared blankly, as if to remind you that, as all humans must, the tenant of the skull had departed to another place. The mad grin of the mouth seemed to say that something in the condition of death was meaningless— for everyone knew that around the family hearth you were always in the company of the dead.

"This was the head of Erc the Warrior," Fergus would tell the visitor proudly. "Killed by my own grandfather."

Deirdre always remembered the day—she had been only a little girl—when the warriors had come by. There had been a fight between two clans to the south and these men had been travelling north afterwards. There were three of them; they had all seemed huge to her; two had long moustaches, the third had his hair shaved except for a high, spiky ridge down the middle. These terrifying figures, she was told, were warriors. They were greeted warmly by her father and taken inside. And from a leather rope slung over the back of one of the horses, she had seen the grisly sight of three human heads, the blood on their necks congealed to blackness, their eyes staring, wide yet sightless. She had gazed at them with horrified fascination. When she had run inside, she had seen her father toasting the warriors with the drinking skull.

And soon she was to learn that the strange old skull should be venerated. Like her grandfather's shield and sword, it was a symbol of the family's proud antiquity. Her ancestors were warriors, fit companions for princes and heroes, and even for the gods. Did the gods in their bright halls drink out of similar skulls? She supposed they did. How else would a god drink if not like a hero? The family might rule only a small territory, but she could still think of the sword, and the shield, and the gold-rimmed skull, and hold her head high.

During her childhood, Deirdre could remember occasional flashes of anger from her father. These were usually brought on by someone trying to cheat him or failing to show him proper respect; though sometimes, she had realised as she got older, his show of temper might be calculated—especially if he was negotiating the purchase or sale of livestock. Nor did she mind that her father sometimes exploded and roared like a bull. A man who never lost his temper was like a man who was never prepared to fight: not quite a man. Life without such occasional explosions would have seemed dull, lacking in natural excitement.

But in the last three years, since her mother had died, a change had taken place. Her father's zest for life had diminished; he had not always attended to his business as he should; his anger had become more frequent, the reasons for his quarrels not always clear. Last year he had almost come to blows with a young noble who had contradicted Fergus in his own house. Then there had been the drinking. Her father, even at the great feasts, had always drunk rather sparingly. But several times in recent months she had noticed that he and the old bard had been drinking more than usual in the evening; and once or twice his moroseness on these occasions had led to outbursts of temper, for which he apologised the next day but which had been hurtful at the time. Deirdre had been rather proud of her position as the presiding woman of the house since her mother's death, and had secretly dreaded the thought of her father taking another wife; but in recent months she had begun to wonder whether that might be the best solution. And then, she thought, I suppose I shall have to marry myself, for there surely won't be room for two women in the house. It was not a prospect she looked forward to in the least.

But could there be another reason for her father's distress? He had never said so—he was too proud for that—but she had sometimes wondered if her father might be living beyond his means. She did not know why he would be. Most major transactions on the island were paid for in cattle, and Fergus had large herds. Some time ago, she knew, he had pledged his most valuable heirloom to a merchant. The golden torc, worn like an amulet round the neck, was the sign of his chiefly status. His explanation to her at the time had been simple. "With the price I've been offered, I can get enough cattle to buy it back again in a few years. I'm better off without it," he had told her gruffly. Certainly there were few cattlemen in Leinster more skilful than her father. But she hadn't been convinced, all the same. Several times in the last year, she had heard him muttering about his debts, and she had wondered what else he might owe that she didn't know about. But it was an incident three months ago that had really frightened her. A man she had never seen before had arrived at the rath and rudely announced in front of the entire household that Fergus owed him ten cows and that he'd better pay up at once. She had never seen her father so angry, though she suspected it was the humiliation of being exposed in such a way that had really infuriated him. When he refused to pay, the fellow had returned a week later with twenty armed men and carried off not ten but twenty cattle. Her father had been beside himself and had sworn revenge. Nothing had come of his threat, but since that time, his temper had been worse than ever. He had struck one of the slaves twice that week.

Would there be other people to whom her father owed debts at the great gathering at Carmun, she had wondered? She suspected that there might. Or would he decide that someone had insulted him? Or, after drinking, start a quarrel for some other cause? It seemed to her that such a thing was only too possible, and the prospect filled her with fear. For at the great festivals, it was an absolute rule: there must be no fights. It was a necessary rule when you had a huge concourse of people competing and feasting. To cause a disturbance was an insult to the king, which would not be forgiven. The king himself could take your life for it, and the druids and bards and everyone else would support him. At other times, you could have a quarrel with your neighbour or go on a cattle raid and get into a fight with honour. But at the great festival of Lughnasa, you did so at risk of your life.

In his present state, she could just see her father getting into a fight. And then? There would be no mercy shown to the old chief from the obscure little territory of Dubh Linn. She trembled to think of it. For a month she had tried to persuade him not to go. But to no avail. He was determined to go, and to take herself and her two young brothers with him.

"I've important business there," he told her. But what that business might be, he would not say.

So she had been taken by surprise by what had happened the day before they were due to leave. He had gone fishing early with her brothers and returned in the middle of the morning.

Even in the distance, you couldn't mistake Fergus. It was his walk. When he was out on the hills with his cattle or moving along the riverbank to go fishing, Fergus was unmistakable. His tall frame moved with an unhurried ease; his long, slow strides ate up the distance. He seldom talked when he was walking, and there was something in his manner, as he moved across the quiet landscape, which suggested that he regarded not only this region but the whole island as his personal estate.

He had come across a stretch of grassland, with a long stick in his right hand and his two sons following dutifully behind. His face, with its big moustache and long nose, was watchful and quietly thoughtful in repose—in which condition, Deirdre realised, it reminded her of a wise old salmon. But as he drew close, his face had broadened and creased into an engaging smile.

"Did you catch something, Father?" she asked.

But instead of answering her question, he had pleasantly remarked, "Well, Deirdre, we're off tomorrow to find you a husband."

❖

For Goibniu the Smith, the strange business had begun one morning the month before. He couldn't really account for what happened that day. But then the place, it was known, was crowded with spirits.

Of all the island's many rivers, none was more sacred than the River Boyne. Flowing into the eastern sea a day's journey to the north of Dubh Linn, its rich banks were under the control of the Ulster king. Slow-moving, stocked with stately salmon, the Boyne flowed softly through the most fertile soil in the whole island. But there was one place—a site on a low ridge overlooking the Boyne's northern bank—where most men feared to go. The site of the ancient mounds.

It was a fine morning when Goibniu came round the side of the mound. He always went up there if he was passing through the area. Other men might be afraid of the place, but he wasn't. To the west, in the distance, he could see the top of the royal Hill of Tara. He had stared down the slope to where the swans were gliding on the waters of the Boyne. A fellow with a sickle was walking along the track by the riverbank. He glanced up at Goibniu and gave a grudging nod which Goibniu returned with ironic politeness.

Not many people liked Goibniu. "Govnyoo" the name sounded. But whatever they felt, the smith didn't care. Though not tall of stature, his restless eye and quick intelligence soon seemed to dominate any group he joined. His face was not pleasing. A chin that jutted out like a rock, pendulous lips, a beak of a nose that came down almost to meet them, protruding eyes, and a forehead that receded under thinning hair: these alone would have produced a face not easily forgotten. But in his youth he had lost one of his eyes in a fight, and as a result, one eye was permanently closed while the other seemed to loom out of his face in a fearsome squint. Some said that he had assumed that squinting expression even before he had lost the eye. It might have been so. In any case, people called him Balar behind his back, after the evil, one-eyed king of the Fomorians, a legendary tribe of ugly giants—a fact of which he was well aware. It amused him. They might not like him, but they feared him. There were advantages in that.

They had reason to fear. It was not just that single, all-seeing eye. It was the brain that lay behind it.

Goibniu was important. As one of the island's greatest master craftsmen, he had the status of a noble in all but name. Though he was known as a smith—and no one on the island could forge better weapons of iron—his calling included working in precious metals. Indeed, it was the high prices that the great men of the island paid for his gold ornaments that had made Goibniu a rich man. The High King himself would invite him to attend his feasts. But his true importance lay in that terrible, devious brain. The greatest chiefs, even the wise and powerful druids, would seek out his advice. "Goibniu is deep," they would acknowledge, before quietly adding: "Don't ever have him for your enemy."

Just behind him was the largest of the huge, circular mounds that lay along the ridge. A sid, the islanders called such a mound—they pronounced it "shee"—and though mysterious, there were many of them.

It was clear that the sid had deteriorated since former times. The walls of the cylinder had subsided or vanished under turf banks in numerous places. Instead of a cylinder with a curved roof, it now seemed more like a hillock with several entrances. On its southern side, the quartz facing that had once flashed in the sun had now mostly fallen down, so that there was a little landslide of pale metallic stones in front of the former doorway. He turned back to face the sid.

The Tuatha De Danaan lived in there. The Dagda, the kindly lord of the sun, lived in this sid; but all the mounds that dotted the islands were the entrances to their otherworld. Everyone knew the stories. First one, then another tribe had come to the island. Gods, giants, slaves—their identities lingered in the landscape like clouds of mist. But the most glorious of all had been the divine race of the goddess Anu, or Danu, goddess of wealth and of rivers: the Tuatha De Danaan. Warriors and huntsmen, poets and craftsmen—they had arrived on the island, some said, riding upon the clouds. Theirs had been a golden age. It had been the Tuatha De Danaan whom the present tribes, the Sons of Mil, had found on the island when they had arrived. And it had been one of them, the goddess Eriu, who had promised the Sons of Mil that, if they gave the land her name, they should live upon the island forever. That was long ago now. Nobody was sure exactly how long. There had been great battles, that was certain. And then the Tuatha De Danaan had withdrawn from the land of the living and gone underground. They were living there still, under the hills, under lakes, or far away across the sea in the fabled Western Isles, feasting in their glittering halls. That was the story.

But Goibniu doubted. He could see that the mounds were manmade; indeed, their construction might not be very different from the earth and stoneworks which men built now. But if it was said that the Tuatha De Danaan had retreated under them, then they probably dated from that former age. So had the Tuatha De Danaan built them? Likely enough, he supposed. Divine race or not, he judged, they had still been men. Yet if this were correct, here was the curious thing: whenever he inspected the carved stones at these old sites, he always observed that the patterns of the carvings were similar to those on the metalwork of his own day. He'd seen pieces of fine worked gold, too, which had been found in bogs and other places, and which he guessed were very old. On these, also, the designs were familiar. Goibniu was an expert in these matters. Did the incoming tribes really copy the designs left by the departed race of the goddess Danu? Wasn't it more likely that some of the former people had remained and transmitted their skills? Anyway, did an entire people, divine or not, really vanish under the hills?

Goibniu cast his cold eye on the sid. There was one stone there that always caught his attention whenever he passed by. It was a large one, a big slab about six feet across, in front of what had once been the entrance. He went over to it now.

What a curious thing it was. The swirling lines with which it was incised made several patterns, but the most significant was the great trefoil of spirals on the left face. As he had so many times before, he ran his hands over the stone, whose sandlike roughness felt pleasantly cool in the warm sun as his fingers traced the grooves. The biggest spiral was a double one, like a pair of eels coiled tightly together with their heads locking in the middle. Follow one of the coils outwards and it led to the second spiral, another double one below it. The third, smaller spiral, a single one, rested tangentially on the swirling shoulders of the other two. And from their outer edges the grooves gathered in the angles where the spirals met, like tidemarks at an inlet, before flowing on in swirling rivers round the stone.

What did they mean? What was the significance of the trefoil? Three spirals, connected yet independent, always leading inward, yet also flowing out into an endless nothingness. Were they the symbols of the sun and moon and the earth below? Or the three sacred rivers of a half-forgotten world?

He had seen a crazy fellow make a design like that once. It was just at this season of the year, before the harvest, when the last of the old grain goes mouldy, and poor folk who eat it act strangely and dream dreams. He'd come upon him by the seashore, sitting alone, big and bare-boned, his eyes fixed upon nothing, a tattered stick in his hand, tracing spirals just like these in the empty sand. Was he mad, or was he wise? Goibniu shrugged. Who knew? It was all one and the same.

Still tracing the swirling grooves in the morning silence, his hand moved to and fro. One thing was certain. Whoever made those spirals, Tuatha De Danaan or not, Goibniu felt he knew him as only a fellow craftsman can. Other men might find the sid grim and fearsome, but he did not care. He liked the cosmic spirals on the stonecold earth.

And then it had come to him. It was a strange sensation. Nothing you could put a name to. An echo in the mind.

The season of Lughnasa was approaching. There would be a number of great festivals on the island, and though he had consid-

ered the big Leinster games at Carmun, he had been planning this
year to go elsewhere. But now, standing by the stone with its spirals,
the feeling had come into his mind that he should go to Carmun,
though he did not know why.

He listened. Everything was quiet. Yet in the very silence, there
seemed to be a significance, a message being carried by a messenger
still far away, like a cloud that is hidden over the horizon. Goibniu
was a hardheaded man; he was not given to foolish moods or fantasies. But he could not deny that, now and again as he had walked
across the island landscape, he had experienced the sensation of
knowing things he could not explain. He waited. There it was again,
that echo, like a dream half remembered. Something strange, it
seemed to him, was going to happen at Carmun.

He shrugged. It might mean nothing, but one shouldn't ignore
these things. His eye travelled along the southern horizon. He'd go
down to Carmun then, at Lughnasa. When had he last gone south?
The previous year, collecting gold in the mountains below Dubh
Linn. He smiled. Goibniu loved gold.

Then he frowned. The memory of that journey reminded him of
something else. He'd crossed by the Ford of Hurdles. There had
been a big fellow there. Fergus. He nodded thoughtfully. That big
fellow owed him a debt—to the value of a score of cattle. A debt
that was long overdue. The chief was in danger of annoying him. He
wondered if Fergus was going to the festival.

Deirdre had not enjoyed the journey to Carmun. They had set off
from Dubh Linn at dawn with a light, misty rain falling. The party
wasn't large: just Deirdre, her father, her brothers, the bard, and the
smaller of the British slaves. The men rode horses: she and the slave
drove in the cart. The horses were short and stocky—in a later age
they would have been called ponies—but sure-footed and sturdy.
They would cover most of the distance by nightfall and arrive the
following day.

The rain didn't bother her. It was the kind that the people of the island disregarded. If you'd asked Fergus he would just have said, "It's a soft day." For the journey, she was dressed simply—a wool dress with a tartan pattern, a light cloak pinned at the shoulder, and a pair of leather sandals. Her father was similarly dressed in a belted tunic and cloak. Like most of the men on the island, his long legs were bare.

For a while, they went in silence. They crossed the ford. Long ago, so the story was, the hurdles had been laid down on the orders of a legendary seer. However that might be, as the chief who controlled the territory, Fergus maintained it now. Each hurdle consisted of a wattle raft held in place with stakes and weighted with heavy stones—solid enough, though they could be washed away if the river flooded. At the far end, where the bridgeway passed over boggy ground, the cart broke some of the wattle that had rotted. "That'll have to be seen to," her father muttered absently; but she had wondered how many weeks would pass before he got round to it.

Once across, they had turned westwards, following the line of the Liffey upstream. Willows grew on the riverbanks. On the dry ground, as in much of the island forest, ash trees and fine oaks abounded. Dair they called the oak tree in Celtic, and sometimes a settlement made in an oakwood clearing was called Daire—it sounded, approximately, "Derry." As they went through the forest track, the rain had ceased and the sun appeared. They crossed a large clearing. And it was only after the track had led them back into the woods again that Deirdre spoke.

"So what sort of a husband am I to have?"

"We'll see. Someone who can meet the conditions."

"And what are they?"

"Such as are appropriate for the only daughter of this family. Your husband will be marrying the great-granddaughter of Fergus the warrior. Nuadu of the Silver Hand himself used to speak to him. Don't forget that."

How could she forget? Hadn't he been telling her since before she could walk? Nuadu of the Silver Hand, the cloudmaker. In Britain, where he was depicted like the Roman Neptune, they had built a great shrine to him by the western river Severn. But on the western island, he was adopted as one of the Tuatha De Danaan— and the kings of that part of the island even claimed him as their ancestor. Nuadu had taken a personal liking to her great-grandfather. Her future husband would have to reckon with that, and all the rest of the family heritage. She glanced sidelong at her father.

"Perhaps I'll refuse," she said. By the ancient laws of the island, a woman was free to choose her husband—and to divorce him later if she wanted. In theory, therefore, her father couldn't compel Deirdre to marry someone, though he would doubtless make it unpleasant for her if she refused ever to marry at all.

Men had made offers for her in the past. But after her mother's death, with Deirdre running the household and acting as a mother to her brothers, the business of her marriage had been put to one side. The last occasion that she knew of had taken place one day when she had been out walking. On her return, her brothers had told her that a man had been asking for her. But the rest of the conversation had not been encouraging.

Ronan and Rian: two years and four years her juniors. Perhaps they were no worse than other boys their age. But they could certainly exasperate her.

"He came by while you were out," Ronan said.

"What sort of man?"

"Oh, just a man. Like father. Younger. He was travelling somewhere."

"And?"

"They got talking."

"And? What did father say?"

"He was just—you know—talking." Ronan looked at Rian.

"We didn't listen much," added Rian. "But I think he made an offer for you."

She looked at them. They weren't being evasive. Just being themselves. Two gangling youths without a thought to share between
them. Like a pair of large puppies. Show them a hare and they'd
chase it. That was about the only thing that would excite them.
Hopeless.

What would they do without her, she wondered?

"Would you be sorry if I left you to get married?" she had suddenly asked.

They had looked at each other again.

"You'll be going sooner or later," said Ronan.

"We'd be all right," said Rian. "You could come to visit us," he
had added, encouragingly, as an afterthought.

"You're very kind," she said, with bitter irony, but they didn't see
it. There was no use, she supposed, in expecting gratitude from boys
of that age.

When she had questioned her father about it later, he had been
terse.

"He didn't offer enough." The marriage of a daughter was a careful negotiation. On the one hand, a handsome young woman of noble blood was a valuable asset to any family. But the man who
married her would have to pay the bride price, of which her father
would receive a share. That was the custom of the island.

And now, with his affairs in the state they were, Fergus had evidently decided he must sell her. She knew she shouldn't be surprised. That was the way things were. But even so, she couldn't help
feeling a little hurt and betrayed. After all that I have done for him
since my mother died, is that really what I am to him? she wondered. Just like one of the cattle, to be kept as long as needed, and
then sold? She had thought he loved her. And indeed, she reflected,
he probably did. Instead of feeling sorry for herself, she should be
feeling sorry for him, and try to help him by finding a suitable man.

She was good-looking. She had heard people say she was beautiful. Not that she was so special. She was sure there must be dozens
of other girls on the island with soft golden hair, a red and generous

mouth with good white teeth like hers. Her cheeks, as the saying was, had the delicate colour of foxgloves. She had pretty little breasts, too, she had always considered. But the most striking feature she possessed was her eyes, which were the strangest and most beautiful green. "I don't know where they come from," her father had told her, "though they say there was a woman with magical eyes somewhere in my mother's family." No one else in the family or anywhere near Dubh Linn had eyes like that. They might not be magical—she certainly didn't think she had any special powers—but they were much admired. Men had been fascinated by them ever since she was a child. So she'd always felt confident that, when the time came, she'd be able to find a good man.

But she wasn't in a hurry. She was still only seventeen. She'd never met anyone she wanted to marry; and in all likelihood, marriage would take her far from the quiet estuary at Dubh Linn, which she loved. And whatever her father's problems with his debts, she wasn't sure she should go away at the moment, leaving her father and her brothers without a woman to run the house.

The festival of Lughnasa was a traditional occasion for matchmaking. But she didn't think she wanted a husband. Not this year.

The rest of the day had passed quietly. She asked no more questions, because there was no point. Her father at least seemed cheerful: that was something to be grateful for. Perhaps, with luck, he wouldn't become involved in any quarrels, and would fail to find her an acceptable suitor. Then they could all return home safely and in peace.

Late in the morning they came to a hamlet in a clearing where her father knew the people; but for once he did not stop to talk. And soon after that, as the Liffey curved away to the south, the track began to rise from the narrowing river plain onto higher ground, taking them westwards. It was towards noon, reaching a break in the trees, that they came out onto a broad shelf of peaty heath, dotted with gorse bushes.

"There," her father pointed to an object a short way ahead, "that's where we'll rest."

The midday sun was pleasantly warm as they sat on the grass and ate the light meal she had brought for them. Her father drank a little ale to wash down his bread.

The place he had chosen was a small earthwork ring beside a single standing stone. These stones, either single or in groups, were a regular feature of the landscape—placed there, it was assumed, by ancestral figures or by the gods. This one stood quite alone, about the height of a man, looking out over a wooded plain that stretched away, westwards, to the horizon. In the great silence under the August sun, the old grey stone seemed, to Deirdre, to be friendly. After they had eaten, and while the horses grazed nearby, they stretched out in the sun to rest a little while. The quiet snoring of her father soon told her that he was taking a nap, and it was not long before Deirdre dozed off herself.

She awoke suddenly. She must have slept awhile, she realised, as the sun had shifted its position. She was still in that hazy condition of having been jolted through the veils of sleep into a too bright consciousness. As she glanced at the sun hanging over the great plain, she experienced a curious vision. It was as if the sun were a spoked wheel, like that of a war chariot, strange and menacing. She shook her head to dispel the last mists of sleep and told herself not be foolish.

But for the rest of that day, and while she lay trying to sleep that night, she was unable to rid herself of a vague sense of disquiet.

⁂

It had been late morning when Goibniu arrived. His single, all-seeing eye surveyed the scene.

Lughnasa: a month after the summer solstice, the celebration of the coming harvest, a festival where marriages were arranged. He liked its patron god—Lugh the Shining One, Lugh of the Long Arm, the magician master of every craft, the brave warrior, the healer.

People were arriving at Carmun from every direction: chiefs, warriors, athletes from tribes all over the island. How many tribes were there, he wondered. Perhaps a hundred and fifty. Some were large, ruled by powerful clans; some were lesser, ruled by affiliated septs; some hardly more than a group of families, probably sharing a common ancestor, but who proudly called themselves a tribe and had a chief. It was easy, on an island which nature had divided by mountain and bog into huge numbers of small territories, for each tribe to have lands of its own in the centre of which there was usually a sacred ancestral site, often as not marked by an ash tree.

And who exactly were these tribes? Where had they come from, these Sons of Mil who had sent the legendary Tuatha De Danaan under the hills? Goibniu knew that the conquering tribes had come to the western island centuries ago from neighbouring Britain and from across the sea to the south. The people of the western island were part of a great patchwork of tribes, whose culture and language, called Celtic, stretched across much of north-western Europe. With their swords of iron, splendid war chariots, and magnificent metalwork, their druid priests and poets, the Celtic tribes had long been feared and admired. As the Roman Empire had spread northwards and across to Britain, the main centres of each tribal territory had usually become a Roman military centre or market town and the Celtic gods of the local tribe likewise put on Roman clothes. Thus in Gaul, for instance, the Celtic god Lugh, whose festival this was, had given his name to the city of Lugdunum, which would one day become transmuted to Lyon. And the tribes in turn had gradually become Roman, even losing their old language and speaking Latin instead.

Except on the outer fringes. In the northern and western parts of

Britain, which the Romans largely left alone, the former tongues and tribal customs had continued. Above all, in the western neighbour island across the sea, where the Romans came to trade but not to conquer, the old Celtic culture, in all its richness, remained intact. The Romans were not always certain what to call these various people. In northern Britain, which the Romans called Alba, lived the ancient tribes of Picts. When colonisers from the Celtic western island sailed over and established settlements in Alba, gradually pushing the Picts back towards the northern British interior, the Romans referred to these Celtic settlers as Scotti, or Scots. But the Celtic tribes of the western island did not call themselves by that Roman name. They knew who they were, ever since they had come to the island and encountered a friendly goddess there. They were the people of Eriu.

⁘

As he watched the Celtic tribesmen approaching the festival, however, Goibniu's stare was cool. Was he one of them? Partly, no doubt. But just as up at those strange old mounds above the Boyne he felt a nameless sense of belonging, at these great Celtic gatherings he could not help an instinctive sensation that he was somehow alien, that he came from some other tribe who had been in this land since long before. Perhaps the Sons of Mil had conquered his people, but he still knew how to make use of them.

His single eye continued to move over the scene, separating, with knifelike precision, the colourful groups into different categories: important, not important; useful, irrelevant; owing him something, or owed a favour. By a large cart he saw two magnificent young champions, arms thick as tree trunks, tattooed—the two sons of Cas, son of Donn. Wealthy. To be cultivated. Some way off stood two druids and an old bard. The old man, Goibniu was aware, had a dangerous tongue, but he had a few pieces of gossip to keep the old man happy. Over to the left he saw Fann, daughter of the great chief Ross: a proud woman. But Goibniu knew that she had slept with one of the sons of Cas, which her husband did not. Knowledge is power. You never knew when such information could be used to secure a piece of future business. Mostly though, as his eye scanned the crowd, what Goibniu noticed were the people who owed him something.

Stately, plump Diarmait: nine cows, three cloaks, three pairs of boots, a gold torc to wear round his neck. Culann: ten pieces of gold. Roth Mac Roth: one piece of gold. Art: a sheep. They all borrowed, all were in his power. Good. Then he saw Fergus.

The tall fellow from Dubh Linn, who owed him the price of twenty cows. Fine girl with him: she must be his daughter. That was interesting. He moved towards them.

❖

Deirdre had also been watching the crowds. The clans and septs were still swinging in from all parts of Leinster. It was certainly an impressive sight. Meanwhile, a curious exchange was taking place between her father and a merchant. It concerned the chief's magnificent golden torc.

It was the custom on the island that, if you had given your jewellery away as security for a loan, you should be able to borrow it back for the great festivals, so that you should not be dishonoured. A kindly dispensation. If Fergus was embarrassed as he retrieved the splendid gold neck ring from the merchant, he certainly did not show it. Indeed, he solemnly took the heirloom from the other man, as though they were performing a ceremony. He had just placed it round his neck when Goibniu arrived.

Whatever the smith thought of Fergus, one couldn't fault his politeness. Goibniu addressed him with all the high-flown courtesy he would have used to the king himself.

"May good be with you, Fergus, son of Fergus. The torc of your noble ancestors looks well upon you."

Fergus eyed him cautiously. He hadn't expected the smith to be down at Carmun.

"What is it, Goibniu," he asked somewhat sharply, "that you want?"

"That is easy to tell," said Goibniu, pleasantly. "I wished only to remind you of your promise to me, before last winter, of the price of twenty cows."

Deirdre looked at her father anxiously. She knew nothing of this debt. Was this going to be the start of a quarrel? So far, the chief's face remained impassive.

"It is true," Fergus conceded. "You are owed it." But then, in a lower voice. "It's a hard thing you're asking, just now. Especially at the festival."

For it was another pleasant custom of the festival that Goibniu could not actually enforce his debt during the proceedings.

"You'll be wanting to deal with the matter when the festival is over, perhaps," suggested the smith.

"Not a doubt of it," said Fergus.

During this exchange, Deirdre had continued to watch her father closely. Was he hiding his anger? Was this the calm before the storm? Goibniu was a man with many important friends. Perhaps that was keeping her father in check. She hoped it would continue to do so.

Goibniu nodded slowly. Then his single eye rested on Deirdre.

"You have a beautiful daughter, Fergus," he remarked. "She has wonderful eyes. Will you be offering her in marriage at the festival?"

"It is in my mind," said Fergus.

"It will be a fortunate man, indeed, who wins her," the smith continued. "Don't dishonour her beauty, or your noble name, by accepting anything but the highest bride price." He paused. "I wish I were a bard," he said, with a polite nod towards Deirdre, "so that I could compose a poem about her beauty."

"You'd do that for me?" she said with a laugh, hoping to maintain the amicable mood of the conversation.

"Certainly." Goibniu's eye looked straight at Fergus.

And then Deirdre saw her father look at the cunning craftsman thoughtfully. Was Goibniu offering to find her a rich bridegroom? She knew that the one-eyed smith had far more influence than her father. Whatever bridegroom Fergus might consider, Goibniu could probably find something better.

"Let us walk together," her father said, with a new softness; and Deirdre watched the two men move away.

So that was it then. Whatever momentary relief she had felt that her father had avoided a quarrel had now been ruined by this new turn of events. With her father, at least, she knew she could still keep some control of the situation. He might shout and rage, but he would not actually force her to marry against her will. But if her fate lay in Goibniu's hands—Goibniu the confidant of kings, the friend of druids—who knew what his deep brain would devise? Against the one-eyed man, she hadn't a hope. She looked at her brothers. They were admiring a chariot.

"Did you see what happened?" she cried. They looked at each other blankly, then shook their heads.

"Anything interesting?" they asked.

"No," she said irritably. "Just that your sister is to be sold."

Lughnasa. High summer. At the ceremonies, the druids would make the harvest offerings to Lugh; the women would dance. And she, quite possibly, would be given to a stranger then and there and, perhaps, never return to Dubh Linn again.

She had started to walk alone across the open ground. Here and there, people at the bright stalls or standing in groups had turned to look at her as she passed, but she had scarcely been aware of them. She passed some tents and pens, and realised that she must be getting near the big track where they raced the horses. There was no big race due yet, but some of the young men would be exercising their horses, perhaps organising an informal, friendly race or two. It looked as if some horses were being led out for that purpose. The late-morning sun was filling the sky with a hard stare as she came to a railed enclosure where a number of riders were preparing to mount.

She stood by the rail and surveyed the scene.

The barebacked horses were skittish. She could hear good-natured taunts and laughter. Over on her right, she noticed a group of men, finely dressed, clustered round a dark-haired young man. He was a shade taller than they were, and as she caught sight of his face she noticed that it was unusually fine. An intelligent, perhaps a thoughtful face—whose quiet expression, despite his smile, suggested that his mind might be a little distant from the activity in which he was engaged. He might, she thought, be a highborn druid rather than a young champion. She wondered who he was. The little group parted and she realised that he must be about to ride in a race since, except for a protective loincloth, he had stripped his body naked.

Deirdre stared. It seemed to her that she had never seen anything so beautiful in her life. So slim, so pale, yet perfectly formed: an athlete's body. He had not a single blemish, as far as she could see. She watched him mount and ride, easily, out onto the track.

"Who is that?" she asked a man standing nearby.

"That is Conall, son of Morna," he replied; and seeing that she had not fully understood: "It's the nephew of the High King himself."

"Oh," said Deirdre.

She watched several races. The men rode bareback. The island horses, though small, were very fleet and the races were exciting. She saw Conall come in just behind the leader in the first race; the second he won. He did not ride in the next two, but meanwhile, more and more people were arriving at the side of the track. One of the main attractions of the day was about to begin.

The chariot races. Already Deirdre could see that the King of Leinster had arrived on the small mound by the track from which vantage point he would preside. For if the racing of horses was the sport of warriors, the riding of chariots represented the highest and most aristocratic of the arts of war. The chariots were strong, lightly built, two-wheeled vehicles with a single shaft between two horses. Each chariot contained a two-man team—the warrior and his charioteer. They were swift and, in the hands of an expert charioteer, wonderfully manoeuverable. Against the disciplined armour of the Roman legions they were not effective, and so in the Roman provinces of Britain and Gaul they had long ago fallen into disuse; but here on the western island, where warfare was conducted along traditional Celtic lines, the ancient art was still practised. Deirdre could see about twenty chariots preparing to enter the track. But first, it seemed there was to be an exhibition. For now two chariots came out, unaccompanied, into the huge, grassy arena.

"There's Conall," remarked the man she had spoken to earlier, "and his friend Finbarr." He grinned. "Now you'll see something."

Conall and Finbarr were both stripped, since it was also the tradition that Celtic warriors fought naked. She noticed that Finbarr was very strongly made, a little shorter than Conall, though thicker in the chest, upon which she could see curls of fair brown hair. Standing just behind their charioteers, each man carried a round shield decorated with polished bronze which flashed in the sun. The chariots went out together into the centre of the arena before wheeling apart to opposite ends. Then they began.

It was astounding. Deirdre had seen charioteers at work before, but never anything like this. Hurtling together at breakneck speed, their spoked wheels, each a blur, almost touched as they passed. Out to the ends they went and turned. This time each hero had taken up a great javelin. As they raced together again, they hurled their spears with devastating skill, Finbarr casting his just an instant before Conall. As the two spears crossed in the air, there was a sudden intake of breath from the crowd. And with good reason: for the aim of each was deadly. Conall's chariot, hitting a small bump in the turf, was slowed just an instant so that the spear thrown by Finbarr would certainly have struck and probably killed the charioteer if Conall had not reached across with lightning speed and deflected it with his shield. Conall's aim on the other hand, was so perfect that his javelin fell precisely on Finbarr's shield as he raced forward so that, holding it up before him, Finbarr could neatly turn the sharp point to one side. There was a roar of appreciation from the crowd. This was warfare as a high art.

The two men were taking up their bright swords as the chariots wheeled round again. Now, however, it was the turn of the charioteers to show their skill. They did not dash straight at each other this time; instead, they began an intricate pattern of pursuit and avoidance, making dizzying circles and zigzags all over the field, swooping down upon each other like birds of prey, chasing and being chased. Each time they came close, sometimes careering along side by side, the two warriors struck and parried with sword and shield. If these fights had been choreographed in advance, it was impossible to tell. As the blades flashed and rang out, Deirdre expected to see blood gush from the pale skin of either man at any moment, and found that she was almost breathless and shivering with nervousness. On and on they went, to the roars of the crowd. It was thrilling in its skill, fearful in its danger.

At last, it was over. The two chariots, Conall's in the lead, made a triumphant circuit of the field to receive their applause, and in so doing, passed in front of Deirdre. Conall had moved forward and was standing, perfectly balanced, on the shaft between the horses. The horses were in a lather, and his own chest was still heaving after the exertion as he acknowledged the applause of the crowd which was so obviously delighted. He was scanning their faces; she supposed he must be pleased. Then, as his chariot drew close, his gaze rested upon her and she found herself staring into his eyes.

But the look in his eyes was not what she'd have expected at all. They were penetrating, yet they did not seem content. It was as if part of him was far away—as though, while he gave the crowd their excitement and delight, he himself had remained apart, lonely, as he balanced so skilfully between life and death.

Why should he have chosen her to look at? She had no idea. But his eyes remained fixed on hers, as if he would like to talk to her, his head turning slowly as he went by. His chariot passed, and he did not look back; but she continued to watch after him when he had gone.

Then she turned and caught sight of her father. He was smiling, and he waved at her, signalling that she should approach.

⁙

It had been Finbarr's idea that they should come to Carmun. He had hoped to lighten his friend's mood. He had also not forgotten the High King's instructions.

"Have you no thought of finding a good-looking woman down here in Leinster?" he had already asked Conall.

The previous evening when they had arrived and gone to pay their respects to the King of Leinster, it was not only the king of the province himself who had shown his delight in welcoming the High King's nephew. There was hardly a woman in the royal company who didn't give Conall a smile. If Conall had noticed these marks of favour, however, he had chosen to ignore them.

Just now, it seemed to Finbarr that he had seen his chance.

"There was a young woman with golden hair and amazing eyes, watching you before you rode," he said. "Did you not see her?"

"I didn't."

"Yet she watched you for a long time," said Finbarr. "I think she had a liking for you."

"I didn't notice," said Conall.

"It was the girl you were staring at yourself just now," Finbarr continued. And it seemed to him that his friend was a little curious, and he noticed Conall glance around. "Stay here," Finbarr said. "I am going to find her." And before Conall could object, he started off with Cuchulainn in the direction in which, moments before, he had seen Deirdre go.

⁙

"Goibniu has the man for you." Her father was beaming.

"How lucky." She said the words drily. "Is he here?"

"No. He is in Ulster."

"That's far away. And what," she asked shrewdly, "is he paying?"

"A handsome amount."

"Enough for you to pay your debt to Goibniu?"

"Enough for that and all my debts." He said it without shame.

"I should congratulate you, then," she said with irony. But he wasn't really listening.

"Of course, he has not seen you. He might not like you. But Goibniu thinks he will. And so he should," her father added, firmly. "A fine young man." He paused, then looked at her kindly. "You'll not have to marry him if you don't like him, Deirdre."

No, she thought. You'll just let me know I've ruined you.

"Goibniu will talk to this young man next month," her father was saying. "You could meet him before winter."

She supposed she should at least be grateful for this slight delay.

"And what can you tell me about the man?" she enquired. "Is he young or old? Is he a chief's son? Is he a warrior?"

"He is," her father said contentedly, "satisfactory in every way. But it's Goibniu who really knows him. He'll tell you everything this evening." And with that he was off, leaving her to her thoughts.

She had been standing quietly by herself for a little time when Finbarr and his hound came towards her.

⁜

Finbarr had collected several men and women, only too glad to meet the nephew of the High King. When he had come up to her, Deirdre had hesitated for a moment, and might not have gone if Finbarr hadn't quietly told her that to refuse would be seen as discourtesy to the prince. And since she was in the company of others, she did not feel embarrassed.

Conall was dressed now, in a tunic and a light cloak. He did not speak to her at first, so she had the chance to observe him. Though still a young man, he moved round the group with a quiet dignity that impressed her. While everyone smiled at him, and his responses were courteous and friendly, there was a seriousness in his manner that seemed to set him apart. As he came towards her, however, she suddenly realised that she had no idea what to say.

Had he sent for her? She didn't know. When Finbarr had asked her if she would like to meet the prince, and indicated that it would be rude to refuse, he hadn't actually said that Conall had sent for her. She would just be one more of the hundreds of faces to be paraded in front of him on an occasion like this—half of them, no doubt, young women eager to impress him. Her pride rebelled against that. She started to feel embarrassed. My family isn't nearly important enough for him to take an interest in me, she told herself; and besides, my father and Goibniu have already found me a suitor. By the time he came to her, therefore, she had resolved to be polite but somewhat cold.

He was looking into her eyes.

"I saw you, after the chariot display." The same eyes, yet instead of that lonely look, they were alive now with a different light. They were searching hers curiously, as though intrigued, interested. Despite all her determination to be cool towards him, she could feel herself starting to blush.

He asked her who her father was and where she came from. He evidently knew about Ath Cliath, but though he said, "Ah, indeed," when she mentioned Fergus as the chief of the place, she suspected that Conall had never heard of him. He asked her a few more questions and exchanged a few words about the races; and indeed, she realised that he had actually spent more time talking to her than to any of the others. Then Finbarr appeared and murmured to him that the King of Leinster was asking for him. He looked into her eyes thoughtfully and smiled.

"Perhaps we shall meet again." Did he really mean it, or was it just an expression of politeness? Probably the latter. She didn't think it was very likely, anyway. Her father did not move in the circles of

the High King. The fact that he couldn't really be sincere annoyed
her slightly, and she almost blurted out, "Well, you know where to
find me." But mercifully she checked herself, and almost blushed
again at the thought of how crude and forward it would have made
her look.

So they parted, and she began to wander back alone towards the
place where her father was likely to be found. Another chariot race
had just begun. She wondered whether to tell her father and her
brothers about her encounter with the young prince, but decided
she had better not. They would only tease her, or gossip, or otherwise embarrass her.

I I

It was autumn and the falling of the leaves was like the slow pluck-
ing of fingers upon a harp. Late afternoon, and the sun was beginning to decline; the ferns were gleaming gold and it seemed as if the
purple heather was melting upon the hills.

The summer quarters of the High King were set upon a low, flat
hill with commanding views of the countryside all around.
Enclosures, cattle pens, and the palisaded camps of the royal retinue
were scattered across the hilltop. It was impressive, for the High
King's royal retinue was large. Druids, keepers of the island's ancient
brehon laws, harpists, bards, cupbearers—not to mention the royal
warrior guards—these positions were highly prized and often inherited within a family. At the southern end was the biggest enclosure,
and at its centre stood a large, circular hall, with timber-and-wattle
walls and a high, thatched roof. A doorway gave entrance to this
royal hall, in the middle of which, on an ingle post, was set a carved
stone head with three faces staring out in different directions, as if
to remind those gathered there that the High King, like the gods,
could see everything at once.

On the western side of the hall there was a raised gallery from which it was possible to look down upon the gatherings inside, or out at the grassy enclosure round the hall and the landscape beyond. And it was in this gallery that two covered benches had been set, a few feet apart, upon which the High King and his queen liked to sit in the late afternoon to watch the sun go down.

In less than a month it would be the magical feast of Samhain. Some years this took place at the great ceremonial centre of Tara; other years it was held at other places. At Samhain the excess livestock would be slaughtered, the rest put out on the wasteland and later brought into pens, while the High King and his followers set off on their winter rounds. Until then, however, it was a slow and peaceful time. The harvest was in, the weather still warm. It should, for the High King, have been a time of contentment.

He was a swarthy man. His dark blue eyes looked out from under the broad crags of a pair of bushy eyebrows. Though his face was reddened by a network of tiny veins, and his square, once closely sinewed body was thickening, there was still a certain vibrant energy about him. His wife, a large, fair-haired woman, had been sitting enveloped in silence for some time. At last, just as the slowly sinking sun had passed behind a cloud, she spoke.

"It is two months."

He did not answer.

"It is two months," she repeated, "two months since you made love to me."

"Is it?"

"Two months." If she had heard the irony in his tone, she ignored it.

"We must do it again, my dearest," he continued, falsely. There had been plenty of lovemaking once; but that was long ago. Their sons were all full grown. A short pause followed while he continued to stare over the temporarily sombre landscape.

"You do nothing for me," she said morosely.

He waited, then made a small click with his tongue.

"Will you look there?" He pointed.

"What is it?"

"Sheep." He watched them with interest. "There's the ram now." He smiled with satisfaction. "It is a hundred sheep he can service."

There was a snort from the queen, followed by silence.

"Nothing!" she suddenly burst out. "A soft, wet little finger of a thing. That is all I get! Nothing a woman can get hold of. I've seen a fish that was stiffer. I've seen a tadpole that was bigger." The outburst was not entirely true, as they both of them knew; but if she hoped to shame him, his face remained serene. She snorted again. "Your father had three wives and two concubines. Five women and he could manage them all." The people of the island saw no virtues in monogamy. "But you . . ."

"That cloud is almost off the sun now."

"You're no use to me."

"And yet," he took his time, speaking meditatively, as though discussing a historical curiosity, "we must remember that I have serviced a mare."

"So you say."

"Oh, the thing was done. I could not be sitting here otherwise."

✤

The initiation ceremony when a great clan elected a new king on the island went back into the mists of time and belonged to a tradition found amongst the Indo-European peoples from Asia to the western outliers of Europe. In this ceremony, after a white bull had been killed, the king-to-be must mate with a sacred female horse. It is explicit both in the legends of Ireland and the temple carvings of India. Nor was the business as difficult as might be supposed. The mare in question was not large. Held by several strong men, her hindquarters suitably spread, she was presented to the future king who, so long as—by whatever means—he could be aroused, would have no great difficulty in penetrating her. It was a fitting ritual for a people who, since they emerged from the Eurasian plains, had depended for their leadership upon men who were wedded to the horse.

⊹

Whether the queen was thinking about the mare or not was hard to say; but after a little time she spoke again, in a low voice.

"The harvest was ruined."

The High King frowned. Involuntarily he glanced back inside the empty hall, where the three-faced head was gazing out from its totem pole into the surrounding shadows.

"That is your fault," she added.

And now the High King pursed his lips. For this was politics.

The High King was very good at politics. When he put his arm round a man's shoulder, that man was always his to command—or to be duped. He knew most men's weaknesses, and their price. His family's success had been remarkable. His royal clan had come from the west and they were hugely ambitious. Claiming descent from mythical figures like Conn of the Hundred Battles and Cormac Mac Art—heroes they may even have invented—the clan had already pushed many Ulster chiefs off their land. Their rise had culminated, in quite recent times, in the successes they ascribed to their heroic leader Niall.

Like many of history's successful leaders, Niall was partly a pirate. He knew the value of wealth. Since his youth he had led raids across to the island of Britain—easy pickings with the Roman legions withdrawing or gone. Mostly he had stolen boys and girls to sell to the slave markets; the profits he could use for himself and his followers. It was the custom, when one king submitted to another— when he agreed to "come into his house," as the saying was—that he would pay tribute, usually in cattle, and give hostages for his continuing loyalty. So many kings were said to have sent their sons as hostages to Niall that he was remembered as Niall of the Nine Hostages. His mighty clan not only had dominated the island and claimed the high kingship but had forced the Leinster kings to give them the ancient royal site of Tara which they intended to make into their own dynasty's ceremonial centre, from which they could rule the whole island.

But mighty though the clan of Niall might be, even high kings were at the mercy of larger, natural forces.

It had happened quite unexpectedly, immediately after the Lughnasa festival. Ten days of drenching rain: the ground reduced to a bog, the harvest utterly ruined. No one could remember a summer like it. And it was the High King's fault. For though the motives of the gods were seldom clear, such terrible weather could only mean that at least one of them was offended with him.

Every place had its gods. They grew out of the landscape and the stories of the beings who had dwelt there before. Everyone could feel their presence. And the Celtic gods of the island were bright and vivid spirits. When a man went up to the island's high places and gazed across the emerald woods and pastures, and breathed the soft island air, his heart almost burst with gratitude to Eriu, the mother goddess of the land. When the sun rose in the morning, he smiled to see the Dagda, the good god, riding his horse across the sky—the kindly Dagda from whose magic cauldron all the good things of life were provided. When he stood on the shore and looked out at the waves, it might seem to him that he almost caught sight of Manannan mac Lir, the god of the sea, rising from the deep.

The gods could be fearsome also. Down off the island's southwestern tip, on a rocky outcrop in the roiling waters, lived Donn, the lord of the dead. Most men feared Donn. And the mother goddess, when she took the form of the angry Morrigain and came with her ravens and screeched over men in battle, she, too, could be a terrifying figure. Was she angry now?

Kings were powerful when they pleased the gods. But a king had to be careful. If a ruler annoyed a god—or even one of the druids or filidh who spoke to them—he might lose a battle. If men came to the High King for justice and got none, the gods would probably send plague or bad weather. Everybody knew: a bad king brought bad luck; a good king was rewarded with good harvests. There was a morality in it. People might not be saying so openly yet, but he knew what they were thinking: if the harvest was ruined, it was probably the High King's fault.

Yet search his conscience though he might, the High King could not think of any great shortcoming on his part that should have brought the wrath of the gods upon him. He possessed all the kingly qualities. He was not mean: he rewarded his followers well; the High King's feasts were splendid. He was certainly no coward. He wasn't jealous or petty. Even his wife could have no complaint about him on that score.

What should he do? He had consulted the druids. Offerings were being made. So far, at least, no one had come up with any further suggestions. The weather at present was fine. A few days ago he had decided that the wisest course for the time being was to wait and see.

"You were shamed in Connacht." His wife's voice punctured the silence surrounding his thoughts like a dagger. Involuntarily, he winced.

"That is not true."

"Shamed."

"It was my shame in Connacht brought the rain. Is that what you mean?"

She said nothing, but, for once, a tiny smile of satisfaction seemed to pass for a moment across her face.

The business in Connacht had been nothing. It was the custom in summer for the High King or his servants to visit parts of the island and receive payments of tribute. Not only did this acknowledge the High King's supremacy but it was an important source of revenue. Large herds of cattle would be collected and delivered back to the High King's pastures. This summer he had gone into Connacht, where the king had received him courteously and paid without question. But there had been a shortfall and the King of

Connacht had explained with some embarrassment that one of the Connacht chiefs had failed to bring his quota. As the man's territory lay on his route home, the High King had said that he would deal with the matter himself. A mistake, he had realised afterwards.

When he had come to the chief's territory, neither the man nor his cattle were to be found, and after a few days' search, he had continued on his way. Within a month, the whole island knew of it. He had sent a party of men back to catch the cheeky fellow, but again the Connacht man had evaded capture. He had meant to go into the whole business thoroughly after the harvest, but the rains had distracted him. So now he was a laughingstock. That chieftain would pay dearly for this in due course, but until he had, the High King's authority was damaged. Nonetheless, he would take his time.

"It will be a poor sort of hospitality we get this winter," she resumed. If the High King collected tribute in summer, in winter he had another way of making his presence felt. He came to stay. And though many chiefs might feel honoured that the High King came to claim some days of hospitality, by the time that the royal party left, they were glad to see them go. "They've eaten almost everything we had," was the usual complaint. If the High King wanted to eat well that winter, he needed to inspire fear as well as love.

"That man who shamed you. That little chief." She laid emphasis upon the *little*. "It is ten heifers he owes you."

"It is. But I shall take thirty now."

"You should not take them."

"Why is that?"

"Because he owns something more valuable, something he is hiding."

It never ceased to amaze the king how his wife could discover the details of other people's business.

"What is it?"

"He has a black bull. They say it's the biggest on the island. He keeps it hidden away because he's planning to breed a whole herd with it and make himself rich." She paused and looked at him balefully. "Since you don't do anything else for me, you could bring me that bull."

He shook his head in wonderment.

"It is like Maeve you are," he said. Everyone knew the story of Queen Maeve, who, jealous that her husband's herd of cattle had a larger bull than her own herd possessed, sent the hero of legend, the great warrior Cuchulainn, to capture the Brown Bull of Cuailnge, and of the tragic bloodshed it led to. Of all the tales of gods and heroes which the bards recited, this was one of the favourites.

"You get me that bull for my herd," she said.

"Do you wish me to get it myself?" he asked.

"I do not." She glowered at him. "It would not be fitting." High Kings did not lead small cattle raids.

"Who should go, then?"

"Send your nephew, Conall," she said.

As he thought about this, the High King, not for the first time, had to admit that his wife was clever. "It may be that I will," he said after a little while. "It would perhaps take his mind off this desire he has to be a druid. But I think," he went on, "that it should be done next spring."

And now it was the turn of the queen, despite herself, to glance at her husband with some respect. For she guessed what was in his mind. It might even be, she realised, that he had deliberately left the business of the Connacht man unfinished. If there was any inclination amongst the island's many chiefs to mount challenges to his authority, he would give them the months of winter to show themselves. They might think they were plotting in secret, but he was sure to learn of it. He was not High King for nothing. Once he knew who his enemies were, he would crush them before they had time to combine.

"Say nothing yet, then," she said, "but send Conall for the bull at Bealtaine."

There was a rainbow. It was not unusual, in that part of the island, to see a rainbow; and now, as the sun came through the filter of moisture after a brief shower, there was a rainbow right across the Liffey's estuary and the bay.

How she loved the Dubh Linn region. With the prospect of leaving it for Ulster ever present now, Deirdre savoured every day. If the haunts of her childhood had always seemed dear, they now seemed to be imbued with a special poignancy. Often she would wander along the river. She loved its changing moods. Or she would go out to the seashore and follow the long, curved sands, scattered with seashells, that led to the rocky hill at the southern end of the bay. But there was one place that she liked even better. It took a bit longer to reach, but it was worth it.

First she would cross by the Ford of Hurdles to the northern bank. Then, following tracks across the low, marshy expanses, she would work her way round to the long, eastwards strand that formed the upper half of the bay. Mudflats and grassy sandbars, a little way out from the shore, accompanied her for a long time; but eventually they ceased and at last ahead of her, at the end of a long spit of land, she would see the big hump of the northern peninsula. And with a new sense of joy she would go forward and start to climb.

Up on the hump of the peninsula, standing all alone, there was a pleasant little shelter. Placed there by men or by the gods long ago, it consisted of a few thickset, standing stones with a huge, flat stone slab laid on top of them at an angle, aslant against the sky. Inside this dolmen, the sea breeze was reduced to a peaceful, hissing sound. But as she sat or lay on its stony roof, Deirdre could daydream in the sun or enjoy the view.

And if Deirdre loved gazing out from the top of the peninsula, it was hardly surprising. For it was one of the finest coastal views in all Europe. Looking southwards across the great sweep of the bay, its grey-blue waters appeared to be molten yet cool—aqueous lava, skin of the sea god, shining softly. And beyond the bay, all the way down the coastline, points and headlands, hills and ridges, and the pleasant sweeps of former volcanoes formed a hazy recessional into the blue beyond.

But much as Deirdre admired this wonderful southern view, what she specially loved was to look across the headland the other way, to the north. Here, too, there was a fine open sweep of the sea, if less dramatic, and the level coastland, known as the Plain of Bird Flocks, was a pleasant region; but what interested her were two objects that lay quite near. For immediately above the headland lay another, smaller bay in the shape of an estuary; and in this estuary were two islands. The larger, more distant, whose long lines reminded her of a fish, seemed sometimes, when the waters were in motion, to be drifting out to sea. Indeed, it was nearly clear of the estuary already. But it was the smaller island which charmed her most. It was only a short way from the shore. You could row out to it quite easily, she supposed. It had a sandy beach on one side and a heathery little hillock at its centre. But on the seaward side there was a small, rocky cliff which had been cleft, leaving a sheltered gap between its face and a pillar of standing stone, with a pebble beach below. How intimate it seemed. The island was not inhabited and had no name. But it looked so inviting. She found it fascinating and would sit on warm afternoons, gazing at it for hours. Once she had taken her father up there, and if she returned late after a long ramble, he would usually smile and say, "Well, Deirdre, have you been looking at your island again?"

She had been there this morning, and had returned in an irritable mood. She had been caught in the rain shower—but that was nothing. The thought of her marriage had depressed her. She hadn't met the man that Goibniu and her father were proposing yet; but whomever she married, it would mean leaving these beloved shores. For I can't marry the seabirds, she thought sadly. And then, on her return, she found that one of the two British slaves had foolishly cracked a barrel of her father's best wine and lost more than half the contents. Her father and brothers were out, otherwise the slave could have expected a whipping, but she cursed him roundly by all the gods. It had irritated her still further that, instead of apologising or at least looking sorry, the wretched fellow, hearing the gods invoked, had fallen on his knees, crossed himself, and started mumbling his prayers.

On the whole, buying the two western British slaves had been one of her father's better ideas. Whatever his shortcomings, he had a wonderful eye when it came to livestock, whether animal or human. Many of the British in the eastern half of the neighbour island couldn't speak anything but Latin, she had heard. She supposed that after the centuries of Roman rule, this was not surprising. But the western British mostly spoke a language very similar to her own. One of the slaves was large and burly, the other short; both had dark hair, shaved close as a mark of their slavery. And they worked hard. But they had their own religion. Soon after they arrived, she had discovered them praying together once and they had explained that they were Christians. She knew many of the British were Christian, and she had even heard of small Christian communities on the island, but knew little about the religion. A bit concerned, she had asked her father about this, but he had reassured her.

"The British slaves are often Christian. It's a slave's religion. Tells them to be submissive."

So she had left the burly slave mumbling his prayers while she went indoors. Perhaps in the peace and quiet of the house her mood would improve. Her hair had become tangled in the rain. She sat down and started to comb it.

The house was a good, solid dwelling—a circular structure with clay-and-wattle walls, about fifteen feet in diameter. Light came in through three doorways which were open to let in the fresh morning air. In the middle of the interior was a hearth; wisps of smoke from the fire filtered out through the thatched roof above. Beside the fire was a large cauldron and, on a low wooden table, a collection of wooden platters—for though they had once done so, the islanders did not use much pottery. On another table near the wall, the family's more valuable household possessions were kept: a handsome, five-handled bronze bowl; a quern for grinding grain; a pair of dice, rectangular in shape with four faces, that you rolled in a straight line; several wooden tankards banded with silver; and, of course, her father's drinking skull.

Deirdre sat there combing her hair for some time. Her immediate irritation had subsided. But there was something else, in the background, something that had been troubling her for the last two months, ever since her return from Lughnasa, and that she did not wish to acknowledge. A tall, pale young prince. She shrugged. It was no use thinking about him.

Then she heard the foolish slave, calling her.

÷

Conall was in his chariot. Two swift horses were harnessed to the central shaft. On his arm, he wore a heavy bronze armlet. Befitting his rank, his chariot contained his spear, his shield, and his shining sword. It was driven by his charioteer. Over the sea, he noticed, there was a rainbow.

What was he doing? Even as the chariot came in sight of Dubh Linn and the ford, Conall had not been sure. He was about to conclude that it was all Finbarr's fault, but had checked himself. It wasn't Finbarr's fault. It was the girl's golden hair, and her wonderful eyes. And something else. He didn't know what it was.

Conall had never been in love. He wasn't without any experience of women. The members of the High King's retinue had seen to that. But none of the young women he had met so far had really interested him. He had felt attractions, of course. But whenever he talked to a young woman for any length of time, he always felt as if some invisible barrier had come between them. The women themselves did not always realise this; if the High King's handsome nephew sometimes seemed thoughtful or a little melancholy, they found it attractive. And he wished it were otherwise. It saddened him that he could not share his thoughts and that theirs, in turn, always seemed so predictable.

"You ask for too much," Finbarr had told him frankly. "You cannot expect a young woman to be as deep and wise as a druid."

But it was more than that. Ever since his early childhood, when he had sat alone by the lakes or watched the red sun go down, he had been overcome by a sense of inner communion, a feeling that the gods had reserved him for some special purpose. Sometimes it filled him with ineffable joy; at other times it seemed like a burden. At first he had assumed that everyone felt the same way, and had been quite surprised to discover that they did not. He had no wish to place himself apart. But as the years went by, these sensations had not passed away but had grown. And so it was that, whether he wished it or not, when he gazed into the eyes of some well-meaning girl, he was troubled by an uncomfortable inner voice that said she was a distraction, taking him away from the path of his destiny.

So why was this girl with the strange green eyes any different? Was she just a bigger distraction? He did not think she was different in kind from the other women he had met. Yet somehow the warning voice that usually troubled him, if it had been speaking, had not spoken loudly enough to be heard. He was drawn to her. He wanted to know more. It would have seemed strange indeed to Finbarr that he should have hesitated so long before he had summoned his charioteer, harnessed a pair of his swiftest horses to his light chariot, and, without saying where he was going, set off towards the Ford of Hurdles and the dark pool of Dubh Linn.

And now he found her alone, with only some of the farmhands for company. Her father and brothers had gone out hunting. He saw at once that the farmstead of Fergus was quite a modest one, and that seemed to make his visit easier. If he had called upon an important chief, the news would have travelled all over the island in no time. As it was, he crossed the hurdles, noted privately that they needed repairing, and came quite naturally to the rath of Fergus to ask for refreshment before he continued on his way.

She met him at the entrance. After greeting him politely and apologising for her father's absence, she led him inside and offered him the usual hospitality for a traveller. When the ale was brought, she served him herself. She recalled their meeting at Lughnasa calmly and politely; yet it seemed to him that there was a quiet, laughing look in her eyes. He had forgotten that she was so delightful. And he was just wondering for how long he should prolong his stay when she asked him whether, after crossing the ford, he had looked at the dark pool that gave the place its name.

"I did not," he lied. And when she asked if he would like her to show it to him, he said that he would.

Perhaps it was the fact that the leaves of the oak tree that stood above the pool had turned golden brown, or perhaps it was some trick of the light, but as he stood with Deirdre and looked down the steep bank to its calm surface, Conall had the momentary apprehension that the pool's dark waters were about to draw him in, ineluctably, down into depths without end. Every pool, of course, might be magical. Hidden passages below its waters might lead down into the otherworld. That was why the offerings to the gods of weapons, ceremonial cauldrons, or golden ornaments were so often thrown into their waters. But to Conall at that moment, the dark pool of Dubh Linn seemed to offer him a threat more mysterious, and nameless. He had never experienced such a sense of fear before, and hardly knew what to make of it.

The girl close by his side was smiling.

"We have three wells here, too," she remarked. "One of them is sacred to the goddess Brigid. Would you like to see it?"

He nodded.

They looked at the wells, which were pleasantly situated on the rising ground above the Liffey. Then they walked back across the open turf towards the rath. As they did so, Conall found himself uncertain what to do. The girl did none of the things that other girls did. She neither moved too close, nor brushed against him, nor put her hand upon his arm. When she looked at him, it was only with a pleasant smile. She was friendly; she was warm. He wanted to put his arm round her. But he did not. When they reached the rath, he said he must go.

Was there a hint of disappointment on her face? Perhaps a little. Was he hoping there might be? Yes, he realised, he was.

"It is this way you'll be coming when you return," she suggested. "You should stay with us for longer next time."

"I will do that," he promised. "Soon." Then he called for his chariot and drove away.

⁛

When Fergus came home that evening and Deirdre told him that a traveller had come through, his curiosity was immediate.

"What sort of traveller?" he demanded.

"It was just a man going south. He wasn't here for long."

"And you didn't think to find out anything about him?"

"He was at Carmun at Lughnasa, so he said."

"And so was half of Leinster," he retorted.

"He said he saw us there," she said vaguely, "but I didn't remember." The idea of seeing a stranger not once, but twice, and still knowing nothing of his business was so far from her father's comprehension that he could only stare at her in silence. "I gave him some ale," she said brightly. "Perhaps he'll come back." And at this, to her relief, her father had turned away, moved to his favourite place near his drinking skull, wrapped his cloak around him, and gone to sleep.

For a long time after that, however, Deirdre had remained awake, sitting with her knees drawn up to her chin, thinking about the day that had passed.

She had been proud of herself that morning. When she had first seen Conall approaching she had let out a little involuntary gasp, and then felt herself tremble. It had taken all her concentration and willpower, but by the time he reached the entrance she had herself completely under control. She had not blushed. And she had kept it up the entire time he was there. But had she given him enough encouragement to return? That was the question. The thought of putting him off was even more terrible than making a fool of herself. As they had walked to the pool she had wondered: should she move closer, should she touch him? She thought not. She believed she had done things the right way. But how she would have liked it, on the way back, if he had put his arm round her. Should she have linked her arm in his? Would that have been better? She didn't know.

One thing she did know was that the longer she could keep her father off the scent, the better. Given his love of talk, he was sure to cause her embarrassment. If there was to be any hope for her with the young prince . . .

And why, for her part, was she so interested in the quiet and thoughtful stranger? Because he was a prince? No, it wasn't that.

It was an old tradition that the High King must be a perfect man. He could have no blemish. Everyone knew the story of the legendary king of the gods, Nuadu. When he had lost a hand in battle, he had resigned his kingship. Then he had been given a hand of silver, which eventually turned back into a natural hand. Only then could Nuadu of the Silver Hand be king again. So it was with the High King, supposedly. If the High King wasn't perfect, then he would not be pleasing to the gods. The kingdom would be blighted.

To her it seemed that the handsome warrior, who, she sensed, had been reluctant to meet her at Lughnasa, had this kingly quality. His body was without blemish—she had certainly seen that. But it was his thoughtful manner, the sense of reserve, even private mystery and melancholy about him, that set him apart in her eyes. This man was special. He was not for any thoughtless, coarse-grained woman. And he had come down to Dubh Linn to see her. She was sure of that. The question was: would he return?

The next day the weather was fine. The morning passed uneventfully, as everyone went about their usual business. It was nearly midday when one of the British slaves called out that there were horsemen crossing the ford, and Deirdre went out to see. There were just two of them, in a light cart with a small train of pack-horses. One man she recognised easily. The other, a tall man, she did not know.

The smaller man was Goibniu the Smith.

Conall awoke at dawn. The evening before, after leaving Deirdre, he had crossed the high promontory at the foot of the Liffey's broad bay and, choosing a sheltered spot by a rock, had spent the night on its southern slopes. Now, in the dawn's early glow, he climbed up the rock and gazed southwards at the misty unveiling of the panorama below.

On his right, catching the first gleams of the sun, the gentle hills and volcanic mountains rose into a pale blue sky in which the stars were still departing; on his left, the white mist and silver sheen of the sea. Between these elemental worlds, the great sweep of open country unrolled like a green cloak down the slopes and along the coastline as far as the eye could see until the mists curtailed it. And like a border along the green cloak's edge ran the little cliffs of the shoreline below which the sea spume spread on the distant waiting sands.

Some way down the slopes before him, he saw a fox lope across open grass and disappear into the trees. All around, the dawn chorus filled the air. Far away, by the edge of the sea, he saw the silent shadow of a heron sliding over the water. He felt the faint warmth of the rising sun on his cold cheek, and turned his face eastwards. It was as if the world had just begun.

It was at times like this, when the world seemed so perfect he wished he could open his mouth like the birds around him to give praise, that Conall would find the words of the ancient Celtic poets coming into his mind. And this morning, it was the most ancient of them all whose words came to him—Amairgen, the poet who arrived on the island with the first Celtic invaders when they took it from the divine Tuatha De Danaan. It was Amairgen, stepping ashore on a coastline like this, who uttered the words that became the foundation for all the Celtic poetry since. As well they might— for Amairgen's poem was nothing less than an ancient Vedic mantra of the kind to be found right across the huge Indo-European diaspora from the western Celtic bardic songs to the poetry of India.

> *I am the Wind on the Sea*
> *I am the Ocean Wave*
> *I am the Roar of the Sea*

So the great chant began. The poet was a bull, a vulture, a dewdrop, a flower, a salmon, a lake, a pointed weapon, a word, even a god. The poet was transformed into all things, not just by magic but because all things, atomised, were one. Man and nature, sea and land, even the gods themselves came from one primal mist, and were formed in one endless enchantment. This was the knowledge of the ancients, preserved on the western island. This was what the druids knew.

And this was what he, Conall, experienced when he was alone— the sense of being at one with all things. It was so intense, so important, so precious to him that he was not sure he could live without it.

It was for this reason that now, in the wonderful silence of the sun's rising, he shook his head. For here was the question he could not solve. Did you lose this great communion if you lived side by side with another? Could you share such things with a wife, or did you somehow lose them? An instinct told him that you did, but he was not sure.

He wanted Deirdre. He was sure of that already. He wanted to return to her. But if he did, was he going, in some way as yet unclear, to lose his life?

⁙

He was a good-looking man, you couldn't deny it. Tall, balding, about thirty years old, she guessed, with a face that reminded you of a mountain crag; eyes black but not unkind. They had talked pleasantly enough and after a time, when he had ascertained her likes and dislikes and, she had to suppose, made some judgements about her character—and she certainly didn't think his judgements would be foolish—she saw him give a little look to Goibniu which must have been a signal. For she saw that the smith soon afterwards took her father by the arm and suggested they walk outside.

So that was it. She was about to be married. She had no doubt the offer would be handsome. And, so far as she could tell, her future husband was a fine upstanding man. She could count herself lucky. The only trouble was that, at the moment anyway, she didn't want him.

She rose. He looked a little surprised. She smiled, said she would return in a moment, and went outside.

Goibniu and her father were standing a little way off. They looked expectantly at her, but when she indicated that she wished to speak with her father, he came across.

"What is it, Deirdre?"

"Is it an offer he's making for me, Father?"

"It is. An excellent offer. Is something the matter?"

"No. Not at all. You may tell Goibniu," she smiled towards the smith, "that I like his choice. He seems a good man."

"Ah." Her father's relief was palpable. "That he is." He seemed ready to go back to the smith.

"But I'm wondering," she continued pleasantly, "if there's something I should tell you."

"What is that?"

There was nothing for it now. Whatever the risk, she must take her chance.

"Have you heard of Conall, son of Morna, Father? He's nephew to the High King."

"I have. But I don't know him."

"But I do. I met him at Lughnasa." She paused as he stared at her in amazement. "It was he that came here yesterday. And I think it was me he came to see."

"You are sure? He is serious?"

"How can I tell, Father? We should need time to find out. But I think it is possible. Is there anything that can be done?"

And now the chief who traded cattle smiled.

"Go inside, child," he said, "and leave it to me."

"She does not dislike him?" Goibniu asked sharply upon Fergus's return.

"She came to tell me she likes him," Fergus said smiling, before adding gently, "well enough."

Goibniu nodded briskly.

"Well enough will do. And the price?"

"It is acceptable."

"We'll take her with us now, then."

"Ah. That will not be possible."

"Why is that?"

"I shall need her with me," Fergus said blandly, "through the winter. But in the spring . . ."

"It's in the winter he'll be wanting a woman, Fergus."

"If his intentions are genuine . . ."

"By the gods, man," Goibniu burst out, "he wouldn't be after coming all the way from Ulster to this miserable spot if he wasn't genuine."

"I am glad to hear it," Fergus said solemnly. "And in the spring she shall be his."

Goibniu's one eye narrowed.

"You've another offer."

"Indeed I have not." Fergus paused. "No doubt I could have had. But seeing it was yourself I was dealing with—"

"I do not like to be crossed," Goibniu cut him short.

"She shall be his," Fergus promised. "There's not a doubt of it."

"And you will have to be his, Deirdre," he said to his daughter later, after their visitors had gone, "if your Conall does nothing before the spring."

III

Though Larine was one of the younger druids, he had a reputation for wisdom. The Peacemaker, they called him. So it did not surprise him, when he came one cold, early spring day to the camp by the Ulster coast where the High King was staying, that as soon as they were alone the king should have turned to him and asked, "Tell me your opinion, Larine. What I should do about my nephew, Conall?"

The druid had always liked Conall and in recent months the young prince had confided in him a good deal. He felt a tenderness and loyalty towards him. He had also been concerned by the increasing sadness he sensed in the young man's mind. He answered cautiously, therefore.

"It is my opinion that he is troubled. His duty is to obey you in all things and to honour his father's memory. He wants to do so. But the gods have given him the eyes of a druid."

"You truly believe that he has a druid's gifts?"

"I do."

There was a long silence before the High King spoke again.

"I promised his mother that he should follow his father's footsteps."

"I know," Larine considered. "But did you swear an oath to do so?"

"No," the king said slowly, "I did not. But that is only because, with my own sister, there was no need."

"All the same, you are not bound."

Again, a long silence fell. And if only they had remained alone to talk quietly a little longer, it seemed to Larine that, there and then, the High King might have granted Conall's wish.

So it must have been fate that the queen should have appeared at that moment. And probably there was nothing Larine could have done when, after the usual greetings, she had looked at him thoughtfully through narrowed eyes and demanded to know what they were talking about.

"Conall's desire to be a druid," he answered quietly.

Did she care whether Conall was a druid or not? He saw no reason why she should. Nor, until the High King explained it to him, had he any idea what she meant when she furiously cried, "Not until he has brought me that bull."

"Your uncle has not yet decided," Larine told Conall later.

"And the queen?"

"The queen was angry," the druid admitted.

It was an understatement. Of course, he knew about the queen's temper, but Larine had still been shocked by the way that she had cursed her husband. He had promised to send Conall, she shouted at him, promised her personally. He was a worthless betrayer. Her husband had tried to say something, but she was in full flood and refused to listen. One thing that the druid did gather from her storm of words, however, was the deeper reason for the planned raid: the assertion of royal authority. And here he couldn't deny the queen's point. Others could be sent, but the handsome and untested young Prince Conall was a clever choice to show the royal family's easy supremacy over the impertinent chief. The thing had style. But she had been foolish all the same. If she had spoken calmly and in private, she might have got her way. By shouting and heaping insults on the High King in front of a druid, she made it hard for her husband to give way and keep his dignity. Larine did not tell all this to Conall, however, but reported only: "The High King says he will decide later. He has promised me," he added, "that he will speak to you privately first."

"I knew nothing of this plan to steal the black bull," Conall confessed.

"It is a secret, and you must not let them know I told you." Larine paused. "You could get the bull, Conall, and then ask the High King to release you from your obligations. The queen would have nothing to say then."

But Conall shook his head.

"Is that what you really believe?" He sighed. "I know them, Larine, even better than you. If I succeed in getting the bull, then sure enough, before a month is out, they'll be asking me to do something else. There'll be task after task. Disgrace if I fail; and if I succeed, honour—for myself, of course, but above all for my uncle the High King. There will never be an end of it, until I die."

"It may turn out otherwise."

"No, Larine. That is how it will be. There is only one way to make an end of it, and that is not to begin."

"You cannot refuse to go."

Conall brooded silently awhile.

"Perhaps I can," he murmured.

It would be best, the druid thought, not to tell the High King about that.

Winter had nearly passed, and still he had not come. Some days, Fergus thought, Deirdre looked paler than the moon. Even her brothers noticed she was moody. It was a bad day, her father thought, that I ever took her to the Lughnasa at Carmun. A sad thing, he saw it now, that she had met Conall.

At first he had supposed Conall would come again. Deirdre was no fool; he did not think she had mistaken the young man's interest. Conall cared for her. But time went by and there was no sign of him. The chief even made discreet enquiries about the young prince. He had discovered, and gently warned his daughter about, the druids' geissi that governed Conall's life. "Men who are marked by the fates like that," he cautioned her, "do not always have easy and untroubled lives." But it was clear that such warnings meant nothing to her.

So why hadn't he appeared? There could be many reasons. But as he saw his daughter silently pining, one thought came into his mind again and again, and each time it came, it grew insidiously. For whose fault was it that Conall did not come? It was not the prince's, nor Deirdre's. The fault was his own. Why should a prince like Conall marry the daughter of Fergus? There was no reason at all. If he were a great chief, if he had riches—it might be another matter. But he had none of these.

Other men on the island, of no greater ancestry than he, had joined in the great raids across the sea or gone off fighting, winning riches and renown. But what had he done? Stayed at Dubh Linn, watched over the ford, entertained travellers at his house.

That had been part of the trouble. When travellers came to the house of Fergus, they were well entertained. Fergus would think nothing of slaughtering a pig, or even a heifer, to provide a lavish meal for a guest. The old bard, who would recite to him most evenings, was always generously paid. The families from the out-lying farmsteads, who called him their chief, would always find food and welcome at his house; and if they were behind with the modest tribute of cattle or hides that they owed him, these debts were often forgiven. It was the simple repetition of these modest displays of sta-tus, so essential to his dignity as he saw it, that had led Fergus in re-cent years to contract a number of debts which he kept hidden from his family. He had managed to get by, because the cattle had always saved him. He had an inborn talent as a cattleman and he thanked the gods for it. But his hidden embarrassment gnawed at him, es-pecially since his wife's death, and now the realisation of his failure in life came to torture him.

Yet what am I? he thought. What can men say of me? There goes a man that's proud of his daughter. There's a girl who'll bring her fa-ther a good price. And what have I ever done, that she should be proud of me? Little enough. That was the truth of it. And now there was his daughter in love with a man who wouldn't marry her be-cause of her father.

She never spoke of it. She went about her daily tasks as usual. Sometimes, before midwinter, he had seen her staring across the cold waters by the ford. Once she had walked over to the headland to look at the little island she loved so much. But by winter's end, she no longer looked at anything but what was to hand, unless it was to stare, dully, at the cold, hard ground.

"You're paler than a snowdrop," he said to her one day.

"Snowdrops wilt. I shall not," she answered. "Were you afraid," she suddenly asked with grim humour, "I should fade away before my wedding day?" And when he shook his head: "You'd best be taking me up to my husband in Ulster."

"No," he said gently. "Not yet."

"Conall is not coming." She sounded resigned. "I should be grateful for the good man you found me."

You should be grateful for nothing, he thought. But aloud he said, "There's time enough yet."

Then a few mornings later, telling them that he'd be gone several days and explaining nothing, he mounted his horse and rode away across the ford.

❖

Finbarr listened carefully when Conall told him about the cattle raid, and his feelings about it. Then he shook his head in wonderment.

"There is the difference between us, Conall," he said. "Here am I, a poor man. What wouldn't I give for such a chance? And you, a prince, are dragged to glory against your own will."

"It is you who should lead this raid, Finbarr, not I," Conall replied. "I shall tell my uncle."

"Do not do that," said Finbarr. "It would only bring down trouble on my head." And then, after a pause, he looked at Conall curiously. "Is there anything else," he enquired gently, "that you wish to tell me?"

It had been at the start of winter that he had noticed the change

in his friend's behaviour. Of course, Conall had been moody anyway, but when he had begun to frown, and purse his lips, and stare
vacantly at the horizon, Finbarr had decided that something new
must be disturbing his friend's thoughts. So now, as Conall told him
about the bull, he assumed that this was the secret problem on his
friend's mind. But when he asked, "How long have you known?"
and Conall replied, "Two days," it was clear that the moods he had
noticed must still have been caused by something else. "Are you sure
there is nothing on your mind?" he tried again.

"Nothing at all," said Conall.

And it was just then that a tall and unfamiliar figure strode into
view.

It had taken Fergus some days to find the camp of the High
King, but once he arrived, a man had directed him to Conall at
once. He looked with secret admiration at the handsome prince and
his good-looking companion.

"Greetings, Conall, son of Morna," he said gravely. "I am Fergus,
son of Fergus, and I have something to say to you in private."

"There is nothing that my friend Finbarr may not hear," said
Conall calmly.

"It concerns my daughter, Deirdre," Fergus began, "who you
came to see at Dubh Linn."

"I will hear this alone," said Conall quickly, and so Finbarr left
them. But he had noticed, with surprise, that his friend was blushing.

It did not take Fergus long to tell Conall about Deirdre. When
he spoke of her love for him, he saw Conall look guilty. When he
explained about the offer that Goibniu had arranged, he saw the
prince go pale. He did not press the troubled young man to declare
himself one way or the other, but simply stated, "She will not be
given until the feast of Bealtaine. Then she must be given." And
with that he strode away.

✛

Finbarr smiled to himself. So Conall had gone all the way down to the Liffey to see that girl he had brought to him at Lughnasa. That was what his friend had been brooding about. Not a doubt of it. For once the mysterious druid prince was behaving like a normal man. There was hope for him yet.

He hadn't hesitated to confront his friend as soon as Fergus had left. And this time Conall gave in and told him everything.

"I think," said Finbarr with some pleasure, "that you'll be needing my advice." He looked at him hard. "Do you truly want this girl?"

"Perhaps. I think so. I hardly know."

Bealtaine. The start of May.

"You have only two months," Finbarr pointed out, "to make up your mind."

IV

Goibniu grinned. All over the landscape he could see little parties of people—some mounted or in carts, but mostly leading cattle—making their way towards the single hill that stood in the middle of the plain.

Uisnech: the centre of the island.

Actually, the island had two centres. The royal Hill of Tara, which lay only a short day's journey to the east, was the greatest political centre. But the geographical centre of the land was here at Uisnech. From Uisnech, said the legend, the island's twelve rivers had been formed in a mighty hailstorm. The island's navel, some people called it: the circular hill in the middle of the land.

But Uisnech was far more than that. If Tara was the hill of kings, Uisnech was the hill of druids, the island's religious and cosmic centre. Here lived the goddess Eriu, who had given the island her name. Here, before even the Tuatha De Danaan came, a mystical druid had kindled the first fire, whose embers had been carried to every hearth in the island. Hidden at Uisnech, in a secret cave, was the holy well which contained the knowledge of all things. At the summit of the hill stood the five-sided Stone of Divisions around which lay the sacred meeting grounds of the island's five kingdoms. At this cosmic centre, the druids had their conclaves.

And it was at Uisnech also, each May Day, that the druids held the great assembly of Bealtaine.

Of all the festivals of the Celtic year, the two most magical were surely Samhain, the original Hallowe'en, and the May Day festival called Bealtaine. If the year was split into two halves—winter and summer, darkness and light—then these two festivals marked the junctions. At Samhain, winter began; at Bealtaine, winter ended and summer took over. The eve of each of these two festivals was an especially eerie time. For during that night the calendar entered a kind of limbo, when it was neither winter nor summer. Winter, season of death, met summer, season of life; the world below met the world above. Spirits walked abroad; the dead came to mingle with the living. They were nights of strange presences and fleeting shadows—frightening at Samhain, since they were leading you to death; but at Bealtaine, less fearsome. For the spirit world in summer was only mischievous, and sexual.

Goibniu liked Bealtaine. He might have only one eye, but he was complete in every other way, and his sexual prowess was well known. As he watched the people gathering, he felt a keen sense of anticipation. How long before he had a woman? Not long, he thought. After all, this was Bealtaine.

By evening, there were thousands gathered in the rosy light, waiting for the ascent. There was a faint, warm breeze. The sound of a piper wound its way round the base of the hill. Expectancy was in the air.

Deirdre glanced at her little family. Both her brothers were carrying sprays of green leaves. She should have been doing the same: it was the custom at Bealtaine. But she wasn't in the mood. Her brothers were grinning foolishly. While they were getting their green sprays, an old woman had asked them if they were going to find themselves girls that night. Deirdre had said nothing. Small chance, in her view. Such things happened of course. By the end of the following night, when everyone had been dancing and drinking, there would be all kinds of illicit couplings in the shadows. Young lovers, wives who had slipped away from their husbands, men who had deserted their wives. It was always like that in the May season. Not that she would ever have done such a thing. As the unmarried daughter of a chief, she had her reputation to think of. She couldn't behave like the farmhands or the slave girls. But what about her father? She glanced at him curiously. Since she was, she supposed, about to be leaving home to be married, her father would no longer have a housekeeper. Would he use the festival of Bealtaine to find himself a woman? There was no reason why he shouldn't, though he had given no indication that such a thing might be in his mind. She wondered how she would feel about it.

Without her wishing it, her gaze wandered amongst the crowd. Conall was there somewhere. She hadn't yet seen him; but she knew he must be there. He had not come to look for her. She had seen that the High King was there with a large retinue; but she had not gone to see if Conall was there. If he wanted to find her, let him do so. If not . . . She could wait no longer. Her bridegroom was coming, and he could not be denied.

Perhaps Conall wanted her, but only in the May Day fashion and nothing more than that. Would he approach her, offer her a night of love, and then leave her to her fate? No. He was too fine for that. But what if he did come to her, up on the hill, in the night? What if, like a phantom, he appeared at her side? Touched her? Asked her, in the dark, with his eyes? What if Conall . . . Would she go with him? Would she give herself to him, like a slave girl? The thought of it. She thought of it.

As the sun was going down, the whole crowd started to move up the hill. There were people climbing hills like this all over the island.

On Bealtaine eve, the whole community kept watch together to guard against the evil spirits who were abroad that magical night. The spirits were up to every kind of mischief: they'd steal the milk, give you strange dreams, bewitch you, and lead you astray. Just for their private amusement. But they liked to take you unawares. They were sly. If you were looking out for them, they usually went away. That was why, in the Celtic world, whole communities kept watch all night on the eve of May.

Deirdre sighed. It was going to be a long vigil until the dawn. Despite herself, not meaning to do it, she glanced around once again.

·⫶·

How strange Conall's face seemed in the starlight. One moment, Finbarr thought, it looked as hard as the five-edged stone that stood only forty paces away at the centre of the hilltop. Yet concentrate upon it for a while, and you might think it was dissolving into the darkness. Could Conall's face be melting? No. It was just the faint flickering glimmer of the starlight upon the dew which was forming on all their faces.

Soon they would see the first hint of dawn. Then the sunrise ritual, and after that, in the full light of day, the great ceremony of the fires of Bealtaine. But as yet it was still night. Finbarr had never seen the sky so clear. The stars blazed out of the blackness; the plain around the hill was covered in a thin shroud of ground mist to which the starlight gave a soft sheen so that the Hill of Uisnech with its standing stone seemed to be set on a cloud at the centre of the cosmos.

"I have seen her," he said quietly, so that only Conall could hear.

"Who is that?" Conall asked.

"You know very well it's Deirdre I mean." Finbarr paused, but getting no reaction from Conall he went on: "She is over there." And he pointed away to the right. Conall had turned his head so that his face was a shadow. "Will you not see her?" In the long silence that followed, the stars moved, but Conall did not answer. "You know these are the last days," Finbarr whispered. "Her bridegroom is waiting. Are you not going to do anything?"

"No."

"Shouldn't you tell her?"

"No."

"So you're not interested."

"It is not what I said."

"You are too complicated for me, Conall." Finbarr said no more, but he wondered: Was it some strange self-denial that his friend was practising, as warriors or druids sometimes did? Was it mere hesitation, the fear that most young men have when faced with commitment? Or was it something else? Why was Conall deliberately pushing this girl into the arms of another man? To Finbarr it seemed perverse. But perhaps, even now, there might be something he could do to help his friend. At least he would try.

⁘

Now half the sky was pale. The stars were fading. There was a golden glow along the horizon.

The High King watched intently. At dawnings like this, he could still feel a tingling inside him, as if he were a young man again. But despite the anticipation of the sunrise, his thoughts remained on the serious matter which had occupied them through the night. He had made up his mind some time ago. His plan was complete. Only one piece, minor but important, was missing before he could put it into action.

Two things had to be accomplished. The first, of course, was to obtain a good harvest. He had handled the druids carefully. Gifts, flattery, respect—he had given these liberally. The priests were on his side. Not that you could trust them very far. It was the nature of priests, in his experience, to be vain. But whatever was required for ceremony or sacrifice, he had promised they should have it. They must all pray to the gods for good weather.

The second was to reassert himself. Some measures were easy. The raid to seize the black bull would be a good beginning. His wife, whatever her faults, had been right to insist upon it, and the timing was perfect. But the matter went deeper than that. When a king's authority was eroded, the process soon became so subtle and widespread that it entered every aspect of his life. The disrespectful way his own wife had spoken to him in front of the young druid, though not important, was evidence of this. And to cure this condition he needed more than a mere demonstration of authority. A king must be respected, a High King dreaded. Like a god, he must be unknowable, deeper than his enemies. Deeper than his friends. They must discover that if they flouted his authority, he had let them do so, watched them expose their disloyalty, known their thoughts and actions all the time. Then he must reveal himself in all his power, fierce and awesome as the rising sun.

It was time to strike where they would least expect it, and he knew exactly what he was going to do. He needed just one more piece to put in place. One person whom he had not yet chosen. Who knew, perhaps he would find that person today.

✢

Conall had not spoken during the rest of the night. If his motives were obscure to Finbarr, to him they were clear enough.

His main worry, when he arrived at Uisnech, had concerned the cattle raid. When Larine had spoken to him earlier that year, he had assured Conall that the High King had not reached a decision on the matter and had promised the druid he would speak to his nephew privately before he did so. For weeks he had waited anxiously for his uncle to broach the matter, but his uncle had never done so. He had gradually come to the conclusion that the High King's plans must have changed. And the growing sense of relief he felt over this had encouraged him in his thoughts about becoming a druid.

But there was still the question of Deirdre. Was she part of his priestly destiny? Was he prepared to make the commitment, to take the irrevocable step of going down to Dubh Linn to claim her? Time and again, as the days and months had passed, he had turned that question over in his mind. Yet each time he had thought about the journey, something had held him back. And finally, just before he set off for Uisnech, he had come to the realisation that had given him some peace of mind. If I still have not gone to her, he thought, then it must be that I did not truly want her. And therefore she is not my destiny.

It was just as the sun was about to rise that Finbarr touched his arm.

"We should move over there," Finbarr murmured, pointing to a place a little way to their left. "The view of the sunrise is better there." It hardly seemed to Conall that it would make much difference, but he didn't argue, and so they moved across.

They waited, with all the thousands of others on the slopes of Uisnech, for the magical moment. The horizon was glimmering. The huge orb of the sun was just breaking free from the liquid embrace of the horizon. Its golden glow spread across the misty plain and set the dew on the side of the hill gleaming. And now began one of the most lovely May Day customs of the Celtic world: the bathing in the dew.

Deirdre did not see him as she stooped down, cupped her hands in the shining wetness of the dew, and washed her face. Nearby, another woman was holding her infant child naked, and gently rolling him in the grass. Now Deirdre stood up straight, and her cupped hands once again spread the dew on her face; and then, stretching wide her arms so that she could feel the warmth of the rising sun on her breasts, she tilted back her head, and her breasts lightly rose and fell as if she were breathing in the sunbeams.

Conall stood, and stared. Finbarr watched his face. Then, realising that Finbarr had tricked him, with a scowl at his friend, Conall turned round and walked away.

⊹

The heat was intense. The line of cattle was long. They had been kept in pens for the night and now they were being led, one by one, towards the fires. They did not like it. The roar of the fires ahead frightened them. A line of smaller fires, arranged like a funnel, guided them to the two great bonfires between which they must pass. They started to bellow; some had to be goaded. But the most fearsome sight, at least to human eyes, was not the burning fire but the strange figures who gathered like a flock of huge, fierce birds just beyond the blazing gateway.

It was the same all across the world. From the druids of Ireland to the shamans of Siberia, from the Persian temples of Mithras to the medicine men of North America, at the time of sacred rituals, those who communed with the gods in trances put on cloaks of feathers. For the plumage of birds was nature's richest array, and contained more than a hint, no doubt, that holy men could fly.

At the ceremonies of Bealtaine, the druids of Uisnech wore huge, brightly coloured cloaks with high bird's-head crests that made them seem almost half as tall again. As each beast was led between the purifying fires, they splashed it with water. This was the May Day ritual that should ensure the health of the all-important live-stock in the coming year.

Larine was standing beside an older druid. His attention should have been on the line of cattle. There were only fifty to go. It was hot work at the fire, and with so many cattle, the druids had taken turns. His turn had finished some time ago and he had taken off the heavy cloak of feathers. But now, while the older druid continued to watch the fires, his own eyes strayed to the plain around the hill.

For Larine had things on his mind. The first, and surely the least important, was a rumour—hardly even a rumour, really, more a whisper on the horizon. He had heard it the month before.

It concerned the Christians.

He knew that there had been Christians on the western island for a generation now. They were small communities—a chapel here, a farmstead there, a scattering of missionary priests ministering to the Christian slaves in the area and, if they were lucky, to some of their masters. As a well-informed druid, Larine had made it his business to know something about them. He had even made the acquaintance of a Christian priest down in south Leinster, with whom he had discussed the Christian doctrine in some detail. And it was the priest who had told him, the previous month, about the rumour.

"They say that the bishops in Gaul are planning to send a new mission to the island to enlarge the community, perhaps make an approach to the High King himself." The priest had been uncertain of the details. Even the names of the missionaries to be sent were unclear. "But they say the Holy Father himself has sanctioned the mission."

The mighty Roman Empire had adopted Christianity as its state religion a century ago. For several generations, therefore, the druids of the western island had been aware that they were the last, isolated stronghold of the old gods beside the vast territories of the Christian Roman Empire. But there were several factors which had given them comfort. The Christianity of the empire was by no means complete: there had still been important pagan temples in Britain, and within living memory the emperor Julian had actually tried to reverse the process and return the empire to its proper pagan tradition. In any case, the western island was protected by the sea. And with the withdrawal of Roman garrisons from Britain and Gaul, there seemed no chance at all that Rome could trouble the realm of the High King now. Without Roman troops, what could the Christian priests do? The little communities in the south of the island were tolerated because they gave no trouble. If any Christian missionary came to trouble the High King, the druids would soon deal with him.

He had said as much to the priest, and perhaps he had said it too bluntly; for the priest had become irritated, muttered words to the effect that it wasn't so long since the druids had performed human sacrifices, and told Larine that he should remember how the prophet Elijah had vanquished the pagan priests of Baal. "He came to their festival," the priest declared, "and built a great fire which burst into flame when he prayed to the Lord, while the priests of Baal could not get theirs to light at all. So take care," he had added severely, "that the missionaries of the true God do not come to shame you at Bealtaine."

"The fires of Bealtaine burn brightly," Larine had replied. The Christian, he judged, was a victim of wishful thinking.

Yet something, he could not say what, had troubled him about the conversation. A vague apprehension. Absurd though it was, he had even glanced about once or twice to see if any of the Christian priests had decided to come to make a nuisance of themselves. But of course they had not. The fires of Bealtaine were burning brightly. As he scanned the horizon, he saw nothing to disturb the sacred ceremonies of the day.

If a feeling of unease continued to afflict him, he decided that it must be on account of the second and more serious of his concerns.

Conall. The prince had just appeared in the crowd that lined the other side of the pathway along which the cattle were led after passing between the fires. He was standing behind the front row, but his height gave him a good view of the fires at which, like the rest of the crowd, he was staring. He did not see Larine. It seemed to the young druid that, while everyone else was obviously enjoying the festivities, Conall's face looked tense.

Several of the beasts being led through the fires were especially fine. Instead of bringing whole herds, farmers who had come a long distance might only bring their best animal, usually a bull, to serve as proxy for the rest. And just now a splendid brown bull was being led through by a tall figure and a girl. The man was a minor chieftain of some sort, Larine guessed, a handsome old fellow with long moustaches. But the girl, with her golden hair, was striking. The druid looked at her with appreciation. Her face was flushed red from the heat of the fire; so were her bare arms. He had the impression that her whole body was glowing. Conall seemed to have noticed the pair as well, for he was staring at them. What a contrast his taut, white face made, the druid thought, with the girl's ruddy glow: like a pale sword before a smithy's furnace. The girl, if she saw Conall, walked straight past without looking at him. She probably did not know who he was. Then another beast came through the fire, and the druid turned his eyes to that. But a few moments later he observed that Conall was still staring straight ahead and looking more like a ghost than ever.

He turned to the older druid beside him.

"What is your opinion of Conall?"

"Why is it you ask?"

"I am concerned about him."

"Ah." The druid glanced at him sharply. "And what is it, Larine," she asked, "that you wish to know?"

Though most druids were men, there had always been female druids, too. Such women, often gifted with second sight and admitted to the mysteries of druidism, could be fearsome. If kings feared the rebuke of the druid men, the scorn of the female druid could be even more dangerous. And this old woman was formidable.

Larine looked down at her thin face. It was wrinkled now. Her hair, which fell almost to her waist, was grey, but her eyes, which were of the palest blue, might have belonged to a young woman and were strangely translucent, as if you could walk through them. As briefly as he could, he tried to answer her. Would his friend find happiness? Would he become a druid? But as he asked, she only shrugged impatiently.

"Foolish questions."

"Why?"

"The fate of Conall is already foretold. It is in his geissi."

Larine frowned. Whatever else you might say, Conall had always been a careful man.

"You know he never wears red because the colour is unlucky in his family. I cannot think he will break any of the geissi."

"Yet he must break them, Larine, since he cannot die until he has."

"That is true," Larine agreed, "but that is far in the future; and it's the present I'm worried about."

"How do you know? Is it for you to decide such things, Larine? As a druid you should know better." She paused and gave him a sharp look. "This I will tell you, and no more. Your friend Conall will break the first of the geissi very soon."

As he stared at the old woman's eyes and then at his friend's pale face, Larine felt a cold shiver pass through him. She had second sight.

"How soon?"

"Three days. Ask no more."

✤

Finbarr was feeling pleased with himself. The cattle had all been led through the fires. The High King's feast would be starting soon. And hadn't he just done Conall a huge favour? Yes, he had. He'd done the right thing. And if his friend didn't rise to the occasion this time . . . Well, he'd done his best.

The High King's feast was no small affair. Starting in early afternoon it would stretch far into the night. A large banqueting hall with wicker sides had been set up. Inside were trestle tables and benches for three hundred people. There would be pipers and harpists, dancers and bards to give recitations. The great chiefs and druids, the law-keepers and the noblest warriors would all be present. Conall, too, of course. Thirty of the most highly born young women, daughters of chiefs every one, were to serve the mead and ale to the company.

And this was where Finbarr had done so well. For Deirdre was to be one of them. It had been a favour from the woman in charge of the girls. Then a quick interview with Fergus and his daughter. Deirdre had held back, embarrassed, but her father had ordered her to do it. Even now she had no idea that she would be directed to serve ale to Conall. Finbarr had made sure of that, too. And more than this, he told himself, he could not do.

-‡-

Noon had passed and the feast had begun when Goibniu the Smith made his way towards the banqueting hall. He was in a very bad temper. The reason was simple: he had failed to get a woman.

He had found one the day before. A handsome buxom woman, wife of a farmer from Leinster. At dusk she had told him, "My husband's sticking like glue. Wait a while." Later in the night she had come and whispered, "Meet me over there, by that thornbush, at dawn." And that had been the last he saw of her—until a short while ago when he had observed her on the arm of a tall man who was certainly not the farmer from Leinster. It had been too late to do anything by then. Those who wanted to find partners had already done so. One girl had approached him, but she was so plain that it offended his pride. He'd been made a fool of, he was tired, and he was frustrated. Another man might have decided to get drunk. But that is not what Goibniu did. His single eye remained watchful. And just now, a moment ago, it had caught sight of something else that reminded him of business.

The big fellow from Dubh Linn. The one with the daughter he'd sold. There was no sign of the girl though. Goibniu went up to him.

What was it about Fergus that made the clever craftsman suspicious? Goibniu did not bother to analyse it. He did not need to. But from the first words of greeting, from the chief's ready smile, from the cheerful way, when asked if Deirdre was there, he replied, "She is, she is," Goibniu knew that something was wrong. His brow darkened.

"I'll be taking her with me, then."

"To be sure, you will. Not a doubt of it."

Fergus was being too obliging. He had to be lying. It was not often that the cunning smith allowed his temper to get the better of him, but the experience of the previous night had affected his judgement. With a sudden burst of irritability in which his contempt was plain, he burst out: "Do you take me for a fool? She is not here at all."

It was the visible contempt which hurt Fergus. He drew himself up to his full height and glared balefully down at Goibniu.

"Is it to insult me you came here?" he demanded with some heat.

"I couldn't care less," the smith retorted, "whether I've insulted you or not."

And now, as his face became suffused with blood, it would have been obvious to anyone who knew him that Fergus, son of Fergus, was about to become very angry indeed.

She knew she looked well. She could see it in the curious glances of the other girls as they all swept in their flowing gowns across the grass to the entrance to the banqueting hall. And why shouldn't I look fine, she thought, for weren't my ancestors as good as theirs? She felt like a princess anyway, whatever they might think.

She hadn't wanted to do this. She had been so embarrassed and mortified when Finbarr had come to her father. "I can't," she had cried. How was it going to look if she turned up where she wasn't supposed to and pushed herself in front of him for all to see? But they had made her, and having got so far, she was determined about one thing. She wasn't going to take any special notice of him. He could take notice of her if he pleased. She'd hold her head high and let the other men see her for the princess she was. Didn't she already have a husband waiting for her anyway? It was with this thought firmly in her mind that she stepped through the entrance into the banqueting hall.

It was a rich smell that pervaded the air: ale and mead, stewed fruits, and, above all, the aroma of well-fatted roasted beef. In the centre of the hall was a huge cauldron full of ale. On tables beside it, small bowls of mead. Around the walls ran the tables where the company sat. Reds and blues, green and gold—the bright dress and gleaming ornaments of the chiefs and their wives gave the hall a splendid air. There was conversation and laughter, but the gentle strains of the three harpists in the corner could still be heard.

She felt the eyes of the men upon her as soon as she entered, but she didn't mind. She went about her business, moving gracefully, pouring ale and mead as required, with a polite word or a pleasant smile but, apart from that, scarcely troubling to look into their faces at all. Once she had to pass in front of the High King himself, and she was aware, out of the corner of her eye, of his swarthy figure, which she found rather distasteful, and of the large presence of the queen. They were both deep in conversation and she was careful not to stare at them. Indeed, she was kept so busy that at first she hardly noticed when she was directed to serve at the place where Conall was sitting.

How pale he looked, how serious. She served him exactly as she had everyone else, even gave him a smile.

"I am glad to see you, Deirdre, daughter of Fergus." His voice was gentle, grave. "I did not know you were to be at the banquet."

"It was as much a surprise to myself, Conall, son of Morna," she answered pleasantly. Then she swiftly passed on without looking at him again.

She had to return to the table several times, but they did not speak again. Once she saw his uncle the High King beckon him to come over, but then her attention was distracted by a piper who began to play.

⁕

Conall returned from the interview with the High King feeling disconcerted. Under those heavy, swarthy black brows, his uncle's eyes, dark blue and somewhat bloodshot, glittered in a way that made you realise he had missed nothing.

"So Conall," he had begun. "It is the feast of Bealtaine, yet you are sad."

"It is only the way my face looks."

"Hmm. Who is that girl—the one you spoke to? Have I seen her before?" In answer, Conall explained as best he could who she was and about her father, the chief at Dubh Linn. "This Fergus is a chief, you say?"

"It is true." Conall smiled. "A small one. His ancestors were of some note."

"It's a fine-looking daughter he has, anyway. Is she betrothed?"

"There is an agreement, I believe. Someone in Ulster."

"But," the king's eyes looked up shrewdly, "it's for yourself you'd like her?"

Conall had felt himself blush. He couldn't help it.

"Not at all," he had stammered.

"Hmm." His uncle had nodded, then ended the conversation; though after he had returned to his seat, he had noticed the king give Deirdre a thoughtful glance. Was his uncle giving him a message? Hinting that he should marry her? At the very least he was telling him that his love for the girl was obvious. And wasn't he now, whatever his reasons, in the act of letting her marry another? Without the decency of giving her even a word of explanation? There was no denying it. And why was he doing this? Was it really what he wanted?

For a while he sat there, speaking to no one. Then at last he looked up and saw that she was approaching. She came so close that if he reached out his hand, he could have touched her golden hair.

"Deirdre, daughter of Fergus." He said the words quietly, but she heard them. She turned her head. Did he see, just for a moment, a look of pain in her wonderful eyes? "I must speak with you. Tomorrow morning. At dawn."

"As you wish." She looked hesitant.

He nodded. Nothing more. And she was just moving away when the shouting began.

All heads turned; druids frowned; the High King glared; even the piper ceased. On the sacred site of Uisnech, at the feast of Bealtaine, someone was daring to disturb the High King's peace.

The shouts continued. Then there was silence. One of the king's personal attendants came into the banqueting hall and said something to the king, who gave a bleak nod. And a few moments later two figures were ushered in. The first, looking irritable but cautious, was Goibniu the Smith. Behind him, the very picture of an affronted chief, stalked Fergus. Conall glanced across to where Deirdre was now standing and saw her go very pale. When the two of them were in front of him, the king spoke. He did so quietly, to Goibniu first.

"The quarrel?"

"I had words with this man."

"About?"

"His daughter not being here. She is promised to a man in Ulster, and I am to take her there. Then," he glanced contemptuously at Fergus, "the fellow struck me."

The High King turned his eyes on Fergus. So this was the chief from Dubh Linn. One glance and he understood Fergus entirely.

"Yet as you see, his daughter is here." He indicated Deirdre. Goibniu looked and registered astonishment. "What have you to say, Fergus?"

"That the man called me a liar," Fergus said hotly, and then, more humbly, "but that my daughter is worthy of a prince and now I have brought disgrace upon her."

Out of the corner of his eye the king saw several of the great nobles give the poor, proud chief a look of approval. He rather agreed.

"It seems, Goibniu," the king said gently, "that you were mistaken about the girl. Is it possible, do you think, that you were mistaken also about the blow? Perhaps you only thought he was about to strike you?" And the king's dark blue eyes looked up at the smith steadily.

Whatever Goibniu was, he was never stupid.

"It may have been so," he conceded.

"You might have been confused."

"Confused. That would be it."

"Take your place at our feast, Goibniu. Forget this matter. As for you," he turned to Fergus, "you will wait Fergus, son of Fergus, for me outside. For it may be that I have something to say to you." And with that, he gave a nod to the piper, who began to blow his pipes at once, and the banquet resumed.

But as the festivities continued, and Fergus waited outside, and Deirdre, uncertain what the king had in mind for her poor father, did her best to attend to her duties, no one present, glancing at the bushy eyebrows and red face of the island's monarch, had any idea what in truth was passing in his mind.

It was perfect, he thought. His plan was now complete. He had only to see this fellow from Dubh Linn and the trap for them all was set. What an unlikely bearer of good fortune the gods had sent. He would make the announcements at the height of the feast. At sundown.

⁜

Late that afternoon, in front of an amused crowd, a small ceremony took place, witnessed by one of the senior druids.

With a decent show of politeness, Fergus and Goibniu stood facing each other. At the druid's order, Goibniu went first. Pulling open his shirt, he bared his chest for Fergus who solemnly stepped forward, placed one of the smith's nipples in his mouth, and sucked it for a moment or two. Then, stepping back, he offered his own chest, and Goibniu stepped up and returned the compliment. After this, both men nodded to the other and the druid pronounced the ceremony complete. For this, upon the island, was the way that two men who had quarrelled sealed their reconciliation. Fergus and the smith, whatever their differences, were now linked by a bond of friendship. Other lands sealed such bargains with a handshake, or the smoking of a pipe, or the mingling of blood. On the island it was done by kissing the nipple.

It was done upon the express order of the High King. For nothing, he told them, was to mar the peace and general happiness of the royal banquet.

⁘

They stood, Conall and Finbarr, at the top of Uisnech. The sun was on the horizon and its fiery light put a red glow on Conall's pale face as he turned to his friend and said they should go down. It was time to return to the feast. And now, having stood in silence for so long, Finbarr ventured, "Did you see the girl?"

"I saw the girl."

"And what will you do?"

"It was you who arranged for her to be at the banquet?" Conall had just realised.

"It was. Do you forgive me?"

"It was the right thing to do." Conall smiled gently. "Will you always be my good friend, Finbarr, whatever happens?"

"I will," Finbarr promised. "So what will you do about Deirdre?"

"Ask me tomorrow."

Finbarr sighed. He knew it was useless to pursue the matter further. Instead, he reached out his hand and gave his friend's arm an affectionate squeeze.

They came down the hill as the darkness fell. Torches were being lit around the base. As they made their way towards the banquet they saw an old druid woman, who gave a nod to Conall, which Conall politely returned. By the entrance to the hall they parted and Finbarr watched his friend go in. A moment later he saw Fergus and his daughter also enter. The chief looked cheerful now. Obviously the High King had taken pity on him; but it seemed to Finbarr that Deirdre looked strangely unwell.

⁘

The High King stood, and the banqueting hall fell silent.

He began quietly, a slight smile on his heavyset face, and welcomed them to what was always a happy occasion. He thanked the druids. He thanked the chiefs for the loyal tribute they had paid. Indeed, he remarked, he was glad to say that there had not been a defaulter anywhere on the island. He paused.

"Except for a man in Connacht." They were all watching him now. Watching for signs and signals. Slowly he allowed a look of wry amusement to form on his face. "It seems he was out when we called."

There was laughter. So, the High King was amused. But what was he going to do? The look of amusement lingered just long enough to become threatening.

"My nephew Conall," he nodded towards the pale prince, "together with some others, will be paying him a visit." He glanced around the hall. "They'll be leaving at dawn." He gave them all a friendly nod. He turned to his wife and nodded to her. Then he sat down.

There had been a tiny intake of breath around the room. Now there was laughter, nervous for a moment, then more robust. Men began rapping on the tables in applause. "At Bealtaine," a voice called out. "The Connacht man will not be expecting that." More laughter. "He'll be sorry he wasn't there before."

He had them. It was the firm smack of authority, mixed with devious cunning. They respected that. They liked the grim humour of the thing. And when, instead of tribute, the prize bull itself was brought back, the whole island would admire his revenge. Some, who knew of Conall's desire to be a druid and his distaste for such ventures, saw deeper. Even the favourite nephew must bow his head under the royal yoke. "The king is right, though," these murmured. "It had to be done."

The High King glanced across to where poor Conall was standing. His nephew looked shocked. No doubt Larine had told the young man of his promise to consult him before taking such a decision. Well, that was too bad. It would be a lesson to Larine and his nephew. Kings use princes: they should both know that. Besides, his uncle considered, the young man seemed so uncertain what he really wanted that by sending him out like this he might be doing the boy a favour. Then he looked at his wife. She was beaming at him, as he had hoped and expected. She had got her way. He smiled back at her.

There was some surprise, a little while later, when he rose again to speak. Perhaps someone was to be honoured. They listened politely.

"I have a further announcement to make. A happy one." He looked round them slowly so that they knew clearly that happiness was a requirement.

"As you know, I have been fortunate indeed to have the company of my lovely wife for many years." He inclined his head towards her, and there was a murmur of not entirely heartfelt assent. "However," he continued, "it is the custom amongst us, from time to time, to take an extra wife." A deathly hush fell now. "And so I have decided, in addition to my dear wife, to marry again."

There was a gasp. All eyes turned on the queen, who looked stunned, as if she'd been hit by a rock. Husbands, who knew about her domineering ways, glanced at each other. Wives, some of them, were shocked. Yet not a few had suffered at the queen's hands at one time or another. And in just a moment or two, all round the hall, like mist condensing in droplets on the leaves of the trees, the communal thought was forming itself: she had it coming to her.

But who was the bride? At a sign from the king, they now saw a tall figure step forward, with long moustaches, accompanied by a handsome girl who, until shortly before, had been serving the ale and mead. People looked at each other. What did this mean?

"Deirdre, daughter of Fergus, son of Fergus, of Dubh Linn," announced the king. And smiling at Deirdre, he drew Fergus close and put his arm round the older man's shoulder so that the chief, who now looked as pleased as if he'd defeated an army single-handed, found himself held, by his kingly son-in-law, in a grip like a vice.

It was Goibniu, while the company was still collecting its thoughts, who quickly rose to his feet and raising his beaker called out, "Long life, good health, to our king and to Deirdre." To which the company, having seen which way the wind was blowing, assented with a friendly roar.

From under his bushy eyebrows the High King watched them all. He could have divorced the queen. Divorce was common and easy on the western island. But that would have offended her family, who were important, whereas by choosing an extra bride, he merely cut her down to size. The masterstroke lay in his choice. While any man on the island might take extra wives, a king had to be careful. Choose the daughter of one great chief and you offended all the others. You could have concubines, of course, but that was not his purpose. Marriage was a balance of power, whether you liked that fact or not. He had needed to undercut the queen and he had done it. The cleverness of the choice was that the girl was noble and looked a princess, but that her father was of no account at all. Lord of a marsh, a no-man's-land, a deserted ford.

The prospective husband in Ulster would give no trouble. He would send one of his men to give the fellow a generous present. The Ulster man would understand: a High King took priority. As for Goibniu, the High King had already secretly compensated the cunning smith for his loss of a marriage fee late that afternoon. So everyone who needed to be was happy; except perhaps Conall and the girl.

"The marriage feast will be tomorrow evening," he said.

✢

It was dark that night; the stars had hidden their faces behind the clouds. Not even a pinpoint of light was offered from above to help Deirdre as she groped her way through the blackness that, creeping close, seemed to pore over her, smothering in its attentions.

Sometimes she felt the ox-hide flaps of the wagons and other temporary shelters that dotted the grounds; several times she disturbed sleeping bodies wrapped in their cloaks. She heard snores or other more intimate murmurs all around. Her father was back in the hall, lying contentedly in sleep along with fifty others. But she could not bear to remain there, and so she had left him, gone out past the dying torches, and begun to wander towards the place where their cart should contain her two younger brothers. It was strange that, in this moment of crisis, she should have sought out the comfort of their two, probably drunken bodies; but at least they were her family. For better or worse, that was something. One last night with her family.

And then? Marriage to the king. She didn't blame her father. There was nothing he could have done about it. She didn't even blame him for being so pleased. It was natural. And how could she tell him that, as she stood with him facing the king, she had felt nothing but a physical horror? It wasn't just that the High King could have been her father. Older men could be attractive. But his swarthy face with its bloodshot eyes, his thickening body, the hands which, to her, seemed like hideous hairy paws, all filled her with revulsion. Would she really have to offer her body to him the following night? Was this the only loving she was ever to know, year after year, until he died? Or she did? It had taken all the self-control she possessed, in front of that company, not to shudder openly. Even the man from Ulster, she had thought bitterly, would not have been so bad. He hadn't repelled her. She could probably have learned to love him.

And Conall? What had he been planning to say to her in the morning? Had he decided, after waiting so long, to ask for her in marriage after all? The thought was so painful she could hardly bear it. Useless. Too late.

It seemed to her now that, in the blackness ahead, she could just make out the shape of their cart. She moved forward cautiously. She reached it. Yes. She was sure this was the one. She listened for the sound of her brothers' snores. She started to raise the leather flap at the back.

And froze, as a hand clamped onto her arm.

"Out walking?" The voice was a low hiss. She gave a little gasp
and tried to break free, but the grip on her arm was too strong. "I've
been waiting for you." This time the voice was more like a growl.
She still wasn't sure who it was who held her so fast. Only with the
next words did she realise. "You think you can challenge me?"

It was the queen.

"No." She stammered it out. In her misery and fear she had forgotten about the queen. "This was no choice of mine," she said
hoarsely.

"Little fool." She could feel the queen's breath on her cheek. It
smelt of ale, stale. "Do you think I shall let you live? Speak softly
now. Do you?"

"I . . ." Deirdre wanted to say something, but no words came.

"Poison, drowning, an accident . . ." the terrible hiss went on.
"Easy to arrange. If you marry the king, young lady, I can promise
you, it's not a month you'll live. Do you understand?" The grip on
her arm was now so tight it was all Deirdre could do not to cry out.

"What can I do?" her whisper was almost a wail.

"I will tell you." The queen's lips pressed against her ear. "Flee,
young Deirdre. Flee for your life. Flee from Uisnech. Flee from
Dubh Linn. Run to a place where no one can find you. Run tonight
and never stop running. For if the king finds you he will bring you
back; and if he does, I will have your life. Run."

The grip was suddenly relaxed. There was a rustling sound; and
then the queen was gone.

Deirdre gasped for breath. She was shaking violently. She wanted
to run, somewhere, anywhere, to a place of safety. It was no good
going to her brothers or her sleeping father. She started to move,
hurrying, tripping, almost running, she hardly knew where until in
the darkness she found a path that seemed to lead somewhere. The
path was rising. There was a sweet smell of long grasses. And then,
above, a handful of stars burst through the clouds and she realised
that she was climbing the Hill of Uisnech.

✜

Conall sat with his back against the big five-sided stone and stared blankly ahead from the top of Uisnech into the darkness. His mood was as black as the night.

First that announcement about the cattle raid. It was the intent behind the thing which so enraged him. Instead of speaking with him beforehand as he had promised Larine, his uncle had made a public announcement that left Conall in an impossible position. Any argument would now be a defiance of the High King. His uncle had meant to outmanoeuvre him, use him, treat him with a cynical contempt. He hated him for it.

But even this was nothing compared to the shock of the second announcement. Deirdre was gone. At this last moment, after the months of difficulty, of agonising, his love was suddenly impossible. She belonged to the High King. She was unobtainable. Clearly she didn't want his uncle. A glance at her face had told him that.

As he had contemplated the terrible fact that she could never be his, Conall had experienced a new and intense emotion. It was as if his doubts had never been. Deirdre. He could hardly take his eyes from her. All the rest of that evening, whenever she was in the hall, he had found himself watching her every gesture. She, for her part, had never looked at him. How could she? Although once, when he had been turning away, he thought he had caught sight of her glancing in his direction. Would she still try to meet him at dawn? Probably not. What could they say? He was not sure. But even after he had left the banquet, the sense of her presence had stayed with him, like a shadow.

And then, behind the stone, he heard a faint sound, and a shadow came and sank to rest against the other side so that, had he wished, he could have reached his hand across to touch it; and next the shadow started softly weeping, before, in a voice he recognised, it murmured: "she will kill me." And then, realising who it was, and trying not to startle her, he whispered, "Deirdre."

It was not long before he was holding her in his arms. Soon she had told him about her interview with the queen.

"Tell me, Conall, what I should do," she cried. "How can I run, and where would I be running to, with the king looking for me, and myself all alone in the world?" Then, tearfully, "Is she really meaning to kill me? Tell me it is not true."

But Conall was silent. For he knew the queen.

So for some time they remained there, she trembling in his arms, while he, afraid for her, too, considered the impossibilities of his own life. Until at last he came to a decision. And as soon as he had made it, he felt a huge new warmth in his heart and a sense of exultation that seemed to him to fill his world with a visionary light. At last, he thought with relief, at last, he knew what he must do.

"We'll run together," he said then, "if need be, to the end of the world."

÷

Finbarr waited nervously, while Fergus hesitated.

"Well?" The High King fixed the man from Dubh Linn with an unyielding stare.

The answer to the first question—Did he know anything of his daughter's plan to run away?—had been easy. He did not. Indeed, Fergus had been horrified, and the fact was obvious. But did he know that Conall was courting Deirdre? He decided honesty was the best policy.

"It would have been a fine thing for me," he confessed, "but it was hard to tell if he was serious. He never came for her," he explained.

They were all turning to Finbarr now: the king, the queen, the two chiefs who had been summoned to the banqueting hall that morning. So Finbarr did the only sensible thing. He told them what he knew of Conall's feelings, and how he himself had arranged for Deirdre to encounter Conall at the feast the day before. Bowing his head respectfully to the king—and trying not to look at the queen—he added: "I had no knowledge, then, of your interest in her." To his relief, the king accepted this with a brief nod.

"It's clearly with Conall the girl's run away," the king concluded.

Nobody spoke. Given the insult to his pride and authority, Finbarr considered, you had to admire the king's calmness. But the king was also looking thoughtful. "I am wondering," he said quietly, "if there may have been some other reason that caused them to run away." They all looked at each other. Nobody knew. The queen's face was impassive. Then she cut in.

"What about that bull?"

"Ah. The bull." The king glanced around. "Finbarr shall fetch it." He gave Finbarr a cold look. "Be sure you succeed," he added.

Finbarr again bowed his head. The message was clear. The king accepted that he was not directly to blame and was even giving him a chance to distinguish himself. But if he failed to bring the king what he needed, he could expect an end to all favours.

"And the runaways?" It was one of the chiefs who spoke.

"Take fifty men," the king answered shortly, "and find them. Bring the girl back."

"And Conall?"

The king looked at him, surprised.

"Kill him," he said.

TWO

TARA

I

THE FIRST NIGHT had been kind to them. They had taken
two strong, swift mounts and two good packhorses. They
prepared in a hurry; Conall had not taken his sword or spear, but
only a hunting knife; he also brought a small bar of silver, concealed
in his belt. It was deep night when they made their way out of the
encampment where everyone was sleeping. It would probably be
long after dawn before anyone even noticed their absence. And
though their pursuers would no doubt move fast, they would not
know which way they had gone.

Which way should they go? Up into the wilds of Connacht?
Over into Ulster, where they could find a ship across to Alba? No,
Conall decided: that would be the first thing the king would think
of; within days he'd have spies on the lookout in every harbour. If
they wanted to escape across the sea, they'd better wait. So where
could they evade the long arm of the High King?

"Our best hope lies south," he told her. "In Munster." The huge,
lovely coastline of the south-west, with its innumerable hills, inlets,

and islands, gave endless opportunities for concealment, as well as being less under the control of the High King than any other part of the island.

Through the first night, they took the track southwards. The country was flat, the forest frequently broken by open pasture. As dawn broke they found a landscape around them of empty bog and continued cautiously for a little while, fording a small river, until they reached some dry ground, where they rested. It was already early afternoon when Deirdre awoke, to find Conall standing beside her. "I've scouted ahead," he told her. "We should keep moving on."

All afternoon they rode carefully. The island's main tracks were usually kept passable. In many places, the undergrowth beside them was so thick that it was only the work of a few moments to find concealment; but this meant that the tracks were the only way to travel. And so even in the least populated areas, there was always the risk of meeting someone on the road. Once, they came to some undulating heathland, where they encountered an empty shepherd's hut. Later, discovering there was a farmstead ahead, they made a wide circuit to avoid being seen; but the branches whipping across their faces made progress so slow that they lost valuable time. It was midafternoon when they came over a ridge and Conall paused. "There." He pointed southwards. And in the distance Deirdre could just make out a long, thickly wooded range of hills rising up out of the plain. "The Slieve Bloom Mountains," he explained. "If we can reach them tomorrow without being seen, we'll be hard to find." And they were well within sight of them when, at nightfall, they wrapped themselves in their cloaks and lay down under the stars. Deirdre remained awake for some time, however, and when she did fall asleep, her sleep was fitful. Twice during the night, she thought she heard the distant howling of wolves.

Deirdre woke at the first grey glimmer of dawn and shivered. A cold, damp breeze had sprung up. Conall was already awake, and nodded to her. "It will be raining soon. That's good, as we have to cross some open ground."

The rain was not heavy, but it persisted all morning, screening them as they followed a track that led across open grassland and heath until, around the middle of the day, it began to rise up a long slope. Trees appeared on either side, the track began to twist, and Deirdre realised with relief that they had reached the safety of the mountains. Soon after this, the rain began to clear, and from the occasional rocky outcrops she could see magnificent views of the countryside spreading out below. They paused and she discovered that she was very hungry. She had brought bread and meat with them when they left. Some of each remained. Now, sitting by a small mountain stream, they ate the last of the meat and drank water from the stream, which tasted sweet.

"From here," Conall said, "we can follow the forest tracks deep into Munster."

"And what will we be eating, may I ask?" she enquired.

"I saw a hare." He smiled ruefully. "Hazelnuts will keep you going. There are fish in the rivers, and deer in the woods. I could go down to one of the farmsteads, tell them I'm a poor traveller and beg a little bread."

"You'd better not be wearing that cloak then," she laughed. "Or even be seen with it," she added more seriously. "It's the cloak of a prince."

And as Conall looked at his cloak, its rich material and its trimming of fur, he knew she was right.

"What a fool I am," he exclaimed, "running across the country with a thing like this." He shook his head, went to one of the packhorses and pulled out a light axe. Then, scraping away some leaves from a bare spot behind a tree, he began to dig a shallow pit. It wasn't long before he had dug a good enough trench to receive the cloak, covered it over, and scattered the leaves across the place again. Satisfied with his work, he returned, replaced the axe, and gave her a smile.

"So, you've buried your fine clothes now, have you?" She returned his smile.

"Yes." But suddenly the smile left his face and he looked thoughtful.

"What is it?" she asked.

"Nothing," he said. "Nothing of importance. Shall we ride on?"

And then she remembered the three geissi of which her father had told her.

Conall shall not die until:
>   He has laid his own clothes in the earth.
>   He has crossed the sea at sunrise.
>   He has come to Tara through a black mist.

He had just broken the first.

She started, a little uncertainly, to say something. But he was already riding ahead.

⁛

Only one thing puzzled Deirdre. He had made no physical advances yet. They had been travelling, of course: the circumstances were hardly convenient. But he had not so much as touched her. She supposed he would in his own time. Meanwhile, she wasn't sure whether to do anything to encourage him or not. She tried holding his arm, or standing with her back to him waiting for him to put his arms round her. She tried standing facing him, waiting to be kissed. All she got was a smile.

She remembered her mother once remarking, "All it takes with a man is a little time and a good meal." So she was doubly hopeful when, as they made their way along the high tracks of the Slieve Bloom Mountains, Conall told her, "Tomorrow, I'll be away looking for food."

The next morning, leaving her with the last of the bread, he set off early, promising to return by evening. The day passed pleasantly. The weather was fine. From a gap in the trees, she could enjoy a magnificent view. Apart from the twittering of the birds, it was silent.

Not a soul came near. The sun was already sinking onto the horizon when Conall appeared. He was carrying a bag containing bread, wheat cakes, and other provisions. He looked pleased with himself.

"I got food from a farmstead," he explained. "Told them I was a messenger going to the King of Leinster."

They ate well that evening. Conall made a small fire. When it was done, she lay contentedly on her back beside it. The firelight, she knew, was playing on her face. She smiled at him. But Conall only smiled back, yawned, remarked that it had been a long day, and, wrapping himself in a woollen blanket, rolled over and went to sleep.

⁙

He had not told her about the message he had sent.

It had been luck, finding the traveller on the road. There were travellers on the island, of course, as there were in most places in the world: merchants, messengers, holy men, entertainers. These last in particular, in the Celtic world, were always roaming. Musicians, dancers, bards. He supposed it was in their nature. Sometimes they would stop at a farmstead for the night and entertain the company in return for food and lodging. At the court of a great chief, however, they would be well rewarded.

He saw the man from a distance. He was on foot, walking down the woodland track with an easy, swinging gait. Concealing his horse in the trees, Conall came towards him.

The traveller was a bard. They fell into conversation easily, and Conall was able to exhibit such a knowledge of poetry that the stranger quickly took him for another bard like himself. Conall judged the man to be a good practitioner of his craft, but it was not long before he learned that the bard was leaving Munster to escape trouble of some sort. So when Conall suggested that he might be able to help his new acquaintance find employment at the court of the High King, he was not surprised to see the fellow's eyes light up.

"You must go to Uisnech, while the king is still there," he told him. "I have a friend, a druid named Larine. If you go to him and say

I sent you, he may be able to help you. But I have enemies myself, so you must tell nobody who sent you. Just go straight to Larine."

"But how will he know who sent me?" he asked.

"I shall give you a token," Conall replied. And breaking a small branch from a nearby tree, he whittled it with a knife and after carefully making marks on it in ogham script, he gave it to him.

"Show him this and say that I told you he would help you."

"I shall indeed," the man promised, and went on his way.

What Conall had written on the stick was a request. He had just asked Larine to come and meet him. He had to get a message to the king.

In the days that followed, they went sometimes southwards, sometimes westwards, at a more leisurely pace. They dropped down to move cautiously past some scattered farms, before finding high ground and forest again. They also fell into a new mode of travel.

It was his meeting with the bard that had given Conall the idea. Each day he would scout ahead, then lead Deirdre forward to a place he judged to be secure. Moving off by himself, then, he would travel until he saw a farmstead. He had some days' growth of beard now. His shirt was not too clean. By walking with a slight stoop, he made himself seem older. Taking care always to arrive on foot, he had no difficulty in passing himself off as a bard and in obtaining food and shelter for the night. In the morning he would beg some extra food for his journey, and this he would bring back to Deirdre. Not only did this solve the problem of feeding her but it also allowed him to keep informed of any news in the countryside. So far there was no word about his flight, nor any sign of a search party. This method of travelling also had another advantage for Conall. He was often away from Deirdre at night.

When a man is withholding himself from a woman, or a woman from a man, the most effective avoidance lies in the arrangement of circumstances. The method of travelling safely which Conall had chosen was so entirely logical that Deirdre could hardly question it. Some nights Conall stayed with her, but when he did he was tired; and so, although she was still puzzled, she supposed that he meant to put off the consummation of their love until they reached a place where they could safely remain, and that she need only be patient.

He had told Larine to meet him in fifteen days. It should take the fellow three, perhaps five days to find the druid; and another three for Larine to reach the meeting place. Allowing a generous margin for error, fifteen days had seemed sensible. He had picked the meeting place carefully. It lay on open ground where he could watch the approaches. To reach it from the north, the druid would have to take a winding path across a bog. He had told him to come alone, but even if his friend were followed, Conall would be able to make his escape before any pursuers could come close. The only problem he had not yet solved was what to do with Deirdre while he went there. Perhaps he would find a farmstead where she could await him; but that was risky. More likely he would have to find a safe place where he could leave her with provisions for a few days. Until then, he did not want to get too far from the meeting place. So it was that their journey was following a large westwards curve, rather than plunging due south into Munster.

His choice of Larine had been natural. If there was one person he could trust, and whom the king might listen to, it was the druid. It was Larine who must convey the all-important messages: first, that they had fled because of the threat from the queen. And second, that he had not touched the girl.

It had been that first day, as they were looking out at the Slieve Bloom Mountains, when he realised how important his abstinence was.

He had known, even that dark night when they had set out, that as soon as he got Deirdre out of danger, he would have to send his uncle some word of explanation. He must tell him about the threat from the queen. He was fairly confident his uncle would know he was telling the truth. He had taken Deirdre only to save her life. For if the queen was determined to cause her death, sooner or later she would find ways of doing so, and surely his uncle couldn't want that. Perhaps, through Larine, they could reach an understanding. After a token pursuit, his uncle might even let him escape discreetly across the sea, and leave it at that.

It was during the morning that he saw other, more complex possibilities. What if his uncle sent the girl away for her safety, but demanded his own return? Or he might divorce the queen and send for Deirdre. Both unlikely, but possible. Of course, he reminded himself, he could never go along with either. After all, he loved Deirdre, and he knew she couldn't abide the king.

But all the same, as he had stood with Deirdre looking at the mountains, the implication had suddenly hit him. For the negotiations to have any hope of succeeding, he must not touch her. Until then, she was still the king's woman, and his flight with her had been for her protection. Unless he could swear to Larine, with a druidic oath of the most solemn kind, that the girl was untouched, then all his explanations of his conduct would fall to the ground.

So it was that, for the time being at least, he avoided contact with the woman he loved. It was not something he thought he could explain to her.

Larine read the message on the stick. It was terse: a name, a place, a date, and the word "alone." Then he turned back to the messenger. It would not be difficult to find the fellow some employment. There were three or four chiefs still at Uisnech who, at a word from Larine, would give this bard a try and pay him something. If he was good, word would travel quickly enough.

"I can help you," he told him.

But the message from Conall was more difficult. The festivities had been continued, as they had to be, but the air was tense. The High King was outwardly calm, but to those like Larine who knew him, he had never seemed so angry. And therefore dangerous.

Even though he had the protection of being a druid, did he dare go on such an errand to the fugitive? If Conall wanted to meet him, it might be to ask his advice, but it might also be to deliver a message. Did he really want to return and tell the king he had gone to see Conall behind his back? Was his friendship with Conall worth that much?

He pondered long and hard that day before deciding he would go. He was a brave soul.

⁘

They had rested three days now by the pool. It was a quiet spot, a little lake in a mountain declivity, fed by a stream, and from which, under an ash tree at the far end, a slip of clear water poured over a stone lip before descending through a gorsy gully into a winding ravine below. The slopes all round were thickly wooded. Nobody came there. Conall had built a shelter. They had fished in the pool, finding trout—small but good to eat. The first day they had rested there Conall had gone out, returning late the next morning with plentiful supplies and with wood he had cut for a fire. Deirdre, meanwhile, had washed their clothes in the stream.

The weather had been getting warmer for several days. Overhead, the sky was clear blue. The light breeze of the morning was growing faint. Conall was whittling a stick to spear fish when she asked him casually if he was going down into the valley that evening.

"No," he answered quietly. "We have plenty of food. But tomorrow," he added, "I shall be going away for several days." Shortly afterwards, he waded into the pool and stood with his spear poised, waiting for fish.

Then she knew what she had to do. She did not know why, but she knew it must be that day.

It was early afternoon when they ate. She had cooked the two fish he had caught over the fire, which sent tiny wisps of blue-grey smoke into the still air. As well as the fish, she had cooked beans and lentils. He had brought a flagon of ale with him the day before, so they drank from that. To follow, she had made honeyed oatcakes. And it was as he lay back contentedly after this meal that she gently remarked, "It is lucky for me that we escaped, Conall. You saved my life."

"That is probably true," he agreed, staring up at the sky. "The queen is a fearsome woman."

"Even without her, I'd not have gone back to the king. It was only you I wanted."

"And yet," he tilted his head forward to look at her, "if ever the king's men catch us, they may kill me. Then you'd have to go back, you know." He smiled. "Maybe the king would divorce the queen and send her away. It's possible. You'd be safe enough then."

But she only shook her head.

"The king will never have me, Conall. I'd kill myself." She said it so simply he supposed it must be true.

"Oh," he said, and leant his head back again and stared at the sky.

They remained silent after that, lying in the sun. There was not a breath of motion in the air now. The wisp of smoke from the fire was not dispersed, but rose straight up until it invisibly dissolved in the blueness above. It was silent all round the pond. Some way off, Deirdre saw a bird on an overhanging bough, its plumage gleaming like gold in the sun; but if it uttered any song, that sound, too, was stopped, as though the passing of time itself had ceased in the general silence of the afternoon.

Then, knowing what she must do, she quietly rose and, while he lay where he was, still staring up, went to the pond's edge and, slipping off her shift and underclothes, stepped quickly into the tingling cold water and swam out towards the middle where she could tread water.

Hearing the sound, but unaware that she was naked, Conall glanced at the pond and, after a little time, sat up to look at her. She stayed where she was, making no suggestion he should join her, but quietly smiling at him, while he continued to look and the golden light was playing on the little ripples in the water that she made around her. They stayed like that, the two of them, for some time.

She swam a few strokes to the shallows and slowly rising up, with the water dripping from her hair and breasts, walked towards him.

And then Conall, with a little gasp, rose to his feet and took her in his arms.

For three days Larine waited at the meeting place. But he had only the birds, sweeping watchfully overhead, for company. Conall never came. And after waiting two more days, just to be certain, the druid returned, sorrowfully.

Despite his sadness over the disappearance of his friend, Finbarr could not help feeling elated as, with Cuchulainn bounding along beside him, he approached the Hill of Uisnech.

He had the black bull. It was certainly a most magnificent beast. While few of the island's shaggy cattle came much above the midriff of a man, the black bull's shoulder was level with his own. Its red and angry eyes glowered down at him. With both arms spread, he could only just touch the tips of the huge creature's horns. Its coat was jet-black, the mighty tangle of its forelock as heavy as a man's head.

The raid had been expertly carried out. Concealing themselves, he and his men had watched for two days until they were fairly certain that one of the cowmen who regularly disappeared into the woods must be the bull's keeper. Following him the third day they found the huge beast, cleverly hidden in a small enclosure where the fellow was filling a trough to feed him.

"We shall need you to lead the bull," Finbarr told him.

"What if I refuse?" the man enquired.

"I shall cut off your head," Finbarr answered, pleasantly. So the man had come.

Following a circuitous route, they had brought the bull safely out of Connacht, and as they drew towards Uisnech, Finbarr sent one of his men back to the owner with the following message.

"The High King was sorry you were not there when he came to collect tribute, but he thanks you for the fine bull you have sent him instead."

Their arrival could hardly have been more encouraging. There were still a number of chiefs remaining with the High King and his retinue at Uisnech. Quite a crowd, including many druids, lined the path as they made their way towards the High King's quarters. But it was the queen who came towards them first, her face wreathed in smiles.

"That's my bull," she cried. And coming closer, in a quieter tone she repeated, "That's my bull," with rich satisfaction.

From the king, however, his reception was less warm. He did receive a nod and a grunt, which seemed to indicate that the success of his mission was accepted. But evidently there were other, more important matters on the king's mind.

"Conall and Deirdre have been sighted." It was Larine who told him. Of his own abortive journey the druid said nothing, and nobody had guessed about it. He had been puzzled and secretly rather hurt when, upon his return, he learned that Conall, at the very time he was waiting for him at their meeting place, had apparently been seen heading south into Munster with the girl. The search parties were still out, he now informed Finbarr. "But there's been no word of him yet."

It was a little before sunset when the king sent for Finbarr. He found the king sitting on a covered bench by a tree. From under his heavy brows the king eyed him thoughtfully.

"You performed your task well." He waited as Finbarr politely bowed his head. "Now I shall give you another. First, however, tell me: do you know where Conall is?"

"I do not know."

"Find him. And bring him back." He paused and then with sudden anger burst out: "He was my sister's son, Finbarr. I showed him nothing but kindness. Do you think he has the right to behave like this to me?" Finbarr could only bow his head again, for the king had said no more than the truth. "He is to return, Finbarr, and then he may tell me why he did this thing. But if he will not come, you will return with his head or not at all. I am sending two chiefs with you. They have their orders."

To watch me, Finbarr thought. Aloud he asked: "And Deirdre?"

"She is not to be harmed." The king sighed. "It would be a mockery for me to take her now. She will be returned to Dubh Linn. You may tell her that."

"Perhaps we shall not find him."

"Your parents and your brothers and sisters are poor, Finbarr. Succeed in this and I promise they will be poor no longer. Fail, and they will be poorer by far."

"Then I have no choice," Finbarr said bitterly, and left.

The High King watched him, but without anger. He would, he reflected, have felt the same in his place. But kings cannot always afford to be kind. Nor can they afford to be entirely honest.

If Conall came with Finbarr, the two chiefs were to kill Conall on the journey. As for the girl, she would be returned to Dubh Linn. But before she reached there, she would be handed over to her new master. For the king had already sold her, as a concubine, to Goibniu the Smith.

It could not be otherwise, when you thought about it.

⁂

Slowly and carefully they travelled now, never venturing out onto open ground in the plain light of day.

It had been a close thing, the day they had been seen. They had just crossed a patch of heathland when two of the king's riders, emerging onto it behind them, had caught sight of them and started to give chase. There had been nothing to do but run. Racing into the forest, they had left the track and managed to elude the king's

men; but the experience had shaken them both. The king would
know they were hiding in Munster now. With its innumerable hills,
creeks, and islands, it might be hard to find them, but he would be
relentless.

It was Deirdre who had the idea.

From the hills of Munster, travelling eastwards, there were forest
and hillside tracks for most of the way until one came to the ranges
of hills that swept up the island's eastern coastline and culminated
in the magnificent heights of the Wicklow Mountains.

"While they go looking into every hill and valley in the south-west,
we could be on our way up there," she pointed out. It was a clever
bluff—to return to the coastal edge of the very regions from which
they had fled—and it was unlikely anyone would think of it. She
also made another suggestion which surprised him: "We should leave
the horses and go on foot." But he soon saw the wisdom of this, too.
No one would be looking out for Conall the prince on foot. And then
she made two further suggestions which surprised him even more.

So it was the middle of June when a single druid, walking slowly
with a staff and accompanied, a few steps behind, by a servant boy,
made his way at dusk down from the Wicklow Mountains and took
the track towards the crossing of Ath Cliath at Dubh Linn. Fergus
and his sons, as Deirdre had told him they would be, were out on
the grasslands far away, with their cattle. But it was deep night in
any case when, skirting some way from the rath, in case there should
be any dogs about, they made their way across the wooden causeway over the shallows of the Liffey. As they did so, Deirdre noticed
that the rotted planks had still not been replaced. Then they passed
onto the broad Plain of Bird Flocks.

Up to now, her plan had worked. When, at her suggestion,
Conall had shaved his head in the druid tonsure, she had smiled to
herself because he looked, it seemed to her, even more himself than
he had before. When she in turn shaved her head like a slave, he
burst out laughing. She had wondered whether the loss of her splendid hair would make her less attractive to him and interfere with

their lovemaking which, since the afternoon at the pool, had been frequent. She discovered within moments of completing the operation that it would not.

But why had she suggested they should seek their hiding place so near to her home? Was it, at this time of crisis, that she was craving the security of her childhood and family? Perhaps. As they passed by her father's rath in the dark, she felt a sudden stab of emotion; she longed to creep in, sniff the familiar scent of the hearth, see the pale shape of her father's drinking skull on its shelf. If only the proud, talkative old man were there, so that they could take each other in their arms. But he was not there and she could not enter; and so she could only peer towards the rath's faint outline as she went by in the dark. Yet her choice of hiding place was also clever. For nobody ever went there.

The first day Conall left her in the dolmen shelter up on the promontory. He went along the shore but had no luck. The second day he came back smiling. He had found an old widow woman living alone in a hut by the shoreline. Telling her he was a single druid seeking greater solitude, he had explained his needs and she was glad to provide them: a bit of food when he came for it, and the use of the small curragh that had belonged to her husband, who had been a fisherman.

Late that night, and quite unseen, Conall and Deirdre came down to the shore and set out in the curragh, upon a still and starlit sea, for the little island with the cleft rock that lay below the headland Deirdre loved. No one, she hoped, would find them there.

II

For a year the search continued. Spies from the High King watched the harbours; on several occasions they also secretly watched Fergus and his rath in case he was concealing his daughter; but each time they returned to report: "No sign."

And for a year Finbarr travelled.

Day by day the pattern was unchanging—Finbarr, with Cuchulainn bounding along beside, rode first. The two chiefs followed behind. Sometimes they took winding tracks; sometimes they would journey along one of the island's great slige highways. It might be a broad cattle drove across the upland pastures, a pathway cut through the forest, or a stout wooden track through a bog, but whatever the terrain, the three riders pushed ahead relentlessly. They asked at every farmstead; they questioned the boatmen at every river. Even in the great wildernesses of the island's interior, it was hard for people to move amongst the tribal territories without encountering anybody. Someone must have seen them. But after the sighting reported by the king's men down in Munster, they seemed to have vanished completely.

It was a grim time. The failure of the harvest the year before was a serious matter. It had not brought starvation to the land, so far. The chiefs of each territory usually saw to that. There was still milk and meat, vegetables and berries. As they led their people out onto the communal grazing lands, they knew that despite the failure of the crops at the farmsteads, they could still live in the manner of their distant ancestors before the raising of crops had come to supplement the tribe's resources. But hardship there was. Oatmeal, bread, and ale, too, with the destruction of the barley, were all in short supply. In most cases on the farmsteads, Finbarr noticed, the chiefs had been ruthless in keeping back grain for sowing. It was as well, he thought, that the land of the island was rich, and that the chiefs had good authority. But if the people looked to their chiefs, and the chiefs to their kings, then the focal point of all their hopes was, more than ever, on the High King and his favour with the gods.

Just after Lughnasa, the rain began to fall. Not the usual rain that might be expected in the warm, wet coastal regions of ocean-bordered Munster, but driving storms and howling winds, day after day without ceasing. This year, too, it was clear the harvest would be ruined. And seeing this terrible evidence of the gods' displeasure, though Finbarr loved his friend, he could not help wondering if Conall's humiliation of the High King might not be the cause.

Fair weather or foul, they searched the coasts and hills of Munster; they scoured Leinster; they went up into Ulster. Sometimes they found shelter at a farmstead; sometimes they slept in the open and heard the howling of wolves. They crossed the rich pasturelands where great earthwork walls and ditches marked the divisions between the lands of one tribe and another; they ventured into the dark bogs where people lived in brannog settlements built on wooden platforms in the water. Everywhere they asked, and everywhere the answer was the same: "We have not seen them here."

Once, just once, Finbarr had a feeling that they might be close. It was on the eastern coast, just above the Liffey's bay. There, by a deserted strand of beach, he had met an old woman and asked if she had seen any strangers.

"Only the druid," she had said, "who lives on the island."

"Has he companions?" Finbarr had asked.

"He has not. None at all. He lives alone."

Yet an instinct might have made him go out to the place, but for his two companions, who called to him: "Finbarr, come on. He is not here." And so they departed.

At last they had come to Connacht, with its mountains and lakes and wild coastline. They do well, he thought, to call it the land of the druids. And thinking of his friend's lonely spirit, it seemed to him that this was where he might be. So for months they searched, but there was not a whisper of him. Until one day as they were standing on the great, sheer cliffs of Moher, staring out at the wild ocean in which somewhere, it was said, lay the Isles of the Blessed where the spirits of the great warriors went to their eternal rest—and Finbarr was just wondering whether perhaps his friend might have died and his spirit gone out there—one of his two companions spoke.

"It is time to return, Finbarr."

"I cannot," he replied. "I have not found him."

"Come with us," said the other. "You can do no more."
And he realised that it was a year since they had set out.

···

Sometimes it seemed to Conall that he had never been happy before. His life with Deirdre had been a revelation to them both. It had not taken her long to become, in their lovemaking, even more adventurous than he. Often she would take the initiative, straddling him, controlling him, or making him lie still while she explored new ways to give him pleasure or arouse him again. As her slim body entwined with his, it was hardly surprising that Conall, for so long beset by doubts and inner tensions, should have learned what it was to feel very happy indeed.

Their life on the island worked surprisingly well. The late-summer rains had not troubled them. The cleft in the cliff provided protection as well as concealment and there, above the tiny cove and beach, Conall used branches from the island's small supply of trees to build a cabin of mud and wattle that would certainly see them through the mild winter. The widow was glad to supply Conall with simple food which he could supplement by periodic trips inland where, as a wandering druid, he could purchase supplies without difficulty. On the island he could catch fish and he also planted beans and peas. Two other necessities were dealt with in the following way. To collect water for drinking, he found several places where rainwater ran off the rock face and dug three good-sized pits which he lined. For boiling vegetables or meat, which he was sometimes able to obtain, he constructed another, much smaller pit. Filling this with water, he would then transfer stones, heated red-hot in the fire, into the pit, which would bring the water to the boil and maintain it at that heat for some time. Those boiling pits were a speciality of the island people and were as effective as they were simple.

No one came near them. There was no reason why they should. The nearby headland was deserted. On the main shore opposite, there was no one but the widow. A little farther up the coast there was a much larger island opposite an inlet. Nobody lived on the island, and the few fishermen by the inlet only occasionally went out to it.

Even if anyone had thought of venturing in their direction, Conall had taken care to tell the old woman that he wanted to be alone, and she had no doubt passed this information on to the fishermen at the inlet. Druids who lived as hermits were not unknown; and it would be a foolhardy person indeed who risked a druid's curse by disturbing him when he wanted to be left alone.

The only thing, for the time being, that concerned Conall was that their island was so small. There was a beach to walk around, a grassy headland to climb, and a few trees, but that, and some rock pools, was all. Wouldn't Deirdre grow restless? Surprisingly, it did not seem so. She appeared to be content. But several times, on moonlit nights, he had taken her in the curragh across to the headland, and they had climbed up to the top and from there they had gazed together not only northwards, at their little refuge, but southwards across the whole sweeping bay past Dubh Linn and the Liffey's estuary to the southern headland and the silent, volcanic shapes of the Wicklow Mountains stretching down the coast, bathed in the silver moonlight.

"It is a pity you cannot visit them," he had remarked the first time, gesturing towards her family's rath, dimly visible above the estuary.

"It does not matter," she said. "I have you." And he hoped that it was true.

Yet as the months went on, in addition to his happiness with Deirdre, Conall was surprised to discover another profound contentment. For if he had always supposed that the company of a woman would somehow interfere with the contemplative thoughts that occupied his mind, so far this had not proved to be the case. Quite the reverse in fact. Partly it was the silence of the place; certainly the fact that she instinctively understood that he needed to be left alone with his thoughts; and perhaps also, more than he realised himself, the fact that he was now free of his old identity. But whatever the causes, in the rhythm of their life he found a sense of peace, of freshness and renewal. His disguise, indeed, had become a new reality; for effectively he had now become a druid. Each day, in his mind, he would go over the vast stock of knowledge he already possessed. Each morning and evening he would watch the sea and listen to the waves. And sometimes, losing his sense of personal identity entirely, he would stand in a trance and, like the poet Amairgen, quietly recite: "I am the Wind on the Sea, I am the Ocean Wave."

So autumn passed into a mild winter, and winter into spring. Then, in late spring, Deirdre told him she was pregnant.

By the midsummer after Finbarr's return, it seemed the harvest would be a good one. In the little fields by farmsteads all over the island, the grain was ripening. The weather was fine. Lughnasa came and immediately afterwards, the High King began a tour of Leinster. He was encamped near the Slieve Bloom Mountains when the great darkness fell.

Larine would always remember how it began. He had noticed the long banks of cloud along the horizon at sunset, but it was not until he awoke in the middle of the night that he noticed that the stars had been snuffed out. Then the night ended, but it still remained dark. "The dawn," men called it afterwards, "which was no dawn." All morning the sky remained not grey but black. Then it turned brown. Then it rained.

It was not a storm; it was a downpour. But unlike any downpour that he had seen before, it lasted seven days. Every stream became a torrent, every riverbank a lake. Swans floated across the meadows; and in the fields, turned into muddy swamps, stood only the crushed and sodden stalks of harvest's ruin. The High King went north into Ulster.

It was early September when he sent for Larine. The druid found him subdued.

"Three harvests lost, Larine." He shook his head. "It's myself they blame." He relapsed into silence.

"What is it you wish?"

"When Conall shamed me . . ." the king began heavily, then sighed. "The Dagda, they say, punishes kings who are mocked. Is it true?"

"I do not know."

"I must find him, Larine. But it isn't easy. My men failed. Finbarr failed. None of the druids or the filidh can tell me where he is." It had been a source of profound relief to the druid that the High King had not killed Finbarr for his failure as he had threatened. Larine had had the chance to question them closely, especially Finbarr, after their return, on the course their travels had taken and the places they had searched; but though he had considered carefully, he had not so far received any definite sense of where his friend Conall might be.

The High King looked up bleakly from under his heavy eyebrows. "Can you tell me, Larine?"

"I will try," the druid promised, and went away to prepare himself.

He had to wait a day or two, for the days in the druid's calendar were clearly marked as lucky or unlucky for rituals of this kind. But as soon as the time was propitious, he got ready.

The holy men of the Celtic world used many methods to see into the future. "Imbas" they called it: divining. The salmon, it was said, could impart wisdom and prophecy to some. Ravens could speak, if you knew what spells to use and how to listen. Even ordinary men, sometimes, could hear voices from the sea. But the method particularly favoured by the initiated class made use of the act of chewing. Some druids achieved powers of vision simply by chewing their thumb; but this was only a quick substitute for the proper method which was a version of one of the most ancient ceremonies known to man: the taking of a sacred meal.

Upon the day, Larine got up, washed himself carefully, and put on his druid's cloak of feathers. Next, he spent some little time in prayer, attempting to empty his mind of anything that might interfere with his receiving whatever message the gods were pleased to send him. Then he went to the small hut where, the night before, he had prepared everything in readiness. Two other druids were guarding the entrance to ensure that nobody disturbed the sacred rite.

Inside the hut was bare except for a small table and three stands. On one stand was a little figure of the sun god, the Dagda; on another, the goddess Maeve, patroness of royal Tara; and on the third, Nuadu of the Silver Hand. On the table, on a silver dish, were three strips of meat. This might be the flesh of pig, dog, or other animal, and Larine had chosen dog. At a nod from him, the two druids outside drew the door at the entrance closed and after standing in silent prayer a few moments longer, Larine went to the dish. Taking one of the strips of meat, he chewed it carefully, showed it to one of the gods, and placed it behind the door. The process was repeated two more times, before he made a polite obeisance in front of each of the gods and said another prayer. Then, lying down on the floor, he placed the palms of his hands on his cheeks and closing his eyes, prepared to receive their message.

There were many techniques, but the aim of all holy men, from the druids in the west to the shamans of Siberia, was always the same: to enter a trance in which the gods could communicate. For some time Larine lay still. It was silent. He emptied his mind. And then—he could not say how long it was—he felt himself beginning to float. Whether he had actually left the ground he had no idea. It was irrelevant. His body was no longer important. He was smoke from a fire, a cloud. He drifted.

When he came out of his trance, he went to the door and tapped three times. The two druids opened it and he stepped out. Then he went to the king.

"I saw the place," he explained. "They are there." And he described the little island with its cleft rock. "But whether it is on the north coast or the south, the east or the west, I did not see."

"Is there anything else you can tell?"

"I saw Fergus led by Nuadu of the Silver Hand walking across the sea in moonlight to speak with Deirdre while she slept."

"So he knows where she is?"

"That I don't know. Perhaps."

"I shall send Finbarr to him," said the High King.

It was evening when Finbarr came to Dubh Linn. He came with only his hound and his charioteer for company.

He came sadly, but also with determination in his heart. The High King had made his position brutally plain. "You failed before, Finbarr, and there was no punishment. This time there will be." They both knew why. When he had returned from his long search with the two chiefs, they had been so emphatic about his efforts to find Conall that to punish him would have looked petulant and weak. But the case now was different. He was being sent alone to find his friend. A respected druid had described the place where Conall was. The High King, after three failed harvests, could not afford any more failures.

And truth to tell, after so many months of searching and of trouble, Finbarr was beginning to feel some resentment towards his friend.

Fergus was at his rath and greeted him in a friendly manner. They went inside and even before any refreshment was brought Finbarr said to the old man, quietly but firmly, "Fergus, we know that you know where Deirdre is."

Yet, carefully though he observed him, Finbarr could have sworn that the chief was sincere when he looked at him sadly and replied, "I wish that I did."

So Finbarr told him of the druid's vision and described the island that Larine had seen. And then Fergus knew where his daughter was.

"I do not know that place," he said.

"I shall stay here until you do," Finbarr replied.

Fergus hesitated, considering his options.

"There may be an island like that some way along the coast," he said at last. "We could look for it tomorrow." He ordered food and wine; and since Finbarr was tired after his journey, when darkness had fallen, he slept. When everyone in the rath was asleep, Fergus silently got up and went out. He took a little curragh of skins and put it on his back; because he was afraid of waking his visitors, he did not take a horse, but went down to the hurdles on foot and crossed the Liffey and started towards the headland that Deirdre had loved. His long legs easily covered the distance, but whenever he could, with the curragh on his back, the old man ran.

It was late in the night when Fergus came to the shore. A three-quarter moon was high in the sky and the sea was calm. Then he put his curragh in the water and crossed to the island and found Deirdre and Conall asleep in each other's arms. And he woke them, and when Deirdre saw him, she flung her arms around him. And seeing how they were, and that his daughter was to have a child, Fergus wept.

It did not take the chief long to tell them what happened and to warn them, "You have only till morning before he finds you." But what were they to do? "You'll have to leave here tonight," he said, though as he looked at his daughter he could not help adding, "for how long, Deirdre, can you run?"

It was the problem that had concerned Conall all summer. Deirdre was not due to have her child until after midwinter, and she seemed strong and well. Conall had hoped that by now it might have been possible to cross the sea, but his secret trips along the coast had not been encouraging. Every harbour was still being watched. More than once he had wondered if she should go to her father. Surely, even if discovered, the king would not harm a help-less mother and child. But Deirdre was against it, and it had been she who hit upon an ingenious solution.

"Take me to the shore when my time is near. I will tell the old widow I am an abandoned woman. She will help me." She smiled.

"Then perhaps the druid from the island will pass by and look at me."

"And then?"

"You will find a way for us to leave, in due course."

Conall had supposed that this plan of action might work, but he was not sure; and as each day went by his secret misgivings had grown. So now, almost before he had time to think about it, he heard himself say, "Perhaps if I can draw Finbarr away, Deirdre can remain with you."

Fergus, for a moment, said nothing. Though he saw her pale and anxious face, he was lost in his own thoughts. What would be the consequences for him, and his two sons, if he were discovered hiding Deirdre? Did he really want the daughter he loved back in his house? And thinking how little he had managed to do for her, he felt ashamed.

"Dubh Linn is her home," he said, "and always will be." But taking Conall by the arm he added, "You must get her off the island by dawn. For in the morning, I shall have to bring Finbarr along the coast. Once Finbarr has gone, let her come to the rath at night and I'll find a way to hide her." Then, anxious to return to the rath before he was missed, he set off back across the water.

The moon was still some way above the horizon when he started to walk back along the shore. On his left, the high hump of the headland rose darkly; hurrying as best he could, it was not long before he reached the foot of the low ridge from the top of which he would see the broad expanse of the Dubh Linn bay. Pausing only for a moment to take a few, deep breaths, the old man started up. The track was easy going. He saw the line of the ridge ahead, outlined against the starry sky. There were a few clumps of trees and bushes along the way.

He was nearing the top when he heard the jingle of a harness and the snort of a horse just ahead. He stopped and stared at the clump of bushes from behind which the sound had come. Then from the shadow, a large shape emerged.

It was a chariot. It wheeled to face him down the slope, and from the chariot came Finbarr's voice.

"Thank you, Fergus, for showing me the way."

⁘

At last she was ready. She knew she could delay no longer; the sky was still full of stars, but there was now a hint of paleness in the east across the sea.

She had taken as long as she could. The island was her sanctuary: once she left it, she sensed, she would never be safe again. Perhaps, Conall had told her, they might be able to return there. Was it possible? She glanced at Conall. He had been standing with his back to her for a long time now, staring silently across at the shore.

The plan they had formed was simple enough. They would cross to the shore now, make their way inland, and hide in the woods. If Finbarr came to inspect the island, he would find only the little hut. The old woman at the shore would tell him that she had never seen anyone but the wandering druid at the place. In due course he would give up and go away. And then? Perhaps they might return to the island. Or Deidre might go to her father. Or they might still escape across the sea. Who knew?

She rose and walked over to Conall. He did not move. She stood beside him, and touched his arm.

"I am ready," she whispered. But Conall only shook his head.

"Too late," he said, and pointed. As she stared into the darkness she saw the shadow of Finbarr's chariot waiting on the shore; and before she could catch the words, they came out: "Oh Conall, I cannot go back. I should die."

They stood there watching, as the light grew and the sea turned grey, and the chariot became a hard, dark shape on the beach. Then Conall said, "I must go to him now." She managed to keep him with her a little longer; but though she still tried to hold him back, as the lightness on the horizon grew he finally pulled himself away, and took the curragh and went across alone.

He was halfway across when she saw the fiery edge of the sun break over the horizon and realised that Conall, breaking the second of the geissi, was crossing the sea with the rising sun behind him. She cried out, "Conall! The sun!"

But if he heard her, he did not turn back.

❖

Finbarr did not move. He had been standing in his chariot, still as a stone, since long before the dawn. During this time, he had pondered: would he feel any of the old love for his friend? Did he feel sorrow or only frustration? He hardly knew. But he did know what had to be done and so, perhaps afraid of his own emotions, he had hardened his heart. Yet now, as Conall came across the water and drew closer, it was none of these, but an entirely different emotion that he felt. It was surprise. And wonder.

He should have realised, he remembered, after what the old woman had told him when he came that way before, that the figure who came from the island would look like a druid. But it was more than that. As Conall reached the beach and started walking towards him, Finbarr experienced the strangest sensation. Seeing him now, coming out of the waves, with his head shaved like a druid, dressed simply as a hermit, it was as if he were looking not at Conall but at Conall's ghost. For if Conall had died and returned from the Isles of the Blessed, then surely this was how he would have appeared. It was the inner spirit, the very essence of the man he had loved, who now drew near like a sorrowful shade. A few paces away, Conall stopped and calmly nodded.

"You know, Conall, why I am here." Finbarr found his voice was husky.

"It is a pity you came, Finbarr. It can do you no good."

Was that all his friend had to say to him?

"It's more than a year I've been looking for you," he burst out.

"What are your orders from the High King?" Conall asked quietly.

"To bring you both safely back."

"Deirdre will not come, and I shall not leave her."

"That is all that matters—yourself and Deirdre?"

"It seems so."

"It does not concern you, Conall," he could not keep the bitterness out of his voice, "that there have been three years of bad harvests, that poor people are only kept from starving by what the chiefs can give them, and that all this is blamed upon you for the way you have shamed the High King, your uncle?"

"Who says this?" Conall looked a little shaken.

"The druids say it, Conall, and the filidh, and the bards." He took a deep breath. "And I say it, too."

Conall paused thoughtfully before replying, and when he did so it seemed to be with sadness.

"I cannot come with you, Finbarr."

"There is no choice, Conall." Finbarr indicated his chariot. "You can see that I am armed."

"Then you must kill me." It was not a challenge. Conall just stood quietly, looking in front of him, as though waiting for the blow to fall.

For long moments, Finbarr gazed down at his friend. Then, reaching down, he took three objects and threw them at his friend's feet. They were Conall's spear, and his shield, and his shining sword.

"Defend yourself," he said.

"I cannot," replied Conall, who did not pick his weapons up.

And now Finbarr lost patience with his friend entirely.

"Is it afraid to fight you are?" he cried. "Then here's what we'll do. I'll wait at the Ford of Hurdles, Conall. You can come and fight me there like a man—and if you win you can leave. Or you can run away with your woman and I'll return to your uncle and tell him I let a coward go free. Please yourself." And with that he wheeled his chariot away.

Then, after a long pause, and having no alternative, Conall picked up his weapons and sadly followed him.

It was on a grassy strand, with the ford across the Liffey just be-hind them, that Conall and Finbarr prepared for battle.

There was a ritual to be followed before a Celtic warrior fought. First, the warrior should be naked, though he might paint his face on his body with the bluish dye called woad. But more important than any outward decoration was the inward preparation. For men did not go into battle cold. Armies worked themselves up with fear-some war chants and terrifying battle cries. Druids would shout to the enemy, telling them they were doomed. As the druids cast spells and warriors hurled insults, men from the camp would sometimes throw mud or even human excrement at the faces of their oppo-nents to discourage them. But above all, each warrior had to work himself into that heightened state where strength and skill became something more than mere bone and muscle—where he drew strength from all his ancestors, too, and even the gods. This was the warrior's sublime inspiration, his battle rage, his "warp spasm," as the Celtic poets called it.

To achieve this heightened state, a Celtic warrior would go through ritual movements, standing on one leg, twisting his body and contorting his face until it seemed to have been transformed into a living war mask.

Finbarr prepared in the classic manner. Drawing up his right knee, he slowly arched his body as if it were a bow. Closing his left eye, he half tilted his face so that his master eye, wide and glaring, seemed to bore into his opponent in a piercing squint. Conall, meanwhile, stood very still, but it seemed to Finbarr that he was communicating with the gods.

"It will be the worse for you, Conall," he cried, "that you came here. I am a boar who will gouge you, Conall. A boar."

But Conall said nothing.

Then they took up their spears and shields, and Finbarr hurled his spear with huge force straight at Conall. It was a perfect throw. Once before, with such a throw, his spear had gone clean through his opponent's shield and pinned the man to the ground through his chest. But Conall, stepping aside so fast that Finbarr scarcely saw him move, let the spear glance off his shield. With only a moment's pause, Conall then hurled his in return. It flew from his hand, aimed straight at Finbarr's heart. And if some other warrior had thrown it, Finbarr would have judged it a fine cast. But he knew the incredible force of Conall's cast when he really tried and, letting the spear crash into his shield, he inwardly cursed. Then, taking up his sword, he rushed at Conall.

There were few who could match Finbarr with the sword. He was brave, he was swift, and he was strong. As he forced Conall back, it was hard for him to tell whether his friend was deliberately giving ground or was out of practice. As iron rang on iron, the sparks flew. They reached the edge of the shallows. Still Conall was giving ground; but though Conall was soon ankle-deep in the water, Finbarr realised that neither of them had yet drawn blood.

And the more he struck, the more mysteriously Conall seemed to elude him. He shouted a war cry, rushed splashing through the water, hacked and lunged. He used every move he knew. Yet strangely his sword either struck uselessly against the defending blade or shield of Conall, or it missed entirely. Once, when Conall's shield was lowered and his sword hung wide, Finbarr made a lightning lunge—and encountered nothing at all. It was as if, for an instant, Conall had turned into a mist. I am not fighting a warrior, Finbarr thought, I am fighting a druid.

For some time this strange contest went on, and who knew how it might have ended if, by a stroke of fate, Conall had not slipped as he stepped back onto a stone. In a flash Finbarr had struck, catching him on the arm. As Conall fell back and raised his shield, Finbarr hacked at his leg, opening a gash. In a moment Conall was up and parried the next blows, but he was limping. There was blood in the water at his feet. He gave more ground, but this time Finbarr knew it was because he was in trouble. A quick feint and he caught him again, on the shoulder. They continued, blow for blow, but skilful though Conall was, Finbarr could feel him getting weaker.

He had him. He knew it. The end was only a question of time. Long moments passed. They went back another twenty paces, Finbarr advancing through the watery shallows that were red with the other man's blood. Conall was slipping. He seemed about to fall.

And now, close to triumph, all the frustration of the last year and, though he scarcely realised it himself, the many years of jealousy spoke for themselves when he cried out, "Do not think I shall kill you, Conall. I shall not. It'll be tied and walking behind my chariot that you and Deirdre will come with me, this day, to the king." And swinging his sword high, he leaped forward.

He never saw the blade. It moved so fast, he did not even feel it for a moment, in his battle fury. But it smashed through his breast and severed every tissue just above the heart, so that Finbarr frowned, first in puzzlement as he became aware that something had stopped. Then he felt a huge, red, aching pain, and found that he was choking, that his gorge and his mouth were full of blood, and that everything was running away from him like a river as he crashed into the shallow water. He felt himself being turned and saw Conall's face looking down at him, infinitely sorrowful. Why was he so sorrowful? His face was becoming blurred.

"Oh Finbarr. I had no wish to kill you."

Why did Conall say that? Had he killed him? Finbarr tried to say something to the blur.

"Conall . . ."

Then the light grew bright as his eyes opened wide.

Conall and the charioteer carried his body to the chariot, to be taken back to the king. Only now did Conall realise that Cuchulainn the hound was tied up in the chariot, waiting for his master. With a last sad look over the wide waters of the Liffey, Conall limped back towards Deirdre and the island.

⁂

Goibniu's single eye surveyed them all: the High King, the queen, the chiefs, and the druids. He listened but said nothing.

It had been that afternoon, after two days' hard driving, that the exhausted charioteer had arrived at the High King's camp with Finbarr's body. The women were preparing it for burial. And in the big hall, with its wicker walls, they were all talking.

There were at least twenty young men who wanted to go after Conall. They would, of course. Kill the hero who had killed noble Finbarr—what a chance for young men eager for glory. The druids, on the whole, seemed to think this was the best plan. Larine was there, Conall's friend. He was looking sad, but saying nothing. The queen, however, was talking. She had never, it seemed to Goibniu, taken much interest in the hunting of Conall; but now she was adamant. Conall and Deirdre should be killed. "Let her father bury his daughter at Dubh Linn," she cried. "And bring me the head of Conall." She looked round the chiefs and young heroes. "The man who brings me Conall's head shall have twelvescore cows." One thing was clear: she did not want them back. But what interested Goibniu far more was the thought process of the king who, though he sat on his large covered bench looking depressed, had still not spoken. Was he, perhaps, thinking as Goibniu thought? Did he look for deeper causes?

As so often happened when Goibniu listened to men talking, it seemed to the smith that their words were empty, signifying nothing. For what was the king's real problem? The failure of the harvests. And what caused the bad harvests? Were they really the fault of the High King? Could they be cured by the death of Conall? Goibniu did not know, but he doubted. Nor, in his private estimation, did anyone else know. But they believed. That was what mattered: their belief. The killing of Conall would achieve revenge for the mocking of the king. But what if, after that, the next harvest failed as well? Wouldn't the druids still blame the High King? They would. Not a doubt of it.

He noticed that the High King was looking at him now.

"Well, Goibniu," he asked, "and what have you to say?"

Goibniu the Smith paused for a moment, considering carefully before he answered.

"It seems to me," he said quietly, "that there is another way. May I speak with you alone?"

She had even dreamed they might go free, once or twice, during those days.

Nothing, she supposed, could be worse than that first morning, waiting on the island to see whether it was the chariot of Finbarr or Conall's handsome form that would come along the strand to fetch her. For her waiting was ended by neither, but by the bent, bloody shape of Conall, limping like a dying animal across the sand, so that at first she scarcely knew him. And when, finally, he fell out of the curragh onto the shingle in front of her, it was all she could do to hide her revulsion at the sight of his wounds.

She tended him as best she could. He was weak, and once or twice he fainted; but he told her what had happened and how he had killed his friend. She hardly liked to ask him what they should do next. Late that afternoon her father had arrived.

"They will come for him. Finbarr's charioteer will show them where he is. But it will take a few days, Deirdre. We can think about what to do tomorrow." They debated whether to move Conall back to the rath at Dubh Linn, but Fergus decided: "Let him stay where he is for the moment, Deirdre. He's as well here as he can be any-where." In the evening he left. And though Conall grew feverish in the night, in the morning he seemed better, and she fed him some broth and a little mead that her father had brought.

Towards midday, Fergus came again. After inspecting Conall and remarking that he would live, he addressed them both seriously.

"It's impossible for you to remain here any longer. Whatever the risks, you have to cross the sea." He gazed out at the water. "At least you can thank the gods the weather is fine." He gave Conall a smile. "In two days I'll be back with a boat."

"But father," she cried, "even if you found one, how would I manage a boat all alone, with me in the state I'm in and Conall hardly strong enough to lift an oar?"

"There'll be a crew," said her father, and left.

The next day was anxious for Deirdre. At first she was grateful. Though almost every wave caused her to glance at the shore, expecting to see the king's men, nobody came. Physically, Conall seemed better. He even took a turn around their little island and she was relieved that his wounds did not open again. But his mental state was another matter. She was used to his moods, and when in the late afternoon he went to sit alone on the shingle beach and stare out to sea, she did not at first attach any particular significance to it; but after a while, he looked so unusually sad that she went and stood beside him. "What are you thinking about?" she asked. For a few moments he did not reply.

"It was Finbarr I was thinking of," he said quietly at last. "He was my friend."

She wanted to put her arms round him but he seemed distant, so she did not dare. She touched him on the shoulder, then withdrew her hand.

"He knew the risks he took," she said softly. "It isn't you who's to blame."

He did not answer, and they fell into silence.

"He told me," Conall said quietly, "that the druids say the bad harvests are my doing—because of my humiliation of the High King."

"Then it would be my fault, too, Conall."

"It would not." He frowned. "It is mine."

"That is foolishness."

"Perhaps." He was silent again while she watched him anxiously.

"You must not think it, Conall," she said, and in return he touched her hand.

"It is not to be thought of," he murmured. But he did not look at her. After a time, uncertain what to do, she moved away; and

Conall remained there, sitting on the shingle, staring at the water until the sun went down.

Her father arrived the next morning. There was still a mist on the sea, as the boat came round the headland. It was a small vessel, with leather sides and a single square sail with which it could run, in a somewhat ungainly fashion, before the wind—hardly different from the curraghs in which her distant ancestors had first come to the western island. Her father had bought it from a fisherman at the southern end of the bay. He sailed it himself, accompanied by her two brothers. They all stepped ashore, looking pleased with themselves.

"Here is your boat," her father said. "The wind's from the west but it's light; the sea is calm. You needn't worry about making the crossing."

"But where is the crew you promised?" she demanded.

"Why it's your father and your brothers, Deirdre," he said, as if it were the most obvious thing in the world. "Put your trust in your father, Deirdre, and I'll put mine in Manannan mac Lir. The sea god will protect you. Is that not good enough for you?"

"Perhaps with just yourself," she suggested, looking doubtfully at her brothers. "The boat is small."

"Would you have me leave your brothers behind," he asked, smiling, "all alone in the world?"

And then Deirdre understood. "You mean you won't be coming back?"

"To face the king after I helped you escape? No, Deirdre, we'll go together. I've always had a mind to go on a voyage. I just left it a little late."

"But the rath, your lands, the cattle . . ."

"At Dubh Linn?" He shrugged. "It's not much of a place, I dare say. It's too marshy. No, Deirdre, I'd say it's time to move on." And looking into the little boat, she saw that it was stocked with provisions, and a small sack of silver, and her father's drinking skull. So she kissed her father and said not another word.

There was only one problem. Conall wouldn't go.

He was very quiet about it. The depression he had exhibited the evening before seemed to have subsided into something else. He appeared sad, perhaps a little absent, but calm. And adamant. He would not go.

"By all the gods, man," cried Fergus. "What's the matter with you? Do you not see what we're doing for you?" And when this did not work: "Must we carry you into the boat by force?" But a look from the prince told him that, even in Conall's weakened state, this would not be a good idea. "Would you at least tell us why?" Fergus finally asked in despair.

For a few moments it was not clear whether Conall would answer, but in the end he said quietly, "It is not the will of the gods that I should go."

"How would you know that?" Fergus demanded irritably.

"If I cross the sea with you, it will not bring you any luck."

While her father cursed under his breath, Deirdre's two brothers looked at each other anxiously. Had the gods cursed their sister's man? Since Conall looked like a druid, it seemed to them that he would know.

"There's no point in getting drowned, Father," one of them said.

"Are we to take Deirdre then, and leave you behind?" Fergus almost shouted. Conall did not answer but Deirdre took her father's arm.

"I cannot leave him, Father," she murmured. And though he cast his eyes up at the sky with impatience, she led him to one side and continued, "Wait one more day. Perhaps he will feel differently tomorrow." And since there seemed to be no alternative, Fergus could only shrug his shoulders and sigh. Before he left, however, he warned, "You have not much time. There's yourself to think of Deirdre, and the child."

For some while after her father and brothers had gone, Deirdre said nothing. There was a flock of seagulls on the shingle beach. Again and again they rose up, crying into the blue September sky, while Conall sat watching them as though in a trance. Finally they departed, and then she spoke.

"What is to become of us, Conall?"

"I do not know."

"Why wouldn't you leave?" He did not reply. "Was it a dream you had in the night." He did not answer, but she suspected he had dreamed. "Is it that you have spoken with the gods? Tell me the truth, Conall. What is it you know?"

"That I am to wait here, Deirdre. That is all."

She looked at his pale, handsome face.

"I shall stay here with you," she said simply.

He reached out and held her hand, so that she would know he loved her; and she wondered whether, perhaps, he might change his mind before the morning.

When she awoke, the sky was clear, but there was a thin layer of mist on the ground. Looking across the water to the shore, it seemed to her that everything was still. It was surely, in any case, too soon for anyone coming from the High King to have reached them. Then something caught her eye.

At first, in the distance, the little shape that was advancing across the misty plain seemed like a flapping bird. All over the wide expanse of the Plain of Bird Flocks, the mist lay in torn veils or hovered in wisps like phantoms, and this whiteness poured over the shore and the intervening sea so that it was impossible for Deirdre to tell whether it was earth or water that lay beneath. As for the seeming bird, she could only surmise that it might be a man with a trailing cloak, borne swiftly by a chariot, unless perhaps it was one of the gods or their messengers who had taken the form of a raven or swan or some other flying thing to visit them.

Then, where the shore would be, the ghostly presence turned and stopped. And now, as Deirdre stared, she could have sworn it was a graceful deer. But after a pause, it disappeared into the mist only to emerge once more, as if it could change its shape at will, floating very slowly, still and grey, like a standing stone, towards her little island.

She glanced round, hoping to see her father's boat coming past the headland. But instead she saw Conall, standing behind her, looking grave.

"It is Larine," he said.

"He seemed to change shape as he came."

"He is a druid," he remarked. "He could probably make himself disappear if he wanted to." And now she saw that it was Larine, in a small curragh, being rowed towards them by his charioteer.

"Come Conall," he said quietly, as he stepped ashore, "we must talk." And as Deirdre turned anxiously to Conall, she was surprised to see that he looked relieved.

They were a long time together, at some distance from her, like two shadows hovering in the wreaths of mist that swirled along the water's edge; and the sun had just broken above the horizon when they returned to her, and she saw that Conall's face had become transformed. All his unhappiness had disappeared and with a gentle smile he took her hand.

"All is well. My uncle and I are reconciled."

III

Samhain: ancient Hallowe'en, when the spirits of the dead walk for one night amongst the living. Samhain, the turning point, the entrance to the dark half of the year. Samhain, when the beasts are slaughtered, Samhain the sinister. Yet in the western island with its gentle climate, the month that led to Samhain was usually a pleasant season.

Deirdre always found it so. Sometimes the days were soft and misty, sometimes the clear blue sky seemed so hard you could touch it. She loved the autumnal woods, the oak leaves brown on the trees or crisp underfoot. And when there was a chill in the air, she felt a tingling in the blood.

Larine had remained with them on their island for three days. He had brought herbs to cure Conall. The two men would spend hours together in conversation and prayer; and even if she felt excluded, Deirdre could see that Conall was being healed in body and spirit. After this time, Larine departed, but before he left he explained to her kindly, "It will be a little time, Deirdre, before Conall is entirely well. Rest here, or at your father's. No one will trouble you. The High King wishes to be reconciled at the festival of Samhain, so you will come to him then." And, guessing her thoughts, he added with a smile, "You need not fear the queen anymore, Deirdre. She will not hurt you now."

The next day, her father brought them home.

The month they spent at Dubh Linn was a happy time. If she had any misgivings about whether Conall would tolerate her family, they were soon set at rest. He listened to her father's ancestry every evening without the slightest sign of boredom; he played hurling with her brothers and indulged in mock swordplay without killing them. He even persuaded Fergus to replace the broken planks at the Ford of Hurdles and helped him do it. She noticed that his wounds had not only healed but that one could scarcely see where they had been. As he lay down beside her at night, it seemed to her that his pale naked body was, once again, as perfect as before. As for herself, she could feel the child growing within her, and growing strong.

"He will come at midwinter," she said happily, "like the promise of spring."

"You say 'he,' " Conall remarked.

"It will be a boy, Conall," she replied. "I can feel it."

They would walk together along the Liffey where the willows trailed their branches, or into the groves of oak and beech. Each day they would also visit one of the three little sacred springs and Conall would gently anoint her swelling belly with water, running his hand over its roundness. There were days of mist and days of sunshine, but the breezes were very light that month, so that only a sprinkling of leaves had fallen from the trees still heavy and thick with the rich gold and bronze of mellow autumn. Only the gathering of the migratory birds foretold that the inevitable coming of winter was close.

It was two days before Samhain, when crowds of starlings were wheeling around the trees at Dubh Linn, that the three chariots arrived.

⁘

Deirdre could see her father was pleased; he had never travelled like this before. The three chariots, each with a charioteer, were splendid indeed. He and his two sons were carried in one, Deirdre in the second; the third chariot, the finest of all, was Conall's own with its two swift horses harnessed to the shaft.

The day was fine. The sun glinted on the Liffey's wide shallows as they crossed the ford. Their path lay north-west. All afternoon they made swift and easy progress past rolling grasslands and wooded slopes. In the early evening they found a pleasant place to camp in an oak grove. The next morning the weather had changed. It was dry, but the sky was overcast. The light was leaden and grey; the slanting shafts of sunshine that sometimes broke through the clouds seemed to Deirdre to be vaguely sinister and threatening. But the rest of the party were in good spirits as they continued north-west towards the valley of the River Boyne.

"We shall be there by afternoon," her charioteer remarked. "We shall be at royal Tara."

And just afterwards, her father called out cheerfully, "Do you remember, Deirdre? Do you remember Tara?"

Of course she did. How could she forget? It had been years ago, when her younger brother was eight, that Fergus had taken them all, one summer's day, on the road to Tara. It had been a happy time. The great ceremonial centre had a magnificent site—a large, broad hill with gentle slopes that rose above the valley of the Boyne half a day's journey upstream from the ancient tomb with its midwinter passage where the Dagda dwelt.

Except for a guardian, the huge site had been deserted at that summer season, for apart from their inauguration, the High Kings usually only came to Tara for the festival of Samhain. Fergus had led his little family up as proudly as if he owned the place, and shown them its principal features—the big earthwork circles in which the shrines and banqueting hall would be erected for the festival. He had also shown them some of the magical aspects of the site.

"This is where the druids choose the new High King," he explained at one small earthwork. "One of them drinks bull's blood and then the gods send him a vision." Showing them a pair of stones set close together: "The new king has to pass between these in his chariot. If he gets stuck, then he's not the rightful king." But the most impressive feature to Deirdre had been the ancient standing stone near the top of the hill, the Stone of Fal. "When the true king's chariot comes and touches the Stone of Fal," he explained solemnly, "the druids hear it cry out."

"And after that," one of her brothers had demanded, "doesn't he have to mate with a white mare?"

"He does indeed," said Fergus proudly.

But if these details of the king's inauguration had fascinated her brothers, the magic of Tara for Deirdre had been its situation. It was not only the magnificent views in every direction during the day, but at sunrise and sunset, when the mists lay over the valleys all round, and the Hill of Tara seemed like a floating island in the world of the gods.

She should therefore have been happy as they drew towards it.

Midday was past when they came in sight of Tara. As the three chariots sped along the broad track, the charioteers drew into a triangular formation with Conall in front, her chariot behind his left wheel, and her father's behind his right. Though the sky was still a dull, metallic grey, with only silvery glints of sunlight, the day was not cold. Ahead of them, lining the route, she noticed a scattering of people, many of them with baskets. Seeing them, Conall suddenly cast off his cloak so that now, with his pale body stripped, he looked like a warrior going into battle. In their arrowhead formation, the three chariots raced forward and as they drew level with them, the welcoming people reached into their baskets and threw handfuls of wild autumn flowers into Conall's chariot. And although Conall was the High King's nephew, Deirdre was surprised that he should receive such a hero's welcome.

The hill was looming above them now. She could see crowds of people on the long earthwork wall that enclosed the summit. In the middle of the wall stood a line of priests, holding long bronze trumpets and the great bull horns that were the sign of kingship. Behind them were the wicker-walled structures that had been erected for the festival. There were a few fires sending thin trails of smoke into the air. They reached a patch of flat, grassy ground, dotted with trees at the base of the hill, the track up the long slope just ahead of it. The priests were raising their trumpets. From these now came a huge, deep-throated, darkly pulsating blast that grew into a terrifying roar.

And then the black mist arose.

It was so sudden and so violent that she screamed. The starlings rose up in front of them with a huge whirr that was almost a roar. Starlings, thousands of them, enveloped the chariots in a swirling black cloud. They wheeled round them as though both they and the travellers were caught in the strange, dark vortex of a whirlwind. Turning and turning, their myriad flapping was so loud that Deirdre could not even hear her own screams. In front of them, all round, behind, the dark cloud rose, fell, rose again and then, just as suddenly veered away with a great rush to descend in a swoop on the nearby trees.

Deirdre looked across. Her father and brothers were laughing. Conall's face she could not see. But glancing at the crowds on the earthwork walls above, she realised, with a new, foreboding horror what they had witnessed.

Conall had just passed through a black mist, as he came to Tara. The geissi were complete.

There was no time to think of that now as they raced up the slope and into the huge enclosure of Tara. There were burning torches lining the route which led to the crest of the hill. As they reached the final stretch, two of the chariots halted, leaving Conall to proceed alone up the short ceremonial avenue with its earthwork walls at the head of which, flanked by his chiefs, the High King was standing.

Deirdre saw Conall step down from his chariot and go to the king. She saw the king bare his breast for his nephew to kiss and then return the gesture of reconciliation. Next Conall kneeled before his uncle, who placed his hands on the younger man's head in a blessing. Though she might have been glad of these signs of love and forgiveness, she was still so shaken by the swarming birds that she felt only a sense of unease. It seemed to her, now, too good to be true. And why, after they had finished their greeting, did the High King and his men step to one side, as though honouring Conall, as he walked through their midst towards the group of druids who, she saw, had been waiting behind the royal party? Why was Conall, the runaway prince, suddenly a hero?

"You are to come with me now." She looked down and was surprised to see Larine smiling beside her chariot. "A place has been prepared for you to rest. You will be in good hands." Seeing her look at him doubtfully he added, "You carry Conall's child. You will be greatly honoured. Follow me." And leading the way, he took her towards a small lodging. Just before they reached it she noticed Goibniu the Smith. He was standing alone, watching her. She did not acknowledge him, nor did he make any attempt to greet her. He just watched her. She didn't know why. As they reached the lodge she asked, "Where is Conall?"

"I shall bring him to you shortly," Larine promised.

There was a slave girl there who gave her refreshments. Her father and brothers, she supposed, were being given lodgings elsewhere. There were plenty of people moving about in the huge encampment, but nobody came over to her when she stood in her doorway. She had the sensation they were politely ignoring her, as if she had been set apart.

Then, at last, Conall came. He came with Larine, who lingered a few paces away.

How at peace Conall seemed. Grave, but at peace. She supposed it was relief at having been reconciled with his uncle. How kindly and lovingly he looked down at her.

"I have been with the druids, Deirdre," he said gently. "There were things to be done." He paused. "They are going to do me a great honour."

"That is good, Conall," she said, without understanding.

"I am to go on a journey, Deirdre, that only a prince can make. And if it is pleasing to the gods, it will bring better harvests." He paused, gazing at her thoughtfully. "If it were necessary for me to travel across the sea to the blessed isles in order to speak with the gods, would you try to prevent my departure?"

"I should await your return. But the blessed isles," she added nervously, "are far away, Conall, in the western sea."

"That is true. And if I were shipwrecked, you would mourn me, but you would be proud, would you not? You would tell my son to be proud of his father?"

"How could your son not be proud of his father?"

"My father died in battle, with honour. So my mother and I did not grieve for him, because we knew he was with the gods."

"What is this to me, Conall?" she asked, confused.

Now Conall was beckoning Larine to draw close.

"Deirdre," he said, "you know that you alone are the love of my life and that you carry my son. If you love me as I love you, do not grieve if I depart upon a journey. And if you love me, remember this. Finbarr, whom I killed, was my dearest friend. But Larine here is an even better friend. I must leave you now because it is the will of the gods. But let Larine be your friend and counsellor always and you will never come to harm." With that, he lovingly kissed her; then he turned and strode away, leaving her with the druid.

And then Larine told her what was going to happen.

❖

Dawn was approaching. Was he afraid? He did not think so.

When Conall was a child, the eve of Samhain had seemed a magical but a dangerous time. People left food for the visiting spirits, but they put out their fires to make sure the dangerous visitors did not linger there. His mother would always make him sleep close to her that night when he was a little boy. After the long night, would come the culling of the animals—the cattle, pigs, and sheep selected for winter slaughter. There was always something melancholy to Conall in the lowing of the cattle as they were led towards the pen where the cattlemen were waiting with their knives. The other little boys always used to think it a great joke when the pigs were seized and the ropes tied round their trotters while they squealed. After the men had hauled them by their hind legs up a tree would come the throat slitting, with more squealing and red blood flooding out and splattering everywhere. Conall had never enjoyed the butchery, however necessary, and took his comfort from the druid blessing the scene.

On Samhain eve, when he was somewhat older, he used to slip out and sit by himself outside. All through the night he would watch for the vague shadows, and listen for soft footfalls as the spirits came to visit, sliding into wicker huts or brushing against the autumn trees. One in particular he had waited for. Surely, he had thought as a little boy, his heroic father would come to visit him. Again and again he would conjure pictures of his father in his mind—the tall figure his mother had told him about, with flashing blue eyes and flowing moustaches. Wouldn't his father come? Yet he never had. Once, on the Samhain eve when he was fourteen, he had experienced something: a strange sense of warmth, a presence near him. And because he had longed and ached for it to be so, he believed it was his father.

But this last night had been different. He had been glad of Larine for company. He had asked that Larine should take him through the ordeal and the request had been granted. They had sat together, talked and prayed a little, recited from the sacred sayings. Then, towards the middle of the night, Larine had left him alone for a while.

So hard had he been concentrating on the ordeal ahead that he had even forgotten that the spirits were abroad that night. Sitting alone in the darkness of the druid's house, he was not sure whether he had fallen asleep or whether he was awake; but it was sometime in the deepest part of the night that he saw the figure enter. He was as plainly visible as Larine, which was strange perhaps, as there was no light; and he knew at once who it was. His father stood just in front of him, with a grave but kindly smile.

"I have waited so long for you, Father," he said.

"We shall be together soon, Conall," his father replied. "We shall be together always, in the lands of the bright morning. I have many things to show you." Then he went out again, and Conall felt a sense of great peace, knowing that he was going to his father with the blessing of the gods.

It had been a long time since they had sacrificed a man at Tara. Not for three generations at least. That made the ceremony all the more solemn and important. If anything could lift the curse that had seemingly fallen upon the High King and the whole land, surely it must be this. If he hoped to purge his own sense of grief and guilt after his elopement with Deirdre and the killing of Finbarr, such a sacrifice would atone. Yet his overwhelming sense, as he prepared to pass through the portals into the next world, was not one of personal sacrifice. It was hardly even one of sorrow or joy. Sorrow was needless, joy not enough. What Conall felt now was a sense of destiny. It was not just that the three geissi and the prophecy about Finbarr had all been fulfilled, but rather that, in this act, all that he was—prince, warrior, druid—found their perfect expression. It was the noblest

death, the finest. It was what he had been born for. To be at one with
the gods: it was his homecoming. He remained at peace until, just as
the first hint of dawn appeared in the east, Larine returned.

They fed him a little burnt cake and crushed hazelnuts, for the
hazel tree was sacred. He took three sips of water and, when he was
finished, stripped. Then, after washing him carefully, they painted
his naked body red with dye. This took a little time to dry. When it
had, Larine tied an armlet of fox fur round Conall's left arm. After
that, he had to wait, but only for a little time. For already it was
growing light outside the door. And soon enough, with a smile,
Larine said to him, "Come."

⁘

There must have been a thousand people watching. The circle of
druids stood on the mound, where all could see them. On another
mound, the High King was standing. The crowd had just fallen
silent. They were bringing Conall.

The High King gazed across the crowd, thoughtfully. It had to be
done. He was not sure he liked it, but the thing had to be done. He
caught sight of Goibniu. There was no doubt, the smith had been
clever. The return of the penitent prince and his willing sacrifice was
a masterstroke. Not only did it restore the royal prestige—the royal
house was giving one of its own to the gods—but it left the druids in
a difficult position. This was their sacrifice, too, the most important
they could make. If the island suffered another bad harvest, it would
be difficult for them to blame it all on the king. He knew it and they
knew it. Their own credibility would be at stake.

At his side stood the queen. She had been silenced as well. Ever
since Larine had seen Conall on the little island, the king had
known about her threats to poor Deirdre. He'd half suspected it all
along. No words had needed to be spoken, but she knew that he
knew. There'd be no more trouble from the queen for a good while.
As for the girl, he frankly felt sorry for her. She would be allowed to
return to her father and have Conall's child. Even Goibniu agreed

about that. One day perhaps he'd do something for the child. You never knew when a child from the fringes of the family might come in useful.

A path was clearing through the crowd. Conall, Larine, and two other priests were passing along it. He wondered if Conall would glance up at him, but the young man's face was staring straight ahead with a rapt expression. Thank the gods for that. They reached the druids' mound and went up. The druids in their feather cloaks stood at one end of the mound, while Conall's naked, red-painted figure stood for a moment alone and apart, so that everyone could see him. The High King glanced towards the east. The sky along the horizon was clear. That was good. They would see the sun as it rose. The horizon was starting to gleam. It would not be long now.

Three druids came across to Conall. One was Larine. At a word from one of the older druids, Conall knelt down. From behind, the senior druid placed a garrotte around Conall's neck, but he left it loose. The second held up a curved bronze knife. Larine held up a club.

There had to be three deaths in a Celtic sacrifice: one for the earth, one for the air, one for the sky—the three worlds. In a similar manner, some offerings were burned, others buried, and others thrown in rivers. Conall, therefore, would undergo three ritual deaths. But the actual process was merciful. For Larine would deliver a blow with the club that would stun him; while Conall was scarcely conscious, the senior druid would apply the garrotte that would kill him. Then the curved knife, slitting his throat, would release the blood to be scattered.

The High King glanced at the horizon. The sun was coming. Any instant. On the druids' mound there was a movement as the other druids came across to form a circle around the victim. All the audience could see now was the backs of the druids covered with bright feathers, and in the centre, the club that Larine held high.

And now the king saw the sun flash brightly towards Tara, and turned just in time to see the club fall and vanish with a crack that sounded across the enclosure, followed by a long silence broken only by the rustling of feathers from within the druid's circle.

He thought of the boy and the youth he had known, of Conall's mother—his sister. It was hard, he thought, and he wished it could be otherwise. But Goibniu was right. The thing had to be done. In life there was always sacrifice.

It was over. The druids pulled back, except for the first three. Larine had a large silver bowl in his hands. Conall's red body, its head lolling forward at a curious angle, was lifeless. While the senior druid pulled back the head to expose the neck, the druid with the curved knife moved in swiftly, gashing the throat, while Larine, holding the silver bowl in front of Conall's chest, filled it with his friend's flowing blood.

The High King watched. The blood, it was to be hoped, when scattered on the ground would ensure a better harvest. As he glanced round the crowd, it seemed to him that they were satisfied. That was good. By chance he noticed the girl, Deirdre, standing by her father.

⁘

It was early afternoon when Deirdre announced that instead of remaining for the king's feast, she wanted to go home to Dubh Linn.

Rather to her surprise, nobody raised any objection. The High King, informed of her wish by her father, sent her his blessing and a ring of gold. Soon afterwards, Larine came to let her know that he would visit Dubh Linn soon and that two chariots were ready at their disposal. Her brothers, she was well aware, would have liked to stay for the feast, but their father had made them be silent. She knew she must go now. She could not remain at Tara any longer.

Yet strangely, during the killing of Conall, it was neither grief nor horror that she had felt. She had known what it would look like. Hadn't she seen the culling of the animals at Samhain all her life? No, the emotion she had felt was entirely different.

It was anger.

She had started to feel it almost as soon as Larine had left her the day before. She was alone. Conall had gone and would remain with the druids until the ceremony. She understood their strength, and the king's, and the terrible power of the gods. But with a simple instinct she knew something else: no matter how it was explained, he had deserted her. And as she brooded about it during the night, it came to her again and again: all that time on the island, and even after Larine's visit, he could still have escaped. He had given his word, of course. The king and the gods themselves had demanded it. But he could have escaped. Conall would never have considered such a thing; her father would have told her not to be foolish. But they could have fled together across the sea. He had had the chance. And he had not taken it. He chose the gods, she thought. He chose death, over me. That was all she knew. In her mind she cursed him, and the druids, and even the gods themselves. And so she watched his death with bitterness and anger. It protected her, for a while, from the pain.

It was just before they left that afternoon that she had an unexpected encounter.

She was standing alone by one of the chariots when she saw the queen coming in her direction. Thinking she had better avoid her, Deirdre looked for a means of escape; but the older woman had seen her and was coming straight towards her. So Deirdre stood her ground and hoped for the best. To her surprise, as the queen came close, she gave her a nod that did not seem unfriendly.

"It's a sad day for you, Deirdre, daughter of Fergus. I'm sorry for your trouble." Her eyes stared at Deirdre without any malice. Deirdre wondered what to reply. It was the queen after all. She must show respect. But she couldn't bring herself to do it.

"It's not your good wishes I'm wanting," she said bitterly. It was no way to speak to a queen, but she didn't care. What else had she to lose?

"You're still angry with me," the queen remarked, quite calmly. Deirdre couldn't believe it.

"Didn't you tell me you were going to kill me?" she burst out.

"It is true," the queen agreed, then added, "but that was long ago."

"By the gods," cried Deirdre, "you're a strange woman." But the older woman seemed to accept this, too.

"He made a noble death, at least," she said. "You can be proud of him."

Deirdre only had to bow her head or mumble something polite, but her anger was on her now and she couldn't help herself.

"Proud of a dead man," she cried. "A lot of use to me, sitting all alone in Dubh Linn."

"He had no choice, you know."

"He could have chosen," she said furiously. "He did choose. But it was not myself and his child he chose, now was it?"

She had gone too far this time, and she knew it. She was insulting the High Kingship, the druids, Tara itself. Half defiant, half afraid, she waited for the queen's wrath to fall.

For a moment or two the queen was silent. Her head was bowed, as though she was deep in thought. Then, without looking up, she spoke.

"Did you not know about men, Deirdre? They always let us down."

Then she walked away.

I V

On the day of the midwinter solstice in her father's rath at Dubh Linn, looking over the ford called Ath Cliath, Deirdre, as she had expected, had a son. To her, even at birth, he looked like Conall. She was not sure if she was glad or not.

The weather was fine that spring, and also that summer. The harvest, though not especially good, was not ruined. And men said that it was thanks to Conall, son of Morna, nephew to the High King, who had influence with the gods.

THREE

pATRick

≒ AD 450 ≒

H IS FIRST VISIT had been inauspicious, and few of those
who had sent him back imagined that he would achieve very
much on the distant western island. Yet after his coming, everything
was changed.

He left an account of his life; yet that account, being chiefly a
confession of faith and a justification of his ministry, leaves many
details of his life a mystery. The stories about him were numerous,
but they were mostly inventions. The truth is that history knows
neither the date of his mission, the names of the Irish rulers he encountered, nor even where, exactly, his ministry was based. All is
uncertainty; all is conjecture.

But Saint Patrick existed. There is not a doubt of that. He was
born a minor British aristocrat. As a boy, he was taken from near his
home, somewhere in the western side of Britain, by an Irish raiding
party. Kept on the island as a slave for some years, during which he
mostly tended livestock, he managed to escape and find his way
back across the sea to his parents. But by now he had already de-

cided to follow the religious life. For a time he studied in Gaul; he may have visited Rome. He suggests that certain churchmen considered his learning to be below standard, no doubt because of his interrupted education. But there may be some irony in these statements, for his writings suggest a literary as well as a political sophistication. In due course he was sent, at his own request, as a missionary bishop to the western island where he had once been a slave.

Why did he want to return there? He states in his writings that he had a dream in which he heard the voices of the islanders calling to him, begging him to bring them the Gospel. There is no reason to doubt the authenticity of the record: accounts of supernatural visions and voices abound in the early Church, and have been recorded from time to time ever since. In Saint Patrick's case, the experience was decisive. He begged to be given the thankless and possibly dangerous mission.

The traditional date of his arrival in Ireland, AD 432, is only a guess. It may be too early. But at some time during the decades that followed the collapse of the Roman Empire in the west, Bishop Patrick began his mission. He was by no means the first missionary to reach Irish shores: the Christian communities in Munster and Leinster had already been there for perhaps a generation or more. But he was probably the first missionary in the north if, as seems likely, his base of operations was near Armagh, in Ulster, where the king of the ancient Ulaid, bullied into a reduced territory by the mighty clan of Niall, liked the missionary bishop enough to give him his local protection.

Of Saint Patrick's actual preaching, no reliable record remains. His famous sermon, in which he explained the mystery of the Holy Trinity by comparing it to a shamrock, is a delightful legend, but there is no evidence that he ever said such a thing. Equally, it may be added, no one can say with certainty that he did not. More can be inferred about Saint Patrick's personality and missionary style. Humble himself, like all those who live the life of the spirit, as a bishop of the Holy Church he demanded and received the respect due to a Celtic prince. From his base in Ulster, he may have gone westwards and set up a second missionary front in Connacht. No doubt he was also in contact, from time to time, with his fellow Christians in the southern half of the island.

And did he, upon his travels, descend the ancient road that led across the Liffey at the Ford of Hurdles, and come to the little rath beside Dubh Linn? History can only say that the record, upon this point, is silent.

⁘

It would be any day now. They all knew. Fergus was dying. The autumn leaves were falling and he was ready to go.

And now he had summoned his family to a meeting. What was he going to say?

Fergus had ruled so long that he was the only chief that most of the folk in the area had ever known. With increasing age, his shrewdness and wisdom had continued to develop. Men came to him for justice from all over the Liffey Plain; and the territory around Ath Cliath had come to be known, in much of Leinster, as the Land of Fergus. And for the last twenty years, ever since the death of Conall, she had kept house for him faithfully. Day after day she had nursed him this last, long year, as his splendid old frame gradually broke down. Even now, at the very end, she always kept him clean. And he had been touchingly grateful. "If I've reached such a great age, Deirdre, it's thanks to you," he had told her more than once, in front of her brothers.

Yet it was herself, thought Deirdre, who should be thanking him—for the peace that he had given her. Twenty years of peace beside the Liffey. Twenty years to walk beside its waters, out to the great open sands of the bay and the promontory she loved. Twenty years to bring up her son, Morna, safe under the gentle guardianship of the Wicklow Mountains.

Morna, son of Conall. The one they all loved. The one they protected. The one they had hidden. Morna: the future. He was all she had.

After Conall's death, she had never taken up with any other man. It wasn't that she hadn't felt the need. Sometimes she could have screamed with frustration. The problem had been the men. At first she had supposed that she might find someone at one of the great festivals. "You won't find another Conall," her father had warned her. But she had hoped that perhaps some young chief might take an interest. Her time with Conall had at least given her confidence with men. She held her head high. She could see that she created a stir. But though people were polite—after all, she had been chosen as the bride of the High King himself—they were cautious. The prince who had gone to sacrifice was a figure of strange honour and awe. But his woman, the cause of the trouble, made people nervous.

"You think I'm a bird of ill omen?" she laughingly challenged one young noble. "Are you afraid of me?"

"I'm afraid of nobody," he'd retorted indignantly. But he'd avoided her all the same.

She'd stopped going to the festivals after a year or two.

So what did that leave? A few brave souls in the Dubh Linn region. Two sturdy farmers, a widowed fisherman with three boats: they didn't inspire her. Once her father had brought home a merchant from Britain, who'd sold him some slaves. He was more interesting. But she would have had to go and live across the sea. She was touched that her father should have suggested such a thing, for she knew that he needed her and that he loved his little grandson; when she hadn't wanted to go, he had not looked too sorry.

Morna, they had called him, after Conall's father. His first two years, for her, had been especially difficult. Perhaps if he had not looked so like Conall it would have been easier. He had her strange, green eyes; but in all other respects he was the image of his father. She couldn't help it. Every time she looked at his little face, she had visions of his father's fate awaiting him. She had been troubled by nightmares: nightmares about Tara, nightmares of blood. She had developed a terror of druids—a terror that they would somehow snatch her baby from her and destroy him. A year after Morna's birth, Larine had come, as he had promised that he would. She knew he meant it kindly. But she could not bear to see him and told her father to ask him to go away. Fergus was concerned that if Larine took offence, this might bring on a druid's curse, but Larine had seemed to understand. She had not seen him since.

Morna: he was such a sunny boy. He liked to play, to go hunting with her father. Fergus doted on him. To her relief, he showed no signs of going off alone or of moodiness. He was a lively, affectionate little fellow. He loved to fish, find bird nests, and swim in the waters of the Liffey or the sea. By the time he was four, she had taken him on her favourite walks up to the headland overlooking the island and along the shore where the seabirds cried. Her brothers were kind to him, too. When he was little, they seemed content to play with him all morning. They taught him to fish and drive the cattle. He laughed at their jokes. By the time he was ten, he would cheerfully go off with them on the long cattle drives that might last a month or more.

But above all, it was Fergus who took the boy's education in hand. Once, when Deirdre had started to thank him, he had cut her short. "He's my only grandson," he had growled. "What else would I do?" Indeed, the boy had seemed to give his grandfather a new lease on life. Fergus had seldom been depressed once he had Morna to look after. He drank sparingly. He had seemed to find a new vigour. But she knew there was more to it than that. For he had sensed a special quality in the boy. Everybody did. His quickness at learning delighted Fergus. By the time he was six, Morna knew all the tales of Cuchulainn, and the island's legendary kings, and the ancient gods. He could relate the stories of his mother's family, too, of the slaying of Erc the Warrior. It delighted Fergus to let Morna hold the old drinking skull in his hands while he told it. He taught the boy to use a sword and throw a spear. And, of course, Morna had demanded to know if his own father had been a great warrior, too.

Deirdre had been uncertain what to say, but Fergus had satisfied him without any difficulty. "He fought all kinds of battles," he would say airily. "But the greatest was against Finbarr. A terrible man. Your father killed him near here, on the shores by the Plain of Bird Flocks." Morna never tired of hearing details of the battle, which in due course included the additional slaying of a sea monster. It was hardly surprising, then, that Morna should dream of becoming a warrior and a hero himself. But Fergus had handled this quite well. "I wanted the same thing when I was a boy," he told his grandson. "But warriors mostly go across the sea to plunder other men's goods; whereas look at all the cattle we have here. You will have to defend this place, though." If, as he grew to be a man, Morna sometimes dreamed of being a warrior, he did not speak of it.

It was not, in any case, his potential as a warrior that had so impressed his grandfather. It was his quality of mind. It showed in all he did. By the time he was ten, Fergus made him sit at his side whenever people came to him for justice. After some years, the boy knew almost as much as he did of the island's ancient brehon laws. He delighted in the knottier kinds of problem. If a man sold a single cow and then a month later she produced a calf, to whom did the calf belong: the new or the former owner? If a man built a water mill powered by a stream that came down from another man's land, did the latter have a right to use the water mill free of charge? And subtlest of all, which of two twins was the elder, the firstborn or the second? Elsewhere in Europe, it was the firstborn, but not always on the western island. "For if he comes out behind the other," Morna reasoned, "then he must have been in there first. So the second-born is the elder."

His sons would never have worked that out, Fergus thought. Unless the case concerned themselves, such abstract problems did not interest them.

There was something else about Morna, something hard to define. It showed in his love of music, for he played beautifully on the harp. It showed in his bearing—and it went beyond his dark good looks. Even as a youth, he had the dignity of old Fergus; but there was something more, a magical quality which drew people to him. He was royal.

It had not been easy, deciding what to tell Morna about his royal ancestry. Deirdre had wanted to tell him nothing. "He'll get no good from that quarter," she had argued, "anymore than his father did." Royal blood was a curse, rather than a blessing. Her father didn't disagree with that assessment.

"But we have to tell him something," he said. Morna was ten when his grandfather finally broached the subject.

"Your father had royal blood on his mother's side," he informed him one day. "But it didn't do him any good. The High King took a dislike to him. It was the king who sent Finbarr to kill him."

"Would the High King hate me, too?" the boy had asked.

"He's probably forgotten you exist," Fergus replied, "and you're better off if he has. You're safe enough here at Dubh Linn," he added; and since Morna nodded quietly, the old man assumed he had accepted what had been said.

As for his mother's role in the quarrel with the king and the sacrifice of Conall, Fergus gave orders to his sons and all his people that these things were never to be mentioned in the boy's presence. And indeed, few people would have been inclined to do so anyway. The subject of the prince who had been sacrificed was something to be spoken of sparingly, in hushed tones. Many felt a sense of awkwardness about it; some openly said that the druids had been wrong to do it. The matter, by common consent, was best forgotten. A gentle and protective conspiracy of silence had arisen in the area. And if, occasionally, a traveller were to ask what had become of Conall's woman, nobody even seemed to have heard of her.

As the years had passed, and nobody came to trouble them, Deirdre had found a sense of peace. Her position as matriarch of the family was assured, for neither of her brothers had wives, and Fergus relied upon her entirely. People in the area treated her with respect. And when, that summer, news came that the old High King had died, she had felt at last that she was free: the past could be laid to rest; Morna was safe. Morna—the future.

⁘

She did not know why her father had called them together. At his summons, however, her brothers had obediently come in from the pasture and Morna from the river, and they had all gone into the house. Now they waited to hear what he had to say.

He was a stately old figure, sitting upright, wrapped in a cloak by the fire. His face was pale and gaunt, but his sunken eyes were still piercing. He motioned Morna to stand on his right, and Deirdre on his left, while his two sons stood facing him. Whatever he intended to say, Fergus took his time, gazing at his sons thoughtfully as if he were gathering his strength. While she waited, Deirdre gazed at them also.

Ronan and Rian. Two lanky men. Ronan a little taller than his younger brother, his hair black where Rian's was brown. His face showed some of the same proud features as her father's, but had none of his strength; her brother had also developed a slight stoop at the shoulders, which gave him a hangdog look. Rian looked merely placid.

How was it, in all these years, that neither of them had managed to get a wife? At least one of them could have married. Yet had they even tried? It wasn't as if they had no interest in women. There had been that British slave girl for a while. Certainly Ronan had slept with her. She thought they both had. There had even been a child, except that it had died. Then the girl had become sickly and in the end Deirdre had sold her. She'd offered to buy them another, but somehow the business had lapsed and they'd never brought it up again. She heard that they found women when they were away on the cattle drives or at the festivals. But never a wife. "Too much trouble," they had told her. And more gratifyingly, "No one else could ever keep house like you." In a way, she supposed, she should be grateful not to have rivals in her little domain. The years had passed anyway, and her brothers had seemed happy enough, hunting and minding Fergus's herd of cattle which, it must be said, had grown.

Hadn't her father been disappointed, though, at the failure of his sons to provide him with grandchildren? He probably had, but he never said so; and since during all the years that went by, he had never put any pressure on them to marry, she had realised that he must have come to his own private conclusions about his sons.

At last Fergus spoke.

"My end is drawing close. A few more days. Then it will be time for a new chief of the Ui Fergusa."

The Ui Fergusa: the descendants of Fergus. It was the custom on the island for a clan to elect its chief from the inner family—normally the male descendants, down to second cousin, of a single great-grandfather. In the case of the little clan who held Dubh Linn, there were no surviving male descendants, apart from Deirdre's brothers, of Fergus's father, Fergus, nor even of his grandfather who had supplied them with the old drinking skull. After Deirdre's brothers, therefore, unless they provided male heirs, the clan would have a problem. The rules, however, were not absolute. Survival was the key.

"Old though I am," Fergus pointed out, "there has never been a designated Tanaiste." This was the recognised heir to a chief. It was quite common for a clan to name an heir during a chief's rule, even from the moment the chief was chosen. "Assuming one of you two, Ronan or Rian, should succeed me, there is no one to inherit after you except Deirdre's son."

"It would have to be Morna," they both agreed. "Morna should be chief after us."

"Would he make a good chief?" he asked.

"The best. No question," they both replied.

"Then here is what I propose." He gazed at them calmly. "Let Morna be chief instead of you." He paused. "Consider. If you choose him yourselves, no one can argue as to his right. You both love him like a son and he thinks of you as a pair of fathers. Unite behind Morna, and the clan of Fergus will be strong." He stopped and looked carefully from one to the other. "This is my dying wish."

Deirdre watched them. She had no idea that her father was going to propose such a thing. She had assumed that Morna might inherit from his uncles in due course, even though not in the male line. But she saw the deep logic in the old man's words. The truth was that neither of them was really fit to be a chief, and in their heart of hearts they both probably knew it. But to have their hands forced like this, to give up their claims to their sister's son, who was still a youth? That was a hard thing. In the long silence which now followed, she wasn't even sure how she felt about it herself. Did she want such a thing so soon? Would this cause bad feelings, and even expose Morna to danger? She was just wondering whether to intervene and ask her father to reconsider, when her brother Ronan spoke.

"He is too young," he said firmly. "But if I am chief, then he can be named as my Tanaiste. What can be the objection to that?"

Deirdre stared. Ronan had gone pale; Rian was looking uncomfortable. Morna glanced at her, uncertain and concerned.

"I should prefer to wait," he said to his grandfather respectfully. "Ronan's suggestion would make me happy."

But the old man, though he smiled at his grandson, shook his head.

"It is better this way," he answered. "I have considered this matter carefully, and I have made up my mind."

"You have made up your mind?" Ronan burst out bitterly. "And what does that signify? Isn't it for us to decide after you've gone?"

Deirdre had never heard her brother address her father with such disrespect, but Fergus took it very calmly.

"You are angry," he said quietly.

"Let Morna have it, Ronan." It was Rian who interposed now, his voice gently pleading. "What would either of us do with the chiefdom anyway?" It suddenly occurred to Deirdre that Rian might prefer having Morna as chief, to being ruled by his brother. As she looked at the two of them, she saw how deftly her old father had handled the business. For not only would Ronan have made a poor chief, but once they heard that Fergus had designated Morna, none of their people at Dubh Linn would accept her brother as chief anyway.

And in the silence that followed, Ronan must have realised this, too. For after a while he sighed.

"Let the boy have it then, if that is your wish." He gave his nephew a wry smile. "You'll make a good chief, Morna. I won't deny it. With a little guidance," he added, to save his face.

"That is what I had hoped to hear," said Fergus. "You have shown wisdom, Ronan, as I knew you would."

And now, placing a hand on Morna's arm, the old chief slowly rose. Since he hadn't walked unaided for nearly a month, Deirdre could only guess what the effort must be costing him, and she almost moved to help him; but she understood that this was not what he wished. With the cloak still wrapped round him, Fergus stood there like a statue, his gauntness only adding to his dignity.

"Bring the drinking skull," he quietly ordered her; and when she had done so, and held it in front of him, he placed his hand upon it and indicated that Morna and his uncles should do the same.

"Swear," he commanded them. "Swear that it is Morna who shall be chief."

So they swore. And when the thing was done, they embraced each other, and agreed what a fine thing it was that they had done; and then Fergus rested. And Deirdre, uncertain whether she was glad or not at what had just come to pass, could only wonder one thing: Ronan had given way to Morna gracefully, but would he keep his word?

✤

The single chariot arrived the following afternoon. It was a swift and splendid vehicle. Morna and his uncles, as it happened, were away with the cattle; Fergus, feeling weak after the events of the previous day, was resting inside; but Deirdre, who had been sitting in the sun outside the rath mending a shirt, had watched its approach with interest. It was not often such a noble equipage came that way. Standing in it, beside the charioteer, was a young nobleman of about Morna's age, with long dark moustaches and a fine green cloak, who glancing down at her called out to know if this was the house of Fergus.

"It is, but he is sick. What is your business with him?"

"None of yours, I should think," the young warrior, who obviously thought she was a servant, replied casually. "But it's Morna, son of Conall, I have come to find."

"Morna?" She was suspicious at once, and was wondering what to reply when her father's voice came faintly from within.

"Who is it, Deirdre?"

"Just a traveller, Father," she called, "passing upon his way."

"Let him come in, then," he cried weakly, but this was followed by a cough and the sound of the chief struggling to catch his breath again, so that it was easy for her to give a firm reply.

"I am Deirdre, daughter of Fergus. As you can hear, my father is very sick. Indeed," she lowered her voice, "it cannot be many more days now that he will live. You may give your message to me."

The messenger looked put out, but he could hardly argue.

"It's a message from the High King I'm to deliver. He is to hold the feis at Tara. And he asks that your son, Morna, attend."

"Tara?" Deirdre looked at the young noble with alarm. "Why should Morna rather than Fergus go to the feis?"

And now it was the visitor's turn to look surprised.

"It would be strange if he didn't," he replied. "His being the High King's own cousin."

The feis—the inauguration at which the king would mate with a mare—was not until Samhain. That was still some way off. She told herself she had a little time. But why should the new king have taken this sudden interest in Morna? Was it just an act of kindness to a relation whom the old king had ignored? Or was there some other purpose behind it? She had no way of knowing. What should she do?

And then she was almost astonished to hear her own voice calmly replying.

"This is wonderful news indeed." She gave the young noble a smile. "My son will be honoured. We are all honoured. There is only one problem."

"What is that?"

"He is not here. He is away." She gestured towards the estuary. "On a sea voyage. He has promised to return before winter, but . . ." She sighed. "If I knew where he was I could send after him. He would be heartbroken indeed to miss such a great event."

"You think he will return in time though?"

"He knows his grandfather is not long for this world. We hope he will return before his grandfather departs. But it is in the hands of the gods."

She offered him refreshment, but indicated that it would be better not to go into the sickroom where her father lay.

The messenger stayed only briefly before departing. With him he carried messages of loyalty from the old chief and the clear impression that young Morna would hasten eagerly to the feis if he reached the island's shores in time. Her performance, Deirdre told herself afterwards, had been rather impressive. There was only one problem.

She had just lied to the High King.

Why had she done it? She could hardly say. But Morna must not go. She felt sure of it. Even during the brief time the messenger had stayed at the rath, she had sat there in a state of misery. When he left, it seemed to her as if a dark and dangerous presence had departed from the place. That night, she had a nightmare in which she and Morna were approaching Tara and the starlings were rising up from the ground again in a black mist. She awoke in a cold panic. No, he must not go.

The next day, Morna and her brothers returned. She had given the slaves instructions to say nothing of the messenger's visit. But in any case, no one had heard what had been said. None of them— Morna, her brothers, nor the chief himself—had any idea what she had done.

There was risk, of course. If the new High King ever discovered the lie, he would consider it an insult. But at least the lie was hers. He could do to her what he liked. She didn't care. Indeed, there was only one small, niggling doubt that briefly troubled her conscience. Was it possible that she was wrong, that the new High King meant only courtesy or friendship—that in truth there was no danger to Morna in the invitation at all? Could it be that her fear was not so much for his safety, but rather that if he went to the High King and found favour at his hands, he might not want to return to her at Dubh Linn? Was she being not only foolish but even selfish? No. That wasn't it. She put the unwelcome thought out of her mind.

⁘

The final decline of Fergus the chief began three days later.

They were trying times. There was the sadness of watching her father slipping away; the sadness, too, of seeing Morna's grief at his passing. Her two brothers were subdued; several times Rian had seemed close to tears, and if Ronan felt anger at being passed over, even that seemed to be forgotten now. She nursed the old man as-siduously. She was determined that his passing should be as gentle and as dignified as possible. But she had to admit that there was also one other consideration in her mind.

If she could just keep Fergus alive until Samhain. Let him die, if die he must, just after that. Even if the High King found out that Morna had been at Dubh Linn then, he would hardly complain about the young man remaining to attend his chief and grandfather on his deathbed. Live, she willed him. Live another month for me. "Let him live," she prayed silently to the gods of her people, "at least past the festival of Samhain." And when, instead, he had slipped from her in early October, her grief was made even sharper by her desperate anxiety.

They gave a fine wake for him. Nobody could fault the family of Fergus for that. For three days the guests had drunk and talked, eaten and sung. They had drunk as only the friends of the dead can do. Chiefs, farmers, cowherds, fishermen, they had all turned up to drink him into the better world beyond. "A fine wake, Deirdre," they said.

They buried him, perhaps not quite as he might have dreamed— standing upright, fully armed, staring across the ford at his invisible enemies—but honourably enough, under a handsome mound beside the estuary waters. And at the same time, they proclaimed that Morna was the new chief.

With the wake over, Dubh Linn returned to its customary quiet and settled into the rhythms of autumn. Morna and his uncles brought the cattle in from the summer pasture. In the woods, the pigs were getting fat on the fallen acorns. Down the road towards the mountains, one could hear, from time to time, the roar of a stag in the rutting season. At the rath, all was quiet. A morning might pass with only the sound of the stream splashing into the dark pool below and the gentle rustle of the falling leaves. The weather was fine, but Deirdre was conscious of the days drawing shorter and of a sharpness in the air.

She was also conscious of the date. Samhain was not far off. The river crossing might be deserted now, but soon there would be parties of travellers making their way up the road from the south towards the feis at Tara. And now a further realisation came to her which, with everything else on her mind, she had not thought about before: the travellers would be passing by the rath. As chief, Morna would be expected to give them hospitality and to entertain them. Such a handsome young chief would be remarked upon. Someone arriving at Tara was bound to mention the successor to old Fergus at the Ford of Hurdles. Could it really be hoped that no word of Morna's presence would reach the ears of the High King? No, it could not. The case was hopeless. Unless she could think of something, her lie was going to be discovered.

What else could she do? She couldn't think of anything. Send Morna away? On what possible pretext? Common sense said that there was only one thing to do. She must tell him about the High King's summons at once and let him decide what to do for himself. Yet the autumn season made it even worse. The sights, the smells, the feel of the chill autumn air, all seemed to be conspiring to drag her back to that season when she had gone so unwillingly on that terrible journey with Conall to Tara. She felt very lonely. She wished Fergus were there to give his advice, but she suspected that she knew what that advice would be. Tell Morna.

So why didn't she do it? She couldn't. That wasn't an answer. She knew it. With every day that Samhain drew nearer, her predicament grew. Days passed. She began to promise herself, each night, that on the following day she would tell him. Each morning she would awake and decide to wait, just until that evening, in case something—she had no idea what—but something should turn up during the day to resolve the situation. And each evening, when nothing had changed, she had promised herself, once again, to tell him in the morning.

One of the British slaves saw them first. By the time she reached the entrance to the rath, the party of horsemen was halfway across the Ford of Hurdles. There seemed to be four of them. One, close to the leader, seemed to be carrying a spear or trident of some kind, which, when it swung behind the leader's head, gave him a strange appearance, as if he were a deer with antlers. She watched curiously as they drew closer. And then, with a sudden, sickening sense, like that of a dream returning, she realised who the leader was.

It was Larine.

He must have come from the High King.

He rode up the path to the rath slowly. He was not much changed. His hair was grey now, but shaved in the same tonsure. He looked fit. His face was still quiet and thoughtful. She watched his approach with a sinking heart. And he was nearly at the entrance when the strangest thing occurred. The British slaves—there were half a dozen of them now—all ran forward and fell on their knees before him. He turned as he passed and gravely made a sign over them. A moment later he dismounted and stood in front of her.

"What is it you want, Larine?" she asked him, trying to keep the dread out of her voice.

"Only you, and your son," he answered quietly.

That was it, then. He had come to take them to Tara. Only one thing struck her as odd. The slaves were standing round, with smiles on their faces.

"What are my slaves doing?" she demanded. "Why were they kneeling?"

"Because they are British, Deirdre. They are Christians."

"Then why would they be kneeling to a druid?"

"Ah." He smiled. "You did not know. You see, I am a Christian, Deirdre." He paused. "In fact, I am a bishop."

She gazed at him, confused.

"But haven't you come from the High King?"

He looked at her in mild surprise.

"The High King? Not at all. I haven't seen the king in many years." He took her gently by the arm. "I see that I had better explain. May we go inside?" And indicating to his men that they should wait for him, he led the way.

She was still trying to comprehend his words as they went in. The tall staff she had mistaken for a trident turned out to be a cross. The young man who held it proudly in his hands remained outside with the two servants as she followed Larine in. But Larine the druid now a Christian? How could that be? What did she know about Christians anyway? She tried to think.

The Romans were Christians. Everyone knew that. Like many on the western island, she had vaguely supposed that with the breaking down of all things Roman across the seas, they would hear less of Christianity as the years went by. Strangely, however, the opposite had been the case.

It was her father who always picked up the news. From the occasional merchant ships that came to the landing place at Dubh Linn, he learned that far from giving up, the Christian churches in Gaul and even in Britain seemed to see the troubles and invasions as a challenge to their religion, and they were fighting back. She knew there were some Christians on the island, in the south. And once in a while her father used to return from one of his journeys and report: "Would you believe it, but we've another group of Christians in Leinster now. There's only a few of them, but the King of Leinster has allowed them to be there. There's no doubt of that." But if the Christian priests had originally come to minister to the slaves, as the years went by Fergus had started to bring other scraps of news. A chief, or his wife, had been converted. One year he had heard of a development which made him shake his head. "A group of Christians are planning to set up a place of worship in sight of a druid sanctuary. Can you believe it?"

Yet if she had supposed that Fergus would have been passionately against these foreign encroachments, she was surprised to find that his reaction was quite muted. The worst he would say about the affront to the druids was that it was "unwise." When she challenged him about this and asked him how the King of Leinster could have allowed such a thing, he had given her a thoughtful glance and remarked, "The king might be glad of them, Deirdre. If the druids get too powerful, it's a way of keeping them in order. He can frighten them with the Christian priests." His cynical attitude had rather shocked her.

But even her old father would surely have been astonished to see

Larine the druid entering the rath now as a Christian bishop. As they sat down, Larine gave her a friendly but searching look, expressed his regret at the passing of her father, remarked that she looked well, and then, in a matter-of-fact way, observed, "You are afraid of me, Deirdre."

"It was you who came to take Conall away," she reminded him with a quiet bitterness.

"It was his wish to go."

She stared at him. He might be a grey-haired bishop now, but all she could see at that moment was the quiet druid, the supposed friend who had persuaded Conall to desert her and give up his life to the cruel gods at Tara. If the autumn season had recently brought back the memories of that terrible time, now, in Larine's presence, the day of the sacrifice itself, the sight of Conall walking out with his naked body daubed in red, the druids with their clubs and strangling ropes and knives—all these came rushing back to her with a vividness, an actuality that made her shudder.

"You druids killed him," she cried, with a passionate anger. "May the gods curse you all!"

He sat very still. She had insulted him, but he did not seem angry. He only looked sad. For a moment or two he did not reply. Then he sighed.

"It is true, Deirdre. I helped perform the sacrifice. Forgive me if you can." He paused while she continued to stare at him. "I have never forgotten it. I loved him, Deirdre. Remember that. I loved Conall and I respected him. Tell me," he asked quietly, "do you have nightmares about that day?"

"I do."

"So did I, Deirdre. For many years." He looked down, thoughtfully. "It was a long time since the druids had sacrificed a man, you know." He raised his eyes to hers again. "Do you approve of the sacrifices the druids make?"

She shrugged. "They have always sacrificed. Animals."

"And men, too, in the past." He sighed. "I confess to you,

Deirdre, that after the death of Conall, I began to lose my desire for sacrifices. I wanted no more of them."

"You do not believe in the sacrifices?"

He shook his head. "It was a terrible thing, Deirdre, that was done to Conall. Terrible. I am stricken with grief, I cringe for shame whenever I think of it. Yet when it was done, we all supposed we were acting for the best. I thought so, Deirdre, and so, I can assure you, did Conall." He shook his head sadly. "That is the way with the old gods, Deirdre. It has always been the same: always those terrible sacrifices, whether of men or animals; always the shedding of blood to placate gods who, if truth be told, are no better than the men who make the sacrifices."

The thought seemed to depress him. He shook his head sorrowfully before taking up his theme again. "It is only here, Deirdre, that such things are still done, you know. In Britain, Gaul, and Rome, they have long since turned to the true God. Our gods are held in contempt. And rightly so." He gazed at her earnestly. "Think of it, Deirdre, can we really suppose that the sun, the sky, the earth, and the stars were made by such beings as the Dagda with his cauldron, or the other multiplicity of gods behaving, often as not, like foolish, cruel children? Could this world be made by anything other than a supreme being so great, so all-embracing, that He passes our understanding?"

Did he expect her to reply? She wasn't sure. She was so astonished to hear him speaking in this way that she would hardly have known what to say in any case.

"When I was a druid," he continued quietly, "I often felt such things. I felt the presence of an eternal God, Deirdre, I felt it when I performed the morning and evening prayers, I felt it in the great silences when I was alone, yet without truly understanding what it was that I felt." He smiled. "But now, Deirdre, I do understand. All these feelings come from the one, true God which the whole of Christendom knows.

"And the wonder of it is," he went on, "that there is no need for any further sacrifice. You know, I suppose, why we are called Christians." He briefly outlined the life of Jesus Christ. "God gave His only Son to be sacrificed on a cross. That sacrifice was made for all men and for all time." He smiled. "Think of it, Deirdre: there is no need for any blood sacrifice, neither of man nor of beast. The ultimate sacrifice has already been made. We are free. All sacrifices are over." He watched her as he gave her this news.

She was silent for a moment.

"And this is the message you preach now, in contrast to the druids?"

"I do. And it is a comforting message. For the true God is not a greedy or a vengeful god, Deirdre. He is a loving God. He wants only that we should love one another and live in peace. That is the finest faith I can think of, and I want no other. I have no doubt," he added, "that it's the truth."

"Are you the only druid to become a Christian?"

"By no means. Many of the priests of the old religion are violently opposed. That is what you would expect. But some of the most learned of us have taken an interest for a long time. The Christian Church, you know, holds all the learning of the Roman world."

Deirdre frowned. She still wasn't sure what to make of this.

"But you had to abandon everything you had believed before."

"Not entirely. For some of us, as I said, the new faith was really what we had been looking for all the time. As a Christian priest, I experience the same sense of things. The world is just as full of poetry. Do you remember the words of Amairgen's great poem?

I am the Wind on the Sea

"One of our bishops has made a hymn, to the Creator of Creation—the one God, that is—and one of its verses is rather similar. Listen to this:

I arise today
Through the strength of heaven:
Light of sun,
Radiance of moon,
Splendour of fire,
Speed of lightning,
Swiftness of wind,
Depth of sea,
Stability of earth,
Firmness of rock.

"The inspiration is the same, but we recognise the true source of it." He smiled and pointed to his shaven head. "You see, as a Christian priest, I didn't even have to change my druid's tonsure."

"I suppose so." She frowned. "And who," she asked, "converted you?"

"Ah. A good question. A man called Bishop Patrick. A great man. It was he who made the poem, actually."

Deirdre received this information but made no further comment. The fact was that her mind was working rapidly. The visit of Larine, with his startling new identity and his still more surprising message, might take a little time to sink in, but certain things seemed clear. There could hardly be any doubt of his sincerity; and whatever her feelings about the past, she was touched by his obvious goodwill. As for his religious message, she was less certain. Perhaps she was tempted by it; certainly she had little love for the sacrifices of the druids and their cruel gods. But it was another thought now that was forming in her mind.

"You said you had come to see me and my son. You wish to convert us?"

"Certainly." He smiled. "I have found the light, Deirdre, and it has brought me joy and peace of mind. Naturally I wish to share that joy with others." He paused. "But there is more than that. After all that has passed, I owe it to Conall to bring the Gospel to you and to his son."

She nodded slowly. Yes, she thought, yes, this might be the way. The persuasive bishop, his father's old friend, might be the one who could offer her a way out of her dilemma about Morna. At least, she considered, it was worth a try. So now, gazing at him steadily, she informed him: "You should understand something, Larine. Morna has never been told about how his father died. I couldn't bear to. We all thought it was for the best. So he knows nothing."

"I see." Larine certainly looked surprised. "Do you mean," he asked, "that you don't want me to say anything either?"

"No." She shook her head. "No, Larine, I think it is time that he should know. And I want you to tell him. Will you do that?"

"If that is what you wish."

"Tell him what really happened, Larine. Tell him how the High King and his druids murdered his father. Tell him of the evil of it," she continued passionately. "Tell him of your new and better God, if you like. Tell him, above all, to avoid the king and his druids. Will you do that for me?"

Did Larine look awkward for just a moment? She did not see why he should. Wasn't this what he wanted? And wouldn't it solve her greatest difficulty if Morna was sufficiently impressed with Larine's Christian message to want to avoid the druids' rites? If she told him about the High King's invitation after that, he probably wouldn't even want to go to the pagan feis at Tara. With luck, if they could keep him out of sight for a while, he should be able to avoid the attention of the High King in the future.

"I will do what I can," said Larine, cautiously.

"That is good." She smiled. And she was just wondering whether to tell Larine the whole story of the royal invitation and to ask for his advice, when their conversation was brought to an abrupt halt by the sudden appearance in the doorway of Morna himself.

"Who are these visitors?" he asked cheerfully.

And Larine gasped.

···

How strange, Larine thought, as he walked beside the young man down the slope towards the water. He had come to Dubh Linn expecting, in a sense, to put a painful memory to rest; yet instead, the past was coming alive before his very eyes with a vividness that was almost frightening.

For it was Conall himself who was walking beside him. True, young Morna had his mother's strange green eyes. But his dark hair and his aquiline good looks were Conall to the life. It was as if his friend had arisen from the dead. Dear God, he even had his father's gentle voice. And when the young man smiled at him, Larine felt as though someone had struck a druid's knife into his heart.

It was easy enough to introduce the subject he had come to speak about; for as soon as Morna learned that Larine had been a friend of his father's, he was eager to know all that the former druid could tell him. He was fascinated to hear about the prince's poetic and religious nature. "I thought of him only as a warrior," he said.

"He was a warrior, and a fine one," Larine assured him, "but he was far more than that." And he explained how Conall had wanted to be a druid. From there, it was only a little while before he told Morna about the sacrifice. The young man was astounded.

"And you yourself took part?"

"I was a druid. I was his friend. It was his own wish, Morna. He gave himself up as a sacrifice for the people of the island. The noblest thing a man can do. Your father died a hero's death," he told him. "You can be very proud. But now," he continued, seeing that Morna was much impressed, "let me tell you about another person who gave himself up as a sacrifice."

It was with great feeling that Larine explained to his friend's son the powerful message of the Christian faith. "The old gods," he concluded, "have yielded their place to the Supreme Deity. Just think of it, Morna: instead of a sacrifice to save a harvest, Our Saviour sacri-

ficed Himself to save the whole world, not for a season but for all
eternity."

If Larine's presentation of the faith to this young man, so obviously hungry to emulate the heroic father he had never known, was
subtly different from the case he had made to Deirdre, he was
pleased to see that it seemed to be effective.

"Do you think my father would have been a Christian," he
asked, "if he'd had the chance?"

"There is not a doubt of it," Larine replied. "We'd have been
Christians together. How I wish," he sighed, "that he were here to
join with me now. We'd have walked this path together." He said it
with real emotion.

"I could take his place," Morna said eagerly.

"You are so like him," Larine answered. "That would bring me
great joy." He nodded reflectively. "You might say, the circle would
be complete."

They were standing beside the river. Now they turned to go back
to the rath. Morna was clearly excited. As the former druid glanced
at him, did he feel, just for a moment, a pang of guilt at what he was
doing? He thought of his plan. Was he making use of the son of
Conall for his own ends? No, he told himself. He was bringing the
family of Conall into the light. If, in so doing, he was serving the
larger cause of the mission, then so much the better. For that was an
even greater cause. And his sense of mission was strong.

By the time they entered the rath again, Deirdre and the slaves
were preparing the meal, and Ronan and Rian had returned. The
two brothers were already engaged in a conversation with the young
priest who had accompanied Larine. He was a decent man from
Ulster whom Larine had converted a few years ago, and the brothers seemed to like him; but when they saw Larine, they were careful
to be respectful. As a former druid, the bishop was clearly not a man
to be crossed. They chatted for a while. He made the usual small
conversation, spoke about Ulster and the harvest up there; and this

led easily enough to a brief account of his mission. They listened politely as he outlined some of the essentials of the Christian faith. It was hard to tell what they thought, but he had the impression that they would probably follow Morna and Deirdre in most things. Before long they were called inside to eat.

It was when the household had all gathered in the big thatched hut, and Larine had blessed the food, that he made the announcement.

"Tonight, my friends, we eat together, and enjoy the excellent hospitality of this house. But now I must tell you that tomorrow you will receive a far greater guest than I. For I have come only to prepare the way for him; whereas he will come to preach and to baptise." He paused impressively. "It is Bishop Patrick himself I am speaking of."

This was a technique that Larine had used before with success. He, the former druid, would go into an area where Bishop Patrick was not known to prepare the path for the great man and make sure the audience understood the importance of their visitor. Briefly, he said a few words about the missionary. He outlined the bishop's ancestry—for it was always important, in the ancient society of the western island, that his hearers should know that Patrick was a man of noble birth in his own right. That, for a start, would gain their respect. He gave them some account of how he was captured, of his years on the island as a slave, and of his subsequent return. He also named some of the princes in the north who had given Patrick their protection and had even been converted. This information, too, would impress his hearers. He also gave some indications of the great man's character.

"He is a prince of the Church; to his followers, his word is law," he explained. "And yet, like other men who have reached the high places of the spirit, he has a great simplicity. He is austere. He honours all women, but he is entirely celibate. He is humble. He is also quite without fear. People have sometimes threatened him for preaching the Gospel, but it never has any effect."

"He has a terrible temper," the young priest added with some relish.

"It is not often seen," Larine gently corrected, "but it is true that his rebuke is terrible. But now," he said with a smile at Deirdre, "let us attend to this feast."

⁘

Deirdre was proud of the meal she had prepared. There was a watercress salad; several meat dishes, including the traditional pork for an honoured guest; stewed apples; cheese; and ale—the best of the island's fare. When Larine complimented her warmly on the food and was joined by a chorus of approval, she knew that she had deserved it.

If it was strange that the Christian bishop should be sitting amongst them while in the background the drinking skull of Erc the Warrior gave a pale and ghostly glimmer in the firelight, it did not seem to strike anyone. Larine talked easily to the men, speaking of everyday things. He told them about events up in Ulster, and encouraged them to tell him stories about old Fergus. The conversation was light and cheerful. The only time he mentioned the subject of religion came after they had already finished the main courses, when he turned to her and remarked: "It may take a generation or two, Deirdre, but once it has established a sound foundation, it's inevitable that the true religion will triumph here on the island, just as it has in every other land where it has come. The communities down in Munster and here in Leinster are still small and scattered, but they have protectors and they are starting to grow. And now Bishop Patrick is making great strides in Ulster, especially with the princes." He smiled. "Once the princes are convinced, you see, their people will follow."

"You do not think the druids could bring people back to the old faith, once they have known the new?" she asked.

"I don't. At the end of the day, our pagan gods are only superstition. Idols. Before the higher understanding, they must fall away."

Deirdre was not so sure about this last assertion. It seemed to her that the druids and their gods would not so easily retreat, but she said nothing. She would have liked at this point to have told Larine about the invitation of Morna to Tara and to have asked his advice, but the others would have heard, and so she said nothing. But shortly afterwards, watching the bishop and her son conversing happily and seeing the admiration in the young man's face, it seemed to her that it shouldn't be a difficult matter for Larine to persuade him to avoid the pagan ceremonies. And so she sat back with a sense of comfort and well-being and let the talk go on around her. Her mind even wandered a little. She saw Larine say something to Morna and saw her son look surprised. Then, suddenly, she was all attention. What was he saying? She stared.

At first, when he said it, she thought she had misheard.

"The High King's feis," Larine repeated. "I wondered when you were leaving for Tara. As you're taking part."

"Myself? Taking part?" Morna was looking slightly bemused. "The keeper of the ford provides hospitality to the important men on their way up to Tara," he explained, "but I wouldn't be going there myself."

Now, however, it was Larine who was confused.

"But you can hardly fail to obey your kinsman the High King when he has summoned you," he said.

"The High King has summoned me?" Morna looked blank.

Deirdre went cold. Larine appeared strangely put out. But nobody was looking at her yet. They hadn't guessed. How, she wondered, had Larine known of the king's summons to the young chief at Dubh Linn? Hadn't he told her he never went near the High King now? She supposed that, as in times past, Larine probably had sources of information in many places. But what should she do? Was this the moment to confess the truth? She couldn't see a way out. But she decided, just for a few more moments, to play for time. Besides, there was something that was puzzling her.

"At the feis," she pointed out quietly, "it will be the druids who conduct the ceremonies."

"Of course," agreed Larine.

"There will be sacrifices."

"Of animals. Yes."

"And the king will mate with a mare?"

"I imagine he may."

"Would you take part in such a pagan rite yourself?" she asked Larine.

"It would not be appropriate."

"So if Morna becomes a Christian, he should avoid such a pagan rite, surely?"

Larine hesitated only a moment.

"If the High King summoned Morna to come, it would be difficult, I should say, for him to refuse. I should not insist upon it. In fact . . ." He stopped. Then he looked at her shrewdly. "So tell me, Deirdre, how is it that Morna does not know that he has been summoned by the High King?"

They were turning to her now. She was silent. Morna was frowning.

"Mother?"

Her brothers were staring, too. It was no good. She was going to have to confess what she had done. She was going to be humiliated in front of them. She could see it. Her brothers were going to blame her. And Morna . . . much as he loved her, he would curse her, too. She knew it. Her hopeless, desperate plans, her plans that suddenly looked so foolish, were all unravelling. She gazed miserably at Larine, and saw a little glint of expectation in his eye.

And then, suddenly, she understood.

"This is why you're here," she cried. "This is what you came for. You came for Morna because you thought he was going to Tara."

Yes, a faint shadow of guilt had passed across Larine's face. Morna was about to intervene, but she cut him off.

"You don't understand," she snapped at her son. "He's using you."

She saw it all. Larine might be a bishop, she thought, but he was still Larine; and he had come again, in a different guise, as he had come before. All her old memories came flooding back: the black mist of birds, the raucous trumpets, the body of Conall daubed in red. "You're just another sacrifice," she said bitterly.

Larine was clever. You couldn't deny it. What was it he'd said? Convert the princes first. That was his game. If you couldn't get to the prince, then get to his family circle. He'd heard that the new king was taking an interest in young Morna. So of course he wanted to convert him. Then he could insinuate a convert into the circle of the High King himself.

"What's the plan?" she demanded. "For Morna to reveal that he's a Christian at the feis?" Morna, the image of his father, Conall, the kinsman of the High King who had given his life for the druids and their pagan gods—Morna was to arrive and say he was a Christian? At Tara itself, the sacred royal site? At the inauguration? It would create a sensation. "Or do you prefer he should conceal his faith until he has made the High King his friend?" That might be even better for Larine. If the High King and his family took a liking to the handsome boy. Of course they would. How could they not? Then in due course he would reveal he was a Christian.

Either way it was a brilliant move, an insidious undermining of the ancient pagan order.

And what would become of Morna? If he revealed his religion at Tara, the High King could hardly tolerate it, and the druids would probably kill him on the spot. If he gained the king's friendship and confessed his new faith later, he would still, at the least, incur the druids' undying enmity.

"They'll destroy you," she cried to her son. "They'll kill you just as they killed your father."

Larine was shaking his head.

"Mother," the young man protested, "Larine is our friend."

"You don't know him," she answered furiously.

"He is our guest."

"No more!" She struck the table and rose to her feet. "Traitor!" She pointed her finger at him. "You can change your shape but never your nature. You are always the same, and I know you. The same cunning fox. Leave!"

Now Larine had risen to his feet also. He was white and shaking with fury. The priest who accompanied him had risen, too.

"This is no way to treat a guest in your house, Deirdre," Larine protested. "Especially a Christian man of peace."

"A man of blood!" she shouted.

"I am a bishop of the Holy Church."

"Deceiver."

"We'll not sleep in this house," Larine said with dignity.

"Sleep with the pigs," she rejoined, and watched as, followed by his people, he stalked out into the darkness. Her brothers, after a moment's pause and a rather bewildered look at her, followed after them, presumably to arrange their sleeping quarters in one of the other huts. That left herself and Morna.

He did not speak. She wondered what to say. For a moment, she almost said, I'm sorry. But she was afraid to do so. In the end, she said, "I'm right, you know."

He did not reply.

She began, angrily, to help the slaves clear up the remains of the meal. He silently helped her, but kept at a distance. Neither of them spoke. After they had finished her brother Ronan returned.

"They're in the barn," he said, and seemed about to say more; but she silenced him with a look. Only then did Morna speak.

"There is something, Mother, you seem to have forgotten."

"What is that?" She suddenly felt weary.

"It is not for you to tell our guests to leave. I am the chief now."

"It was for your own good."

"I will be the judge of that. Not you."

Out of the corner of her eye she saw Ronan smirk.

"You have also deceived me, Mother," Morna went on quietly. "It is true, isn't it, that the High King summoned me to Tara?"

"I was going to tell you." She paused. "I was afraid. After your father . . ." She trailed off. How could she ever explain it all to him? "You do not know the danger," she said.

"I must go to Tara, Mother."

She nodded her head sadly. Yes, he would have to go.

"But do not go as a Christian, Morna. I beg you. At least do not do that."

"I will decide that also." His words felt like a heavy stone hung round her neck. She sagged. "I am going outside now, to apologise to Larine. If he comes back inside, you will be courteous to him. But it may be better if you sleep in the barn yourself." He left.

Ronan remained. He was looking at her curiously. She supposed that after all the years in which she had been the dominant force in the household, and after his humiliation at being passed over for the position of chief, he probably took some satisfaction in her own. In a little while, Morna came back.

Not surprisingly, Larine had declined to return.

⁜

The situation the following morning was not good. The Christians were outside, but had announced that they would not be leaving until Bishop Patrick arrived. No doubt they were looking forward to watching the missionary from the north exhibit his famous temper. Deirdre knew that she should apologise, but since her brothers were standing truculently with the visitors, she could not bring herself to do so. She had told the slaves to feed them and a large bowl of porridge had been prepared. Morna was outside also, but had tactfully decided to occupy himself with the animals. She had no idea what he was thinking.

The morning wore on. Larine seemed to be spending his time in prayer. His followers were talking to her brothers. At one point Ronan came in and remarked: "There's a lot in what these

Christians say, Sister. They tell us you'll be going to eternal hellfire."
Then he went out again.

⁘

It was nearly midday when one of the slaves announced that a chariot was approaching. Larine rose, looked through the gateway of the
rath, and went out. A long pause followed. Obviously the two bishops were conferring. Perhaps, Deirdre thought, as she followed
Larine to the gateway, Bishop Patrick would go away.

The cortege which had halted a short distance in front of the entrance to the rath consisted of a chariot, a large wagon, and several
horsemen. The chariot, which led the way, was magnificent and
could have been a king's. Deirdre had to admit she was impressed.
From the wagons, a number of priests were emerging; there seemed
to be five of them, along with the several young men on the horses
who, by their rich dress and golden ornaments, were clearly sons of
princes. They were forming a little procession. The priests were
dressed in white. From the chariot she now saw a grey-haired man
descending, also in white. He was not especially tall, but he stood
very upright. He took his place just behind the priests, with Larine
behind him and followed by the rest of the party. The single priest
who led the procession now raised a tall staff in the air. It was not a
cross, such as Larine had brought, but at the end of the long shaft
was a curved head, like a shepherd's crook, polished so that it shone.
When the priest raised it high in the air, it gleamed in the sun.

Slowly the procession came towards the gateway. Deirdre and
the family watched silently. She noticed that all the slaves had come
out to the side of the track and that they were kneeling. The procession reached the gateway and started to enter the rath. But when
the bishop from the north reached the entrance, he stopped, knelt
down, and kissed the ground. Then, straightening, he passed inside.
They drew up in front of the doorway to the house. There was nothing else, in courtesy, that she or her family could do but welcome
him and offer him the usual hospitality. As soon as this was done,

the man from Ulster gave her a kindly smile, and in a clear voice announced: "Gratias agamus."

Deirdre realised that this was Latin, but did not know what it meant.

"Let us give thanks," Larine called out.

So this, thought Deirdre, was Bishop Patrick.

There was no mistaking his authority. He had a fine, aristocratic face. His eyes were very clear and sharp, but there was something special—she could see it at once—an aura of spirituality that seemed to radiate from him, and which was impressive. With two priests close behind him, he started on a little tour of inspection. First he went over to where two of the female slaves were still kneeling, briefly inspected their hands and their teeth, nodded, apparently satisfied, and proceeded to her brothers. He looked at them only briefly, then he moved on. He came to Morna and looked long and hard at him, while Morna blushed. Then he said something in Latin to Larine. Deirdre had not known the clever druid spoke Latin nowadays.

"What does he say?" she demanded.

"That your son has an honest face."

Bishop Patrick was coming to her now. She was conscious that before he reached her, she had already been keenly observed. She was aware of his thinning grey hair as he bowed his head courteously before her.

As he moved on to inspect two more of the slaves, Morna was standing at her side. She could see that the bishop had greatly impressed him.

Bishop Patrick had completed his circle. He glanced across to Larine, nodded his head in a way that indicated that Larine should stay where he was, and then returned to Deirdre and Morna.

"I am sorry for your trouble, Deirdre, daughter of Fergus," he said to her. He was speaking in her own tongue now. His eyes, looking out from under a thatch of grey eyebrows, seemed to see everything. "I hear you were a good daughter."

"I was." She couldn't help it, whether the man was her enemy or not, she was touched.

"And it's yourself, I should say," Bishop Patrick continued, "who holds everything together here. Isn't that so?"

"It is," she said with feeling.

"Thanks be to God for that." He smiled at her kindly. "You are afraid for your son's safety?" She nodded. "What good mother would not be?" He paused thoughtfully. "Tell me, is it God that you fear, Deirdre, or is it the druids?"

"The druids."

"You do not think that the God who made all things can protect your son?"

She was silent; but he did not seem offended. Then he turned to Morna.

"And so, young man." He was staring keenly into Morna's eyes. "You are the young man who this is all about. The kinsman of the High King." He took a step back as though to survey the youthful chief. "You have been summoned to him, have you not?"

"It is true," Morna answered respectfully.

Bishop Patrick appeared to be meditating. His eyes seemed to be half closed as he considered the subject before him. There was no question, she thought, he might have been some royal druid prince. Was he going to encourage Morna, or perhaps rebuke him? She had no idea.

"And you would like to go to the High King's feis at Tara?"

"I should." Morna wasn't certain whether this was the correct response, but it was the truth.

"It would be a strange young man who did not," said Bishop Patrick. "And you have quarrelled with your mother?"

"It is . . ." Morna was about to explain, but the bishop went on gently.

"Honour your mother, young man. She is the only one you possess. If it is God's will that you should do a certain thing, she will be led to understand the rightness of it." He considered for a moment. "You wish to serve the one true God. Is that correct?"

"I think so."

"You think so." Bishop Patrick paused. "His service, Morna, is not always easy. Those who follow the Christian path have to try to do God's will, not their own. Sometimes we have to make sacrifices." At the mention of sacrifices, Deirdre tensed; but if Bishop Patrick saw this, he took no notice. "Are you prepared to make sacrifices to serve the God who gave His only Son to save the world?"

"Yes." He said it quietly, but he did not seem to hesitate.

"From those who follow me, Morna, I expect complete obedience. My followers have to trust me. These young men," he indicated the princes standing nearby, "obey my commands, which are sometimes hard."

Morna glanced at them. They looked a noble group, the sort of group to which any young chief would be proud to belong. But having told him this, the bishop did not seem to be expecting any reply. For turning round abruptly, he went over to where one of the priests was holding his staff. Taking it from him, he held it firmly in his hand and in a clear voice addressed them.

"This is the staff which gives me strength, for it is the staff of life, the staff of Jesus, the only Son of God the Father, who died for our sins. Jesus who sacrificed his life that each of us may live eternally. I, Patrick, bishop, humble priest, penitent sinner," he continued solemnly, "I, Patrick, come here not on my own authority—for I have none—but at the command of God the Father, made known to me through His Holy Spirit, to bear witness for His Son and to bring you the good news, that you, too, if you believe in Him, may have eternal life in Heaven and not perish into nothingness or the terrible fires of Hell. I shall not try to impress you with great learning, for my own is modest. I shall not persuade you with eloquent words, for I have no eloquence unless it be that given to me by the Holy Spirit. But listen to my poor words carefully, for I have come to save your souls."

✦

It was strange: Deirdre could not afterwards remember exactly what he had said. Some of it she recognised from what Larine had told her; but when Patrick spoke, it was different. He told them the story of Christ, and how he had gone to sacrifice. He described the cruel old island gods and explained that they were not real. They were stories, he told them, to give pleasure or to frighten children. How much greater, he explained, was the single, all-powerful God, who created the whole world.

One part of the sermon she did recall in detail. He had made much of the fact that, like so many of the gods from the ancient days, this Supreme Being had three aspects: Father, Son, Holy Spirit—the Three in One, he called it. Nor should this be surprising, he explained. All nature was full of triads: the root, stem, and flower of a plant; the spring, stream, and estuary of a river; even the leaves of plants, like that of the tripartite shamrock, for instance, showed this principle of Three in One. "This," he explained, "is what we mean by the Holy Trinity."

But above all, it was the way he spoke that impressed her. He had such passion, such certainty, such warmth. He brought her a sense of peace. Even if she did not exactly understand why this God of love of whom he spoke should necessarily be all-powerful, she found that she wanted it to be so. The cruel old gods were being chased away, like dark clouds fleeing over the horizon. And good riddance to them, she thought. The sense of warmth emanating from the preacher enveloped her. His confidence told her that he must be right. She glanced across at Morna. His eyes were shining.

By the time Bishop Patrick had finished speaking, the idea of doing as he wished did not seem so strange. When he asked if they would join in fellowship with him and be baptised, she realised that she wished he could stay with them longer. She did not want him to depart. Joining his new faith seemed a way of keeping his comforting presence with them. If she followed her heart, she was ready to do as he wished. But she had followed her heart once before, and so had Conall. The heart was a dangerous thing. Dangerous for Morna.

"Baptise me," she suddenly cried out. "Baptise the rest of us. But spare Morna." She couldn't help it.

"*Spare* him?" Bishop Patrick was glaring at her. "*Spare?*" She saw the terrible flash of anger in the old man's eyes. He took several steps towards her and for a moment she thought he might even be about to strike her, or curse her like a druid. Instead, to her surprise, he stopped in his tracks, shook his head, apparently at himself, and then, to her utter astonishment, went down on his knees in front of her.

"Forgive me, Deirdre," he said. "Forgive my anger."

"Why . . ." She didn't know what to say.

"If I failed to touch your heart, the fault is mine, not yours. It is my own shortcomings that made me angry."

"It was beautiful, what you said," she protested. "It's just . . ."

He had got to his feet again and he cut her off with a gesture of his hand.

"You do not understand," he growled. He turned to Morna. "It is you who are chief of the Ui Fergusa now," he said solemnly. "Is it your wish that your family should be baptised?"

"It is," said Morna.

"And if you accept baptism from my hands, will you submit to my authority in matters concerning religion, and follow my instructions, as these young princes do?"

"I will," said Morna.

"Come then," the bishop commanded, "and I will tell you what we must do."

The baptism they were to undergo required a simple immersion in water. A glance at the shallows of the Liffey had convinced Bishop Patrick that the river was not a very convenient place. The three local wells, which he now briefly inspected and blessed, were not suitable either. But the dark pool of Dubh Linn would do very well, he decided, and he told them to assemble there at once.

And so a little group of Deirdre, her two brothers, and Morna, dressed in only linen shifts under their cloaks and attended by their half-dozen slaves, trooped down on that fine but slightly chilly September afternoon to the edge of Dubh Linn to be baptised. And one by one they stepped into its dark waters, where Bishop Patrick was standing, and sank down under its surface for a cold moment to emerge back into the light, baptised by Patrick's own hand, in the name of Christ.

They dried themselves quickly. Everyone except Deirdre seemed cheerful. And they were just starting back up towards the rath when they were brought to an unexpected halt by Deirdre's youngest brother, Rian. He had just thought of something.

"Is it true that only Christians go to the good place?" he asked.

"It is," they assured him.

"And the others all go to the fiery place?"

That was so, too, they said.

"Then what about my dad?" he asked, with genuine concern. "That means he'll be going to the fire." And after a few moments of consultation with his brother, they both agreed. Their logic might be a little strange, but it was held with conviction. Their father was resting with the family's gods. Right or wrong in the visitors' eyes, those gods had always been there and, somehow, would protect their own. But if Dubh Linn and the rath of Fergus became Christian, then the family would have turned their backs on the gods. Insulted them. Fergus would be left, as it were, stranded. The old gods would probably want nothing more to do with him, while the Christian God, apparently, would consign him to hellfire.

"We can't let that happen to him," he protested. His brother, Ronan, was looking worried, too.

Yet if Deirdre felt embarrassed, she observed that none of the priests seemed in the least surprised.

For this was by no means an uncommon problem for Christian missionaries. If we are to be saved, their converts would ask, then what is the fate of our revered ancestors? Are you telling us they were wicked? The normal answer to this question was that God would make at least a partial dispensation for those who, through no fault of their own, had not the opportunity of accepting Christ. Only for those hearing Christ's message and then refusing it could there be no salvation. It was a reasonable explanation, but it did not always satisfy. And it was typical of the great northern bishop that he had, upon occasion, employed a method of dealing with this problem which was all his own.

"How long is he dead?" he asked.

"Five days," they replied.

"Then dig the man up," he ordered. "I'll baptise him now."

And that is what they did. With the help of the slaves, the brothers disinterred their father from his mound down by the Liffey's edge. While the pale form of Fergus lay stiffly on the ground, looking remarkably dignified in death, Bishop Patrick splashed some water upon him and, with the sign of the cross, brought him into the Christian world.

"I cannot promise you he will reach heaven," he told the brothers with a kindly smile, "but his chances have greatly improved."

They reburied the old man in his mound, and Larine placed two pieces of wood, joined in the sign of the cross, above it.

They had returned to the rath and were about to enter the big thatched hall where the fire was burning, when Bishop Patrick stopped and turned to the members of the family.

"There is now," he announced, "a small kindness that you can do for me." They asked him only to tell them what it might be. He smiled. "You may not like it. I am speaking of your slaves." At these words the slaves standing around looked up hopefully.

"Your British slaves." He smiled. "My fellow countrymen. They are Christians, you know. Part of my flock." He turned to Deirdre. "The life of a slave is hard, Deirdre, daughter of Fergus. I know because I was one myself. Seized from their homes. Stolen from their families and their Church. I wish you to set your British slaves free." He smiled again. "They do not always leave, you know. I see you treat your slaves well. But they must be free to return to their homes if they wish. It's a barbarous trade," he added with sudden feeling.

Deirdre saw Larine and the priests nod automatically. Obviously they were used to these strange proceedings. For herself, she wasn't sure what to say. Morna looked astonished. It was Ronan who spoke up.

"Are you saying we should set them free without payment?"

Patrick turned to him. "How many slaves have you?"

"There are six."

"The raids produce so many. They cannot have cost you much."

Her brother thought a moment.

"But three of those are women," he pointed out. "They do all the heavy work."

"Lord preserve us," the bishop murmured, and turned up his eyes to heaven. A silence followed. With a sigh, Bishop Patrick nodded to Larine, who reached into a small pouch hanging from his belt and produced a Roman coin.

"Will that do?" Larine enquired. It seemed he was used to making such bargains to help the British Christians.

"Two," said Deirdre's brother quickly. He might be stupid, she thought, but he was still her father's son when it came to bargaining for livestock.

Larine glanced at Bishop Patrick, who nodded. A moment later, the British slaves were on their knees before the bishop kissing his hands.

"Give thanks to God, my children," he told them kindly, "not to me." Deirdre wondered how much he spent like this each year.

⁜

But none of these events, as far as Deirdre was concerned, did anything to lessen her agony.

Morna was a Christian. He was going to Tara. The missionary bishop might possess the tongue of an angel, he might be sent by God, but he was still going to place her only son in mortal danger. And there was nothing she could do about it. A heavy gloom descended upon her.

Bishop Patrick had indicated that he would depart the following day. Until then, he and all his party must be treated as honoured guests. The bishop retired for a while to rest by the fire. Larine wandered down to the estuary and paced about there for a time, before returning to sit alone by the entrance to the rath. Deirdre and the slaves set to work to prepare a feast. Morna, meanwhile, had joined the company of the young princes who formed the bishop's retinue. She heard them laughing together outside, and it was obvious that Morna was impressed with them. Once he appeared and told her, "They are splendid fellows. Every one is a prince. They travel about with Bishop Patrick and treat him like a king."

It was only after he had rested that Bishop Patrick, looking much refreshed, sent one of his priests to summon Larine and Morna, and called upon Deirdre to join them. When the four of them were gathered by the fire, he turned to Morna.

"You will recall that you promised to obey me," he began.

Morna bowed his head.

"Very well, then," the bishop continued. "Let me tell you what I wish you to do. You are to accompany me tomorrow. I wish you to join these young men who are travelling with me. I want you to remain with us for a time. Would you like that?"

"I should indeed." Morna's face lit up with delight.

"Do not be too pleased," Bishop Patrick cautioned him. "I also told you that there would be sacrifices, and there is to be one now." He paused. "You are not to go to Tara."

Deirdre stared. Not go to Tara? Had she heard him correctly? Evidently she had. Morna's face had fallen, and Larine was looking horrified.

"I may not go to the feis?"

"You may not. I forbid it."

Larine opened his mouth to say something, but Bishop Patrick gave him one look and he was silent.

"But the High King . . ." Morna began.

"He will probably notice your absence. But as you will have gone tomorrow, any travellers to Tara who come across the ford will say you were not here. And if in time the High King hears that you have gone away with me," he smiled, "he is used to me making a nuisance of myself. It was I, after all, who took away Larine. It is I who would be blamed, not you. You may be sure of that." He turned to Deirdre. "You will miss him, I dare say."

Yes, she would miss him. She would miss him desperately. But he would not be at Tara. That was all that mattered. She could scarcely believe it was happening.

"Where would he be?" she asked.

"In the north and west with me. I have protectors, Deirdre. He'll be safe enough."

"And would he . . . would I . . ."

"See him again? You would indeed. Didn't I tell him to honour his mother? I would send him to you after a year. You and your brothers could manage at Dubh Linn until then, I should think, could you not?"

"Yes," she said gratefully. "We could."

Morna was looking utterly downcast, but the bishop was firm.

"You swore to obey," he reminded him sternly. "Now you must honour your oath." Then he smiled kindly. "Do not grieve for Tara, my young friend. Before the year is out, I promise you, I will show you even better things."

It was a pleasant little feast that they all enjoyed in the rath that night. The company was in a cheerful mood. Deirdre was so relieved that she was radiant. Her brother Ronan, with the prospect of acting as chief for a year, was looking pleased with himself. And even Morna, in the company of the young nobles, was visibly brightening. The food was well prepared, ale and wine flowed. And if the old drinking skull that gleamed softly in the corner might have seemed inappropriate at such a Christian feast, no one appeared to think of it. Not only did the kindly bishop prove to have a rich store of good stories and jokes, but he even insisted upon Larine reciting some of the tales of the ancient gods.

"They are wonderful stories," he told them, "full of poetry. You must not worship the old gods anymore. They have no power, because they are not real. But never lose the stories. I make Larine recite them whenever I spend an evening with him."

As she looked back over the day's extraordinary events and the wonderful turn that they had taken, there was only one small thing that puzzled Deirdre. Towards the end of the evening, she confided it to Larine.

"You say that Bishop Patrick is austere? He never touches a woman?" It was one aspect of the new religion she found a little strange.

"That is true."

"Well, when I went into the water, I was just wearing my shift, you know. So when I came out, it was all stuck to me." She glanced across to make sure the bishop could not hear her. "And . . . I saw his eyes light up. He noticed me, you know."

And now, for the first time since his arrival, Larine threw back his head and laughed.

"Oh, I'm sure he did, Deirdre. He would indeed."

⁂

They left soon after dawn. Bishop Patrick gave his blessing to them all, and promised Deirdre once more that he would send her son back to her safely again. Morna, for his part, bade his mother a tender farewell, and likewise promised to return.

So it was with relief and happiness, rather than grief, that Deirdre watched the great chariot with its accompanying wagon and riders, with their cross and staff, sweep away across the Ford of Hurdles and take the track northwards towards Ulster.

Indeed, everybody involved in the day's work was pleased, with the possible exception of Larine who, around midday, when they were resting, ventured to make a small complaint to Bishop Patrick.

"I was a little surprised that you decided to override my counsel," he remarked. "In fact, I was somewhat embarrassed. I had hoped to send a young Christian to the High King at Tara. But all I achieved was to bring you a few converts at a rath by a ford."

Bishop Patrick watched him calmly. "You were angry."

"I was. Why did you do it?"

"Because, when I saw them all, I thought the woman was right. I returned to this island to bring the Gospel's joyful message to the heathen, Larine. Not to make martyrs." He sighed. "The ways of God are inscrutable, Larine," he said gently. "We do not need to be so ambitious." He patted the former druid's arm. "Morna is a chief. The ford is a crossroads. Who can tell what Dubh Linn may be worth?"

FOUR

VIKINGS

⊰ 981 ⊱

I

T HE RED-HAIRED BOY stared at the ship.
It was nearly midnight. The sea was like dusted silver, the sky pale grey. He had met men who had sailed beyond the islands in the distant north, where the sun shone at midnight and for long weeks in summer there was no darkness at all. But even here at Dyflin, in July, the night was almost banished. For an hour or so there was enough darkness to see a few stars, but for the rest of the sun's short absence, the world was full of the strange, luminous greyness that is special to midsummer nights in the northern seas.

The ship was moving silently. It had come up the coast from the south. Instead of using their oars, the crew were letting the breeze bring them into the Liffey estuary along the northern shore where the pale sandbars lurked.

Harold was not supposed to be down by the sandbars; he was supposed to be asleep in the big farmstead. But sometimes, on summer nights like this, he would sneak out and take his pony from the field and come here to the coast to watch the huge, silver-grey waters of the bay which seemed to draw him to them, as the tides are invisibly drawn by the moon, with a magic he did not understand.

It was the biggest ship he had ever seen. Its long lines were like a great sea snake; its high, curved prow cut through the water as smoothly as an axe through liquid metal. Its big, square sail rose over the sandbar, blocking out a patch of sky, and even in the twilight he could see that it was black and ochre like dried blood. For this was a Viking ship.

But Harold was not afraid. For he was a Viking himself, and these were Viking waters now.

So he watched the blackening sea snake with its brutal sail as it passed by and glided away into the awaiting Liffey's stream, knowing that it carried not only armed men—for these were dangerous times—but rich merchandise. Perhaps, the next day, he could persuade his father to take him down to see it.

He didn't notice the other boy at first. There were so many people at the waterside below Dyflin's dark wall. He didn't even see him until he spoke.

He had been in luck. His father, Olaf, had agreed to take him to the port. The day had been bright when they had set out from the farmstead and started to ride across the Plain of Bird Flocks. The damp breeze had felt refreshing as it pressed against his cheek; the sky was blue, and the sun was shining on his father's red hair.

There was no one like his father: no one so brave, no one so handsome. He was firm. When Harold was helping on the farm, his father would often push him to work a little longer than he wanted. But if you were down, he'd soon tell you a story to make you laugh. And then there was something else. When Harold was with his mother and sisters, he knew he was loved, and he was happy. But he couldn't feel free. Not quite. Not nowadays. When his father scooped him up in his strong arms, though, and put him on his pony, and let him trot along beside his own splendid horse, then Harold felt something beyond happiness. A surge of strength seemed to flood through his small body; his blue eyes shone. That was when he knew what it was to feel free. Free as a bird in the air. Free as a Viking on the open sea.

It was nearly two centuries since the Vikings of Scandinavia had begun their epic voyages around the northern seas. There had been greater land migrations in the ancient world; sea traders, Greek and Phoenician, had set up ports and colonies round most of the shores known to classical civilization. But never before in human history had there been such a huge adventure as that of the Viking sea rovers upon the world ocean. Pirates, traders, explorers—they set out from their northern inlets in their swift longships and soon, all over Europe, men learned to tremble when they saw their square sails approaching by sea, or their great, horned helmets coming up from the riverbank. From Sweden they travelled down the huge rivers of Russia; from Denmark they first ravaged and then settled the northern half of England. Vikings sailed south to France and the Mediterranean: Normandy and Norman Sicily were their colonies. They voyaged westwards to the Scottish isles, the Isle of Man, Iceland, Greenland, even America. And it was the fair-haired Vikings from Norway who, coming to the pleasant island west of Britain, explored its natural harbours and, converting its Celtic name—Eriu, which they pronounced Eire—into their own tongue, first gave the place the Nordic name of Ire-land.

Harold knew how his ancestors had come to Ireland. The story was as wonderful to him as any of the Nordic sagas his father told. Almost a century and a half had passed since the great fleet of sixty longships had sailed into the Liffey's estuary. "And my father's grandfather, Harold Red-Hair, was in one of them," his father had told him proudly. When a large party had rowed upstream to the Ford of Hurdles, they had been rather disappointed. After passing a burial mound, they had found a small rath protecting a jetty, a dark pool, and, on the high bank above it, a little monastery to which the head man of the rath seemed to attach great importance. The pagan Norsemen hadn't thought much of it. Twenty armed men could scarcely fit into the stone chapel which contained only a modest gold cross and a chalice to take away for their trouble.

But if the trading post and its little monastery provided poor pickings, the Vikings could see at once that the site had potential. The old Celtic road system converged nearby, to use the river crossing; the tidal harbour was protected and the land was good. The area around the rath was defensible, too.

The Norwegians had settled. Though known to history as Vikings, or Norsemen, they often referred to themselves as Ostmen—men from the east. Soon, a little way upstream from the ford, a huddle of their timber-and-wattle huts and a Viking cemetery had appeared by the riverside. Learning that the dark pool was called Dubh Linn, the Norsemen produced their own version of the name: Dyflin. Nor was the Viking presence limited to their small port. Scandinavian farmsteads had spread across the territory north of the Liffey estuary. The farmstead of Harold's family was one of them. And so it was that the old Plain of Bird Flocks had acquired an additional Celtic name: Fine Gall, the Foreigner's Place—Fingal.

When Harold's ancestor and the Norwegian fleet had arrived at Dubh Linn that day, the men at the rath had not tried to give battle. Since a single Viking longship carried anywhere from thirty to sixty fighting men, resistance would have been futile. And it was thanks to this reception that from that day on, the fair-haired Norwegians had taken the people of the trading post under their protection.

Not that the last century and a half had been peaceful. Life was seldom peaceful for long in the Viking world. But to Harold, the coastal plain of Fingal and the small town of Dyflin were delightful places. And when today, as they rode down the long slope towards the Liffey, a bank of grey clouds moved across the sky, darkening the landscape, it had not affected his happy mood a bit.

The merchant ship had arrived from the harbour of Waterford, on the island's southern coast. There were a number of ports round the coasts of Ireland—nearly all of them settled by Vikings and bearing Viking names. Though Viking fighting ships were long and sleek, their merchant vessels had a bulge at midship which allowed them to carry a considerable amount of cargo in their bellies. The Waterford ship had brought a cargo of wine from south-western France, and Harold's father was going to buy a few barrels. While his father talked to the merchants, Harold had been admiring the ship's handsome lines when he heard a voice from somewhere behind him.

"You. Hey. Cripple boy. I'm talking to you."

As Harold turned, he saw a pale, black-haired boy, of nine or ten he guessed—about his own age—standing in a crowd. Though one or two of the crowd glanced in his direction when they heard the boy call out, nobody seemed particularly interested, but the boy's eyes were fixed upon him intently. He had spoken in Norse, not Irish, and as Harold had never seen him before, he supposed he must have arrived on the ship. He wondered whether to ignore the rude stranger, but that might look like cowardice, so he limped over to him. The boy's eyes were gazing at his legs as he approached.

"Who are you?" Harold asked.

"That's your father, isn't it?" the boy said, ignoring his question and nodding towards Harold's father, who was standing some way off. "The one with red hair, like you."

"Yes."

"I didn't know," the boy said thoughtfully, "that you'd be a cripple. Your other leg's good, isn't it? Just your left that's bent."

"That's right. Not that it's any of your business."

"Perhaps not. Or perhaps it is. What happened?"

"A horse fell on me." A horse his father had told him not to go near. The horse had bolted with him, then jumped over a ditch and fallen. His left leg, trapped under the horse, had been smashed.

"Have you any brothers?"

"No. Only sisters."

"That's what they told me. It'll always be crooked, your leg, won't it?"

"I should think so."

"Pity." He gave Harold a strange smile. "Don't misunderstand me. I don't care about your leg. I hope you're in agony. I'd just prefer if you weren't a cripple when you grow up."

"Why?"

"Because that's when I'm going to kill you. My name's Sigurd, by the way."

Then he turned round and walked swiftly back through the crowd; and Harold was so astonished that, by the time he tried to hurry after him, the dark-haired boy had vanished.

"So you know who he was?" Harold had been telling his father about the strange incident. Now his father was looking grave.

"Yes." Olaf paused. "If this boy is who I think he is," he explained, "then he comes from Waterford. He's a Dane."

The first Norwegian settlement at Dyflin had only been in existence ten years when the Danish Vikings arrived. With the northern half of England in their grip, they had been prowling round the Irish coast looking for places to raid and settle. The trading post that their fellow Vikings from Norway had established on the Liffey looked appealing. They arrived in force and told the Norwegians: "We've come to share this place." For a generation after that, the port had gone about its business under various masters: sometimes Norwegian, sometimes Danish, sometimes both ruling together. Though there were still plenty of fair-haired Norwegian settlers like Harold and his family in the area, it was the Danish Vikings who ruled in Dyflin and many other Irish ports nowadays.

"But why should he want to kill me?" the boy asked. His father sighed.

"It goes back a long way, Harold," he began. "As you know, the Ostmen of Dyflin have always had an enemy. I mean the High King."

Even now, six centuries after Niall of the Nine Hostages had laid claim to the High Kingship of Tara, his descendants, the O'Neill as they were called, still held the High Kingship and dominated the northern half of the island. The Vikings had never been able to settle on the northern and western coasts which the O'Neill directly ruled; and the existence of the independent Viking port on the Liffey had always annoyed them. For it hadn't been long before the Viking ruler there had started behaving like one of the provincial Irish kings. The last King of Dyflin, as he called himself, had married a princess of Leinster; his territory had included all of Fingal. "And he would have liked to control all the land up to the River Boyne and beyond," Harold's father had once told him. No wonder the mighty O'Neill looked at the newcomers with distaste. Every ten years or so, since the settlement began, the O'Neill High King had come to try to kick the Vikings out. Once, eighty years ago, the Irish had managed to burn the place down and the Vikings had left, though only for a few years. On their return, between Ath Cliath and the pool of Dubh Linn the Norsemen had built a new settlement on the ridge with a strong wall and stockade, and a stout wooden bridge across the river. But the present O'Neill king was a determined man. A year ago, in a big battle up at Tara, he had beaten the Norsemen of Dyflin. Harold's father had not gone to that fight; but afterwards, he and Harold had watched the Irish king's line of chariots crossing the long wooden bridge over the Liffey. The king had stayed in Dyflin for several months; but then he had left, taking away whole cartloads of gold and silver, and Dyflin was back under a Viking ruler. The port had to pay tribute to the Irish king now, but otherwise it was business as usual.

"Long ago," his father began, "when Dyflin was still Norwegian, the High King attacked us one year. And he paid some Danes to help him. Did you ever hear the story?"

Harold frowned. There were many sagas about Viking battles and heroic deeds, but he could not recall hearing this one. He shook his head.

"It's recorded," his father said quietly, "but it's not a popular story nowadays." He sighed. "There was a particular party of Danes who'd been raiding the northern islands. They were bad people. Even the other Danes avoided them. The High King got word to them, and offered them a reward if they'd help him attack Dyflin."

"And they came?"

"Oh yes." Olaf grimaced. "We beat them off. But it was an ugly business. My grandfather—he was a child at the time—lost his father in that raid." He paused. Harold listened carefully. He hoped that his ancestor had not died dishonourably.

"He was killed after the battle was over," his father went on. "A Dane came up and stabbed him in the back, then ran away. The Dane's name was Sigurd, son of Sweyn. Even his own men despised him for that deed."

"It wasn't avenged?"

"Not then. They got away. But years later, when my grandfather was on a ship trading in the northern islands, he saw a longship in a harbour and was told it belonged to Sigurd and his son. So he challenged them to fight. Sigurd was an old man by then, though still strong, and his son was my grandfather's age. So Sigurd agreed to fight on condition that, if he was killed, my grandfather would fight his son as well. And my grandfather swore: 'I will have both your heads, Sigurd, son of Sweyn, and if you had more sons I would take those away with me, too.' As it was evening then, they agreed to fight the next morning, as soon as the sun was over the sea. So at dawn my grandfather went to where their ship was; but as he came near, they pushed away from the shore and started rowing out to sea. And they laughed at him and shouted insults. Then my grandfather ran back to his own ship and begged them to follow Sigurd. They refused and as he was only a young man, there was nothing he could do. But they'd all seen what happened, and Sigurd and his son were known as cowards all over the northern seas.

"My grandfather got word of them from time to time down the years. They were on the Isle of Man, that lies between ourselves and Britain, for a while, then in England, in York. But they never came to Dyflin. And after my grandfather died, we heard no more of them. Until five years ago when a merchant told me that Sigurd's grandson was in Waterford. I thought about going down there, but . . ." He shrugged. "It's been too long. I thought that the grandson in Waterford mightn't even know about the business. I put it behind me and I've never worried about it again—until today."

"But Sigurd's family didn't forget."

"It seems not."

"If you choose to forget, why doesn't this boy?"

"It's his family who were disgraced, Harold, not ours. He seems to be prouder than his ancestors, at least. They never cared about their evil reputation, but he obviously does. So he must avenge their shame by killing you."

"He wants to cut off my head and show it to everyone?"

"Yes."

"So I'll have to fight him one day?"

"Unless he changes his mind. But I don't think he will."

Harold considered. He felt a little frightened, but if this was his fate, then he knew he must be brave.

"So what should I do, Father?"

"Prepare." His father looked down at him gravely for a moment. Then he smiled and clapped him on the back. "Because when you fight, Harold, you're going to win."

⁑

Goibniu the Smith glared at the mound. Then he grabbed his son's arm.

"Will you look at that!"

The sixteen-year-old boy stared. He wasn't sure what he was meant to see, but it was obvious that his father was furious about something. He tried, surreptitiously, to discover what point exactly his father's eye was fixed upon.

The prehistoric mounds above the River Boyne had not greatly altered since the time of Patrick. Here and there a further subsidence had occurred. The entrance doorways were all hidden now; but in front of them, a quantity of white quartz stones were still strewn across the ground, glistening when the sunlight caught them. In the River Boyne below, the salmon and swans went about their quiet business as if they themselves had been there when the Tuatha De Danaan had gone to their bright halls within the ridge. But something had evidently displeased the eye of Goibniu. Unlike his distant ancestor, Goibniu had the use of both his eyes. But when he was considering something, he had a trick of closing one eye and squinting through the other, which seemed in the process to become unusually large. Men found his gaze disconcerting. And not without reason. He never missed anything.

"Look at the top, Morann." Goibniu held his son's arm in a vice-like grip, as he pointed impatiently.

And now the young man saw that the top of one of the mounds had been disturbed. Near the middle of the grassy dome, several ragged piles of stone indicated that someone had tried to break into the tomb from above.

"Barbarians! Heathens!" the craftsman cried. "It was the cursed Ostmen who did that."

About a century ago, a party of Vikings, curious to discover how the great tombs were constructed and whether they contained any treasure, had spent several days trying to break into one of them. Unaware that there was an entrance hidden in the side, they had tried to come in through the top.

"Did they get anything?" Morann asked.

"They did not. The stones are huge as you go farther down. I looked. They gave up." He relapsed into silence for a moment and then burst out, "How dare they touch the gods!"

Strictly speaking, this was inconsistent. Though the craftsman's family, like many others, had held out for several generations after Patrick's ministry before they grudgingly took the new religion, they had been Christians for nearly four centuries now. On feast days, Goibniu went to the church of the little monastery nearby and solemnly took communion. His family had always supposed that the smith was a faithful son of the Church—though you could never be sure with Goibniu. But like most of the faithful on the island, he still felt an affection and a need for the ancient ways. Paganism never dies entirely. Most of the pagan rites of seedtime and harvest, of course, had already been incorporated under new names into the Christian calendar; and even some of the old inauguration rites of the kings, including that of mating with a mare, were still a fond memory. As for the old gods, they might not be gods anymore—"idols and lies," the priests declared. They might be only myths, to be recited by bards. Or they might, with the Church's blessing, be accounted for as ancestral heroes, extraordinary men, from whom dynasties like the mighty O'Neill could claim descent. But whatever they were, they belonged to Ireland, and it was not for the Viking pirates to profane their sacred places.

Morann said nothing. His father had dismounted, and together they walked round the tombs in silence. In front of the largest stood the great stone with its strange carved spirals, and the two of them paused to stare at the mystical object.

"Our people used to live near here," the smith remarked moodily. It had been an ancestor two centuries ago who had moved two days' journey away, to the north-west, into the region of small lakes which the family presently occupied. Evidently, for Goibniu, the stone with its cosmic spirals represented a kind of homecoming.

And it was only now that his son ventured to ask the question which had been puzzling him since his father's outburst began.

"If you hate the Ostmen so much, Father, then why are you taking me to live with them?"

It seemed a natural question; but in answer, the smith looked at him bleakly, muttered, "It's a fool I have for a son," and relapsed into silence. Only after a long pause did he deign to explain himself further.

"Who is the greatest power on this island?" the smith asked.

"The High King, Father."

"He is, indeed." He nodded. "And isn't it true that for generation after generation, the High Kings have tried to kick the Ostmen out of Dyflin?" He pronounced the Norse name sullenly.

"They did, Father."

"But last year, when the High King won a great battle at Tara and came down to the Liffey—when he could have kicked them out, and they could have done nothing about it at all—he let them stay and took tribute instead. Why would he do that, do you think?"

"I suppose because it suited him," his son suggested. "He'd be better off taking their tribute than kicking them out."

"That is true. A port is a valuable thing. The Ostmen's ports bring in wealth. You're better off keeping them than destroying them." He paused. "I will tell you something else. Is the power of the O'Neill as great today as once it was?"

"It is not."

"And why is that?"

"They quarrelled amongst themselves." Up to a point this was true. Long ago, the mighty royal house had split into two branches, known as the Northern and Southern O'Neill. Generally these two had skilfully avoided dissension by alternating the High Kingship between them. But in recent generations there had been bickering. Other powers on the island, especially the kings of Munster in the south, had been chipping away at the authority of the O'Neill in the time-honoured manner. One young Munster chief, named Brian Boru, seemed ready to stir up trouble with scant respect for any of the settled kingships. The O'Neill were still strong—hadn't they just defeated the Vikings of Dyflin?—but the lesser Irish kings were watching. Like a huge bull, the great power in the north was show-ing signs of age.

"Perhaps. But I will suggest to you a deeper cause. The O'Neill are not to be blamed. They could not have foreseen the conse-quences of their actions. But when the Ostmen first began to attack our shores, the O'Neill were so strong that the Ostmen could not establish a single port on the coasts of their land. Not one. All the

Ostmen's ports lie farther south. Yet that strength may have been a curse. Can you tell me why?"

"The ports bring wealth?" his son offered.

"And wealth is power. How do you imagine Niall of the Nine Hostages became so mighty before Saint Patrick came? By raiding Britain. He had treasure and slaves to reward his followers. The Ostmen are pirates and heathens, mostly. But their ports are rich. The more ports a king has, if he can control them, the more riches and power he has. That is the weakness of the O'Neill now. The ports are not on their lands. That's why they need Dyflin, the richest port of all."

"So that's why you want me there?"

"It is." Goibniu looked at his son seriously. Sometimes he thought the boy was too cautious, too careful. Well, if so, it might be for the best. He gestured to the tomb and its broken roof again. "I'll never like the Ostmen. But Dyflin is the future, Morann, and that is where you're going."

She was dancing. Such a slim, dark little thing—white legs like sticks and a tangle of black hair tumbling down her back—a shuffle it was, she danced, this way and that; and he, watching her all the time, the child in the street. Caoilinn was her name; his, Osgar. And as he watched her, he wondered.

Was he to be married that day?

Wherever you looked in the Viking town of Dyflin, you saw wood. The narrow streets that rolled up and down the uneven slopes were made of split tree trunks; in the winding alleys and footpaths you walked on planks. All the lanes were lined on both sides with blank-faced wattle or picket fences behind which, in their narrow plots, could be seen the thatched roofs of the rectangular wicker-walled dwellings or timbered halls of the Norsemen. Some tenements contained pens for pigs, hens, and other livestock, some were given over to workshops; and the wooden walls around them were to deter thieves or attackers or, like the sides of a ship, to keep out the winter wind from the wide, grey estuary and the open seascape beyond. Enclosing this twenty-acre wooden village was an earth rampart topped with a wooden palisade. Beyond the palisade, on the waterfront, was a stout wood quay, against which several long-ships were tied. Just upstream was the long wooden bridge and past that the Ford of Hurdles. The Irish people still mostly called the place by its old name, Ath Cliath, even if they often crossed by the Viking bridge instead of the Celtic ford. But though Caoilinn was Irish, she called the wooden township Dyflin, because she lived there.

"Shall we go over to the monastery?" She suddenly turned her green eyes on him.

"Do you think you should?" he said. She was nine and he was eleven. He had a better sense of what was fitting.

"Come on," she cried; and, with an amused shake of his head, he followed her. He still didn't know if he was to be married.

The little monastery stood on the slopes just south of the ridge where the old rath of Fergus had overlooked the dark pool of Dubh Linn. It had been there when first the Vikings came—a small religious house protected by the Ui Fergusa descendants of the old chief. In the centuries after the death of Fergus, other small chiefs had set up raths here and there in the broad plain of the Liffey's estuary and their names had survived. Rathmines, Rathgar, Rathfarnham all lay within a few miles' distance. The old rath of Fergus now lay within the walls of Dyflin, but the little clan of the Ui Fergusa were still recognised as chiefs in the area, and they had a farmstead nearby.

As he gazed across to the dark pool and the walled Viking settlement beyond, Osgar felt a comforting warmth spread through him. This was home.

When the Norwegian Vikings first arrived, his ancestor, the Ui Fergusa chief of the day, had wisely decided not to put up a futile resistance. It was also fortunate that, like Fergus long before him, this master of the rath had been an excellent cattleman. The Vikings had no sooner arrived on the Liffey than they began to look for supplies. Having dispersed his livestock to places where they would be hard to find, the cattleman made himself useful to them in every way, supplying them with grain, meat, and cattle at prices which were fair. The Vikings might be pirates but they were also traders. They respected him. Despite his Christian religion, this descendant of Fergus had still proudly preserved the family's ancient drinking skull. The Vikings could relate to that. He soon learned enough of their language to conduct business and made sure that none of his people gave them trouble. He became quite a popular figure. There was open land all around: there was no need to throw the old chief off his territory. And if he wanted to keep the little monastery, whose only object of value they had already taken, the pagan Norsemen had no objection. The monastery paid them a small rent. The monks often had skill in medicine. Vikings from the settlement would trudge over there for cures from time to time. And so it was that the family of Osgar had held on, by ancient Ath Cliath, down the centuries.

The two children were nearing the monastery gate, from which an elderly monk was emerging, when Caoilinn declared her intention.

"I think," she said, "I should like to get married in church today." And approaching the old monk, she asked politely, "Is the abbot in, Brother Brendan?"

"He is not," came the gruff reply. "He's gone fishing with his sons."

"We can't use the chapel, then," Osgar told her firmly, "or we'll be in trouble with my uncle." The abbot was strict about such things. If he allowed the children into the little chapel when there was no service, well and good. But if they sneaked in there without permission, they could expect to feel his strap across their backsides.

The fact that Osgar's uncle the abbot was a married man with children was not an indication of moral laxity at the monastery. Ever since, about two centuries after Bishop Patrick's visit, the Ui Fergusa had allowed a party of monks from a great religious community to the south to settle near their rath, the family had associated itself with the monastery. From time to time down the generations, if some member of the family felt a desire for the contemplative life, what could have been more natural than for him to enter their own religious house? Indeed, it even added to their prestige: for just as their ancestors had sometimes become druids, so the greatest families in the island would often have one of their number in holy orders at any given time. And it was only natural, also, that the Ui Fergusa should think of themselves as guardians of the monks.

Not that the little monastery was in need of much protection. Some of the great monasteries on the island had grown so rich that the chiefs in the region, for whom cattle raiding, after all, was an ancient and honourable tradition, could not resist the temptation to plunder the religious houses upon occasion. In the last two centuries, the Viking raiders had also plundered some of the monasteries when they came upon them near the island's coasts and navigable rivers. There had even, on some memorable occasions, been pitched battles between the monks from rival monasteries, over their possessions, precedence, or other matters. But the little religious house above the dark pool had suffered few of these troubles for the simple reason that it was too small and possessed no great treasures.

Nonetheless, it suited the family's pride that they should be its guardians, and in recent generations the chief of the family or one of his brothers had generally taken the position of lay abbot, which allowed the family to benefit from the modest living afforded by the place as well as giving it their protection. Such arrangements were quite common, both on the island and in many other parts of Christendom.

"Well," said Caoilinn crossly, "if we can't use the chapel, then it'll have to be somewhere else." She thought for a moment. "We'll go to the mound," she then announced. "Have you got the ring?"

"I have the ring," he replied patiently, and reaching into the leather pouch hanging from his belt he pulled out the small ring, made of deer antler, with which he had already wed her at least a dozen times.

"Come on, then," she said.

The game had been going on for almost a year now: the game of getting married. She never seemed to tire of it. And still he did not know—was it just a little girl's game, childish and without meaning, or was there some serious intention behind it? He was always the one she chose to be the bridegroom. Was that just because he was her cousin and he played along, and she was afraid the other boys might have laughed at her? Probably. Wasn't he embarrassed? Not really. He could shrug it off. She was just his little cousin. Anyway, Osgar might be slim, but he was taller than most of the other boys of his age, and he was sinewy. The other children treated him with a cautious respect. So he usually indulged her. Once when he was busy, he'd refused, and seen her face fall and watched her grow silent. Then, with a defiant toss of her head, she'd come back at him.

"Well, if you won't marry me, I'll have to find someone else."

"No, I'll marry you," he had relented. Better himself, after all, than another.

The mound wasn't far off. It stood on a grassy platform a little way back from the mudflats that lay downstream of the dark pool's inlet. When the Vikings first saw it they had named the place Hoggen Green, which meant "graveyard"; and as the Nordic people often did when they found a sacred place near a settlement, they used Hoggen Green for their assemblies where the freemen of the town came together to hold counsel and elect their leaders. And so it was that while the graves of his descendants, including Deirdre, Morna, and his children, gradually sank down until they were level with the rest of the grass at the Viking meeting place, the mound that was the last resting place of old Fergus was built up to be used as the platform on which the Viking headmen would stand to conduct their assemblies. The assembly was called the "Thing." Old

Fergus's grave, therefore, had nowadays acquired a new name. It was known as the Thingmount.

Before the Thingmount, the two children stood and prepared to get married. The marriage, they both knew, was appropriate. They were second cousins: Caoilinn's grandfather had become a crafts-man and moved into Dyflin, while Osgar's had remained at the family farmstead by the monastery.

The stately old Thingmount by the quiet river was also an ap-propriate place. For both knew that it was from under it that their ancestor Fergus had emerged to be baptised by none other than Saint Patrick himself. And both Osgar and even nine-year-old Caoilinn could recite with familiar ease the twenty-five generations that joined them to the old man.

As he always did, Osgar had to act the part of both bridegroom and priest. He did it very well. Since his father had died four years ago, his uncle the abbot had taken charge of his education. To the great joy of his mother, who went down on her knees in prayer four or five times every day, he not only knew his catechism and many of the Psalms by heart, but he could recite large parts of the Church services, too. "You have a talent for the spiritual life," his uncle in-formed him. He could also read and write, haltingly, in Latin. Indeed, his uncle told his proud mother, young Osgar had shown more aptitude for these things than his own sons.

Standing beside Caoilinn, but also just in front, he rather con-vincingly intoned the priest's part and gave the bridegroom's re-sponses. The antler ring was fitted, the bride duly but chastely kissed on the cheek, and Caoilinn, delighted with herself as always, walked about with her arm linked in his and the ring on her finger. She would wear it until the end of their games when, upon parting, she would give it back to him, to be put safely in the pouch until the next time.

What did it all mean? She might not know herself, but Osgar supposed that indeed, one day, they would marry in earnest.

You could see they were cousins. They had the same dark hair and good looks that had usually run in the family. But whereas Osgar's eyes were deep blue, hers were a startling green. He knew that green eyes ran in the family, but of all his cousins, she was the only one to have them, and that had made her seem special to him, even when she was only an infant. There was something about a cousin, too. Their shared ancestry seemed to form a strange bond between them—familiar, yet magical. He couldn't quite explain it, but he felt as if they were destined to be together in a world from which other families were somehow excluded. Yet even if they hadn't been cousins, he would have been fascinated by her wild, free spirit. The grown-ups, his uncles and aunts, had always considered him the most responsible of all the children of the extended family. The boy who was most likely to lead. He wasn't sure why, but it had been so even before the death of his father. Perhaps that was why he felt a special protectiveness towards his little cousin Caoilinn, who always did what she wanted, and climbed the tallest trees, and insisted that he marry her. For in his heart he knew that he could not think of marrying anyone else. The bright little spirit with her green eyes had long ago enchanted him.

They stayed there for a while, playing by the Thingmount and along the banks of a little stream that crossed the grass nearby; but at last it was time to return. And Caoilinn had just slipped off the ring and handed it to Osgar when they noticed two figures coming in their direction. One was a tall red-haired man on a splendid horse; the other a red-haired boy on a pony. They rode slowly along the riverside edge of Hoggen Green.

"Who are they?" Osgar asked Caoilinn. She always knew everybody.

"Ostmen. Norwegians. They've been here a long time," she said. "They live out in Fingal but they come into Dyflin sometimes. Rich farmers."

"Oh." He thought he knew the farmstead, and gazed at the two riders curiously, supposing they had come to visit the Thingmount. But to his surprise, though they glanced in the mound's direction, the two figures abruptly turned away towards the estuary and started heading into the shallows. "They must be going to the stone, then," he remarked.

It was a strange sight. Out on the watery mudflats, a single standing stone stood like a lonely sentinel, with only the crying seabirds for company. Behind it, bare mud and sea pool; before it, the breeze-blown waters of the estuary: the Long Stone, as it was called, had been set there by the Vikings to mark the place where, a century and a half earlier, their leading longship had first run aground on the Liffey's shore. For the two Norwegians, Osgar supposed, the Long Stone at the sea's edge might evoke the same ancestral echoes as the tomb of old Fergus did for him.

There was no question, he thought, that the tall Ostman with his red hair was a fine-looking man. And as if catching his thought from the wind, he heard Caoilinn beside him remark, "The boy's name is Harold. He's handsome."

Why should that strike a discordant note? No doubt she'd noticed him in Dyflin. Why shouldn't the Norwegian boy be handsome?

"Are they Christian or heathen?" he asked casually.

Many of the Vikings in Dyflin were still pagan. But the situation was fluid. The Irish living within the walls, like Caoilinn and her family, of course, were all Christian. Over the water, in England, Normandy, and the lands where they had taken their place beside other Christian rulers, the Viking chiefs and their followers had mostly availed themselves of the prestige and recognition that came with membership in the universal Church. But in Ireland, you still had to ask. Those who live and trade on the high seas often learn to show respect to different gods in different lands. The old Viking gods like Thor and Woden were very much alive. So if a merchant in Dyflin had something like a cross hanging round his neck, you could never be sure whether it was a crucifix or the hammer symbol of Thor.

One thing was certain, though. His cousin Caoilinn's family

were as devoutly Christian as his own. Caoilinn would never be allowed to marry a pagan, however rich or handsome he might be.

"I don't know," she said, and a brief silence fell between them. "The boy's a cripple," she added casually.

"Ah. Poor fellow," said Osgar.

I I

⊰ 9 9 1 ⊱

"You'd better go and collect him, Morann. You know what he's like."

Morann Mac Goibnenn looked up at his wife, Freya, with a smile and nodded.

It was the end of a warm and quiet summer. All the world, it seemed, was at peace this year. Seven years ago, the rising warlord from Munster, Brian Boru, along with some of the Waterford Vikings, had tried to raid the port. Two years ago, the High King had paid the place another brief and terrifying visit. But last year and this, everything had been quiet. No warships, no thundering of horses' hoofs, no threatening fires or clash of arms: the port of Dyflin under a new king, Sitric, had gone quietly about its business. It was time to think of family pastimes and of love. And since Morann had these things for himself, it was time to think of them for his friend Harold.

What was the matter with him? Was it forgetfulness, as he pretended, or shyness that caused him to miss appointments with pretty girls? "Just so long as it isn't to meet some woman," he'd said, when Morann had invited him. They'd tried introducing him to a girl about a year ago. He'd remained silent for the whole evening. "I wouldn't want her getting any ideas," he'd explained afterwards, while Morann had shaken his head and his wife, behind Harold's back, had cast her eyes up to heaven. Now it was time to try again.

Freya had selected the girl, whose name was Astrid and who was a kinswoman of her own. She'd spent a whole morning talking to her about Harold, told her everything about him, good and bad. Though the Norwegian knew nothing about it, the young woman had already been down to where he worked and observed him several times. In order to get round the problem of Harold's shyness, they had agreed to say that she was on her way to Waterford, where she was betrothed.

Morann would have been glad to see his friend married to a good woman like his own wife. He looked up at her fondly. There might be two communities in Ireland, Celtic and Scandinavian, and in describing their battles, the bards might like to build them up as heroic adversaries—Celt against Viking, Gaels against Foreigners, "Gaedhil and Gaill" in the poetic phrase—but in reality, the division had never been so simple. Though the Viking ports were certainly Nordic enclaves, the Norsemen had been marrying island women since they first arrived, and Irish men wed Nordic women.

Freya was dressed as a good Scandinavian wife should be—plain woollen stockings, leather shoes, a full belted dress over a linen shift. From the tortoiseshell clasp at her shoulder, on a silver chain hung two keys, a little bronze needle case, and a small pair of scissors. From her broad brow, her light brown hair was tied back severely under a hairnet. Only Morann knew the fires that burned beneath this demure exterior. She could be quite as wanton, he thought approvingly, as any harlot. That was the sort of wife his friend needed.

This Astrid girl was pagan, too. Though most of their Fingal neighbours were Christian, the family of Harold had remained quietly true to their old gods. Morann's wife had also been pagan, but converted to Christianity when she married him. He'd insisted upon that because he felt it showed respect to his family. Indeed, when she'd asked him what it would mean to become a Christian, he had given her an answer worthy of his one-eyed ancestor from six centuries ago: "It means you'll do as I say." He smiled when he thought of it. Five years of happy marriage and two children had taught him better.

Freya had certainly prepared a splendid meal. They lived in the Viking style: a modest breakfast in the morning, then nothing until the main meal of the day in the evening. Pickled herring and fresh fish from the estuary to start; two sorts of freshly baked bread; a main course of stewed calf, served with leeks and onions; cheese curds and hazelnuts to finish. All washed down with mead and a good wine shipped in from France. The stew was in its pot, hanging over the central hearth in the big main room. He could smell it from his workshop.

"You want me to go now?" he asked Freya. She nodded. Slowly, therefore, he began to gather up the objects on the table in front of him.

They were the various tools of his trade: the gimlets, tweezers, hammers that proclaimed he was a metalworker. More interesting was the small, flat piece of bone—the trial piece—upon which he had been carving rough designs for future items of metalwork. His talent was obvious. Even in this rough work, with its complex, interlacing forms, one could see the skilful blending of the abstract, swirling patterns of the island's ancient art, with the snakelike animal forms so popular with the Norsemen. Under his clever hands, rude Viking sea snakes would be caught in cosmic, Celtic patterns that delighted men and women equally.

In a strongbox beside his table, which was neatly divided into compartments, were all kinds of curiosities. There were pieces of the dark stone known as jet imported from the British Viking city of York; another compartment contained bits of coloured Roman glass, dug up in London and used by Viking jewellers for decoration. There were beads of dark blue, white, and yellow for making bracelets. For Morann could make anything: copper buckles, silver sword handles, gold arm rings; he could decorate with gold filigree and pattern silver, and make jewellery and ornaments of every kind.

Also in his box were some small piles of coins. As well as the old ring money and hack silver, the Viking traders of Dyflin were used to transacting business with coins from all over Europe, although there was talk of setting up their own mint, like the English did in their towns, there in Dyflin. Morann owned one or two old coins from the mints of Alfred the Great in England, and even one, of which he was especially proud, two centuries old, of the Holy Roman Emperor Charlemagne himself.

Carefully, now, he put the contents of his worktable away in the iron-banded box, which he then locked and gave to his wife for safe-keeping inside the house.

It was nearing the end of the working day. He made his way past the premises and workshops of comb makers and carpenters, harness makers and sellers of precious stones. Everywhere the busy prosperity of the Viking town was evident. He passed a blacksmith's glowing forge and smiled—the occupation of his ancestors. But it had to be admitted, the Norse invaders were better craftsmen with iron and ringing steel than even the warlike men of the island had been. Turning down the street known as Fish Shambles, where the fish market was already closed, he saw a merchant who gave him a respectful nod. The merchant dealt in the most precious commodity of all—golden amber that came all the way from Russia in a ship of the Baltic trade. Only a few of the craftsmen in Dyflin could afford to buy amber, and Morann was one of them.

Morann Mac Goibnenn. In Irish it sounded "Mocgovnan"—son of the smith—for both his father and grandfather had borne the name of Goibniu. It was only in the last generation or two that this form of individual family name had begun to be used. A man might be called Fergus, son of Fergus, and might belong to a great royal tribe, like the O'Neill; but the tribe was not, as yet, a family name. Morann and his children, however, were now the Mac Goibnenn family.

And it was used, by both Irish and Viking townsmen alike, with respect. Young though he still was, the maker of jewellery had shown himself to be a master of his craft. He was also known to be cautious and canny, and already he was a man who was listened to in the Viking port. His father had died two years after he had first come to Dyflin and it had been a great grief; but it gave Morann pleasure to think of how proud his father would be if he could see him now. Almost unconsciously, as though to keep alive the memory of his father, he had begun since the old man's death to imitate his trick of fixing people with one eye when he was negotiating or studying them for some reason. When his wife had complained of it, he had only laughed, but had not stopped doing it.

At the bottom of Fish Shambles, he came out onto the big wooden quay. There were still plenty of people about. A party of slaves, chained together with iron rings round their necks, was being led along it from one of the boats. He glanced at them quickly, but with a critical eye. They looked strong and healthy. Dyflin was the main slave market for the island and there were regular shipments from the great British slave port of Bristol. The English, in his opinion, being somewhat slow and docile, made good slaves. Swiftly, he made his way along the quay to the end where he knew his friend would be. And there, sure enough, he was. He waved. Harold saw him, and smiled.

Good. He suspected nothing.

It took a little while to get Harold away from the quay; but he seemed quite happy to be coming, which was all that mattered. His real concern, however, seemed to be that Morann should admire the great project upon which he was working, and of which he was obviously very proud. Nor had Morann any difficulty in doing so.

"It's magnificent," he agreed. In fact, it was awesome.

It was a Viking ship. All over the Viking world, nowadays, the port of Dyflin was famous for building ships. There were many shipyards around the coasts of Scandinavia and Britain; but if you wanted the best, you went to Dyflin.

Like everyone else in the town, Morann knew that the latest boat was special; but today they had been taking down some of the scaffolding which had surrounded it, and the ship's sleek outlines were now visible. It was massive.

"A yard longer than anything built in London or York," Harold said proudly. "Come, see inside it." And he led the way to a ladder, while Morann followed.

It always amazed Morann that, despite his limp, Harold could move as fast, indeed faster than other men. Watching him run up the ladder and then, with a laugh, leaping lightly over the ship's side, the craftsman could only marvel at his agility. Having known him only since the young Norwegian came to work in the port, however, he had no idea of the years of painful training and hard work that had achieved this result.

Ever since the meeting with Sigurd, it had been the same. Early in the morning, he would be up to help his father on the farm. But by midday he was always free, and then his regimen would begin. First came the physical training. He would drive himself ruthlessly. Ignoring the pain and humiliation of his stumbles and falls, the little boy at the farmstead would force himself to walk as fast as he could, dragging his crippled leg along, pushing it into use. In due course, with an erratic, hopping kind of action, he could run. He could even jump, leaping with his good leg and tucking the damaged one under him as he cleared an obstacle. In the afternoons his father would usually join him. And then the fun would begin.

His father had made him little wooden weapons first: an axe, a sword, a dagger and shield. For two years it was like a game he would play, teaching Harold to strike, parry, thrust, and dodge. "Move away. Hold your ground. Strike now!" he would call. And, weaving, ducking, or whirling his toy axe, the boy would go through every exercise his father could devise. By the age of twelve, his skill was remarkable and his father would laugh: "I can't catch him!" At thirteen, Harold was given his first real weapons. They were light, but a year later his father gave him heavier ones. At the age of fifteen, his father confessed he could teach him no more, and sent him to a friend up the coast, whom he knew was highly skilled. It was there that Harold learned not only greater agility but even to make use of his physical peculiarities to strike unconventional blows that would take any opponent by surprise. By the age of sixteen, he was a killing machine.

"Strangely enough," his well-meaning father once remarked to him, "by threatening your life, that Dane may have done you a favour. Think what you were then, and look at you now."

And Harold kissed his father affectionately and said nothing, because what he knew was that he had developed extraordinary skills, but that he was still a cripple.

"The lines are fine," Harold called to Morann, as the craftsman clambered over the ladder. And indeed they were. The long clinker-built lines of the ship swept forward to the huge prow so smoothly and with such power that when you imagined it in the water its swift passage didn't just seem natural, it seemed inevitable—as inevitable as fate, in the hands of the pagan Nordic gods themselves. "The space for the cargo," Harold was gesturing towards the empty centre of the huge vessel, "is nearly a third larger than anything else on the water." He pointed down to the bottom of the ship, where the mighty spine of the keel ran like a blade. "Yet the draught is still shallow enough for all the main rivers on the island." The Liffey, the massive Shannon waterway in the west, every major river in Ireland had seen the Viking oarsmen come skimming up their shallow waters into the interior. "But do you know the real secret of a ship like this, Morann? The secret of its handling under sail, on the sea?"

They were strong. They never capsized. The craftsman was aware of these. But with a grin, the Norwegian went on: "They bend, Morann." He made a wiggling motion with his arm. "As you feel the power of the wind on the sail, running down the mast, and you feel the power of the water against the sides, you can feel something else. The keel itself bends, it follows the water's curve. The whole ship, braced against the wind, becomes at one with the water. It's not a ship, Morann, it's a snake." He laughed with delight. "A great sea snake!"

How handsome he looked, the craftsman thought, with his long red hair, like his father's, and his bright blue eyes, so happy on his ship.

Once Freya had asked Morann, "Did you never wonder why Harold left the farmstead and came to work in Dyflin?"

"He loves building ships," he'd answered. "It's in his blood," he had added. It was obvious to any man.

And indeed, if there was more to the matter than Morann Mac Goibnenn supposed, he had never heard of it from his young friend.

⁘

Harold had been almost seventeen the summer when they presented him with the girl. She came from over the sea, from one of the northern islands—a girl of good ancestry, they told him, whose parents had died leaving her in the care of her uncle. "He's a fine man," his father told him, "and he has sent her to me. She'll be our guest for a month and you're to look after her. Her name is Helga."

She was a fair, slim girl, blue-eyed, a year older than he was. Her father had been Norwegian; her mother, Swedish. Yellow hair framed her cheeks, pressing them close, like a pair of hands taking her face between them before the lips were kissed. She did not smile much, and her eyes had a slightly distant look, as if half her mind was somewhere else. Yet there was a hint of sensuality in her mouth that Harold found a little mysterious, and exciting.

Around the house, she seemed placid and content. Two of Harold's sisters were married and away by then, but his remaining sisters got on with her well enough. No one had any complaints. His own duties, apart from joining in whatever entertainments the girls devised for themselves in the evenings, were to take her riding from time to time. Once he had shown her round Dyflin. More often they would ride out or walk along the sandy shore. On these occasions, she would talk to him in her strangely detached yet easy way about the farmstead, the cheese they were making, the shawl that she and his mother were weaving for his aunt. She would ask him his likes and dislikes, nodding calmly and saying, "Ja, ja," as she elicited each piece of information so that, he began to think, if he had told her his favourite pastime was cutting people's heads off, she would probably have nodded and said, "Ja, ja," just the same. But the process was still very pleasant.

When he questioned Helga about her own life, she told him about her uncle's farmstead and also her early life in the north. What did she miss, he asked. "The snow and the ice," she told him, with a hint of real enthusiasm greater than any he had seen before. "The snow and ice is very good. I like to fish through the ice." She nodded. "And I like very much to go in boats on the sea."

Once, in order to take her in a boat, he had rowed her out on a sunny day from the beach to the little island with its high, cleft rock, opposite the headland. She had been pleased. They had sat on the beach together. And then, to his great surprise, she had calmly remarked, "I like to swim now. You also?" And stripping off all her clothes as if it were the most natural thing in the world, she had walked into the sea. He hadn't followed her. Perhaps he was shy, or ashamed of his body. But he had looked at her slim body, and her small, high breasts, and thought to himself that it would be a pleasant business indeed to possess them.

It was a few days afterwards that his father and mother had called him into the house when the girls were all busy outside, and his father with a smile had asked him, "How would you feel, Harold, if Helga were to be your bride?" And before Harold could formulate an answer he continued: "Your mother and I think she would do very well."

He stared at them hardly knowing what to say. The idea was certainly exciting. He thought of her body as he had watched her coming back out of the sea, and of the water running down her breasts in the sun.

"But," he stammered at last, "would she want me?"

His father and mother gave each other a warm, conspirational smile, and it was his mother who answered, "She does indeed. She has spoken to me."

"I just supposed . . ." He thought of his leg. His father cut in.

"She likes you, Harold. This all comes from her. When her uncle asked me to have her here, I dare say he may have desired a match with our family; but you're young and I hadn't considered it was time to think of such things for you yet. But we like this girl. We like her very much. And so when she came to talk to your mother . . ." He smiled again. "It's up to you, Harold. You're my only son. This farmstead will be yours one day. You can have the pick of the girls, and you certainly shouldn't marry one you don't like. But this one, I have to say, isn't bad."

Harold looked at his happy parents and felt a great warmth run through him. Could it really be that this girl had chosen him? He knew that he was physically strong, but with this wonderful knowledge, he experienced a new, thrilling sense of strength and excitement unlike anything he had ever known before.

"She has asked for me?" They nodded. His infirmity was not of consequence, then? It seemed not. "You think I should?" What would it mean to be married? He wasn't sure. "I think," he began, "I think I should like it."

"Splendid," Olaf cried, and was about to get up and put his arm round his shoulders; but it was his wife, now, who gently laid her hand on his arm, as if to remind him.

"He should wait a few days," she said quietly. "We discussed this."

"Oh." His father looked a little disappointed, but then smiled at her. "You are right, of course." And then to Harold: "you have only just heard of this, my son. It's all very new to you. Consider the whole thing for a few days. There's no hurry. You should do that in fairness to yourself."

"And to the girl, too," his wife gently reminded him.

"Of course, yes. Her, too." And now his father did rise and put his arm round him, and Harold felt the great warmth of his loving presence. "Well done, my son," he murmured. "I'm so proud of you."

And had it not been for the merest chance, Harold supposed, he would have been married by that very winter.

It had been two days later. He had just left his father out in the field and was coming in a little earlier than expected. He had seen his sisters disappearing into the big wooden barn some time ago. Apart from a slave making a basket by the woodshed, there was no one about as he came to the entrance of the high, thatched house. And he was about to stoop under the doorway into the shadowy space inside, when he heard his mother's voice.

"But Helga, are you sure you will be happy?"

"Ja, ja. I like this farm."

"I'm glad you do, Helga. But perhaps liking the farm is not enough. Do you like my son?"

"Ja, ja. I like him."

"He is my only son, Helga. I want him to be happy."

"Ja, ja. I make him happy."

"But what makes you think so, Helga? Marriage is about many things. It's about companionship. About love . . ."

Was there a hint of impatience, a hardness in the girl's voice that he had not heard before, as she answered?

"It was your husband who came to my uncle, ja? When he hears my uncle has a niece he wants to get out of the house, to make more room for the four daughters he have of his own? He pays my uncle to bring me here. Because he wants to marry his son, who is a cripple? This is true, ja?"

"That may be, but . . ."

"And I have come, and I do all that you want, and then your husband three days ago say to me, 'Will you marry him?' and I say, 'Ja, ja?' Because he wants grandchildren from this only son and he is afraid nobody want to marry his cripple son."

There was a pause. He waited for his mother to deny all this, but she did not.

"Do you find my son . . ."

"His legs?" It was as though he could hear her shrug. "I thought I would marry a boy with both legs straight. But he is strong."

"When two people marry," his mother's voice was anxious now, almost pleading, "there must be truth between them."

"Ja? You and your husband say nothing. My uncle say nothing. But I hear my uncle tell my aunt that your husband is afraid someone coming to kill your son before he gives you grandchildren, and that is why your husband wants to buy me quickly from my uncle. Is that true? We speak of truth, ja?"

"My son can defend himself."

Harold turned away from the doorway. He had heard enough.

The next day he had gone into Dyflin. Because of his work about the farm, he was a tolerably good carpenter. He had been able to get a job in the boatyard. And by late afternoon he had found temporary lodgings in the house of a craftsman. On his return to the farmstead that evening he had told his astonished parents, "I'm leaving."

"But what about this girl? Your marriage?" his father had demanded.

"I've changed my mind. I don't want her."

"In the name of all the gods, why?" Olaf roared.

There are so many things that children cannot say to their parents. Could he really tell his father that he knew the truth, that the trust between them was broken, that he was humiliated? If he was ever to marry, and he doubted now that he would, he'd find the girl for himself—that was for sure. "I don't want to marry her. That's all," he said. "It's my choice. You said so."

"You don't know what's for your own good," his father snapped. His frustration was so visible that his son was even sorry for him. But it was no good.

"You don't have to leave," his mother urged.

But he did, even if he neither then nor ever afterwards said why.

And so he had come to Dyflin. He had lodged for a year with Morann Mac Goibnenn. He had made himself so useful in the boatyards that he was nowadays a foreman. It was known that he was heir to a big farmstead out in Fingal; but he seldom went there, and it was said that his father and he were on poor terms. He worked hard, was a good companion, but though he seemed comfortable enough with women, he was never seen out walking with one.

·╬·

The sunset was already sending a red glow over the water when Harold and Morann left the great Viking ship and began to stroll along the wooden quay. Several other longships were tied up there. One, the ship that had brought the slaves from Bristol, had just finished loading with huge bales of hides and wool. The turning to the Fish Shambles was just ahead.

"Remember me?"

Morann looked at the black-haired young man who was leaning casually against some bales that lay almost in their path. He was wearing a dark leather jacket that came down to his knees. His leather belt was drawn tight so that the jacket hugged what was evidently a lean, muscular body. His dark beard was trimmed to a jagged point over his chest. The craftsmen wondered who he was.

"Still a cripple I see."

Harold had stopped and Morann stopped with him.

"I just happened to be in Dyflin." He hadn't moved. He just stayed there, leaning casually against the crates, apparently unguarded, as if the man he was insulting could be of no more danger to him than a passing fly.

"Good evening, Sigurd," said Harold, with a calmness that surprised the craftsman. "Have you come about our business then?"

"I considered it," said the stranger coolly. "But I think I'll wait."

"I supposed I wasn't in danger as soon as I saw you in front of me," Harold remarked. "They tell me the men of your family only attack from behind."

Just for a moment, it seemed to Morann, the stranger winced. His hand moved, perhaps unconsciously, to the dagger on his belt. But though his long fingers briefly clasped it, they then slowly stretched out, and his hand went back to rest on his leg.

"I made enquiries about you," he remarked. "And I was very disappointed. It seems you haven't a woman at all. Would that be on account of your being a cripple, would you say?"

Morann had had enough.

"I can't imagine any woman but a whore looking at you, you dirty black creature," he snarled.

"Ah, the jeweller." The stranger made a slight bow with his head. "A man of respect. I've no quarrel with you, Morann Mac Goibnenn. Does he know," he asked Harold, "who I am?" And seeing Harold shake his head, "That is what I thought."

"I could fight you now," Harold said easily. "It's no use my saying I'll fight you in the morning; when we last agreed that, your grandfather ran away."

"And yet," the dark fellow said musingly, as though he had not heard this last remark, "it seems to me that I should be happier to kill you when you've a family to grieve for you. Children to be told that their father has been defeated and killed. Perhaps in time, then, we would be killing them, too." He nodded thoughtfully, and then in a brighter tone, "Do you not think there's a chance of your marrying?"

Harold had a knife in his belt. He took it out, flicked it expertly from hand to hand, and motioned for Morann to stand away to one side.

"I will kill you now, Sigurd," he said.

"Ah." The dark man straightened himself, but instead of moving forward, he took a step to one side. "I'd rather you had time to think about it though. Like on your wedding day." He took a step back-

wards now, with the crates to one side of him. As he never looked
behind him, Morann assumed he already knew where he was going.
And sure enough, a moment later, "Goodbye for now," he said, and
quick as a flash, he was behind the crates, to the side of the quay,
and with an easy leap he was in a small boat which, until that moment, the craftsman had not noticed.

"Row, lads," he called out to the two men already in the boat;
and as Harold and Morann watched from the side of the quay, the
boat raced swiftly out into the waters. From the dark man there
came a contemptuous laugh, and then, from the reddening waters,
as the black shape of the boat slipped away downstream, his voice
came calling again. "I'll try to come to your wedding."

For some time the two men stood there.

"What was that about?" Morann finally asked.

"An old family quarrel."

"Does he really mean to kill you?"

"Probably. But I'll kill him." Harold turned. "So are we going to
your house for supper?"

"We are. Of course we are." Morann forced a smile.

But as they made their way up Fish Shambles in the lengthening
shadows he wondered what to tell his wife. And the girl. If the
black-haired fellow comes to the wedding, he thought, I'd better kill
him myself.

⁘

It was early the following morning that Osgar received a visit from
Caoilinn's father. It had been made to seem like a casual encounter,
but Osgar suspected that the craftsman had been waiting near the
monastery wall for some time before he happened to walk by.
Though his kinsman from Dyflin had similar aquiline features, he
was shorter and more thickset than Osgar and, unusual for the family, he was balding. As he stood there before the aristocratic young
man, it seemed to Osgar that he detected a trace of awkwardness in
his manner.

But he was not the only one, thought Osgar, who is feeling awkward. There was nothing to be done, however. He must wait for the man to speak. They went through a few of the usual pleasantries which must precede any important matter. Then, as he knew it must, it came.

"We shall be thinking of finding a husband for Caoilinn soon."

It had begun. He knew it couldn't be avoided. He gazed at the older man, wondering what to say.

"She'll have a good dowry," his kinsman went on. It was more than two centuries since any father on the island had been able to secure the ancient bride price. Fathers had to find dowries for their daughters now, which was often a heavy burden—though an important son-in-law could always be a valuable asset.

Osgar certainly represented a good catch. There was no doubt about that. Twenty-one years old, he was a strikingly handsome young man. Sparely built but athletic, with his finely drawn face and natural elegance, Osgar also had a quiet dignity, almost a reserve, that impressed people. Many thought he would be the future chief of the Ui Fergusa. Not only to the family but to the monks at the monastery as well, he had become a figure to respect.

Osgar loved the family's little monastery. He was almost as proud of it as his uncle. "Let us never forget," his uncle would say, "that Saint Patrick came here."

It was remarkable how, in the last few centuries, the legend of Saint Patrick had grown. Largely because the diocese in the north where he had been based—Armagh—wanted to be considered the oldest and most important bishopric in Ireland, a great medieval propaganda campaign had been launched, through the chronicles and other documents and records, to prove Armagh's point. Earlier bishops and their communities were practically written out of the story; bishops from Patrick's own time were turned into his disciples; the northern mission was now said to have covered the whole island. Even the snakes, who were never there, were supposed to have been banished by the saint. At Dubh Linn, one of the three ancient wells had been named after him and a chapel built at the site. "And let us not forget, either," Osgar's uncle would remind them, "that our ancestor Fergus received baptism from Saint Patrick himself."

"He was dead at the time," his eldest son had rudely remarked upon one occasion.

"Raised from the dead," the abbot had roared. "The greater the miracle. And remember also," he would admonish, "that there have been no better Christians and no finer scholars than those of this island. For it was we who kept the flame of the faith alive when all the rest of Christendom was in darkness, we who converted the heathen Saxons of England, and we who built monasteries with libraries when half of Christendom could hardly read or write."

If these lectures were intended to encourage his sons in the paths of piety and learning, however, they had no effect. His uncle's boys had little interest in the family monastery. They constantly found excuses to avoid lessons. And while Osgar had enjoyed memorising the hundred and fifty Psalms in Latin—a feat which any illiterate novice had to master—they could only pretend to mouth the words on the occasions when they joined the monks at their prayers.

But one thing was very clear: the monastery and its Ui Fergusa patrons grew out of the sacred dawn of Irish Christianity. This was a tradition which the family had a duty to uphold. And Osgar did so. When he was twelve, his mother had died, and thereafter he had gone to live in the little monastery with his uncle. It had been Osgar who had organised the monks to refurbish the inside of the monastery chapel; Osgar who had persuaded some Dyflin merchants to donate a new cross for the altar. It was Osgar who always seemed to know exactly what was due from the monastery's tenants, who sold the cattle or bought the things they needed; Osgar who knew how many candles they had in stock, and which Psalms should be sung on any given day. On these, as on all issues, he was both businesslike and very precise. Even his uncle, secretly, was slightly nervous of forgetting something in front of him. And a year ago his uncle had taken him to one side and told him, "I think it's you who should take my place at the monastery one day, Osgar." And then, as an afterthought, he had added, "You could marry, you know."

Not only could he marry, but with a prospective position that carried such respect, he would be a very attractive catch for the daughter of his kinsman in Dyflin.

He could marry Caoilinn. How wonderful that had felt. For days he had gone about in a state of such happiness that it had seemed to him as if the whole of Dyflin and its bay was bathed in a divine and golden light.

They had grown up together. Even during the awkward years of adolescence, there had never been a day when they hadn't been friends. There had been times when they had seen less of each other, but she had never been far away. If he was in Dyflin, it was natural that he should call in at her father's house. She was family. The lively girl he had known as a child had never entirely disappeared. If they were walking together, she would suddenly point to the clouds and see the strangest comic shapes in them. Once, standing on the southern headland of the bay, she had insisted that she had just seen the old sea god Manannan mac Lir out in the waves; and for half an afternoon she had periodically cried, "There he is!" Caught off his guard, he had several times looked out, while she collapsed into peals of laughter.

But on one occasion, she had gone too far. They had been walking along the estuary's northern strand and they had wandered far out onto the sands which at low tide stretched for hundreds of paces into the bay. When the tide had started to come in, he had told her they must turn back, but she had refused. Impatiently he had started back, and with equal obstinacy, she had remained where she was. But even he had not foreseen the swiftness and strength of the tide that day. The sea had come in with the speed of a running horse. From the shore, he had seen her standing defiantly on a sand-bar, laughing at first as the incoming water swirled round her, then trying to wade her way back and finding that the waters were already deeper than she thought. Suddenly he, too, realised that the water was moving with a powerful current; the surface was frothing with choppy little waves. He saw her lose her balance; her arms were thrown up; and he had run forward through the shallows and dived into the flowing current. It had been fortunate that he was a strong swimmer. The current had almost swept him along, too. But he had managed to reach her and, swimming for both of them, with her slender body pressed against him, bring her back to the shore, bedraggled and very pale. She had sat there, coughing and shivering for some time, while he put his arms round her to warm her and helped her get dry. Finally, she had got up and then, to his astonishment, she had laughed. "You saved me," she cried. And when they got back, she told everyone delightedly, "Osgar saved my life!" She was a strange girl. But after that day he had always felt a warm sense of protectiveness towards her that pleased him.

Apart from small adventures like this, he could not say that his own life during the years from childhood to manhood had been particularly eventful. Once, the Irish king had come to demand tribute from the Norsemen of Dyflin and had camped outside the walls until he got it; but though there had been a brief skirmish, this had been exciting rather than frightening. Osgar's life had not been so very different from the lives of all the other boys he knew. But he had developed one passion. It had started as a child. He would amuse the adults by returning from his walks along the shore with bags of shells he had picked up. At first it was just a childish game, picking up strangely shaped or brightly coloured shells that had pleased him. Then he had begun to sort his shells into a collection, until he had an example of every one of the different sea creatures whose shells could be found in the area. If any strange or unusual shell appeared on the beach, he would know it at once. As time went on, however, looking over these childish treasures, he began to be fascinated by the shape and structure that each exhibited. He would examine their lines minutely, observing the simplicity and purity of the basic forms within them, admiring the elegance and complexity with which each shell achieved its necessary and harmonious whole. Their colours fascinated him, too. Sometimes, hardly knowing that time was passing, he would gaze at his shell collection, completely absorbed, for hours. In due course, he added other kinds of objects: pressed leaves, strange stones, complex knotted branches from fallen trees. He brought them all home and studied them. It was a solitary activity, only because he never found anyone else to share his enthusiasm, though his uncle, in a kindly way, was always amused to see what strange thing he had found. Even Caoilinn, when he periodically showed her the collection, would glance around at the treasure trove with a quick nod, but would soon get bored.

Occasionally he would also pay a visit to one of the churches in Dyflin. Here there was a Psalter, not especially fine, but with some handsome illuminations; and the priests there, knowing he was the nephew of the abbot of the little monastery on the slope, would allow him to turn its pages and stare at them by the hour. He had waited a long time before he brought Caoilinn to see the Psalter, thinking that she might be too young to appreciate such a thing. But finally, when she was sixteen, he had brought her there and reverently turned the pages for her. One, in particular, in greens and golds, he thought was fine.

"Do you see," he showed her, "how it glimmers? It's as if you could step right into the page; and once you are there, you encounter . . ." he searched for words for a moment, "a great silence." He had gazed at her, hoping she felt the same thing. But though she smiled briefly, he detected a faint frown of impatience as well.

After what she felt was a proper pause, she said, "Let's go outside."

The transformation that had taken place in Caoilinn had been remarkable. The thin little girl he had known and loved had all but disappeared, and in her place there was now a dark-haired young woman with a well-rounded figure. Subtler changes had also occurred. It was to be expected that her interests would change. She would speak of domestic matters now, or show delight at the fine cloth at a merchant's stall—things which he did not especially care for himself but which he knew were the matters that women liked to discuss. But there was something else about her now, something in her eyes, something about her whole person that was different, and which he found exciting and even a little mysterious. It had been last year, at Lughnasa, that he had finally recognised it.

There had been dancing on the night of the old festival. Most of the young people in Dyflin, Irish or not, had taken part. Osgar was a good dancer himself. He had watched with pleasure as some of the older women danced in a stately manner. But when Caoilinn had got up to join the dance, he had been astonished. He knew she would be lively and graceful; but now he found himself confronted with a new Caoilinn, a vigorous young woman who moved her body this way and that, with a warm and confident allure. Her face was slightly flushed, her eyes gleaming, her mouth open in a laughing smile in which he thought he detected a hint of rich sensuality. She was dancing among the young men. She danced no more than the steps they danced, yet as Osgar watched their faces, it seemed as if she had touched each one of them, giving them a little part of her warmth; and for a while he hung back from the dance, feeling almost shy. Was his cousin behaving in a way that was almost too full-blooded, too earthy for his taste?

But then she had beckoned to him, and he had joined in. And suddenly he was in front of her, aware of the closeness of her body; the warmth and the scent of her flesh were intoxicating. She smiled to see him dance so well. At the end he had bent to kiss her on the cheek, but she, instead, had kissed him chastely but softly on the mouth and, just for a moment, she looked straight into his eyes and he saw the green-eyed Caoilinn he had loved all his life. Then she laughed and turned away.

The next day, he went for a long walk along the seashore, alone. It was Caoilinn who had brought up the question of their marriage. He had been out walking one spring Sunday with her whole family. They had gone down to Hoggen Green by the old Thingmount, and he and Caoilinn had been standing a little apart when she had turned to him.

"Do you remember how we used to get married down here?"

"I do."

"Do you still have the ring?" The little antler ring.

"Yes."

She was silent for a moment.

"It wouldn't fit on my finger now," she said with a quiet laugh. "But when I get married—whoever will marry me—I'd like to put it on my little finger." She smiled up at him. "Will you promise to give it to me for my marriage?"

He gazed at her affectionately. "I promise," he said.

He had understood. Assertive though she was, she couldn't go further and keep her dignity. She had dropped the hint. It would be up to him to make the next move after that.

And now here was her father, looking at him expectantly.

"We shall be seeking a husband," he repeated.

"Ah," said Osgar. There was a pause.

"I could have found her a husband before," her father pointed out. "There would be no shortage of offers." This was undoubtedly true. "But I had an idea," he pressed on, "that she might be waiting for you." He stopped and smiled encouragingly at Osgar.

"We have been getting married ever since we were little children," Osgar said with a smile.

"So you have. Indeed you have," said her father, and waited for Osgar to continue. But nothing happened. "Young men," he continued patiently, "often have difficulty when it comes to committing to marriage. They are afraid. It seems like a trap. And this is only natural. But there are compensations. And with Caoilinn . . ." He trailed off, allowing Osgar to imagine for himself the delights of being married to his daughter.

"Oh, indeed," said Osgar.

"But if they do not offer when the time is right," he gave Osgar a warning glance, "they may lose the girl they love to someone else."

Lose Caoilinn to another? It was a terrible thought.

"I shall come and speak with Caoilinn," Osgar promised, "very soon."

⁙

Why should he have hesitated, he asked himself when her father had gone? Wasn't this what he had always wanted? What could be better than living with Caoilinn at the family's little monastery, enjoying the things of the spirit and of the flesh, for the rest of his life? It was a delightful prospect.

So what was missing? What was wrong with it? He scarcely knew himself. All he did know was that he had been feeling a strange disquiet in recent months. Ever since the incident.

The disquieting incident had occurred at the turn of the year. He had been riding back across the Plain of Bird Flocks after delivering a message from his uncle to a small religious house in that area. As it was a fine day, one of his uncle's sons had decided to ride out with him, accompanied by one of the slaves. There were several Viking farmsteads in that part of Fingal, with large open fields, and they had passed one of them and gone into a small wood when, suddenly, half a dozen men had jumped out onto the track.

Osgar had just time to think. Robberies were not unknown in the area, and travellers usually went armed. His cousin had a sword with him, but Osgar was only carrying a hunting knife. The robbers would be after their valuables if they had any; then they'd take their horses. Whether they meant to kill them he couldn't guess, but it certainly wasn't worth waiting to find out. He saw his cousin slash at two of the men with his sword and wound them. Two more were coming at him. The slave had already been dragged from his horse. One of the men was standing over him with a club. He raised it.

Osgar never really knew what happened. He seemed to be flying through the air. His hunting knife was out of its sheath and in his hand. He landed on top of the man with the club. They crashed to the ground, struggled, and a moment later Osgar's knife was through the robber's ribs and the fellow was coughing blood. Meanwhile, the rest of the robbers had decided not to risk the fight any longer and were running away through the trees. Osgar turned to the man he had stabbed. The robber had gone grey. A few moments later, he started to tremble, then he shuddered and became still. He was dead. Osgar stared at him.

They rode back to the farmstead they had just passed, where the big, red-haired owner called his men together at once to organise a hunt for the robbers. "It's a pity my son, Harold, isn't here," he remarked, and Osgar realised that this must be the big Norwegian he had once seen at the Thingmount years ago. When Osgar explained who he was, the big Viking was delighted. "I'm honoured to meet one of the Ui Fergusa," he said cheerfully. "You did well today. You can be proud of yourself." When they got back to the monastery late that evening and told their tale, his uncle congratulated him, too. By the next morning, the story was all round Dyflin and meeting Caoilinn, she had come up and squeezed his hand. "Our hero," she had said, with a proud smile.

There was only one problem. He didn't feel like a hero at all. In fact, he had never felt worse in his life. Nor, as the days went by, did he feel any better.

He had killed a man. He wasn't guilty of any crime. He had done what he had to do. Yet for some reason the dead man's face with its staring eyes seemed to haunt him. It came to him in his dreams, but also when he was awake—pale, horrible, and strangely insistent. He assumed that after a while it would go away, but it hadn't; and soon he found himself imagining the rotting body as well. But the worst thing was not so much the memory as the nagging thoughts that accompanied it.

Revulsion. Absurd though it was, he experienced all the horror and disgust he would have felt if he'd committed murder. He never wanted to do such a thing again. He vowed to himself that he would not. But in such a violent world, how could you be sure of keeping such a vow? And with the revulsion came another disturbing thought.

He had been a hair's breadth away from death. What if he had died? What would his life have been? A few meaningless years, ended by a stupid brawl. It had nearly happened then; it could happen tomorrow. For the first time, he was afflicted by a terrible, urgent sense of his own mortality. Surely his life must have some purpose; surely he should be serving some cause. When he thought of the passion he experienced when he was studying the natural forms or the illustrations that he loved, the daily, humdrum life he was leading at Dyflin seemed to be lacking an essential ingredient. He yearned for something more, something lasting, that could not be so pointlessly snatched away. He didn't quite know what it was; but his sense of unease had continued to grow, as if a voice deep inside him were whispering, "This is not your true life. This is not your destiny. This is not where you belong." He had heard it, again and again, but he hadn't known what to do.

And now, suddenly, this business with Caoilinn seemed to be bringing matters to a head. He wasn't sure why, but an instinct told him that his decision about their marriage was going to decide everything else, too. If he married now, he was going to settle down with her at Dyflin, have children, and live there for the rest of his days. An honourable life of domestic bliss. It was an attractive option. It was what he had always wanted. Wasn't it?

✣

The two monks came by the little monastery the week after his interview with Caoilinn's father. They had been staying in Dyflin for a few days and were returning southwards to their monastery at Glendalough.

Osgar had only been to the great lakeside monastery in the Wicklow Mountains once. The abbot of Glendalough had the right

to visit and inspect their own little monastery, and when he was a
boy of eight, his uncle had taken him there; but it had rained for the
entire time, Osgar had been bored, and perhaps because of this depressing memory, he had never made the effort to journey down
there again. Now, however, feeling the need for a change of scene
while he made up his mind about the question of Caoilinn, he asked
if he might accompany them to visit the place, to which they readily agreed; and so, telling his uncle that he would be back in a few
days, he set off in their company.

The journey was delightful. They had chosen the lower road that
led southwards along the slopes of the great volcanic hills below the
Liffey estuary, with wonderful views eastwards over the coastal
plain. They went about twenty miles before resting for the night and
then continued the climb that led to the high ground. It was midmorning when, pausing by a turn in the mountain track, one of the
monks beckoned to him and pointed.

There was still a morning mist over the floor of the narrow
mountain valley, and the wooded sides which rose steeply from the
waters appeared to be floating in the clouds. The two small lakes
were invisible under the mist, but the treetops around them,
drenched in dew, emerged into the morning air. From where he
stood, Osgar could also see the roofs of several of the stone buildings:
the main chapel, which they called the abbey, with its little turret;
some smaller churches, the high arch of the gatehouse; and a few
small chapels. And dominating them all, rising a hundred feet into
the air, stood the solitary guardian of the valley, the round tower.

So this was Glendalough—the valley of the two lakes—the
loveliest monastery in all Ireland.

The secluded position of Glendalough was not unusual. Irish
monasteries were sometimes founded on former pagan holy places;
but, as in other parts of Christendom, they were often set up on
lands that had not been much used before—marshy riverbanks,
borderlands, and isolated mountain places. It had been founded,
about a century after the mission of Saint Patrick, by a hermit.

The tradition of the Church in Ireland, ever since the days of Saint Patrick, had been a kindly and peaceable one. Saints there had been, and scholars too numerous to mention, but few if any martyrs. There had also been hermits. There were many hermits in the Celtic Church. The practice had come to the island, through Gaul, from the early Christian anchorites, as these solitary desert dwellers were called, of Egypt. And as there had never been much need for Christian martyrs in Ireland, it was natural, perhaps, that the role of a mountain or woodland recluse should have appealed to men, heirs to the druids of older times, who wanted to make a radical commitment to their religious faith.

Like many holy men, Kevin the hermit monk had attracted followers; and so it was that the mountain refuge had been arranged in two parts. Beside the upper lake, which lay deeper in the narrow valley, was the hermit's cell, overlooked by a tiny cave in the steep hillside, known as Kevin's Bed. A short walk down the valley, past the lower lake and where the stream from the lakes was joined by another, lay the main monastic community with its various buildings stoutly constructed, nowadays, of stone.

When they reached the entrance, Osgar had received his first surprise. Isolated the monastery might be, but small it was not. Its huge, impressive gateway proclaimed its power. "Don't forget," his companions reminded him, "the bishop has a house up here as well as the abbot." The bishop, Osgar knew, oversaw most of the churches in the Liffey valley.

And yet, as soon as they had passed through the impressive gateway into the great, walled enclosure, Osgar felt as though he had entered another world. Resting on the grassy meadow between the two streams as they joined each other below the smaller lake, the monastery's grounds seemed like an enchanted island. After they had made themselves known to the prior, one of the novices was summoned to show him round.

There were a number of churches and chapels, a sign of Glendalough's long standing and importance; nearly all were solidly built of well-dressed stone. As well as the big main church with its handsome doorway, there was a church dedicated to Saint Kevin and a chapel for another Celtic saint. They inspected the dormitory where many of the monks lived; though, in the usual Celtic manner, some of the senior monks had small, free-standing timber and wattle cells of their own on the grounds.

The most impressive building in the lower monastery was the huge tower. The two young men had gazed up at it solemnly. The tower was circular and very tall. Sixteen feet in diameter at its base, tapering gradually towards its conical top a hundred feet above, the sheer sides of the great stone tube seemed to dwarf everything else.

"We call it the bell tower," the novice explained. Osgar thought wryly of the modest hand bell that summoned the monks to prayers at his family's monastery. "But it's a watchtower, too. There are four windows at the top, under the cone. You can see the approaches in every direction from up there."

The round towers of Ireland were becoming a notable feature of the landscape in the last few generations, and that of Glendalough was one of the finest. These towers with their corbel-constructed cones had been invented by the Irish monks. They were mostly about a hundred feet high, the circumference of their base being almost exactly half their height. As long as the foundations were good, these proportions made for a very stable structure. The walls were sturdy—at Glendalough they were three and a half feet thick.

"If there's an attack, we put the valuables inside," his guide explained. "And most of us can get in, too. It has six floors." He pointed to the doorway. It was twelve feet off the ground, reached by a narrow wooden ladder. "Once the door's barred, it's almost impossible to break in."

"Is Glendalough attacked much?" Osgar asked.

"By Vikings? Only once in the last hundred years, I believe. There have been other troubles. The lands around here have been disputed by several of the lesser kings. A few years ago they came and made a terrible mess of the mills down the valley. But you won't see any sign of it today. We're mostly pretty quiet up here." He smiled. "We don't seek a martyr's death." He turned. "Come and see the scriptorium."

This was a long, low building in which half a dozen monks were at work copying texts. Some, Osgar noticed, were written in Latin, others in Irish. His uncle, of course, had several books, but though Osgar and one of the old monks could write a fair hand, they did not make any new books. He observed the expert calligraphy with admiration. But it was a single monk, sitting at a table in a corner, who now caught his attention. In front of him was an illustration he was working on. The outline of the design was already complete and he was beginning to fill in one corner with coloured inks. The broad abstract border fascinated Osgar. Its lines seemed geometric, but his practised eye saw clever visual hints everywhere of natural forms, from the gentle geometry of a scallop shell to the powerful stress lines of a knot of gnarled oak. How complex the thing was, yet how pure. He gazed at it, rapt, and thought how wonderful it must be to spend one's life in such a way. He had been there for some time when the monk looked up, gave them a frown for disturbing him, and they tiptoed away.

"Come," said the novice when they got outside. "You haven't seen the best yet."

He led Osgar across a little bridge over the stream and turned right, onto a track that led up the valley.

"We call this the Green Road," he explained. As they proceeded past the lower lake, the valley narrowed. On their left, the steep wooded slope was almost a cliff and Osgar could hear the sound of a waterfall. On his right, he noticed a grassy earth circle, like a little rath. And then, just as they passed through some trees, suddenly: "Enter paradise," his companion said softly.

For a moment, Osgar caught his breath. The upper lake was large, about a mile long. As its quiet waters stretched before him between the high, rocky slopes that rose through the trees, it seemed as though they might have emerged from an entrance into the mountain itself.

"There's Kevin's cell." The novice indicated a small stone structure some way off by the lakeside. "And up there," he pointed to where Osgar could just see the entrance to a small cave under a rocky ledge overlooking the water, "is Kevin's Bed." It looked a hard place to reach; the rocky slope beneath it was almost a cliff. He noticed there were banks of sorrel growing down below, and nearby those, a swathe of stinging nettles. Following his gaze, his companion smiled. "Some people say that's where the saint threw himself in the nettles."

Everyone knew the story of Saint Kevin's youth. Tempted by a girl who wanted to seduce him, the young hermit had driven her away and, stripping himself naked, had rolled in a bed of stinging nettles to cure his lust.

"He used to stand in the shallows of the lake to pray," the young monk went on. "Sometimes he'd stand there all day." It wasn't hard, Osgar thought, to imagine such a thing. In the perfect peace of the lake he, too, he felt sure, might do the same.

For some time, the two young men stood together, drinking in the scene, and it seemed to Osgar that he had never known such a sense of perfect peace in all his life. Indeed, he hardly noticed the sounding of the bell from down the valley until his companion gently touched his arm and told him it was time to eat.

His interview with the abbot had taken place the next day. He was a tall, handsome man, with curly grey hair and a kind but stately manner, who came from an important family. He knew Osgar's uncle, and welcomed the young man warmly and asked after the affairs of the family monastery.

"What has brought you to us at Glendalough?" he enquired.

As best he could, Osgar explained to the abbot his situation, his hesitation about his marriage, his sense of disquiet and uncertainty; and he was relieved to see that the older man listened in a manner that suggested he did not think his concerns were foolish. When he had finished, the abbot nodded.

"Do you feel called to the religious life?"

Did he? He thought of his life at the family's little monastery beside Dyflin, and of his possible future there. Was that what the abbot meant by the religious life? Probably not.

"I think so, Father Abbot."

"You think that if you marry, it will . . ." the abbot considered a moment, "take you away from the conversation you wish to have with God?"

Osgar looked at him in wonder. He had not formulated the thought in that way, yet it was just how he felt.

"I feel . . . a need . . ." he trailed off.

"You do not think your uncle is drawing closer to God?"

What should he say? He thought of his uncle's easygoing family life, his long fishing expeditions, his frequent sleep during the divine service.

"Not much," he answered awkwardly.

If the abbot suppressed a smile, Osgar did not see it.

"This girl," the older man asked, "this Caoilinn, whom you feel you have a duty to marry. Have you ever . . ." He glanced at Osgar and saw that he was not understood. "Have you ever had carnal knowledge of her, my boy?"

"No, Father. Never."

"I see. Ever kissed her?"

"Only once, Father."

"You have urges, perhaps?" the abbot probed and then, apparently losing patience with this line of questioning: "Well, no doubt you do." He paused, eyeing the young man thoughtfully. "You think you might like it here?"

In this earthly paradise? This mountain retreat halfway to Heaven?

"Yes," he answered slowly. "I think I should."

"You mightn't be bored, perhaps, up here in the mountains?"

"Bored?" Osgar stared at him in astonishment. He thought of the churches, of the scriptorium, of the wondrous silence of the big lake. Bored? Not, he thought, in a hundred lifetimes. "No, Father Abbot."

"The path of the spirit is not easy, you know." The abbot's look was somewhat stern. "It isn't just a case of finding a life that's congenial. There has to be a renunciation, sooner or later. Here at Glendalough," he continued, "our rule is strict. We live, you might say, like a community of hermits. The way is hard. Straight is the gate. And," he nodded slowly, "you will not escape temptations of the flesh. Nobody does. The devil," he smiled ironically, "does not give up so easily. He places temptations in our path: sometimes they are obvious, sometimes insidious. Beware. You will have to overcome them." He paused. "I cannot tell you what to do. Only God can do that. But I shall pray for you. And you should pray, too."

That day and the next, he joined the monks at all the daily offices sung in the big church, and spent the rest of the time in prayer.

He tried to follow the abbot's bidding. He prayed as he had never prayed before. He knew the proper technique. He tried to empty his mind of all other considerations, to listen only to God's silent prompting. He asked to be shown his duty. What did God require?

Would God speak to him? For nearly two days he wondered, but no word came.

Yet how strangely God chose to reveal His will. Osgar was standing by the upper lake as the sun was dipping towards the mountains in the late afternoon of the second day. He hadn't been praying just then, but was lost in the beauty of the place, when he had felt a tap on his shoulder and turned to see the friendly face of one of the monks who had brought him there.

"So have you discovered what you want?" the older man asked.

Osgar shrugged.

"What I *want* is to stay here, of course," he said, as if this was not what really mattered.

Then suddenly he realised. The thing was so simple, he had missed it. He wanted to be at Glendalough and nowhere else. He had never felt so at home in his life. This was where he was meant to be. And Caoilinn? Greatly though he loved her, he knew now, with a certainty, that he did not want to marry her. And here—he saw it with a wonderful sense of illumination—here was the wonder of the business: God in His kindness had not only sent him a sense of belonging, He had even taken away his desire for the girl he had loved. To help him on his way, that old desire had been replaced with a new desire, a passionate wish for Glendalough. He was sure. It was meant to be. He loved Caoilinn as much as he had ever done before; but that love must be the love of a brother. It had to be so. He knew he was going to have to cause her pain, but it would have been crueller by far to have married her when he could not have given her his whole heart. For some time he stood there, gazing out over the water, filled with a strange new sense of peace and understanding. That evening, he informed the abbot, who nodded quietly and made no comment.

He left the following morning.

He had chosen to go back by the most direct route, which led straight over the high ground. At noon, he passed the great central gap in the Wicklow Mountains where, not far from the track, lay the spring which was the tiny source of the River Liffey. The view was magnificent. Below, the stream rushed down the mountain to be joined by others, and he could see the growing river winding its way another thousand feet below into the broad Liffey Plain, that stretched for twenty miles into the distance.

The day was fine. As he followed the path across the high plateau, he felt a great sense of peace. Indeed, the only concern he could think of was that he might be too happy. What was it the Abbot of Glendalough had said about the religious life? There must be renunciation. He wasn't sure he felt a sense of renunciation at the moment. Was it possible that the devil, who laid such subtle snares, might be laying one now? Was he following the desires of his own heart and will? He did not think it was so; but he resolved to be watchful. And it was, on the whole, with a light heart that he made his way northwards.

It was late afternoon when, descending the track on the mountains' northern edge, he paused by a gap in the trees and saw the great slopes falling away for hundreds of feet to the huge, open panorama of the green Liffey estuary and its broad bay.

He stopped and stared. The afternoon sun was slanting from the west down the Liffey's waters. Past the river's mouth he could see the sandbar in the bay and the curving headland beyond. He could see the broad marshes; he could see the far side of the long wooden bridge across the river. He could even make out—or was he deceiving himself?—the walls of the little family monastery. Forgetting everything else for a moment, he felt a rush of joy. And he had been staring affectionately at his childhood home for several minutes before the realisation hit him. Once he went to Glendalough, he would be cut off from all this. Cut off forever. Cut off from the broad bay, cut off from his family, cut off from Caoilinn. And at the thought of Caoilinn, memories of the little girl he had always known came to him with a haunting vividness: the games they had played; how he had married her at the tomb of old Fergus; how he had rescued her from the sea. And now he would not see her anymore, little Caoilinn, who was to have been his wife.

Who could still be his wife.

And now it came to him, with a flash of understanding. This was the test. God had not made it so easy after all. He would have to give up Caoilinn. Caoilinn whom he loved and who, God knew, if it were not for his calling, he would happily marry. Yes, he thought, this is it. This is my renunciation.

And with a new sense of dedication, where desire was tempered with pain and joy with sadness, Osgar continued on his way down towards Dyflin.

His interview with Caoilinn the next day was not all he might have hoped. He arrived at her father's house in the town quite early.

Her parents and all her family were there and so he asked her if she'd walk out with him. He noticed the look of anxiousness on her father's face. So he and Caoilinn walked to the Thingmount. And there, at the tomb of old Fergus by the Liffey's flowing waters, he told her everything.

If she looked a little surprised, she listened carefully as he explained the situation. He explained everything: how much he loved her, the sense of uncertainty that had troubled him, and his calling to the monastic life. He explained, as gently as he could, his need to go to Glendalough, and his inability to marry her. When he had finished, she was silent for a few moments, gazing at the ground.

"You must do what you think is right, Osgar," she murmured at last. Then she looked up at him with her green eyes, a little strangely. "So, if it weren't for going to Glendalough, you'd be marrying me?"

"With all my heart."

"I see." She paused. "What makes you think I'd have said yes?"

For a moment he stared at her in surprise. But then he thought he understood. Of course, she was preserving her pride.

"Perhaps you would not," he replied.

"Tell me, Osgar," she seemed curious, "do you desire to save your soul?"

"Yes," he confessed. "I do."

"And would you say that I have a chance of getting to Heaven?"

"I . . ." He hesitated. "I do not know." He had never thought about it.

"Because I don't think I'll become a nun."

"That is not necessary," he assured her. And he started to explain to her how good Christians may reach the heavenly seat by following their proper calling. But he was not sure she was really paying attention. "I shall always think of you," he added. "I shall remember you in my prayers."

"Thank you," she said.

"Shall I walk you home?" he suggested.

Why had the interview seemed unsatisfactory, he wondered as they walked back together. What had he expected? Tears? Confessions of love? He didn't quite know. It was as if her mind was drifting elsewhere, away from him, though into what region he could not tell. When they came to the gateway to her house, she paused.

"I'm sorry," she said a little sadly, "that you prefer Glendalough to me." She smiled kindly. "I shall miss you Osgar. You'll come and see us sometimes?"

"I will."

She nodded, looked down for a moment, and then to his great surprise suddenly looked up with what, if the occasion had not been so solemn, might almost have seemed like her old mischievous humour.

"Do you ever feel the lusts of the flesh, Osgar?"

He was so surprised that for a moment he did not know what to say.

"The devil tries us all, Caoilinn," he replied a little awkwardly; and then, kissing her chastely, for the last time, upon the cheek, he departed.

It was another week before Osgar departed for Glendalough. His uncle was not best pleased, but suggested that in due course, he might still return from the mountain monastery to take his place and maintain the family rule. Caoilinn's father took the trouble to come out and, putting the best face on it, wished him happiness, even declaring that he would be there to see him off; and Osgar was touched by this magnanimous kindness. Caoilinn he did not see, but as they had said goodbye there was no need.

The morning he left, he decided to follow the lower route instead of crossing the mountain gap, and so, with a satchel of provisions on his back, a letter from his uncle to the abbot promising a handsome payment to the monastery on his account, and the blessings of friends and neighbours, he set out southwards across the fields from Dyflin. His uncle had offered him a horse to take him there, which could be delivered back in due course, but Osgar had thought it more appropriate to walk.

The day was fine. In the clear morning air, the great crescent of the Wicklow Mountains to the south seemed so close that you could touch them. Osgar made his way towards the slopes on the seaward side with a cheerful, swinging stride. On his left, marshy ground gave way to scattered woodland. On his right, fields and clumps of trees. He passed an orchard and was just approaching a ford across a stream named the Dodder, when to his great surprise, by a tree beside the path he saw Caoilinn. She was leaning against the tree and had wrapped herself in a long cloak. He supposed she must have been waiting some time if she was cold. She smiled.

"I came to say goodbye," she said. "I thought you might like to see me before you go."

"Your father was back there."

"I know."

"It's very kind of you, Caoilinn," he said.

"You're right," she said. "It is."

"Have you been here long?" he asked. "You must be cold."

"It's been a while." She was looking at him thoughtfully, as if she was considering something about him. "Did you keep the ring?"

"I did. Of course."

She nodded. She seemed pleased.

"And you're on your way to be a monk in the mountains?"

"I am indeed." He smiled.

"And you haven't been tempted by any lusts of the flesh, have you, Osgar?"

"I have not. Not recently anyway," he said kindly.

"That's good. Because you have to overcome them, you know."

And he was just thinking of something to say when, to his astonishment, she opened the cloak and he found himself looking at her naked body.

Her skin was creamy pale; her breasts young and firm, but a little larger than he had supposed, a rich darkness at the nipples making him involuntarily gasp. She was entirely naked. He found himself staring at her stomach, her thighs, at everything.

"Will you remember me now, Osgar?" she asked, and then closed the cloak again.

With a cry, he ran past her. A moment later, he was splashing across the ford. At the other side he looked back, half afraid she might be following him. But there was no sign of her. He crossed himself. Dear God, why would she do such a thing?

As he walked on, he realised he was trembling as if he had seen a ghost; he could hardly believe it had actually happened. Had he imagined it all? No. She had been real enough. What had possessed her? Was this Caoilinn the child, indulging in a last wild and foolish joke? Or was it a young woman, smarting from a rejection, trying to shock and humiliate him? Perhaps both. And was he shocked? Yes. Not by the sight of her body, but by her crudity. He shook his head. She shouldn't have done it.

Only as he hurried farther along the path did it occur to him that there was also another, profounder explanation. The temptations of the flesh. The devil and his snares again. The abbot had warned him. This was what really lay behind the encounter. Was he tempted? Surely not. Yet, as he went on, to his horror, the vision of her body kept rising before his mind. Scarcely knowing whether he was afflicted by lust or by fear, he tried to shut the vision out; but it only returned, each time more vivid than before. Worse yet, after a little while, he saw that she was starting to do lewd things—things he did not think she even knew about—and the more he tried to dismiss them from his mind, the worse they got. He even tried to return to the simple, pure nakedness with which he had begun, but it was no use. The more he struggled, the worse she got, as he found himself watching, half fascinated, now, and half repelled.

This was not Caoilinn. She had not done these things. It was he, not she, who was imagining them: he, not she, who was in the devil's grip. A hot sensation of guilt swept over him, then cold panic. He stopped.

The devil had prepared a challenge for him on his way to Glendalough. How should he meet it? A short way ahead, he saw that beside the path there was a bank on which bushes were growing, and beneath it a dark green patch. As he hastened forward he saw that it was just as he had supposed: the dark green vegetation had been placed there by God who, in His wisdom and kindness, had foreseen everything. Stinging nettles.

For what had Saint Kevin of Glendalough done when he was tempted by a woman? Driven the girl away and mortified his flesh. With nettles. It must be a sign.

He looked around. There was nobody in sight. Quickly he stripped off his clothes and, hurling himself into the nettles, rolled in them over and over, again and again, wincing with the pain.

⁜

The wedding of Harold and Astrid took place that winter. It was a happy occasion for several reasons.

In the first place, and most important of all, it was clear that the young couple were well suited to each other. Secondly, they were obviously in love.

If there had been a spark between them the first evening they met, at the house of Morann and his wife, his future bride had realised that it would take time and effort to break down his resistance. So she had set about it patiently. She had asked to see over the ship, and when he had taken her round she had asked to see his own handiwork, after which she had remarked appreciatively, "You're good at what you do, aren't you?" A week later, Astrid had met him and offered him some sweetmeats wrapped in a napkin. "I think they are the kind you like," she had said hopefully. And when he had replied, with some astonishment, that indeed they were his favourite kind, she had explained, "You said so when we were at

Morann's." He had forgotten. "I wanted you to have them," she added and then, affectionately, she had touched his arm.

Astrid had waited three weeks before, out walking one day, she had turned and casually enquired, "Does your leg hurt you?"

"No. Not really," he had answered, then shrugged. "I wish it was straight, but it isn't," he had added, before falling silent.

"It doesn't worry me," she replied simply. "To tell you the truth," and now she allowed herself to gaze into his eyes for a moment, "I like you the way you are."

But perhaps her wisest move was the one she made in the third month of their courtship. They were standing on the wood quay, beside the site where work had already commenced on a new, smaller ship, and looking towards the river where the great ship Harold had built was now moored. What, she had asked him, would he most like to do in his life? What was his dream?

"I think one day," he confessed, "of sailing in that vessel." He pointed to the ship, which was soon to leave on a voyage to Normandy.

"You should," she said, and gave his arm a squeeze. "You should do it."

"Perhaps." He paused, almost glanced at her, but didn't. "The voyages are long. The seas are dangerous."

"A man must follow the call of his spirit," she said quietly. "You should be sailing away over the horizon on an adventure and returning to find your wife waiting for you on the quay. I can see you doing that."

"You can?"

"You can do that," she said frankly, "if you marry me."

It had not taken long after this for Harold to realise he should marry Astrid, and so her courtship of him was brought to its conclusion. It had been a very successful courtship. For him, the discovery that he was respected and loved opened the floodgates of his passion. For her, though she did not tell him so, the process of overcoming his hesitancy had produced a transformation: at the start, he

was the man she had decided to love; by the end, he was the object
of an intense desire.

The marriage also had the happy effect of reuniting Harold with
his family. To say they were delighted with his bride was an understatement; and if, on Harold's part, there was any lingering resentment, he was far too happy to worry about it now. The marriage was
celebrated at the family farmstead in the old pagan way and the couple received his father's heartfelt blessing.

Only one person at the wedding was not smiling. Morann Mac
Goibnenn, God knew, was pleased enough at his friend's happiness.
His present to the couple had been a silver bowl, beautifully inlaid
and decorated by his own hand; he and his family were there to eat
and to dance at the wedding feast. But all the time, as the fires
burned high outside and the guests went in and out of the Viking
hall, Morann stood quietly apart, watching. He watched the late arrivals to the feast; he looked down the lane and across the Plain of
Bird Flocks towards Dyflin; he scanned the horizon eastwards towards the sea. He felt the long knife, concealed in his cloak, ready
for use if the dark-haired Dane should come.

Morann did not like taking chances. Unknown to Harold, as
soon as his marriage had been decided, the craftsman had made
some careful enquiries about the Dane. He learned that he had become involved in a fight in Waterford and soon afterwards had left
with a crew of fellows like himself and sailed northwards. The rumour was that they had gone to the Isle of Man. Did he know about
the wedding of Harold? He might have heard. Would he come now
to disrupt it? Morann kept up his watch until after dusk had fallen;
and after that, inside the hall, his eyes continually moved to the
doorway until late into the night. But at last, when they departed in
the morning, there had still been no sign of Sigurd.

A week after this another marriage took place, in Dyflin, which
also gave the families concerned great pleasure. For some time now,
Caoilinn's father had been in negotiation with the family of a young
man from the nearby settlement of Rathmines. Not only was his

family prosperous, but he was descended, by only four generations, from the kings of Leinster. "Royal blood," Caoilinn's father had announced proudly; and he had been quick to let the bridegroom's family know that Caoilinn herself, by her distant descent from Conall, had royal blood as well. Caoilinn's cousins from the old rath by the monastery were all at the wedding, of course, including Osgar who had come from Glendalough, and whom the bride greeted with a calm and modest kiss upon the cheek. Osgar's uncle conducted the marriage service and everyone agreed that the bride and groom made a very handsome couple.

But the highlight of the wedding, it was generally agreed, was when Osgar the monk gave the couple an unexpected wedding gift. It came in a wooden box.

"My father always kept this," he explained. "But it surely belongs better to you and your husband," he said with a wry smile, "than it does to me."

And from the box he drew a strange, ivory-yellow object with a gold rim. It was the drinking skull of old Fergus.

Caoilinn was very pleased.

And if she noticed, she did not mention the fact that, whether through tact or because he had forgotten, Osgar had not kept his promise to produce the little antler wedding ring.

FIVE

BRIAN BORU

I

A T FIRST, when he had warned them, his neighbours had laughed at him. Everyone in Dyflin knew that Morann Mac Goibnenn didn't like taking chances, but surely his fears were unjustified. "We're in no danger at all," the King of Dyflin had announced. How could the craftsman still doubt? Some people even called him a traitor.

"He's not an Ostman," an elderly Dane remarked. "What can you expect?" And though, given the situation, this reasoning was completely illogical, there were plenty of people to nod their heads wisely in agreement. Not that Morann cared much, whatever they thought. But it was not long before all Dyflin was in a state of panic. The question was: what to do? One thing could be agreed upon, and soon the entire Liffey Plain was empty of livestock, which had all been driven to places of safety on the high ground. But what about the human population? Some went with the cattle and took refuge in the Wicklow Mountains; some remained on their farmsteads; others came into Dyflin to seek the protection of its walls. Osgar's uncle and his sons retired into the little monastery and closed the gates. Meanwhile, a huge force was gathering. Eager sons of chiefs from all over Leinster were arriving to camp in the orchards near the city walls. Longships were arriving from other Viking ports, the men drinking heavily and roaring cheerful battle cries down on the quay. King Sitric of Dyflin, in a splendid cloak, his long beard and red face making him look very jolly, rode around the town with a retinue that grew larger every day. Finally, when the first frost of winter was on the ground, the King of Leinster arrived and, with King Sitric beside him, they all set off towards the south with the happy assurance that the enemy would never even get close to the Liffey Plain.

The next day, as Morann was walking through the streets, which seemed very quiet now after the previous busy weeks, he saw one of the town's senior craftsmen walking along with a handsome, dark-haired woman who looked vaguely familiar. Pausing to greet him the craftsman remarked, "You remember my daughter, Caoilinn, who lives out at Rathmines."

Of course. He did not know the family well, but he remembered the dark, green-eyed girl who married a man from Rathmines, of the royal house no less. She smiled at him.

"My father tells me you had doubts about this business of the king's."

"That may be so," he answered.

"Well, my husband's gone away with them. He's very confident."

"He would know, then, I should say."

"But my father wanted myself and the children to come into Dyflin." There was now a hint of uncertainty in her eyes, he noticed. "We're safe enough in Dyflin, I suppose," she remarked. "I see that you're still here."

"You do," he said. "You do."

He loaded the wagon that night. Early the next morning, the

wagon, containing his family and all their valuables, lumbered across the long wooden bridge over the Liffey and disappeared into the mists on the other side. Morann was gone.

His first objective was not far away. Across the Plain of Bird Flocks lay the farmstead of Harold.

Though he had no reason to doubt that his friend was happily married, Morann couldn't help wondering whether Harold's wife, Astrid, might sometimes regret encouraging him to go to sea. It had brought them wealth, of course. Harold the Lame, as he was called, had already become a notable sea trader; but his voyages sometimes kept him away for weeks at a time. More than a month had passed since he had set out on a voyage that was to take him to Normandy and England. Since his father had died in an accident three years ago, Harold and his wife had taken over the running of the farm-stead as well. But as Harold's wife and children came out to greet him that morning, Morann's message was blunt.

"You must leave the farm," he told them, "and come with us." And when Astrid was unwilling, and remarked, "They have come here before," he shook his head and urged her to pack up at once.

"This time," he said, "it will be different."

⁘

It was six centuries since Niall of the Nine Hostages had founded the mighty dynasty of O'Neill, and in all that time, despite the ebbs and flows of power amongst the island's Celtic chiefs, no one had ever dislodged the O'Neill from the High Kingship. Until now.

Brian: his father's given name was Kennedy, so he was properly called Brian, son of Kennedy. But like Niall of the Nine Hostages many centuries earlier, Brian was so well known for the tribute he collected that he was called "Boruma," the cattle counter, or Brian Boru. He had astounded all Ireland by his rise.

His people, the Dal Cais, had only been a small and unimpor-tant Munster tribe in his grandfather's day. They lived on the banks of the Shannon just upstream from where it opens out into its long western estuary. But when the Vikings founded their settlement nearby at Limerick, Brian's grandfather had refused to come to terms with them. For three generations, the family had conducted a guerrilla war against the Vikings' river traffic. The Dal Cais had become famous. Brian's grandfather had called himself a king; Brian's mother had been a princess from Connacht; his sister had even been chosen as a wife by the king at Tara—though this hadn't done the family much good after she was executed for sleeping with her husband's son.

The Dal Cais were ambitious. They had a hardened fighting force. Brian's brothers had already tested their strength against several of the other rulers in the region. But no one could have imagined what they did next. All Ireland gasped when the news of it came.

"They've taken Cashel."

Cashel—the ancient stronghold of the Munster kings. True, the Munster kings were not what they were. But the cheek of it! And when the King of Munster got the Vikings of Limerick to join him to punish these insolent upstarts, the Dal Cais beat them all, and plundered Limerick, too. A few years later Brian Boru took over as King of Munster.

A minor chieftain's family had taken one of the four great kingships of Ireland—where the Celtic royal dynasties went back into the mists of time. And indeed, to go with their new position, the Dal Cais decided to improve their ancestry. Suddenly it was discovered, and declared in the chronicles, that they had an ancient, ancestral right to share the old Munster kingship with the previous dynasty—a claim that would certainly have surprised Brian's grandfather. But these alterations to the record were not as rare as might be supposed: even the mighty O'Neill had falsified large parts of their genealogy.

Brian was in his prime. The tides of fortune were with him. He was King of Munster. Where else could ambition take him? Only gradually did it become clear that he had decided to aim at nothing less than the High Kingship itself.

He was bold, methodical, and patient. One year he moved against the nearby territory of Ossory; another, he took a great fleet into Connacht; a dozen years after becoming King of Munster, he even moved into the island's central heartland and camped by the sacred site of Uisnech. He had taken his time, but the message to the O'Neill was clear: either they must crush Brian Boru or give him the recognition he asked for. Two years ago the High King had come to meet him.

It was fortunate for Brian, and probably for Ireland, that the O'Neill High King at this time was of a noble and statesmanlike mind. The choice was clear, but not easy: either he must challenge the Munster man to a war, which could only involve a huge loss of life, or he must swallow his pride and come to terms with him, if the thing could be done with honour. He chose the latter course. And reviving the ancient division of the island into two halves, the upper Leth Cuinn, and the lower Leth Moga, he declared, "Let us rule jointly: you in the south, and I in the north."

"I should rule Leinster as well as Munster then, while you keep Connacht and Ulster," Brian solemnly agreed. "Which means," he pointed out to his followers afterwards, "that I shall control all the chief ports, including Dyflin." Without having to strike another blow, he had just gained all the richest prizes in Ireland.

Or thought he had.

✛

Morann stayed two days at the farmstead. He tried his best, but nothing that he or his wife could say would persuade Astrid to come with them. She did agree to bury some of their valuables. "Leave some for the Munster men to find," he advised her grimly, "if you don't want the farm burned down." Morann stayed there as long as he could in the hope that Harold might return; but when he could stay no longer, he begged her a last time at least to seek a place of sanctuary.

"There's Swords nearby," she remarked. This was a fine little monastery with stout walls and a high round tower, which might have offered sanctuary. "But we aren't Christian. Or there's Dyflin. That's where Harold will be coming. I don't mind going there."

Morann sighed.

"Dyflin will have to do then," he answered. And it was agreed that the family would occupy Morann's house in the city.

The following day, he continued on his way. They passed the monastery at Swords—secure enough, but too close to Dyflin for his liking—and headed north. They did not stop until that evening, when they slept below the Hill of Tara.

The High King might have meant well, but when he gave the overlordship of their kingdom to Brian, the proud men of Leinster were unimpressed. Nobody had asked them. The king and the chiefs in particular were incensed. The new overlord, you could be sure, would be wanting tribute and taking their sons as hostages for their good behaviour, in the usual way.

"Give our sons to the man from Munster?" they cried. The upstart? "If the O'Neill can't defend us, what right have they to give us to this fellow?" they demanded.

Whatever the Leinster men might have felt about the Vikings of Dyflin when they first arrived, the two communities had been living together for generations now. They'd intermarried. Indeed, King Sitric of Dyflin was actually the King of Leinster's nephew. True, many of the Vikings were still pagan, but even religion had to take second place where matters of honour were at stake. As for the Vikings themselves, they had been stubbornly resisting the control of the High King for a long time. They were hardly likely to submit to Brian Boru just because the O'Neill High King, who was too weak to fight, told them that they should.

So it was that autumn that the King of Leinster and the King of Dyflin had decided to refuse to recognise the Munster man. "If he

wants a fight," they declared, "he'll get more than he bargained for."
And now the Munster man was coming, and they had gone out to
meet him.

The sky was overcast the next morning when Morann and his
family crossed the River Boyne; it was still dull grey at noon. Their
spirits were not high. To the children, the journey seemed long; and
he suspected that his wife would secretly have preferred to remain
inside the walls of Dyflin with her neighbours and Harold's wife.
More than once she had asked him doubtfully about the place to
which they were going. Could it really be any more secure than
Dyflin? "You'll see. We'll be there before nightfall," he promised
them. The afternoon wore on, the horse pulling the wagon seemed
to plod more slowly, and though his children dared not say so, they
were wondering whether they would be spending another night out
in the empty landscape when, as the darkness was closing in, a shaft
of vivid evening sunlight suddenly pierced the cloud and they saw,
illuminated upon a hill some way ahead, the great walled sanctuary
that was their destination.

"The monastery of Kells," Morann announced with satisfaction.

If the journey had been gloomy, the effect of the great monastery
upon his family made up for it now. The children gazed at it with
awe. Even his wife turned to him with a look of respect.

"It looks like a city," she remarked.

"It is a city," he said. "And a sanctuary. You can sleep easy
tonight," he added, pleased by the impression he had made. "It's almost as big as Dyflin, you know," he said. Soon, while it was still
light, he would give himself the pleasure of showing them around.

But they had only gone a hundred paces when they heard the
sound of horse hoofs cantering behind them, and turned to see a
man wrapped in a cloak, his face pale as a ghost, his horse all in a
lather, about to overtake them on his way to the monastery. He
hardly seemed to see them as he came past, but in answer to
Morann's calling out to ask him if he had news, he cried back, "We've
lost. Brian Boru has smashed us. He's on his way to Dyflin now."

✤

The room was silent. Looking at the monks in their woollen habits, sitting stooped over their desks, you might almost have taken them for five huge mice trying to burrow into the vellum before them.

Vellum—skin of the newborn calf—pale and smooth; for the hair had been removed by soaking it in excrement or lime before scraping it with a sharp knife. Everyday documents and accounts were written on ordinary cattle skins, which were plentiful and cheap on the island. But for copying sacred texts like the Gospels, only costly vellum would do. And they could afford the finest vellum here, in the scriptorium of the great monastery of Kells.

Glancing outside now, Osgar saw flakes of falling snow; swiftly, with only a faint scratch, his hand moved to and fro. It was nearly two months since he had come to Kells; soon he'd be leaving.

But not just yet. Not if he could help it. He stared at the snow outside. The weather had changed abruptly that morning, as if in reaction to the news of the night before from Dyflin. But it was not the snow that concerned Brother Osgar, but the person who was waiting for him out there. Perhaps the snow would be a deterrent. If he waited in the scriptorium until the bell for prayers, he could make his escape without getting caught. At least, he hoped so.

He had changed in the last decade. There were some grey hairs now, a few stern lines on his face, a quiet dignity.

His eyes went back to his work. The pale vellum had been neatly ruled into lines with a stylus. He dipped his pen in the ink. Most scribes used a quill pen, made from the tail feather of a goose or swan; but Osgar had always favoured reeds and he had brought a good supply with him, cut from the edge of the lake at Glendalough. The ink was of two kinds: either a brownish colour, made from oak apples and sulphate of iron; or a jet-black, made from holly.

Osgar was a skilful calligrapher. Writing in the clear, rounded script of the Irish monasteries, he could copy a text at roughly fifty

lines an hour. Working six hours a day, which was certainly the max-
imum possible during these short winter days—for good calligraphy
needs natural daylight—he had almost finished copying the book of
the Gospels for which he had come there. Another day and it would
be done.

He paused to stretch. Only those who had tried it understood—
the calligrapher might seem only to be moving his hand, but in
fact the whole body was engaged. It was hard on the arm, the back,
even the legs.

He settled back to his task. Another dozen lines, a quarter-hour
of silence. Then he looked up again. One of the other monks caught
his eye, and nodded. The light was fading; it was time to stop work.
Osgar started to clean his pen.

On the floor at his side were two bags. One contained a small,
workmanlike text of the Gospels, another of the Pentateuch. The
Psalms, of course, he knew by heart. There were also two little de-
votional books that he liked always to have with him. The other
bag, into which he now dipped his hand, contained his writing ma-
terials and one other item. And it was upon this object that his fingers fastened.

His secret sin. Nobody knew about it. He had never even mentioned it in the confessional. Oh, he had confessed the sin of lust itself, a hundred times. He was rather proud of it—the pride was a
sin, too, of course. And yet, wasn't his concealment of the secret in
a way even worse for having been repeated so many times? Was
there anything else, his confessor would ask? No. A lie. A hundred
lies. Yet he had no intention of confessing his secret, for the good
reason that if he did, he would be told he must part with it. And
that he could not do. His talisman. Caoilinn's ring.

He had always kept it. There wasn't a day when he didn't take it
out and look at it. Each time, he would give a little smile and then,
with a sweet sadness, put the ring away again.

What did she mean to him now? She was the dark-haired child
he had planned to marry; the girl who had shown him her naked-

ness. He wasn't shocked anymore. If, for a little while, he had thought of her as a crude woman, a vessel of sin, her marriage soon afterwards had obliterated the idea. She was a respectably married woman, a Christian matron. Her body would have thickened now, he supposed. Did she sometimes think of him? He felt sure she did. How could she not, when he thought of her every day? The love he had given up.

The ring was not just a sentimental mascot though. In a way it helped to regulate his life. If at times he thought of leaving the monastery, he had only to look at the ring to remind himself that, since Caoilinn was married to another, there was hardly any point. If, as had happened once or twice, he found himself attracted to a woman, the ring reminded him that his heart was given to another. And if perhaps some monk—like the young novice who had first shown him round Glendalough—if such a one seemed to be drawing too close, and if he, out of kindness, was drawn to return a gentle look or a touch, he had only to take out Caoilinn's little memento to relive the feelings he had experienced for her all those years ago, and to know that he would not be going down that other road which some of his fellow monks were travelling. So if he had first denied her by entering the monastery, and she had then made herself unavailable through marriage, it seemed to him that in this impossible relationship he had been granted a protection against greater evils; and he even dared to wonder whether, in his present small disobedience and sentimental lust, he might perceive the hand of providence itself gently helping him, poor sinner that he was, along his sometimes lonely way.

There was still an hour before the bell for prayers. The other monks were shuffling towards the door, but he did not follow them. For he knew exactly how to employ the time. In the corner, on a lectern, lay a large volume. It was kept in the sacristy of the big stone church normally, but it had been brought into the scriptorium for the time being. It was encased in a silver cover which was set with gems. Taking up a candle from a table now, he advanced towards it.

As he did so, he noticed with pleasure that one of the gems caught a glow from the candle's flame.

The greatest treasure in the monastery of Kells: the Gospel book. It was the chance to spend time with the magnificent illuminated text that had brought him to Kells two months ago. His skill in calligraphy had advanced so rapidly at Glendalough that he had branched into illustration, at which he had shown talent also. In return for two months' work copying texts, he had been granted leave to study the treasury of illustration in the Kells collection, and in particular the great Gospels, which he normally did for two hours every morning. This extra hour was a bonus, therefore. He reached the lectern and was just stretching out his hand when he heard a hiss at his ear. It was the elderly brother in charge of the scriptorium.

"I'm locking up now."

"I could lock up later and give you the key afterwards, if you like."

The old man treated this suggestion with silent contempt. Osgar knew better than to argue. He sighed and, after lingering hopefully a few more moments, went outside.

Silence. The light wind had stopped. The snow fell softly, caressing his face. The last remains of daylight gave the pale scene an eerie glow. His eyes scanned the street and peered down the slope towards the monastery gateway. There was no sign of Sister Martha. Nobody about at all. He sniffed. The air wasn't very cold. Perhaps instead of returning to the dormitory where he was staying, he'd stretch his legs and go down to the gateway. Pulling his hood over his head, more to hide his face than to protect it from the light snow, he began to walk down the street.

There was no doubt that it was comforting, in these dangerous times, to find oneself safe within the great walls of Kells. Even in the snow shower, it was an impressive place. Extending all over the low hill, with its stout buildings, stone churches, and well-laid streets, not to mention the market and suburbs that lay just outside its high walls, the monastery was not only a walled sanctuary, like Glendalough, but like several of the other great religious houses, it was really a medieval city.

As Osgar knew, this idea went back to the early days of the Christian mission on the island. For when Saint Patrick had begun his mission, he had come as a bishop. All over the crumbling Roman Empire, the pattern was the same: Christian priests and their flocks were guided and led by a bishop, who would be based in the nearest important Roman town. It had been vaguely assumed, therefore, that even in the distant western island, matters would be organised in a similar way. The trouble was, of course, that the island, never having been part of the empire, did not possess such things as towns; and though the first missionary bishops tried to attach themselves to the tribal kings, these Celtic chiefs were always moving about their territories. It didn't suit the Roman priests at all.

But a monastery was a permanent, year-round centre. You could build a church, living quarters, even a library there. It could be protected with walls. It was self-sustaining, providing workers, priests, and leaders from within the community. The abbot could act as the local bishop himself, or provide a house for a bishop within the safety of the monastery's walls. For a long time the bishop who oversaw Dyflin had kept his house up at Glendalough. Craftsmen and traders were attracted to settle by monasteries. Markets appeared; whole communities grew up in suburbs around the walls. No wonder that within a century of Patrick's mission, these monasteries were rapidly becoming the main centres of the Christian community on the island. Until the first Viking coastal settlements, centuries later, the larger monasteries were the only towns in Ireland. Kells had been built upon this pattern.

He went through the gateway into the marketplace. It was empty. Near one side, like a priest at a snowbound offertory, stood a handsome stone cross, and behind it several covered wagons, already white. He looked around. All the stalls and workshops were closed. A solitary lamp shone from a cowshed, but the only signs of human life were the wisps of smoke from the thatched roofs of the surrounding cottages, shuttered against the snow and the dying day. Osgar turned round, took three deep breaths, decided this was enough exercise for the present, and would have been gone in another moment if he hadn't noticed, just then, a figure emerging from one of the wagons. It wasn't Sister Martha, yet the figure looked vaguely familiar.

It was Morann, the goldsmith from Dyflin. It had been years since he'd seen him, and he'd only known the man slightly, but his face wasn't one you'd forget. The craftsman was surprised but seemed glad to see him and explained his own reasons for seeking sanctuary there.

"I supplied the abbot with some fine candlesticks last year," he added with a grin, "so they're glad to give me shelter."

"And you really think Brian Boru will destroy Dyflin?" Osgar asked.

"He's too clever for that," Morann answered. "But he'll teach them a terrible lesson."

"You think the religious houses are safe, don't you?" Osgar asked, thinking of the little family monastery.

"He has always respected them in the past," said Morann.

They had paused now, in front of the great market cross. Kells had several of these elaborately carved stone crosses which, like the round towers, had become a feature of the island's monasteries. The arms of the cross were set in a ring of stone—an arrangement which, though known as a Celtic cross, went back to before the time of Saint Patrick, to the Roman wreaths of triumph, and echoed the symbol of the sun god earlier still. But the truly remarkable feature of the island's crosses was their carving. Some were incised with the interlaced patterns and swirling spirals of the ancient days. But the crosses at Kells were typical of the finest work: arranged in panels, every surface, even the plinths on which they stood, seemed to be covered with sturdy reliefs: Adam and Eve, Noah and his Ark, scenes from the life of Christ, angels and devils; the base of the market cross showed a striking scene of warriors going into battle. Like the statues and carvings inside the churches, the figures on these great ornamental crosses were brightly painted. The spears of the warriors were even tipped with silver. Morann looked at it with approval. Though on a much bigger scale, the arrangement of its parts was not unlike the jeweller's art.

They were about to return when they saw her, standing in the gateway. Sister Martha. Osgar cursed under his breath.

He liked her. With her broad face and kindly grey eyes, the middle-aged nun was a good soul. Sister Martha, the nun from Kildare. The Abbess of Kildare had given her permission to visit Kells to attend to an aunt who was thought to be dying there. But the old lady in question had recently made an unexpected recovery, and Sister Martha was now anxious to return. If only, in a moment of weakness some time ago, he hadn't promised that he would accompany her back.

There was certainly every reason why he should do so. He had almost finished his own work at Kells; he could, without going much out of his way, travel back to Glendalough by way of Kildare; and it was unquestionably his duty to accompany the single nun across the countryside in troubled times like these. He had originally expected to be ready to leave by now, but his work had taken a little longer than he had thought. When he had explained this, she had accepted it cheerfully enough, but he knew very well that she was anxious to be gone, and she had been gently asking him for some days when he thought he might be ready to depart. He suspected that she knew he would complete his copying the following day, so she must reasonably be expecting to go the day after that.

The trouble was, he didn't want to go. Not just yet. For when he had completed his task, he had been looking forward to spending a week alone with the treasures of the Kells library, especially, of course, the great Gospel book. A week of blissful private study, undisturbed. He had worked hard; it was a treat he had well deserved. And now the thought of warding off her enquiries and keeping her waiting for days longer filled him with a thoroughly tire-some sense of guilt. Yesterday, with the latest turn of events disrupting the countryside, he had suggested that she might want to wait for a while before setting out. But unfortunately she had given him a shrewd look and then answered gently, "I'm sure that God will protect us." He'd been trying to avoid her ever since.

Hearing his muttered curse, Morann asked him the reason; and as they walked towards the gateway, Osgar briefly told him.

So it was with delight, after introducing the craftsman to the kindly nun, that he heard Morann remark: "I hear you are both travelling down to Kildare, Sister Martha. I should tell you that the countryside may be a little unsafe at the moment, but if you could wait, I shall be going down that way myself in five days, and we could all travel together." He smiled at her. "There is safety in numbers." It was hardly an offer that anyone would reasonably refuse; and after the nun had accepted, and the two men had walked on, the craftsman turned to him. "Will that give you enough time?"

Three clear days in the library. Morann's company across what might, indeed, be dangerous terrain. "I can't believe my luck," Osgar replied with a smile.

Morann's own plans, he learned, were to settle his family at Kells and then return to Dyflin where he wanted to check on the safety of Harold's family. "But I have a piece of business I'd been meaning to do in Kildare," he explained, "and so I may as well go down that way first." Osgar remembered the big farm in Fingal where he had encountered Harold's father after being attacked by the robbers years before, and he was impressed by the craftsman's loyalty to his friend.

"Are you not afraid of the danger at Dyflin?" he asked.

"I'll be careful," Morann replied.

"If you get to Dyflin," Osgar remarked, "you might see my uncle and cousins at the monastery. I hope they are safe. You could give them my greetings."

"I will, certainly," Morann answered. "By the way," he added, "I saw another cousin of yours, I believe. She was coming into Dyflin just before I left, to be safer while her husband was away at the fighting."

"Indeed? And who was that?"

"She's married to a rich man out at Rathmines. Wasn't her name Caoilinn?"

"Ah." Osgar stopped and looked at the ground. "It was," he said quietly. "Caoilinn."

⁂

It was the last day before leaving. For the first hour of the day, Osgar liked to practise his illustration. If calligraphy was painstaking, illustration was even more intricate. Of course, there was the design first. That could be simple or complex. Only those skilled in geometry should even attempt the making of a Celtic pattern. But once the design was made in rough, then carefully fair copied and transferred onto the vellum as a drawing, the intricate business of choosing the colours and of slowly painting them in with needle-thin brushes required extraordinary patience and skill.

The pigments themselves were rare and valuable. He dipped his brush in a red, to colour part of the scalloped design of an eagle's feathers. Some reds were made from lead, but this came from the pregnant body—it had to be pregnant—of a certain Mediterranean insect. He checked a proportion on the design with a pair of dividers. Purple next, from a Mediterranean plant. The greens were mostly from copper. You had to be careful. If the page got wet afterwards, the copper could eat through the vellum. The whites were usually made with chalk. Cleverer were the golds. The pigment for gold was actually a yellow—arsenic sulphide—but when applied it would develop a metallic shine so that it looked like gold leaf. Most precious and rare of all was the blue lapis lazuli. That came from the farthest Orient, from a place, it was said, where the mountains, higher even than the Alps, rose into the blue sky until they touched it. A country without a name. Or so he had heard.

The greatest art of all, in Osgar's opinion, was the delicate layering of colours one on top of the other so that one achieved not only subtle gradations of tone but even a relief, like a landscape as it would be seen from above, as by the eye of God Himself.

But when he entered the scriptorium that morning, Osgar did not trouble to practise his own poor art. He went straight to the great book on the lectern. It was, after all, his last opportunity to do so.

The wonder of it. As he stood before the masterpiece, it was hard for Osgar to believe that he might not see it again. For two months now he had explored its creamy vellum pages and discovered its wonders so that, like a pilgrim to a holy city who has come to know all its byways and secret places, he felt almost as if the great treasure belonged to him personally.

And indeed, wasn't the book laid out like a celestial city? Four Gospels: four points of the compass, four arms of the holy cross. Hadn't Ireland four provinces? Even the mighty Roman Empire, in the later days when it was Christian, had been divided into four parts. At the start of each of the Gospels came three magnificent full-page illuminations: first the winged symbol of the evangelist— Matthew the man, Mark the lion, Luke the calf, and John the eagle; second came a portrait page; third, the first words of the Gospel were worked up into a huge design. A trinity of pages to start each of the four Gospels. Three and four: the seven days of the week. Three times four: the twelve apostles.

There were other full-page illuminations at appropriate places, like the eight-circle double-cross design, the Virgin and Child, and the great Chi-Rho symbol that began Matthew's account of the birth of Jesus.

The splendour of the pages was in their colour: deep, sumptuous reds and mauves, the purples, emerald greens, and sapphire blues; the pale tinctures of the saints' faces, like old ivory; and everywhere the gleaming yellow that made them look like gold enamelled screens.

But their magnificence was in their construction. Trefoil spirals enclosed in discs, borders of interlacing ribbons and knots, and motifs from the island's most ancient past were joined to Christian symbols—the eagle of John; the peacock, symbol of Christ's incorruptibility; fish, snakes, lions, angels and their trumpets—all stylised into geometric patterns. There were human figures, too, grouped in spandrels in the corners, or round the bases of golden letters, men with arms and legs lengthened and interlaced so that human body and abstract design became one and the same in this Celtic cosmos. And these patterns were endless: repeating interlacings of such Oriental complexity that the eye could never unravel them; discs of spirals set in clusters like jewels, circle and stipple, snakelike forms and filigree—the rich riot of Celtic decoration seemed likely to run completely out of control were it not for the massive, monumental geometry of the composition.

Ah, that was the thing. That, Osgar thought, was the wonder of it. For whether it was the great cruciform image of the four evangelists, or the mighty sinuous curve of the Chi-Rho, the message of the illuminated pages was unmistakable. Just as, in its later days, the stolid empire of pagan Rome had tried with its numbered legions and massive walls to stem the tides of barbarians, so now the Roman Church, with the still greater power and authority of the true religion, was imposing its monumental order on the anarchy of the heathen, and building not just an imperial but a celestial city—timeless, eternal, comprehensive, and bathed in spiritual light. He would gaze at the pages by day and, sometimes, dream of them at night. Once he had even dreamed that he had come into the monastery church and found the book open. Two of its pages, having detached themselves, had grown huge: one a gold mosaic on the wall; the other, like a great Byzantine screen of gold and icons across the choir, barring his way towards the altar. And as he had approached it the golden screen had glowed, as though burnished by a dark and holy fire; and he had softly touched it and it had sounded, harshly, like an antique gong.

But now he had to leave with Morann and Sister Martha. He would accompany the nun to Kildare, then make his way into the mountains and back to Glendalough. And Morann would go to Dyflin and perhaps see Caoilinn. Well, he shouldn't complain. This was the life he had chosen.

"The hand of Saint Colum Cille."

Osgar started at the voice behind his shoulder. It was the old monk who was in charge of the scriptorium. He hadn't heard him come up.

"So they say," he replied. Many people ascribed the Kells Gospels to Saint Colum Cille. The royal saint, direct descendant of Niall of the Nine Hostages himself—his name meant the Dove of the Church—who had founded the famous island monastery of Iona off the coast of northern Britain, was a noted calligrapher, certainly. But Colum Cille had lived only a century after Saint Patrick, and it seemed to Osgar, who had examined a number of books in the monastery library, that the great book was of a later date. Two centuries ago, Kells had been founded as a refuge for some of the monks of the Iona community after the island monastery had been attacked by Vikings. A few of the illustrations were incomplete; so perhaps the great book had been prepared in Iona and the Vikings had interrupted its completion.

"I have been watching you, you know."

"You have?" In the two months since he'd been there, the keeper of the scriptorium had hardly said a word to him beyond what was necessary, and when once or twice he had seen the old man looking at him severely, he had the feeling that the Kells man probably disapproved of him. He wondered what he'd done wrong. But to his surprise, when he turned his head, he saw that the old monk's mouth was drawn into a smile.

"You're a scholar. I can see it. The moment I saw you I said to myself, 'Now there's a true scholar of our island race.' "

Osgar was as pleased as he was surprised. Ever since his uncle's lectures to him on the subject when he was a child, he had felt a justifiable pride in the achievements of his countrymen. For with barbarians occupying much of the world, it had been the missionary monks from the western isle who had gone out into the old Celtic areas of the ruined Roman Empire to reassert Christian civilization. From Colum Cille's Iona they had established other notable centres, like the great western monastery of Lindisfarne, and converted most of the northern part of England. Others had gone to Gaul, Germany, and Burgundy, and even over the Alps into northern Italy. In due course, the founders of monasteries had been followed by Celtic pilgrims, in remarkable numbers, making their way southwards down the pilgrim routes that led towards Rome. Not only had the Celtic Church carried back the torch of truth; it had become one of the greatest guardians of classical culture. Latin Bibles and their commentaries, the works of the greatest Latin authors—Virgil, Horace, Ovid—even some of the philosophers: all these were copied and treasured. English princes sent their young men to study on the western island, where some of the monasteries were almost like academies; the island's scholars were known in courts all over Europe. "These island Celts," it was said, "are the finest grammarians."

Personally, Osgar thought this proficiency owed much to the great tradition of the island's complex but poetic Celtic tongue. Indeed, he privately doubted whether the speakers of Anglo-Saxon could ever really appreciate classical literature. And he remembered how another of the monks at Glendalough had once remarked, "Anglo-Saxon: that's how a thatched house would talk if it could." And he was glad that the monastic chroniclers had also taken care to record the old Celtic tradition in writing. From the ancient brehon law codes of the tribes and the druids to the old oral tales sung by the bards, the island's monks had set them down with their chronicles of past events. The stories of Cuchulainn, Finn mac Cumaill, and the other Celtic heroes and gods were now to be found in monastic libraries, alongside the classical texts and scriptures. Not only that. A new literary tradition had arisen as the Irish monks, steeped in the sonorous tradition of their Latin hymns, had taken the rich alliteration of the ancient Celtic verse and transformed it into a written Irish poetry more echoing, more haunting than even the pagan original had been. Admittedly, the stories had often been changed a bit. There were things in some of those old tales, Osgar thought, that no Christian would want to commit to writing. You couldn't leave them as they were. But the grand old poetry was still there, the Celtic soul of the thing.

One thing he regretted: the old druidical tonsure of the island monks had been given up. Two centuries after Saint Patrick, the Pope had insisted that all the monks in Christendom should shave just the tops of their heads, in the Roman manner, and after some protest the Celtic Church had gone along with it. "But we're still druids underneath," he liked to say, only half in jest.

"And tomorrow you're leaving?" the old monk asked him.

"I am."

"When there's so much trouble in the world." The old man sighed. "There'll be Brian Boru's men wandering all over Leinster and God knows what they'll be up to. You should stay here awhile. Wait until it's safe." Osgar explained to him about Sister Martha, but the old man shook his head. "'It's a terrible thing for a scholar such as yourself to be out in the world, on account of a nun from Kildare." Then he turned and moved away. A few moments later, he came back.

He had a small piece of parchment in his hand, which he laid on the table in front of Osgar.

"Look at that," he said.

It was a design, traced in black ink. Osgar had never seen anything quite like it before. It was a trefoil of three loosely connected spirals, reminding him somewhat of the trefoils to be seen in some of the great illuminations. But unlike those, in which the spirals were arranged into a completed geometric design, the swirling lines seemed to wander away towards the edges, as if they had been caught in the midst of some endless, unfinished business.

"I copied that," the old monk said proudly.

"From what?

"A big stone. By the old tombs above the Boyne. I used to walk over there sometimes." He looked at his handiwork with satisfaction. "That's how it is carved. The copy is exact."

Osgar continued to gaze at it. The wandering design seemed ancient.

"Would you know," asked the old monk, "what it means?"

"I wouldn't. I'm sorry."

"Nobody knows." The old monk sighed, then brightened. "But it's a curious thing, wouldn't you say?"

It was. And strangely enough, after he had left the library that evening, it was the curious design, even more than the magnificent Gospels, which seemed to remain, haunting his imagination, as if the wandering spirals contained an undeciphered message for those about to set out on journeys as to their fate.

They left at first light. The snow had already vanished the day before; though it was cold, there was no frost and the ground was damp. They travelled in a small cart which Morann had provided. They met nobody else travelling. Each time they came upon a farmstead, they would ask for news of the forces from Munster, but nobody had seen or heard anything. It seemed that this part of the country, at least, was still quiet. Early in the afternoon, they reached the Boyne at a point where there was a ford. Once past the Boyne, they continued southwards, under a leaden sky.

The day passed quietly. They kept a careful lookout for raiding parties, but saw none. As dusk was drawing in, they saw smoke coming from a farmstead by an old rath, and found a shepherd and his family. Glad of the warmth of a fire and shelter, they stayed the night. The shepherd told them that Brian Boru, together with a huge force, had all gone to Dyflin and were camped there now. "It's said he means to stay through Christmas," the shepherd reported.

Had there been any other trouble? "Not around here," he told them.

The next morning, when they set off again, the weather was overcast. Ahead of them stretched a large, flat terrain. On their right-hand side, to the west, began a huge area of bog. To the east, two days' journey away, lay Dyflin. Ahead, to the south, the plain consisted of woodland interspersed with large open spaces. By late afternoon, if they travelled at a reasonable rate, they would come to the largest of these open spaces, the bare tableland of Carmun where, since time out of mind, the people of the island had gathered for the pagan festival of Lughnasa and the racing of horses. And it was only a short distance from the ancient racing grounds to their destination, the great monastery of Kildare.

The afternoon was almost over and darkness nearly falling when they reached the edge of Carmun. A strange greyness pervaded the sky. The huge, flat, empty spaces seemed eerie and vaguely threatening. Even Morann was uneasy, and Osgar saw him looking anxiously about. It would be dark before they arrived at Kildare. He glanced at Sister Martha.

The kindly nun had certainly been an excellent travelling companion. She did not talk unless someone indicated that they wished to, but when she did talk, she gave evidence of a fund of cheerful good sense. She must be very good, he thought, at tending the sick. Was she a little nervous now? He was quite ready to admit, at least to himself, that he was. But she gave no sign of it. A few moments later she smiled at him.

"Would you like to recite something with me, Brother Osgar?" she suddenly asked.

He quite understood. It might help them all not to be nervous.

"What would you like?" he asked. "A Psalm, perhaps?"

" 'Patrick's Breastplate,' I think," she replied.

"An excellent choice." It was a lovely poem. Tradition said it was composed by Saint Patrick himself, and it could have been so. It was a hymn of praise but also of protection, and it had not been composed in Latin but in Irish—which was fitting, for this great Christian chant, so full of a sense of the wonder of God's earthly creation, had a druidical character that recalled the poets back to Amairgen from the ancient Celtic tradition.

Osgar took up the first verse, chanting it firmly:

> *I arise today,*
> *My spirit mighty;*
> *I call on the Three,*
> *The Trinity;*
> *I confess the One*
> *Creator of Creation.*

Then Sister Martha took up the second:

> *I arise today*
> *By the birth of Christ . . .*

Her voice had a cheerful strength. It was almost musical. She was a good companion, thought Osgar, as they went across the open space together. And as they came to the great druidical centre of the poem, they found themselves naturally taking turns, line by line, alternating the chant between them:

> *I arise today*
> *By the power of heaven:*
> *Light as the sun,*
> *Bright as the moon,*
> *Splendid as fire,*
> *Quick as lightning,*
> *Fast as wind,*
> *Deep as the sea . . .*

The evening air was growing cold; but as they chanted the stirring poem together in that echoing place with the harsh green turf all round, and feeling the cold air raw on his reddening cheeks, Osgar experienced a quickening of the spirits; there was a boldness and manliness in his voice, and Sister Martha smiled. And they did not finish their hymn until, in the gathering darkness, they saw the walls of Kildare looming ahead of them.

⁂

The following morning, having said goodbye to the nun, the two men prepared to go their separate ways. The weather had changed. It was cold, but the sky was clear and the day was crisp and bright. The journey from Kildare to Glendalough was not a difficult one, and as they had encountered no trouble upon the way, Osgar was happy enough to continue alone. First he would go to a small religious house that nestled below the western slopes of the Wicklow Mountains, not a dozen miles away. By good fortune, the monks there had recently lent a horse to one of the abbey's servants, and it was agreed that Osgar should return it. After a night there, he proposed to take the mountain path that led up to Glendalough, a familiar path that would easily bring him there by the next afternoon.

Morann, meanwhile, intended to spend the morning conducting his business at Kildare, then leave on the road that went past Carmun. He, too, would break his journey, and arrive at Dyflin the following day.

As there was no need to hurry, Osgar spent a pleasant couple of hours looking around the monastery town of Kildare.

The place had always been a holy site. Osgar was aware that, before Christianity came to the island, there had been a shrine there, in an oak grove, sacred to Brigid, the Celtic goddess of healing, whose festival was Imbolc, at the start of February. A patron of crafts and poetry, Brigid had also protected the province of Leinster, and to make sure of this favour, the priestess at the shrine kept a sacred fire always alight, night and day. The exact details had never been clear, but it seemed likely that, a generation or so after Saint Patrick's activities in the north, the then high priestess of the shrine, who would have been known by her title, the priestess of Brigid, had taken the new Roman religion. In the centuries that followed, not only had the shrine acquired a new name—Kildare, Cill Dara, the church of the oak—but the nameless priestess had been transformed into a Christian saint with the same associations as the old pagan goddess, and a life story and attendant miracles on the usual pattern. As a learned man, Osgar knew that the chroniclers always had such biographies preprepared for the necessary manufacture of the lives of saints. But that did not take away from the essential point, which was that Saint Brigid, the patron saint of poets, blacksmiths, and healing, had entered the Christian calendar, along with her saint's day, February 1, the ancient pagan festival of Imbolc.

It was a great place nowadays, bigger even than Kells. A large township—with a sacred centre, an inner ring of monastic buildings, and outer secular quarters—it contained a double monastery, one for monks and another for nuns, under the rule of a single head. Rich and powerful, Kildare even had its own retinue of armed men for its protection.

It was while he was inspecting one of the town's fine crosses that Osgar decided to change his plans.

The idea had first occurred to him while he was still working at Kells, but he had dismissed it as unnecessary. During the journey, it had once or twice come into his mind again. But now, perhaps because of the sun shining so cheerfully on the frosty ground, and doubtless also because Morann was already going there, he suddenly felt an urge to visit Dyflin.

After all, he reminded himself, it wasn't as if he was expected on any particular day at Glendalough. If he hadn't gone down to Kildare on account of Sister Martha, he'd probably have been returning to Glendalough through Dyflin anyway. It was surely his family duty, with all the present troubles going on, to check on the well-being of his old uncle. Moreover, since the little family monastery was nominally under the auspices of Glendalough, he could imagine that the Abbot of Glendalough would be grateful for a report on the state of things there. And if he should happen to see Caoilinn, whom Morann had told him was staying with her father in the city now, there could surely be no harm in that. So when Morann emerged from his meeting, Osgar asked the surprised craftsman if, instead of going to Glendalough, he might ride in his cart with him into the city.

The craftsman gave him a cautious look.

"It could still be dangerous out there," he warned.

"Yet you are going." Osgar smiled. "I'm sure I shall be safe with you."

They set off an hour before noon. For the first two hours, their journey was uneventful. There was a sheen of frost on the ground, and as they passed across the huge open spaces of Carmun, the terrain was sparkling green in the reflected sun. Osgar felt a strange happiness and a sense of tingling excitement that grew with every mile they passed. And though at first he told himself that this was because he was going once again to see his family at the monastery, he finally gave up and admitted, with an inward smile, that it was because he might be seeing Caoilinn. By early afternoon they had started up a wide track that led northwards, with the sweeping slopes of the Wicklow Mountains rising up some miles away to the west.

It was Osgar who spotted the first horseman. He was riding along a track about a mile away to their right. Even as he pointed him out to Morann, he saw that there were others not far behind. There were men on foot as well. Then he saw a cart in the distance, and more horsemen. And gazing southwards he realised that they were about to encounter a great stream of people flowing raggedly up the edge of the plain below the Wicklow Mountains. It wasn't long before they came close enough to hail one of them. He was a middle-aged man, with a blanket wrapped round him. One side of his face was streaked with dried blood. What had happened, they asked.

"A big battle," he called out. "Down there." He waved towards the south. "At Glen Mama, by the mountains. Brian smashed us. We were destroyed."

"Where is Brian now?" asked Morann.

"You've missed him. He and his men would have passed this way long ago. He'd have been riding like the devil," he cried grimly. "He'll be in Dyflin already by now."

Morann pursed his lips. Osgar felt a little stab of fear, but said nothing. The horseman moved away. After a short pause, Morann turned to Osgar.

"I have to go on. But you've no need to. You could walk back to Kildare now and be there before dark."

Osgar considered for a moment. He thought of his uncle at the family monastery. He thought of Caoilinn.

"No," he said. "I'll come with you."

As the afternoon went on they found themselves merging into a stream of men returning home. Many were wounded. Here and there were carts carrying those who could not walk or ride. There was not much talking. Those who did speak all told the same story. "We left more dead than living down there at Glen Mama," they said. The short afternoon was drawing to a close when they came in sight of a small religious house beside a stream. "That's where we'll stop," Morann announced. "If we leave early from here tomorrow, we'll be in sight of Dyflin before the end of the morning." Osgar could see that there was already a large collection of people resting there.

⁘

Morann was worried. He hadn't really wanted to bring the monk with him. Not that he didn't like him; but he was a complication, an additional responsibility, possibly a risk.

What lay ahead? A conquering army after battle is a dangerous animal. Looting, pillage, rape: it was always the same. Even a king as strong as Brian would not necessarily be able to control his men. Most commanders let their troops do what they wanted for a day or two and then reined them in afterwards. The religious houses with their walled compounds would probably be safe. Brian would see to that. But going into the area round Dyflin would be perilous. How would the quiet monk cope with these things? What use could he be? Was he just going to get in the way and need to be looked after? There was another consideration, too. Morann's first objective would be to find Astrid and her children and, if necessary, help them escape. He certainly didn't want the monk taking up valuable space in the cart. He wished that Osgar hadn't come.

And yet you couldn't help admiring him. The religious house where they had broken their journey was a small place, with less than a dozen inmates. The monks there were accustomed to giving shelter to travellers, but by nightfall, their resources were completely overwhelmed. There must have been fifty or sixty tired and wounded men, some of them close to death, camped in the little yard or outside the gates; the monks were giving them what food and bandaging they could. And Osgar was aiding them.

He was impressive. Moving about amongst the wounded and the dying, giving food and water to one, bandaging the wounds of another, sitting quietly talking to some poor fellow whom food and bandages could no longer help, he seemed to possess not only a quiet competence but an extraordinary, gentle grace. During the night—for he appeared to be able to do without sleep—he sat with two men who were dying, praying with them and, when it was time, giving them the last unction. And you could see from their faces that he brought them peace and comfort. It was not only what he did, Morann concluded, but something in his manner, a quietness that radiated from his elegant, spare body, of which he himself was probably not conscious. "You have a gift," the craftsman remarked to him once during a break in his vigil, but Osgar only looked surprised.

When morning came, the monks would obviously have been glad if he remained. A number of the men resting there were unfit to go on and others were still arriving.

"There will be raiding parties about this morning," Morann pointed out to Osgar. "Are you sure you would not do better to stay here?"

"No," said Osgar, "I'll come with you."

⁘

The morning was crystalline. The sky was blue. There was a dusting of snow, shining in the sunlight on the tops of the Wicklow Mountains.

Despite the sad scenes of the night and the possible danger ahead, Osgar felt a sense of excitement mixed with a glow of warm joy. He was going to see Caoilinn. The first part of their journey was quiet, and he allowed his mind to wander a little. He imagined her in danger; he imagined himself arriving, her look of surprise and joy. He imagined himself saving her, fighting off assailants, bringing her to safety. He shook his head. Unlikely visions, boyish dreams. But he dreamed them all the same, several times, as the little cart bumped along below the gleaming mountains.

Then he felt Morann nudge him.

There was a small rise ahead. Just below it was a farmstead. And by the farmstead there were horsemen.

"Trouble." Morann was looking grim.

"How do you know?"

"I don't, but I suspect." He narrowed his eyes. "It's a raiding party." He glanced at Osgar. "Are you ready?"

"Yes. I suppose so."

⁘

As they went forward, they could see what was happening. The raiding party consisted of three horsemen. They had come to collect cattle, and finding only a few at the farmstead had evidently decided to take them all. Osgar could see a woman standing at the entrance to the farmstead. There was a child behind her. A man, her husband presumably, was trying to argue with the raiders, who were taking no notice of him.

"Osgar," Morann's voice was low, "reach down behind you. There's a blanket there with a sword underneath it. Put the blanket over your knees and keep the sword between your legs."

Osgar felt for the sword and did as Morann had asked.

"Let me know when you want it," he said quietly, as they drew closer.

The man at the farmstead was shouting now, as the cattle were being driven out of their pen. Osgar saw the man run forward and catch one of the riders by the leg, remonstrating with him. He was tugging at the leg, wildly.

The movement was so swift that Osgar never saw the horseman's hand move at all. He saw the blade though, a single, sudden flash in the morning sun. Then he saw the farmer falling, saw him crumple on the ground.

The horseman did not even cast an eye upon him, but rode on, driving the cattle, as the woman with a scream ran forward with the child.

He was dying when they reached him. The raiders were already moving away. Osgar got down. The poor fellow on the ground was still conscious, aware that Osgar was giving him the last rites. Moments later, with the woman and the child weeping on the ground beside him, he died.

Osgar slowly rose and stared down. He did not speak. Morann was saying something to him, but he did not hear. All he was conscious of was the dead man's face. A man he did not know. A man who had died for nothing, in a foolish moment, in a foolish way.

And then it came back to him. The same ashen face. The same staring eyes. The blood. The horror. It was always the same. The endless human cruelty, and the violence without a cause. The uselessness of it all.

The memories that had troubled him once, after the killing of the robber in his youth, had long ago subsided. They had returned once in a while, but as recollections, as things that belonged in the past. And up in the safety and quiet of Glendalough, there was little enough reason why it should be otherwise. But now, as he stared suddenly at the terrible, bloodied flesh and human waste before him, his old horror came upon him with all the fresh, raw urgency that he had experienced long ago.

And I, too, have killed a man, he thought. I have done this, too. Whether in self-defence or not still seemed to make no difference. And just as he had then, all those years ago, he felt a huge need to turn away, to take no more part in these evil and tragic things. Never again, he had vowed to himself. Never again.

He realised that Morann was pulling at his arm.

"We must move on," the craftsman was saying. "There is nothing we can do here."

Osgar was almost in a daze as he found himself sitting in the cart again, with the sword between his knees. Morann was driving along the track. The raiders were a little way off on their left, but seemed to be watching them. For after a few moments, deserting the cattle, the three horsemen came towards them. He heard Morann telling him to stay calm. He felt his hand involuntarily tightening on the sword, still concealed under the blanket between his legs. The horsemen reached them.

Of the three of them, two wore heavy leather jerkins and carried swords. These were obviously soldiers. The third, a thin, broken-toothed fellow with a cloak wrapped round him, didn't look as if he belonged with them. The soldier who had struck down the farmer spoke.

"We shall be needing that cart." It was an order. But as Osgar was reluctantly starting to move, Morann placed his hand on his arm and prevented him.

"That's impossible," he said.

"Why is that?"

"The cart's not mine. It belongs to the monastery." He indicated Osgar. "The monastery in Dyflin to which I'm taking this good monk." He gazed at the soldier calmly. "I don't think King Brian would be wanting you to take the monastery's cart."

The soldier considered. His eyes appraised Osgar carefully and seemed to conclude that he was indeed a monk. He nodded slowly.

"Have you any valuables?"

"No." Morann's face was confident. Apart from some silver concealed in his clothes, he hadn't.

"They lie!" It was the broken-toothed man who had cried out. His eyes seemed a little wild. "Let me search them."

"You'll do as you're told and help drive the cattle," the soldier ordered him curtly. He nodded to Morann. "Drive on."

They continued along the track. The horsemen and their cattle receded. Morann smiled grimly. "Just as well I had you along," he grunted. They went over a small rise and were just pausing at the top when, in the distance, they saw a grim sight. Smoke was rising into the sky. Smoke that must be coming from a large fire, perhaps many fires. Judging by the direction, it could only be coming from Dyflin. Osgar saw Morann shake his head and glance a little doubtfully at him. But he continued driving forward.

The sound of a galloping horse behind them came just moments later. Osgar turned. To his surprise he saw it was the thin fellow with the ragged teeth. He seemed to be making straight towards them. Evidently he had broken away from the soldiers. To his horror, as the fellow drew close, Osgar realised that he was brandishing a sword. The fellow's eyes seemed even wilder than ever. "Pull out the sword," he heard Morann's voice say, quietly but firmly, beside him. But though he understood Morann perfectly well Osgar remained motionless. He seemed to be frozen. Morann nudged him impatiently. "He's going to swing at you. Pull out the sword."

And still he did nothing. The fellow was only paces away now. Morann was right. He was preparing to strike. "For God's sake defend yourself," Morann cried out. Osgar could feel the sword in his hand. Yet his hand did not move.

He wasn't afraid. That was the strangeness of it. His paralysis was not one of fear. He scarcely cared, at that moment, if the fellow struck at him. For if he struck this fellow himself, he would probably kill him. And all he knew, just then, was that he was determined not to kill another man. He wanted no part of it. None.

He hardly felt it as Morann seized the sword out of his hands. He was only conscious, for a moment, of Morann's strong left arm banging against his chest as, throwing his body across Osgar's, the craftsman thrust at their assailant. He heard the clang of steel on steel, felt Morann's body twist violently, and then heard a terrible cry as the thin fellow tumbled from his horse. A moment later, Morann clambered over him, jumped down from the cart, and plunged his sword into the wounded man's breast.

The thin man lay on the ground. Blood was frothing from his mouth. Morann was turning. And now the craftsman was cursing.

"What were you thinking of? You could have had us both killed. Dear God, you are useless to man or beast. Are you the greatest coward that was ever born?"

"I'm sorry." What could he say? How could he explain that he had not been afraid? What difference did it make anyway? Osgar hardly knew himself.

"I shouldn't have brought you," the craftsman was crying. "I shouldn't have done it, against my judgement. You're no use to me, Monk, and you're a danger to yourself."

"If it happens again . . ." Osgar heard himself saying weakly.

"Again? There'll be no again." Morann paused, and then declared with finality. "You're going back."

"But I can't. My family . . ."

"If any place in Dyflin is safe, it's your uncle's monastery," Morann told him.

"And Caoilinn . . . She'll be in the city, probably."

"Dear Heaven," Morann burst out, "what in the world can a useless coward like yourself do for Caoilinn? You couldn't save her from a mouse." He took a deep breath, and then, a little more kindly, went on reasonably. "You are wonderful with the sick and dying, Osgar. I have watched you. Let me take you back to the place where you are needed. Do what God made you for, and leave the saving of people to me."

"I really think—" Osgar began, but the craftsman firmly stopped him.

"I'm not taking you any farther in my cart." And before Osgar could say anything more, Morann jumped in, turned the cart round, and headed back the way they had come before.

They saw no one along the way. The cattle raiders had disappeared. The people at the farmstead had already dragged the corpse of the farmer back inside. They could see the little religious house where they had spent the night in the distance when Osgar asked the craftsman to stop.

"I suppose you are right," he said regretfully. "The place ahead is where I should go. They seem to want me. So put me down and I can walk from here. The sooner you get to Dyflin, the better." He paused. "Would you promise me one thing? Would you call in at Rathmines. It's on your way. Call in and make sure that Caoilinn isn't there, in need of any help. Would you do that for me?"

"That," Morann agreed, "I can do."

Osgar had just got down, when a sudden thought occurred to him.

"Give me the blanket," he said.

With a shrug, Morann threw it down.

"Good." And removing his monk's habit, Osgar wrapped the blanket around himself. Then he tossed the habit up to Morann. "Put it on," he called. "It might help you get into Dyflin."

❖

The flames and smoke arising before Dyflin had been growing greater by the hour; but they were not the result of destruction: they came from the huge bonfires that the Munster men had built in their camp on the open ground between the town ramparts and the open spaces by the Thingmount.

Caoilinn was looking anxiously towards them and wondering what to do when she saw the two men appear. She wondered if they could help her.

She had gone to Rathmines the evening before. As soon as she had heard the news of Glen Mama, she had decided to ride out to the farmstead, leaving her children with her brother in Dyflin, to wait for her husband in case he should come that way. She had seen Brian's men pass by, and a few of the defeated army, seeking their homes. Though the huge camp of the Munster men lay outside the walls, the gates of Dyflin were open. People were going in and out. But for a long time there had been no sign of Cormac.

She had expected to find some of her people at the farmstead, but fearing Brian's men, presumably, they had all disappeared, and she had found herself quite alone. The farmstead stood at some distance from the main track, at the end of a lane of its own, so nobody had come by. She had gathered her courage, however, and stayed the night out there by herself, all the more anxious that, if her husband should come that way, he would find someone at the place.

And it was as well that she had.

He had arrived half an hour ago, alone. If she had not recognised his horse, she would not have guessed, until he fell at her feet, that the ragged, bloodstained figure who was approaching was the man she loved. His wounds were terrible. It seemed to her that he probably would not survive. God knows what effort of will had kept him on his horse at all as the animal walked slowly back. She had managed to prop him up just inside the gateway, and bathe and bandage some of his wounds. He had groaned softly and let her know that he knew who she was and that he was home. But he could scarcely speak. And having done what little she could, she had been wondering how to get him to her brother's in Dyflin, or whether she should leave him here alone while she went for help, when she saw the two men approaching the farmstead up the little lane.

They were soldiers. From Brian's army. They seemed friendly and came into the farmstead with her. One of them took a look at Cormac and then shook his head.

"I don't think he's going to make it."

"No," the other agreed. "He hasn't a chance."

"Please," she cautioned them, "he may hear you."

The two men looked at each other. They seemed to be considering the situation. One of them, who appeared to be the senior, had a large, round face, and had been the most smiling and polite of the two. It was he, finally, who spoke.

"Shall we finish him off, then?" he genially enquired.

"If you like," said the other.

She felt her heart sink.

"We could kill him after we've had her. He might like to watch." The round-faced man turned to her. "What do you think?"

A terrible fear overcame her. She could scream, but would anyone hear her? Not a chance. If she'd had a weapon, she'd have tried to use it. They had swords and they'd kill her, but she'd rather go down fighting. She looked about.

Of course. Her husband, Cormac, had a sword. He was staring at her from his position by the gate, as if he were trying to tell her something. That he had a weapon? That he'd sooner they both went down fighting? That he wasn't prepared to watch her raped? Yes, she thought. That was the only way. She lunged towards him.

But they had her. They had her by the waist. She couldn't move. She heard a cry from the lane. She screamed.

And a moment later, to her great astonishment, a monk appeared. He had a sword in his hand.

✢

It was Morann's idea to take Caoilinn and her husband to the little family monastery. "That's a place where he will be well looked after, and you would be safer under the protection of the monks than anywhere else I can think of." He wished he could hunt Caoilinn's second assailant down. The man with the round face he had wounded mortally, but he was sorry the other fellow had managed to run away. However, first things came first.

Osgar's uncle had been delighted to take them in, and was full of praise for his nephew when Morann tactfully told them all that it had only been thanks to the monk that he had come there. The abbot had also been full of information. Though he was getting very old and frail now, the excitement of the events of recent days seemed to have made him quite lively. Yes indeed, he confirmed, Brian was staying within the ramparts of Dyflin. "He means to spend the whole Christmas season there." The battle of Glen Mama had been a catastrophe for Leinster. The death toll had been heavy; wounded men were still coming in all the time. The King of Dyflin had fled north into Ulster; but search parties had been sent out after him. Brian hadn't taken a bloody vengeance on the people of Dyflin, but he had taken a huge tribute.

"He stripped them," the old man said, with the grim satisfaction of a bystander at a good fight. "Dear God, he has stripped them. Not less than a cartload of silver from every house." And though this was clearly an exaggeration, Morann was doubly glad that he'd removed his own valuables. The Munster king had also lost no time in impressing his political authority on the province. "He's already holding the King of Leinster, and he's taking hostages from every chief in the province, every church and monastery, too. He's even taken my own two sons," the old man added, with some pride. It was not unusual for kings to take hostages in this way from the great religious houses. For even if these monasteries were not in the hands of a powerful local family who needed to be controlled, they had the wealth to hire fighting men, and might even possess regular armed retainers of their own. Taking both the old abbot's sons as hostages, however, was to accord the family and its little monastery an importance that would have made his ancestor Fergus proud.

The old man asked Morann if he was intending to go into the town, and the craftsman replied that he was.

"It's the Ostmen who are seen as the real enemy," the abbot remarked. "But though you're not an Ostman, you're a well-known figure in Dyflin—even dressed in a monk's habit!" he added wryly. "I don't know what the Munster men will feel about that. I'd stay out if I were you."

Morann thanked him for the advice, but couldn't take it. "I'll be careful," he promised; and leaving his cart at the monastery, he walked down into the town.

The streets of Dyflin were much as he had left them. He had expected to see fences down, perhaps some thatched roofs burned; but it looked as if the inhabitants, wisely, had accepted their fate without resistance. Groups of armed men lounged here and there. The Fish Shambles was crowded with carts of provisions, and the presence of pigs and cattle in many of the little yards indicated that the occupiers meant to feast well over Christmas. Many of the houses had obviously been taken over by the Munster men, and he wondered what had happened to his own. He had told Harold's wife to take her family there in his absence; so that was his first destination.

When he reached his gate, he saw a couple of armed men leaning on the fence, one of them apparently drunk. Turning to the other, he asked if the woman was in there.

"The Ostman's woman, with the children?"

Morann nodded. The fellow shrugged.

"They took them all away. Down by the quay I think."

"What are they doing with them?" Morann asked casually.

"Selling them. Slaves." The fellow grinned. "Women and children. It'll make a change to see some of the Ostmen being sold, instead of selling us. And every one of us that fought for King Brian will get a share. We're all going home rich this time."

Morann forced himself to smile. But inwardly he was cursing himself. Had he brought this on his friend's family, by persuading them to go into Dyflin from the farmstead?

His first impulse was to go down to the wood quay to try to find them, but he quickly realised that this might be unwise; nor was it yet clear how he could help them. He needed to find out more. Next, therefore, he went to the house of Caoilinn's father, and told him where his daughter was.

"Brian's men have already been here," the old merchant declared. Caoilinn's husband, he explained, had already been fined in his absence. "He's to pay two hundred cattle and give his eldest boy as a hostage," he said gloomily. "I've already lost half my silver and all my wife's jewellery. As for you," he cautioned the craftsman, "if these Munster men discover who you are, you'll suffer like the rest of us."

When Morann told him about his problem with Harold's family, the older man was not encouraging. There were already several hundred, mostly women and children, being kept in a big compound under close guard down by the quay. And they were bringing in more each day. He advised Morann not to go near the place for the moment.

A short while after leaving the merchant, Morann was moving carefully down towards the wood quay. Though he was shocked by what had happened to his friend's family, he knew he shouldn't be entirely surprised. The slave markets were always being fed with people who had lost battles or been caught in Viking raids. Hard though it was, King Brian was simply making a point that the whole northern world would understand.

The craftsman's first objective was to discover where Harold's family was being held. If possible, he would try and make contact with them, at least to give them a little comfort and hope. The question then would be how to get them out. It was unlikely that he

would be able to sneak them away from their captors. To make
things more difficult, it was possible that Astrid had been separated
from her children, if they were to be sold in different markets. He
might, of course, be able to bribe the guards; but he thought it unlikely. He stood a better chance of buying them outright from the
Munster men at the full market price. But then he'd have to explain
who he was, and that could prove to be troublesome. He could even
finish up, he thought grimly, in the slave market himself.

The quay was in front of him now. It was crowded with ships.
Nobody took much notice of him as he started to make his way
along. A group of armed men came swinging down from an alley on
his right. He paused to observe them as they went past.

But they didn't go past. Hands suddenly seized his arms. He
struggled, tried to protest, but realised at once that it was useless.
Immediately, therefore, he became very calm.

"What is it you want, boys?" he enquired. "Where are you taking me?"

The officer in charge was a swarthy figure, with a look of quiet
authority about him. He came to stand in front of the craftsman
and smiled.

"What we want, Morann Mac Goibnenn, is the pleasure of your
company. Where are we taking you? It's to King Brian Boru himself." He turned. "And you wouldn't want to keep the man waiting,
now, would you?"

÷

It was Morann who was kept waiting. He was kept waiting all afternoon. Whatever his fate was to be, he was curious to see the
Munster king, whose talent and ambition had raised him almost to
the pinnacle of power; and while he waited, he went over what he
knew about him.

He'd been born the youngest son of his father, Kennedy, beside
the River Shannon by a ford. Morann had heard somewhere that
quite early in his life, Brian had been told by a fili that he was a man

of destiny and that, having been born by a ford, he'd die by a ford also. Well, he was by Ath Cliath now, but he was very much alive. "He likes the women." They all said that. But then who didn't? He'd had three wives so far. The second had been a tempestuous woman, the sister of the King of Leinster. She had already been married to both the Viking King of Dyflin and the O'Neill High King. But she'd given Brian a fine son before he'd discarded her.

There were many people, Morann knew, who thought that this divorce had led to the bad feeling behind the revolt of the Leinster and Dyflin kings against Brian; but a chief who knew the King of Leinster well had assured Morann that the rumour wasn't really correct. "He may not have been pleased, but he knows his sister's trouble," he'd told the craftsman. And God knows, divorce was common enough amongst the royal families of the island. More likely, in Morann's opinion, the bad feeling against Brian was the inevitable jealousy against a man who rises so far and so fast. What nobody denied was the Munster king's prowess. "He's as patient as he's daring," they acknowledged. He would be in his late fifties now, but full of vigour, it was said.

And so it proved to be. It was nearly dusk when Morann was finally brought into the big hall of the Dyflin king, which Brian had taken over. There was a fire in the centre, where several men were standing. One of these, he noticed, was the rich merchant who imported amber. Beside him, turning to look at him, was the figure he guessed must be Brian Boru.

The king was not a tall man, hardly above middle height. He had a long face, thin nose, intelligent eyes. His hair, where it was not greying, was a rich brown. The face was fine, almost intellectual; he might have been a priest, Morann thought. Until Brian took a few steps towards him. For the southern king moved with the dangerous grace of a cat.

"I know who you are. You were seen." He wasted no time. "Where have you been?"

"To Kells, Brian, son of Kennedy."

"Ah, I see. And you hope your valuables will be safe from me there. They tell me you left nothing much in your house. Those who rebel have to pay the price, you know."

"I didn't rebel." It was the truth.

"Did you not?"

"That man could tell you." Morann indicated the amber merchant. "I told the Dyflin men that it was a mistake to oppose you. They were not pleased. Then I left."

King Brian turned to the amber merchant, who nodded his confirmation.

"So why did you come back?" the king demanded.

Morann related the exact details of parts of his journey, how he had set out with Osgar and the nun, and his discovery that Harold's wife and children had been taken. He discreetly omitted the incident at Rathmines and his flight with Caoilinn and her husband to the monastery, and hoped that Brian was unaware of it.

"You came back for your friends?" Brian turned round to the others and remarked, "As this man's not stupid, he must be brave." And then, turning back to Morann again, he coolly observed, "You are a friend to Ostmen, it seems."

"Not especially."

"Your wife's family are Ostmen." It was said quietly, but it contained a warning. This king was not to be deceived. "That must be why you came to live here in the first place: your love of Ostmen." Was King Brian playing with him, like a cat with a mouse?

"In fact," Morann replied evenly, "it was my father who brought me here, when I was little more than a boy." For a moment he smiled at the memory of that journey down, past the ancient tombs above the River Boyne. "My family were craftsmen, honoured by kings since before Saint Patrick came. And my father hated the Ostmen. But he made me come to Dyflin because he said that Dyflin was the place of the future."

"Did he now? And is he alive, still, this man of wisdom?" It was hard to tell whether this was sarcastic or not.

"He's long dead."

King Brian was silent. He seemed to be thinking to himself. Then he moved close to the craftsman.

"When I was young, Morann Mac Goibnenn," he spoke so softly that Morann was probably the only person who heard him, "I hated the Ostmen. They had invaded our land. We fought them. I once even burned down their port of Limerick. Do you think that was wise of me?"

"You had to teach them a lesson, I should think."

"Perhaps. But it was I, Morann Mac Goibnenn, who needed to learn a lesson." He paused, and then he took a small object from his hand and placed it in Morann's. "What do you think of this?" It was a small silver coin. The King of Dyflin had started minting them just two years ago. In Morann's opinion, the workmanship was not especially fine, but passable enough. Before waiting for his reply, Brian continued. "The Romans minted coins a thousand years ago. Coins are minted in Paris and in Normandy. The Danes mint coins in York; the Saxons have mints in London and several other towns. But where do we mint coins on this island? Nowhere, except in the Ostmen's port of Dyflin. What does that tell you, Morann?"

"That Dyflin is the island's greatest port, and that we trade across the sea."

"Yet even now our native chiefs still count their wealth in cattle." The king sighed. "There are three realms on this island, Morann. There is the interior, with its forests and pastures, its raths and farmsteads, the realm that goes back into the mists of time, to Niall of the Nine Hostages, and Cuchulainn and the goddess Eriu—the realm from which our kings have come. Then there is the realm of the Church, of the monasteries, of Rome, with its learning and its riches in protected places. That is the realm our kings have learned to respect and love. But now there is a third realm, Morann, the realm of the Ostmen, with their ports and their trading across the high seas. And that realm we still have not learned to make our own." He shook his head. "The O'Neill High King thinks he is a great fellow because he holds the right to Tara and has the blessing of Saint Patrick's Church. But I tell you, if he does not command the Ostmen's fleets and make himself also the master of the sea, then he is nothing. Nothing at all."

"You think like an Ostman," the craftsman remarked.

"Because I have observed them. The High King has a kingdom, but the Ostmen have an empire, all over the seas. The High King has an island fortress, but without ships of his own, he is always vulnerable. The High King has many cattle, but he is also poor, for the trade is all in the Ostmen's hands. Your father was right, Morann, to take you to Dyflin."

As Morann considered the implication of these words, he looked at Brian with a new curiosity. He had realised that, by taking the southern half of the island, the Munster king had already taken control of all the major Viking ports. He was also aware that, on some of his campaigns, Brian had made extensive use of water transport on the River Shannon. But what Brian had just said went far beyond the sort of political control that kings had exercised up to now. If the High King without Viking fleets could be dismissed as "nothing," then this was confirmation that Brian, as many people suspected, did indeed intend, sooner or later, to take over as High King. But more than that, it sounded as if, once he had made himself master of the island, he meant to be a different sort of king. Dyflin seemed to interest him more than Tara. Morann suspected that the Ostmen of Dyflin would be seeing more of this new kind of ruler than they had been used to, and that this foolish revolt had probably given Brian just the excuse he was looking for to assert his authority in the place. He looked at the king respectfully.

"The Ostmen of Dyflin are not easy to govern," Morann remarked. "They are used to the freedom of the seas."

"I know that, Morann Mac Goibnenn," the king replied. "I shall need friends in Dyflin." He watched the craftsman shrewdly.

It was an offer. Morann understood at once. He could hardly believe his luck. After his arrest down at the quay, he had not known what to expect. And now here was Brian Boru offering him friendship in return for his loyal support. No doubt there'd be a price to pay, but it would surely be worth it. He couldn't help admiring the vision of the Munster king as well. Just as Brian looked beyond his present position, to the time when he would be master of the whole island, so even here, when he had just crushed the opposition in Dyflin, he was already laying the groundwork for a peaceful and friendly rule of the port in the future. Perhaps, Morann thought, he even meant to base himself there one day.

And he was just about to assure the king of his loyal friendship, when there was a disturbance at the entrance, the sound of raised voices, and then the leader of the armed guard who had brought him there burst into the hall. His face was covered in blood.

"I have been attacked by an Ostman, Brian, son of Kennedy," he called. "I ask for his death."

Morann saw the king's brows close and his eyes grow dark.

"Where is he?" he demanded.

And now, at the entrance, Morann saw the men drag in a figure who looked familiar; and as they pulled back his red hair to raise his head, he saw by the firelight that it was Harold.

Morann had not caught the dark fellow's name, but evidently he was well known to King Brian; and at a curt nod from the king, he related his tale. Despite the fact that his head was bleeding quite a lot, he was brief and to the point.

Harold's ship had entered the Liffey estuary just after dark. It seemed the crew had seen the bonfires by the Thingmount, but had assumed they must be connected with the celebration of the Christmas feast. They had tied up at the wooden quay and immediately been held by the watch, who had taken Harold's name and sent for their officer who had gone up to the royal hall.

"As I came down onto the quay," the dark fellow explained, "my men told the Ostman," he indicated Harold, "to stand forward. But the moment I got close, he turned round and grabbed a spar that was lying there; I put my hand to my sword, but before I could get it out, he caught me in the face with the spar. He's very fast," he remarked, not without respect, "and strong. It took three of my men to hold him down."

It was obvious that they'd done more than hold Harold down. They'd clubbed him over the head and given him a severe beating. He'd been unconscious when they brought him in, but now he groaned. The king went over to him, took him by the hair, and raised his face again. Harold opened his eyes, but they were glazed; he stared at the king dully. It was evident that he did not see Morann, or anyone else in the place.

"It is the king who speaks to you," Brian said. "Do you understand?"

A mumble indicated that Harold did.

"It's my own officer that you've attacked. He wants you dead. What have you to say?"

"I'd kill him first." Harold's voice was slurred, but the words were unmistakable.

"Are you defying me?" the king cried.

By way of answer, Harold suddenly twisted himself free of the two men holding him. God knows, Morann thought, where he finds the strength. He caught sight of the officer now and made a lunge towards him. It was Brian himself who caught him, before the two surprised guards seized him again and pushed him to the ground, while one of them pulled out a small club and brought it down heavily on Harold's head. Reflexively, Morann started forward to intervene; but at this moment, Brian held up his hand and everybody froze. It was obvious that the king was furious.

"Enough. I'll hear no more. It seems that some of these Ostmen still haven't learned their lesson." He turned to the officer. "Take him away."

"And?" the dark fellow enquired.

"Kill him." King Brian's face was set, hard and implacable. Morann realised that he was now looking at the man who had destroyed the Viking port of Limerick and won a score of battles. When such a man had lost patience, it would be a foolish person who started to argue with him. However, there seemed little other option.

"Brian, son of Kennedy," he began. The king rounded on him. "What is it?"

"This man is my friend. The one I told you about."

"The worse for you, then. And for him. And his cursed family in the slave house." The king's eyes stared at him angrily, daring him to say more. Morann took a deep breath.

"I'm only thinking that this isn't like him at all to do such a thing. There must be a reason."

"The reason is that he is a fool, and a rebel. He gave no other. And he is going to die. If it's my friendship you want, Morann Mac Goibnenn, you will speak of this no more."

The guards were starting to drag Harold out. After the blow from the club, he was unconscious again. Morann took another deep breath.

"Would you not let me speak with him? Perhaps . . ."

"Enough!" Brian shouted. "Do you want to join him in death?"

"You will not kill me, Brian, son of Kennedy." The words came out, cold and hard, almost before he had time to think what he was saying.

"Will I not?" The king's eyes flashed dangerously.

"No," said Morann quietly, "because I am the best silversmith in Dyflin."

For a moment, Morann wondered if he was about to discover that he was wrong. The hall had fallen very silent. The king was looking at the ground, apparently considering the matter. After a long pause, he murmured, "You have nerves of iron, Morann Mac Goibnenn." Then he looked up and eyed him coldly. "Do not presume upon my friendship. My rule is to be respected."

"That is not to be doubted." Morann bowed his head.

"I will give you a choice then, Morann Mac Goibnenn. Your friend may keep his life and join his family in the slave house; or he may lose his life, and I will set his family free. Let me know which you prefer before I sit down to eat tonight." Then he turned away. Morann knew better than to say anything more. They dragged Harold out of the hall and Morann followed sorrowfully behind.

It was a terrible choice, thought Morann; a cold, Celtic dilemma, as subtle and cruel as anything in the stories from the ancient days. That was why Brian had done it—to let him know plainly that he was dealing with a master of the kingly craft. He did not think that there was any hope of the Munster king changing his mind. A hard choice: but who should make it? If Harold came round, Morann had no doubt what his friend would choose. Freedom for his family, death for himself. So if Harold did not come round, was that the choice he should make for him? Or should he save his life and leave them all in slavery? The latter course might be preferable, if he could buy them out afterwards himself. But what if the king refused to let him do that, or they were shipped over the seas to the foreign markets. Would Harold ever forgive him for that?

As they left the hall, the officer went off to tend to his wound while they were led across the yard in silence to a small wooden building. Morann had hoped that perhaps the cold night air might bring his friend round, but it did not. They were pushed into the room and a guard placed at the door.

There was a single taper in the room and a small fire. Morann sat by the fire. Harold lay on the floor with his eyes closed. Time went by. Morann asked for water, and when it came, he dashed a little on Harold's face. It had no effect. After a while, Harold groaned. Morann raised his head and tried to get some water through his lips. He thought he got a few drops in, and Harold groaned again; but though his eyes flickered, he did not come round.

After perhaps another hour, one of the guards arrived and an-

nounced that King Brian was waiting for his answer. Morann told
him that his friend had still not come round.

"You're to bring an answer regardless," the fellow said.

"Dear God, what am I to say?" Morann burst out. He looked
down at Harold. He seemed to have fallen into a restful sleep.
Thank God at least that the Norwegian was so strong. Morann had
a feeling that he might come round if he could only wait a little
longer. He still wasn't sure what answer he was going to give the
Munster king. "I can't make any sense of the business at all," he said
in exasperation. "Why would he attack your man anyway?"

"I don't know," the fellow replied. "But I can tell you this: Sigurd
did nothing to him. Come on."

"If I must," Morann muttered absently, and started to follow.
And he had already walked halfway across the yard to the big hall
when he stopped and turned to the man. "Just a moment," he said.
"What did you say his name was—the officer that my friend attacked?"

"Sigurd. Officer of the watch."

Sigurd. A Viking name. The dark fellow wasn't a Viking, as far
as Morann knew; but then it wasn't uncommon these days, especially around the ports, to find Vikings who had taken Celtic names
and vice versa. Sigurd. Until this moment it had never occurred to
him that the officer's name could be significant. He tried to imagine it—the confusion on the quay, the swarthy figure suddenly advancing . . .

"Were you there on the quay when it happened?" he asked the
guard.

"I was."

"Did someone call out a name?"

The fellow considered.

"Sigurd arrived. We said to the Ostman, 'Step forward. Our man
wants to see you.' Then I called out, 'Here's your man, Sigurd.' And
then as Sigurd got close, the Ostman took one look at him
and . . ."

But Morann was no longer listening. He was already striding into the hall.

"I know, Brian, son of Kennedy," he called out. "I know what happened."

He ignored the king's look of irritation when he began his story. He did not obey when the king told him to be quiet. He continued even when it looked as though the guards would remove him. And by this time, in any case, the king was listening.

"So he thought my fellow Sigurd was this Dane who had vowed to kill him?"

"I have no doubt of it," cried Morann. "Imagine it: in the darkness, a similar-looking fellow, he hears the name called out—and in the very place, remember, where they had met before . . ."

"You swear that this story is true?"

"Upon the Holy Bible. Upon my life, Brian, son of Kennedy. And it is the only explanation that makes sense."

King Brian gave him a long, hard look.

"You want me to spare his life, I suppose."

"I do."

"And free his wife and children, too, no doubt."

"I would ask it, naturally."

"They have a price you know. And after all that, you would be my loyal friend, would you, Morann Mac Goibnenn?"

"I should indeed."

"Even to the death?" He looked Morann in the eye.

And just for a moment, because he was honest, Morann hesitated.

"To the death, Brian, son of Kennedy," he answered.

Then Brian Boru smiled.

"Will you look at that," he called out to the company gathered in the hall. "Here's a man, when he swears to be your friend, who really means it." He turned back to Morann. "Your friend's life, Morann, I will give you if you vouch for his future loyalty also, and if he pays five of those silver coins you mint here to my man Sigurd, who never did him any harm. His wife and children you may buy from me yourself. I shall be needing a silver chalice to give to the monastery at Kells. Could you make me such a thing by Easter?"

Morann nodded.

"No doubt it will be a fine one," the king said with a smile.

And it was.

II

⊰ 1013 ⊱

There was no doubt about it, at the age of forty-one, with her dark hair and brilliant green eyes, Caoilinn was still a very striking woman; and it was also generally agreed, by summer's end, that she was looking for a new husband.

She had earned some happiness. Nobody would have disputed that. She had looked after her sick husband devotedly for more than a dozen years. Cormac had never recovered his health after the battle of Glen Mama. With one arm missing and a terrible wound in his stomach, it was only thanks to Caoilinn's nursing that he had lived at all. But worse even than his physical disabilities had been his melancholy. Sometimes he was depressed, sometimes angry; increasingly, as the years went by, he drank too much. The last years had been difficult indeed.

To get through them, Caoilinn had clung to her memory. She did not see before her the broken man that he now was. She managed instead to see the tall, handsome figure he once had been. She thought of his courage, his strength, his royal blood. Above all, she had wanted to protect his children. Their father was always presented to them as a fallen hero. If he lay idle for weeks on end, or suddenly burst out in a rage over nothing, these were the tribulations of his heroic nature. If his mood in the last days descended into a morbid darkness, it was not a darkness of his own making but one created by the evil spirits who had surrounded him and were dragging him down. And from what quarter did these spirits come? Who was the evil influence behind them, and the ultimate cause of all this misery? To be sure, it could only be one person: who else but the instigator of the trouble, the upstart who had come deliberately to humiliate the old royal house of Leinster to which her husband and her children were proud to belong. It was Brian Boru who was to blame. It was not her husband's weakness but Brian's malevolence that was the cause of their misery. So she taught her children to believe. And as the humiliations gathered with the passing of the years, she even came to believe it herself. It was Brian who had caused her husband's sickness, his sadness, his rage, and his dissolution. It was Brian who was the evil presence in their family life. Even when their father started a drinking bout, it was Brian Boru who drove him to it, she told them. It seemed the Munster king had a personal animus against the family at Rathmines. So perfect was her belief that, in the course of time, it had transformed itself into something that was almost tangible, as though King Brian's enmity had solidified into a stone. And even now, when she was a free woman again and her children grown, she still carried her hatred of Brian like a flint in her heart.

Cormac had died at midwinter. It had been a relief. Whatever painful memories she had, her conscience was clear. She had done her best. Their children were healthy. And thanks to her good stewardship—for in fact, if not in name, she had been running his estate for years—she and the children were now almost as rich as they had been before the battle of Glen Mama. By spring, the wound of her sadness had begun to heal. By early summer, she felt quite cheerful. By June, people were telling her that she was looking younger than she had for years. And after a careful private inspection of her own body, she concluded that some confidence was justified. As the long, warm days of August saw the harvest ripen, she began to feel that perhaps one day she might think of marrying again. And as the harvest was gathered in, she began, in a calm and cheerful way, to look about.

·ૐ·

Osgar hardly knew what he felt, that October, as he approached the family monastery at Dyflin. Samhain was approaching, an appropriate time he supposed for his uncle to have departed for the world beyond. The old abbot had taken his leave very peacefully; there was no need to feel pain on that account. As he had descended the path from the mountains on that clear autumn day, Osgar had felt only a gentle melancholy as he thought affectionately of the old man. But as he came to the monastery gates, there was another thought on his mind. For he knew very well what they were going to ask of him. And the question, which he had not yet answered in his own mind, was what he was going to do?

They were all there. His uncle's sons, friends, and family he had not seen for years. Morann Mac Goibnenn was there. And Caoilinn, too. The wake was just ending when he arrived, but they asked him to conduct the final ceremonies as they placed the old man in his grave. It was kind of Caoilinn, afterwards, to have invited him to visit her at Rathmines the following day.

He arrived at midday. He had asked for only the simplest meal to be provided. "Remember I am only a poor monk," he had told her. He was rather glad to find that she had arranged for the two of them to eat alone. Looking at the handsome, dark-haired woman opposite him he realised with a slight shock that he had not sat alone with a woman for twenty-five years. It wasn't long before she came to the main issue on everybody's mind.

"Well, Osgar, are you coming back?"

That was what they all wanted. Now that his uncle had gone, it was obviously Osgar who should come and take his place. His uncle's sons wanted it, since neither of them had any real desire to take on the role. The monks wanted it. He would probably be the most distinguished abbot the little place had had in generations. Wasn't it his duty? Probably. Was he tempted? He wasn't sure.

He didn't answer her question just yet.

"It is strange to be back," he remarked. "I suppose," he went on after a thoughtful pause, "that if I had remained here, I might be sitting in the monastery now with a brood of children and my wife opposite me. And I suppose," he added with a smile, "that the wife in question might have been you." He glanced at her. "But then, perhaps you would not have married me."

Now it was her turn to smile.

"Oh," she said, reflectively, "I would have married you."

She looked at the man before her. His hair was grey. His face was thinner, and rather severe. She studied the way the lines on his face ran: ascetic, intellectual, but not unpleasing.

She remembered how close they had been when she was a little girl. He'd been her childhood playmate. She remembered how he'd saved her from drowning. She remembered how she had admired his fine, aristocratic ways and his intelligence. Yes, she had always supposed he would marry her. And how shocked she had been, she remembered, how hurt and furious when he had turned away from her. And for what? For a monastery in the mountains when he already had one at home. She couldn't understand it. That day when she had met him on the path, she had wanted to shock him, attack his choice of life, show her power over him was greater even than the religious vocation that was so humiliatingly stealing him away. I'd have been happy at that time, she realised with wry amusement, if I'd seduced him into denying God Himself. She shook her head at the memory. What a devil I was, she thought.

She almost asked him if he regretted his decision now, but decided she had better not.

After their meal, they went for a short walk. They talked of other things. She told him about the improvements she had made to the estate and about her children. It was only as they were returning to the house that she pointed to a place and casually remarked, "That's where I was nearly killed. Or worse."

Osgar stared at the spot.

"You know about that, I expect?" she asked. "It was Morann who saved my life. He was wonderful. Brave as a lion. Dressed in your habit, too, I might say!" And she laughed.

But Osgar did not laugh.

How could he even smile? It had been a while before he had heard all the details of the events of that fateful day. It was his uncle who had sent him a long and glowing letter on the subject of Morann Mac Goibnenn's valiant rescue of his cousin and how she and her wounded husband had been brought to the little monastery. And it was thanks to Osgar's concern and foresight, his uncle had been careful to add, that Morann had gone to Rathmines at all. But for that, he pointed out, Caoilinn would have been raped and probably butchered. They were all very grateful, he assured his nephew.

Such praise. Such a role he'd played. It had been like a knife through his heart. Caoilinn had been saved. But by Morann, not him. His own monk's habit, even, had attended her rescue, but it was Morann who had been wearing it. Morann, who was a better man than he.

He could have been there to rescue her himself, of course, if he hadn't shown what the craftsman took to be panic. Perhaps Morann had been right and that was all his hesitation had been— mere cowardice. He could have been there if he had refused when Morann sent him back, if he'd insisted on accompanying him whether the craftsman liked it or not. If he'd been a stronger man. If he'd been a man at all. For weeks after receiving the letter he had felt a sense of shame and self-disgust. Humiliated, he had gone about his daily tasks at Glendalough like a person with a guilty secret he cannot share. And in the end, he had decided that there was nothing more to do except admit to himself that his love for Caoilinn, the little ring he kept, and all his thoughts about her were nothing but a sham.

When it came to the one time that he should have gone to her, he had failed, shamefully, to do so. Involuntarily, he shook his head.

✥

He had not even realised that she had been speaking. She was talking now of something else. He tried to pay attention. She was speaking of her marriage.

"I was very angry at the time," she was confessing, "but as the years passed, I came to see that you were right. We are all happy enough now, I dare say. You did what you had to. You made your choice."

Yes, he thought, that was it. He had had his chances down the years and each time, he had made his choice. His choice to leave. His choice to desert her in her hour of need. His choice. And once such choices were made, you could not go back. You could never go back.

"I shan't be returning to Dyflin," he said. "I can't go back."

"I'm sorry," she said. "I shall miss you."

Not long afterwards, he took his leave. As he did so, he enquired, "Do you think you'll marry again?"

"I don't know," she said with a smile. "I hope so."

"Have you someone in mind?"

"Not yet." She smiled again, confidently. "I shall please myself."

✥

It was years since Harold had thought about Sigurd the Dane. It was not as if, even back at the time of Glen Mama, the man had actually appeared; and the embarrassment that his delusion had caused on that occasion made Harold even less willing to trouble himself by thinking about the fellow again. He assumed that, as the years had passed, the Dane had probably forgotten about him anyway.

And the years had been good to Harold. Dyflin and Fingal had been at peace. Brian Boru had succeeded in all his ambitions. Two years after the submission of Dyflin, the head of the proud O'Neill had acknowledged him as High King of the whole island, though, as the head of the mighty O'Neill, he was still usually referred to as the King of Tara. The northern chiefs in Connacht and Ulster had been grudging about the business, but Brian had gone up and made them submit. Cleverly, he had also made a pilgrimage to the great church of Saint Patrick at Armagh and secured the blessing of the priests there with a huge present of gold. Meanwhile, in the peace of Fingal and the busy port of Dyflin, Harold had enjoyed an ever-increasing prosperity.

It was not until after a decade that Harold's happiness had been marred by a loss: in 1011 Astrid, his wife of more than twenty years, had died. The blow had been great. Though, for the sake of his children, he had forced himself to go about his business as usual, the heart was gone out of him. He had continued almost like a sleep-walker all through that year, and it was only thanks to the affection of his children that he had not fallen into a worse state than he did. Not until the next spring did his spirits begin to rise again. Late in April, he went into Dyflin to stay with his friend Morann.

Caoilinn first caught sight of him one April afternoon. She was visiting her family in Dyflin. Her father having died some years before, her brother and his family occupied her old home now. She and her brother's wife had gone for a walk to the Thingmount, and they had just started across Hoggen Green when they caught sight of two figures riding towards them from the direction of the Long Stone out on the mudflats. One she recognised as Morann Mac Goibnenn. The other was a tall figure, splendidly mounted. She asked her sister-in-law who he was.

"That's Harold the Norwegian. He has a big farmstead in Fingal."

"He's handsome," Caoilinn remarked. She remembered hearing about the Norseman in the past. Though he was middle-aged, she saw that his hair was still red, with only a few streaks of grey, and that he had a pleasant air of vigour and health about him.

"He has a limp. A childhood accident, they say," her kinswoman remarked.

"That's nothing," said Caoilinn. And as he came up, she smiled at him.

The four of them had a pleasant conversation. When Morann glanced at his friend, the handsome Norwegian seemed to be in no hurry to move on. Before they had finished, he had suggested that Caoilinn might like to ride over to the farmstead with him the following week, and she had accepted. The following Tuesday, they did so.

By the month of June, the progress of their courtship had become a subject of some amusement to their families. Their children also welcomed it. Caoilinn's eldest son, Art, was more than ready to take his father's place and would not be entirely sorry if her energetic presence were removed from the management of the family's affairs. And for all the children, the prospect of having the kindly Norwegian as a new father was, if truth were told, an improvement on the gloomy memory of Cormac. As for Harold's children, they loved their father, found Caoilinn agreeable enough, and were glad if she brought him happiness. So it was made clear to both parents that they should conduct their courtship as they pleased.

It had begun easily enough, the day they rode out to Fingal, when Caoilinn asked him about his crippled leg. The question was casual and friendly, but they both understood: she'd spent years looking after one sick man and she didn't want another. He told her the story and explained how, after his life had been threatened, he had worked so hard to prepare himself for a fight. "My lame leg's probably even stronger than the other."

"It doesn't ache at all?" she asked solicitously.

"No," he said with a smile, "it doesn't."

"And what about this Dane who wants to kill you?" she demanded.

"I haven't seen him for twenty years," he said with a laugh.

The farmstead was impressive. She didn't need to count the cattle—though of course she did, and discovered that she only had a dozen more herself. She was too proud to marry far beneath her former station; and besides, her children might have been suspicious of a poor man. She did, however, notice some small improvements that could be made in the running of the farm. She would say nothing yet, of course, but it pleased her to think that she would be able to make her mark upon the Fingal estate and garner some admiration. Not that she would try to overshadow Harold. He was too much of a man for that, thank God. But it would be pleasant for him, she thought, to be able to say to his friends, "Look at what my clever wife has done."

For some weeks she made further observations and enquiries. And as she satisfied herself as to the Norseman's suitability, she also took care to make herself desirable.

When Harold looked at the handsome, green-eyed woman who was taking such an interest in him, he had to admit that he was flattered. Though he had been attracted to her from the moment they met by the Thingmount, it was a small incident the next week which had really caught his attention. They had just arrived at the farmstead, and he had reached up to lift her down from her horse. As he took her in his strong arms, he had hardly known what to expect. Unconsciously, he had braced his crippled leg to take her weight.

And she had floated down, light as a feather. Before her feet touched the ground, she had half turned in his arms, smiling, to thank him, and as well as her lightness, he had become instantly conscious of her wiry strength. So strong, yet so light in hand: such a woman promised many sensual delights.

As the weeks went by, her attraction grew. He soon discovered the strength of her intelligence: he respected that. She was proud: her pride did him honour. She was also cautious. It was not long before he noticed that if she offered to spend time in his company, it was partly so that she could observe him. Sometimes she would start seemingly innocent conversations. She might say, "I felt sad last night and the sadness would not leave me. Do you ever feel like that?" And only afterwards would he realise that she had been testing him to find out if he was subject to moods. When he visited her at Rathmines, she had the servants bring him wine repeatedly, to see if he would drink too much. He did not mind these little traps she set for him. If she was careful, so much the better. And it was gratifying that, beyond the cautious enquiries, she let him see that she was starting to care for him.

He, of course, knew all about her. He hadn't needed to make his own enquiries; his friend Morann had seen to that, and the silversmith's investigations had led to only one conclusion.

"You could hardly do better," Morann told him. It would certainly look well to have such a wife at his side; and though Harold was too sensible to be much swayed by such things, he saw no reason why he shouldn't cut a handsome figure in the world.

In fact, there was only one obstacle to their marriage. It did not appear until halfway through June, when he proposed to her. For after the usual expressions, instead of answering at once, she told him that she must first ask him a single question.

"What is that?" he asked.

"Would you mind my asking, what religion it is you follow now?"

The question was not strange. She had known that, at the time of his marriage, Harold had been a pagan, but it was harder than ever to know, nowadays, what religion people followed in Dyflin. Though some of the Vikings in Dyflin had remained faithful to Thor, Woden, and the other gods of the north, since her childhood the old Norse gods had been in steady decline. There had been too many marriages with Christians. The King of Dyflin was the son of a Christian Leinster princess. Besides, if the pagan gods protected their own, people might ask, then how was it that every time the men of Dyflin had challenged the High King, they had lost? And Brian Boru, the patron of monasteries, was their master now. The old wooden church had been rebuilt in stone, and the Viking King of Dyflin had openly worshipped there. So it was not surprising if the Ostmen nowadays were often vague about their religious beliefs. Harold, for instance, wore a talisman round his neck that might have been taken for a cross or a symbol of Thor; and certainly few of the varied folk who came into the busy port would have pressed him as to which it was.

In truth, like most middle-aged men, Harold no longer had any strong feelings about the gods, and it would have mattered little to him whether he were Christian or not. But faced with her sudden question, he hesitated.

"Why is it you ask?"

"It would be hard for me to marry a man who was not a Christian." She smiled. "It is easy to be baptised."

"I will think about what you say," he replied.

She waited for him to say more. He watched her instead. She flushed a little.

"I hope you will do it," she said.

He waited to see if she would concede any more, but she did not.

Soon afterwards, he returned home. A week passed before they met again.

Harold considered the matter carefully during those days. The business of baptism, as such, was nothing. He didn't mind that. But it was the way Caoilinn had brought it up that concerned him. Why, if it was so important to her, had she waited this long? It could only be because she thought that, once he had committed himself so far, he could be manipulated. True, the fact she'd waited also showed that she had been anxious not to put him off. She wanted to secure him. But look at it however you liked, she was raising her price. If he loved her, of course, he could pay the price and laugh it off. But if she was going to play a trick like that once, mightn't she do it again? He was old enough to know that, however subtle the game, marriage was a balance of power; and he wasn't sure he liked the way she played. By waiting a week, he was indicating his displeasure and giving her a chance to back down.

But what if she didn't. What was he going to do? Did he really intend to give her up on account of her god? If he did, and she married someone else, wouldn't he regret it? Each time he went over the matter in his mind, he found that it came down to the same thing. It's not what she asks for, he thought, that I care about, but how she asks for it. What matters is her attitude.

It was late in June when he rode back again to Rathmines. He had no definite plan, even then. He did not know whether he was going to offer to be baptised, and whether he'd be married or not. As he approached the big earth wall and palisade of her rath, he had no other plan than to watch, and listen, and follow his instincts, and see what happened. After all, he told himself as he rode up to the entrance, I can always leave and come back again another day. Only one thing worried him a little: how was he going to open the conversation on such a delicate subject? He still didn't know when he saw her coming to the gateway. I'll just trust, he supposed, to luck.

She met him with a smile. She led him inside. A slave brought him mead. She told him how glad she was that he had come. Was there something new, something almost respectful in her manner? It seemed to him there was.

"Oh, Harold, son of Olaf," she said, "I am so relieved that you have come. I have been feeling so embarrassed by my impudence— truly impudence—to you when we last met."

"It was not impudence," he said.

"Oh, but it was," she cut in earnestly. "When you had done me the honour—the *honour*—to make the offer you did. And I never expect it to be repeated now. But that I should have *dared* to impose conditions on a man I respect so much . . ."

"Your god is important to you."

"It is true. Of course. And because I believe He is the true God, I was anxious to share . . . I certainly won't deny," she allowed her hand lightly to touch his arm, "that if you were ever to come to the true faith, I should rejoice. But that is no excuse for what I did. I am not a priest." She paused. "I was so anxious to say this to you and to ask for your forgiveness."

It was admirably done. He might not be entirely deceived, but it was agreeable, very agreeable, to be so flattered.

"You are kind and generous," he replied with a smile.

"It is the respect you are owed, nothing more," she said, placing her hand on his arm again. She waited a few moments. "There is something else," she said. She led him towards a trestle table on which there was an object of some kind, covered with a cloth. Supposing this might be a platter of food, he watched as she carefully pulled away the covering. But instead of food, he saw an arrangement of small, hard objects that glinted in the weak, interior light. And coming closer, he stared in surprise.

It was a chess set. A magnificent chess set, the pieces carved of bone tipped with silver and set on a polished wooden board. He had seen it before, in Morann's workshop.

"It is for you," said Caoilinn. "A token of my respect. I know," she added, "that the Ostmen like to play chess."

It was perfectly true that the marauding Viking traders had developed a liking for the intellectual game, though this may partly have been because the carved chessmen were often objects of great value. Though Harold seldom played the game himself, he was touched that Caoilinn should have gone to such trouble on his account.

"I wanted you to have it," she said, and he scarcely knew what to reply.

He realised, of course, that she had outmanoeuvred him. He guessed that she was betting that sooner or later he would convert to the faith of the Christians to please her. And he supposed that he probably would. By raising the issue, moreover, and then giving way so graciously, she had placed him in her debt. He saw through her, understood, but didn't mind. For hadn't she also signalled clearly that she knew when she had gone too far? That, he reckoned, was good enough.

"I have only one request," she continued, "though you may refuse it if you wish. If ever you should wish to marry me at some future time, I should ask if there could be a ceremony conducted by a priest. Just for my sake. He would not be asking you what you believe, you may be sure."

He waited a few more days, then he came back to ask her, and was accepted. Since she wanted to complete the harvest at Rathmines before she left that estate, it was agreed that they would marry, and she would come to his house in the autumn.

For Harold, the days that followed began a period of both anticipation and contentment. Rather to his own surprise, he had already started to feel younger; and he looked forward to the autumn eagerly.

For Caoilinn, the prospect of marriage meant that she was ready to fall in love. Although, when she had first asked him to be baptised, she had fully intended that Harold should give in, she realised afterwards that she was glad that he had fought her. She respected him for it, and she had rather enjoyed the challenge of bringing him round. The vigorous, red-haired Ostman was like a spirited horse that one could only just control, she thought. Yet at the same time, he was a sensible man. What could be better? He was safe and he was dangerous and he was where she wanted him. By July, as the fields were ripening in the summer sun, she enjoyed some very pleasant fantasies about the times they would spend together. By the time he next came to call, her heart was quite in a flutter.

And it was just then that she had another happy thought.

"I shall ask my cousin Osgar to marry us," she told Harold. "He's a monk at Glendalough." And she explained to Harold about Osgar and their childhood marriages, though she left out the incident on the path.

"Does this mean I have a rival?" he asked cheerfully.

"Yes and no," she answered, smiling. "He probably still loves me, but he can't have me."

"He certainly cannot," said Harold firmly.

She sent a message to Osgar the very next day.

⁜

The blow fell two days after that. It fell without warning, from the summer sky.

The northern headland of the Liffey's bay, with its lovely view down the coast to the volcanic hills, was a pleasant place to hold a quiet conference. As well as its Celtic name of Ben Edair, the Hill of Edair, it had acquired a Norse name also nowadays, for the Ostmen called it Howth. Often as not, therefore, the local people mixed the two languages together and referred to it as the Ben of Howth. And it was on a warm day in early July that Harold and Morann Mac Goibnenn met upon the Ben of Howth to discuss the situation.

It was Harold, in his genial way, who summed it up when he remarked, "Well, Morann, I think we may say that the men of Leinster have finally proved that they are insane."

"It cannot be doubted," Morann wryly replied.

"Thirteen years of peace, thirteen years of prosperity, put at risk for what? For nothing."

"And yet," Morann added sadly, "it was inevitable."

"Why?" The Leinster men had never forgiven Brian, of course, for daring to be their master. But why, after years of peace, should they have decided to challenge him now? To Harold it made no sense.

"An insult was offered," said Morann. The rumour was that the King of Leinster and Brian's son had fallen out over a game of chess, and that Brian's son had taunted the king with his humiliation at the battle of Glen Mama more than a decade before. "That could start a war," the Celtic chiefs of Leinster cheerfully agreed. "That would do it." Worse, the Leinster king had left Brian's camp without permission and struck the messenger Brian had sent after him. "And then," Morann added, "there was the woman." Brian's ex-wife, the King of Leinster's sister, longing to see Brian humbled: like a vengeful Celtic goddess, like the Morrigain herself, she was reputed to be stirring up trouble between the parties.

"Why is it," the Norseman burst out, "that the men of Erin allow their women to make so much trouble?"

"It has always been the practice," said Morann. "But you know very well," he added, "that it's your own Ostmen who are behind this as well."

Harold sighed. Was he getting old? He knew the call of the high seas; he'd sailed them half his life. Those adventures were past though. All he wanted was to live on his farm at peace. But around the seaborne settlements of the Norsemen, a restlessness had arisen that year, and now it had come to Dyflin, too.

The trouble had begun in England. More than a dozen years ago, at the very time that Brian Boru had crushed the Dyflin men at Glen Mama, the foolish Saxon king of southern England, known to his people as Ethelred the Unready, had unwisely attacked the Vikings of northern England and their mighty port of York. He had soon paid for his foolishness. A fleet of Viking longships had crossed the sea from Denmark and returned the compliment. For the next decade, the southern English had been forced to pay Danegeld—protection money—if they wanted to live in peace. And now, this year, the King of Denmark and his son Canute had been assembling a great Viking fleet to smash poor Ethelred and take his English kingdom from him. The northern seas were echoing with the news. Every week, ships had come into the port of Dyflin with further reports of this adventure; small wonder, then, if some of the Dyflin men were growing restless. Ten days ago, in the middle of a drinking session by the quay in Dyflin, Harold had heard a sea captain from Denmark call out to a crowd of local men, "In Denmark, we make the King of England pay us. And now we're going to throw him out. But you Dyflin men sit around paying tribute to Brian Boru." There had been some angry murmurs, but nobody had challenged him. The taunt had hit home.

Because of the excitement caused by the English business, every Viking troublemaker and pirate in the northern seas was on the lookout for an adventure.

And now the men of Dyflin were going to get their chance. If the Celtic King of Leinster wanted to revolt, his Viking kinsman the ruler of Dyflin was ready to join him. That, at least, was the word in the port. Had they learned nothing from their defeat at Glen Mama? Perhaps not; or perhaps they had.

"They won't try to fight Brian in the open again," Morann told Harold. "He'll have to take the town, which won't be so easy." He paused thoughtfully. "There may be a further consideration."

"What is that?"

"The north. Ulster hates Brian. The O'Neill King of Tara was forced to resign the High Kingship and swear an oath to Brian, but the O'Neill are still powerful, and just as proud as they ever were. If they could get back at Brian . . ."

"But what about the old king's oath? Would he break it?"

"He would not. He's an honourable man. But he might allow himself to be used."

"How?"

"Suppose," said Morann, "that the men of Leinster attack some of the O'Neill lands. The old King of Tara asks Brian for help. Brian comes. Then Leinster and Dyflin and others too perhaps, combine to destroy Brian, or at least to weaken him. Where does that leave the old King of Tara? Back where he was before."

"You think the whole business is a trap?"

"It may be. I do not know."

"These devious tricks don't always work," the Norseman remarked.

"In any case," Morann pointed out, "there will be fighting and looting all around Dyflin, and your farm is one of the richest."

Harold looked grim. The thought of losing his livestock at his time of life was deeply depressing. "So what should I do?"

"Here is my suggestion," the jeweller replied. "You know that I have sworn a personal oath to Brian. I cannot fight against him, and the King of Dyflin knows that. I can hardly fight against my own people in Dyflin either. But if I were to go to the O'Neill king, who's also bound by oath to Brian, then my obligations are fulfilled. I avoid," he smiled wryly, "embarrassment."

Yes, thought Harold, and if a trap had been set for Brian as his friend suspected, he would still finish up with the winning side. "You are a cautious and a devious man," he said admiringly.

"I think therefore that you should stay on your farmstead," Morann advised. "Do not let your sons join any raiding parties that go to attack Brian or the O'Neill King of Tara; since I have vouched for your loyalty to Brian, you can't do that. Keep your sons with you. The danger to you will be when Brian or his allies come to punish Leinster and Dyflin. And I will tell them that you feel bound by the oath I made on your behalf and that you stand with me. I can't guarantee that this will work, but I think it's your best chance."

It seemed to Harold that his friend was probably right, and he agreed to do as he suggested. There was only one other thing to consider.

"What about Caoilinn?" he asked.

"That is a problem." Morann sighed. "Her estate at Rathmines will undoubtedly be at risk; and I don't know what we can do for her."

"But I could help her," Harold said. "I could marry her at once."

And he set off for Rathmines that afternoon.

✜

It was a pity that Morann's knowledge of Caoilinn had been imperfect. But then it was scarcely his fault that, when he had told his friend Harold about her, he could not see into all the secret places of her heart. As for Harold, during their courtship he had avoided any discussion about her former husband; he had no idea of the handsome widow's passionate fixation with the person of Brian Boru. It was a pity, also, that instead of talking outside in the daylight, where he might have gauged the expression on her face, they had gone into the privacy of the thatched hall in whose penumbra he could hardly tell what she was thinking.

He began by remarking in a cheerful way that there was a good reason why they should marry at once. She had seemed to be interested. Remembering how careful and practical she was, he set out his case in a businesslike way.

"So you see," he concluded, "if we marry now and you came across to Fingal, you could bring at least some of the livestock and keep them with me until the trouble is over. I believe there's a good chance that we could save them. With luck, thanks to Morann, we might even be able to protect the estate at Rathmines, too."

"I see," she said quietly. "And by marrying you, I'd be giving my loyalty to Brian Boru." If there was a new coldness in her tone, he missed it.

"Thanks to Morann," he answered, "I think I can guarantee it." Knowing the misfortunes she had suffered when her husband had opposed Brian before, he imagined she'd be glad for a way of staying out of trouble now. In the shadow, he saw her nod slowly. Then she turned her head and glanced into a dark space near the wall where, on a table, the yellowed old drinking skull of her ancestor Fergus glimmered like a savage Celtic ghost from a former age.

"The men of Leinster are rising." Her voice was faint, almost distant. "My husband was of royal blood. And so am I." She paused.

"Your own Ostmen are rising, too. Does that mean anything to you?"

"I think they are very stupid," he said, frankly. He thought he heard a little intake of breath from her, but he wasn't certain. "Brian Boru is a great war leader." He said it with admiration. "The Leinster men will be crushed, and they deserve to be."

"He is an impostor." She spat the word out with a sudden venom that took him by surprise.

"He has earned respect," he said soothingly. "Even the Church . . ."

"He bought Armagh with gold," she snapped. "And a despicable thing it was, to be bought by such a man." And before he was quite sure what to say next: "What were his people? Nothing. River raiders no better than the pagan savages of Limerick they fought with." She seemed to forget that these insulting expressions about the pagan Norsemen in Limerick might have been applied to Harold's antecedents, too. Perhaps, he thought, she didn't care. "He is a pirate from Munster. Nothing more. He should be killed like a snake," she cried with contempt.

He saw that he had touched upon a raw nerve, and that he must tread gently, though he could not help feeling a little annoyed.

"Whatever may be said of Brian," he said quietly, "we have to consider what to do. We both have our estates to protect. When I think," he added, hoping to please her, "of all that you have done, so splendidly, here at Rathmines . . ."

Had she heard him? Was she listening? It was hard to tell. Her face had become hard and pale. Her green eyes were flashing dangerously. He realised, too late, that a rage was upon her.

"I hate Brian," she cried. "I'll see him dead. I'll see his body cut to pieces, I'll see his head upon a spike for my sons and daughters to spit upon; I'll have their children drink his blood!"

She was splendid in her way, he thought. And he should, he knew, have waited for her rage to subside. But there was, he sensed, a disregard for him in it which displeased the powerful Norseman.

"I shall protect my own farm in Fingal, anyway," he said grimly.

"Do what you like," she said contemptuously, turning her head away from him. "It has nothing to do with me."

He said nothing, but waited for some word of concession. There was none. He rose to go. She remained as she was. He tried to see in her face whether she was angry and hurt, waiting perhaps for some word of comfort from him, or whether she was merely contemptuous.

"I am going," he said at last.

"Go to Munster and your friend Brian," she replied. Her bitter voice fell like death in the shadow. She looked at him now, her green eyes blazing. "I have no need for traitors and pagans to be limping into this house again."

With that, he left.

The events of the weeks that followed fell out very much as Morann had supposed they would. The men of Leinster made a raid into the O'Neill king's territory. Soon after this, the King of Tara came down to punish them and swept across Fingal to the Ben of Howth. Thanks to Morann, however, who came with the old king, Harold and his big farmstead were not touched. Within days, more parties, reinforced by men from Dyflin, struck back. The King of Tara sent messengers south to ask Brian for help. And by mid-August the frightening rumour was spreading through the countryside.

"Brian Boru is coming back."

Osgar glanced quickly around. There was smoke drifting up the valley. He could hear the crackle of flames.

"Brother Osgar." The abbot sounded impatient.

Behind him, the monks were going up the ladder into the round tower—a quite unnecessary precaution, the abbot had told them. But their faces looked white and scared. Perhaps he looked like that, too. He didn't know. He suddenly wondered if the brothers would pull up the ladder as soon as he and the abbot were out of sight. How absurd. He almost smiled at his own foolishness. But the image remained—he and the abbot, running back through the gateway with the Munster men chasing behind, reaching the round tower, looking up, seeing the door closed and the ladder gone, and running round the sheer walls helplessly until the swords of the plunderers raised, and flashed, and . . .

"I am coming, Reverend Father." He hurried towards the gateway, noticing as he did so that all the monastery's servants had miraculously vanished. He and the abbot were alone in the empty precinct.

He had heard that Brian Boru's raiding parties were sweeping the countryside as the Munster king came north to punish the Leinster men, but he had never supposed that they would come here, to disturb the peace of Glendalough.

He caught up with the abbot at the gateway. The track was deserted, but from down the little valley he saw a flash of flame.

"Couldn't we bar the gates?" he suggested.

"No," said the abbot. "It would only annoy them."

"I can't believe that King Brian's men are doing this," he said. "They're not pagans or Ostmen." But a bleak look from the older man silenced him. They both knew from the chronicles of the various houses that more damage had been done to the island's monasteries in princely disputes than had ever been inflicted by the Vikings. He could only hope that Brian's reputation as a protector of the Church would hold good on this occasion.

"Look," the abbot said calmly. A party of about twenty men was coming up the track towards the gateway. They were well armed. In the centre of the group walked a handsome, brown-bearded man. "That's Murchad," the abbot remarked, "one of Brian's sons." He stepped forward, and Osgar kept by his side.

"Welcome Murchad, son of Brian," the abbot called out firmly.

"Did you know it's the monastery's property you're burning down there?"

"I did," said the prince.

"You'll surely not be wishing to do harm to the sanctuary of Saint Kevin?" said the abbot.

"Only if it's in Leinster," came the grim reply, as the party came up to them.

"You know very well that we've nothing to do with this business," said the abbot reasonably. "I have always held your father in the highest regard."

"How many armed men have you?"

"None at all."

"Who is this?" The eyes of the prince rested on Osgar with a level stare.

"This is Brother Osgar. Our finest scholar. A wonderful illuminator."

The eyes looked at him sharply now, but then lowered with, it seemed to Osgar, a hint of respect.

"We'll be needing supplies," he said.

"The gates are open," the abbot replied. "But remember this is a house of God."

They all started to walk through the gateway together. Osgar glanced at the round tower. The ladder had disappeared. The door was shut. At a nod from the prince, his men began to move towards the storehouses.

"You will give my respects to your father," the abbot remarked pleasantly, "unless he means to favour us with a visit himself." He paused a moment for a response, which was not forthcoming. "It's wonderful how he keeps his health," he added.

"Strong as a bull," the prince replied. "I see your monks have run away," he noted. "Or more likely all in the tower with your gold."

"They do not know your pious character as well as I," the abbot answered blandly.

While his men collected a small cartload of cheeses and another two cartloads of grain, the prince went round the monastery with the abbot and Osgar. It was soon obvious that he was looking for valuables. He eyed the golden cross on the altar of the main church, but did not take it, nor any of the silver candlesticks he saw; and he was starting to mutter to himself irritably when at last, making a desultory inspection of the scriptorium, his eye fell on something. "Your work?" he suddenly enquired of Osgar, and Osgar nodded.

It was an illustrated Gospels, like the great book at Kells, though much smaller and less elaborate. Osgar had only started it recently and hoped to complete it, including all the decorated letters and several pages of illumination, before the next Easter. It would be a handsome addition to the minor treasures of the Glendalough monastery.

"I think my father would like to receive it," the prince said, gazing at the work thoughtfully.

"It is really for monastic—" Osgar began.

"As a mark of your loyalty," the prince continued with emphasis. "He'd like it by Christmas."

"Of course," said the abbot smoothly, "it would indeed be a fitting gift to so devout a king. Do you not agree, Brother Osgar?" he went on, giving Osgar a look.

"Indeed," said Osgar sadly.

"So there we are then," said the abbot with a smile like a benediction. "This way." And he led his royal visitor out.

It was after the prince and his men had departed and the monks had started to come down from the tower that a thought had occurred to Osgar. "I was supposed to have been going down to Dyflin to marry my cousin," he remarked to the abbot, "though with all this going on, I suppose it may be delayed."

"Out of the question anyway," the abbot cheerfully replied. "Not until you have finished the book."

"I'll have to send a message to Caoilinn, then," said Osgar.

✣

She received it just as the gates of Dyflin were closing. And if, in the weeks that followed, she was unable to send any message in return, it was because she was trapped inside.

It was September 7, the feast of Saint Ciaran, when King Brian, at the head of an army drawn from Munster and from Connacht, arrived before the walls of Dyflin. No attempt was made by the Dyflin defenders to give battle; instead, with a large contingent of Leinster men to help them, they fortified the ramparts of the town and dared the Munster High King to fight his way in. Brian, ever cautious as he was bold, inspected the defences thoroughly and camped his army in the pleasant orchards all around. "We'll starve them out," he declared. "Meanwhile," the ageing king remarked, "we'll take in their harvest and eat their apples while they watch." And that, as the warm weeks of autumn passed into a pleasant October, is what the besieging army proceeded to do.

In Dyflin, meanwhile, Caoilinn had to confess that life was rather boring. In the first days, she had expected an attack. Then she had at least supposed that the King of Dyflin or the Leinster chiefs would make some attempt to harass the enemy. But nothing happened. Nothing at all. The king and the great men kept mostly to the royal hall and the enclosures round it. The lookouts maintained their lonely vigil on the ramparts. Each day in the open space of the marketplace in the western corner the men practised with their swords and spears, in a desultory fashion; the rest of the time they played dice or drank. So it went, day after day, week after week.

The food supplies held up well. The king had shown foresight and brought a large quantity of cattle and swine within the ramparts before the siege began. The granaries were full. The wells within the town supplied ample water. The place could probably hold out for months. Only one important part of Dyflin's usual diet was missing: there was no fish. Brian's men were watchful. If anyone set foot outside the defences to place nets in the river, by day or night, they were unlikely to return. Nor, of course, could any boats enter or leave the port.

Each day, Caoilinn would stand upon the ramparts. It was strange to see the wood quay and the river empty. On the long wooden bridge a short way upstream, there was a guard post. Looking out towards the estuary, she could see a dozen masts on the north side of the water, where a stream called the Tolka came down to the Liffey. Brian had placed his longships there, with a command post at a fishing hamlet called Clontarf close by. The longships effectively blockaded the port and had already turned away dozens of merchant vessels trying to enter. She had never realised before how entirely the life of the place depended upon the arrival of ships. The unending silence was eerie. She would also go round to the rampart on the southern side and gaze towards her home at Rathmines.

It had been her eldest son, Art, who had insisted that she and the younger children stay with her brother in the greater safety of Dyflin while he remained at Rathmines. A mistake probably. She felt sure she could have saved the livestock from that cursed Brian just as well, probably better than he. She had looked towards Rathmines every day and never seen any sign they were burning the place, but since the Munster men's camp lay across the orchards and fields between them, she didn't know what was happening. What annoyed her particularly was that she had a suspicion that her son had not been entirely sorry to get her safely out of the way. Anyway, here she was, trapped in Dyflin.

Osgar's message, arriving the day she had gone into Dyflin, had come as a surprise. The truth was that with so many other matters on her mind since the summer, she had forgotten all about him.

Since the day she had thrown Harold out of her house, she had not seen the Norseman. She was not sure that her son had been pleased about her break with Harold. The worse for him then. Every day now, as she looked out at the hateful Munster king's camp, her fury was rekindled. She wished she had stayed at Rathmines if only to curse Brian as he passed. What could he have done to her, the snake? Let him kill her if he dared. And for Harold to have supposed she would lend support to such a devil—it made her white with anger to think of it. Even her own son had tried, once, to argue with her about it. "Harold is only doing his best for you," he had dared to suggest.

"Are you forgetting who your own father was?" she snapped back. That had silenced him.

The only mistake she admitted to herself was her choice of parting words to the Norseman. To have called him a pagan and a traitor was no more than the truth. But telling him not to limp into her house again—calling him a cripple—that was wrong because it was beneath her. She would even have wished to apologise, if the circumstances had been different. But, of course, that was impossible. No word had come from Harold since that day; in all likelihood, she thought, she would never see him again.

Morann Mac Goibnenn was still uneasy. As the next months passed, he had ample opportunity to observe the forces ranged against Dyflin, and he was still convinced that his own estimation of the situation had been correct.

When, back in the late summer, he had taken his family north to the O'Neill King of Tara, he had been well received. Tall, handsome, with a flowing white beard, the old king had a noble air about him, though his eyes, it had seemed to Morann, were still watchful. It had not been difficult to secure a protection for the farmstead of his friend Harold; but his plan to stay safely out of trouble with the O'Neill king had not been so successful, since the old monarch had required him to accompany the party that had gone, in August, to summon Brian to his aid. So anxious was he that the craftsman should go, and so fervent were his expressions of loyalty to Brian, that Morann suspected O'Neill was using him to convince the Munster king that the call for help was genuine.

Brian Boru had welcomed him warmly. "Here's a man who keeps

his oath," he had told the chiefs around him. It was ten years since Morann had seen the Munster king in person. He found him still impressive. He was grey; his teeth were long and yellow, though remarkably he had kept most of them. A quick calculation reminded Morann that Brian must be more than seventy years old, but even so, a sense of power exuded from him. "I am slower, Morann," he confessed, "and I get aches and pains that I never had before, but this one," he indicated the young woman who was now his wife, "keeps me younger than my years." This was the fourth wife, by Morann's count. You had to admire the old man.

"You shall accompany me," Brian told him, "on my way up to Dyflin."

It had been early in September, on a bright day when Brian's advancing army, on its way to Dyflin, had just emerged onto the Liffey Plain. Morann had been riding not far from the Munster king, in the vanguard of the army, when to his surprise he saw, coming towards them, the splendidly mounted figure of Harold, quite alone. He had been even more surprised when he had learned why the Norseman was there.

"You want me to ask King Brian to spare Caoilinn's estate? After all she has done?" He had been shocked, the previous summer, by the treatment his friend had received from Caoilinn. At first Harold had only given him a general idea of the interview; but it was his wife who, after a long walk with the Norseman, reported back, "She as good as called him a cripple and threw him out." Freya had been furious. "Whatever her reason," she had declared, "she had no cause to behave so cruelly." And it soon became obvious to Morann that his friend had been seriously hurt. He had even wondered whether to go and see Caoilinn himself. But Harold had been so definite in saying that the affair was over that Morann had concluded that there was nothing to be done.

The Norseman had only shrugged.

"It would be a pity to destroy what she built up."

Morann wondered if perhaps the two of them had made it up

and that Harold had a stake in the business; but the Norseman explained that this was not the case, that Caoilinn and he had never
spoken and that even now, she was behind the ramparts of Dyflin.

"You are a generous man," Morann marvelled.

To his relief, when he explained the matter to King Brian, the
king was not angry but amused. "This is the Ostman who hit my
fellow over the head in Dyflin? And now he wants me to save a lady's
farm?" The king shook his head. "It is more, perhaps, than I should
have done." He smiled. "Men with great hearts are rare, Morann.
And they are to be cherished. In times of danger, keep big-hearted
men about you. Courage brings success." He nodded approvingly.
"What sort of place is this Rathmines and where exactly?" Morann
gave him an account of Caoilinn's estate and its handsome hall. The
situation, he explained, was close by Dyflin, and her herd of cattle
was large. "The cattle will all be hidden in the hills by now," Brian
remarked.

"Where your men will sooner or later find them," Morann
pointed out.

"No doubt." Brian nodded thoughtfully. "Very well," he continued briskly, after a short pause. "I will stay at Rathmines myself. The
estate will supply me and my personal household. The sooner
Dyflin is given to me, the sooner I leave and the more of this lady's
livestock will be left. Those are my terms, Morann. Will you agree
to them?"

"I will," said the craftsman. And he rode ahead with Harold to
prepare the house at Rathmines. Caoilinn's son might not have rel-
ished having Brian Boru in the house, but he could see the merit of
the deal. "You can thank Harold if you have any livestock at the end
of this," Morann told him.

Brian kept Morann with him at Rathmines until nearly the end
of October. During that time, Morann had the chance to see how
the great warlord conducted himself—his ordered camp, his well-
trained men, his patience, and his determination. Then Brian sent
him back to the King of Tara with some messages.

"This game will play out peacefully in the end," he remarked to the craftsman as he was leaving. But Morann was not so sure.

⁂

The message did not come until December—in the form of a single horseman arriving on a cold, grey day at the gates of Glendalough. Over his shoulder was slung an empty leather satchel which he laid on the abbot's table as he announced: "I have come for the book."

The prince's book: the present for Brian Boru. Christmas was approaching. It was due.

"Unfortunately," said the abbot with some embarrassment, "it is not quite ready. But when it is," he added, "it will be very fine."

"Show it to me," said the messenger.

Osgar had been working hard. By the end of October he had prepared the vellum, laid out the book, and copied the entire Gospels in a perfect hand. The decorated capital letters came next. He had left spaces for each of these and in the first ten days of November he planned a schema: while each letter would be treated differently, certain details—some purely geometric, others in the form of serpents, birds, or extended human figures—would subtly repeat themselves or balance each other in an exotic counterpoint, thus producing a hidden, echoing unity to the whole. He also intended to add little decorations to the text, as the spirit moved him. Finally, there would be four, full-page illuminations. He had rough sketches for three of these pages, and knew how they would come together; but the fourth was more ambitious, and about this he was more uncertain.

By mid-November Osgar had made a good start on the drawing and painting of the capitals, with more than a dozen completed by the end of the month, and when the abbot had inspected the work he had pronounced himself pleased; but the abbot had nonetheless made one complaint.

"Every year, Brother Osgar, you seem to take longer to complete each illustration. Surely with so much practice, you should be getting more proficient, not less."

"The more I do," Osgar had answered sadly, "the harder it gets."

"Oh," said the abbot, irritably. It was at times like this that he found the perfectionist calligrapher tiresome and even rather contemptible. And Osgar had sighed because he knew that he could not explain such things to any man, however intelligent, who had not practised the druidic art of design himself.

How could he explain that the patterns the abbot saw were not the result of simple choice or chance, but that often as not, as he worked upon them, the strands of colour would mysteriously refuse to conform to the pattern he had first envisaged. And that only after days of obdurate struggle would he discover within them a new, deeper, dynamic pattern, far more subtle and powerful than anything his own poor brain would have been able to design. During these frustrating days, he would be like a man lost in a maze, or unable to move as though caught in a magic spider's web, trapped within the very lines he drew. And as he came through, each discovery revealed to him new rules, layer upon layer, so that like a ball of twine that is slowly growing, the artefact he was making, simple though it seemed, had a hidden weight. Through this exhausting process, from these unending tensions, were the elegant patterns of his art constructed.

And of nothing was this more true than the fourth of the full-page illuminations. He knew what he wanted. He wanted, somehow, to echo that strange spiral which the old monk had copied from the stone and shown him up in Kells. He had only seen it once, but the strange image had haunted him ever since. Of course he had seen trefoils and spirals in many books; but this particular image was haunting precisely because it was subtly different. Yet how could you capture those swirling lines when their mysterious power came from the very fact that they were wandering, indeterminate, belonging to some unknown but profoundly necessary chaos? Every sketch he made was a failure, and common sense, especially when he was labouring under such lack of time, should have told him to give it up. Something conventional would do. But he couldn't. Each day he puzzled over it, while he continued with the rest.

Fortunately, when the prince's messenger was shown the partly completed book, it was already clear that it would be handsome.

"I will tell the prince it is in hand," the messenger said, "but he won't be pleased it isn't finished."

"You will have to work faster, Brother Osgar," said the abbot.

⁙

The siege of Dyflin was raised at Christmas. Brian and his army retired southwards to Munster. No attack upon the ramparts had been made by the besiegers and no one had come out to fight them. When the men of Dyflin saw the Munster king depart, they congratulated themselves.

In early January, after Brian had departed, Morann decided to leave the O'Neill King of Tara for a while and pay a visit to Dyflin. He was not surprised to receive a summons to attend the Dyflin king and his council in the royal hall. They welcomed him cheerfully. "We all know you were under oath to Brian," the king reassured him. They had numerous questions about the Munster king and the disposition of his forces, which Morann answered. But the craftsman was surprised by the air of truculence he detected in some of the younger council members.

"You might as well have stayed with us, Morann," said one. "Brian came to punish us, but he's had to give up."

"He never gives up," Morann replied. "He'll be back. And you had better prepare yourselves."

"What a gloomy fellow he is," the king answered with a smile, and the others had laughed. But when Morann had happened to meet him in the street the next day, the king had taken his arm and told him quietly, "You're right about Brian, of course. But when he comes back, we'll have a different reception ready for him." He gave Morann a friendly nod. "Be warned."

It was two days after this conversation that Morann went out to Fingal to visit his friend Harold. It was four months since he had seen him.

He was pleased, on his arrival at Harold's farmstead, to find the Norseman looking fit and cheerful. They spent a pleasant hour looking over the farmstead, which was in excellent order, in the company of his children. Only when they were alone did Morann broach the subject of Caoilinn.

"I hear that Rathmines was left with more than half its livestock."

"I heard it, too. And that other farmsteads there were stripped. I am grateful to you, Morann."

"You have not been over there?"

"I have not." It was said firmly, and grimly.

"Have you received any word of thanks? I told her son, at the time it happened, that it was you who should be thanked."

"I have heard nothing. But I do not expect to. The thing was done. That is all." It was clear to Morann that his friend had no further wish to discuss the subject, and he did not bring it up again during his stay that day. When he left the following morning, however, he had come to a private decision. It was time he went to see Caoilinn himself.

She was not alone, the next day, when he arrived at Rathmines. Her son was with her. Was it for that reason, he wondered, that she was guarded?

It was certainly clear that she had no wish to see him. When, sitting in the big hall, he politely mentioned that he was glad to hear her livestock had survived the trouble at Dyflin, her son gave a nod of acknowledgement and murmured, "Thanks to you." But Caoilinn stared straight ahead, as though she had not heard him.

"I was out in Fingal recently," he said. His words fell like a stone on the ground. There was silence. He thought that she was about to move away, and he was ready to follow her if she did; but then an interesting thing happened. Her son abruptly got up and went outside, so that he was left alone in the hall with Caoilinn. Without breaking all the rules of hospitality, she could not very well do the same and desert him. He saw her frown with vexation. He didn't care.

"I was at Harold's farmstead," he said calmly. Then he waited, practically forcing her to respond.

But whatever response he might have expected, it was not the one he got. For after a prolonged silence, in a voice that was quiet with anger, she remarked, "I am surprised that, in the circumstances, you would mention his name in this house."

"In the circumstances?" He stared in disbelief. "Didn't he save you from ruin? Have you no word of thanks for his kindness?"

"Kindness?" She looked at him with scorn and also, it seemed, incomprehension. "His vengeance, you mean." Though Morann's face still registered bewilderment, she did not appear to see it. Indeed, she seemed to be talking to herself rather than to him as she went on. "To have Brian Boru, the filthy devil, living in my own husband's house. Eating his cattle. Waited upon by his own children. Wasn't that a fine revenge for my calling him a cripple?" She shook her head slowly.

And for the first time, Morann realised the extent of her pain and sadness.

"It was not Harold," he said simply. "He never had any dealings with Brian. He is under the protection of the O'Neill king, you know. But he asked me to persuade Brian not to destroy your husband's estate. So it was I that caused Brian to come here." He shrugged. "It was the only way." He saw Caoilinn make a gesture of impatience. "You must understand," he went on more urgently, even taking her by the arm, "that he only tried to save you and your family from ruin. He admired what you had done. He told me so. You do him an injustice."

She was very pale. She said not a word. He couldn't tell whether he had got through to her or not.

"You owe him," he quietly suggested, "at least some thanks, and an apology."

"Apology?" Her voice was rising sharply.

He decided to go on the offensive.

"Dear God, woman, are you so blinded by your hatred of Brian that you cannot see the generosity of spirit of the man from Fingal? He ignores your insults and tries to save your children from ruin, and still you cannot see anything but a malice that is of your own imagining entirely. It's a fool you are," he burst out. "You could have had the man for a husband." He paused. Then in a lower voice and, apparently with satisfaction, he added, "Well, you are too late for that, anyway, now that there are others."

"Others?"

"Of course." He shrugged. "What would you expect?" Then, suddenly and unceremoniously, he left.

⁂

It was February when the news began to arrive at the port. Remembering the King of Dyflin's warning, Morann had been expecting it.

The Vikings were coming. From the Isle of Man, just over the horizon, its Viking ruler was bringing a war fleet. From the faraway Orkney Islands in the north, another great sailing was coming. Warrior chiefs, merchant adventurers, Nordic pirates—they were all making ready. It would be another great Viking adventure. Who knew, if they defeated old Brian Boru, there might even be a chance to take over the whole island, just as Canute and his Danes were doing in England. At the least, there would be valuable pickings.

In Dyflin, by the middle of the month there were all kinds of rumour. It was said that the King of Leinster's sister, the turbulent former wife of Brian, had even offered to marry again if it would help the cause. "They say she's been promised to the Isle of Man king and to the Orkney king as well," a chief close to the family told Morann.

"She can hardly marry them both," Morann remarked.

"Don't count on it," answered the other.

As yet, there was no word from King Brian in Munster. Was the old warrior aware of the preparations in the northern seas? Undoubtedly. Would he hesitate to return against such odds, as some in Dyflin still supposed? Morann did not think so. He had no doubt that the cautious conqueror would, as usual, take his own time. At the end of February, a ship arrived from the Orkneys with definite news.

"The fleet will be here before Easter."

✢

It had been in early January, as he had been despairing of ever finishing his work in time, that Osgar had received news of a very different kind, from Caoilinn. She apologised for failing to send a message before, but explained that she had been trapped in Dyflin throughout the siege. A little guiltily perhaps, she sent him tender expressions of affection. And she let him know that, for reasons she did not explain, she would not be marrying again, after all. "But come to see me, Osgar," she added. "Come to see me soon."

What could he feel, at such a message? He hardly knew. At first he received it calmly enough. He realised that it had been some time since he had even given her a thought. During that day, he had gone quietly about his business as usual; only at the end of the afternoon, as he put his pens away and his fingers encountered the little wedding ring that still resided in the bag, did he suddenly experience a sharp stab of recollected emotion at the thought of her.

She came to him that night in his dreams and again when he awoke in the dark January dawn, bringing with her a strange sense of warmth, a tingling of excitement—he hardly remembered when he had last felt this way. Nor did the sensation depart, but remained with him throughout the day.

What did it mean? That evening Osgar reflected carefully. When he had returned to Glendalough after his uncle's death, he had suffered from melancholy moods for some time. His inability to go back to Dyflin and his abiding sense of failure over Caoilinn had been hard to bear. With the news of her forthcoming marriage, however, a door in his mind seemed to have closed. She was departing once again into the arms of another. He was still married to Glendalough. He told himself to think of her no more, and was at peace. But now, with the knowledge that she was not, after all, to marry, it was as if, in some strange and unexpected way, she belonged to him again. They could renew their friendship. She could come to Glendalough to see him. He could visit Dyflin. He would be free to indulge in a relationship as passionate as it was safe. In this way, whether through the agency of good or evil powers, the sorrow of Brother Osgar was converted to a new kind of joy.

He noticed a difference the very next morning. Was there more sun in the scriptorium that day, or had the world grown brighter? When he sat down at his desk, the vellum before him seemed to have acquired a new and magical significance. Instead of the usual, painful struggle with an intricate pattern, the shapes and colours under his pen burst into life like the bright new plants of spring. And more extraordinary still, as the day progressed, these sensations grew stronger, more urgent, more intense; so utterly absorbed was he that by the late afternoon he did not even notice that the light outside was fading as he worked, with a growing fever of excitement, immersed in the rich and radiant world he had entered. It was only when he felt a persistent tap on his shoulder that he at last broke off with a start, like a man awoken from a dream, to find that they had already lit three candles round his desk and that he had completed not one but five new illustrations. They almost had to drag him from the page.

And so it had continued day after day as, lost in his art, in such a fever that he often forgot to eat, pale, absentminded, outwardly melancholy yet inwardly ecstatic, the middle-aged monk—inspired by Caoilinn if not by God—now in the abstract patterns, verdant plants, in all the brightly coloured richness of sensual creation, for the first time discovered and expressed in his work the true meaning of passion.

Late in February, he began to trace the great, triple spiral of the last full page, and stretching it out and bending it to his will, found to his astonishment that he had formed it into a magnificent, dynamic Chi-Rho, unlike any that he had seen before, that echoed on the page like a solid fragment of eternity itself.

Two weeks before Easter, his little masterpiece was completed.

⁘

She was not expecting him; and that was what he intended. Harold was counting on an element of surprise. Though the real question was, should he be going there at all?

"Stay away. She's more trouble than she's worth." That had been Morann's advice. Twice since he had gone to see Caoilinn, the craftsman had let her son know that Harold would be visiting him on a particular day in Dyflin. It would have been easy enough for Caoilinn to come in from Rathmines and encounter the Norseman, seemingly by chance, on the quay or in the marketplace. Indeed, her son, who was quite ready for his mother to move out of the house, was anxious to help. But she had neither come, nor sent any word at all to Harold. And though, originally, Morann had hoped to see a reconciliation of the lovers, he had now changed his mind. "Find another wife, Harold," he counselled. "You can do better."

So why was he going? In the months since her rejection of him, the Norseman had often reflected upon the subject of Caoilinn. She had hurt him, of course. Indeed there had been times when, thinking about her contemptuous treatment of him, he had clenched his strong hands in rage and sworn to himself that he would never set eyes on her again. But in his generous way, he had still tried to understand what might have caused her to behave in such a manner; and after learning more of the details about her husband from other people familiar with the household, he had formed a shrewd idea of what might be in Caoilinn's mind. He made allowances; he was ready to forgive. But he was also mindful of the inner contempt for his own feelings that her behaviour had shown. Morann had let him know of his visit to Rathmines. As he thought about the matter in the early months of that year, Harold had agreed with his friend that he should wait for her to make a move, but she never did.

When Morann had warned Caoilinn that she had rivals, he was not entirely bluffing. There were two women who had made it clear to Harold that, if he showed an interest in them, that interest would be returned. One of these, Harold was sure, had a genuine affection for him; the other, though he thought her a little foolish, was certainly in love with him. Did Caoilinn love him? Not really. He had no delusions. Not yet, anyway. But he would make either of the other two women happy and his life with them would be pleasant and easy.

And perhaps, in the end, that was the trouble. Whatever their attractions, the two women offered a life that was just a little too easy. Caoilinn, for all her faults, was simply more interesting. Even in middle age, it seemed, Harold the Norwegian was still looking for the excitement of a challenge.

So having considered the whole business very carefully, on the last day of March, he rode out once again towards Rathmines. Had he decided exactly what to say? Depending on how he found her, yes. But just as he had in his encounter with her before, he knew he would rely on his instincts. And he was still half curious about what he would do as the gates of the rath came in sight.

If he had meant to surprise her, he succeeded. For as he rode through the gateway, she was in the act of milking a cow. As she turned and rose from the stool on which she had been sitting, her dark hair fell across her face; with a single gesture she swept it back;

her two hands smoothed down her dress, and her large eyes stared at him as at an intruder. For a moment he thought she might be going to say something insulting, but instead she remarked, "Harold, son of Olaf. We did not know you were coming." Then she remained dangerously silent.

"It's a fine day. I thought I'd ride this way," he replied blandly, gazing down from his horse.

Then, without dismounting but making casual remarks as if he might move on at any moment, he began to talk. He spoke quietly, about his farmstead, events in Dyflin, a cargo of wine that had just arrived at the port. He smiled now and then, in his friendly, easy way. And never once did he allude to the fact, by word or look, that she had insulted him or that she owed him an apology. Not a word. Nothing. He was magnificent. She could not deny it.

But what had really shaken her was something else entirely. It was the one thing, in the turbulent months since their separation, that she had forgotten. She had forgotten he was so attractive. The moment he had ridden through the gateway and she had turned to see him, it had hit her almost like a blow. The splendid horse with its gleaming harness; Harold's figure, powerful, athletic, almost boyish; his red beard and his eyes, those bright blue eyes: for a moment, as she smoothed down her dress to deflect his attention, she had found she could hardly breathe; she had fought down a flush and stared at him with a furious coldness so that he should not know her heart was beating faster, far faster than she wished. Nor was she entirely able to subdue these sensations which, like little waves, continued to form and break all the time he was talking.

It was then that Harold, gazing at her calmly, made his move.

"There was talk last year," he observed with perfect coolness, "that you and I would get married."

Caoilinn looked down and said nothing.

"Time passes," he remarked. "A man moves on." He paused just long enough to let this message sink in. "But I thought I would come by." He smiled charmingly. "I should not wish to lose you through carelessness. After all," he added graciously, "I might do as well, but I could never do better."

She had to acknowledge the compliment. What else could she do? She bowed her head.

"There were difficulties," she managed to say. She did not apologise.

"Perhaps they can be overcome," he suggested.

"Several difficulties." For just a moment she nearly brought up the question of religion, but then thought better of the idea.

"It is for you to decide, Caoilinn." He looked at her quite sternly. "My offer is still open. I make the offer gladly. But whatever your decision, I will ask you to make it by Easter."

"Am I understanding you right," she asked, with a trace of irritation, "that the offer will no longer be open after Easter?"

"It will not," he said, and wheeled his horse away before she could say another word.

"Dear God," she murmured, as he went out of sight, "the cheek of the man."

⁘

Morann was not surprised when, ten days into April, no word had come from Caoilinn.

"If she does come," Harold told him, "she'll wait until the last moment." He smiled. "And even then, you may be sure there will be conditions."

"She won't come at all," said Morann, not because he knew but because he did not want his friend to be disappointed.

A few days later, however, events arose which made even Harold's marriage a secondary consideration. A longship arrived at the port with news that the northern fleets were setting out and would soon appear. And two days later came a horseman from the south who announced: "Brian Boru is on his way."

When Morann and his family arrived at Harold's farmstead the next day, the craftsman was very firm. The Norseman wanted to stay and protect his farmstead as he had done before.

"But this time it will be different," Morann warned him. There would be all kinds of men—marauders, pirates, men who killed for pleasure—in the Viking longships. "Nothing can protect your farm if they should come that way." He was going back to join the O'Neill king, as he had done before. "And you and your sons must come with me," he told him.

Still Harold made excuses and prevaricated. Finally he objected: "What if Caoilinn should come?" But Morann had anticipated the question.

"She moved into Dyflin yesterday," he told his friend bluntly. "No doubt she'll stay there, as she did before. But you can leave word for her to follow if she comes." Eventually he persuaded the Norseman of the wisdom of leaving. The farmstead's large cattle herd was split into four parts; and three of them, each under a cowman, were driven away to different places where they might not be found. There was nothing for Harold to do then but hide his valuables and prepare to set out, accompanied by his sons, on the journey north-west. Four days later, they reached the O'Neill King of Tara.

The King of Tara's camp was impressive. For his renewed campaign, he had collected a formidable army from some of the finest fighting tribes in the north. When Morann brought Harold and his sons to him, he welcomed them and told them: "When the fighting begins, you shall stand by me"—an arrangement, Morann noted, which honoured his friends as well as practically guaranteeing their safety.

Morann soon made himself familiar with the military situation. He estimated that there were nearly a thousand fighting men in the camp. It was rare in the Celtic island to see a fighting force much larger; Brian Boru had not brought more than that to the siege of Dyflin. Many were drawn from the most loyal base of the king's power, the central kingdom of Meath; but others were still arriving from farther away. The quality of the men was good. Morann watched, impressed, as they underwent their practice in hand-to-hand combat. The old king was planning to remain at his camp until he heard that Brian was in the Liffey Plain; then he would move south to join him, coming down by way of Tara.

But what would he do when he got there? Everything Morann could see—the daily arms practice, the king's councils of war—all confirmed that he meant to keep his word to Brian, and to fight. Might there be a more devious plan? As Morann looked at the King of Tara's cragged, shrewd old face, he found it impossible to decipher his intentions; perhaps, the craftsman concluded, the truth lay in a conversation he had when the king summoned him the next day. The old monarch seemed in a reflective mood, though Morann had little doubt he had calculated everything he wished to say. They talked quite extensively, of the men he had brought, of the expected Munster army, and of the forces ranged against them.

"You know, Morann, that Brian has many enemies. He wants to rule as High King with more authority than the O'Neill ever had; for we never really subdued the whole island. Those Leinster kings especially resent him. They're almost as proud as we are. And they're not the only ones." He gave Morann a quick, sharp glance. "But if you think about it, Morann," he went on quietly, "you'll see that the truth of this whole business is that we can't afford to let him lose."

"You fear the Ostmen."

"Of course. They have seen Canute and his Danes take over England. If Brian Boru loses this battle now, we shall have Ostmen from all over the northern seas descending upon us. We may not be able to withstand them."

"Yet it's Leinster which has begun this business."

"That is why they are so foolish. Firstly, they are acting out of pride. Secondly, they suppose that, because they have close family ties to the Ostman King of Dyflin, that they will be honoured by any Ostmen who invade. But if all the fleets of the north were to descend, Leinster would be treated just the same as the rest of us. Indeed, being close to Dyflin, they will be the first to be taken over. Then they will be under the rule of an Ostman king instead of Brian." He smiled sadly. "If that occurs, Morann, then it will be our turn to withdraw from the lordship of the land. Like the Tuatha De Danaan, we shall all go under the hill." He nodded thoughtfully. "So you see, Morann, whatever happens, Brian Boru must win."

The messenger from King Brian arrived at the camp the following morning, with a request that the King of Tara should advance forthwith to join the Munster army on the northern bank of the Liffey. He also carried a message for Morann. The silversmith was to join Brian at his camp as quickly as possible; and if his friend the Norseman was with him, King Brian wanted Morann to bring him, too. The first part of the summons came as no surprise to Morann, but he had not expected the one for Harold. Remembering King Brian's amused admiration for the Norseman when he had come to save the estate at Rathmines, however, he thought he understood. What was it Brian had said to him? "In times of danger, keep big-hearted men around you. Courage brings success." Before this greatest of all his battles, the ageing commander was reaching out for loyal and valiant men.

Leaving his family and Harold's sons with the O'Neill king, he and the Norseman set out at once.

They rode easily and made good time. They did not speak much, each no doubt occupied with his own thoughts. Morann was glad to think that he could give Brian a detailed account of the King of Tara's forces and their conversation, which he had no doubt the Munster king would ask for. Harold, as far as Morann could see, was rather excited by the prospect ahead. His normally ruddy face looked a little pale and his blue eyes were gleaming.

The road led south towards Tara; but at a certain point, a track turned away to the left, towards the south-east.

"If we go that way, the road is less good, but it leads more directly to Dyflin," Morann suggested. "Which way would you rather take?"

"The direct route," said Harold, easily; so that is what they did. And for several hours more, they rode towards the River Boyne.

Why had he chosen to go that way? From some instinct—he scarcely knew what it was—he had given Harold the decision. But by telling him, correctly, that this was the more direct way, he had known it was this one that the Norseman would choose. And why had he wanted to go that way? Morann did not know. Perhaps because it was the way his father had brought him when he had come to Dyflin for the first time, all those years ago. But whatever the reason, he felt a strange, inner compulsion to return to that path again.

It was late afternoon when the two men approached the great green mounds above the Boyne. The place was silent, not a living soul to be seen; the sky was dull and grey, and in the waters below, the swans had acquired a pale luminosity, like gleaming specks upon the iron waters.

"This," Morann said with a smile, "is where the Tuatha De Danaan live." He pointed to the damaged roof of the biggest mound. "Your people tried to get in there once. Did you know that?"

The Norseman shook his head. "This place is grim," he said.

They walked around the tombs, staring at the carved stones and the fallen quartz. Then Harold said he wanted to walk along the ridge a little way, but Morann chose to remain, in front of the entrance of the largest of the tombs, where the stone with the three great spirals stood. From somewhere came the cry of a bird, but he heard no other sound. The light was imperceptibly fading.

Grim. Was the place grim? Perhaps. He was not sure. He stared over the river. He remembered his father. And he had been waiting like that for some time, he supposed, when it seemed to him that he sensed something moving up the slope from the river towards him.

The strangest thing was that he felt neither fear nor surprise. He knew, as did all men upon the island, of the many forms the spirits may take. There were the ancient gods who might appear as birds or fish, or deer or lovely women; there were fairy folk and dwarfs; before the death of a great man, you might hear a terrible wailing—this was the keening of the spirit they call a banshee. But what he sensed, though he suspected at once that it might be a spirit, was none of those things. It had no form at all; it was not even a floating mist. Yet he was nevertheless aware of it moving up the slope towards him, as though it came with a definite intention.

The invisible shadow passed close beside him and Morann felt a curious sensation of coldness before it drew away towards the mound and, passing by the stone carved with spirals, entered it.

When the spirit had gone, Morann remained perfectly still, staring over the Boyne; and though he could not say how, he knew with certainty what was to come to pass. He was not afraid, but he knew. And when some time later Harold returned, he told him, "You must not come with me. Go to your farm in Fingal."

"But what about Brian Boru?"

"It is me he wants. I will make an excuse for you."

"You told me it was dangerous to remain at the farm."

"I know. But I have a presentiment."

The next morning, the two men rode southwards together, but as they came to the northern edge of the Plain of Bird Flocks, Morann pulled up his horse.

"This is where we part, but before we do, Harold, I want you to make me a promise. Stay on your farmstead. You cannot go back to the O'Neill king after Brian summoned you; in any case, your sons will be safe enough with him, I think. But you must promise not to follow me into this battle. Will you do that?"

"I do not like to leave you," said Harold. "But you have done so much for me that I don't like to refuse you either. Are you sure this is what you want?"

"It is the one thing I ask," said Morann.

So then Harold departed to his farmstead while Morann turned westwards to seek King Brian to whom he had just denied the company of a big-hearted man.

❖

"The monk is to bring the book himself. King Brian was very definite," said the messenger. "Is it ready?"

"It is," said the abbot. "Ten days ago. This is an honour for you, Brother Osgar. I expect the king wishes to thank you in person."

"We're going down to Dyflin, where the fighting will be?" asked Brother Osgar.

"We are," said the messenger.

Osgar understood the abbot's need to oblige King Brian. Though the Leinster king was preparing for a conflict he thought he could win, not everyone was so certain of the outcome. Below the Wicklow Mountains, down the coastal plain, the chiefs in the south of Leinster had failed to join their king and the Leinster men. The unprotected abbey at Glendalough, though it was one of the noblest in the Leinster kingdom, could hardly be expected to insult King Brian by refusing what was, in any case, owed.

It was the Friday before Easter week, in the middle of April, when the messenger arrived. On Saturday morning at dawn, the messenger and Osgar rode out of the great gateway of Glendalough, and headed northwards into the long pass that would take them over the mountains towards Dyflin. By the time they reached the open high places, the sky was clear and blue. It seemed it would be a fine day.

With the damp breeze catching his face, Osgar was suddenly reminded of the day he had crossed these mountains, so many years ago, when he went to tell Caoilinn he was joining the monastery. For a few moments he felt exactly as if he were that same young man again; the sharpness of the sensation surprised him. He thought of Caoilinn now, and his heart was racing. Would he see her?

Yet there was danger down there on the Liffey Plain: he was approaching a battlefield. Would he be able to deliver the book to Brian and withdraw to safety, or would he be caught up in it?

Tomorrow was Palm Sunday: the day of Jesus's entry into Jerusalem. A day of triumph. He had ridden into the Holy City on a donkey; they had strewn palms in His way to signal their respect, sung His praises, called Him the Messiah. And five days later, they had crucified Him. Was that, Osgar wondered as they crossed the mountains, to be his own fate? Was he about to descend from this deserted place, have his praises sung on account of his little masterpiece, and then perhaps fall to a Viking axe? There would be irony in that. Or, it even occurred to him, might he happen to encounter Caoilinn and meet his end heroically after all, saving her from a burning Dyflin or a Viking marauding party? A surge of warmth accompanied this vision. He had failed in such a business once before; but that was long ago. He was another man.

And indeed, in a way, Osgar was a changed man. The little book of Gospels was a vivid masterpiece. There was no doubt that King Brian would be delighted with it. The passion for Caoilinn that had produced it, that had driven his work for three months, had left Osgar in a state of elation. He had a compulsive desire to do more, a sense of urgency he had never experienced before. He needed to live in order to create. Yet at the same time, he also knew with a tiny warmth of certainty that if he were suddenly taken from this mortal life, he had now left behind a bright little jewel that, in the eye of God also, he hoped, seemed to make his uneventful life worthwhile.

They passed over the high mountain gap, taking the way that led north-west. By that nightfall they would have descended the slopes, skirted the Liffey's broad basin, and crossed the river by a small monastic bridge a dozen miles upstream from Dyflin. The day was pleasant, the April sky remaining unusually clear. It was past mid-afternoon when they emerged on the northern slopes and saw below them and to the east the wide magnificence of the Liffey estuary and the huge sweep of the bay laid out before them.

Then Osgar saw the Viking sails.

It was the whole Viking fleet, strung out from the northern curve of the bay, past the Ben of Howth, and away into the open sea where, finally, they became indistinct in the sea mist. Square sails: he could see that those nearest were brightly coloured. How many sails? He counted three dozen; no doubt there were more. How many fighting men? A thousand? More? He had never seen such a sight before. He stared in horror, and felt a terrible, cold fear.

⁘

There were no palm trees in Dyflin, so on Palm Sunday Christians went to church with all kinds of greenery in their hands. Caoilinn carried a sheaf of long, sweet grasses.

It was a strange sight that morning to see the stream of worshippers, Leinster and Dyflin people, Celtic Gaedhil and Nordic Gaill, carrying their greenery through the wooden streets, watched by the men from the longships. Some of the warriors from the northern seas were good Christians, she noted with approval, for they joined the procession. But most seemed to be either heathen or indifferent, and they stood by the fences or in the gateways, leaning on their axes, watching, talking amongst themselves or drinking ale.

It had been a remarkable sight when their longships had started coming up the Liffey the evening before. The two fleets had arrived together. The Earl of Orkney had brought with him Vikings from all over the north, from the Orkneys and the Isle of Skye, from the coast of Argyll and the Mull of Kintyre. From the Isle of Man, however, the scar-faced warlord Brodar had brought a fearsome collection, drawn, it seemed, from the ports of many lands. Fair-haired Norsemen, burly Danes; some were light coloured, some dark and swarthy. Many, she judged, were nothing more than pirates. Yet these were the allies that her Leinster king had called upon to strike at Brian Boru. She could have wished he had found other sorts of men.

As she made her way to church, she wondered what to do. Was

she making a terrible mistake? For a start, it was now clear that her move back to her brother's in Dyflin had been premature, and probably pointless. King Brian would not be troubling Rathmines this time, because he was coming up the other side of the Liffey, far away. Her eldest son had already gone back to the rath to watch over the livestock that morning. But the real question was, why hadn't she gone to Harold? Her son had been unequivocal.

"For God's sake go," he had told her. "You've no complaint against Harold. The man has nothing to do with Brian Boru. You've honoured my father's memory longer than you need. Haven't you done enough for Leinster?"

She didn't even know for certain where Harold was now. Was he at his farmstead or with the O'Neill king, perhaps? His offer had been clear. She must come to him by Easter, but not afterwards. If the man was in any way reasonable, she thought, a few days or weeks wouldn't matter, but there was something in the Norseman's nature that indicated he would not budge. Irritating though it was, she rather admired him for it. If she came to him after Easter, his mind would have swung closed, like a heavy wooden gate. The offer would be gone. She knew it.

Even if she could accept what he had done before, even if she could accept that she was in the wrong, Caoilinn didn't like being told what to do. By making the offer in the way he had, he was asserting his authority, and she couldn't see how to get out of it. Her pride still made it difficult for her to let him win and she meant to put off the decision as long as possible until she could think of a way of getting even.

She was also a little nervous. So far, no one had troubled Harold about his equivocal position. People knew that Morann had secured protection for his friend, just as, in turn, Harold had mitigated the damage to her own estate. But now there was going to be a great battle; whoever won would suffer terrible casualties. If she were seen leaving Dyflin now to go across to a man under Brian's protection, and the men of Dyflin were to succeed in smashing Brian, they might not take kindly to her desertion. There could be ugly reprisals. Alternatively, of course, if she stayed where she was and Brian won, she could be trapped in a burning Dyflin. But the worst aspect of the business lay in the bluntly cynical proposition her son had put to her just before he departed.

"As a family, you know, it would be best if we had a foot in each camp, so that we could help each other whatever the outcome. I'm in the Leinster camp, of course, but if you were with Harold . . ."

"You mean," she said bitterly, "you'd want *me* in Brian Boru's camp?"

"Well, not exactly. Only with Harold being Morann's friend, and Morann . . ." He shrugged. "It doesn't matter, Mother, since I know you won't."

Curse them all, she thought. Curse them. For once in her life, Caoilinn truly didn't know what to do.

The church service for Palm Sunday had already started as the solitary figure made his way along the wood quay towards the boat. He walked with a slight stoop. He was alone. His companions in the longship were elsewhere. They were, in any case, only companions for this voyage; after this, he might see some of them again, or he might not. It was all the same to him. He had no use for friends. At this moment, his face wore a twisted smile.

He had lived in many places. His three sons had been raised in Waterford; but he had fallen out with them some years ago and scarcely seen them since. They were fully grown. He owed them nothing. One thing, however, he had given them, when they were still children.

He had been trading at the small harbour on the River Boyne. There had been a woman there; he had stayed awhile. And because he was swarthy, the Celtic-speaking people at the port had called him Dubh Gall—the dark stranger. Even the women had called him that: "My Dubh Gall." It had amused his shipmates. They had car-

ried the name back with them. And before long, even in the Viking
port of Waterford, his children were known as the family of Dubh
Gall. The name had ceased to amuse him now. His companions in
the longship called him by his real name: Sigurd.

For the last few years he had led a wandering life, sometimes
working as a mercenary. He had arrived in Dyflin the night before
with Brodar, who had been hired by the Leinster and Dyflin kings.
And the reason why he was smiling was not because the pay and the
prospects for looting were excellent, but because he had just made a
pleasing discovery.

Harold the Norwegian, the red-haired crippled boy, was still
living.

He had never forgotten about Harold; from time to time down
the years, the lame Norwegian had come into his mind. But there
had been so many other matters to attend to, and fate had not
brought them close again. The nature of his feelings had also
changed. As a boy, he had felt a burning need to avenge his family's
name: the Norwegian had to be killed. As a man, this old desire had
become spiced with cruelty. He took pleasure in contemplating the
pain and humiliation he could inflict upon the young farmer. In recent years, it had just become a piece of unfinished business, a debt
unpaid.

But now he had found himself on the way to Dyflin to take part
in a battle. The circumstances were perfect. Naturally, during the
voyage he had thought about Harold. But it had been when he first
stepped on to the wood quay, where they had met before, that all
the sensations of his boyhood had suddenly come back at him with
a rush. This was destiny, he concluded. The Norwegian must die.
When that was duly accomplished, he thought, he would go back
to Waterford and seek out his sons, who had never known about
this business, and tell them what he had done and why and, perhaps, even be reconciled with them.

It had not taken long to find out about Harold in Dyflin. At
first, when he had asked about a lame farmer, he had received some

blank looks; but then a merchant in the Fish Shambles had smiled in recognition.

"Do you mean the Norwegian? The man with the big farmstead out in Fingal? There's a rich fellow. An important man. Is he a friend of yours?"

Though he had traded, and fought, and stolen all over the northern seas, Sigurd had never become rich.

"He was, many years ago," he had answered with a smile.

The merchant had soon told him all he needed to know: that Harold was a widower, the size of his family, the location of the big farmstead.

"He has powerful friends," the merchant said. "The O'Neill king is his protector."

"You mean he might be fighting against us?"

"I do not think he would do that. Unless he was obliged to. Possibly his sons might."

If Harold and his sons were in the battle on the other side, so much the better. He would make his way towards them. If not, then during or after the battle, he would find them at the farmstead. He would take them by surprise, with luck; kill the sons as well and end their family line. It would be a fine thing indeed to bring not only Harold's head but those of his sons back with him across the sea.

No wonder, then, that Sigurd wore a twisted smile. He was looking forward to the battle.

Morann reached King Brian's camp at noon that day.

The Munster king had decided to encamp on the northern side of the estuary. To the east lay the headland of the Ben of Howth. To the west, not far off, was the Tolka stream, running down to the Liffey's shore, a small wood, and the little hamlet of Clontarf. "The bulls' field" the name of the hamlet meant, though if there had been any bulls in the pasture before, their owners had wisely removed them before the army of Brian arrived. It was a good choice. The ground sloped, giving the defenders an advantage, and anyone approaching from Dyflin across the Liffey still had to wade across the Tolka to reach the camp.

On entering the camp, Morann received his first surprise. For instead of encountering Munster or Connacht men, the first part of the camp he passed through consisted entirely of Viking Norsemen, whose fearsome faces he had never seen before. Seeing one of Brian's commanders whom he knew, he asked him who they were.

"They are our friends, Morann. Ospak and Wolf the Quarrelsome. Fighting bands, much feared on the seas, they say." He grinned. "If the Dyflin king can call in friends from across the water, King Brian's just returning the compliment." He laughed. "You have to admit, the old man's lost none of his cunning."

"They look like pirates," said Morann.

"Dyflin has their pirates, and we have ours," the commander replied, with satisfaction. "Whatever it takes to win, Morann: you know Brian. Where's the King of Tara, by the way?"

"He is coming," said Morann.

He found King Brian at the centre of the camp, sitting on a silk-covered chair in a large tent. With his white beard and deeply lined face, the ageing king looked a little tired, but his spirit, as ever, was sharp and he was in a good humour. Morann apologised quickly for Harold's absence. "His horse tripped when we were crossing a stream and he fell. With his crippled leg, you know, I sent him home." And though King Brian gave him a cynical look, he seemed to have too much else on his mind to pursue the matter further. The first thing he wanted was news of the O'Neill king, and he listened intently as Morann gave him a careful report. At the end, Brian looked thoughtful.

"He will come then. That is clear. He said he could not let me lose. That is interesting. What do you think he means?"

"What he says. No less, and no more. He won't break his oath, but he will sit out the battle and preserve his own strength while yours is wasted. Only if he thinks you're in danger of losing will he intervene."

"I think so, too." Brian gazed into the distance for a moment. He seemed sad. "My son will command the battle," he remarked. "I'm too old." He glanced up at Morann with a flash of shrewd irony. "It is I, however, who will plan the battle."

Certainly the old king seemed confident. He had already sent a large detachment of his army away to raid parts of Leinster that its king had left unguarded. He chatted briefly about these developments with Morann, then fell silent; and the silversmith was about to take his leave when Brian suddenly reached onto a table beside him and took up a small book.

"Look at this, Morann. Did you ever see anything like it?" And opening its pages he showed the craftsman the astonishing illustrations that the monk of Glendalough had done. "Send in that monk," he called out, and a few moments later, Morann was pleased to see Osgar. "You know each other. That is good. You shall both stay by my side." He smiled. "Our friend here wanted to go back to Glendalough but I told him he's to stay here with me and pray for victory." Brother Osgar looked rather pale. "Don't worry," the king said to him genially, "the fighting won't reach here." He glanced at Morann mischievously. "Unless, God forbid, your prayers fail."

At the end of the following day, they saw the great host of the King of Tara arrive from the north. They pitched camp on the slopes below the Plain of Bird Flocks, some distance away but within sight.

The next morning, the King of Tara arrived with several of his chief men. They went into Brian's tent and spent some time there, before returning. That afternoon, as Brian was making a tour of the camp, he saw Morann.

"We have had our council of war," he told him. "Now we have to draw them out to fight on our ground."

"How will you do that?"

"Anger them. By now they'll be getting reports of the damage my raiding parties are doing behind them. Then they'll see the flames here. If the King of Leinster thinks I'm going to destroy his kingdom, he won't sit in Dyflin for long. So, Morann," he said smiling, "it's time to tease him."

✦

Harold saw the smoke on Wednesday morning. There was no sign of Caoilinn. The fires seemed to be coming from the southern edge of the Plain of Bird Flocks. Then he saw the plumes of smoke appearing farther east; then flames, breaking out on the slopes of the Ben of Howth. By the afternoon, the fires extended right across the southern horizon. It was probably as well that Morann had persuaded him to go back to the farmstead. He made what preparations he could. There were a few slaves left there, so he armed them and together they put up a barricade in front of the main house—though whether they could do anything if a raiding party of any size came along, he seriously doubted.

The next morning, the fires were closer. The breeze from the south-west was blowing the smoke in his direction. Around noon, he saw smoke away to his right, then behind him. The firings were encircling him. Early in the afternoon, a horseman came in sight, cantering towards the farmstead. He seemed to be alone. He stopped by the entrance and, cautiously, Harold went towards him.

"Who owns this place?" the man called out.

"I do," said Harold.

"Who are you?" the man demanded.

"Harold, son of Olaf."

"Ah." The man smiled. "You're all right, then." And wheeling his horse round, he rode away. Once again, as he gave a sigh of relief, Harold gave thanks to his friend Morann for protecting him.

But if the farmstead appeared to be safe, there were other urgent matters to worry about. He had to assume that Caoilinn was still in Dyflin. The army of Brian Boru and the fires lay between them.

There was little chance of her reaching him now. If there was a battle and Brian won, he would quite likely burn down the town as well. What would become of Caoilinn then? Even if, as it certainly appeared, she had decided to reject his offer, was he really going to leave her in the burning town and make no attempt to save her?

Then in late afternoon a small cart came towards the gate, and huddled in it he saw the family of a farmer from south of him. Their farm had been torched and they were looking for shelter, so of course he took them in. Had they any news of what was happening at Dyflin, he asked.

"Brian Boru and the King of Tara are both drawn up to fight," the farmer told him. "It could start any time."

Harold considered. Morann had been so insistent he should stay at the farmstead; and Morann always had good reasons for everything he did. But for the moment anyway, the farmstead was safe; whereas his sons were with the O'Neill king who was about to go into battle. Could he really stay here instead of riding to fight beside his sons? Shouldn't he at least arm himself and ride towards the battle. He smiled to himself: there had been a time when he had trained himself to become a formidable warrior.

Should he keep his promise to Morann, or break it? He wasn't sure. That evening, he cleaned and sharpened his axe and his other weapons. Then, for a long time, he remained staring into the darkness at the glow of the fires on the horizon.

Good Friday, 23 April 1014. One of the most holy days of the year. They marched out of Dyflin at dawn.

Caoilinn watched them from the ramparts. She was one of a large crowd. The day before she had watched fearfully as a big raiding party had even had the cheek to cross the Liffey by Ath Cliath, under their very noses, and set light to farmsteads out at Kilmainham and Clondalkin. She had been worried they might go round to Rathmines as well, but they had dashed back across the

river before the Dyflin defenders had managed to get a war party together to stop them. The fires over Fingal and out at Howth had
been bad enough, but this last humiliation had been too much. It
was said that the King of Leinster's sister had given him a piece of
her mind about it. Troublemaker though the royal lady was,
Caoilinn would have agreed with her. During the night, the Fingal
and Kilmainham fires had all died down, but there was no knowing
what fresh ones Brian's men might start. It was almost a relief, therefore, to see the army move out.

But it was a fearsome sight. And most terrifying of all, the
Leinster people agreed, were the Vikings from across the seas.

It was their armour. The Celtic people of the island no longer
stripped for battle as their ancestors had done. The Leinstermen
who marched out of Dyflin wore long, brightly coloured vests or
leather padded tunics over their shirts; some had helmets, most carried the traditional painted shield, strengthened with bosses of iron.
But splendid though this battle gear was, it did not compare with
that of the Vikings. For the Vikings wore chain mail. Thousands of
tiny links of iron or brass, tightly woven and riveted, and worn over
a leather undershirt, that stretched to below the waist or even the
knee, the chain mail was heavy and slowed the warrior down, but it
was very hard to pierce. In their use of chain mail, the Vikings were
only following a practice that had evolved in the Orient and was
now in use across much of Europe. But to the people of the western
island it made them look strangely grey, dark, and evil. This was the
armour worn by most of the men from the longships.

It was a huge force that marched out of Dyflin and went across
the wooden bridge. Though their armour was different, the
weapons carried by Irish Gaedhil and Viking Gaill were not so unlike, for as well as the customary spear and sword, more than a few
of the Celtic warriors carried Viking axes. There were some archers
with quivers of poisoned arrows, and there were several chariots to
carry the great men. But the battle would be fought not by ma-
noeuvre but by massed lines in hand-to-hand fighting. Watching

them go, Caoilinn did not try to keep count, but it seemed to her that there were well over two thousand men.

There was still a pale mist on the water as they crossed the bridge and for a little way on the other side it looked as if they were float-ing, like an army of phantoms, along the opposite bank. To the right, farther off, she detected movements in the camp of Brian Boru; and on the slopes in the distance, she could make out the vague mass of the army of the King of Tara.

The question now was, what should she do? The way was open before her. After the army had passed through, the town gates had been left open. The bridge was clear. On the far bank, the army would soon be two miles away or more and the camp of the O'Neill king was at a similar distance. If she chose to do so, she could take the old road to the north and be at Harold's farmstead in less than two hours. Once the battle started, however, who knew what would happen? At the least, the way could be barred again. This might be her last chance.

Should she go? Her son thought so. Did she want to go? Over the last few days she had thought of little else. If she were to leave to marry someone, she certainly didn't know a better man than Harold. She'd make him a good wife, too; and that knowledge was also an attraction. She desired him. It was futile to deny that. Did she love him? When she had seen the smoke and flames from Fingal and thought of the Norseman and his farmstead, she had experi-enced a pang of fear, and a little wave of tenderness for him, before she had reminded herself that, as he was under the King of Tara's protection, he and his farm were probably safe.

But now, as she watched the men of Dyflin go out to battle, she decided that whatever her own feelings, and whatever her eldest son might wish, her most important duty must be to secure the best chance of success for her younger children. She must be calculating and, if necessary, cold.

Today was Good Friday. With luck the battle would be decided by nightfall. If Brian Boru was defeated, then marriage to Harold would be foolish. But if he won, that would leave one day before Easter in which to go to the Norseman. Harold might be killed, of course. He might also think her timing opportunistic. That couldn't be helped. Easter was Easter. As a mother, there was only one sensible course to follow.

So it was, a short time later, that the lone figure of Caoilinn on a chestnut mare, followed by her two younger children, rode slowly out of Dyflin and across the wooden bridge. Once across, she followed the track up to a vantage point on some raised ground from which she could watch the outcome of events. Depending on how the battle went, she could either go with all haste to the man she loved, or retire discreetly back to Dyflin.

"Let us pray, children," she said.

"What for, Mother?" they asked.

"A clear victory."

✛

They had drawn up the battle in three great lines. In the centre, the front line was made up of the men of Brian's own tribe, led by one of his grandsons; behind them came the Munster host, with the Connacht men in the third line. On the two wings were the Norse contingents of Ospak and Wolf the Quarrelsome. Opposite them, advancing across the Tolka, the Leinster and Dyflin forces were in similar battle lines.

Morann had never seen anything like it. He was only a few feet away from King Brian. Around the old king, his personal guards had formed a protective enclosure, ready to form their shields, if necessary, into an impenetrable wall. The slight slope gave them a good view of the battle which was to take place below them.

The lines of troops were packed so thickly and were so deep, it seemed to Morann that you could have driven a chariot over their helmets from one wing to the other. Both sides had unfurled their battle banners, dozens of them, which were streaming in the breeze. At the centre of the enemy line, a huge wind sock in the form of a red dragon seemed ready to devour the other banners, while over the centre of Brian's line, a black raven banner flapped as though screeching in fury.

It was as soon as the enemy had waded across the Tolka stream that the war cries began, starting with bloodcurdling shouts from individual warriors or groups, but then gathering into a single huge roar from one line, only to be echoed by an answering roar from the other. Again the roar came as the two lines advanced, and again. And then, from the Celtic centre came the great opening shower of javelins. A second shower of spears followed the first; and then, with a mighty roar, the two front lines rushed forward and, with a huge bang, crashed together. It was a terrifying sight.

Morann glanced at the little group in the enclosure. The king was sitting on a broad bench covered with furs. His eyes were fixed on the battle ahead, his face so alert that, despite his lines and his white beard, he seemed almost youthful. Beside him, waiting for an order, stood a faithful servant. Behind him, his face now paler than a ghost, was Osgar the monk. Several of the guards also stood ready to carry any messages he might wish to send. He had already sent one or two messages to his son, as to troop dispositions, but now, for the time being, there was nothing to do but watch and wait.

If Osgar the monk looked frightened, Morann could hardly blame him. Would the enemy break through and sweep towards them? Scar-faced Brodar's fearsome Vikings appeared to be making terrible inroads on one part of the line. But though it seemed to sag, Morann saw the standards from the centre suddenly start to move, creating an internal bulge in the line as they went towards the most hard-pressed point.

"There goes my son," said Brian with quiet satisfaction. "He can fight with a sword in each hand, you know," he remarked to Morann. "Left or right, he strikes just as well."

In a little while the advance of Brodar's men seemed to be contained; but it was soon clear that neither side had a definite advantage. Now and then part of a line would give ground, and troops from the line behind would take their place. Individual warriors could be seen, both by their standards and also by the eddies and swirls they produced as they struck down those around them. Where there were Vikings engaged, Morann could see little flashes as the blows struck against the chain mail produced sparks. The battle cries grew fewer as time went on. The sound of the blows made Morann wince. As for Osgar, his eyes had grown wide in a sort of fascinated horror. And perhaps Brian Boru could sense the palpable fear behind his shoulder, for after a while he turned round to the monk and smiled.

"Sing us a Psalm, Brother Osgar," he said amiably, "since God is on our side." He reached down into a satchel beside him and pulled out a small volume. "You see," he added, "I even have your Gospels here. I shall look at them while you sing." And to Morann's amazement and admiration, that was exactly what the old king did, remarking casually to his servant: "Keep an eye on the battle and let me know if anything happens."

One thing, Morann thought, that should have happened, was that the King of Tara should by now have come to join the fight. But as yet, though he was not far off, he had not moved. The silversmith did not say anything on the subject. To look at King Brian, calmly perusing the book, you would never have guessed he even expected him.

Almost to his own surprise, Morann did not feel much afraid. It was not because he was behind the shield wall with King Brian. For the battle in all its fury was only a few hundred yards away. No, he realised, his calmness was due to something else. It was because he already knew that he was going to die.

⁘

It was past noon when Sigurd saw the movement to his right.

He had looked hard for Harold, as the two forces approached. Though Harold was a Norseman, Sigurd thought it most likely that, if he were in the battle, he would be with Brian's own tribe or the

Munster men. Or alternatively, he might be one of the men guarding the old king in person. He saw no sign of him yet, however, and though he had asked several men in the various detachments to call out if they saw him, he had heard nothing.

He had killed five men so far and wounded at least a dozen others. He had chosen a steel sword to fight with today. In close fighting, he found it better to stab than try to swing an axe. Though good blades were forged in Dyflin, the Viking armaments were still superior to anything made on the Celtic island, and the blue-bladed, double-edged sword he had acquired in Denmark was a deadly weapon. He had known this would be a hard fight, but it had gone far beyond his expectations and he had pulled back now, to take a short rest.

By midmorning a sharp, cold breeze had sprung up from the east. In the heat of the battle he had scarcely noticed it, but now it caught him in the face. It was wet, like sea spray—except, he suddenly realised, that it could not be. It was too warm. It was sticky also, getting in his eyes. It tasted salty on his lips. He blinked, frowned, and then cursed.

It was not from any sea. Each time the warriors in front of him crashed together, each time he heard the huge thud of a blow being landed, the shock of it sent up a little spray of sweat from the combatants. And of blood. And now, like the spume from the sea, it was a mixture of blood and sweat that was being carried back by the wind into his face.

Brodar had been hard-pressed by Wolf the Quarrelsome and his Norsemen. It seemed he was pulling back from the battle line to regroup. He had about a dozen men with him. Sigurd could see the warlord clearly. Brodar was pausing to rest.

Or was he? Unseen by their comrades fighting in front of them, the group was starting to move away towards the small wood near the hamlet.

Sigurd was not a coward; but his reason for being there was straightforward. He couldn't care less whether Munster or Leinster

won. He hadn't come here to die but to fight and be paid for it; and
Brodar was paying. If the scar-faced warrior was going to shelter in
the wood, then so was Sigurd. He started to follow.

❖

Harold watched carefully. It was midafternoon, and he thought he
saw how it would go.

He had ridden out at dawn and stationed himself at a point from
which he could see the King of Tara's camp and the battle down at
Clontarf. He was fully armed and he had decided upon a clear plan.
If the O'Neill army, where his sons were, started to move into battle, he would ride across to join them. And if he saw the army of
Brian being routed and Morann in danger, then despite his promise, he would go over and try to rescue his friend.

All morning he had watched. The King of Tara had not moved.
As usual, he thought, his clever friend had foreseen events. Though
neither battle line had yet given ground, he could see signs that
Brian had the upper hand. He had already seen one of the Viking
warlords sneaking away. The ranks of the Leinstermen were thinning, and though both sides were visibly slowing down, Brian still
had reserves of fresh troops in the third line. He watched a little
longer. The Leinstermen were giving ground.

It was safe to go home. He turned his horse's head. He had not
the least idea that, from a point behind the Leinster line, Caoilinn
also was watching to see how the battle went.

❖

"They're giving ground," murmured Morann.

"It isn't over yet." King Brian's voice was quiet. He had risen and
he was standing beside the craftsman now, surveying the battle.

Breaks in the cloud had allowed slanting rays of afternoon sun to
light up patches of ground, and in the yellowish glow, the field before them looked in places almost like charred woodland after a forest fire with clumps of damaged trees still standing amidst the

tangled mess of the fallen. But in the centre, the great mass of the battle was still heaving. There was no question, the advantage was with their side, but the fighting was stiff.

Catching the sunlight near the centre was a golden banner. This was held by the standard-bearer of Brian's son. Sometimes the banner moved from one part of the fight to another. Though Brian said nothing, Morann knew that his eyes were fixed upon the banner. From time to time he gave a grunt of approval.

Suddenly there was a mighty surge, as another banner from the other side came towards it. The golden banner, apparently aware of the move, also stirred in that direction. There was a sound of shouting, a small roar as the two banners seemed almost to touch. He heard Brian hiss through his teeth, then there was an intake of breath. A long pause followed, as if the whole battle line was holding its breath. Then came a huge cheer from the other side, followed by a moan from the Munster men. And suddenly, like a firefly that has been extinguished, the golden standard fell and was seen no more.

Brian Boru said nothing. He stared straight ahead, obviously trying to see what was taking place in the melee. His son's standard was down and nobody had raised it. That could only mean one thing. He was dead, or mortally wounded. Slowly the old man turned, went back to his former place, and sat down. His head sank forward. Nobody spoke.

Down in the battle line, however, the death of their leader seemed to have inspired the army with a desire to avenge him. They surged forward. For some little time, the enemy managed to make a last stand, but soon they were falling back, first one section of the line then another, until the whole front broke and fled towards the estuary and the Tolka.

Brian's servant and Morann looked at each other. Neither of them liked to interrupt the king at such a moment. But it had to be done.

"The Leinstermen have broken. They're running away."

Did the old man hear? It was hard to tell. Some of the guards who made up the shield wall were obviously itching to join in the fray, now that the danger to the king was past. After a short pause, Morann decided to speak for them.

"May some of the guards go down to finish them off?" he enquired. This was acknowledged with a nod. A few moments later, half the guards went quickly down towards the water, the rest remaining at their posts by the king.

For a little longer, Brian Boru sat silently, his head bowed. If he had just won the greatest victory of his career, he did not seem to care. Suddenly, he looked very old.

Meanwhile, at the water's edge some hundreds of yards away, a truly terrible scene was taking place. The Leinstermen and their allies had fled to the water's edge, but having got there, were trapped with no further escape route. Those running westwards were caught as they tried to wade back across the stream. And in these two places they were slaughtered without mercy. Already the bodies were piling up in the stream and floating out into the estuary.

King Brian Boru did not watch. His head remained bowed, his shoulders stooped in pain. At last, turning his eyes sadly towards Brother Osgar, he motioned him to his side.

"Pray with me, monk," he said quietly. "Let us pray for my poor son." So Osgar came, and knelt at his side, and they prayed together.

Not wishing to disturb them, Morann moved to the edge of the enclosure and stepped out. The remaining guards were watching the events down by the water. Strangely, though it was only hundreds of yards away, the massacre seemed distant, almost unreal, while by Brian's small enclosure there was an eerie quiet.

So the battle was over, and he was still alive. Morann had to admit that he was surprised. Had his intimation back at the tombs by the Boyne been wrong?

It was a few moments later that he saw the movement away to

his right. No one else had noticed. It came from the small wood which ran down to the hamlet. From the top of it, now, a party of Vikings was emerging. There must have been at least a dozen of them. The people down by the water had their backs to them. They were fully armed, and they were running, rapidly, towards King Brian's enclosure.

He let out a shout.

✦

Caoilinn had seen enough. She could not tell exactly what was happening at the water's edge, but the outcome of the battle was clear. The Leinster and Dyflin men had lost and Brian's men were going to massacre them.

"Come, children," she said, "it is time to go."

"Where to, Mother?" they asked.

"Fingal."

They headed north. At first, she urged her horse into a canter. It would look better, after all, if they could arrive at the farmstead quickly, before news of Leinster's defeat reached Harold. She could claim that she had set out that morning and been delayed by troops on the road, rather than admit she had waited to see the outcome of the battle. She'd have to instruct the children in their story, too. But then she shook her head and almost laughed at herself. How absurd. What an insult to Harold's intelligence, demeaning to them both. If they were going to marry, there would have to be more honesty than that.

So as soon as she was certain they were clear of any danger, she slowed her horse to a walk. She would take her time. She might as well look her best.

✦

Osgar had already jumped up by the time Morann was back in the enclosure. The guards, caught unawares, were still snatching their shields and weapons. One of them had let Morann have an axe, and the silversmith was placing himself directly in front of the king. Osgar had no weapon. He felt helpless and naked.

The Vikings were getting near. He could hear their footfalls. He saw the guards tense. There was a loud bang that almost made him jump out of his skin, as a Viking sword struck an upraised shield. Then he saw the Viking helmets—three of them, four, five. They seemed huge, larger than life, looming over the shield wall. Their axes were crashing down. He saw one axe hook itself over the top of a shield, tearing it down while a sword blade stabbed through into the defender's stomach, causing him to scream and then wilt in a welter of blood. Another guard fell, and another, writhing and biting the grass in his agony. The Vikings were through. Three of them, two with axes, one with a sword, were coming straight towards him. To his horror, he found himself unable to move, as in a dream. He saw Morann bravely raise his axe and swing at a Viking with a scarred face. With a clever stoop, the Viking dodged the blow while his companion, a black-haired, swarthy man, moving so quickly that Osgar hardly saw it happen, plunged a great, blue-bladed sword straight into Morann's ribs below the heart. Osgar heard the ribs crack and then saw Morann sink down to his knees, while his axe dropped at Osgar's feet. Efficiently, the dark fellow put one foot on Morann's shoulder, pulled out his sword, and the silversmith fell forward, facedown onto the ground. Osgar saw his body twitching as the life left him.

For a moment the Vikings paused. They were looking at Osgar and Brian Boru.

Osgar had not been watching the king. To his surprise, he realised that Brian was still in the same position, slumped in his seat, where they had been praying together. There was a sword leaning against the back of the seat, but Brian had not bothered to reach for it. Until this moment, paralysed by fear, Osgar had not moved; but now, faced with death, instead of terror he felt an unexpected anger. He was going to die and no one, not even Brian Boru the warrior king, was going to do anything about it. The axe Morann had dropped was at his feet. Scarcely knowing what he was doing, he snatched it up.

The shield wall had collapsed. The rest of the Vikings were coming into the enclosure, but evidently the man with the scarred face was the leader, since they all kept behind him. Then the dark man pointed his sword at Brian and spoke.

"King."

The leader looked from Osgar to Brian, then shook his head.

"No, Sigurd. Priest."

"No, Brodar." Sigurd was grinning as he pointed his sword at Brian's white beard. "King."

And now Brian Boru moved. Quick as a flash, with remarkable agility, he reached back over his head as he sat, grasped the sword behind him; and almost in the same instant it flashed forward, striking Brodar in the leg. As the sword bit, the Viking chief let out a roar and with a mighty swing brought down his axe on the old king's neck, smashing the collarbone and opening a huge gash. Brian rocked, blood burst from his mouth, his eyes opened very wide, and he keeled over on his side.

And now Sigurd stepped forward with his broad, two-edged sword. Somewhere behind the swarthy Viking, Osgar heard someone say, "Priest," but he hardly took it in. As he came towards Osgar, he wore a curious smile. Osgar, clutching his axe across his chest, backed away. Slowly Sigurd brought the blade of his sword up in front of Osgar's face, showing it to him.

Osgar shook. He was going to die. Should he accept death like a Christian martyr? Earlier, he had not been able to bring himself to kill. But now? Even if he raised the axe to strike at Sigurd's head, the swarthy pirate would plunge the fearsome sword through his rib cage before the axe had even started to descend.

As Osgar hesitated, Sigurd, taking no notice of the axe at all, took two steps up to the monk and, lowering his sword so that the flat of the blade caressed Osgar's leg, brought his face so close to

Osgar's that their noses almost touched. His eyes stared into Osgar's with a cold, terrifying menace. Osgar felt the sword blade slowly moving up his leg. Dear God, the pirate was about to stab it, with a terrible force, into his stomach. He would see his own entrails burst out. Only half aware of it, he vaguely felt a warm wetness running down his legs.

And then, suddenly, without warning, opening his mouth wide as though he was going to bite him, Sigurd the pirate let out a huge, bloodcurdling roar, into his face.

"Aarrgh! Aarrgh!"

And before a third was even out, Osgar had turned and fled, fled for his life, running as fast as he knew how, his legs wet, his face cold with terror. He did not even hear the laughter of the men behind him, but ran northwards, away from Sigurd, away from the battle, away from Dyflin. He did not stop until, breathless and panting, he reached the edge of the Plain of Bird Flocks and realised that there was no one behind him and that all was silence.

⁑

Brodar was bleeding badly; Brian's blow had almost severed his leg. Down by the water, the Munster king's forces had still not realised what had happened to him, but there was no time to lose.

Sigurd looked around him. When Brodar had pointed to the enclosure and led the raiding party, Sigurd assumed that the warlord was looking for loot to plunder. That was certainly what Sigurd wanted. Morann had been wearing a gold armband and was carrying some coins. Sigurd had those in a moment. Brian Boru had worn a magnificent clasp on his shoulder. By rights this was Brodar's, but Brodar was no longer in a condition to take it. Sigurd swiftly detached it. The other members of the party were taking what they could. One had snatched a rich damask; another had the furs on which the old king had been sitting. A third had picked up a little book of illustrated Gospels that had fallen to the ground. He had shrugged, but put it in his pouch, supposing it must have some value.

"It's time to go," said Sigurd.

"What about Brodar?" asked one of his men.

Sigurd glanced at Brodar. The lower part of his leg was only hanging by a fragment of bone and fleshy tissue. The warlord was a pale grey colour; his face looked clammy.

"Leave him. He will die," he said. It was no use trying to go back towards Dyflin, but some of the longships there would probably put out and work their way up the coast, looking for survivors. "I will meet you on the beach north of Howth," he said. "If you find a longship, keep it there until nightfall."

"Where are you going?"

"I have a piece of business to attend to," said Sigurd.

It was only a short walk to the tents of the Munster camp where, Sigurd knew, there would be plenty of horses. It was guarded, so he had to move stealthily; but before long he saw a horse tethered to a post, and quietly untying it, he led it away. Moments later, he was on its back and heading north. His sword hung from his belt at his side. For the time being, he took off his heavy metal helmet and let it hang by its strap down his back. The cool breeze on his face felt refreshing. At a stream, he paused and dismounted for a moment to drink. Then, at a walk, he rode on. There were still a few hours of daylight. And thanks to his informants in Dyflin, he knew exactly where Harold's farmstead was.

Only when he stopped running did Brother Osgar discover, to his surprise, that he was still clutching the axe.

There was no danger in sight at the moment, but who knew what threat might be lurking out there in the landscape. The axe was rather heavy, but he decided not to let it go just yet. Where should he seek refuge? Nearby he saw a burnt-out farmstead. No shelter there. Anyway, those pirates might come up here. Tomorrow or the next day, when he was sure there were no more Vikings around, he would go to Dyflin; but for the moment, he would continue until he reached some place of safety. So as soon as he had caught his breath, he pressed on.

He passed another ruined farm, crossed a patch of marshy ground, and had just emerged onto a track with a good view of the surrounding country when he caught sight of the woman and the two children riding some way ahead. When he first glimpsed them, he received a small shock. The woman looked like Caoilinn. Hardly realising he was doing so, he quickened his pace. The three horses reached a slight rise in the ground. Just as she was going over it, the woman half turned and he got a sight of her face. It was Caoilinn: he was almost sure of it. He called out, but she did not hear him and a moment later the three riders passed out of sight. He started to run.

They had cantered across some level terrain and were farther away from him when he caught sight of them again, but he managed to catch glimpses of them for some time. Then he lost them. But he continued in the same direction and, a little while later, passing through a small wood, he realised that he had come to the place where he had been attacked by the robbers when he was a youth. Sure enough, moments later, he saw spread out ahead of him, not a mile away, a large farmstead. The big wooden barn, the thatched storehouses, and the hall were all standing unharmed. They happened, at that moment, to be in a broad patch of sunshine, and bathed in its gentle evening light they seemed to him to glow like an illuminated page. It was Harold's farmstead. A place of refuge. Caoilinn must have gone there. He went forward, joyfully.

The track to the entrance was of short, green turf. In his growing excitement, he felt a new spring in his step.

He was approaching the gateway when he saw her. She was standing in the open space in front of Harold's hall. Her children were waiting by the horses. She was looking around. Apparently nobody was there. Her dark hair had fallen to her shoulders, just as he had pictured it a thousand times. His heart leaped. As a widow, now, she was even more beautiful, more alluring than he had remembered. He hurried forward.

She did not see him. She seemed still to be looking for someone. She came towards the gateway to look outside. And then he saw her staring towards him. He waved. She stared blankly.

He frowned, then smiled. Of course, a bedraggled figure in a monk's habit, carrying an axe: he must look a strange sight. She probably hadn't recognised him. He called out.

"Caoilinn. It is Osgar."

Still she stared. She looked puzzled. Had she understood? Then she pointed at him. He waved again. She shook her head, pointing once more, urgently, to something behind him; so he stopped and turned.

The horse was only ten yards away. It had stopped when he did. It must have been walking behind him, but in his excitement at seeing Caoilinn, he had not heard its hoofs on the grassy track. Sigurd was riding it.

"Well, Monk, we meet again." The pirate gazed at Osgar, apparently considering what to do with him.

Instinctively, clutching the axe, Osgar started to back away. Sigurd moved his horse slowly forward, keeping pace with him. How far was he from the gateway to the farmstead? Osgar tried to remember. He dared not look behind him. Could he make a run for it? Perhaps Caoilinn was closing the gate, trapping him outside with Sigurd. Suddenly he realised that the pirate was talking to him.

"Run away, Monk. It isn't you I'm interested in." Sigurd grinned. "The person I want is in that farmstead." He waved him away. "Go on, Monk. Run."

But Osgar did not run. For Caoilinn was there. The memory of that miserable day when he had let Morann go into Dyflin alone to save her flashed into his mind with bitterness. He had failed to strike a blow then. He had chosen his monk's vocation over her, just as he had been doing for most of his life. And now this devil, this monster was going to take her. Rape her? Kill her? Probably both. The time had come. He must kill. He must kill this Viking or die in the attempt. Terrified of Sigurd though he was, the fighting spirit of his ancestors stirred within him, and calling loudly to Caoilinn behind him, "Close the gate," he took a step back and raising the axe over his head, barred the way.

Slowly and carefully, Sigurd got down from his horse. He did not trouble to cram the helmet back on his head, but he drew out his double-edged sword. He was not going to argue with the monk, but Osgar was in the way. Would the fool really strike? The monk did not know it, but his stance was all wrong. His weight was so distributed that one of two things might happen. Sigurd would make a feint, Osgar would swing down and, meeting only thin air, probably cut off his own leg. If he didn't swing then, Sigurd would take one nimble step to the right and plunge his sword straight into the monk's side. It would be all over before the axe was halfway down. Osgar was about to die, but didn't know it. If he tried to fight, that is.

But would he? Sigurd took his time. He slowly raised the blade of his sword, showing it to Osgar as he had done before. The monk was trembling like a leaf. Sigurd stood two paces away from him. Suddenly he let out a roar. Osgar quivered. He almost dropped the axe. Sigurd took one more step forward. The poor fool of a monk was so frightened that he had closed his eyes. In the gateway behind, Sigurd could see a dark-haired woman with a pale face. Handsome, whoever she was. He measured the distance. No need even to make a feint. He gripped his sword for the thrust.

And just at that moment, coming round the outside of the farmstead fence, he saw Harold. What luck.

Osgar struck. He had sent a single, fleeting prayer to heaven, half opened his eyes, seen the pirate, just for an instant, shift his gaze elsewhere and known that God, for all his sins, had granted him one chance. He struck with all his might. He struck for Caoilinn whom he loved, he struck for his hesitating life, his chances lost, his passion never practised. He struck to end his cowardice, and his shame. He struck to kill Sigurd.

And he did. Distracted for an instant, the pirate did not heed the blow until it was too late. The unexpected blade bit through the bone, cleaving the skull with a sickening crunch and a splatter of brains, shattering the bridge of his nose and smashing the jaw before it buried itself with a thud in the neck bone. The tremendous force of the blow drove the body onto its knees. It knelt there for a moment, like a strange creature with an axe for a head, the haft sticking out in front like a yard-long nose, while Osgar stared in disbelief at what he had wrought. Then it keeled over.

Harold, who had come in from a nearby field, unaware that he had any visitors, gazed at the scene before him with great surprise.

Three weeks later, Harold and Caoilinn were married in Dyflin. At Harold's suggestion, it was a Christian ceremony, the bridegroom, with great good humour, having allowed himself to be baptised beforehand by the bride's cousin Osgar, who also officiated at the marriage. Just before the ceremony, Osgar silently handed the bride a little antler ring. Despite many renewed requests, Osgar did not take up the position of abbot at the family monastery but preferred to return to the peace of his beloved Glendalough. There he produced another book of illustrated Gospels, which was very fine; but it lacked the genius of the one which was lost.

The Battle of Clontarf is rightly regarded as the most important of Celtic Irish history. It has often been depicted as the decisive encounter between the Celtic Gaedhil and the Nordic Gaill: Irish Brian Boru against the invading Vikings, by which Ireland was triumphant against the foreign aggressor. Such was the foolish propaganda of romantic historians. Although it may well have deterred further Viking raids at this unstable time in the northern world, Dyflin itself was left in the hands of its Viking ruler, just as before. The Nordic element in Ireland's ports remained strong and the two communities, the Hiberno–Norse as they are often called, became indistinguishable.

The real significance of the Battle of Clontarf was probably twofold. First, Clontarf and the events surrounding it made clear the strategic importance of the island's richest port. Never a tribal nor a religious centre, its trade and ramparts meant that, while the holding of ancient Tara was symbolic, to rule all Ireland, it was Dyflin that was crucial.

Secondly, and sadly, far from being a triumph, Clontarf was Ireland's great missed opportunity. For though Brian Boru had decisively won the battle, he had also lost his life. The descendants of his grandchildren, the O'Briens, would earn high renown; but his immediate successors were unable to unite and hold all Ireland as, for a decade, the old man had briefly done. Twenty years later, the High Kingship would pass back to the O'Neill kings of Tara; but it was and remained only a ceremonial shadow of the kingship of Brian Boru. Disunited Ireland, like the fragmented Celtic island of ancient times, would always be vulnerable.

So Brian Boru won, but lost; and Harold the Norseman and Caoilinn the Celt, who were not in love, married and were very happy; Morann the Christian craftsman, having received a pagan warning, died like a warrior in battle; and Osgar the monk killed an evil man, even if he did not understand why.

SIX

STRONGBOW

⊰ 1167 ⊱

I

T HE INVASION that was to bring eight centuries of grief to Ireland began on a sunny autumn day in the year of Our Lord 1167. It consisted of three ships which arrived at the small southern port of Wexford.

Yet had anyone told the two young men who eagerly disembarked together that they were part of an English conquest of Ireland, they would have been most surprised. For one was an Irish priest returning home, while his friend, though he owed allegiance to the King of England, had never called himself English in his life. As for the purpose of the mission, the soldiers in the ships had come because they had been invited, and were led by an Irish king.

Indeed, many of the terms found in reports of these events are misleading. Irish chroniclers of the period refer to the invasion as the coming of the Saxons—by which they mean the English—notwithstanding the fact that for three centuries, much of the northern half of England had been settled by Danish Vikings. Modern historians refer to it as the coming of the Normans. But that is also inaccurate. For although the kingdom of England had been conquered by William of Normandy in 1066, it had since then passed, through his granddaughter, to King Henry II—who belonged to the Plantagenet dynasty from Anjou, in France.

So who were these people—apart from the Irish priest—who were arriving in three ships at Wexford on this sunny autumn day? Were they Saxons, Vikings, Normans, Frenchmen? Actually, they were mostly Flemish; and they had come from their home in south Wales.

The young priest was enthusiastic.

"As soon as this business is done, Peter, you'll promise to visit my family, I hope. I know they'll be pleased to welcome you," said the handsome young priest.

"I shall look forward to it."

"My sister must be twelve now. She was a pretty, lively child when I left."

Peter FitzDavid smiled to himself. It was not the first time his Irish friend had mentioned his sister's charms or indicated that she would receive a handsome dowry.

Peter FitzDavid was a pleasant-looking young man. His light brown hair was cut short and he wore a small beard cut into a chiselled edge. His eyes were blue and set wide apart. His chin was square and strong. A pleasant face, but a soldier's face.

Soldiers need to be brave, but as he prepared to step ashore, Peter could not help feeling a little apprehensive. His fear was not so much that he could be killed or maimed, but that he might somehow disgrace himself. There was, however, an even greater fear lurking in the background, and it was this fear which, in the times ahead, would drive him on. It was because of this fear that he had to succeed, to catch the eye of his commander and win fame. Even as the shore drew closer, his mother's words were echoing in his mind. He understood her very well. The last penny she could spare had been spent on his horse and equipment. There was nothing else left. She loved him with all her heart, but she had no more to give.

"God be with you, my son," she had said to him as he left. "But do not come back empty-handed." Death, he thought, would be better than that. He was twenty.

To call Peter FitzDavid a knight in shining armour would not quite be correct. His chain mail, a hand down from his father that had been altered to fit him, was free of rust and if it did not shine, at least it gleamed. In short, like many of the mounted men of that age, Peter FitzDavid, who owned little more than what he carried, was a young fellow in search of his fortune.

And he was Flemish. His grandfather Henry had come from Flanders, that land of craftsmen, merchants, and adventurers which lay on the rich flatlands between northern France and Germany. He had been just one of a stream of Flemings that had flowed across to Britain after the Norman Conquest and had settled not only in England but in Scotland and Wales as well. Henry was one of many Flemish immigrants who were granted land in the south-western peninsula of Wales which, because of its rich mines and quarries, the new Norman kings were anxious to control. But the settlement in Wales had not gone well. The proud Celtic princes of that land had not submitted easily and now the Norman Flemish colony was in trouble. Several castles were taken; their lands were under threat.

Peter's family had been especially hard hit. They were not important tenants in chief—vassals of the king himself—with holdings in many of the Plantagenets' wide domains. They were vassals of his vassals. Their modest lands in Wales were all they had. And by the time that Peter's father, David, had died, they had lost two-thirds of those. What remained was only enough to support Peter's mother and his two sisters.

"You'll have nothing to support you, my poor boy," his father had told him, "except your family's love, your sword, and the good name I leave you."

By the time Peter was fifteen, his father had taught him everything he knew about the arts of war, and Peter was an accomplished swordsman. The love of his family was not in doubt. As for his name, Peter had loved his father and so he loved that, too. For just as in Celtic Ireland, the term "Mac" implied "the son of," so in Norman England, the French term "fitz" had a similar meaning. His father had thus been known as David FitzHenry; and he was proud to be called Peter FitzDavid. Now it was time to seek his fortune as a fighting man for hire.

Warfare has always been an expensive and specialised business, conducted on a temporary basis, and so the instruments of war have always been for hire. Arms and equipment were traded. Transport in particular was hired for the occasion. Only two years earlier, the men of Dublin—as the merchants of Dyflin were usually calling the big port now—had offered their great fleet to King Henry of England for a campaign against the Celtic princes of Wales, a deal which fell through only when Henry changed his mind.

But above all, across the huge patchwork of tribal lands and dynastic lordships that, since the fall of the ordered Roman Empire, now made up most of Christendom, it was armed men who were for hire. When William the Conqueror came to England, it was not just his Norman vassals that he led but a whole collection of armed adventurers from Brittany, Flanders, and other places, and who were granted estates in the conquered country. After their defeat, a large contingent of English warriors travelled right across Europe and formed what was called the Saxon regiment in the service of the Emperor of Byzantium. Adventurers from England, France, and Germany had already gone on Crusade to get land in the kingdom of Jerusalem and other crusader colonies in the Holy Land. Celtic kings in Ireland had been hiring Vikings to fight for them for generations. It was not strange, therefore, that any young man from Wales in search of his fortune should have gone to the Plantagenet King of England to see if that mighty monarch needed some hired help.

÷

When Peter FitzDavid first set out, it was to the great English port of Bristol that he had travelled. His father had once had some acquaintance with a merchant there.

"After I'm gone," his father had advised Peter, "you could pay him a visit. He might be able to do something for you."

Bristol lay more than a hundred miles away, across the huge estuary of the mighty River Severn which traditionally separated Saxon from Celtic Britain. It had taken Peter five days to reach the Severn, and another half day riding up its western bank to a place where there was a horse ferry across. When he arrived at the ferry, however, he was told that on account of the Severn's swift and complex currents, he would have to wait some hours. Looking about he saw that on the slopes just above there was a small fort and, set in an oak grove nearby, there seemed to be some ancient ruins. Making his way up to these, he had sat down to rest.

It was a pleasant place with a fine view over the river. Without particularly thinking about it, he sensed that the ruins had a religious air. And indeed they had, for the site he had come upon was the old Roman temple to Nodens, the Celtic god of healing. Christianity had long since submerged the god as well as his temple: in England he had been quite forgotten, and across the sea in Celtic Ireland, under the name of Nuada of the Silver Hand, he had long since been converted by the monkish scribes from a deity to a mythical king.

And as he was sitting there, gazing across the river to the distant shore, it had struck Peter with a terrible force, that when he crossed the River Severn, he would be leaving everything he knew behind. For whatever his family's troubles, Wales was his home. He had never lived anywhere else. He loved the green valleys, the coastline with its rocky outcrops and sandy coves. Though he spoke French to his parents, the tongue of his childhood was the Celtic Welsh of the local people with whom he had grown up. Once across the Severn, however, the people would speak English, of which he knew not a word. And after he got to Bristol and encountered the English, would he stay in that country or go farther away, across the seas, never perhaps to see his native land again? For a while he felt so sad he almost turned to go home again.

But he couldn't go home. They loved him, but they didn't want him. And late that afternoon, with a heavy heart, he had led his charger and his packhorse onto the big raft that would take them across the river.

Entering Bristol the following evening came as a revelation. He had seen some impressive stone castles in Wales and several great monasteries, but never before had he encountered a city. After London, Bristol was England's greatest port.

He walked through its busy streets for a while before he found the house he was looking for and entered it with some trepidation, for the place had its own stone gateway, a cobbled court surrounded by timbered, gabled buildings, and a handsome hall with a high roof. His father's friend, he saw at once, must be a man of great wealth.

And it was still more disconcerting when, on being ushered into the hall by a servant, it was immediately clear to him that the merchant was not entirely sure who he was. Some anxious moments passed while the merchant asked him not once but twice to repeat his father's name. At last, while Peter felt himself blushing, the man seemed to recall who his father was, if not with great interest, and asked him how he could be of help.

The next two days were interesting, but not enjoyable. The merchant was a swarthy man. His father had been an Ostman, a Dane who had come from Ireland. With him he brought a Celtic name Dubh Gall—"the dark stranger"—which in Bristol they pronounced as Doyle. Though born in Bristol, the merchant had been given neither an English nor a Norman name, but instead had been

christened Sigurd. No one used his first name, though. All Bristol
referred to him as Doyle.

The dark stranger: he was certainly that. Dark and silent. He was
hospitable enough: Peter even had an entire chamber to himself beside the hall. To Peter, as he would to any nobleman or substantial
merchant, he spoke in the courteous tongue of Norman French. But
he spoke little, and smiled not at all. Perhaps it was because he was
a widower, Peter thought. Perhaps when his married daughters visited, or his sons returned home from their business in London, he
would show a better humour. But for the two days that Peter was
there, conversation was minimal. And since the numerous servants,
grooms, and underlings spoke only English, he felt rather lonely.

The first morning, Doyle took him round the port. They visited
his countinghouse, his warehouse, two of his ships down by the
slave pens on the waterfront. Doyle was certainly still in full possession of his vigour; his dark eyes seemed to be everywhere; he spoke
very quietly, but men watched him apprehensively and jumped to
obey his orders when he gave them. By the end of the day, Peter had
learned a good deal about the business of the port, the organisation
of the town with its courts and aldermen, and its trade with other
ports from Ireland to the Mediterranean. But he had also decided
that Doyle was rather frightening.

This feeling was reinforced by a small incident that evening. He
and the merchant had just sat down in the big hall and the servants
were about to bring the food, when a young man of about his own
age entered and, after bowing respectfully to them both, seated himself at some distance from them. Doyle, having given the young
man a curt nod and grunted to Peter, "He works for me," took no
further notice of him. The young man, who was wearing a hood
which he did not remove, was served a goblet of wine, which was
not refilled; and as his host continued to ignore him, and the young
man himself never once looked up, Peter did not know how to address him. As soon as he had eaten, the young man left; he looked

depressed. I should think I'd look depressed, too, if I worked for Doyle, Peter thought.

It was later that evening, when he had retired to his chamber, that he heard their voices out in the courtyard. At least, it was certainly Doyle's voice, low and menacing, that murmured something he could not catch, and then: "You're a fool." It was said in French. "You can never repay."

"I'm completely in your power." The voice was that of a young man, urgent and plaintive. It must be the fellow he had seen that evening. This was followed by a harsh murmur from Doyle. The words were indistinct, but the tone was threatening. "No!" the young man cried. "Don't do that, I beg you. You promised."

They moved away after that and Peter heard no more. But one thing was very clear to him: Doyle was sinister, and the sooner he left the better.

The following morning, without warning, Doyle told him to saddle his horse, take his weapons, and accompany him to an exercise yard near the eastern gate. There he found several men-at-arms practising swordplay, and after some words from Doyle, he was invited to join them. The dark merchant watched him for some time and then quietly departed, leaving him to make his own way home later on. Peter did not see him again until the evening.

It was that evening, however, that Doyle remarked to him, in his usual saturnine way, "There is talk of an expedition. To Ireland."

❖

If nobody had succeeded in dominating all Ireland since the days of Brian Boru, it was not for lack of trying. One after another the great regional dynasts had tried to gain supremacy; Leinster and Brian's grandson from Munster had both had their turn. The ancient O'Neill were always watching for a chance to regain their former glory. At present, the O'Connor dynasty of Connacht claimed the High Kingship. But no one had truly achieved mastery, and the chronicles of the time adopted a telling formula to describe the position of most of these monarchs: "High King, with Opposition." So while the rulers in the huge patchwork of Europe began to amalgamate territories into ever greater holdings—the Plantagenets now controlled a feudal empire consisting of most of the western side of France, as well as Normandy and England—the island of Ireland continued to be split between ancient tribal lands and rival chiefs.

The latest Irish dispute concerned the kingdom of Leinster.

For some time now, the ancient province of Leinster had been controlled by an ambitious dynasty from Ferns in the southern, Wexford part of the territory. But ambitious King Diarmait of Leinster had made enemies. In particular, he had humiliated a powerful king, O'Rourke, by eloping with his wife. Now this cheated husband, together with others, had turned on Diarmait of Leinster and forced him to flee.

It was a considerable surprise to Plantagenet King Henry, who was down on his domains in France, when they told him: "King Diarmait of Leinster has arrived here to see you."

And it was with some curiosity that he answered, "An Irish king? Bring him to me."

The meeting was certainly strange: the Plantagenet monarch, sandy-haired, clean-shaven, quick and impatient in his movements, dressed in tunic and hose, sophisticated, French in language and culture, face-to-face with the provincial Celtic king, with his thick brown beard and heavy woollen cloak. Henry actually spoke some English—an achievement of which he was rather proud—but no Irish. Diarmait spoke Irish, Norse, and some French. But there was no difficulty in communicating. For a start, Diarmait had brought with him his interpreter—Regan by name—and failing that, the clerks employed by both sides spoke Latin, as did every educated churchman in western Christendom. The two men also had things in common: both had eloped with another man's wife; both had uncertain relationships with their own children; both were self-centred and cynical opportunists.

King Diarmait's request was simple. He'd been driven out of his kingdom and he wanted to get it back. He needed to raise an army. He couldn't pay them much, but there would be property and land to be distributed if he was successful. It was the usual deal, upon which the present aristocracy of many parts of Europe, including England, had been founded. He also knew, however, that he couldn't raise men in any of the Plantagenet dominions without getting Henry's permission.

King Henry II was a very ambitious man. He had already built up an empire and his main occupation now was in taking territory away from the rather ineffectual king of France, whom it amused him to bully. As it happened, a dozen years earlier, he had briefly considered the possibility of annexing Ireland as well, though he had dropped the idea and had little interest in the island now. But he was also an opportunist.

"Are you offering to become my vassal?" he gently enquired.

His vassal. When an Irish king recognised the supremacy of a greater monarch and submitted to him, he "came into his house," as the expression was. He gave hostages for his good behaviour and promised to pay tribute. When a French or English feudal lord became the vassal of another, however, the obligations were more comprehensive. Not only did he owe military service, or payment in lieu, but when he died, his heirs had to make payment to inherit their land, and if the inheritance was in dispute, the overlord decided it. In conquered England, moreover, the Normans had been able to take an even stronger line. For if any vassal there gave trouble, the English king could take his lands away and give them to another. A feudal vassal could not, theoretically, fight or travel without his overlord's permission. Beyond even this, Henry Plantagenet was constantly extending the royal power. In England, he wanted to give ordinary freemen the right to go past their own lords and appeal directly to his royal courts for justice. It was the start of a centralised administration undreamed of in the informal world of the Celtic Irish kings.

But King Diarmait needed men. Besides, he knew very well that whatever King Henry's views about feudal vassals might be, Ireland lay far beyond the Plantagenet monarch's reach.

"That would be no trouble at all," he said.

And so the deal was struck. King Henry of England gained for the first time a provincial Irish king who recognised him, however cynically, as his overlord. It might be of no practical value at present. "But," he could point out, "it has cost me nothing." And King Diarmait got a letter in which the ruler of the sprawling Plantagenet empire gave permission to any of his vassals to fight for Diarmait if they wished.

There hadn't been a mad rush. The prospect of helping a dispossessed provincial chieftain from an island out in the western seas was not a great attraction. But one of King Henry's magnates—the mighty lord de Clare, best known to fighting men as Strongbow— met the Irish exile and took an interest. Strongbow had land holdings in several parts of the Plantagenet domains, but the ones in south-west Wales had been under pressure. It was clear that King Diarmait was ready to let him name his own price.

"You could marry my daughter and inherit my entire kingdom," he wildly suggested. As Diarmait had sons, and at present controlled not a yard of his former kingdom, this offer was worth just about as much as his oath of fealty to the Plantagenet monarch. But Strongbow decided to take a calculated gamble. He told the Irish king to recruit in the territories of which he was overlord in south Wales. Perhaps a contingent could be raised which would serve as an advance party. After all, he concluded privately, if they all get killed, it really doesn't matter.

It had been Peter's good fortune that Doyle should have encountered Strongbow that day on one of the magnate's periodic visits to the great port that lay so close to his territories. Strongbow had been speaking to a group of merchants about the Irish king's desire to raise troops in the region.

"There's a young man in my house, the son of a friend, who might like to go along," the Bristol merchant mentioned. "I'm wondering what to do with him."

"Send him," said Strongbow. "Tell Diarmait I chose him."

And so it was that Peter FitzDavid, having crossed the sea in ships supplied by Doyle, found himself disembarking with King Diarmait of Leinster and a contingent of assorted fighting men in Wexford on this sunny autumn day.

⁌⁜⁍

The horses were coming ashore now. From where he was standing on the beach, Peter had a good view of King Diarmait, who had already mounted a horse, and the lord de la Roche, the Flemish nobleman who was directing operations. They were disembarking at some distance from the town of Wexford. Roche had already taken care to set up a defensive position, but no one so far had come out of the town to challenge them. It was a small port with modest ramparts not unlike the ones he had known in south Wales. Compared to a proper castle, or the great city of Bristol, it was nothing: they'd take it easily. For the time being, however, there was nothing for Peter to do but wait.

"Well, goodbye then." His friend was bidding him farewell. While the soldiers set up their camp, it was time for him to depart. During their journey together, Peter had had cause to be very grateful to young Father Gilpatrick. The priest was only five years older than Peter, but he knew far more. He had spent the last three years at the famous English monastery of Glastonbury, south of Bristol, and now he was returning home to Dublin, where his father had secured him a position with the archbishop. He had joined the ship to Wexford because he wanted to go up the coast to Glendalough for a brief stay at that sanctuary before he arrived in Dublin.

Seeing that Peter was young and perhaps lonely, the kindly priest had spent much time in his company, learned all about him, and in return told him about his family, Ireland, and its customs.

His learning was impressive. From his childhood he had spoken Irish and Norse, and also become a good Latin scholar. While at Glastonbury in England, he had made himself familiar with English and Norman French.

"I suppose I could be a 'latimer'—that's what we churchmen call an interpreter," he had said with a smile.

"You're probably better than King Diarmait's interpreter Regan," Peter suggested admiringly.

"Oh, I wouldn't say that." Gilpatrick laughed, though not unpleased.

He was able to reassure Peter that he would be able to learn the Celtic that the Irish spoke without much difficulty. "The languages of Ireland and of Wales are like cousins," he explained. "The principal difference is in a single letter. In Wales, when you make a 'p' sound, we make a 'q' sound. So in Ireland, for instance, if we say 'the son of,' we say 'Mac.' In Wales you say 'Map.' There are many differences of course, but in a while you'll find you can understand what is said easily enough."

He gave Peter some account of Dublin—it sounded to Peter more like "Doovlin" when the Irishman said it. The Irish port was almost on a scale with Bristol, it seemed. And he explained some of the politics of the island.

"Whatever success you bring King Diarmait against his enemies, he will still have to go to Ruairi O'Connor of Connacht—that's the High King now, you know—and O'Connor will have to recognise him and take hostages before Diarmait can call himself king of anything in Ireland."

As for his own ambitions, it seemed that they were bound up with the great Dublin bishop to whom he had been recommended.

"He is a saintly man, and of great authority," Gilpatrick declared. "My father is a senior churchman himself, you see." He paused. "My mother is also a kinswoman of Archbishop Lawrence. That's what we call him in the Church. We Latinise his name to Lawrence O'Toole; in Irish that would be Lorcan Ua Tuathail. The Ua

Tuathail are a princely family in north Leinster. In fact, the archbishop is actually a brother-in-law of King Diarmait as well.
Though I don't know that he much likes him," he added confiden-
tially."

Peter smiled at this complex web of relationships.

"Does this mean your family is princely, too?" he enquired.

"We are an old Church family," Gilpatrick said, and seeing Peter
look a little puzzled, he explained. "The custom in Ireland is somewhat different to that of other countries. There are ancient ecclesiastical families, greatly honoured, with ties to monasteries and
churches; often those families are the kinsmen of kings and chiefs
whose histories go back into the mists of time."

"Your family is linked to a particular church?"

"We endowed our monastery, as you would say, at Dublin."

"And your family history goes back into the mists of time?"

"The tradition," Gilpatrick said impressively, "is that our ancestor Fergus was baptised at Dublin by Saint Patrick himself."

It was the mention of the saint that had prompted Peter to ask
another question.

"Your name is *Gilla Patraic*. That means 'the Servant of Patrick,'
doesn't it?"

"It does."

"I wondered why your father didn't give you the saint's name
without any addition. Why not just 'Patrick'? My name is a single
Peter, after all."

"Ah." The priest nodded. "That is something you should know
if you are going to spend time in Ireland. No good Irishman would
ever be called Patrick."

"They wouldn't?"

"Only *Gilla Patraic*. Never Patrick."

So it had been for centuries. No Irishman in the Middle Ages
would dare to take the name of the great Saint Patrick for himself.
It was always Gilpatrick: the Servant of Patrick. And so it would remain for centuries more.

He was a slim, dark, handsome young fellow. His grey eyes were unusual for they were curiously flecked with green.

It would have been hard not to like the priest, with his kindness, his not quite hidden pride in his family, and his obvious affection for them. Peter learned a little about his brothers, his pretty sister, and his parents. He did not quite understand what sort of senior churchman the priest's father could be if he were married, nor what he meant by "our" monastery, but when he began to raise this subject, Father Gilpatrick hurried on to another subject and Peter had not pressed the matter further. It seemed clear not only that the friendly priest liked him personally but that he by no means disapproved of the presence of these Plantagenet vassals on his native soil. Peter was not sure why.

But it was one night on the ship that Peter saw something more, a deeper side to the Irishman. It turned out that Gilpatrick was a fine harpist, and that he could sing. He proved to be versatile. He knew some popular English ballads. He even gave them a saucy song of the troubadours from the south of France. But finally, as the night had grown deeper, he had turned to the traditional music of Ireland, and another kind of quiet had fallen over his listeners, Flemish though many of them were, as the soft, mournful melodies had come from the strings and floated out to haunt the waters of the sea. Afterwards, he had remarked to the priest, "It seemed to me that I was listening to your soul."

His friend had given a quiet smile and responded, "They are traditional tunes. It's the soul of Ireland you were hearing."

And now the young priest was walking rapidly away. Peter watched him until he was out of sight, then remained on the shore observing the horses, glancing up from time to time at the hills that rose in the distance, and thinking to himself that the place was really not so unlike his native Wales. Perhaps, he considered, I might be happy if I settled here. When the opportunity arose, he would certainly pay a visit to the priest and his family in Dublin.

So he was most surprised, half an hour later, to see his friend returning. Father Gilpatrick was smiling broadly. Beside him, on a small but sturdy horse, rode a splendid and rustic figure: he had a long grey beard; over his head he wore a hood that came down to his chest; he had a loose shirt, not too clean after his journey, and woollen leggings with feet. If he had any boots with him, Peter couldn't see them. He was riding the little horse bareback without saddle, stirrups, or spurs, his long legs hanging down to the horse's knees. He seemed to be guiding the horse with taps from a crooked stick. His face was curious: with its half-closed eyes and sardonic expression, it made Peter think of a wise old salmon. He supposed the fellow might be a shepherd or a cowman whom his friend had hired to guide him up into the mountains.

"Peter," the priest said proudly, "this is my father."

His father? Peter FitzDavid stared. The senior churchman? Peter had known men who had taken vows of poverty, but he did not think that Gilpatrick's father was one of them, nor was he wearing any sort of clerical dress. Wasn't he supposed to be a large landowner? He didn't look like any lord that Peter had ever seen. Had his friend lied to him about his father? Surely not. And if he had, he'd hardly bring him back to meet like this. Perhaps Gilpatrick's father was an eccentric of some kind.

He greeted the older man respectfully and the Irishman addressed a few words to him in his native tongue, some of which Peter understood; but their conversation did not go further than this, and it was clear that Gilpatrick's father wished to depart. As they were leaving, however, Gilpatrick took Peter by the arm.

"You were surprised by my father's appearance." He was smiling with amusement.

"I? No. Not at all."

"You were. I saw your face." He laughed. "Don't forget, Peter, I've been living in England. You'll find a lot of men like my father, here in Ireland. But his heart's in the right place."

"Of course."

"Ah," Gilpatrick smiled. "Wait till you see my sister." Then he was gone.

⁙

"Well?" Father Gilpatrick waited until they were some distance from the port of Wexford before he asked his father's opinion.

"A nice young man, no doubt," his father, Conn, allowed.

"He is," the priest agreed. He glanced at his father to see if the older man was going to say anything more on the subject, but it seemed he was not. "I still have not asked you," he continued, "how you came to be here yourself."

"A Bristol vessel arrived in Dublin last week. They said that Diarmait had set off to pick up men in Wales on his way to Wexford. So I came down to take a look."

Gilpatrick eyed his father shrewdly.

"You thought you'd see if King Diarmait would be getting his kingdom back."

"You saw Diarmait," his father asked, "on your ship?"

"I did."

"Did you speak with him?"

"A little."

The older man was silent for a moment.

"That's a terrible man," he remarked sadly. "There were many in Leinster who were not sorry to see him go."

"Are you impressed with what you have seen?"

"These ships?" His father pursed his lips. "He'll be needing more men than that when he meets the High King. O'Connor is strong."

"Perhaps there will be more. The King of England is behind this business."

"Henry? He has given permission. That is all. Henry has other things to think about." He shrugged. "Irish kings have been hiring fighting men from over the sea for hundreds of years. Ostmen, Welshmen, men from Scotland. Some stay, others go. Look at

Dublin. Half my friends are Ostmen. As for these," he glanced back towards Wexford, "there aren't enough of them. By next year most of them will be dead."

"I was thinking," Gilpatrick ventured, "that Peter might like to meet Fionnuala."

This was greeted with such a long pause that Gilpatrick was not even sure if his father had heard, but he knew better than to press the matter; so for some time they continued on their way in silence. Finally his father spoke.

"There are things you do not know about your sister."

II

⊰ 1170 ⊱

"You aren't going to do anything stupid today, are you?" Fifteen-year-old Una glanced at her friend nervously. It was a warm May morning and it ought to be a perfect day.

"Why would I do something stupid, Una?" Her green eyes wide, innocent, laughing.

Because you usually do, Una thought; but instead she said, "He really means it this time, Fionnuala. He'll send you home to your parents. Is that what you want?"

"You'll look after me."

Yes, thought Una, I always do. And perhaps I shouldn't. Fionnuala was loveable because she was funny and good-hearted—when she wasn't quarrelling with her mother—and somehow when you were with her, life seemed brighter and more exciting, because you never knew what was going to happen next. But when a man as kind as Ailred the Palmer ran out of patience . . .

"I'll be good, Una. I promise."

No you won't, Una could have screamed. You won't at all. And we both of us know it.

"Look, Una," Fionnuala suddenly cried. "Apples." And with her long, dark hair flying behind her, she was running across the little marketplace towards a fruit stall.

How could Fionnuala behave the way she did? Especially when you considered who her father was. The Ui Fergusa might long ago have ceased to be a power in the land, but people still looked up to them with respect. Their little monastery on the slope above the dark pool had been wound up some while ago and the chapel converted into a small parish church for the family and their dependants; but as head of the family, Fionnuala's father, Conn, was the priest and was much respected. With his ancient position and his ancestral lands in the area, he was treated with courtesy by the King of Dublin and by the archbishop equally. With his tall, stately presence and his dignified way of speaking, Una had always held him in awe. But she was sure he was kindly. She couldn't imagine him mistreating Fionnuala. How could Fionnuala think of doing anything to let him down?

Her mother, admittedly, was another matter. She and Fionnuala were always fighting. She wanted her daughter to do one thing; Fionnuala wanted to do something else. But Una wasn't sure she blamed the mother for the constant rows. "If I were your mother I'd slap you," she'd several times told her friend. Two years ago, however, the friction in the household up by the little church had become so bad that it had been agreed that Fionnuala should reside during the week with Ailred the Palmer and his wife. And now even Ailred had had enough.

Una sighed. It would be hard to imagine any nicer people. Everyone in Dublin loved the rich Norseman whose family had owned the big farmstead out in Fingal for so long. His mother had come from a Saxon family who'd left England after the Norman conquest and she had given him the English name of Ailred; but she was blue-eyed like her husband, and Ailred looked just like his red-haired Norwegian ancestors. He was generous and kindly. And he was religious.

The Irish had always made pilgrimages to holy places. There were many holy sites in Ireland. If they went across the seas, they might journey as far as the great shrine of Saint James at Compostela in Spain. But a few, a very few, had gone all the way on the perilous journey to the Holy Land, and if they reached Jerusalem they would enter the Holy City holding a palm. Upon their return, such a pilgrim would be known as a "Palmer." Ailred had done this.

And God it seemed had rewarded him. As well as the big farmstead in Fingal, he had other lands. He had a loving wife. But then their only son, Harold, had gone on pilgrimage, it was said, and never returned. Five years had passed. No word had come; and his unhappy parents had finally accepted that they would not see him again. Perhaps it was to compensate for this loss that Ailred and his comfortable wife had started a hospital on a piece of land he owned just outside the city gate where the ancient Slige Mhor came in from the west. As a pilgrim he had often seen such places, where the sick could be tended and weary travellers could rest; but until now there had never been such a facility at Dublin. He and his wife spent much of their time there nowadays. He named it the Hospital of Saint John the Baptist.

But despite all this activity, Una suspected that Ailred and his wife were still lonely. So perhaps it was that reason as well as their natural kindness that caused them, when Fionnuala's father was lamenting his difficulties with his daughter one day, to offer to take her into their home.

"There will be plenty to keep her busy helping us in the hospital," Ailred had explained. "She'd be like our daughter." And so it had all been arranged. On Saturdays Fionnuala returned to her parents' house and spent Sunday with them. But from Monday to Friday she lived with Ailred and his wife and helped at the hospital.

The arrangement had worked admirably for nearly a week.

Una remembered so well the day when the Palmer had come to see her father. Fionnuala had been at the hospital only a week. "But it's wrong for the child to be alone in our house with nothing but old people," the Palmer had explained. "We'd like her to have a companion, a girl of her own age but a sensible girl, who could help to steady her."

Why did everyone always call her sensible? Una knew they did and she supposed it was true. But why? Was it just her nature? Or was it because of her family? When her eldest sister had died while her brothers were still little boys, she had known that her parents had relied on her. In a way, it had always seemed to Una that her father needed her most of all.

Kevin MacGowan the silversmith was not strong. With his small, spindly body, he was certainly nothing much to look at. And then there was his face: when he was concentrating hard on his work, he would unconsciously twist it into a grimace, so that one of his eyes seemed to be bigger than the other. It made him look as if he were in pain, and she suspected that he sometimes was. Yet within this fragile body lay a fiery soul. "Your father's a strange, poetical fellow," a kindly friend had once said to her. "I only wish he was stronger." Others saw it, too. They certainly respected his work. For that was when Una loved to watch him—while he was working. His fingers, slim and bony like his body, seemed to take on a new strength. His twisted face might be tense, but his eyes shone, and he became transformed into something else, something so fine it was almost like a spirit. Unaware that she was watching him, he would work on, absorbed, and she would be filled with love for her little father and a desire to protect him.

MacGowan. The family name had made a gradual transition down the generations. Some scribes would still have written it MacGoibnenn, in the old manner, but it was mostly written and pronounced MacGowan now.

In the last few years, her father's hard work had brought the family some prosperity. Outside Dublin, men still measured their wealth in cattle. But the wealth that Kevin MacGowan had saved was the little hoard of silver that he kept in a small strongbox. "If anything should happen to me," he would tell Una with gentle pride, "this will see the family through."

He had planned for his family so carefully. The old church in the centre of Dublin had been raised, some years after the battle of Clontarf, to the rank of cathedral and since then transformed into quite a noble building. Western Europe might be moving to the light and delicate Gothic style of architecture, but in Ireland, the heavy, monumental Romanesque style of former times, with its high blank walls and thick curved arches, was still in vogue, and the cathedral in Dublin was a fine example. With its thick walls and its high roof, it towered over the little city. Officially it was the Church of the Holy Trinity, but everyone called it Christ Church. And it was to Christ Church Cathedral that, at least once a month, Kevin MacGowan would take his daughter.

"There is the true cross on which Our Lord was crucified," he would say, pointing to a small piece of wood encased in a golden casket. Christ Church was becoming famous for its growing collection of relics. "There is a portion of the cross of Saint Peter, a piece of the vest of Our Lady, and there, that is a bit of the manger in which Christ was born." The cathedral even had a drop of the Blessed Virgin Mary's milk, with which she had fed the baby Jesus.

But even more revered than these sacred objects were the two treasures that every visitor to Dublin came to see. The first was a great crucifix which, like some ancient pagan stone from earlier times, would sometimes speak. And greatest of all, was the beautiful staff that, it was said, an angel had given to Saint Patrick from Jesus Christ himself: this was the famous Bachall Iosa, the Staff of Jesus. It was kept at a shrine to the north of Dublin but was brought into Christ Church on special occasions.

And as she gazed at these marvels with awe, her father would say to her, "If ever the city is in danger, Una, we shall bring the strongbox to the cathedral monks. In their keeping it will be as safe as are these relics that you see before you." It gave them both comfort to know that their little worldly treasure would be protected by the keepers of the true cross and the Bachall Iosa of Saint Patrick.

Every day, Una knew, her father carried the thought of that box of silver around with him in his mind like a talisman or a pilgrim's amulet.

Thanks to his efforts, her father had an assistant now, and her mother had an English slave girl to help her in the house. Her two brothers were healthy, lively boys. There was no reason, therefore, why Una couldn't spend three days a week at Ailred the Palmer's hospital which, in any case, was only a few hundred yards from her own home. And before long, she was coming in on Mondays and leaving on Fridays. Since Fionnuala was required to spend Sundays with her parents, this meant that the Palmer and his wife only had to keep her under control for one day of the week which, they bravely declared, was no trouble at all.

They were such a loving couple, the tall red-haired Norseman and his quiet, grey-haired, motherly wife. Una guessed what a blow the loss of their son, Harold, must have been; she never mentioned the subject and nor did they. But once, as they were folding blankets in the hospital, the older woman smiled at her gently and said, "I also had a baby daughter, you know. She died when she was two; but if she'd lived, I think she would have been just like you." Una had felt so touched and honoured. Sometimes she would pray that their son would return to them after all; but of course he never did.

Una loved the Hospital of Saint John the Baptist. It contained thirty inmates at present; the men in one dormitory, the women in another. Some were elderly, but not all. They cared for every kind of sickness there, except lepers whom no one would come near. There was plenty to do feeding and nursing the inmates, but above all Una loved to talk to them and listen to their stories. She was a popular figure. Fionnuala's reputation was different. She could be funny when she chose. She would flirt harmlessly with the old men and make the women laugh. But it was not in her nature to work very hard. She might surprise and delight the inmates by suddenly appearing with a delicious fruit tart; but as often as not, in the middle of some tedious chore, Una would find that her friend had vanished, leaving her with all the work to do. And sometimes, if something had annoyed her or if she thought Una wasn't paying enough attention to her, she would suddenly have a temper tantrum, throw down the work she was doing, and rush away to some other part of the hospital where she would sulk. On these occasions, Ailred the Palmer would shake his long red beard, and his kindly blue eyes would look sad, and he would turn to Una and say, "She is good-hearted underneath, my child, even if she does foolish things. We must all try to help her." But Una knew very well that, though they certainly tried, it would be her own efforts which generally brought Fionnuala round.

The last few months had tried even the Palmer's patience. And this time the problem wasn't temper tantrums, though Fionnuala still had those. It was men.

Fionnuala had always looked at men, ever since she was a little girl. She would stare at them with her large green eyes, and they would laugh. It was part of her childish charm. But she was no longer a child; she was almost a young woman. Yet still she looked at them, and it was no longer the wide-eyed gaze of a child. It was a hard, challenging stare. She stared at young men in the street; she stared at old men in the hospital; she stared at married men in the market in front of their wives, who were ceasing to be amused. But it was a visiting merchant who was residing in the hospital after breaking his leg who first complained to Ailred. "That girl's making eyes at me," he said. "Then she came and sat on the end of the bench where I was sitting and opened her shirt so I could see her breasts. I'm too old to play games with girls like that," he told the Palmer. "If I hadn't got a broken leg, I'd have reached over and slapped her."

Last week there had been another complaint, and this time

Ailred's wife had heard about it. Una had never seen that kindly woman so angry.

"You ought to be whipped!" she cried.

"Why?" Fionnuala had answered calmly. "It wouldn't stop me."

She had nearly been sent home there and then, but Ailred had given her one more chance. "There must be no more complaints, Fionnuala," he told her, "of any kind. If there are," he had promised, "you will have to go home. You cannot come here anymore."

That had shaken Fionnuala. She had been very quiet and thoughtful for a day or two. But it hadn't been long before her usual spirits returned; and though she took care not to cause any complaints from the men they encountered, Una could see the flash of mischief back in her friend's eyes.

The market where the two girls now found themselves lay just inside the western gateway. In recent generations, the old ramparts from the days of Brian Boru had been extended westwards and they had all been rebuilt in stone. Besides the cathedral rising over the thatched roofs of the city's busy clusters of timber-and-wattle houses, there were now seven smaller churches. Across the river on the north side of the bridge an extensive suburb had also arisen. The Norse-Irish kings of Dublin now ruled over a walled city quite as impressive as most others in Europe.

Though not as big as the market where the slaves were sold down by the waterfront, the western market presented a lively scene. There were food stalls of every kind: meat, fruit, and vegetables. And there was a colourful collection of people crowding the place. There were merchants from northern France: they had their own church, called Saint Martin's, that overlooked the old pool of Dubh Linn. There was an English colony from the busy port of Chester that lay due east across the Irish Sea. The Chester trade had been increasing in recent generations. They had a Saxon church in the mid-

dle of the town. The Scandinavian sailors had their chapel, called
Saint Olave's, down by the waterfront. And there were often visitors
from Spain or even farther off adding brightness and colour to the
marketplace. Even the native population were a very mixed people
now: huge burly fellows with Nordic red hair and Irish names;
Latin-looking men who would tell you they were Danish—you
could speak of Ostmen and Irishmen, Gaedhil and Gaill, but the
truth was that you could hardly tell one from the other. They were
all Dubliners. And they were proud of it. There were at this date between four and five thousand of them.

Fionnuala was standing by the fruit stall. Una watched carefully
as she followed after her. Was Fionnuala flirting with the stall
holder, or the people close by? She didn't seem to be. A handsome
young French merchant was strolling towards the stall. If Fionnuala
made eyes at him, Una supposed it wouldn't matter. But as the
young man came close, it seemed to her that for once Fionnuala
wasn't taking any notice. Una gave a little prayer of thanks. Perhaps
Fionnuala was going to behave herself today.

For several moments after she saw what Fionnuala did next,
Una didn't understand. It seemed the most natural thing in the
world. All that Fionnuala had done was to stretch out her hand
and take a large apple from the stall, inspect it and put it back.
There was nothing strange about that. The young Frenchman was
speaking to the stall holder. For a few moments, Fionnuala hung
around by the stall, then she moved away. Una caught up with
her.

"I'm bored, Una," said Fionnuala. "Let's go down to the quay."

"All right."

"Did you see what I got?" She looked at Una and gave her a slow
mischievous smile. "A nice juicy apple." She reached into her shirt
and drew it out.

"Where did you get that?"

"From the stall."

"But you didn't pay for it."

"I know."

"Fionnuala! Put it back at once."

"I can't."

"Why?"

"Because I don't want to."

"For God's sake, Fionnuala! You stole it."

Fionnuala opened her green eyes wide. Usually when she did that and made a funny face it was difficult not to laugh. But Una wasn't laughing now. Someone might have seen. She had a vision of the stall holder rushing towards them, of Ailred being called.

"Give it to me. I'll put it back."

Slowly and deliberately, her eyes still wide in their fake solemn look, Fionnuala raised the apple as if she were going to hold it out to Una; but instead of proffering it, she calmly took a bite. Her mock-serious eyes were fixed on Una.

"It's too late."

Una turned on her heel. She walked straight over to the stall, where the stall holder had just finished speaking to the Frenchman, and took an apple.

"How much for two? My friend's already started hers." She smiled pleasantly and indicated Fionnuala who had followed her over. The stall holder smiled at them.

"You work at the hospital, don't you?"

"Yes." Fionnuala gazed at him with her large eyes.

"That's all right. Have them for nothing."

Una thanked him and led her friend away.

"He gave them to us." Fionnuala gave Una a sidelong glance.

"That's not the point and you know it." They walked a little farther. "I'm going to murder you one day, Fionnuala."

"That would be bad. Don't you love me?"

"That's not the point either."

"Yes, it is."

"You don't know the difference between right and wrong, Fionnuala, and you'll come to a bad end."

Fionnuala didn't answer for a moment.

"I expect I shall," she said.

⁙

It was fortunate that Fionnuala's father was unaware of her behaviour, since it might have spoiled a very pleasant morning. For at the same time that the two girls were leaving the marketplace with their apples, that eminent churchman was walking at a dignified pace towards the hostel where his son Gilpatrick now lived. His mood was serious, because there was important family business to discuss. But the business was not unpleasant, the morning was fine and sunny, and he was looking forward to seeing Gilpatrick. As he came in sight of his son, therefore, he raised his stick in a solemn but friendly greeting.

The hostel of Saint Kevin's was a small fenced enclosure containing a chapel, a dormitory, and some modest wooden buildings, which lay only two hundred yards south of the family's ancient monastery. It belonged to the monks of Glendalough, who used it when visiting Dublin, and Gilpatrick had often resided here in the last two years. He was standing at the gateway and now, seeing his father approach, he moved forward.

But was there something in his manner, some hesitancy, which suggested he was not as glad to see his father as he should have been? It seemed to the older man that there might be.

"Are you not pleased to see me, Gilpatrick?" he enquired.

"Oh I am. Of course. Indeed I am."

"That is good," said his father. "Let us walk."

They could have taken the roadway south, through the orchards. To the east, crossing a footbridge over the stream, they would have come out onto a large area of marshy meadows, dotted with trees. Instead, however, they took the roadway northwards that followed the gentle curve of the family's ancient monastic enclosure before it continued, past the dark pool, towards the Thingmount and Hoggen Green.

Walking this route with his father, Gilpatrick thought, was always rather like a royal progress. As soon as they saw his father coming, people would smile and bow their heads with respect and affection, and his father would acknowledge them like a true tribal chief from ancient times.

And indeed, Conn probably had more prestige now than any chief of the Ui Fergusa had enjoyed before. His mother had been the last of the family of Caoilinn who had held the lands at Rathmines. Through his mother, therefore, the two strands of the descendants of Fergus were rejoined, and he inherited the blood of the ancient royal house of Leinster. As well as the family's ancient drinking skull, his mother had also brought, as her dowry, some of those valuable Rathmines lands. By his own marriage, moreover, to a kinswoman of Lawrence O'Toole, he had allied himself with one of the noblest princely houses of northern Leinster. The Viking settlement might have taken over Fergus's final resting place and the Church might have encroached upon many of the ancient grazing grounds in the region, but the present chief of the Ui Fergusa could still run his cattle over a huge tract of land down the coastal strip towards the Wicklow Mountains. More than this, the generations of family rule of the little monastery had given the chiefs a sacral role. And although the little monastery had been wound up and its chapel turned into a parish church, Gilpatrick's father was still the vicar and as such he was, his son thought, that curiously Irish phenomenon, the druidical chief. No wonder his parishioners treated him with a special and tender respect.

Since he was dreading the conversation that was to come, Gilpatrick was glad that, as they walked down the roadway, his father seemed to feel no need to converse. When his father did speak, it was only to make a casual enquiry.

"Did you ever hear from that friend of yours, FitzDavid?"

At first, Gilpatrick had been a little disappointed that no word had ever come from Peter FitzDavid, and as time went by he had almost forgotten about him. Perhaps he had been killed.

The progress of King Diarmait and his foreign troops had been slow. The O'Connor High King and O'Rourke had gone down to Wexford to deal with him; there had been two skirmishes, neither very decisive. Diarmait had been forced to give hostages to the High King and pay O'Rourke a large fine in gold for the theft of his wife. He'd been allowed back into his ancestral lands in the south, but that was all. For a year he'd stayed down there and nobody had heard a squeak from him.

Last year, however, he'd managed to procure another, larger contingent of troops—thirty mounted men, about a hundred men-at-arms, and more than three hundred archers. They included several knights from prominent families that Gilpatrick had heard of, such as FitzGerald, Barri, and even an uncle of Strongbow himself. FitzGerald and his brother had been given the port of Wexford, which probably hadn't pleased the Ostmen merchants there; and thanks to the mediation of Archbishop O'Toole of Dublin, the High King had agreed to a new deal.

"Send me your son as hostage," he'd told Diarmait, "and—excluding Dublin, of course—you can have all Leinster." To which he had quietly added, "If you can get it." Diarmait had also had to promise that once he'd secured Leinster, he'd send all his foreigners back across the sea again.

But that had been a year ago, and still Diarmait hadn't ventured into the northern part of the province. "You've no friends here," he was firmly told.

"I doubt," Gilpatrick's father now remarked, "that you'll be seeing your Welshman any time soon."

They rounded the bend in the roadway above the pool and gazed down to the old burial ground. It was, Gilpatrick thought, a pleasant prospect. For if in former times the waterside site of Hoggen Green had been starkly bare, the spirits of the dead, perhaps, almost too free to wander as they liked, the Church had now placed its own sanctuaries beside the place, enclosing the spirits, as it were, with invisible barriers so that, if wander they must, they would have to go eastwards, past the old Viking stone and into the Liffey's waters to be carried, no doubt, on the ebb tide, out into the long draw of the estuary and the open sea. To the left, just across the pond from the city wall, stood the small church of Saint Andrew's, attended by a sprinkling of timber houses. To the right, a little above the Thing-mount, lay the walled enclosure of the city's only nunnery; and on the bankside of the Liffey, on reclaimed marshland, a small Augustinian friary.

"I dare say," his father remarked, indicating the nunnery, "that I should put your sister in there."

"They wouldn't keep her," Gilpatrick replied with a smile.

If only his wayward sister were the subject for discussion. That would have been easy. The real business of the day, however, had still not been mentioned; and they had walked out onto the old grave-yard and were almost at the Thingmount before his father finally brought it up.

"It's time your brother married," he said.

It seemed such a harmless statement. Until the previous year, Gilpatrick had been blessed with two brothers. His elder brother who had been married for some years lived several miles down the coast and farmed the family's great tract of land. He had loved his farm and seldom came up to Dublin. His younger brother, Lorcan, who had helped on the farm, was still unmarried. But at the start of the previous winter, after getting chilled on his way back from a journey into Ulster, his elder brother had taken a fever and died, leaving two daughters with his widow. She was a pleasant young woman and the family loved her. "She's a treasure," they all agreed. She was only twenty-three and clearly she should marry again. "But it would be a terrible pity to lose her," as Gilpatrick's father had very truly said.

And now, six months after the sad event, a solution had pre-sented itself that promised to be satisfactory to everybody. Last week, his younger brother had come up from the farm and spoken to his father. An understanding had been reached. All the parties were agreeable.

The young man was to marry his brother's widow.

"I couldn't be happier, Gilpatrick," his father said. "They'll wait until the year has passed. And then they will marry with my blessing. And yours, too, I hope."

Gilpatrick took a deep breath. He'd been preparing himself for this. His mother had told him about it two days ago.

"You know very well that I can't," he now replied.

"They will have my blessing," his father repeated sharply.

"But you know," Gilpatrick pointed out reasonably, "that the thing is impossible."

"I do not," Conn replied. "You know yourself," he continued in a conciliatory tone, "that they are perfectly suited. They are the same age. They are already the best friends in the world. She was a wonderful wife to his brother and will be to him, too. She loves him, Gilpatrick. She confessed it to me herself. As for him, he's a fine young man, sound as an oak. As good a man as ever his brother was. There can be no reasonable objection to the marriage."

"Except," Gilpatrick said with a sigh, "that she is his brother's wife."

"Which marriage the Bible allows," his father snapped.

"Which marriage the Jews allowed," Gilpatrick patiently corrected. "The Pope, however, does not."

It was a much disputed passage. The book of Leviticus actually enjoined a dutiful man to marry his brother's widow. The medieval Church, however, had decided that such a marriage was against canon law, and throughout Christendom such marriages were forbidden.

Except in Ireland. The truth was that things were still done differently in Christendom's north-western corner. Celtic marriages had always been fluid affairs, easily dissolved, and even if it did not quite approve, the Celtic Church had wisely learned to accommo-

date itself to local custom. The heirs of Saint Patrick had not withheld their blessing from the four-times-married Brian Boru who was
their loyal patron; and to a traditional Irish churchman like Conn,
such canonical objections as this question of the brother's widow
seemed like nit-picking. Nor did he feel any sense of disloyalty to
his church when he remarked a little sourly, "The Holy Father is a
long way away."

Gilpatrick looked at his father affectionately. In a way, it seemed
to him, the older man represented all that was best—and worst—in
the Celtic Irish Church. Half hereditary chief, half druid, he was an
exemplary parish priest. He was married with children, but still a
priest. These traditional arrangements extended to his ecclesiastical
income as well. The lands with which his family had anciently endowed the monastery—and Conn had added those valuable lands
at Rathmines as well—had passed into the parish, and so they technically belonged to the Archbishop of Dublin now. But as the parish
priest, his father received all the revenues from these lands himself,
as well as those from the family's large estates down the coast. In due
course Gilpatrick himself might succeed him as priest, and in all
likelihood one of his brother's children, assuming this uncanonical
marriage produced sons, might follow on after. It was so in churches
and monasteries all over Ireland.

And, of course, it was a scandal. Or so, at least, thought the Pope
in Rome.

For during the last century or so, a great wind of change had
been sweeping across western Christendom. The old church, it was
felt, had become too rich, too worldly, lacking in spiritual fire and
passionate commitment. New monastic orders dedicated to simplicity, like the Cistercians, were springing up. The Crusades had
been launched to regain the Holy Land from the Saracens. Popes
sought to purify the Church and to extend its authority, even issuing peremptory commands to kings.

"You have to admit, Father," Gilpatrick gently reminded him,
"that the church in Ireland lags behind our neighbours."

"I wish," his father replied gloomily, "that I'd never let you go to England."

For one country in particular that had felt the force of this vigorous new wind had been the kingdom across the water. A century ago, the old Saxon Church had been notoriously lax. When William of Normandy began his conquest, he had easily obtained a papal blessing by promising to clean it up. Since then, the Norman English Church had been a model, with archbishops like the reforming Lanfranc and the saintly Anselm. Not that Gilpatrick was the only Irishman to catch the reforming contagion there. Quite a number of Irish churchmen had spent time in the great English monasteries like Canterbury and Worcester. The ecclesiastical contacts were many. For a while, indeed, the bishops of Dublin had even gone to England to be consecrated by the Archbishop of Canterbury. "Though they only did that," Gilpatrick's father had remarked with some truth, "to show that Dublin was different from the rest of Ireland." As a result, many of the leading churchmen in Ireland now had a sense that they were out of step with the rest of Christendom and that they ought to do something about it.

"In any case," the older man said irritably, "the Irish Church has already been reformed."

Up to a point, it had—the administration of the Irish Church was certainly being brought up to date. The ancient tribal and monastic dioceses had been redrawn and brought under four archbishoprics: the ancient seat of Saint Patrick at Armagh, Tuam in the west, Cashel down in Munster, and lastly Dublin. Archbishop O'Toole of Dublin had set up new monastic houses, including the one at Christ Church, which followed a strict Augustinian rule that couldn't have been bettered anywhere in Europe. In Dublin, at least, many of the parishes now paid taxes, known as tithes, to the Church.

"We've made a start," Gilpatrick said. "But much still needs to be done."

"You would consider my own position needed reforming then, I dare say."

It was a tribute to Gilpatrick's filial respect that he had always managed to avoid discussing this issue with his father. There had been no need to discuss something that wasn't going to change anyway. It was the realisation that the discussion of his brother's marriage might lead to such larger issues that had made him dread this meeting with his father in the first place.

"It would be hard to defend outside Ireland," Gilpatrick said gently.

"Yet the archbishop has made no objection."

It was one of the great wonders of the rule of Lawrence O'Toole that, like many great leaders, he had the genius—there was no other word for it—to live in two contradictory worlds at once. Gilpatrick had been given a number of tasks by the archbishop since his return and had had the opportunity to study him. He was saintly—there was not a doubt of that—and Gilpatrick revered him. O'Toole wanted to purify the Irish Church. But he was also an Irish prince, every inch of him, a poetic soul, full of a mystical spirit. "And it's the spirit that matters, Gilpatrick," the great man had often said to him. "Some of our greatest churchmen, like Saint Colum Cille, were royal princes. And if a people revered God through the leadership of their chief, there surely can be no harm in that."

"That is true, Father," Gilpatrick now replied, "and until the archbishop does object, I shan't say a word about it."

His father looked at him. On the face of it, Gilpatrick was being conciliatory. But did he not realise, his father wondered, how patronising that answer was? He felt a flush of anger. His son was patronising him, telling him he would tolerate his position in life until such time as the archbishop called it in question. It was an insult to him, to the family, to Ireland itself. He felt like hitting out.

"I'm beginning to see what it is you want for the Church, Gilpatrick," his father said with a dangerous gentleness.

"What is that, Father?"

The older man looked at him coldly. "Another English Pope."

Gilpatrick winced. It was a low blow, but telling. The previous decade, for the first and only time in its long history, the Catholic Church had had an English Pope. Adrian IV had been unremarkable, but for the Irish at least he had done one thing that made him remembered.

He had recommended a Crusade against Ireland.

It had been at a time, just after his accession, when King Henry of England had briefly considered an invasion of the western island. Whether to please the English king, or whether he had been misled about the state of the Irish Church by Henry's ambassadors, Pope Adrian had written a letter telling the English king that he would perform a useful service in taking over the island "to increase the Christian religion."

"What could you expect from an English Pope?" men like Gilpatrick's father had asked. But though Pope Adrian had now departed this life, the memory of his letter still rankled. "We, the heirs of Saint Patrick, we who kept alive the Christian faith and the writings of ancient Rome when most of the world had sunk under the barbarians, we who gave the Saxons their education, are to be taught a lesson in Christianity by the English?" So Gilpatrick's father would storm if ever the subject came up.

Pope Adrian's letter, of course, had been an outrage; Gilpatrick wouldn't deny it. But that wasn't really the point. The real issue was larger.

"You speak as if there were such a thing as a separate Irish Church, Father. But there is only one Church and it is universal: that is its great strength. Its authority comes from the one Heavenly King. You speak of the past, when barbarians were fighting over the ruins of the Roman Empire. It was only the Church which was able to bring peace and order because it had a single, spiritual authority beyond the reach of earthly kings. When the Pope calls upon the knights of Christ to go on Crusade, he calls upon them from every land. Disputing kings set aside their quarrels to become warriors and pilgrims together. The Pope, the heir of Saint Peter himself, rules all Christendom under Heaven. There must be only one true Church. It cannot be otherwise."

How could he convey the vision which inspired him and so many others of his kind—of a world where a man might walk from Ireland to Jerusalem, using a common Latin language, and finding everywhere the same ordered Christian empire, the same monastic orders, the same liturgy. Christendom was a vast spiritual machine, an engine of prayer, a universal brotherhood.

"I will tell you what I think," said his father softly. "The thing which these reformers love is not a matter of the spirit. It is power. The Pope does not take hostages like a king, but takes spiritual hostages instead. For if a monarch disobeys him, he excommunicates him and tells his people, or other kings with a power to do it, that he should be deposed. You say such things are done to bring the nations of the earth closer to God. I tell you they are done from a love of power."

Gilpatrick knew that his father had a point. There had been many clashes of will between popes and monarchs, including the kings of France, England, and even the Holy Roman Emperor about whether the Church's vast lands and its army of churchmen were subject to royal control. At this very time King Henry of England was locked in a furious dispute with Archbishop Thomas Becket of Canterbury over just this issue—and there were senior churchmen in England who thought that the king was in the right. It was the ancient tension between king and priest that was probably as old as human history.

"And I will ask you one thing more," said his father. "Have you seen a copy of Pope Adrian's letter in which he tells the king to come to Ireland?"

"I believe I have." The letter had become widely known.

"What is the condition that the Pope makes, what thing must the King of England do to obtain a blessing for his conquest? It is mentioned not once, but twice," he added nastily.

"Well, there is the question of the tax, of course . . ."

"A penny to be levied upon every household in the land, and sent to Rome each year. Peter's Pence!" the older man cried. "It's the money they want, Gilpatrick. The money."

"It's only right and proper, Father, that . . ."

"Peter's Pence." The older man raised his finger and stared so fiercely at his son that Gilpatrick could almost imagine that he was being admonished by a grey-bearded druid from ancient times. "Peter's Pence."

And then, suddenly, the older man turned away from his son in disgust. If Gilpatrick did not understand even now, then what could he say? It was not the money. It was the spirit of the thing which offended him. Could Gilpatrick really not see that? For seven centuries, the Irish Church had been an inspiration to all Christendom because of its spirit. The spirit of Saint Patrick, of Saint Colum Cille, Saint Kevin, and many others. Missionaries, hermits, princes of Ireland. It had always seemed to him that the Irish had been touched in some special way, like the chosen people in ancient times. Be that as it might, Christianity was a mystic communion, not a set of rules and regulations. It was not that he was ignorant of the ways of other countries. He had met priests from England and France in the port of Dublin. But he had always sensed in them a legalistic mentality, a love of logical games that repulsed him. Men like these did not belong in the beloved silences of Glendalough; they could never fashion the Book of Kells. They might be priests but they were not poets; and if they were scholars, then their scholarship was dry.

It was therefore with a sense of bitterness towards more than just his son that the old man now, standing in front of the Thingmount where Fergus himself lay buried, hotly declared, "You will come to Lorcan's wedding, Gilpatrick, because he is your brother and he will be hurt if you do not. You will come also because I order you to do so. Are you understanding me?"

"Father, I cannot. Not if he marries his brother's wife."

"Then you needn't trouble," his father shouted, "to enter my house again."

"Surely, Father . . ." Gilpatrick began. But his father had turned on his heel and walked away. And Gilpatrick knew, sadly, that it was useless to follow him. A week later, the wedding was announced. In June it took place, and Gilpatrick was not there. In July, seeing his father by the entrance of Christ Church, Gilpatrick started towards him; but his father, as he saw him coming, turned away, and Gilpatrick, after a moment's hesitation, decided not to follow him. August passed and they did not speak. September came.

And then there were other, more urgent matters to think about.

⁘

It was still quiet when Kevin MacGowan awoke that September morning. The sky was grey. His wife was already up; from the oven in the yard came the faint smell of baking bread. The slave girl was sweeping near the gate. The two boys were playing in the yard. Through the open doorway he could see the steam of their breath. Autumn had come to Dublin. There was a chill in the morning air.

Automatically, as he always did, he reached under the bed and felt for the strongbox. It was reassuringly there. He liked to sleep with it close to him. There was another place, under the bread oven, where he usually concealed it. Only his wife and Una knew about that. It was a good hiding place. Not as secure as the cathedral perhaps, but cleverly disguised. You could look there a hundred times and never guess there was a hiding place. But when he slept in the house, he kept the box under his bed.

He looked across the room. In the far corner, in the shadows, he could see another form gently stirring. It was Una. Normally she would have been at the hospital, but with all the recent events, she had preferred to remain at home with her family today. She was sitting up now. He smiled. Could she see his smile from over there in the shadows? He wondered if she knew what happiness her presence gave him. Probably not. And probably better if she didn't. One mustn't burden one's children with too much affection.

He got up, went over to her, and kissed her on the head. He turned, felt a slight constriction in his chest, and gave a little cough. Then he walked to the entrance and looked out. It was certainly getting cold.

His gaze went out towards the gateway. He saw a neighbour go past with a wooden bucket of water from the well. The fellow seemed in no hurry. He listened. Some sparrows were chattering in the branches of the apple tree in the yard next door. He heard a blackbird. Yes, everything seemed to be normal. There was no hint of any commotion. That was a relief.

Strongbow. Nobody really thought that he would come. His uncle and the FitzGeralds had stayed down in the south all summer and the people of Dublin had reasonably assumed they would be there for the rest of the year. But then in the last week of August the news had arrived.

"Strongbow is in Wexford. He's arrived with English troops. A lot of troops."

Two hundred fully equipped mounted men and a thousand foot soldiers, to be precise. They were mostly drawn from the family's huge holdings in England. It was a force that only one of the greatest magnates in the Plantagenet empire could have collected. By the standards of feudal Europe, it was a small army. By Irish standards, the armoured knights, the highly trained men-at-arms, and the archers, who shot with mathematical precision, represented a disciplined military machine beyond anything they possessed.

Within days, news came that the port of Waterford was in Strongbow's hands as well; then that King Diarmait had given Strongbow his daughter in marriage. And soon after this: "They're coming to Dublin."

It was an outrage. The High King had allowed Diarmait to take Leinster; but Dublin was another matter, specifically excluded from the agreement. "If Diarmait wants Dublin, then he means to take all Ireland," the High King judged. "And didn't he give me his own son as hostage?" the O'Connor king continued. If Diarmait broke his oath under such circumstances, O'Connor had the right under Irish law to do what he liked with the boy, even execute him. "What kind of man is it," O'Connor cried, "that sacrifices his own son?"

It was time to put a stop to the ambitions of this turbulent adventurer and his foreign friends.

There was no doubt about the feelings of the Dubliners either. Three days ago, MacGowan had watched the King of Dublin and some of the greatest merchants ride out to welcome the High King as he came down to the Liffey. It was said that even Diarmait's brother-in-law the archbishop was disgusted with him. The O'Connor king had brought with him a large force, and it was quickly agreed that the Dubliners would prepare to defend their city while the High King would march a day's journey to the south and block the approaches up the Liffey Plain. A day later, MacGowan heard that not only was O'Connor camped across the route but he had ordered trees felled to make every track in the region impassable. Dublin made preparations, but the consensus was clear; even with Strongbow and all his men, King Diarmait would give them no trouble. "They'll never get through."

Except on the coldest winter days, when he might be forced to retreat indoors, Kevin MacGowan always worked in an open-sided shed in the yard. That way he had daylight to see what he was doing. To stay warm he kept a small brazier at his feet.

He sat down at his workbench that morning with a contented smile. He never ate much, but his wife had given him fresh bread, piping hot from the oven and served with honey. The smell and the taste of it lingered in a delightful way as he set to work. His wife and Una were spinning wool in a corner by the oven. His two sons were busy with a wood carving. It was a perfect family scene.

A merchant came in to talk about a silver brooch for his wife. Kevin asked him if all was quiet in the town and he said that it was. After a while the man left, and for some time Kevin went on with his work in silence. Then he paused.

"Una."

"Yes, Father."

"Go to the south wall, by the main gate. Tell me if you see anything."

"Couldn't one of the boys go? I'm helping Mother."

"I should prefer it if you went." He trusted her more than the boys.

She glanced at her mother who smiled at her and nodded.

"As you wish, Father," she said. She put a saffron-coloured shawl over her head to keep out the cold and set off along the street.

She was glad to be at home. Perhaps she had been spending too much time with the sick at the hospital, but it seemed to her that her father had not been entirely well recently. Normally she would have been busy at the hospital that day, but Fionnuala had agreed to take over her tasks. She believed that recently she had managed to persuade Fionnuala to adopt a more responsible attitude to life and she felt rather proud of that.

She saw nothing unusual along the way. People were going about their business. She passed a cart carrying timber, and she had just reached the Saxons' church when, from the king's hall nearby, she heard a clatter of hoofs and a dozen riders came out towards her. In front rode the king himself. She noticed that none of the riders were dressed for battle, though one or two carried the Viking battle-axe that was a favoured weapon in most parts of Ireland now. The rest, including the king, only had daggers in their belts.

As she drew against the wooden fence to let them pass, the king smiled down at her. He was a handsome, kindly-looking man. He certainly didn't appear in the least worried.

When she went up onto the wall, she found herself quite alone. Although the sky was grey, the day was clear. Beyond the fields and orchards to the south, the rounded humps of the Wicklow Mountains seemed to loom so close that you could almost touch them. She was a little surprised not so see any lookouts posted on the wall, but there was certainly no sign of any enemy approach. The gateway nearby was open. Away on the left, she could see a ship coming in from the estuary. The port had been particularly active of late. Everything seemed to be normal.

Kevin was busy at his work when she returned. A short while ago, he had felt a need to cough and had gone into the house; but that had passed. He smiled as she returned and told him all was well, and the household resumed its peaceful routine.

It was late in the morning that the silversmith put down the piece he was working on and listened. He did not say anything, just sat there very still. Was something wrong? Nothing that he could put his finger on. Could he hear anything out of the ordinary? No, he could not. But still he sat there, puzzled. His wife glanced at him.

"What is it?"

"I don't know." He shook his head. "Nothing."

He went back to his work for a short while, then paused. The feeling had come to him again. A strange sensation. A sense of coldness. As if a shadow had passed just feet away from him.

"Una."

"Yes, Father?"

"Go up to the wall again."

"Yes, Father." What a good girl she was. Never a word of complaint. The only one he could completely trust.

Although the view at the wall was the same as before, Una did not return at once. There had been no need for words between her father and herself. She understood him. If he was worried, she would take good care to check every possibility. For some time, therefore, she scanned the south-western horizon where the Liffey made its winding way towards the city. Was there any sign of dust, any glint of armour, any hint of movement? There was nothing. Satisfied at last, she decided to go back. She glanced towards the estuary, gave a last brief look at the Wicklow Mountains, and then she saw them.

They were pouring out of the hills like a mountain stream. They were flowing down from a small valley that led up into the wooded hills to the south and spreading out onto the slopes above the hamlet of Rathfarnham, less than four miles away. She could see the glimmer of the chain mail of the knights, scores of them. Masses of men, marching in three columns, followed after. At that distance, the columns looked like three huge centipedes. Behind them came still more columns of men; from their slightly bobbing motion she supposed these must be archers.

She understood what must have happened at once. Diarmait and Strongbow must have come over the mountains instead of up the Liffey valley. They had given the High King the slip entirely. In all likelihood, this was the whole army. In a quarter of an hour they would be at Rathmines. For several moments she watched in horrified fascination; then she turned and ran.

There was no need for Una to raise the alarm. Others also had seen the army on the slopes. People were starting to run in the streets. By the time she reached her own gate, the family had already heard the shouting, and it only took a few moments for her to tell them all she had seen. The question was: what to do?

The lane in which they lived ran into the Fish Shambles. They were not far from the quays. When Una went into the street again to see if there was further news, she discovered that their next-door neighbour was loading a handcart. "I'm going to get on a ship if I can," he told her. "I'll not be waiting here if the English come." On the other side lived a carpenter. He had already built a barricade around his house. He seemed to think that he could keep an army out by his own handiwork.

The MacGowan household was hesitant. Her father had closed up his strongbox and her mother had wrapped some possessions in a cloth which she had slung over her back. The two boys and the apprentice were standing beside her and the English slave girl seemed more anxious to go with them than to be liberated by her fellow countrymen.

Kevin MacGowan had never liked taking chances, and he had always tried to plan for every contingency that might threaten his little family. Faced by this crisis now he found himself well able to think rationally. The carpenter might be absurd, but surely his neighbour planning to go down to the quay might be panicking too soon. Even with his English allies, it seemed unlikely that King Diarmait would be able to penetrate stone-walled defences. That meant a siege—days or weeks of waiting, and plenty of time to leave from the quays if necessary. On balance, it seemed to the silversmith that it might be foolish to run down to the waterside now. Less easy was the question of what to do with the strongbox. He did not like to trouble the monks at Christ Church until there was good reason. If there were a siege, he'd probably continue working; so he'd need to keep some of the valuable pieces in the house anyway. If the family had to leave, he might want to take at least some of his silver with him, and perhaps leave the rest in the strongbox at Christ Church. It would depend on the circumstances.

"Go to the Fish Shambles, Una," he instructed. "Find out what's happening."

The sloping market street was full of people hurrying in every direction, some towards the quays, others up the slope to Christ Church. She stopped several people, but no one seemed to have a definite view about what was happening; and she was wondering what to do when she saw Father Gilpatrick coming swiftly towards her. They knew each other slightly and he gave her a friendly nod. She asked his advice.

"The archbishop is already riding out to talk to them," he told her. "He's determined to avoid any bloodshed. I'm going to join him now myself."

When she returned with this news, Kevin MacGowan pondered.

It seemed to him that the chances were good. Whatever you thought of him, even King Diarmait was hardly going to ignore his saintly brother-in-law.

"We can wait awhile to see what happens," he told his family. "Una, you'd better go back to the wall. Let us know at once if anything starts to happen." It was a shock when she got to the wall this time. She could hardly believe they could have come so close, so soon. The nearest line of men was not three hundred yards away. She could see their faces as they stared sternly towards the walls. Detachments of knights, men-at-arms, and archers were drawn up at intervals and seemed to stretch all the way round the walls.

Straight ahead a quarter mile down the main road, she could see Archbishop O'Toole. He was mounted in the Irish style, without a saddle, on a small grey horse. Behind him were several other churchmen, including Father Gilpatrick's father. The archbishop was in deep conversation with a bearded man, whom she took to be King Diarmait, and a tall man with long moustaches and an impassive face. That would be Strongbow. All the way along the lines, the men stood motionless. Towards one corner of the wall, some of the mounted men seemed restless, but she supposed that might be their horses. Occasionally one of the knights would wheel out of the line and make a circle before coming back. She saw Father Gilpatrick ride out from the open gate and join his father and the other priests. Still nobody moved. The archbishop was dismounting now. So were King Diarmait and Strongbow. Men were bringing stools for them to sit on. Obviously the negotiations were going to take some time. She looked away from the scene for the moment and glanced down into the lane behind her. And then she stared in shock.

Fionnuala was walking down the lane below the wall. She wasn't alone either. There were half a dozen boys with her. They were laughing, and she was flirting, too, by the look of it. She'd ruffled the hair of one of the boys and she was just putting her arm round another. They couldn't possibly be unaware of the danger outside the walls. Perhaps they didn't imagine the English would get in. But it wasn't their stupidity, nor even Fionnuala's flirting, that really shocked her. It was the fact that Fionnuala was supposed to be at the hospital. She had promised. Who was looking after the patients? She felt a surge of indignation.

"Fionnuala!" she cried out. "Fionnuala!"

Fionnuala looked up in surprise.

"Una. What are you doing there?"

"Never mind that. What are *you* doing? Why aren't you at the hospital?"

"I was bored." Fionnuala made a funny face. But it wasn't funny.

Una only glanced over the wall long enough to see that the archbishop was still deep in his discussions. Then she raced to the steps, flew down them, and, ignoring the boys entirely, made straight for Fionnuala. She was in a fury. She had never been so angry. Fionnuala, seeing that she was serious, started to run, but Una caught up and grabbed her hair.

"You liar!" she screamed. "You stupid, useless bitch!" She slapped Fionnuala's face as hard as she could. Fionnuala slapped her back, but this time Una hit her with her clenched fist. Fionnuala screamed, broke away, and started running again. Una could hear the boys laughing behind her. She didn't care. She ran after Fionnuala. She wanted to hurt her and she wanted to hurt her badly. Such a thing had never happened to her before. She forgot King Diarmait, Strongbow, even her father. She forgot everyone.

They ran towards Christ Church, then left past the skinners' booths and across town towards the market. Fionnuala was running faster, but Una was determined. She was shorter than Fionnuala, but she reckoned she was stronger. When I've given her a good slapping, she thought, I'll drag her back to the hospital—by the hair if I have to. Then she realised that the western gate might be shut. She'll be lucky if I don't throw her over the wall, she thought grimly. She saw Fionnuala run into the marketplace. The stalls were being closed. A moment later Fionnuala had vanished, but Una knew she must be hiding there somewhere. She'd find her.

Then Una stopped. What was she doing? It was all very well to be getting worked up about Fionnuala and the inmates of the hospital, but what about her own family? Wasn't she supposed to be keeping watch on the wall? She cursed Fionnuala, and turned.

The sounds first reached her when she had gone about a hundred yards along the street. She heard shouting, several big bangs, more shouts. Ahead, people were starting to run in her direction. Then suddenly, from the marketplace behind her, she heard a similar racket, and a moment later saw half a dozen knights in chain mail dash into view. They must have come through the western gate. There were men-at-arms behind them. Fionnuala was there somewhere, she knew, and for an instant she felt an urge to run back and save her friend; but then she realised the uselessness of it. If she can hide from me, she thought, then she can hide from them. She saw horsemen in front of her now. She had to get to her family. She dived into an alley.

It took her some time to reach home, working her way across the town. She didn't know how it had happened, but the English troops were obviously taking the town. They seemed to be all round Christ Church and the king's hall. Their arrival inside the walls had been so sudden that there was scarcely any resistance. She had to go down almost to the waterfront to avoid them.

Her family were waiting anxiously by the gate. Mercifully the English had not come that way yet. She had expected reproaches but her father only seemed relieved to see her.

"We know what happened," her mother said. "Those cursed English. While they talk to the archbishop by the south gate, they break in at the east and west. Shameful, it was. Did you see them?"

"I saw them," said Una, and then blushed. In all her life she had never told a lie. Strictly speaking, it was true. She had seen them in the street. But it wasn't what her mother had meant. Nobody noticed. "It was hard to get here. They're all round the cathedral," she added.

"We're going to the quay," said her father. Una noticed that he wasn't carrying the strongbox. "The cathedral's already surrounded," he explained, "and I daren't carry it through the streets now. So I've hidden it in the usual place. Please God no one will find it." He indicated a pouch tied inside his shirt. "There's enough in here to see us through our journey."

The quay was crowded. The English were flooding through the gates of Dublin now, but they were still in the upper part of the town. People were already swarming across the bridge to the suburb on the Liffey's northern side, but it was far from clear that they would be any safer from the English over there. On the quay, the shipmasters were doing a brisk trade. It was lucky, Una thought, that there were so many vessels in the port that day. A Norse ship had already pulled out into the stream. That would probably be going to the Isle of Man, or the islands of the north. There was a ship ready to leave for Chester. That would be closest, but the ship was already full. Two more were Bristol-bound, but their masters were holding out for such high fares that her father had looked doubtful. Another was going to Rouen in Normandy. A French merchant that MacGowan knew slightly was embarking. The fare was less than it was to Bristol. The silversmith hesitated. Rouen was a longer voyage, more dangerous. He spoke no French. He looked back towards the Bristol boat, but the sailors were already turning people away. There seemed to be no other choice. Unwillingly, he went to the Rouen boat.

He was just paying the captain of the vessel when a familiar figure came in sight. Ailred the Palmer was striding along the quay in the direction of the hospital. As soon as he saw MacGowan, he came swiftly towards him.

"I'm glad to see you safe, Kevin," he said. "Where are you going?"

The silversmith quickly explained the situation and his misgivings.

"You may be right to go." Ailred glanced up the hill. Fires had broken out in one or two buildings. "God knows what kind of people these English are. You'll surely find work in Rouen to tide you over and I'll get word to you of what is happening here." He was looking thoughtfully at Una. "Why not let Una remain here with me and my wife, Kevin? She'll be safe in the hospital. We're under the protection of the Church. She can prepare your house for your return."

Una was horrified. She loved the Palmer, but she didn't want to be separated from her family. Above all, she was sure her father needed her. But both her parents seemed in favour of the idea.

"Dear God, child, I'd sooner you were safe in the hospital than out on the wild seas with us," her mother cried, "and no knowing that we mightn't all be drowned." And her father put his arm round her and whispered in her ear, "You could rescue the strongbox, if you get the chance."

"But Father . . ." she protested. Everything was happening too fast. It was hard to think.

The ship's master wanted to leave.

"Go with Ailred, Una. It's for the best." Her father turned so quickly that she guessed the decision hurt him as much as it did her. But it was his final word, and she knew it.

Moments later, guided by Ailred the Palmer's firm but kindly hand, she found herself moving swiftly in the direction of the hospital.

As it turned out, King Diarmait and Strongbow had not instigated the sudden attack on Dublin. Indeed, they had been rather embarrassed when, in the middle of the negotiation with the archbishop, some of the more hot-headed knights, impatient with the delay, had made a rush at the gates and burst through before the defenders had time to realise what was going on. Of course, it worked out well for them: neither Diarmait nor Strongbow could deny it. While they and the archbishop watched, the city had fallen with scarcely a blow. After apologising to O'Toole, the Irish king and his new English son-in-law had ridden into the city to find that there was nothing left to do. The place was theirs.

A few buildings were burned and there was some looting going on, but that was to be expected. Soldiers must be allowed the spoils of war. They didn't let it go too far, though, and they made sure that none of the religious houses were touched.

More significant was the exodus of inhabitants from the town. This had its good side and its bad side. On the good side, there was accommodation to quarter the whole army. On the bad side, half the craftsmen and merchants in the town had fled across the river or over the sea, and they were a big part of the city's value. It also turned out that the King of Dublin had slipped away. The best information was that he had taken a Norse ship to the northern islands. That was bad news because it seemed likely that he would try to collect forces for an attack. But for the moment, at least, the city was quiet.

It was four days after the occupation when Una MacGowan set out from the Hospital of Saint John to visit her home in the city. The hospital had not been troubled: indeed, two days ago, King Diarmait and Strongbow themselves, accompanied by several knights, had paid a brief visit to inspect the place. Una had been struck by the tall English nobleman. With his finely drawn, oval face and his splendid bearing, he seemed to her quite as impressive as his kingly father-in-law. They had all treated the place with the same respect as if they had been in a church, and Diarmait had politely asked Ailred to take in half a dozen people, two of them English, who had been hurt during the taking of the city.

Una had certainly been busy in the hospital, as Fionnuala had not appeared again. Her father had sent word that he wished her to stay with him for the present; but Una suspected that there was an additional reason for her absence. She's heard that I'm here, she thought, and she doesn't want to face me.

As she passed through the market by the western gate, she noticed that nearly half the stalls were open again and doing a quiet trade. Walking up towards the cathedral, she saw that most of the houses now had troops in them, and some had obviously been abandoned entirely by their owners. The Englishmen seemed strange. With their harsh accents, stout leather jerkins, and padded tunics, they somehow seemed tougher, more compact than the men she was used to. Some of them gave her looks which made her uncomfortable, but nobody molested her. In an open space by the cathedral, a group of archers had set up targets for practise, the arrows thudding into the packed straw with a precision that was almost mechanical. She found it disturbing. Passing down the slope of the Fish Shambles, she turned into the lane that led by her home.

She hesitated. Why had she come here? To see what had happened to the house? What if it had been burned? It was sure to be full of English soldiers anyway. She felt suddenly miserable and had half a mind to turn back. But she couldn't do that. For her family's sake, she had to find out what had become of it.

The lane was rather quiet. She could see behind the fences that most of the houses were being used as quarters for the soldiers. In one yard several of them were sleeping; another seemed to contain only an old woman. When she reached the fence in front of her own house, she glanced nervously at the gateway. It was open. As she drew level, she looked inside. There was no sign of damage, anyway, nor could she see any occupants. She stopped and glanced along the lane. No one was coming. She put her head through the gateway and looked round the yard.

It was a strange sensation, to be peering furtively into her own home. From the wood glowing in her father's brazier, which had been moved a little, and from the scattered possessions in the yard, it was clear that the place was being used. Perhaps the men were asleep inside the house. In any case, she had better move on. But she didn't. Instead, after glancing down the street once more, she stepped into the yard. It was silent.

The strongbox: what a chance! It was sitting there, waiting to be rescued; and no one was looking. If she could just slip through the yard to its hiding place. It would only take a moment. She knew she could carry it. The woollen cloak over her shoulders would cover it. How long would it take to walk up to Christ Church and bring it to safety? Moments. No more. And when might she get another chance like this? Perhaps never.

But were there men in the house? That was the question. To get to the hiding place she would have to go past the open doorway. If anyone was awake in there she'd probably be seen. There was only one thing to do. She started to cross the yard, past the brazier, past the bread oven. She would have to look in through the doorway and see if anyone was there. If they caught sight of her, she'd have to run. She didn't think they'd catch her. But if no one was there, she could get the box and be gone. Her heart was pounding, but she forced herself to keep calm. She reached the doorway.

She looked in. It was hard to see anything, since the only light came from the doorway and the small opening in the roof. Were there eyes in there, watching her, hands reaching out? She strained to see into the shadows. There was no sound. After a few moments, she could make out the benches along the walls. There did not seem to be any human forms on them. Very cautiously, she stepped inside. Now she could see better. She looked at the place where her parents always slept, then at her own corner. No. Nobody was there. She felt a sudden urge to go over to her place, to feel its comforting familiarity again; but she knew she must not. With a sigh, she turned round and stepped back into the yard. She wondered whether to look outside the gate again and decided there was no need. Better not waste time.

She went quickly to the hiding place under the bread oven. If you knew how to push the little stone panel aside and reach in, it was only the work of a moment. She pushed her arm in. Farther. She felt around with her hand. And encountered . . .

Nothing. She couldn't believe it. She felt again, frowning. Still nothing. Surely there must be some mistake. She pulled back her sleeve until her whole arm was bare and tried once more, moving her hand this way and that, pushing it through until she touched the end of the hiding place.

There was no doubt about it. The hiding place was empty. The strongbox had been stolen. She felt a sudden, cold panic, then a sickening sense of misery: someone had found her father's treasure. Her family's entire wealth was gone. She pulled back, glancing around. Where would they have put it? Inside, perhaps? It was worth a try, at least. She glanced at the gateway, still empty. She ran back inside, into the darkness.

She didn't worry about the mess. There was no time to think of that. It didn't even matter that the room was dark: she knew every foot of it with her eyes closed, every crevice and hiding place. With furious speed, she went round the walls, pulling benches back, throwing off cloaks, blankets, and even a chain mail shirt, scattering them on the floor. In her irritation, she even sent two metal bowls flying with a clatter across the room. She worked rapidly and thoroughly, and at the end of it all, standing with her back towards the doorway and gazing miserably around at the silent shadows, she knew for a certainty that the strongbox was not there. She had come too late. The cursed English troops had found it and she would never get it back. Her father had lost all that he had. Her head fell forward. She wanted to cry.

And wasn't there something even worse? She suspected there was. What if, instead of chasing after that stupid Fionnuala, she had watched on the wall and seen the English attack? What if she'd run, then, straight to her father? Mightn't he have had time to get the box safely to Christ Church? Or at least, if she'd got home earlier, he might have felt safer taking the box with him down to the quay. It was waiting for her that had caused him to panic and make his disastrous decision. Even if her brain told her that all these suppositions might be false, her heart told her otherwise. It is my fault, she thought. My family is ruined because of me. She stood there in the quiet emptiness of her home, stunned by grief. And so, for a moment, she did not even feel the hand upon her shoulder.

"Looking for something?"

The voice spoke in English. She didn't completely understand, but it made no difference. She whirled round. His grip shifted instantly to her arm and tightened.

A studded leather jerkin, a jagged scrape on the right-hand side. A face covered with several days' dark stubble; a large brutal nose, bloodshot eyes. He was alone.

"Looking for something to steal, are you?" She didn't understand him. He held up a silver coin in front of her face. She wasn't sure, but it looked like one she had seen in her father's strongbox. He chuckled as he put the coin away. She saw a strange, soft gleam in his eyes. "Well, you found me."

Holding her arm in one hand he started to loosen his tunic with the other. She might not understand the words, but there was no doubt about what he wanted. She struggled to get free. His hand was large and calloused. As he jerked her back, she felt how easily he did it and realised how much stronger he was. She had never known the fear of feeling physically powerless before.

"The punishment for stealing's much worse than what I'm going to do to you," he said. He could see that she didn't understand, but that didn't stop him going on. "You're lucky, that's what you are. Lucky to be getting me."

Una had been so startled and frightened that she had forgotten even to scream.

"Help!" she shouted, as loud as she could. "Rape!" Nothing happened. She shouted again.

The soldier didn't seem to be bothered. His jerkin was loose now. Una suddenly realised that, even if they cared, no one would be taking notice of her cries. The nearby houses were probably all taken by English troops, and they wouldn't even understand her. She took a deep breath, to scream.

And then he made one mistake. Stripping off his jerkin, just for a moment, he let go of her arm. It was only a moment, but that was all she needed. She knew what she must do. She had never done such a thing before, but she wasn't a fool. He saw her opening her mouth to scream, but he didn't see her kick until it was too late.

She gave it everything she had. He felt a sudden, searing flash of pain in his groin. He doubled over, his hands clutching his stomach in agony.

She fled. Before he could even straighten up, she was through the gate. She started to run down the street, hardly knowing which way she went. She saw a group of soldiers in her path. It seemed they were parting to let her through. She heard his voice behind her.

"Thief! Stop her!"

Powerful arms were holding her. She tried to get free, but they lifted her off the ground. There was nothing she could do. The soldier was coming along the street now. He was limping and his face was contorted with fury. She didn't know whether he was going to try to rape her again, but he obviously meant to get even. He had come up with them now. He was thrusting his face into hers.

"What is this?" Another voice. Peremptory. From behind her. The men were drawing apart.

"A thief." Her accuser's voice, shaken but surly. She saw a dark robe, looked up.

It was Father Gilpatrick.

"Rape." It was all that she could say. She indicated the man with the unshaven face. "He tried . . . I'd gone into our house . . ." It was enough. The priest turned on them furiously.

"Villains!" he shouted. She did not understand all of what he said, because he was speaking in English. But she heard several things she recognised. Hospital of Saint John. Archbishop. King Diarmait. The men were looking confused. Her attacker, she saw, had gone very pale. Moments later, Father Gilpatrick was leading her away.

"I told them you're under Church protection at the hospital. I shall complain to the archbishop. Are you hurt?" he gently enquired. She shook her head.

"I kicked him in the groin and got away," she told him frankly.

"Quite right, my child," he said. Then she told him about the missing strongbox and the coin in the soldier's hand. "Ah," he said sadly. "I'm afraid there's nothing to be done about that."

He accompanied her all the way to the hospital, talking to her quietly as they went, so that by the time they got back, she was not only feeling better but even had the chance to observe, which had never struck her before, how uncommonly handsome the young priest was. When they arrived at the hospital, the Palmer's wife put her straight to bed and brought her warm broth and comfort.

By the next morning, Una was over her fright and seemed to all the inmates at the hospital to be her usual self. But she wasn't. Nor in the weeks and months that followed would she ever feel easy with herself again. It was not the near escape she had experienced that troubled her: that was soon enough forgotten. It was another thought, insidious as it was unfair, which would not leave her.

My father has lost everything he has. And it is all my fault.

III

⊰ 1171 ⊱

Peter FitzDavid smiled. A summer's day. The soft, warm light seemed to be rolling down from the Wicklow Mountains and drifting in from the wide blue curve of the bay. Dublin at last.

He'd been waiting a long time to come to Dublin. Last autumn, when Strongbow and King Diarmait had come up here, he'd been left down south guarding the port of Waterford. Peter had performed his tasks well, but by the time Strongbow had retired to Waterford in the winter he seemed to have nearly forgotten who Peter was.

The port of Waterford stood on a handsome site overlooking a large river mouth. The original Viking settlement there had been nearly as old as that of Dublin and traders came there from the south-western ports of France and even farther away. Strongbow had set up extensive winter quarters there but the very size of the camp had only reminded Peter of his next problem. The English lord had so many knights—relations, followers, friends, and sons of friends—to look after that it was going to be a long time, or take some extraordinary deed on his part, before his own turn came to share the rewards. By late spring, moreover, some of the young men like himself were wondering what the future of the expedition was going to be. There were two opinions in the camp.

"Diarmait and Strongbow are going to take the whole island," said some. Peter thought it quite likely that the Irish king hoped to do this; and with Strongbow's well-equipped army, he probably could. The Irish chiefs, fine fighting men though they were, had nothing that could withstand the devastating effect of an armoured cavalry charge; nor had they anything like the massed archers. Even the High King, with all his followers, might have difficulty stopping them.

But equally there were others who thought that the mission might be near completion. If so, then most of them would be paid off and sent home. And I'll be sure to be sent back, Peter thought, with little enough for myself or to give to my mother. He wondered where he'd find employment after that. But then, in the month of May, an unexpected change occurred.

King Diarmait of Leinster, having regained his kingdom, suddenly fell sick and died.

What would happen next? It was true that when he gave Strongbow his daughter, the Leinster king had promised to make him his heir. But was that promise worth anything? Peter had learned enough of the customs of the island by now to know that any new king or chief in Ireland was chosen by his people from amongst his close kin. Diarmait had left a brother and several sons, and under Irish law there should be no question of their sister's foreign husband taking their inheritance. Yet it soon became clear that Diarmait's sons, at least, were going along with the idea.

"They've no choice," a Waterford merchant had remarked to

him. "Strongbow has three hundred knights, three hundred archers, a thousand men. He has the power. Without him they're nothing. If they stick with him, they're still in with a chance of keeping part of what they lost."

"But I can see another difficulty," Peter had replied. By the feudal law of Plantagenet England, a great lordship like Leinster would pass to the eldest son; or if it devolved upon an heiress, there would be no question of her marrying without the king's permission—and kings usually made a point of giving such heiresses to their faithful friends. Since Diarmait had actually acknowledged King Henry of England as his overlord, and Strongbow was in any case a vassal of the Plantagenet king, the English magnate would be placing himself in a dangerous legal position by taking up this Leinster inheritance. "He would really need King Henry's permission," Peter had explained to the Waterford merchant. "And I wonder if he has it."

Just at that moment, however, King Henry II of England had other things to worry about. Indeed, it seemed to Peter that the English king would scarcely dare to show his face.

The shocking news from England had come quite early in January. By the following month it had spread all over Europe. The King of England had killed the Archbishop of Canterbury. No one had ever heard of such a thing before.

The quarrel between the English king and Archbishop Thomas Becket had been the usual one over the Church's power and jurisdiction. Henry had insisted that those in religious orders should answer to regular courts if they committed crimes like murder or theft. Becket, his former friend and Chancellor, who owed his position as archbishop to King Henry, had obstinately set his face against the king in a bitter and long-running dispute. Some of the senior English clergy actually thought that Becket had let his new position go to his head. But after years of strife, a group of Henry's knights, supposedly hearing the king burst out in irritation "Who will rid me of this turbulent priest!" thought it was an order to kill him and went and did so in front of the high altar in Canterbury cathedral.

All Europe was scandalised. Everyone blamed Henry. The Pope denounced him. People were saying he should stand trial and that Becket should be made a saint. Peter supposed that the English king was far too busy dealing with this crisis to pay much attention to events in a place as far away and marginal as Leinster.

Strongbow had wasted no time. He had gone straight to Dublin. But Peter, once again, had been left behind. The news from Dublin had sounded exciting. The ousted King of Dublin had returned with a fleet from the northern isles, but the Norsemen had botched the whole business: as they started to attack the eastern gate, the English had raced out of the southern gate, caught them in the rear, and cut them to pieces. They'd killed the King of Dublin, too. But though the former Dublin king might have failed to grab his city back, nobody imagined that the High King of Ireland was going to stand by and see this English intruder take over a quarter of the island and its greatest port.

"The High King won't be long coming," the messenger from Dublin had told him. "All possible reinforcements are to go to Dublin right away. And that includes you."

So here he was at last, on a sunny summer day, coming into Dublin. And as soon as he had reported to Strongbow and quartered his men, he knew what he would do.

He would call upon his old friend Gilpatrick and his family. Did his friend still have a pretty sister, he wondered?

It was not often that Gilpatrick's mother had to find fault with her husband; but sometimes she knew it was necessary to put pressure on him. When Gilpatrick failed to come to his brother Lorcan's wedding, she had been as angry as her husband. It was a public insult and a humiliation for the entire family. If her husband wouldn't see Gilpatrick after that, she didn't blame him. But at some point the rift had to end. After a year she had finally decided that it was better for everyone if the priest allowed his son to visit the house again; and following some weeks of judicious coaxing and tears, she had persuaded her husband, somewhat grumpily, to allow him to visit once more. "And you're lucky," she had told Gilpatrick firmly, "that he does."

Nonetheless, as he awaited the arrival of his son and his son's friend three days later, old Conn was not in a very good humour. Perhaps it was partly the weather, which had been strangely changeable in the last two days. But the priest's mood had been irritable for much longer than that.

It had been one thing to have English mercenaries in the pay of Diarmait, but it was quite another to have Strongbow himself and his army setting up as a power in the land. He knew that some people in Dublin were quietly cynical about the situation. "We're probably no worse off with Strongbow than we were with that rogue Diarmait," a friend had remarked to him the day before. But the chief of Ui Fergusa was not so sure. "There's been nothing like this in Ireland since the Ostmen first came," he grumbled. "Unless the High King can stop them, this will be an English occupation."

"Yet even the Ostmen never really went beyond the ports," his friend reminded him.

"The English are different," he had retorted.

Now his son Gilpatrick, with whom he had only recently begun to speak again, was bringing this young soldier of Strongbow's to his house. Irish courtesy and hospitality demanded that he give the stranger a polite welcome, but he was hoping that the visit would be short.

And if all this wasn't enough, his wife was choosing this day to bother him again with a subject he didn't wish to discuss.

"You've done nothing," she was saying, with perfect truth. "Though you've been saying you would for these last three years."

They were a curious couple to look at: the priest, tall and rangy, his wife short and stout; but they were devoted to each other. Nor did Gilpatrick's mother blame her husband for putting off this part of his duty for so long. She understood very well that he was afraid. Who wouldn't be, when the problem was Fionnuala?

"If we don't marry her soon, I don't know what people will say. Or what she'll do," she added.

It should have been the easiest thing in the world. Wasn't she good-looking? Wasn't she the daughter of the chief of the Ui Fergusa? Couldn't her father afford to give her a handsome dowry? It wasn't as if she had a bad reputation. Yet.

But in her mother's view it was only a matter of time. If when she first returned from the Palmer's, her father remarked that Fionnuala seemed to have improved, her mother had watched her with more scepticism. She had tried not to quarrel with her daughter and she had kept her busy; but after a few weeks the signs of stress had begun to occur again. There had been tantrums and sulks. More than once Fionnuala had run out of the house and not come back all day. Her parents had suggested she should return to the Palmer's, but she had refused; and on the occasions when they met Una in the town, it was clear that a coolness had developed between the two girls. "We'd better get her safely married," her mother declared.

It wasn't as if no thought had ever been given to the subject. Fionnuala was sixteen now. Her father had been talking about finding her a suitor for years. But if he'd been lazy when she was younger, she suspected he was nervous now. There was no knowing how Fionnuala would react to anyone they proposed. "She'll certainly know how to put them off if she wants to," her father remarked glumly. "God knows whom she'll insult." There was also the question of dowry. Negotiating with the future husband was always an anxious process. If word got out that Fionnuala was difficult, "twelvescore cattle won't be enough," her father said bitterly. The whole business seemed so likely to lead to costly embarrassment that the priest had to admit he had been secretly putting it off every month.

"Anyway," his wife now said coaxingly, "I might have a candidate."

"You might?"

"I was talking to my sister. There's one of the O'Byrnes."

"O'Byrne?" This was promising news indeed. His wife's sister had done well when she married into that family. The O'Byrnes, like the O'Tooles, were one of the finest princely families in northern Leinster.

"It wouldn't be Ruairi O'Byrne?"

"It would not." Even the O'Byrne family, amongst its many members, had the occasional weak link. Ruairi, as it happened, belonged to the senior branch of the family; but young though he was, he had already acquired a dubious reputation. "I am speaking," she continued, "of Brendan."

This was quite another matter. Though only a junior member of the princely clan, the priest had always heard that Brendan was a sound fellow. For his daughter in her present state to marry any O'Byrne, apart from Ruairi, should be counted a blessing.

"Have they ever met?" he enquired.

"He saw her once in the market. It seems he asked my sister about her."

"Let him come here," said her husband, "as soon as he likes." And he might have said more had not one of the slaves appeared to tell them that Gilpatrick was approaching.

⁘

Of course Gilpatrick had been glad to see his old friend when Peter had turned up at his door.

"You told me to come to see you if ever I came to Dublin," FitzDavid said with a smile.

"I did. Aha. I did," said Gilpatrick. "Once a friend, always a friend."

It wasn't quite true. You couldn't ignore the fact that things had changed. Even amongst the churchmen with the closest English connections, the murder of Becket had soured their view of the English king. Gilpatrick's father never missed the opportunity to remark to him, "Your English king is still a friend to the Church, I see." And the disturbing new presence of Strongbow and his army had begun to worry many of the bishops. Gilpatrick had accompanied Archbishop O'Toole to a council up in the north where the elderly Archbishop of Armagh had declared, "These English are surely a curse sent by God to punish us for our sins." The assembled churchmen had even passed a resolution suggesting that all the English slaves in Ireland should be freed. "For perhaps," some had suggested, "it is our making slaves of these English that has caused offence to God." Gilpatrick hadn't noticed many people freeing their slaves on this account, but the perception remained in the community: the English were a penance. Nonetheless, it would have been unnatural not to greet his former friend and he did so warmly.

"You haven't changed at all," he cried.

That wasn't true either. And now, as they made their way up to his parents' house, he glanced at Peter FitzDavid and thought that, though he could see the same boyish face and innocent hope, there was something else in his friend now. A hint of anxiety. For the fact was that, although Peter had been on active service for three years, no one had rewarded him with so much as a single cow.

"You must get yourself some land, Peter," he remarked kindly. It was strange, he realised, that he, an Irishman, should be saying such a thing to a foreign mercenary. In traditional Ireland, of course, a warrior would be rewarded with livestock which he could pasture on the open lands of his clan; but at least since Brian Boru, Irish kings like Diarmait of Leinster had been known to reward their followers by granting them estates which lay on what would formerly have been considered to be tribal lands. Yet if you failed to obtain material rewards, he reflected, the traditional system was kinder. A brave warrior returned to his clan with honour. A feudal knight, though he might have a loving family, had no clan system to support him. Until he got an estate, though he might be a man of honour, he had no substance. The Irish priest felt a little sorry for his foreign friend.

If Gilpatrick had also been a little uncertain what sort of reception FitzDavid would receive from his father, he needn't have worried. His father welcomed Peter with stately dignity. And for his part, Peter observed that the priest's stone house was well furnished and comfortable enough, even if he did notice with wry amusement that the churchman kept a gold-rimmed drinking skull in the corner.

No mention was made of Becket. His parents asked the visitor about his family and his experiences with King Diarmait in the south. And when at last his father couldn't resist remarking that, as a priest, he felt a little nervous of the English king, "seeing what he does to archbishops," Peter passed this off by laughing. "We're afraid of him, too."

If any proof of his father's friendliness were needed, it came when he remarked to his son, "I would not really say your friend was English."

"My family was Flemish, in fact," Peter said.

"But you were born in Wales? And your father before you?"

"That is true," Peter agreed.

"You speak Irish almost like one of us, I would say. That would be because you speak Welsh?"

"All my life."

"Then I think," said the Irish chief, "that you are Welsh." He turned to his wife.

"He is Welsh." She smiled.

"You're Welsh." Gilpatrick grinned.

"I am Welsh," Peter wisely agreed.

And it was just as this fact about his identity had been established that a new figure appeared in the doorway.

"Ah, Welshman," said the chief, his voice suddenly lowering, "this is my daughter, Fionnuala."

It seemed to Peter FitzDavid, as she stepped through the doorway, that Fionnuala was the most beautiful girl he had ever seen in his life. With her dark hair, her pale skin, her red mouth: wasn't she the perfect object of any man's desire? If her brother Gilpatrick's eyes were curiously flecked with green, Fionnuala's were an astounding pure emerald. Yet what struck him most, after only the briefest acquaintance, was her modesty.

How demure she was. Most of the time her eyes were downcast. She spoke to her parents and her brother with a respectfulness that was charming. When he addressed her himself, she answered him so quietly and simply. Only once did she allow a little animation to creep into her voice, and that was when she spoke about the Palmer and his good works at the hospital where, until recently, she had been working. He was so fascinated by this virtuous young woman that, if any looks of surprise passed between her family, he did not see them.

Gilpatrick's parents indicated after a while that they wished to have some words with their son alone, so it was suggested that Fionnuala should show their guest round the little church. He duly admired it. Then Fionnuala took him across to Saint Patrick's Well, and pointing to the dark pool and to the Thingmount in the distance, she told him the story of her ancestor and Saint Patrick and explained how old Fergus was buried there. Listening respectfully, Peter now understood what Gilpatrick had meant about his family's ancient status. Looking at the girl, observing her beauty, her gentle seriousness, and her piety, he wondered if she might be contemplating the religious life—and hoped that she was not. It seemed a waste that she should not be married. He was sorry when it was time to return.

It had been agreed that this was to be only a short visit, but Gilpatrick's parents were warm in their invitation that they should both return to be feasted and entertained in the Irish manner in the near future. Gilpatrick's mother pressed a gift of sweetmeats upon him. As he escorted them to the gateway, Gilpatrick's father gazed out over the estuary and remarked, "Take care tomorrow, Welshman, there'll be a mist." As the sky was entirely clear, Peter thought this unlikely, but he was too polite to say so.

As he and Gilpatrick walked away, Peter could not help bringing up the subject of Fionnuala.

"I see what you mean about your sister."

"Oh?"

"She is altogether remarkable. A pious soul."

"She is?"

"And very beautiful. Is she to be married soon?" he added, a little wistfully.

"Probably. My parents were telling me they have someone in mind." He sounded rather vague.

"A lucky man. A prince, no doubt."

"Something like that."

Peter secretly wished he were in a position to ask for her himself.

✢

When he opened his eyes the next morning, Peter glanced towards the open doorway and frowned. Had he woken too early? It seemed still to be dark.

There were six people in the place where he lodged. He and another knight occupied the house. Three men-at-arms and a slave slept in the yard outside. He'd heard that the place had belonged to a silversmith called MacGowan who had left the city when it was first taken. Nobody seemed to be stirring. Beyond the doorway there was a strange, pale greyness in the yard. He got up and went out.

Mist. Cool, damp, white mist. He couldn't even see the gate a few yards away. The men were awake and sitting huddled under their blankets in the little shelter where the silversmith had presumably worked. They had stoked up the brazier. The slave was preparing some food. Peter found the gate. If there was anyone about in the lane, he could neither see nor hear them. The mist clung to his face, kissing him wetly. He supposed the sun would burn the mist away later; there'd be nothing much to do until then. Gilpatrick's father had been right. He shouldn't have doubted him. He returned to the yard. The slave had some oatcakes by the oven. He took one and munched thoughtfully. The oatcake smelled and tasted good. He thought of the girl. Though he had no recollection of dreaming during the night, it seemed to him that she had been in his thoughts while he slept. He shrugged. What was the point of thinking about a girl who was unattainable? He'd better put her out of his head.

There hadn't been many women in Peter's life. There was a girl with whom he'd spent some happy nights in a Wexford barn. In Waterford, he had experienced some weeks of vigorous lovemaking with a merchant's wife while her husband was away on a voyage. But in Dublin the prospects did not look good. The place was full of soldiers and half the inhabitants had fled. The knight he shared the house with had told him about his exploits across the river in the suburb on the northern bank.

"Ostmanby they call it, because so many of the Norse families went over there when we arrived. They had to build shelters beside the existing houses. Some of the poorer craftsmen and labourers are struggling to feed their families, so their wives and daughters come over here . . . I had a delicious one last week."

Peter had soon come to the conclusion that most of his companion's exploits were invented. Certainly the women he had seen on his brief visit across the bridge to Ostmanby hadn't offered themselves to him, and the few loose women he had seen in the streets hadn't looked very appetising. He'd decided he'd sooner do without.

The morning was spent sitting by the brazier playing dice with the men. He had expected the summer sun to burn off the mist, but though by late morning there was a faint brightness overhead, he couldn't see thirty paces down the lane. As for the girl, her image was still there, floating vaguely like a spirit in his mind. And partly in the hope that this vaguely unsettling presence would float away and get lost in the mist, he decided at noon to go for a walk.

As he left the Fish Shambles, he intended only to go a short distance, keeping careful note of how he went, so that he could find his way back again; but he soon realised that he had failed to do so. He was fairly sure he was going westwards and after a while he supposed he might be getting close to the market by the western gate. The hospital where Fionnuala had been working lay outside that gate, he remembered. He might take a look at it. He'd probably get a sense of the place, even in the mist.

But after a while, he still hadn't found the market. From time to time, figures appeared in the mist and if he'd been sensible he could have asked the way. But he hated asking directions. So he continued until at last he saw it. There were a couple of men-at-arms on sentry duty.

The mist outside the gate was so thick that he decided that, in order to see anything of the hospital, he'd have to go inside it. He almost turned back, but the sentries were watching him, so sooner than admit his mistake he continued past them casually, remarking: "I think I'll see if the mist is lifting across the river." And he made his way down the track towards the river.

It was silent on the bridge. He was alone. He could hear his own footfalls sounding dully on the timbers over the water. On his right, the ships by the wood quay appeared in the shrouds of mist like insects caught in a dewy spider's web. He could see a hundred yards down the river, but as he went over he realised that the mist was finally starting to lift. Halfway across, he saw a patch of blue sky. Then he could see the mudflats on the Liffey's northern side, and the scattered thatched roofs of the suburb beyond. To the left of the bridge end he caught sight of green, grassy banks in the sunlight. There was a sprinkling of yellow flowers. Then he saw . . .

Horsemen. All along the bank, coming out of the mist. Scores of them. Then footmen, carrying spears and axes. Hundreds. God knows how many. And in a few moments, they would be on the bridge.

It could mean only one thing. The High King had come. And he was about to take Dublin by surprise.

He turned. He started to run. He ran faster than he had ever run before, back across the misty bridge. He heard his own footfalls and he thought he heard his heart. Did he also hear the drumming of hoofbeats on the timbers, too? He didn't think so but he didn't dare look back. He reached the end of the bridge, raced up the track, came to the gate, and saw the two sentries staring at him in surprise. Only when he was through the gate did he turn, glance back at the empty path behind him, and order the sentries, "Close the gate. Quick." And he told them what he'd seen. Then he set to work.

In the next few minutes, Peter FitzDavid acted quickly and decisively. Gathering some men-at-arms, he sent them flying to their tasks. One he despatched immediately to Strongbow. "Go straight to him. Don't stop." Two more went to alert the riverside defences and the eastern gate. Taking one more as a guide, he set off for the southern gate himself. If the High King's men used the ford as well as the bridge, it would be the big western gate they made for. When he arrived, no troops had yet come in sight. He got the gate closed and barred and, stirring up the garrison there, he hurried along the street towards Christ Church and the royal hall.

When he reached the old hall where Strongbow had taken up residence, he found the magnate, accompanied by a dozen knights, about to mount his horse to find out what was going on. He was looking angrily round, demanding answers and receiving none.

"Who started this alarm?" he had just demanded of a nervous-looking commander.

"I did," Peter called out as he came towards him.

A pair of cold blue eyes fixed upon him.

"And who the devil are you?"

It was his moment.

"Peter FitzDavid," he said boldly. Quickly and succinctly he told Strongbow what he'd seen. "I've closed the bridge and western gate and sent men to all the others."

"Good." The great man's eyes narrowed. "You were with Diarmait, weren't you?" He gave Peter a nod to let him know he was remembered. Then he turned to his knights. "You know what to do. Raise the garrison. Go!"

By midafternoon the weather was clear and bright. The people of Dublin looked over their walls to see the forces of the High King on every side. As well as the clans under his direct control, there were those of the great chiefs who acknowledged his authority. The ancient Ulaid of Ulster were camped out at Clontarf. The O'Brien, descendants of Brian Boru, had their forces on the city's western boundary. King Diarmait's brother, who had decided not to support Strongbow like Diarmait's sons, had brought his forces and was camped across Dublin's southern coastal approaches. Every supply route to the city by land or sea was blocked. The High King's army was camped in a great ring round the walls with forward posts to watch each gate for any sign of an English attempt to break out.

Late in the afternoon, from a vantage point above the wood quay, Peter saw Archbishop O'Toole ride across the bridge with a party of priests to begin the negotiations. He noticed that Gilpatrick was one of them.

The next morning the city was shrouded in mist again. Strongbow had every wall manned. Peter was sent out on foot with a scouting party to look for any sign of the besiegers mounting a surprise attack. When he'd asked Strongbow if he meant to mount a surprise breakout himself, however, the magnate had shaken his head.

"No point," he said. "I can't direct an army if I can't see it."

Peter returned from his patrol without finding any sign of enemy movement. It was eerie walking about in the city afterwards. Though the sentries on the wall were silent, every time a figure loomed out of the mist in the street, he half expected it to be an enemy. News came that once the mist cleared, the archbishop would go out to negotiate again. Peter went back to his lodgings and found them empty. He sat down by the brazier, and waited.

Time passed. The mist did not seem to be lifting at all. In the quietness, everything felt slightly unreal. As he looked across the yard to the gate, Peter could see only the whiteness beyond, as if the little yard had been transported, by some strange magic, into a separate world that was hidden in a cloud.

When the shape appeared outside the gateway, he assumed it was the knight. When it hovered there like a ghost instead of coming in, he wondered if it might be a thief, and glancing across to the bench where his sword was lying, he prepared to spring. Sitting where he was, he realised that he was not easily visible from the gate, so he kept still, making no sound. The figure continued to hover, obviously looking into the yard. Finally, it glided in. It had a hood over its head. It came towards the brazier. Only when he could almost reach out to touch it did he recognise the figure.

The girl. Fionnuala. She gave a little start as she saw him, but nothing more. He admired her control. She smiled.

"I thought I'd see if you were here." She was amused, it seemed, by his astonishment. "Gilpatrick told me where you were lodging. It was my friend's house, until this year."

"But how did you get into the city?" He thought of the guards on the city gate.

"I came in by the door." There was usually a small door in the big gates, through which single people could pass. "They know I'm the priest's daughter." She glanced around. "Are you all alone?" He nodded. "Can I sit by the fire?" He placed a stool for her and she sat on it. She peeled back her hood and her hair cascaded down.

"Gilpatrick says you gave the alarm." She gazed into the embers in the brazier. "So now the High King will sit outside Dublin, and you will sit inside, and he'll wait until you starve."

He watched her, wondering what she wanted and why she had come, and how it was possible to be so beautiful. Her assessment of the situation was probably right. The High King had all the rich produce of Leinster in his hands. He could feed his army for months. But the city was well stocked with provisions. It could be a long siege.

"Perhaps your brother and the archbishop will negotiate a peace with the High King," he suggested.

"Gilpatrick says the archbishop wants to avoid bloodshed," she agreed. "But the O'Connor king doesn't trust Strongbow."

"Because he's English?"

"Not at all." She laughed. "It's because he's Diarmait's son-in-law."

Why was she there? Was she a spy of some sort, perhaps sent by her father to find out about Strongbow's defences? Gilpatrick could do that better, but perhaps as a mediator he would refuse such a role. He decided that, beautiful and pious though she might be, he had better keep a careful eye on her. Meanwhile they talked of this and that, she spreading out hands and her slim, pale arms towards the fire, and he answering when required and watching her.

After a time, she stood up.

"I must go back to my home now."

"Shall I accompany you to the city gate?"

"No. There's no need." She gave him a curious little look. "Would you like it if I came to see you again?"

"I . . ." he stared at her. "Why certainly," he stammered.

"Good." She glanced at the gateway to the street. It was empty. "Tell me, Peter FitzDavid," she said quietly, "would you like to kiss me before I leave?"

He gazed at her. The demure priest's daughter, the Irish princess, was asking to be kissed. He checked himself. He was being stupid. Politely he kissed her on the cheek.

"That wasn't what I meant," she said.

It wasn't? What was all this about? He almost blurted out, "Aren't you about to be married?" Then he told himself not to be a fool. If she was asking, who but an idiot would refuse? He moved closer. Their lips met.

⊹

Una was surprised the next day to find Fionnuala at the entrance of the hospital, and still more so when Fionnuala informed her why she'd come.

"You want to work here again?"

"I've nothing to do at home, Una. I can't just sit around being useless. My parents want me to live at home, but I could spend the days here and some nights. That is," she smiled ruefully, "if you don't mind." She paused, and then continued seriously, "You were quite right to be angry with me, Una. But I think I've grown up a bit now."

Had she? Una stared at her. Perhaps. Then she told herself not to be stupid. Didn't they always need help at the hospital? She smiled.

"The floor needs washing," she said.

The only person who was doubtful was Ailred the Palmer. He was concerned for her safety. But Fionnuala was able to convince him without too much difficulty.

"I can come down through the small gate into the town," she told him. For there was a small gate in the city wall almost directly below her father's church. "Then I can come out of the west gate and walk across to the hospital. Nobody's going to hurt me coming from the church or going to the hospital." It had to be said that neither the English nor the High King's forces had troubled any of the religious houses round the city. The priest's daughter could go about unmolested even in the middle of a military siege.

"I will talk to your father," the Palmer promised.

And so by that evening it was agreed. Fionnuala would come down several days a week to the hospital. Sometimes she would sleep there.

"Who knows," her father remarked to Ailred, "perhaps she is growing up."

⊹

The offer from the High King came the third day that the arch-bishop and Gilpatrick rode out.

"Let Strongbow keep Dublin, Wexford, and Waterford," he said, "and we need not quarrel."

In many ways it was a handsome offer. The High King was ready to give up the most important port in Ireland to the English lord. But it seemed to Gilpatrick that it was also a very traditional offer. The archbishop summarised it when, on their way back, he re-marked: "I suppose, in a way, it's just exchanging the English for the Ostmen in the ports."

That was it, Gilpatrick thought. Even now, after three centuries of living side by side, the Irish still saw the old Viking ports, crucial though they were to Ireland's wealth, as places apart. To the ancient clans, and to the O'Connor High King from Connacht, it hardly mattered who held the ports so long as they did not encroach upon the green and fertile Irish hinterland.

But the O'Connor king was no fool. There was cunning in the offer, too. If he was willing to give up Dublin, he had also wanted to ensure that Strongbow reduce the size of his army. Therefore he must deny them the one thing that would allow them to remain: land. The feudal grants of land for military service. That was what they had all come for, from poor young Peter FitzDavid to the fam-ily of Strongbow himself. The High King's offer did not give them that.

"Let us hope Strongbow will accept," the saintly archbishop said. But Gilpatrick had his doubts.

It was the next day, before any answer was returned, that he saw Peter FitzDavid in the Fish Shambles. They greeted each other in a friendly way but with a trace of awkwardness. With the siege in progress, a visit to his parents' house outside the walls was inadvis-able. Besides, since his father was naturally on the side of the High King, he might not have cared to meet Peter again just now. They chatted pleasantly enough, however, until Peter casually asked, "And how are the plans for your sister's betrothal?"

Gilpatrick frowned. Why did the question strike a false note? Could it be that his young friend entertained a hope in that direction? After all, he had once had that idea himself, some years ago. But Peter's prospects did not seem very bright at present. Hardly a good match. He smiled ironically to himself. He wasn't sure it would be such a kindness to wish his temperamental sister onto young FitzDavid anyway, come to that.

"You'd have to ask my parents," he said curtly, and moved away.

✛

There was no doubt, Una had to concede, that Fionnuala had changed. She might not be able to come every day, but when she did come, she worked hard and without complaint. There was only praise now, from the inmates. Ailred was pleased and made a point of telling her father how much she'd improved. Sometimes she stayed the night at the hospital, sometimes she had to leave during the afternoon. But she always let Una know in advance.

There was never any trouble from the English soldiers. Their forward sentries were quite close, but they knew who she was and where she was going. Once she and Una even went for a walk on the bridge, but nobody troubled them and after exchanging a few words with the English soldiers on the far side, they had been free to return.

Nonetheless, as the second week of the siege turned into the third, the cordon round the city was beginning to have its effect. As well as the various forces round the walls, the men of Ulster out at Clontarf had successfully turned away all ships wanting to enter the Liffey. No supplies were reaching Dublin by any of the roads, and stocks of everything were slowly running down. Nor could news get through.

It had been months since she had heard from her father in Rouen. A sailor had come to the hospital and delivered a message from MacGowan, saying that he and the rest of the family were well, that he had found work as a journeyman under another master, but that life was hard and that if she was safe with the Palmer,

Una should stay where she was. The sailor had also been told to ask if she had found the dog she had lost when the family left.

The dog. She realised that her father meant the strongbox. This was the moment she had been dreading. For weeks after she had made her terrible discovery, she had wondered what to tell her father. She couldn't bear to think of the misery and anxiety it would cause if he knew the truth. But the Palmer had been firm with her.

"You must tell him, Una. Imagine if he were to return believing he had this wealth behind him, and then discovered he had nothing. That would be a shock far worse." So she had sent back a message: "The dog is lost." And she had not heard from her father since. She had no means of knowing if he was alive or dead.

Despite the fact that he had kissed her, Peter hadn't really expected to see Fionnuala again. But two days after her visit, one of the soldiers in the yard came into the house to tell him that there was a young lady at the gate who said she had a message for him from one of the priests. Seeing her there, he assumed that she had indeed brought a message from Gilpatrick. His greeting was as formal as it was friendly; and when she asked him if he could accompany her to Christ Church, he politely agreed. He was much astonished, as they entered the Fish Shambles, when she turned to him with a smile and remarked: "I haven't a message from Gilpatrick, you know."

"You haven't?"

"I was thinking," she went on calmly, "that I might be coming by your lodgings again, when it isn't so crowded."

"Oh."

She paused by a stall, looking at the fruit to see if it was fresh, then passed on.

"Would you like that?"

There could be no mistaking her meaning. Unless she was playing some kind of game with him, and he didn't think she was, the girl was making an assignation.

"I should like it very much," he heard himself say.

"I could come tomorrow, late in the afternoon perhaps?"

The men-at-arms, he knew, would be on sentry duty then. The knight with whom he shared the house might be there, but he could probably make some arrangement with him.

"Tomorrow would be convenient," he replied.

"Good. I must go home now," she said.

The next day, waiting alone in the house, he had some anxious moments. He didn't think the girl was a spy. Yet there was no chance that her father or her brother would allow her to lose her virtue for any reason at all. The other possibility was that, behind a demure mask, she concealed a quite different character. For all he knew she'd already slept with half the men in Dublin.

Did he mind? He thought about it. Yes, he did. He was a healthy young fellow with all the sexual appetites of any man his age; but he was also quite fastidious. He didn't want to be seduced by the town whore. Why, she might even be unclean. Sexual diseases existed, especially in the ports, all over Europe. It was said that there had been more since the Crusades began. Peter had never heard of anyone being infected in Ireland, but you never knew.

Then he told himself that his fears were foolish. She was just an ordinary girl who happened to be the daughter of a priest. But that in itself contained further dangers, which he tried not to think about. As a result of all these doubts, by the time she arrived the next day, he was considerably nervous.

When Fionnuala arrived, somewhat late, it seemed to him that she was pale, and nervous, too. She asked him if they were alone and when he said they were, she seemed pleased but somewhat distracted, as if she was not certain what to do next. He had prepared warm mead and oatcakes and asked her if she would like some. She nodded gratefully and sat down with him on the bench by the bread oven to eat them. She drank the mead. He gave her more. Only when she had drunk that and was starting to look a little flushed did

she turn to him and demand, "You have made love to women before, haven't you?"

And then he understood, and smiled kindly.

"Yes," he said, "I have. You needn't worry."

So he led her into the house where it was shadowy except for the
patch of afternoon sunlight coming through the doorway. And he
was going to help her off with her cloak, but she motioned him
back; and then, in front of him, she calmly stepped out of her
clothes and stood before him naked.

He caught his breath. Her body was pale and slim, her breasts a
little fuller than he had expected—she was the most beautiful
woman, he thought, that he had ever seen. He moved towards her.

Two days later, they met again. It was necessary this time to take the
knight in his lodgings into his confidence. With some amusement,
and a congratulatory pat on the back, his companion assured Peter
that he would be gone until nightfall, and he was as good as his
word. Before she left this time, Fionnuala had arranged to return the
following evening. How could she make these arrangements to visit
him in the town without arousing suspicion, he had asked her. It
was simple, she had explained. She had started working at the hospital again, and passed through the town on her way. "So when I
want to come here, I tell them at the hospital that I need to go
home; and when I get home, I say I've just come from the hospital.
Nobody will ever be the wiser."

Soon they were making passionate love every other day. And
then Fionnuala suggested: "I could spend the night tomorrow."

"Where would we meet?" he asked.

"There's a storehouse down by the quay," she said.

It turned out to be a delightful place. The storehouse stood at the
end of the wood quay. It had a loft containing bales of wool. There
was a large double door at one end of the loft that opened over the

water, with a view eastwards down the river towards the sea. The summer night was short and warm; the bales of wool made a pleasant bed; and at dawn, they opened the doors and saw the sun rising over the estuary, flooding the Liffey with light, while they made love again.

Later, after they had eaten the provisions they had brought with them, Fionnuala slipped away towards the western gate, where they would assume that she had just come through the town from her home. Peter waited awhile and then, just as the first people were stirring on the quay, he made his way back towards his lodgings.

He had started up the Fish Shambles when he saw Gilpatrick.

For a moment, he wondered if he could avoid him. But Gilpatrick had already seen him. He was coming towards him, smiling.

"Good morning, Peter. You are up early." Gilpatrick was surveying him with some amusement. Peter realised that he probably looked a mess after last night. He put his hand up to his hair to smooth it. "You look as if you had a rough night," Gilpatrick said, with a twinkle in his eye. "You had better go to church and make a good confession." But behind the gentle teasing, Peter also sensed a hint of priestly reproof.

"I couldn't sleep actually," he said. "Have you ever stood on the quay and watched the sun come up the estuary? It's beautiful."

He could see that Gilpatrick didn't believe him.

"I saw my sister just now," Gilpatrick said.

Peter felt himself going pale. He fought it.

"Your sister? How is she?"

"Working hard at the hospital, I'm glad to say."

Was the priest looking at him in a different way? Had he guessed? Peter yawned and shook his head to cover his confusion. What was Gilpatrick saying?

"She and Una were coming in from the hospital. Do you know Una MacGowan? It's her house you're living in."

"Ah, no. No, I don't."

Fionnuala must have moved fast. Gratefully, he muttered that he had to go, and made his escape.

But as he sat in his lodgings soon afterwards, Peter had some uncomfortable moments. His affair with Fionnuala had been so unexpected and so exciting that until now he hadn't thought much about the risks. The encounter with Gilpatrick had suddenly shaken him into a new awareness. The young priest had guessed he had spent the night with a woman. The people in the house knew it, too. He had seen them exchange glances as he came in. That meant that soon most of the English troops in Dublin would have heard. Within the army, of course, this would only enhance his reputation. But it was also dangerous. People would be asking who the girl was. They might try to find out.

And if they did discover? A terrible, cold panic came over him at the thought of it. Consider who the girl was. The daughter of a churchman close to Lawrence O'Toole, and chief of an important local family. The sister of a priest involved in the negotiations with the High King. These were exactly the people that, if he was to take Diarmait's place in Leinster, Strongbow needed as his friends. No matter that it was the girl who had practically seduced him. By sleeping with her he had dishonoured her family. For he had no doubts about the behaviour required of the unmarried daughter of an important family like this. He had abused his friendship with Gilpatrick and the hospitality of his parents. They would never forgive him. They'd demand his head and Strongbow would sacrifice him without blinking an eye. He was finished.

Was there any way out? What if he ended the affair now, and if nobody found out? The memory of the night he had just spent with her filled his thoughts: the scent of her, the warm, intense passion they had shared, the long, erotic passages of time as her pale body entwined with his, the things they had done. A man, he thought, would almost face death itself for such nights as these. Did he have to give this up?

Perhaps not. For now another calculation came into his mind.

Even if he got caught, the outcome needn't be so bad. What if he were to brazen it out? Treat the whole business like a military engagement? That, he felt sure, was what a man like Strongbow would do. If Fionnuala were discovered, if word got out that she had been dishonoured, her chances of marriage to an Irish prince wouldn't be too high. To keep her reputation, her family would have to consent, however unwillingly, to her marrying him. He considered her father's situation: the income from the Church properties, the great tract of land he owned down the coast, his many cattle. Fionnuala was bound to receive a handsome dowry, if only to preserve her family honour. As the husband of a girl from such a prominent Leinster family, wouldn't Strongbow, who was married to a Leinster princess himself, be likely to take an interest in him? If he kept a cool head, this business could turn out to be the best thing he ever did.

Two days later, he spent the night with Fionnuala again.

⁕

The siege of Dublin continued for weeks. Around the city, the besiegers had a pleasant time. The cattle and livestock, the gardens, orchards, fields, all the produce of the area were in their hands. In their camps, they could enjoy the warm summer and wait for the harvest to ripen.

Inside the city, however, things were not so pleasant. Although the watercourse from the south was cut off, there was plenty of water; there were fresh fish from the Liffey, though not enough. There were still the city's grain stores; there were vegetable patches and some pigs. But by the time six weeks had passed, it was clear to Strongbow that, even keeping his troops on short rations, he could only hold out another three or four weeks at most. After that, they would have to start killing the horses.

It was not a surprise to Gilpatrick, therefore, in the sixth week of the siege, to be summoned by Archbishop O'Toole to join him on a mission to the High King's camp. On this occasion, it seemed, he was to be the only person accompanying the great man. They set out at noon, riding across the long wooden bridge to Liffey's northern side and then westwards a little way along the stream, to a point where the king had said he would meet them.

The archbishop looked tired. His ascetic, finely drawn face was showing lines of stress around the eyes; and Gilpatrick knew this was not only because he felt the weight of his responsibilities but because his sensitive, poetic nature suffered almost a physical pain when he contemplated the suffering of others. When the King of Dublin had been killed after his unsuccessful attack the previous year, the saintly bishop had been visibly distressed. He was clearly concerned now, since the offers made by the High King to Strongbow had still not been accepted, and he saw only suffering and bloodshed ahead. "He blames himself," Gilpatrick told his father. "It isn't his fault, of course; but that's his nature."

When they reached the meeting place, they found that a handsome reception had been prepared for them. A big thatched hall had been set up with a wicker wall on the north side and the other sides left open. Inside this were benches covered with woollen cushions and cloths, and tables piled with a splendid feast. The High King, accompanied by some of his greatest chiefs, gave them a warm and respectful greeting and invited them to eat, which Gilpatrick, at least, was glad to do. Nor, for all its genuine kindness, was the significance of the feast lost upon him. The High King was letting them know that he had ample supplies, while the sight of Gilpatrick's face had told the king what he had suspected, that food was getting short in the city.

The O'Connor king was a tall, powerful man, with a broad face and a mass of curly black hair that fell with an almost oily thickness to his shoulders. His dark eyes had a soft glow that, Gilpatrick had heard, was fascinating to women.

"I've been here for six weeks," he told them. "But as you can see, we are out of sight in the city, so please don't tell them where we are.

I can go down and bathe in the Liffey every morning." He smiled. "If Strongbow likes I'd be happy to stay here a year or two."

Gilpatrick ate heartily. Even the ascetic archbishop consented to take a glass or two of wine. And to Gilpatrick's delight they were entertained by a skilful harpist; and better yet, a bard recited for them one of the old Irish tales, of Cuchulainn the warrior and how he got his name. It was in a mellow mood that the little group of men got round to discussing the problem of the English.

"I have a new offer," the archbishop began, "and it will surprise you. Strongbow still wants Leinster. But," he paused, "he is prepared to hold it from you in the proper Irish manner. He'll swear an oath to you, give hostages. In English terms, you would be his overlord." He looked at the High King carefully. "I know you believed he was intending to conquer the whole island, but it isn't so. He's ready to accept Leinster from your hands, and give you the respect that is your due. I think this has to be taken seriously."

"He would hold it as Diarmait did?"

"He would."

The High King sighed, then he stretched his long arms. "But isn't that just the problem, Lorcan?" They were speaking in Irish and he used the archbishop's Irish name. "You wouldn't have trusted Diarmait. The man was ready to sacrifice his own son to break his oath. Are you saying that Strongbow's any better?"

"I don't like the man," O'Toole answered frankly, "but he is a man of honour."

"If that is so, Lorcan, then will you tell me this: how is it that this man of honour can be ready to swear an oath to me as his overlord when he has already sworn one to King Henry of England? Is there not a contradiction in that?"

The archbishop looked flummoxed. He glanced at Gilpatrick.

"I think," Gilpatrick said, "that I can explain that. You see, technically, I don't believe Strongbow has actually given homage to King Henry for his Irish lands. So you would be his overlord for Leinster, and Henry for his lands in England." And seeing the other two men look blank, he explained: "Over there, every yard of land has a lord, and so you may do homage to a different lord for each piece of land you hold." He smiled. "Many of the great lords, like Strongbow, for instance, do homage to Henry for their lands in England, and to the King of France for their lands in France."

"So where does their loyalty lie?" demanded the High King.

"It depends on where they are."

"Dear God, what sort of people are these English? No wonder Diarmait liked them."

"An oath is not so much a personal matter with them," Gilpatrick said. "It's more a legal form." He searched for a characterisation that would convey the spirit of Plantagenet feudalism. "You might say, I suppose, that they are more interested in land than in people."

"God forgive them," murmured the archbishop as he and the O'Connor king exchanged looks of horror.

"Do you think that if he had Leinster and the ability to reward all his armed men, and any others he might import, that Strongbow could be trusted not to attack the other provinces of Ireland?" the O'Connor king asked. And before the saintly archbishop could even formulate a reply, he continued: "We have him safely walled up in Dublin, Lorcan. There's nothing he can do. Let him stay there until he accepts our offer to keep the ports. It's either that or starvation. We've no need to bargain with him or to accept these English oaths that are not made with the heart."

⁜

For Fionnuala, the heady weeks of summer had been a revelation. She had never realised how boring her life had been before.

She had known she was bored, of course: bored by her parents, bored by her brothers—not that she saw so much of them, thank God—bored by her life in Dublin and at the hospital. Bored by the kindly Palmer and his wife. She was even bored with Una, who meant well but was always trying to restrain her. In Una's company, she felt like a horse, bred to race, that is being forced into pulling a sturdy little cart.

What was it she wanted? She hardly knew. Something else: a bigger sky, a brighter light.

What did a girl do when she was bored? Stealing apples wasn't much fun. There were the local boys to flirt with. She knew it would annoy her parents. But the truth was, the local boys bored her. And those old men in the hospital had just been a joke. More recently there had been the English soldiers to think about. The men mostly seemed coarse; she was more afraid of being raped than seduced. Some of the knights were quite handsome, but they seemed too old and she was a little afraid of them.

But when Gilpatrick's friend, the knight from Wales, had appeared in their house, she thought he was the most beautiful young man she had ever seen in her life. And she knew at once that it was he who could be the one to open the gates to life's next great adventure. The result had been beyond her wildest dreams.

"Welshman," she called him as her father had done. "My Welshman." She knew every curl of his hair, every inch of his proud young body. She was almost lost in wonder, sometimes, that she could be in possession of such a thing.

Was she in love? Not exactly. She was too excited, too pleased with herself even to be in love. The sexual awakening, of course, was wonderful, quite the best thing, she told herself, that had ever happened to her. But the adventure, the game was the greatest thrill. It was knowing that she was deceiving them all that aroused her excitement as she made her way towards her assignations. It was knowing she had just come from his bed while Una went about her serious business that made the mornings in the hospital seem full of light and life. It was knowing that what she did was dangerous and forbidden that made her tremble with anticipation as her young lover came to her and which brought the fire and climax to her passion.

There was the other risk, too, beyond being discovered. Even in medieval times women knew of barriers to conception, but they were imperfect, permeable, uncertain. She knew the risk, yet tried not to know. She would not give it up. And so the affair continued. It was love, it was passion—it was something to do.

It was three days after her brother's unsuccessful mission to the High King that Fionnuala, standing by the hospital entrance, saw Una hurrying from the city's western gateway. It was nearly noon. Fionnuala had spent the night before with Peter by the quay, arriving as usual at the hospital in the early morning. An hour ago, Una had gone on an errand into the town. Her friend was scurrying back now, Fionnuala thought, as if she'd been stung by a bee. It didn't take long to find out why.

"I was after visiting the cathedral to say a prayer for my poor family—and for you, too, Fionnuala—when who is it sees me but your father." She had dragged Fionnuala to the corner of the building where they couldn't be overheard. "And he says to me, 'It's a fine thing that Fionnuala's spending so much time at the hospital. But as she was with you last night, I couldn't tell her to be sure to be back at the house before this evening. We have visitors. Will you tell her that?' And there's myself, standing there like an idiot and saying, 'Yes, Father, I will.' And it was almost out of my mouth to say you weren't at the hospital at all." She was staring at Fionnuala now in wide-eyed reproach. "So if you weren't here and you weren't there, then in the name of God where were you?"

"I was somewhere else." Fionnuala looked at her friend enigmatically. She was enjoying this.

"What do you mean you were somewhere else?"

"Well, if I wasn't here, and I wasn't there . . ."

"Don't play games with me, Fionnuala." Una flushed with anger now. She looked at her friend searchingly. "You don't mean . . . Oh God, Fionnuala, was it with some man you were?"

"I may have been."

"Are you out of your wits? In the name of Heaven, who?"

"I'm not telling."

The slap that struck her face took Fionnuala by surprise and almost sent her reeling. She struck back, but Una was ready for her and caught her hand.

"You childish fool!" Una cried.

"You're jealous."

"Isn't it like you to think so? Have you no thought for what will become of you? Not a care for your reputation and your family?"

Fionnuala flushed. She felt herself starting to get angry now.

"If you shout any more," she said crossly, "the whole of Dublin's going to know anyway."

"You must stop it, Fionnuala," Una dropped her voice almost to a whisper. "You've got to stop it at once. Before it's too late."

"Maybe I will. Maybe I won't."

"I'll tell your father. He'll stop you."

"I thought you were my friend."

"I am. That's why I'll tell him. To save you from yourself, you stupid child."

Fionnuala was silent. In particular she resented her friend's patronising tone. How dare she order her about like this?

"If you tell, Una," she spoke slowly, "I'll kill you." It was said so quietly, and with such force, that Una, despite herself, blanched. Fionnuala looked at her steadily. Did she mean it? She hardly knew herself. Was she in the act of destroying their friendship? Anyway, she realised, it wouldn't do any good to threaten Una.

"I'm sorry, Fionnuala. I have to."

Fionnuala paused. Then she looked down. Then she sighed. Then she stared longingly towards the west gate. Then she looked down and did not move for a minute or so. Then she groaned. "Oh it's so hard, Una."

"I know."

"You really think I have to?"

"I know you must."

"I'll stop seeing him, Una. I will."

"Now? You'll promise?"

Fionnuala gave her an ironic smile. "You'll tell my father if I don't. Remember?"

"I'd have to."

"I know." She sighed again. "I promise, Una. I'll give him up. I promise."

Then they hugged each other and Una cried and Fionnuala cried, too; and Una murmured, "I know, I know," and Fionnuala thought, you know nothing at all you little prig, and so the matter was settled.

"But you mustn't tell on me now, Una," Fionnuala said. "Because even if I never set eyes on the man again in my life, you know what my father would do. He'd whip me till I couldn't stand and then he'd put me in the convent over at Hoggen Green. He already threatened me with it before, you know. Will you promise Una?" She looked at her pleadingly. "Will you promise?"

"I will," said Una.

Fionnuala was in a thoughtful mood that evening when she went home. If she was to continue the affair without interference from Una, then she'd have to take some fresh precautions. Perhaps she should come to the hospital with her father or her brother one morning, to show that she'd been at home. She'd have to meet Peter in the afternoon a few times. Once she'd allayed Una's suspicions, then no doubt the affair could resume its previous pattern. She was so busy thinking about these arrangements that she almost forgot the reason that she had to be home in good time.

She came to the gateway to the house, which stood just beside the little church. She noticed the two horses there and remembered the visitors, but without curiosity. She had the good sense, however, to straighten her clothes and brush her hand over her hair before she walked through the gateway. As it was summer, they had set out benches and trestles upon the grass. Her father and mother were both there and they were smiling. So was her brother Gilpatrick.

They turned in a way that suggested they had all been waiting for her, talking about her.

Her mother was coming towards her now, smiling still, but with a strange look in her eye.

"Come Fionnuala," she said, "our guests have arrived already. Come and give a fitting welcome to Brendan and Ruairi O'Byrne."

⁜

A week after Una's threat, Peter FitzDavid was still seeing Fionnuala. They had been careful, meeting in the afternoons or early evenings, not spending the night together. The arrival of the O'Byrne cousins had helped. Fionnuala had cleverly encouraged her father to bring them both to visit her while she was working at the hospital one day. They had seen her, demure and pious, working with Una and the Palmer's wife; and Una in turn had seen that Fionnuala now had a serious suitor in prospect. "She can't even imagine," Fionnuala had told Peter laughingly, "that I could look at another man when I've a chance to marry an O'Byrne."

Peter did not treat the new arrivals so lightheartedly. From Gilpatrick he learned that Brendan O'Byrne was the one his parents wanted for their daughter; but whether he would like her, and whether the princely O'Byrnes might feel Brendan could do better, remained to be seen. His cousin Ruairi was another matter, and Gilpatrick's parents had not been best pleased to see him. "Brendan's a fine upstanding man, but Ruairi's the taller of the two." Gilpatrick gave Peter a wintry look. "I don't know why he's here," he muttered.

Peter thought he could guess. Brendan had probably brought his cousin, whatever his reputation, for cover. If he'd come alone, it looked too obvious; if he decided not to make an offer for Fionnuala, it might disappoint or even give offence to the chief; but if the two cousins paid a friendly visit and then left again, nobody could say anything against him.

Should he be jealous of this cautious young prince? Peter wondered? Probably. O'Byrne had all the wealth and position that he himself lacked. He was an excellent match for Fionnuala. If I've any decency at all, he thought, I ought to step aside and stop wasting this girl's time. You're nothing better, he angrily told himself, than a thief in the night. But then she had come to his lodgings again, and pressed up against him, and he had given way at once.

Besides her body, Fionnuala also brought him food. For food was getting scarcer in the city all the time. Even Gilpatrick was going hungry. "My father's got plenty at the church," he explained. "And nobody stops me going to see him. But the difficulty is the archbishop. He says we must suffer with the people in the city. The trouble is, he never eats more than a crust of bread anyway." Peter could hardly tell him that Fionnuala was smuggling food to him from her father's house almost every day.

He was coming in from his sentry duty on the walls one morning, having dismissed his men, and looking forward to the rendezvous he had with Fionnuala that afternoon, when passing Christ Church he saw Strongbow. The great lord was standing alone, staring down towards the river, apparently lost in thought; and Peter, supposing that Strongbow was unaware of him, was walking quietly past when he heard the magnate say his name. He turned.

The magnate's face was impassive, but it seemed to Peter that Strongbow looked depressed. It was hardly surprising. Though the besiegers were comfortably camped well back from the walls, they were keeping a sharp eye on the gates. It had been impossible to send out patrols. Two days ago, Strongbow had sent a boat under cover of darkness to see whether any supplies could be sneaked in by water; but the enemy had caught it opposite Clontarf and sent it back, on fire, on the incoming tide. Amongst the remaining Dublin inhabitants, and the English soldiers as well, the word was the same: "The High King's got him." But Strongbow was a seasoned commander; Peter didn't think he'd give up on him yet. Strongbow's eyes were surveying him as if he were considering something.

"Do you know what I need at the moment, Peter FitzDavid?" he asked quietly.

"Another fog," Peter suggested. "Then at least we could sneak out."

"Perhaps. But what I need more than that is information. I need to know where the High King is and the exact disposition of his forces."

So, he's planning a breakout, Peter thought. There was no other option, really. But to have any hope of success, he'd need to take the besiegers by surprise.

"Do you want me to go out tonight and scout?" he asked. If he came back successfully that would certainly put him in high favour.

"Perhaps. I'm not sure you'd get through." His eyes fixed on Peter's, then lowered. "The archbishop and the young priest probably know. What's his name? Father Gilpatrick. But I can't ask them, of course."

"I know Gilpatrick, but he'd never tell me."

"No. You might ask his sister, though." Strongbow's gaze moved back towards the river. "Next time you see her."

He knew. Peter felt himself go pale. He and how many others? But worse than the fact that he knew about the illicit affair, was what he was asking him to do. To use Fionnuala as a spy, or at least dupe her into revealing information. She probably didn't even know anything, he thought; but that was hardly the point. If he wanted Strongbow's favour, he'd better discover something.

Amazingly, his chance came that very afternoon, and it turned out to be easier than he could have imagined. They had made love in the house. They had an hour before she had to leave. They were talking casually about the O'Byrnes, who were due to come again the next day, and about her life at home. "I think," he had remarked, "that Strongbow will have to give in to the High King soon. I can't see this going on another month, and there's no chance of anyone coming to help us." He grinned. "I'll be glad when it's over. Then I can come and eat at your house as your father promised. If you haven't already married Brendan O'Byrne by then, that is," he added uncertainly.

"Don't be silly." She laughed. "I shan't marry Brendan. And the siege is bound to end."

It was his opportunity.

"Really?" He seemed to be looking for reassurance. "Does Gilpatrick think so?"

"Oh, he does. I overheard him telling my father only yesterday that the High King has a camp only a short way upstream. He knows so well the English haven't a chance that his men go bathing in the Liffey, every day."

"They do?"

"With all the great chiefs. They haven't a care in the world."

Peter gasped. His face was just about to register his delight but he checked himself, looked glum, and murmured, "We haven't a chance then. It's as good as over." He paused. "You'd better not tell anyone I said that, Fionnuala. If Strongbow ever heard it . . . they'd doubt my loyalty."

"Don't worry," she said.

But already his mind was working fast.

The following afternoon, the sentries at the Irish forward posts saw Fionnuala leave the hospital and walk back as usual to the city's western gate. Since they could not see the southern gate they never knew how long she spent in Dublin before returning to her home, and so they had no idea that she had proceeded to Peter's lodgings and remained there until it was nearly dusk, at which time the look-out post near her father's house observed her leave the southern gate and walk home.

It was almost dark when the sentries on the west side observed Fionnuala, with her saffron shawl wrapped over her head, returning to the hospital. It was unusual for her to leave and return the same day, but they saw her go through into the hospital yard and thought no more about it. They were puzzled therefore the following evening, when they saw her going to the hospital yet again. "Did you see her go back into Dublin today?" one of the sentries asked his companion. Then he shrugged. "Must have missed her." At dawn the next morning, she flitted back from the hospital to the western gate. But then, an hour later, she made the same journey again. This was clearly impossible. The sentries concluded that there was something odd. They decided to maintain a closer watch.

When Peter had reached the hospital the first evening, he had passed through the gateway and then sunk down with his back to the fence. Nobody could see him. The inmates were all inside at this hour. He unwrapped the shawl from his head and waited. The darkness fell slowly. At this time in the summer, there would be only about three hours of real darkness. The sky was full of passing clouds but there was a sliver of moon. That was good. He needed a little light but not too much. He waited until well after midnight before he made his move.

Outside the hospital ran the broad track of the ancient road, the Slige Mhor that led towards the west. There was a large contingent of men less than a mile along the road, blockading it. He intended to avoid the Slige Mhor entirely. He knew that on the river side of the hospital enclosure there was a small gate. Stealing round to this, he went out. In front of him lay open ground, dotted with bushes, leading to the marshy banks of the river. With luck, in the darkness, he might be able to slip through there.

It took him an hour, working his way carefully, moving only when clouds covered the moon, to get past the Irish camp that straddled the road. After that he was able to move more quickly, but always with caution, following the line of the river until he came opposite the place where he guessed the High King's encampment might be. Then, finding concealment in some bushes on a slope which made a little vantage point, he prepared to wait the rest of the night.

It turned out that he had been nearly right. The next morning he could see the High King's camp, only about half a mile farther upstream. Early in the morning he saw the patrols go out. A few hours later they returned. And soon afterwards, he saw at least a hundred men come down into the water. They remained there quite a long time. They seemed to be throwing a ball between them in some sort of game. Then they all went up the bank again. He could see the sun glinting on their wet and naked bodies.

He spent the rest of the morning in his place of concealment. He had brought half a loaf of precious bread with him and a small leather flask of water. He also took good care to note the terrain around. That would be essential if he was to carry out the rest of his plan. In the early afternoon he realised that there was one more thing he would have to do that day, which was dangerous. An hour later he left his hiding place and very cautiously worked his way across some meadows to a patch of wooded higher ground. He did not return to his hiding place until evening; but by the time he did so, he was satisfied that his plan could work. Not until it was dark did he make his way back to the hospital again. It was strange waiting at the hospital gate because he knew that Fionnuala was working there that night, only yards away from him; but he remained there until dawn and then, wrapped in his shawl, returning past the Irish forward post at dawn where he was taken for Fionnuala by the sentries. By midmorning he had seen Strongbow.

He told Strongbow everything, how he had gone out scouting and discovered the High King bathing, with one small difference: he omitted all reference to Fionnuala. If Strongbow guessed the truth, he said nothing. When he had finished, Strongbow was thoughtful. "To get the best advantage from this information," the magnate said, "we need to catch them when they're bathing and their guard is down. But how can we know?"

"I have thought of that," said Peter. And he told Strongbow the rest of his plan.

"You can get out, past the sentries again?" Strongbow asked, and Peter nodded. "How?"

"Do not ask me," Peter replied. "It will be low tide tomorrow morning," he added, "so you could use the ford as well as the bridge to send the men across."

"And where should we station the man to receive your signal?"

"Ah." Peter smiled. "On the roof of Christ Church Cathedral."

"So," Strongbow summarised, "the plan is by no means without risk." He ran over the details, step by step. "But if it works, you will have done well. It is, however, contingent upon one other thing. A clear and sunny morning."

"That is true," Peter admitted.

"Well," Strongbow concluded, "it's worth a chance."

⁂

It was sunset that day when the sentries at the forward post saw a figure leave from the western gate and start walking towards the hospital. They had already stopped both Una that morning and Fionnuala an hour ago to make certain who they were. Once again, they decided to check, and one of them rode quickly forward. The figure was dressed as a priest, but the sentry was suspicious. It could be a disguise. The fellow wore a hood over his head.

"Who are you and where are you going?" The sentry addressed him in Irish.

"Father Peter is my name, my son." The answer was delivered in a comfortable Irish also. "On my way to visit a poor soul in the hospital there." He pulled back his hood, to reveal a tonsured head and gave the sentry a pleasant smile. "I am expected, I believe."

At this moment, the gate of the hospital opened and Fionnuala appeared. She gave a sign of recognition to the priest and waited respectfully by the entrance.

"Proceed, Father," said the sentry, a little embarrassed.

"Thank you. I do not expect to be returning until tomorrow. God be with you, my son." Pulling his hood on again, the priest continued on his way and the sentry saw Fionnuala usher him through the gate, which closed behind them.

"A priest," the sentry reported. "He'll be going back tomorrow." And no one thought any more about it.

Inside the hospital, meanwhile, Fionnuala was leading Peter to the room they were to use—a separate compartment, entered by an outside door, at the end of the men's dormitory, where kind, gullible Una had promised her they would not be disturbed.

As they got inside and Peter pulled back his hood again, Fionnuala could hardly restrain her laughter.

"You've got a tonsure," she whispered, "just like Gilpatrick."

"It's as well, or I might have been in trouble with that sentry."

So far, Peter congratulated himself, everything had worked out perfectly. His quick thinking and foresight two days ago had made everything possible. He was sorry that it had meant that he must deceive Fionnuala, as he was doing now, and make use of her; but he told himself that it was for a greater cause.

His calculations had been precise. Discovering that she was due to be in the hospital the next two evenings, he had decided it would be unwise to attempt the female disguise twice. On the assumption that, after his return from his scouting expedition, he would want to go straight back out again, he had hit upon this new device.

"The day after tomorrow, we'll spend the night together," he'd said.

"By the wharf?" She'd looked uncertain.

"No, in the hospital."

"The hospital? You're mad!" she had cried.

"Is there a quiet place there, somewhere?" he asked. She had thought and said there might be. "Listen, then." He had grinned. "This is what we're going to do."

And now, as Fionnuala looked at him in wonderment, she decided this was the most daring thing she had ever done. Amazingly enough, it hadn't even been very difficult. Once she had told Una that she felt the need for spiritual counselling, her friend had been sympathetic. "I want to make my confession to a priest, Una," she told her. "And then I need to have a long talk with him." She smiled apologetically. "It's those O'Byrne boys. I don't know what to do." When Una asked how she could help, Fionnuala explained: "I don't want to be seen going to a priest's house. It always feels as if people are watching me in Dublin. So I asked the priest to come here." The Palmer and his wife always went to sleep early. The priest could visit, see her alone, and leave as late as necessary. To her relief, Una had agreed that this was a good idea. It was Una who had suggested the room at the end of the men's dormitory. She had even offered: "If anyone asks, I'll say the priest came to see me." She had taken Fionnuala by the arm and murmured, "I do understand, Fionnuala." And Fionnuala had thought: it's as well you don't.

There was no one about. If Una was watching from somewhere, she had made herself scarce. They entered the room, in which Fionnuala had already lit two candles and placed a little food. She reached up and stroked his tonsured head. "Now I shall think," she said slyly, "that it's a priest I have for a lover." She gazed at him, puzzled. "How will you explain your bald head in the next few days?"

"I'll cover it," he said.

"And you did all this for me?"

"I did," he lied. "And I'd do it again."

They talked for a while. Before they made love, Peter removed his priest's robe. Fionnuala noticed that he also took off a stiff pad that was strapped round his lower back. "Backache," he explained sheepishly. "I'll massage it," she said.

It was nearly dawn when she awoke to find that he had gone.

Peter had moved carefully, but swiftly. After letting himself out of the hospital's northern gate, he had followed the same route as before. By dawn, he was approaching the little wooded rise he had marked out the day before. His vantage point was already chosen: a tall tree with a commanding view. In the early light of the day, he climbed up to the branch he had selected. From there, parting the leaves, he could see the opposite riverbank, down which the Irish king's men would come; he also had a clear view eastwards towards Dublin. In the distance, he could see the southern headland of the bay. The city's low ridge was mostly obscured by the intervening woods. But it was possible to make out, quite clearly, the roof of Christ Church Cathedral. Slowly now, he loosened the straps round his waist and pulled the pad from his back. Taking his time, he un-wrapped the cloth covering and extracted the thin, hard object from its centre. He inspected it carefully. Not a mark or a blemish.

It was a metal plate of polished steel. Strongbow had given it to him. It was so highly polished that you could see every pore of skin on your face in its reflection. The magnate used it as a mirror. Peter held it, keeping its polished surface towards him. He did not want to risk giving his position away. He looked eastwards and smiled. The sky was clear. Time passed. The eastern sky grew lighter, then red, then gold: it began to shimmer. And then, over the distant bay, he saw the fiery orb of the rising sun.

Everything was ready. There was a risk, of course, that when he sent the signal he would give himself away. If the Irish besiegers caught him, they would surely kill him. He'd have done the same in their place. But that was a small risk compared to the favours he could expect from Strongbow if the operation succeeded. He was excited, but he waited patiently. It grew warmer. The sun was rising over the bay.

The High King's patrols would be out now. He had seen some of them leaving the royal camp. Midmorning passed and there was no sign of activity. The patrols were out later than yesterday. Perhaps they would not bathe after all. He cursed under his breath. Another hour went by; it was nearly noon. Then, at last, he saw that some-thing was happening at the camp. Above the riverbank, he saw a group of men appear, bearing a large object; but he couldn't decide what it was. They set their burden down at the top of the slope. Now more men were coming. It looked as if they were carrying buckets. They kept coming and going, swarming round the big object. And now he understood what they were doing. It was a huge tub they were filling. He knew that the Irish liked to have a bath in a tub whose water had been heated with hot stones. The setting up of this great tub, therefore, could only mean one thing.

The High King of Ireland was about to take a ceremonial bath.

So it proved. Before they had finished filling the tub, the first patrols started to return. There seemed to be even more of them this time. Peter guessed that at least two hundred were going down into the river, and others were still arriving. And as soon as everything at the top of the slope was ready, he saw a single figure emerge from the camp, accompanied by about a dozen men, who lifted the figure into the great bathtub. While his men splashed about in the river below, the O'Connor king, surrounded by his companions, was performing the royal ablutions.

It was perfect. Peter couldn't believe his luck. He turned the steel reflector over, carefully judging the angle. He started to rotate it, back and forth.

On the roof of Christ Church, the waiting sentry saw the tiny flash of light, greenish from the tree, reflecting the brightness of the burning sun. And moments later, the southern and western city gates burst open; a hundred lightly armed horsemen, with five hundred more foot soldiers running behind them, made for the ford, while two hundred armoured knights thundered at a gallop across the wooden bridge.

⁘

The sudden breakout of the English from their trap in Dublin that summer's day proved to be the pivotal event in the history of England and Ireland. The Irish besiegers, perhaps complacent after the weeks of inaction, were caught completely off guard. As the English forces burst through the Irish lines and stormed along the

Liffey towards where the High King was bathing, the O'Connor king had only time to gather his clothes and make a dash for safety to avoid them. The Irish foot soldiers round his encampment were slaughtered. Within hours, all the besieging forces knew that the High King had been humiliated and that Strongbow's army was out in the open. The English war veterans now moved with the utmost speed. The approaches to the city were secured. Spearhead attacks by the armoured cavalry devastated each of the various encampments. The Irish were unable to cope with the highly trained European fighting machine once it was free to operate in the open field. Opposition melted away. For the time being at least, the High King wisely withdrew. Leinster, its rich farmland, its cattle, and its great harvest lay in Strongbow's ruthless and capable hands.

For Peter FitzDavid, it seemed the future would be bright. That very night, Strongbow had rewarded him with a small bag of gold. No doubt still better things would follow. He was not a public hero. After all, he had only been a secret scout. It was the bold breakout of Strongbow and the humiliation of the High King caught bathing in the Liffey that would be everywhere reported and engage the attention of the chroniclers.

But if the role of Peter FitzDavid was to be quickly forgotten, the part that Fionnuala played in these great events was never to be known at all. Peter never referred to it once, not even to Strongbow. It was only the next day, as the rumour of Peter's role reached her, that she guessed some of what had happened. After half an hour spent in tears, she also understood that she could never tell anyone, not even Una, of his infamous conduct, since it would also implicate herself. Indeed she realised, with a terrible coldness, he had the power to do her terrible damage if he ever chose to reveal what she had done.

Two days later, she caught sight of him in the market. He came towards her smiling, but she could see the embarrassment in his eyes. She let him come up to her, then, mustering all the dignity she could, she said with quiet coldness: "I never want to see your face again."

He seemed to want to say something, but she turned her back on him and walked away. He had the good sense not to follow her.

⁜

In his calculations of the likely benefits that would accrue to him from Strongbow's triumph, there was one thing that Peter FitzDavid forgot.

One month after the defeat of the High King, Peter happened to be walking past the king's hall when he saw Strongbow coming out. He bowed his head to the great man and smiled, but Strongbow didn't seem to see him. He looked distracted, almost haggard. Peter wondered what the reason could possibly be. The next day, he heard that Strongbow had gone. He had taken a ship during the night. Where had he gone, Peter asked one of the commanders, who gave him a strange look. "To find King Henry, before it's too late," the man replied. "Strongbow's in trouble."

King Henry Plantagenet was the most dynamic ruler of his age. His genius for exploiting situations to his own advantage, his success in expanding his sprawling Plantagenet empire, his highly aggressive administration—all these made him feared. Henry also had one other, devastating ability. He moved with incredible speed. All medieval kings had peripatetic courts which moved about their domains. But the itineraries of Henry were dizzying. He would move to and fro across the English Channel several times in a season, seldom stopping anywhere for more than two or three days. He would race from one end of his empire to the other just when you least expected it. And anyone who imagined that this ruthless and mercurial monarch would tolerate one of his vassals setting up a rival power base anywhere within his empire would be in for a shock.

For some time Henry had been watching the progress of Strongbow in Ireland. While King Diarmait was alive, the English magnate remained effectively a mercenary, no matter what Diarmait might have promised. Hard on the heels of Diarmait's death came news that Strongbow was trapped in Dublin. But now, suddenly, Strongbow had a kingdom in Leinster and obviously the possibility to conquer the whole island. It was both a threat and an opportunity.

"I did not give Strongbow permission to become a king," he announced. He'd already had enough trouble from one subordinate after he'd made Becket Archbishop of Canterbury. "He is my vassal. If Ireland is his, then it is mine," he judged. And soon the word reached Strongbow: "King Henry is not pleased. He is coming to Ireland himself."

With the ending of the siege, Una received word of her father. It made her sad. The continual fretting over the loss of the strongbox, it seemed, was taking a toll on his health; and she knew he was not robust. The fact that she blamed herself for the business and that they were separated made her still more distressed. The message he sent had, once again, asked her to remain where she was. She considered disobeying and going to see him in Rouen, but the Palmer told her she should not. She did, however, send word that, depending how events turned out, it might be possible for him in a few months to return and that she and the Palmer would surely be able to help him make a start again. So she worked hard at the hospital and waited to see what would come.

One thing that pleased her was the change in Fionnuala. There's no doubt, she thought, that visit from the priest did her good. In the days that followed, Fionnuala had looked so sad and thoughtful. A new quietness and seriousness seemed to have descended upon her. "You have changed, Fionnuala," she once ventured with a gentle approbation, "and I was thinking it would be the long time you spent with the priest that was the cause." And she was so glad when Fionnuala murmured, "That would be it."

It was during this time that two new people came into her life. She had heard from Fionnuala that the two O'Byrnes were making a second visit and had been to see her father, but she had not somehow expected them to call in at the hospital. They did so, however, one morning and were conducted round by the Palmer, who showed great respect to Brendan O'Byrne and, it seemed to Una, slightly less to his cousin Ruairi. At the end of the visit, since it was time for Fionnuala to leave, the two O'Byrnes were going to accompany her when she turned to the Palmer and asked whether Una could be spared a little while to walk with them. "Of course, she may," cried that kindly man. And so the four of them set off. The day being fine, they decided to walk some way along the Slige Mhor.

Una had a chance to observe them all. Fionnuala was behaving beautifully. She was demure, serious, her head down, but looking up to smile pleasantly at Brendan from time to time. Una felt so proud of her. Brendan himself she found impressive. Dark-haired, with an early touch of grey, good-looking, he had an air of serious solidity about him that she liked immensely. He talked quietly but well. He considered before uttering an opinion. He asked thoughtful questions about the hospital. If Fionnuala could just get him for a husband, she thought, wouldn't that be a wonderful match?

His cousin Ruairi was very different. He was taller than Brendan, longer boned. His hair was light brown and trimmed short. He had a few days' growth of light stubble on his face, which made him seem manly, like a young warrior. He did not appear to be as heavy and serious as Brendan; but rather than ask questions as they went round the hospital, he had seemed content to listen and watch with a half smile on his face so that, after a time, one became curious about what he was thinking. Though his pale eyes sometimes seemed unfocussed, as though he was engaged in an interior dialogue with himself, Una also had a sense that he had noted everything he saw. She wondered what he had noted about herself and Fionnuala.

At first they walked as a group, side by side, along the track, talk-

ing easily. Ruairi said something about one of the hospital inmates
he had observed which made them all laugh. Then they fell into two
pairs, Brendan and Fionnuala walking ahead, Ruairi and Una behind.

For a while Ruairi seemed content to walk along, making the occasional chance remark. Una, who still felt a little shy, was glad to
find everything so easy. When she asked him some questions about
himself, however, he did begin to talk, and then he talked well.

He appeared to have been everywhere, and done everything. She
was amazed that anyone of his age—he surely wasn't twenty-five—
could have done so many things, even for a short time. He told her
about the horse traders and cattlemen he knew in Ulster and
Munster, and some of their tricks. He described the coasts of
Connacht and the islands there. He told her about his voyages with
the merchants "from the time I was down in Cork." He'd been to
London and Bristol, and France, too. She asked him eagerly if he
had been in Rouen. He hadn't, but he told her a good story about a
merchant from there who was caught in a shady deal.

"Does your cousin Brendan travel so much, also?" she enquired.

"Brendan?" A look she could not read crossed his face. "He
prefers to stay at home and tend to his affairs."

"And you? Do you not tend to your affairs at home?"

"I do." He stared ahead of him as if he were thinking of something else for a moment. "But I've another voyage to make shortly.
I'll be going to Chester."

For some reason Una was sorry to learn this. It seemed to her
that, for all the wonders he might see upon his travels, there was
something missing in the life of this fine young man with his restless soul.

"It's by a warm fire in your own home that you should be," she
said. "At least some of the time."

"It's the truth," he said. "And perhaps when I return that's what
I'll do."

Brendan and Fionnuala were turning round now. It seemed that they still wished to walk together, and Una was anxious to encourage this, so she quickly turned round herself so that she and Ruairi would be walking in front of them for the journey back. Ruairi talked less during the return, but she didn't mind. Though she hardly knew him, it was strange how comfortable she felt in his company. She had never known such a feeling of ease, not even with the Palmer. And he was a good man, none better. She couldn't account for it at all. Exchanging a few words now and then, they made their way back to the hospital; and although it was a considerable distance, she had no sense of time passing. As they parted, she couldn't help wishing, though she knew it was foolish, that they might meet again someday.

On the seventeenth day of October in that year of 1171, King Henry II of England arrived in Ireland, the first English monarch ever to do so. He landed at the southern port of Waterford with a large army. His intention in coming was not at all to conquer Ireland, in which he had little interest, but to take away the power of his vassal Strongbow and reduce him to obedience. To an extent, he had achieved his object before he arrived, because a worried Strongbow had already managed to intercept him in England and had offered him all his Irish gains. Now, however, Henry meant to inspect the place and see to it that Strongbow's submission to him was made good.

The army that King Henry brought with him was truly formidable: five hundred knights and nearly four thousand archers. With this, let alone with the addition of Strongbow's already large forces, the English king could, if he chose, have swept across the entire island and devastated any and all opposition in open battle. Henry knew this very well. But as his subsequent actions were to show, the ruthless Plantagenet opportunist intended to proceed cautiously, and with limited objectives. Try to subdue an island whose native population are against you? He was far too clever. Would he watch, though, for signs and situations that might be of advantage to him? Of course he would.

⁘

Gilpatrick stood with his father and gazed at the extraordinary scene before him. He didn't know what to think. There, on the edge of the ancient Hoggen Green, between the city's eastern gate and the Thingmount where their ancestor was buried, a huge wicker-walled hall had been erected. It was the sort of great hall that would have been put up for the High King in days of old, but it was bigger. "It makes the Thingmount look like a pimple," he had heard a work-man remark. And in that huge hall was the King of England.

He hadn't wasted any time. Twenty-five days after he had landed at Waterford, he had settled all the affairs in southern Leinster and arrived at Dublin. Now he was holding court there in perfect safety, surrounded by an army of thousands. Even Gilpatrick's father was awestruck.

"I didn't know," he quietly confessed, "there were so many sol-diers in the world."

And the kings and chiefs of Ireland had all been coming to sub-mit to him, ever since he arrived on the island. The High King and the great men of Connacht and the west held aloof, but from every other province, willingly or unwillingly, the chiefs of the great Irish clans were seeking him out.

Gilpatrick's father was contemptuous, but fatalistic.

"They'll come into his house now, even quicker than they did to Brian Boru, because he has an army to compel them. But once he's gone, they'll forget their pledges quick enough."

Gilpatrick, however, had noticed a subtler process at work. Henry, he realised, was a canny statesman. As soon as he arrived in Ireland, he had announced that he personally would take over Dublin and all its territories, Wexford, and Waterford. Strongbow was allowed to hold the rest of Leinster as his feudal tenant; but another great English magnate, the lord de Lacy, whom Henry had brought with him, was to remain in charge of Dublin as Henry's personal representative or viceroy. So on the face of it, any Irish chief looking to the eastern part of the island would see a traditional Irish arrangement: a king of Leinster, a king of Dublin, and some partly foreign ports. Behind them, however, would be a rival High King—far more powerful even than Brian Boru—a High King across the water. And if they wanted protection against the O'Connor High King in Connacht, as they might, or if Strongbow, or even de Lacy, started to behave as they themselves had always done and tried to encroach upon their territory, then wouldn't it be wise to come into the house of King Henry and have him as a protector against their neighbours, Irish or English? That was how things had always been done on the island. You paid tribute in cattle; you got protection. He's using his own lords to keep an eye on each other and to frighten the other chiefs into his camp as well, he thought.

"The man's very clever," Gilpatrick muttered. "He's playing our own game even better than we do."

Then there was the question of Dublin city. It was being given to the merchant community of Bristol, apparently, but no one was quite sure what that would mean. The Bristol men would have the same trading rights in Dublin as they had at home. The mighty city of Bristol had ancient privileges, huge fairs, and was one of the great gateways to the English market. Its merchants were rich. Did this mean that the port of Dublin would enjoy a similar status? The word was that the king also wanted the merchants and craftsmen who had left to return.

"It's very hard to know at this stage," the Palmer had remarked to him the day before, "but if the Bristol men bring in extra money and trade, this could actually turn out to be good for Dublin."

What had really surprised Gilpatrick, however, was the news that he had learned that morning. And now, as they gazed at the huge royal camp, he imparted it to his father.

"You cannot be serious."

"I had it from Archbishop O'Toole this morning."

"The man murders an archbishop and then summons the bishops to a council? To discuss Church reform?" His father looked at him in stupefaction. "What does O'Toole say?"

"He's going. He's taking me with him. It's not certain, you know, that King Henry was at fault."

The question of whether King Henry had ordered the killing of Thomas Becket the previous Christmas was still being eagerly discussed all over Europe. The general feeling was that even though he probably hadn't actually ordered the killing, he was still responsible for the fact that it happened, and therefore culpable. The Pope had not ruled on the matter yet.

"And where and when is this council to be?" asked his father.

"This winter. Down in Munster, I believe. At Cashel."

During the autumn months, Una watched Fionnuala with interest and with concern. Ruairi O'Byrne had gone to Chester, but in the weeks before the arrival of King Henry, Brendan made two visits to Dublin. On each occasion he went to see Fionnuala before departing, but his intentions remained unclear. Fionnuala continued to spend time helping her at the hospital, perhaps to keep her mind off the situation. Una couldn't tell. She could quite imagine that Brendan had other things on his mind than marriage at such a time.

It was soon after King Henry's arrival that Brendan's cousin reappeared in Dublin. They did not see him at first, but they heard that he had been spotted in the town. Whether he was just there for a few days before leaving again or whether he had some other plans, she did not know.

"I saw him down at the quay," the Palmer's wife told her one morning.

"What was he doing there?" she asked.

"Wasn't he just playing at dice with the English soldiers?" she answered. "As if he'd known them all his life?"

Una met him the next day. Though the gates were open and the market was busier than ever, with all the English troops in the vicinity, Una did not feel inclined to go into the city usually; and when she did, she made a point of avoiding the lane where her own house was because it brought back memories that were too painful. But for some reason, as she came down from the Fish Shambles in the darkening afternoon, she decided to turn across that way for a quick look. And she had just glanced in through the gateway and observed her father's little brazier, when she noticed, in the lane just in front of her, a figure sitting on the ground with his back to the fence. He was staring thoughtfully at the ground in front of him, but as she was about to go past, something about the hang of his head and the smell of ale told Una that he was drunk. She wasn't in the least afraid, but as she skirted him so as not to step on him, she glanced down at his face and saw with astonishment that it was Ruairi.

Had he seen her? She didn't think so. Should she speak to him? Perhaps not. She wasn't shocked. Most young men got drunk once in a while. She walked on a little way and then realised that she was going in the wrong direction, and so she'd have to retrace her steps anyway. With the November darkness drawing in, it was getting cold, and she thought she could feel a biting wind beginning. As she drew close to Ruairi she saw that now his eyes were closed. What if he stayed there in the darkness and nobody saw him or took any notice of him during the night? He'd freeze to death. She stopped and spoke his name.

He blinked and looked up. In the darkness, she supposed he could not clearly see her face. His eyes were blank.

"It is Una. From the hospital. Do you not remember me?"

"Agh." Was it the beginning of a smile? "Una."

Then he keeled over sideways and lay entirely motionless.

She stood there several minutes to see if he came round. He didn't. Then a man came along the lane, pulling a handcart from the

Fish Shambles. It was time to take action. "I am from the hospital," she told him. "This is one of our inmates. Could you help me get him home?"

"We'll have him home in no time at all. Open your eyes, me darlin'," he shouted into Ruairi's ear. But when this had no effect he bundled him, not without a few jarring bumps, into the cart and started off behind Una, who led the way.

✢

Father Gilpatrick was rather surprised, late in November, to find Brendan O'Byrne at his door. He wondered for a moment whether, for some reason, Brendan wanted to discuss his sister with him and tried to think what he could say in her favour that would not be at variance with the truth.

But it seemed that Brendan had more important business to discuss. Explaining that he had felt in need of advice, Brendan let him know further that he had come to him in particular because of his discretion and his knowledge of England after his residence there.

"You will know," he continued, "that the O'Byrnes, like the O'Tooles, with their territories to the south and west of Dublin, have always had to take careful note of events both in Dublin and in Leinster. Now it seems we are to have English kings in both. The O'Byrnes are wondering what to do."

Gilpatrick liked Brendan O'Byrne. With his quiet precision, he had the brain of a scholar. As far as Gilpatrick knew, the chief of the O'Byrnes had not yet come down to King Henry in his wicker palace. He told Brendan, therefore, exactly the game he thought Henry was playing in tempting the Irish kings into giving him homage by threatening them with Strongbow. "And note the man's cleverness," he added, "for as well as de Lacy in Dublin as a counterweight, Henry has Strongbow's other lands in England and Normandy which he can threaten any time Strongbow gives him any trouble."

O'Byrne listened carefully. Gilpatrick could see that he had immediately appreciated all the finer points of the assessment. But his next question was even more impressive.

"I am wondering, Father Gilpatrick, to what it is exactly that our Irish chiefs are swearing. When an Irish king comes into the house of a greater king, it means protection and tribute. But across the sea in England, it may mean something different. Can you tell me what that is?"

"Ah. That is a good question that you have asked." Gilpatrick looked at him with admiration. Here was a man who looked for deeper causes. Wasn't this exactly the conversation he had started with the O'Connor High King and with the archbishop, neither of whom, he realised, had really understood what he was trying to tell them. Carefully he outlined to Brendan how the feudal system operated in England and in France.

"A vassal of King Henry swears loyalty to him and promises to provide military service each year. If a knight cannot appear fully equipped and armed himself, he pays for a mercenary instead. So you might think that this is similar to the cattle tribute an Irish king would receive. A vassal also goes to his lord for justice, just as we do. But there the similarity ends. Ireland since time out of mind has been divided into tribal territories. When a chief swears an oath, he does so for himself, his ruling clan, his tribe. But over there, the tribes have long ago disappeared. The land is organised into villages of small farmers and the serfs, who are almost like slaves or chattels. They go with the land. And when a vassal there does homage, he isn't offering loyalty in return for protection, he's confirming his right to occupy that land, and the payments made will depend on its value."

"Such arrangements are not unknown in Ireland," Brendan remarked.

"That is true," Gilpatrick agreed. "At least since the time of Brian Boru, we have seen Irish kings grant estates to their followers on what would formerly have been thought of as tribal lands. But these are exceptions; whereas across the sea, everybody has to hold their land that way. Nor is that all. When a vassal dies, his heir must pay the king a large sum in order to inherit—it's called the relief fine. There are numerous other obligations as well.

"And in England in particular, an even harsher system operates. For when William the Norman took England from the Saxons, he claimed that all of it belonged to him personally by right of conquest. He had every square yard of England assessed for what it could yield and had it all written down in a great book. His vassals there only occupy their land on sufferance. If anyone gives trouble, he doesn't just come to punish them and take tribute. He takes the land away and gives it to anyone else he chooses. These are powers far beyond anything any High King in Ireland has ever dreamed of."

"These English are harsh people."

"The Normans are, to be precise. For some of them treat the Saxon English like dogs. An Irishman is a free man, within his tribe. The Saxon peasant is not. It has generally seemed to me," Gilpatrick confessed, "that these Normans care more for property than they do for people. Here in Ireland, we dispute, we fight, we sometimes kill, but unless we are truly angry, there is a human kindness and consideration among us." He sighed. "Perhaps it is just a question of conquest. After all, we ourselves are content to own English slaves."

"Do you think any of our Irish princes imagine they could be making these English commitments when they come into Henry's house?" asked Brendan.

"I don't suppose so."

"Has Henry told them?"

"Surely not."

"Then I think I see," Brendan said thoughtfully, "how it will go. At a later date, the English—not Henry, who is clearly very devious—but the English lords will genuinely believe the Irish have sworn to one thing, and the Irish will think they have sworn to another, and both sides will mistrust the other." He sighed. "This Plantagenet king comes from the devil."

"It has been said of all his family. What will you do?"

"I do not know. But I thank you, Father, for your counsel. By the way," he said smiling, "I have not had the chance to see your family and your sister. Will you give them my greetings. Fionnuala especially, of course."

"I will," Gilpatrick said as Brendan left. And a fine thing for this family it would be, he thought, if you married her. But you're far too good for her, Brendan O'Byrne. Far too good.

It didn't take Una long to see the good in young Ruairi O'Byrne. After the first night's sleep at the hospital he appeared well enough in the morning, and she had supposed he would leave. But by the middle of the day he was still there. Indeed, he was quite content to talk to the inmates, who seemed to like his company. Fionnuala was not there, and seeing Una in need of assistance, he more than once stepped over to help her with her tasks. The Palmer's wife thought him a very pleasant young man. The Palmer himself, though not unfriendly, muttered that a young man of that age ought to have better things to do, for which his wife rebuked him.

Ruairi showed no desire to move on that day, but said he would be glad to sleep in the men's dormitory. The next morning he told Una that he must buy a horse in Dublin so that he could return to the O'Byrnes. Fionnuala was due in, but he left early before she arrived and did not return until after she had left. When he came back, he was looking a little pale. The trader he had been dealing with had tried to sell him a horse that was unsound, but he had spotted the weakness just in time. He seemed irritated at not being able to leave, but spent another night at the hospital.

The next morning Ruairi seemed to be depressed. He sat in the yard looking gloomy and it wasn't clear if he meant to go anywhere. When she could spare a little time from her duties, Una came and sat with him. For a while he didn't say much, but when she gently asked him why he seemed sad, he confessed that he was trying to make a difficult decision. "I should go back." He indicated southwards towards the Liffey valley and the Wicklow Mountains, so she assumed he meant back to the O'Byrnes. "But I have other plans."

"Is it another voyage you'll be making?" she asked, thinking to herself that he had only recently returned from one.

"Perhaps." He hesitated, and then said quietly, "Or a greater journey."

"Where would you go?"

"It's a pilgrimage I'm thinking of," he confessed. "To Compostela maybe, or the Holy Land."

"By all the saints!" she exclaimed. "That's a long and perilous way to go walking the world." She looked at him carefully to see if he was serious. "Would you really go, like the Palmer, all the way to Jerusalem?"

"It would be better," he muttered, "than going back there." And once again he indicated the direction in which his family lived.

She couldn't help feeling sorry for him and wondered why he should be so unwilling to be with his family.

"You should stay here a few days," she counselled. "This is a quiet place in which to rest your mind as well as your body. Have you prayed about it?" she asked, and when he seemed uncertain, she begged him: "Pray and your prayers will surely be answered." Secretly she already intended to pray for him herself.

So he stayed another day. When she told the Palmer about poor Ruairi's troubles and his plans, he only gave her a wry glance, and remarked, "You can waste a lot of time with a young man like that."

She was surprised that so good a man, and a pilgrim himself, would say such a thing, and she could only conclude that he didn't understand. She bridled also, a little, at his tone which she thought was patronising. The Palmer, seeing her annoyance, quietly added, "He reminds me of a boy I used to know."

"And perhaps," she said testily, "you didn't know that boy so well either." She had never spoken to the Palmer in such a tone before and she wondered if she had gone too far. But to her surprise, he gave no sign of anger.

"Perhaps," he said, with a sudden sadness for which she could find no explanation.

The next morning, Fionnuala was back. She greeted Ruairi politely, but she did not seem particularly interested in talking to him. When Una remarked on this Fionnuala gave her a look and said quietly, "It's Brendan I'm interested in, Una." So they discussed the matter no further.

But in the afternoon, while Fionnuala was speaking to one of the inmates, Una came upon Ruairi sitting gloomily in the yard. It had occurred to her since their conversation that it must be different being part of a princely family like the O'Byrnes, especially when you had to measure yourself against the reputation of a man like Brendan. A pilgrimage to the Holy Land would certainly have the effect of making Ruairi a notable figure. But was it, she wondered, what he truly wanted to do?

"They torment me! They despise me!" he suddenly broke out. Then he relapsed into gloom. "Ruairi's a poor thing! That's what they say. 'Brendan's the man.' He is. It's true. And what have I ever been doing all my life?"

"You must have patience, Ruairi," she urged. "God has a plan for you as he does for us all. If you would pray and listen, Ruairi, you'll discover what it is. I'm sure you have it in you to do great things. Is that what you desire?" she asked, and he confessed that it was.

She felt honoured as well as touched that he should have shared such intimate thoughts with her. At that moment, with his long body stooped and his handsome young face sunk in sadness, he seemed to her so noble and so fine that her heart within her swelled at the thought of what he could become. If only he can find himself, she thought, he will do greater things than people imagine. Hardly thinking what she did, she took his hand in hers for a moment. Then she heard Fionnuala calling her, and had to go.

If only she had not spoken to Fionnuala. If only she had kept Ruairi's confidence to herself, as indeed she should have done. She could never forgive herself, afterwards, for her foolishness. But so it was. For while they were working together, didn't she like an idiot have to tell Fionnuala that young Ruairi was thinking of going to the Holy Land, and that she was worried about him.

Yet even then, she asked herself, what could have possessed the stupid girl to blurt out to him that very evening: "So it's to Jerusalem you are going, is it Ruairi? And will there be plenty of drinking along the way?" Then she had laughed, and Ruairi had said nothing to Fionnuala, but he'd given Una a look of reproach that almost broke her heart. The next morning, he was gone.

And as if all this wasn't bad enough, who could ever have supposed the reaction of Fionnuala when Una rightly rebuked her for treating poor Ruairi so shamefully. She laughed in Una's face.

"You're in love with him, Una," she cried. "Don't you know?"

"You're a liar! Are you mad?"

"No more than you, Una, for falling in love with such a poor useless fellow."

"He is not. I am not!" Una was so flustered and angry that she could hardly speak. And Fionnuala was still laughing, which made Una hate her even more. Then the foolish girl ran off and Una could only wonder, in her fury, how it was possible for people so completely to misunderstand.

She did not see Ruairi again until December. It was the day after Father Gilpatrick had gone down to Cashel for the big council there. Many of the royal camp had also left and Dublin was quieter than it had been recently. The Palmer's wife had gone into the market. Just before Fionnuala was due to return home, she and Una were surprised to see the Palmer's wife returning with a young man. It was Ruairi.

"I met him in the market," she explained. "I wasn't going to let this good young man leave us without coming to see our two girls here."

If Ruairi had not particularly wanted to come, he had the good grace not to show it. He went to greet one or two of the inmates, which gave them pleasure; and he explained that he had been with his family recently. Una wanted to ask him about his plans for going on pilgrimage, but she didn't like to. It was Fionnuala, after a few moments' awkward pause, who made the conversation.

"Have you seen your cousin Brendan?" she asked. "He's not been here this last few weeks."

"I have." Did he look a little uncomfortable? Una thought he did; and when she glanced at Fionnuala it seemed that she had thought so, too.

"He's keeping well, then, is he?" Fionnuala pursued.

"Oh. Ah, he is, indeed. Always well is Brendan."

"Is he getting married yet?" Fionnuala continued boldly. And now it was clear that Ruairi was truly embarrassed.

"There is talk of it, I believe. One of the O'Tooles. But I couldn't say if the thing is definite. No doubt," he added wryly, "I'll be one of the last to know."

No, Una thought, it's Fionnuala who'll be the last to know; and she looked at her friend with compassion. But Fionnuala was putting a brave face on it.

"Well he's a fine man to be sure," she said. "His wife may not have cause to laugh very often; but so long as she's of a serious disposition she'll be happy I'm sure." She smiled brightly. "Are you going back into Dublin, Ruairi?"

"I was."

"Then you can walk with me, as I'm on my way home."

Fionnuala never mentioned Brendan after that. As for Ruairi, Una didn't see him again. She heard once or twice that he'd been in Dublin and asked Fionnuala if she'd seen or heard of him; but Fionnuala said that she hadn't.

⁘

The rock of Cashel. It was seventy years since an O'Brien king had granted the ancient Munster stronghold, with its dominating views over the countryside, to the Church for the use of an archbishop. It was certainly a magnificent place to hold such a council, and appropriate, too, thought Gilpatrick: for a number of the Munster churchmen he knew were as keen reformers as he was. It was to be a great gathering. Most of the bishops, many abbots, and a papal legate were to be there. Yet even so, as he approached its grey stone eminence, he had felt a sense of unease.

It had been interesting to watch King Henry.

For the most part, though he had convened the council, he had asked the papal legate to take the chair, outwardly deferring to him in everything and sitting quietly to one side of the great hall where they met. Most days he dressed without ceremony in the simple green hunting tunic he favoured. His hair, which he cut short, had a faint reddish tinge, reminding one of his Viking Norman ancestors. But his face was sharp, devious, watchful; and Gilpatrick couldn't help thinking that he was like a fox watching so many ecclesiastical chickens.

As well as the legate, there were several distinguished English churchmen present, and it was one of these, on the first day of the proceedings, who gave Gilpatrick and Lawrence O'Toole some interesting information.

"You have to understand," he told them quietly, during a break in the proceedings, "that King Henry is very anxious to make a good impression. This business with Becket . . ." Here he dropped his voice. "There are bishops in England, you know, who think Becket just as much to blame as Henry. And I can tell you, for reasons of statecraft if nothing else, it is inconceivable that Henry would have ordered the murder. Howsoever that may be," he continued, "the king is anxious to display his piety—which I assure you is genuine," he added hastily, "and he is most determined that the Pope should see him making every effort to aid the Irish Church in the reforms we know you both wish to make. Of course," he went on with a faint smile, "not all Irish churchmen are as dedicated to purifying the Church as you."

The legate desired them first to compile a report on any present shortcomings of the Irish Church. As in previous councils of this kind, the bishops were generally keener to bring Irish practice closer to that of the rest of western Christendom, where power resided in bishoprics and parishes rather than in the monasteries. The hereditary abbots, not unreasonably, argued that the old monastic and tribal arrangements were still better suited to the country as it was. Gilpatrick was fascinated to hear Archbishop O'Toole, an abbot as well as a priest, and a prince like many of them, give the abbots a qualified support. "There is still room, I think, for both systems, depending on the territory." As for the demand that there should be no more hereditary churchmen, he again was kindly. "The real issue surely," he pointed out, "is whether a churchman is qualified for his post. If he is unsuited, then he must give it up; but the fact it has been passed down his family should not be a disqualification. In ancient Israel, all priests were hereditary. The spirit comes from God, not from the making of arbitrary rules." He pressed them further on other matters, however: on reform within their houses; the ordering of parish priests, who were often lax; the extension of parishes; and the collection of tithes. It was wonderful to see how amongst these men, many of whom came from families as noble as his own, this saintly and unworldly man could command such respect through his spiritual authority alone. In due course they produced a report which, it was generally felt, would suit the case.

It was the English priest who took the archbishop and Gilpatrick aside.

"The report is promising," he said, "but incomplete. It lacks," he searched for a word, "conviction." He looked seriously at the archbishop. "You, of course, Archbishop, are a reformer. But some of your colleagues . . . The report as it stands could be used by the legate, or even by King Henry were he so minded—and I do not say he is—to claim that the Irish Church is not serious about reform. In Rome they might even say, perhaps, that other bishops are needed, from outside Ireland."

"I think not," said O'Toole.

"What is in your mind?" Gilpatrick enquired.

"This question of hereditary churchmen," the English priest said to O'Toole, "will be a problem. And married priests," here he glanced at Gilpatrick, "were stopped in England a century ago. The Pope won't stand for it." Gilpatrick thought of his father and blushed. "But the most important thing is the care of our flock. Can we really turn our eyes away from the laxities that have been permitted in so many parts of the island? Why, even in Dublin, we are told, marriages are contracted openly that are clearly outside canon law. A man marrying his brother's wife, for instance? Intolerable." He shook his head while Gilpatrick went even redder. "Yet not a word of it in this report."

"What do you think we should do?" asked Gilpatrick.

"I suggest," said the Englishman smoothly, "that a small committee of us see what we can do to strengthen those parts which need to be strengthened while leaving in place those parts which are excellent already." He turned to Archbishop O'Toole. "I wonder whether Father Gilpatrick, as your representative, might work with us in preparing a revised draft for your consideration?"

And so the thing was done. And a few days later a new report emerged which the legate himself recommended to the council. It took some days to persuade the Irish churchmen to agree to this, which was hardly surprising. For the report was damning. Every vice, every malpractice, every Irish deviance from the accepted continental code was ruthlessly laid bare. When Gilpatrick and the English priest showed it to O'Toole, the archbishop was doubtful.

"This is harsh," he said.

"It is. I agree," said the English priest. "But think of the zeal it shows." He smiled. "No one could accuse the Irish Church of any lack of conviction now."

"Should there not be some mention of the reforming work already done in Ireland, and of what we intend to do in the future?" O'Toole queried.

"Absolutely. That is the key to the whole business. And that is what we must address in the second of our reports. The sooner we can get on to that," he added encouragingly, "the better."

So the damning report was approved, and the legate moved them on to consider what reforms had already been done, and how the good work could best be forwarded. This part of the council was by no means easy, but by the start of February the work was done and a second report produced. The legate thanked them, and King Henry, who had remained modestly watching, rose to congratulate them upon their great work. So ended the Council of Cashel.

Archbishop O'Toole was by no means happy with all the details; but Gilpatrick felt, on the whole, that they had done rather well.

The sailor arrived on a grey March morning. Wet clouds were sweeping over the Liffey. The Palmer and his wife had gone to the king's camp, leaving Una and Fionnuala in charge of the hospital until they returned. There were raindrops in the sailor's hair. He was asking for Una.

"I have a message from your mother," he informed her. "Your father has been very sick. But if he is able to walk again, he will return to Dublin, because he wants to see Ireland before he dies."

Una's eyes filled with tears. She had so longed to see her family, but not like this. Practical questions also crowded into her mind. How would they live? If her father died or was too sick to work, her brothers were still too young to be successful craftsmen. She and her mother would have to support them as best they could. And where would they lodge? If only, she thought, they could get their old house back upon whatever terms. If anything might help her father recover, she thought, it would be that. She wondered if perhaps the

Palmer would do something for them, and decided to ask his advice as soon as he returned.

She discussed the problem with Fionnuala meanwhile. Her friend had been a little subdued since the loss of Brendan in the winter. Sometimes she had been her lively self, but in the last two or three weeks she had seemed abstracted, as if something was secretly worrying her. To her credit though, she was sympathetic today, putting her arm round Una and telling her that everything would be all right.

When the Palmer and his wife returned soon after noon, however, it was clear that he was in no mood to talk; for as she went up to him he smiled sadly and saying, "Not now, my child," he went past her into his quarters, accompanied by his wife. Two hours passed and neither of them came out again. The girls could only wonder what was amiss.

Fionnuala was in the yard when she saw the figure coming through the gate. The sky had cleared somewhat, but the March breeze was making a cross, hissing sound in the thatch and caused the gate to bang as the figure entered. Una appeared from the women's dormitory at just that moment and Fionnuala was conscious of her eyes upon them both. She realised that Una probably didn't know who the figure was. Fionnuala stared at him.

Peter FitzDavid looked at her. His face was grave. If he felt embarrassment under her stony gaze, he was being careful not to show it.

"Your brother Gilpatrick asked me to fetch you," he said quietly. "I'm to take you home. I met him at the king's camp," he added, to explain his presence.

Fionnuala felt a little stab of fear. Was one of her parents hurt? Una was at her side now.

"Why?" she asked.

"You have not heard? The Palmer has not told you?" He looked surprised, then nodded slowly. "It's King Henry," he explained. "He's finished his business in Ireland. He's ready to leave. There are just the affairs of Dublin to put in order and that's what he's doing now. I'm afraid, Fionnuala," he paused a moment, "that this has not been good for your father; although he has been treated with special consideration," he added. "He keeps the southern part of his lands, down where your brother is. Those, of course, he will hold directly from the king as his vassal. But all the northern part of his land, near Dublin, has been granted away to a man called Baggot. Your father is very upset." He stopped. "I'm afraid," he added, "these sort of grants and regrants are quite normal in the circumstances."

The two girls stared at him, stunned. It was Una who was the first to recover.

"Is that what has happened to the Palmer?"

"He has fared worse, you might say. The king has taken all his lands in Fingal for his knights. He's left the Palmer with his land near Dublin, which is just enough to support himself and the hospital. The king is mindful, of course, that the Palmer hasn't any heirs. It's only the hospital he really cares about."

Una was silent. After such a blow as this, how could she trouble the Palmer with her own poor family's difficulties?

"There have been charters floating down upon the fortunate like leaves in autumn," said Peter. "For the houses inside the city, too."

"And what are you getting out of it?" Fionnuala asked coldly.

"I?" Peter shrugged. "I am getting nothing, Fionnuala. Strongbow has his own relations to think of, and once King Henry came, Strongbow's power to give was greatly reduced. King Henry scarcely knows me. I've received nothing in Ireland. I'm probably leaving when King Henry does. Strongbow persuaded him to take me on, so perhaps I'll make my fortune in some other land."

Fionnuala took this information in. Then she gave a sad smile.

"We shan't be seeing you again then, Welshman," she said more gently.

"No."

"Well, I hope you enjoyed your time here."

"I did. Very much."

They looked at each other silently for a moment. Then Fionnuala sighed. "You've no need to escort me to my home, Welshman. I've a few things to do here and then I'll be on my way."

During this little exchange, which she thought rather pointless, Una's mind had focussed on one thing Peter had just said.

"I wonder what has happened to my father's house," she murmured to Fionnuala.

"Welshman," Fionnuala said. "This is Una MacGowan whose family lived in your lodgings. She's wondering what's to become of them."

"I do know, as it happens," Peter answered. "There are a number of Bristol merchants coming over and that house, along with others, has been granted to one of them. A man I met, actually. His name's Doyle."

Una had expected Fionnuala to leave almost at once after Peter FitzDavid had gone. Rather to her surprise, half an hour passed and she realised that Fionnuala was still there. When she went to look for her, she found her in the room at the back of the men's dormitory where once she had had her private meeting with the priest. She was kneeling on the floor, silently weeping. Thinking to comfort her, Una sat down beside her.

"It could be worse, Fionnuala," she reminded her. "Your family is still richer than most. I'm sure your brother will be a bishop one day. And there'll be no shortage of fine young men wanting to marry you."

But none of this seemed to help. Fionnuala's shoulders still shook. She murmured, "Brendan's gone. My Welshman's gone. Everyone." This seemed a little beside the point to Una; but wishing to comfort her she suggested: "Perhaps you should see that priest again." This only caused poor Fionnuala to weep the more. At last, however, she raised her head and turned her face, streaked with tears, towards her friend.

"You don't understand, Una, you poor silly creature. You don't understand at all. I'm pregnant."

"You are? In the name of God, Fionnuala, by whose doing is that?"

"By Ruairi O'Byrne. God help me. By Ruairi."

There were all kinds of people on the ship: potters, carpenters, saddlers, stonemasons, artisans, and small traders. He'd brought many of them from Bristol himself. The ship was his, too, of course. The April day was breezy but bright as the ship came in from the greenish sea.

Doyle's dark eyes watched the wood quay as Dublin grew nearer.

"Are you ready?" Doyle did not turn round to ask the question.

"As ready as I shall ever be," said the younger man standing behind him. If he had been youthful when he had first come into Doyle's house half a dozen years ago, his close-cut, pointed beard was wiry now; and his face was weather-beaten from the sea voyages on which he had been sent.

"You'll take the consequences for your crime?"

"I'll have to. You gave me no choice." He smiled grimly. "Once I do, you won't have a hold over me anymore."

"You'll be working for me still, don't forget."

"True. But I'll make my fortune in Dublin and then I'll be rid of you."

Doyle did not reply. Who knew, thought the younger man, what resided in the deep, dark passages of that devious brain? And indeed, the Bristol merchant had much to think about. Though he had traded with Dublin, he had not visited the place himself in years. In taking up the new opportunities opened by King Henry, who had just departed, he was going to have to move carefully. It was a compliment to the young man standing behind him that Doyle should have chosen him to run the Dublin operation. When he had first come to his house, he had been a youthful wreck, good for nothing at all. But over six years Doyle had turned him into a competent merchant and a man. If things went well in Dublin, then in due course one of Doyle's grandsons might come and take over; but that would be years away. Before he left this young man in charge, however, Doyle knew he would need to get a good feel of the place and its present trade. Many of the merchants he had dealt with until recently had gone, at least for the time being; but there were a couple he trusted. And then, of course, there was that kindly man with whom, years ago, he had struck up an acquaintance on a previous visit. Ailred the Palmer. He would be going to see him first.

The moment she saw him, Una's heart sank.

When she had discovered earlier that day who Ailred's visitor was to be, she had still hesitated to speak to the Palmer. She was so anxious not to ask him for help which she knew he could no longer give that, even now, she hadn't told him about her father's return. But since he was going to find out anyway in due course, and think it very strange then if she'd never mentioned it, she had plucked up her courage and gone to him that afternoon.

"So this Bristol merchant that wants to see me has your father's house? And you say your father may shortly return." Ailred looked thoughtful. "I shall certainly explain to him the facts of your situation. But what he will do is another matter." He sighed. "I've never had to beg before, Una, but I must learn how to do it." How her heart went out to him when he said that.

But when Una saw the merchant come through the hospital gate and disappear into the small hall at the back with the Palmer and his wife, any hope she might have harboured in her heart had sunk. Tall, hard, swarthy, with a fearful dark-eyed stare: one look at Doyle and she knew she was lost. A man like that does no kindnesses, she thought. A man like that takes what he wants and strikes down anyone in his path. She could see her father being left to die at his own door, and her mother forced to beg in the street, at least until the Palmer gave her shelter.

So what would she do when Doyle turned the Palmer down?

This was the question she brooded on while the Bristol merchant ate alone with Ailred and his wife that evening. The case seemed hopeless, but she couldn't let it go at that. If necessary, she decided she would seek the man out and plead with him herself. She had no choice.

She tried to imagine it. Merely begging for charity was obviously a waste of time; but what could she possibly offer him? To work free for him as a servant? That would hardly be enough to get the house back. Sell herself as a slave? Probably no better. What else?

There was only one thing she could think of. Her body. What if she were his servant and gave him that as well? She supposed a man like Doyle would want some such condition. If he even found her attractive: she had no idea as to that. She thought of his tall, swarthy form, and his hard face, and shuddered. To give her body, like a harlot, to a man like that: could she bring herself to do it? For a girl like Fionnuala, she imagined, it mightn't be so difficult. She almost wished she were like that herself. But she wasn't, and she knew she never could be. Then the thought of her poor little father came to her, and biting her lip she told herself, Yes, if I must, for him I will do it.

Ailred the Palmer remembered Doyle well enough, although their business dealings, which had taken place six or seven years ago, had not been extensive. He was aware of the man's importance in Bristol and somewhat flattered that Doyle should have come to seek his counsel at such a time.

"Since I started this hospital," he informed the merchant, "I have hardly taken any part in the trade of the port, and so I'm not sure I shall be able to help you much."

As Doyle looked at the fine old Norseman and his kindly wife, he felt sorry that the man should have fallen on such evil times and wondered whether, as an incomer, the Palmer might somewhat resent him. However, he had his own mission to accomplish and he was not a man to be deflected from his purpose. Politely but firmly, therefore, he plied Ailred with questions about the city, what craftsmen it contained, what was bought and sold, which merchants were to be trusted. And as he had expected, the Palmer in fact knew a great deal. By the time they had finished their meat, and fruit pies and cheeses were brought in, the Bristol merchant could relax, drink his wine, turn to more general subjects, and answer some of the questions which Ailred had for him.

In particular the Palmer wanted to know about the city of Bristol and its organisation—its aldermen, its trading privileges, and what taxes it paid the king. "For this, I suppose," he said, "is what we must now expect in Dublin." On these and other points, Doyle was able to satisfy him.

While they were talking, Ailred had also been observing the Bristol merchant carefully. He was not sure exactly what he was looking for: something perhaps to give him an insight into his visitor's mind; some clue as to his character that he might be able to use, for instance, to persuade him to do a kindness to Una and her family. Doyle's name suggested an Irish origin, and Ailred thought he had heard the man had family in Ireland. Perhaps that might provide a way in.

"Will you be moving to Dublin yourself, to live?" he enquired.

"Not at present," Doyle replied. "I've a young partner who'll be looking after things for me here, for the time being. He's very competent."

"You've no family in Dublin, then?" the Palmer ventured.

"Waterford's where we came from. I have a few relations there," Doyle answered. Then, for the first time, he smiled. "The last of my family that was in Dublin left his body here. At the battle of Clontarf. A Norseman like yourself, but Danish. One of the old sea rovers."

"There were many brave men died in that battle," Ailred agreed. "I might have heard of him."

"You might. To tell you the truth," Doyle continued, "the family in Waterford never knew a great deal about him except that he was a tremendous fighter. He was one of those that attacked the camp of Brian Boru. He may have struck a blow at the king himself for all I know."

It was evident that the swarthy Bristol merchant, dour though he was, felt pride in this ancestor.

"And what happened to him?" the Palmer asked.

"We never discovered. They say he went off in pursuit of the enemy and was never seen again. Killed by the guards of Brian Boru, I dare say."

"And what was his name?"

"Sigurd," the merchant said proudly. "The same as mine. Sigurd."

"Ah," said Ailred.

"You have heard of him?" Doyle was almost eager.

"I might have," said Ailred. "I would have to think, but I might have."

There seemed little doubt of it. This must be the Sigurd who had come out to his ancestor Harold's farmstead and been killed by the priest. Who would know of him now, he wondered? Probably only himself, and the family of Fionnuala, no doubt. Evidently Doyle had no idea of his ancestor's evil reputation. And here the Palmer was, his honest fortune lost, about to beg a favour from this descendant of a vicious murderer, who thought his ancestor a hero. For a moment, just for a moment, he was tempted to humiliate this man who had gained power over him; but then he thought of poor little Una, and his own good nature prevailed.

"I think I heard," he said without lying, "that he was a devil of a man."

"That would be him," said Doyle, with satisfaction.

In the slight lull that followed, it seemed that the Bristol merchant might be about to introduce another topic of conversation, but seeing that the discussion about his ancestor had brought him so much pleasure, Ailred now seized the opportunity to raise the delicate subject of Una.

"I have," he proceeded, "a small kindness to ask of you." He saw Doyle's eyes grow wary, but he pressed on and briefly explained the sad case of Una and her father. "You see my situation here," Ailred continued. "I could give the family temporary shelter but . . . Could you see your way to helping them?"

Doyle looked at him steadily. It was hard to tell what he was thinking, but somewhere in his dark eyes Ailred thought he saw a faint gleam of amusement. He didn't know the reason, unless perhaps the Bristol man was reflecting on the irony of his own fall from prosperity and his having to beg like this. But those who ask favours cannot afford resentments, so he waited patiently for Doyle's response.

"I was going to put my young partner in there," Doyle remarked. "He mightn't like to lose his lodgings. I am not in the habit," he added quietly, "of doing favours for people I don't know and to whom I owe nothing."

If this was a warning to the Palmer not to presume too far, Ailred took it and said nothing in reply. But his wife, ever kindly, went on.

"We have always felt," she said sweetly, "that we gained more happiness from the work we do in this hospital than we ever did from our former good fortune. I am sure," she smiled at him gently, "that you have given and received kindnesses before in your life."

Ailred had glanced at Doyle rather nervously while she made this little speech, afraid that their visitor might not like it. But whether it was her innocent manner, or something else in her words, the Bristol man did not seem to mind.

"It is true," he acknowledged, "that I have received kindnesses once or twice in my life." He gave her a wry look. "Whether I've returned them is another matter." Then he fell silent and it seemed he had no further wish to discuss the issue. But Ailred's wife was not to be so easily put off.

"Tell me," she pressed him, "what is the greatest kindness you ever received?"

Doyle gazed at her thoughtfully for a few moments, as if he were considering something else; then, having apparently reached a conclusion of some kind, he spoke again.

"I could tell you of one. It happened many years ago." He nodded slowly, as if to himself. "I've two sons. My eldest has always been steady, but my second, when he was young, fell into bad company. I never worried about it, because I thought, being my son, he'd have too much sense to do anything stupid." He sighed. "That shows you how much I know. So one day, he disappeared. Just like that. Days went by and I'd no idea where he was. Then I found out that he'd been stealing money from me, for gambling, mostly, and other things. A large sum, too. He couldn't repay it, of course. He was so afraid of me—with reason—and so ashamed, he'd run away. Left Bristol. Not even his brother knew where he'd gone. Months went by. Years." He stopped.

"What did you do?" Ailred's wife asked.

"Actually," Doyle confessed, "I lied. I wanted to protect his name, but my own pride, too, I dare say. So I gave out that he'd gone to France on family business. But as we never heard from him, I thought he might be dead.

"Finally, we did hear. He'd been taken in by a London merchant. Funnily enough, I only knew the man slightly. But he'd taken my son into his house, acted as a father to him—quite a stern one—and helped him set up in business so he could start to pay me back. Then this merchant had made him come to me and ask my forgiveness. That was a kindness, if you like." He paused. "You can't really repay a thing like that. You just have to accept it."

"And did you forgive your son?" asked Ailred's wife.

"I did," the dark Bristol merchant replied. "To tell the truth, I was just grateful he was alive."

"He returned to live with you?"

"I made two conditions. He was to let me forgive him the rest of what he owed me. It was my own guilt which made me do that, I should think. I blamed myself, you see, for being such a stern father. I drove him away."

"And the other condition?"

"He was to marry a wife I chose for him. Nothing unusual in that. I found him a good, steady girl. They're happy." He rose abruptly. "It's getting late. I thank you for your hospitality." He turned to Ailred's wife. "One good turn deserves another, I dare say. I'll think about this girl and her family and let you know in the morning."

When he had departed, the Palmer and his wife sat alone in their hall.

"I'm sure he will help her," she said.

"Say nothing to Una," he replied. "Let's wait and see what he does."

For some time after that, they sat together, saying nothing. It was she who finally broke the silence.

"How strange that his son did the same as Harold. He even gave out a story, the same way we did. Except we said Harold had gone on pilgrimage."

"He got his son back," said Ailred grimly. "I suppose I drove Harold away, too."

"You were never stern."

"No. I was too kind." He gestured towards the dormitories. "What can you do when you steal from your father and he is Ailred the Palmer?"

She was about to say, Perhaps Harold is alive, too, but she realised that the subject was too painful for him.

"Let us hope," she said instead, "that Doyle will do something for Una."

Una was in the road outside the hospital the next morning when the man arrived. A tall, handsome, red-haired man with a weather-beaten face. He asked for the Palmer, but she did not realise that he had come from Doyle the Bristol merchant.

She started to show him the way, but he seemed to know it. He went through the gateway just as it happened that Ailred had come into the yard from the hospital doorway. She was following behind. She saw Ailred look at him, puzzled, but she did not think he knew him. And certainly the Palmer stared with the utmost astonishment when the man went suddenly down on his knees and called him, "Father."

⁂

It was the following midwinter, nine months after King Henry of England had departed the island, that Archbishop O'Toole of Dublin summoned Father Gilpatrick to his private quarters and handed him three documents. When he had finished reading them, the young priest continued to stare at the parchments as though he had seen a ghost.

"You are sure this is genuine?" he asked.

"There is not a doubt of it," replied the archbishop.

"I wonder," Gilpatrick said quietly, "what my father will say."

It had been a trying year. The marriage of Fionnuala to Ruairi O'Byrne had been necessary, of course. Her father had been unshakeable, and rightly so. The O'Byrnes themselves had been equally insistent. "Ruairi will not dishonour the Ui Fergusa," they had declared. Indeed, Gilpatrick suspected that the presence of Brendan O'Byrne at the wedding was partly to make sure that Ruairi turned up and that the business was successfully concluded. Everyone had put the best face on it. Gilpatrick's father had officiated. But there had been no mistaking the bride's condition and though, as a mark of friendship, Archbishop O'Toole had attended, the whole family felt they had been lowered in everyone's eyes. After the king taking their lands, it had been a bitter blow.

Indeed, these had been grim times for most of the old families in Dublin, with one notable exception.

Ailred the Palmer had got back his son. That had been a wonderful thing to see. Though he had not succeeded in making a pilgrimage to Jerusalem, as his father had done, he had returned as the partner of Doyle the Bristol merchant and thereby ensured himself a position of some wealth in the port of Dublin. He was nowadays living in a house on the Fish Shambles. But most remarkable of all had been his marriage, not long after his return, to Una MacGowan. It seemed that he had taken her in deference to the wishes of his father, and more particularly his mother. And as a happy result of this union, when Una's father had returned, a sick man, with his family that summer, his new son-in-law had been able to install him in his own house once again, since it was now in the ownership of Doyle the merchant. Though he did not know them intimately, Gilpatrick was happy for the family, and especially for Una, whom he had once rescued from a worse fate. But if this turn of events had reminded him that God was always watching over the lives of men, the parchment in his hands now seemed to show—if it were not sacrilege even to suppose it—that the eyes of God must be resting elsewhere.

The documents in question were letters from the Pope in Rome. One was addressed to the archbishop and his fellow bishops; the second was addressed to the kings and princes of Ireland. The third was a copy of a letter to King Henry of England.

The shortest was to the Irish princes. It commended them for submitting to "Our most dear son in Christ, Henry." This was how the Pope referred to the man who caused the murder of Becket! He told them that Henry had come to reform the Church in Ireland. And he warned them to be humbly and meekly obedient to the English king, or risk the papal wrath. To the bishops, he commended Henry as a Christian ruler who would rid the Church in Ireland of its terrible vice and corruption, and urged them to enforce obedience "with ecclesiastical censure."

"Does he mean we should excommunicate any of our chiefs who don't obey him, do you think?" O'Toole asked in wonder. "The Holy Father also seems to think," he added crossly, "that every prince in Ireland has come into King Henry's house, which they haven't."

But it was actually worse than that. For as he had read the letters, Gilpatrick had noticed something else. It was the terminology. For the Pope had used exactly the terms of feudal obedience and obligation that he would have used to French or English barons. And remembering his conversation with the intelligent Brendan O'Byrne, he realised how difficult it would be to explain all these differences to the archbishop.

"The Holy Father does not understand Irish conditions," he said sadly.

"He most certainly does not," O'Toole burst out. "Look at this," he pointed to a phrase in the first letter, "and this!" He jabbed his finger at the second. "As for this . . ." He picked up the third letter, then threw it down on the table in disgust.

There was no question, the letters were not only inappropriate, they were downright insulting. The Irish, according to the Pope, were an "ignorant and undisciplined" race, wallowing in "monstrous and filthy vice." They were "barbarous, uncultured, ignorant of the divine law." You might have thought that the seven hundred years since the coming of Saint Patrick, the great monastic schools, the Irish missionaries, the Book of Kells, and all the other glories of Irish Christian art had never existed. And the Holy Father was quite content, it seemed, to address the Irish bishops and princes and say it to their faces.

"What can he mean? What can he be thinking of?" the saintly archbishop demanded.

But Gilpatrick already knew. He saw it very clearly. The answer lay in the third letter, the letter to King Henry.

Congratulations. There was no other word for it. The pontiff sent the English king congratulations for this wonderful extension of his power over the stubborn Irish, who had rejected the practice of the Christian faith. Furthermore, to obtain complete forgiveness for his sins—these, no doubt, would chiefly be his complicity in killing the Archbishop of Canterbury—the king has only to keep up the good work. So Henry had got everything he wanted: not only a pardon, it seemed, for killing Becket but a blessing for his crusade against the Irish. "It might," O'Toole complained, "have been written by the English Pope."

And how had Henry done it? The text of the letter made it plain. The Pope had heard, he explained, of the disgraceful state of morals on the western island from an unimpeachable source: namely, the very churchman whom King Henry had sent him! And were not his words confirmed by the very report which they, the Irish churchmen, had sent him? He enumerated some of the abuses: improper marriages, failure to pay tithes, all the very things which the Council of Cashel had taken good care to address. Yet the Pope made no mention of the Cashel council. He was evidently quite unaware that it had taken place and of the reforms enacted there; just as he seemed also to be ignorant of all the fine work already done by Lawrence O'Toole and others like him.

And now at last Gilpatrick saw the cunning of the Plantagenet king. He had tricked the Irish churchmen into issuing that damning report, then run to Rome with it as proof of the state of things in Ireland. He'd suppressed all word of the council. The officials in Rome, who only knew a little of Ireland anyway, had found Pope Adrian's earlier letter. And the trick was completed. The English king's foray into Ireland to sort out Strongbow was now a papal crusade. "And we gave him the pretext. We condemned ourselves by our own hand," Gilpatrick murmured.

It was devious. It was a betrayal. It was a brilliant lesson in politics from a master at the game.

I V

⊨ 1192 ⊨

On Saint Patrick's Day in the year of Our Lord 1192, an important ceremony took place at Dublin. Led by the city's archbishop, a procession of ecclesiastical dignitaries emerged from Christ Church Cathedral and made its way out through the city's southern gate. Among them was Father Gilpatrick. Two hundred yards away down the road was the Well of Saint Patrick beside which, for a long time, there had been a tiny church. But today, on its site, there now stood a large though still uncompleted structure. Indeed, its size and its handsome proportions suggested that it might almost be intended to rival the great cathedral of Christ Church itself. Nor was it to be only a church; for the foundations of the accompanying school could already be seen. One thing might have struck the onlookers as incongruous about the procession to this fine new foundation dedicated to Ireland's patron saint. The Archbishop of Dublin who led it was named John Cumin: and he was resolutely English.

Indeed, everything about the new Saint Patrick's was to be English. It was being built in the new Gothic style, now in fashion in England and France. Unlike the important Irish foundations, which were monastic, the new college of Saint Patrick was to be a collegiate church for priests, not monks—in the latest English fashion. Most of the priests were English, not Irish. And it could hardly have escaped anyone's notice that this new English headquarters of the English bishop was situated outside the city wall and several hundred yards distant from the old Christ Church, where the monks still remembered the saintly Archbishop O'Toole with reverence and affection.

The wet March breeze caught Father Gilpatrick in the face. He should, he supposed, have felt grateful. It was, after all, a compliment that the English archbishop should have chosen him, an Irishman, to be one of the new canons. "You are held in high regard by everyone," Cumin had told him frankly. "I know you will use your influence wisely." Given the circumstances as they were nowadays, Gilpatrick had no doubt that it was his duty to accept. But as he glanced across at the site of his family's old monastery on the rise to his left, and as he thought of the man he had asked, most reluctantly, to meet him as soon as the consecration was over, he could only think: thank God at least that my poor father is no longer alive to see this.

His father's last years had not been happy. After the visit of King Henry, the old man had seen his world gradually being butchered, like a body losing limbs, one at a time. The final blow for him had been when a new Church council had declared that all the hereditary priests like himself should be thrown out of their positions and dispossessed. Archbishop O'Toole had utterly refused to let such a thing happen to him, but the heart had gone out of the old man after that. The end had come only half a year after the death of Lawrence O'Toole himself. His father had gone for a walk down to the old Thingmount. And there, by the tomb of his ancestor Fergus, he had suffered a single, massive seizure and fallen dead on the spot. It was a fitting end, Gilpatrick thought, for the last of the Ui Fergusa.

For his father had turned out to be the last chief. He himself, as a celibate priest, had no heirs. And his brother Lorcan, whether by chance or as divine punishment for marrying his brother's widow, had been granted daughters but no son. In the male line, therefore, the family of the chiefs who had guarded Ath Cliath since before Saint Patrick came was about to die out.

There was one final indignity, however, which had been reserved for this day. It was a mercy, indeed, that his father was not there to see what he must do after the consecration.

⁘

The service was well done, you couldn't deny it. And afterwards they were all very friendly to him, complimentary indeed. But it gave him no pleasure. He had no illusions. The Church was still predominantly Irish, so they needed a man like him as a go-between. For the time being. Until the English were in the majority. The present archbishop was not a bad man, in his way. He'd encountered other churchmen like him during his time in England. An administrator, a servant of the king: intelligent, but cold. How he longed, sometimes, for the less worldly spirit of O'Toole. When the business was over, he went outside and looked around. After a moment or two, he saw the lordly figure approaching, and inwardly he cringed. It was all his brother's fault.

For a brief time, after King Henry had completed his visit to the island, it had seemed that the two parties occupying the land might live in an uneasy peace. The Plantagenet monarch and the O'Connor High King had even made a new treaty dividing the island between them, rather as it had been divided into the two halves of Leth Cuinn and Leth Moga, north and south, in times before. All over the English-occupied territory, the Norman motte and bailey castles started to appear. Big wooden palisades enclosed a high earthwork mound crowned with a timber keep. These stout little working forts certainly dominated the estates, the new manors that Strongbow and his followers had set up. But had it stopped at that? Of course not. The Irish were unhappy; the settlers were greedy for still more land. Before long the truce had broken down and the lords of the borderland manors were raiding into the High King's domain, stealing territory. Ironically, during this process, Strongbow, who had been the cause of it all, had died. But that had made no difference. The land grabbing had developed a momentum of its own. One aristocratic adventurer named de Courcy had even raced into Ulster and seized a little kingdom for himself up there.

These events in the borderlands had not much affected Gilpatrick's family in the relative quiet of Dublin; but a new development was to have profound consequences for his brother. For in the year 1185, Ireland had received a second royal visit; not from Henry, this time, but from his youngest son.

Prince John had none of the glamour of his elder brother, Richard the Lionheart. All his life he seemed to make enemies. He was clever but tactless; he did everything by fits and starts. Arriving in Ireland and meeting Irish chiefs whose dress and flowing beards he thought funny, the young man mocked them to their faces and cheerfully insulted them. But behind this arrogance and vulgarity lay another, darker calculation. Prince John cared nothing for the feelings of the Irish: he had come to impose order, and with him he brought ruthless henchmen with names like de Burgh, and the family of administrators known as the Butlers, who were very good at imposing order indeed.

For occupied Ireland was to be administered on English lines: ancient tribal territories were to be administered as baronies; townlands, like the English hundreds, were to be set up. The seats of modest chieftains would become the fortified manors of English armed knights. English courts, English taxes, English customs, even English counties were planned. There were also the further contingents of knights, many of them friends of the prince, who must be given Irish estates. And if that meant kicking a few more of the Irish off their land, Prince John couldn't have cared less.

Amongst those who had suffered had been Ailred the Palmer. One day he had suddenly been informed that his holdings to the west of the city, which supported the hospital, had been given to two Englishmen of Prince John's acquaintance; and although both his son, Harold, and the grandson of Doyle were by now important men in Dublin, not even their influence had been able to prevent it. But within months, the kindly Palmer and his wife, instead of giving way to anger, had persuaded both the men who had obtained his land to grant most of it back to the hospital, which received a formal blessing from the Pope himself soon afterwards. "So you see," his wife sweetly declared, "in the end everything turned out for the best."

If only his brother could have been as wise, thought Gilpatrick. But was it, he asked himself, partly his fault? Had he been too busy with Church affairs to realise the danger his brother was in?

When King Henry had taken the ancient lands of the Ui Fergusa, he had split them into two great manors, north and south. The northern manor was still held by Baggot; the southern had remained in his brother's hands. To his brother's way of thinking, therefore, he was still the chief. And the fact that he had never fully understood his new status, Gilpatrick considered, was partly because of wishful thinking, but also because, as an Irishman, he could not comprehend one important feature of European feudal life: the absentee landlord.

It was a commonplace in England or France. The king gave his great lords scattered territories to hold; they in turn had tenants. The lord of the manor might be resident there; or he might be away; or he might hold several manors and be represented by a steward to whom the various people on the estate, from the tenants of the larger farms to the humblest serf, would answer.

In the case of the Ui Fergusa lands, the lord of the manor was the king himself, represented by the Justiciar. A steward handled the daily business. For convenience, so far, Gilpatrick's brother had been left as the sole tenant farmer of the place; during the first few years, the rents demanded by the steward had been modest and Gilpatrick's brother had rationalised these as the customary tribute due from an Irish chief to his king. With the arrival of Prince John's new administrators, however, the situation had changed, and the trouble had begun. When the steward had demanded payments for the knight service due from the estate, Gilpatrick's brother had failed to pay. Summoned to the lord of the manor's court, he had failed to turn up. When the steward, a patient man, had come to see him, he had treated the royal servant with contempt.

"We have been chiefs here since before your king's family was ever heard of," he told the steward with perfect truth. "A chief does not answer to a servant. When the king is in Ireland again," he had conceded, "I will come into his house." The steward had said no more, but had gone away.

Yet was it, perhaps, his own fault, Gilpatrick now asked himself, that his brother had behaved so stupidly? If he hadn't been busy with Church affairs, could he not have made sure that his own family's position was secure and in proper order? It had been three weeks ago that his brother had arrived at his house. And the moment he had asked his question, Gilpatrick's heart had sunk.

"Explain to me, Gilpatrick," he had demanded, "what is a tenant-at-will?"

There were various kinds of men on any manorial estate. The lowest were the serfs, tied to the land, and little better than slaves. Above these came various classes, some of them specialist workers with clearly defined rights and duties. At the top of the hierarchy were the free tenants, holding a farm or two on formally contracted rents. These might be free farmers of substance, or even another feudal lord or a religious foundation with a cross-holding or part share in a manor. But below the free tenant lay a precarious class. The tenant-at-will was normally a freeman, able to come and go as he pleased, but he held his land in the manor on no fixed contract. The lord had the right to terminate his tenancy at any time.

When King Henry had taken the Ui Fergusa land, no one had ever bothered to obtain a proper charter. Because they had been left in place, Gilpatrick's family had assumed they had security of tenure. After all, they'd been there a thousand years. Didn't that make their position plain enough? Of course it didn't, Gilpatrick thought, and he of all people should have known it.

The steward had struck a double blow. He had reminded the Justiciar that the next time the king needed to reward one of his men, the southern Ui Fergusa manor was still available. And now that the manor had just been granted, the steward had informed the new lord that he had a troublesome tenant. "However," he had explained, "as there has never been any formal agreement, we can consider him as a tenant-at-will." Last week the steward had gone down to see Gilpatrick's brother and calmly informed him, "The new lord will be coming here shortly. He wants you out before he arrives. So pack up and leave."

"And where am I to go?" Gilpatrick's brother had furiously demanded. "Up into the Wicklow Mountains?"

"As far as I'm concerned," the steward coolly answered, "you are free to go to hell."

So now it was up to Father Gilpatrick to try to save the situation.

The realisation that the ancestral lands would probably be lost to the family, even in the female line, for the rest of time was a bitter one. Mercifully, most of his brother's daughters were safely married by now; but there were two still to be provided for. At least, Gilpatrick thought, I may be able to buy him a few more years. For, as his brother had quite rightly pointed out, if anyone had a hope of persuading the new lord of the manor to relent, it must be himself. After all, he knew him.

So he did his best to smile as the once familiar figure reached him and gazed down at him from his horse.

"It has been a long time," Gilpatrick said, "since last we met, Peter FitzDavid."

It had been a long time. Peter FitzDavid would not have denied it. A quarter century since he had first set out; twenty years and more that he had been hoping for his reward. Some of those years had been spent outside Ireland; but he had found himself back there often enough. He had fought in the west, in Limerick; he had organised garrisons, commanded under the Justiciar. He had become well known and well respected amongst the armed men on the island. Peter the Welshman, the Irish called him; and the English-speaking troops and lesser settlers similarly referred to him as Peter Welsh or, as it often sounded to the ear, Walsh.

Peter FitzDavid, better known as Walsh, had been kept hard at work down the years because he was trusted. He had learned to be patient and watchful. But at the right time, he had let it be known that a reward should be forthcoming; and now, when it had finally come, it was better than he had dared to hope. A fine estate, not on the borderlands where the angry Irish were always likely to raid in revenge for what had been stolen from them, but here in the rich, safe, coastal farmland of Leinster, close by the garrison of Dublin itself.

It was time to settle down. Time, late though it was, to marry

and produce an heir. Years of service followed by a late marriage—
it was not an uncommon career for a knight. He had already found
a bride—a younger daughter of Baggot, the knight whose estate
marched with his. He had every intention of enjoying the good fortune he had earned.

He had thought of Gilpatrick, of course, when he learned he was
to be given the Ui Fergusa estate; but he wasn't embarrassed to meet
him. He had reached the point of middle age where he had no more
time or emotion to waste. The land was his now. That was that. The
fortunes of war. The business about Gilpatrick's younger brother,
however, was another matter. He knew perfectly well that this must
be the reason the priest had asked to see him and he knew that, out
of courtesy, he must listen to what Gilpatrick had to say. But perhaps there was an element of calculation in the fact that, on reaching his former friend, he did not dismount. Nor when Gilpatrick
suggested they should walk a little did he do so, but allowed the
priest to walk beside him.

Their route took them a short way eastwards, to the open common from which the stream ran down towards the old Viking stone
at the estuary's edge. Recently a second hospital, a small one for lepers, had been set up there and dedicated to Saint Stephen. It was
past this little foundation beside the marshland that the two figures
went, one still mounted, the other on foot; and Peter listened to the
woes of poor Gilpatrick's brother. And as he listened, he felt . . .

Nothing. He listened to the family story, the extenuating circumstances, the fact—the priest felt sure, he said, that Peter would
understand—that his brother had not fully appreciated the new situation. Gilpatrick recalled to him his old father, and their friendship
in the past. And still, almost to his own surprise, Peter still felt nothing. Or rather, after a while, he did begin to feel something. But that
was contempt.

He despised Gilpatrick's brother. He despised him because he
had not fought, and yet had lost. He despised him for being as arrogant as he was weak. He despised him for being wilfully ill in-

formed, for being unbusinesslike, and for being stupid. Hadn't he himself had to fight, and to endure hardship, and to learn wisdom and patience? Success despises failure. Peter stayed on his horse. And at last, as they gazed down towards the Thingmount and the Viking stone he said: "Gilpatrick, I can do nothing." And he continued to gaze straight ahead.

"You have grown hard with the years, I see," the priest said sorrowfully.

Peter turned his horse's head and slowly wheeled round. The interview was over. He'd had enough. He wanted to kick his horse into a trot and leave his former friend standing. And rude though this would have been, he might have done it if, just then, he hadn't seen a woman coming across the green towards them. For now, instead of moving off, he stared.

Fionnuala. There was no mistaking her. It was nearly twenty years since they had parted, but even in the distance he'd have known her at a glance. As she came up, she gave Gilpatrick a brief nod.

"They told me you'd be here."

"I did not know you were in Dublin," the priest began. He seemed a little put out. "Do you remember my sister, Fionnuala?" He turned to Peter.

"He remembers," she cut in quietly.

"I was explaining to Peter that our brother . . ."

"Has been a fool." She looked straight at Peter. "Nearly as great a fool as his sister once was." She said it simply, without any malice. "They told me you were meeting him," she said to Gilpatrick. "So I thought I'd come up to Dublin, too."

"Unfortunately—" Gilpatrick began again.

"He's turned you down." She transferred her gaze back to Peter. "Haven't you, Welshman?"

The years had been more than kind to Fionnuala. If as a girl she had been lovely, thought Peter, there was only one way to describe her now. She was magnificent. A brood of children had left her body lithe, but fuller. Her hair was still raven black, her head held proudly, her eyes the same astounding, emerald green. At ease with herself and all the world, she looked exactly the Irish princess that she was. And this is the woman, thought Peter, that in different circumstances I might have married.

"I'm afraid that I have," he admitted with a trace of awkwardness.

"He's been dispossessed," she suddenly cried out. "We have all been robbed of the land we have loved for a thousand years. Do you not see that, Welshman? Can you not imagine his rage? We were not even conquered. We were deceived." She stopped, and then in a lower voice continued, "You do not care. You owe him nothing."

He did not reply.

"It is to me that you owe something," she said quietly.

The two of them gazed at each other, while Gilpatrick looked puzzled. He couldn't imagine why the knight should owe his sister anything.

"You are enjoying good fortune now, Welshman," she went on bitterly. "But it was not always so."

"It is usual to be rewarded for twenty years of service," he pointed out.

"Your English king has rewarded you. But it was I, like a fool, who caused you to be noticed when I gave you Dublin."

"It was yourself you gave to me. Not Dublin."

"You betrayed me." She said it sadly. "You hurt me, Welshman."

He nodded slowly. Every word of it was true. He noticed Gilpatrick looking mystified.

"What is it you want, Fionnuala?" he asked at last.

"My brother still has two daughters to find husbands for. Leave him on his farm at least until they're wed."

"That is all?"

"What else could there be?"

Did she, he fleetingly wondered, wish that she had married him? Or could she only hate him now? He would never know.

"He must pay his rents," he said.

"He will."

He pursed his lips. He could imagine the future trouble his tenant would probably cause him. There would be years of sullen looks and anger. How could it be otherwise? Perhaps Fionnuala would be able to keep her brother in order, perhaps not. One day, no doubt, it would end with his kicking her brother off his ancestral land. That was just the way of things. But he supposed he could live with the fellow until these last two daughters had gone to their husbands with suitable dowries.

"You ask nothing for yourself," he remarked. "Will your own daughters not be looking for good husbands? English knights perhaps?" For if they look like you, he thought to himself, that might not be impossible.

She answered with a laugh. "My children? I've seven of them, Welshman, running free with the O'Byrnes in the hills. They won't be marrying English knights. But take care," she added, looking straight into his eyes, "for they may come down from the hills one day, to take their land back again."

"Well, Fionnuala," he said slowly, "that may be. Your brother can stay, at least. I'll do it for your sake. You have my word for that. If you'll trust my word, that is," he added wryly.

She nodded, then turned to her brother.

"So Gilpatrick," she asked, "am I to trust the word of the King of England's man?" And as she said it, she glanced back at her former lover with a faint, ironic smile.

But Father Gilpatrick, confused though he was by their conversation, had witnessed too much since the days when he'd crossed the sea with Peter. And so now, though the knight had been his friend, he could only answer her question with a silence.

SEVEN

Dalkey

THE FALCON flapped its wings and tried to rise; but Walsh's gloved hand held it fast. Its great, curved beak struck down at the hand, but John Walsh only laughed. He loved the bird's fierce, free spirit. A fitting companion for a French or English lord. Its eyes were marvels, too: they could pick out a mouse at a thousand paces.

Walsh stared out from his castle wall. Like most of his family, he had a strong, soldier's face. His blue eyes were keen. They had to be, here in the borderlands. And they narrowed, now, as they fixed upon something. It was a small moving object, of no significance at all. Quite ordinary. Too ordinary. It struck him as odd. Nothing was ordinary in the borderland.

Carrickmines Castle. Carrickmines meant "Little Plain of Rocks." And certainly there were rocks enough, strewn around over the terrain nearby. But the real character of the place derived from the stately slopes of the Wicklow Mountains that rose just in front of the little castle and, behind it, the six leagues of road that led northwards across the rich coastal strip up to Dublin.

The moving object was a young girl. The last time he'd seen her, he remembered, some cattle had gone soon afterwards.

The castle was built of stone; it had already been reinforced several times. Most of the motte and bailey mounds of the original colonists were sturdy stone strongholds now, and they were to be found scattered over huge tracts of the island. Three of the best in the Dublin region lay at the northern and southern ends of the broad bay: there was one on the northern peninsula of Howth; a little way above that lay the stout castle of Malahide; and here at Carrickmines, just below the high headland that marked the bay's southern extremity, the Walsh family guarded their farmlands and the approaches to the great, green centre of the English power.

The territory around Dublin was a huge patchwork of estates. The greatest landowner, by far, was the Church. The Archbishop of Dublin held numerous huge tracts. His big manor of Shankill lay just south of Walsh's castle; below the city, taking in the old lands of Rathmines, was his even larger manor called Saint Sepulchre. But nearly all the religious houses of Dublin—and there were many of these now—had their rich estates in the region: the monks of Christ Church, the nuns of Saint Mary, the knights of Saint John; Ailred the Palmer's hospital had two handsome estates; even the little leper house of Saint Stephen had some rich farmland not far from the Walshes, and known as Leopardstown. Some of the land on these ecclesiastical estates was managed directly by the church landlords themselves; mostly it was let to tenant farmers. The rest of the territory was held by men like Walsh.

"And a great comfort it is," a Dublin merchant had once remarked to him, "to know that the countryside around is safely in the hands of loyal Englishmen."

Was that true, Walsh wondered? Up in Fingal, it probably was. There was a tiny residual element of the ancient Celtic aristocracy still in the region—though a small family called O'Casey was the only example that came into his mind. The former Viking families had almost all been pushed out of Fingal. In their place were Norman and English names—Plunkett and Field, Bisset and Cruise, Barnewall, and the Talbot lords of Malahide. They were all stout Englishmen; they married among themselves or other English families. But elsewhere, the situation was less clear-cut. If the Norsemen were no longer in Fingal, what about the old suburb on the north bank of the Liffey? Oxmantown, people often called it nowadays, but the origin of the name—Ostmanby, the town of the Ostmen—was not forgotten. There were plenty of people of Norse descent around there. And making the great curve round to the west and south of the city, one encountered local lords with names that were anything but English. There were the Harolds, descendants of Ailred the Palmer's son. They were Norse. So were the powerful Archbolds. As for the Thorkyll family, they descended from a former Norse king of the city—loyal to the English Justiciar, no doubt, but hardly Englishmen. And finally, there were the families like his own. There was a cluster of them in the territory south of the city, living on rich, fortified farms. Howell, Lawless, and the several branches of the Walsh family: their names might or might not make it obvious, but they all had come over from Wales. Were they, too, loyal to England? Of course they were. They had to be.

All the same, life down in the southern farmlands was rather different from that above Dublin. Because of the wild Wicklow Mountains which rose close by, and where the old Irish clans still held sway, the area was more of a frontier. John's mother had come from the settled conditions of Fingal, and it had worried her that he was allowed to run wild with the local Irish children, but his father had taken a different view. "If he is going to live beside these people," he would say cheerfully, "then he'd better know them." And know them he did. Even at the Walsh farmstead, a harpist or an Irish bard would sometimes arrive and offer to entertain his father in his hall—an offer his father never refused, and for which he always paid generously. And as for young John, there was hardly a

month when he didn't go out with the fishermen at the nearby
coastal village of Dalkey, or go up into the Wicklow Mountains and
run with the O'Tooles and the O'Byrnes. They all knew who he
was, of course: he was a Walsh, one of the colonists who had taken
their best land from them. But children have a passport into places
where their parents may not go, and for a number of years the boy
was only dimly conscious of the barrier that lay between himself and
his companions. He spoke their language, he usually dressed and
rode bareback as they did. Once he discovered an even closer link.

A party of boys had gone up into the hills and ridden their
ponies over to the lakes at Glendalough. The old monastery there
was a shadow of its former self: the bishopric had long since been
taken over by Dublin and only a small group of monks lived there
now; but John had still been impressed by the quiet beauty of the
place. They had stopped by the little settlement nearby when he had
noticed the dark-haired girl watching him. She was about his own
age, slim; he thought her rather beautiful. She was sitting on a grassy
bank, eating an apple, and silently staring at him with a pair of
bright green eyes. Feeling a little uncomfortable under her steady
gaze, he had gone over to her.

"So what are you staring at?" he had demanded to know; though
he had said it in a perfectly friendly way.

"You." She took another bite out of her apple.

"Do I know you?"

She munched for a moment or two before replying, "I know
who you are."

"And who is that?"

"My cousin." She watched his look of astonishment with interest. "You're the Walsh boy, aren't you?" He agreed that he was. "I
could be a Walsh, too, if I wanted," she declared. "But I don't," she
added fiercely, taking another bite out of her apple. Then she had
suddenly sprung up and run away.

Could this girl really be related? he had asked his father that
night, when he got home.

"Oh she'll be your cousin, all right." His father had looked amused. "Though I've never seen her. Your uncle Henry was a great one for the women. You've more cousins in Leinster than you suppose. There was a beautiful girl once, up in the hills. That would be his daughter by her, I've no doubt. It's a pity your uncle died when he did, but he certainly left a record of his passing." He sighed affectionately. "Is she pretty?"

"She is," John said, then blushed.

"Well, she's your cousin," his father had confirmed. "And I'll tell you something more. Most of the land around here, and right up to Dublin, used to belong to the mother's people. The Ui Fergusa they were called. We've been here since the days of Strongbow, when we were granted the estate. But they have long memories. As far as the descendants of the Ui Fergusa are concerned, we're on their land."

The memory of the girl had fascinated him for a long time. Once he had even gone over to Glendalough to ask after her. But they told him she had moved away, and he had never seen her again.

Indeed, a year later he had wondered if she might have died. For that had been the time of the terrible plague.

The Black Death had finally come to Ireland, as it had to all Europe. From 1347 onwards, for nearly four years, the plague, carried by fleas from the rats with whom, whether they know it or not, humans always share their dwellings, had swept across the whole continent. In its bubonic form, it afflicted its victims with terrible sores; in its even more deadly pneumonic form, it attacked their lungs and was passed, with terrible rapidity, from person to person on their breath. Perhaps a third of the population of Europe died. It had arrived on Ireland's east coast in August 1348.

The Walshes had been lucky. John's father had been going into Dublin on the very day that news came that the plague had arrived there. News of the Great Mortality, as it was called, had already reached them a little earlier from merchant ships coming into the port; so that the moment Walsh heard of a sudden sickness in the city, he had turned back. For more than a month the family had remained on their farm; and God, it seemed, had ordained that they were to survive. For though other farms were struck and the nearby fishing village of Dalkey suffered—they even heard there had been deaths up at Glendalough—the plague had passed them by.

But the effect on the Dublin region had been considerable. In the city and its suburbs, there were whole streets left almost empty. The Church estates had lost numerous tenants. There was a sense of desolation and disorder, as if the land had just been at war. And so it was hardly a surprise to the Walsh family if the O'Tooles and O'Byrnes up in the Wicklow Mountains, sensing the weakness in the plains below, began to come down to see what pickings there were to be had. There were certainly cattle with not enough men to guard them. Nobody familiar with the traditional life of the clans could be surprised if there were a few cattle raids. "They've been tak-ing each other's cattle since before Saint Patrick came," John's father calmly remarked, "so we needn't be surprised if they extend the compliment to us." To young John, and he suspected to his father, too, there was a certain excitement in the prospect of a raid. There was the thrill of the chase, the chance of a little skirmish with peo-ple whom, in all likelihood, one would recognise. It was part of frontier life. But the royal Justiciar in Dublin had taken a bleaker view. To him, and to the citizens of Dublin, these signs of disorder were to be deplored and must be dealt with firmly. Fortifications were needed. And so it was that the castle of Carrickmines—which had been neglected for years—had been repaired and strengthened, and John Walsh's father had been asked to move out of his farmstead and take over as castellan of the place. "We need a good, reliable man," the Justiciar had told him. And young John had been dimly conscious that the change also represented a social promotion for his father. In the eyes of the royal officials at Dublin, he was now one of the king's officers, more of a knight than a farmer, nearer to the status held by his ancestor Peter FitzDavid who had first been granted the land.

It was a small incident at this time which had taught him what all this meant for his own identity.

The family had been installed at the castle only a few months when the officer from Dublin rode up. It was a fine morning and young John had just decided to ride over to see one of his Walsh cousins on a neighbouring farm. As usual when he went about in the locality, he was wearing only a shirt and tunic; his legs were bare and he was riding his little horse without a saddle. He might well have passed for one of the young O'Byrnes. The man riding up the lane from Dublin was as smartly dressed and turned out as any English knight, and John watched him, not without admiration. As the man drew up in front of the castle gate, he glanced at John and enquired curtly whether Walsh was within.

"Who shall I say is looking for him?" John asked.

The knight frowned, uncertain whether this young fellow before him belonged to the castle or not; and meaning only to be helpful, John had smiled and explained: "I'm John Walsh, his son."

He hadn't expected any particular response to this statement; so he was much taken aback by what happened next. For instead of merely nodding, the knight stared at him openmouthed.

"You are Walsh's son? Walsh, the warden of this castle?" A look of disgust crossed his face. "And your father lets you ride about like that?"

John looked down at his legs and his bareback horse. It was already obvious to him that this young knight must be a newcomer, one of a company who had recently arrived from England to help the Justiciar in Dublin. All the same, under the contemptuous gaze of the nobleman, he felt a little shamefaced.

"I was only riding to another farm," he said defensively.

"Dear God, man," the knight cried out, "you don't have to dress like a native." And seeing the youth looking confused, he told him sharply, "Pull yourself together." Then without another word to him, he rode in through the castle gate.

At first, John had intended to continue on his journey; but he had only gone fifty paces when he had stopped and turned back. The knight was rude—he obviously knew little about Ireland—but John did not like to be scorned by a man who was, after all, one of his own kind. A short while later, therefore, he was in his mother's chamber, having his hair vigorously brushed and struggling into a clean white shirt and leather boots. By the time the knight was ready to ride out, he encountered in the yard a young man who might have been a handsome squire in any English castle.

"Better," he remarked tersely as he strode past him; and having mounted, he signalled John to accompany him through the gateway. As they came outside, he pulled up his horse and pointed to the rich pastureland in front of them. "Tell me something, young Walsh," he said in a voice that was more friendly. "Do you want to keep this land?"

"Yes, I do," John replied.

"Then you had better realise that the only way you'll do so is if you remember you're an Englishman." And with that brief advice, he rode away.

Standing on his castle wall today, twenty years later, Walsh would not have disagreed with the knight's assessment. The King of England's rule, in some shape or form, extended over parts of Ireland; but since the early days of colonial expansion in the time of Henry II and his son, there had been a gradual retreat. The island now was divided up between the native Irish and the colonists in a vast patchwork of territories, representing a series of accommodations or stalemates. The English rulers were on the defensive, not only against the Irish ruling clans but even against some of the settlers who, after five or six generations in the borderlands, were more like Irish chiefs themselves, and almost as hard to control. When the English administrators in Dublin looked out at the uncertain world around them, they could draw only one conclusion: "We've got to stiffen the backbone of our people here. Get some English order, or the place will degenerate into chaos. Remind our colonists that they are Englishmen."

What did that mean, to be an Englishman? There was the matter of dress, of course. You didn't go around with bare legs or ride without a saddle. You didn't let your wife wear a bright saffron-coloured shawl like an Irishwoman. You didn't speak Irish except to the natives; you spoke English. In his grandfather's day, Walsh recalled, a gentleman would speak Norman French. It was still used for the more formal court proceedings. But if you went down to Dublin now, the merchants and the royal officials would usually be speaking the Frenchified English that was current in places like Bristol or London. And above all, you weren't supposed to marry the Irish. "Marrying them," one of his Fingal relations had declared to him, "that's where the rot starts."

Indeed, the English government had become so fixated by the subject that four years ago, at a parliament held down in the town of Kilkenny, a series of statutes had been promulgated which actually made all such intercourse between the communities illegal.

Privately, Walsh wasn't impressed with the Statute of Kilkenny. The colonists had been marrying the Irish ever since Strongbow first obtained Leinster by wedding King Diarmait's daughter; and just as the Norse and the Irish had been marrying before that. This attempt to force the two communities into separate worlds might be possible, but he thought it smelled of panic. Laws were no good when they couldn't be enforced.

But even if he didn't think much of the larger issue, Walsh understood perfectly well what it meant to be English here in his own locality. It meant guarding his and his neighbours' farmlands from the O'Byrnes.

Most of the time, it had to be said, everything was quiet. But now and again, things got interesting. Ten years ago, the chief of the O'Byrnes at that time, an unusually ambitious man, had come down with a large force and surrounded the castle. "Do you really

think you can hold the place if you take it from me?" Walsh had
called down from the wall. But he had only received a volley of mis-
siles in return for his pains. The siege had gone on for several days
until the Justiciar, the Earl of Ormond, had come out of Dublin
with a large party of knights and driven the invaders away. "Personally," Walsh had told his wife, "I think O'Byrne is playing a
game. He'll make a nuisance of himself to see how much he can get
out of the Justiciar." And when some months later O'Byrne came to
an agreement with Ormond, and the remarkable news came back—
"That wild man of the mountains has been given a knighthood, no
less!"—Walsh had laughed till he cried. All the same, the walls had
been strengthened again, and from time to time troops of cavalry
had been stationed there. For nearly ten years things had been quiet
after that. But the underlying truth still remained. The farmlands
south of Dublin were safe because the castle protected them; and
the castle was there because the English ruled in Dublin.

As he had pointed out to one of his cousins just recently: "The
English king gave us our lands and our position. He can also
take them away. And you cannot suppose for a moment that the
O'Byrnes and the O'Tooles would leave us in possession of them if
the English power was taken away." Yes, John Walsh thought, that
was what, at the end of the day, it meant to him to be English.

So what the devil was that girl doing? On the eastern side of the little plain where the castle was set, the high hump of the bay's southern headland rose, masking the fishing village of Dalkey from his
view. Half a mile away, with the headland as a magnificent back-
drop, he had set up a large rabbit warren. That was another useful
custom the colonists had brought with them. The warren provided
him with a constant supply of meat and fur. And it was by that warren that the girl was lurking. Was she planning to steal some rabbits?

He knew who she was, of course. She was the daughter of his
beautiful, dark-haired cousin up in the mountains. His cousin had

married one of the O'Byrnes, he'd heard, some years ago. This little girl looked just like her. The same brilliant green eyes. He smiled to himself. If she stole a rabbit, he was certainly going to pretend he hadn't seen. He'd noticed her lurking about on his land once before though, some months back; and shortly afterwards he'd lost those cattle. That was a more serious matter.

But then another thought occurred to him, and he frowned. There had been trouble down in Munster recently, and the Dublin authorities had been concerned enough to send troops. There was a new O'Byrne chief now, and seeing the English forces occupied elsewhere, he had taken the opportunity to move into several small forts down the coast. It was cheeky, but Walsh reckoned that the Irish chief would probably get away with it. At least for the moment. Was this a prelude to another attack on Carrickmines? In Walsh's opinion, that would be ill-advised. The people in Dublin were already nervous. A couple of weeks ago, they'd sent a squadron of horsemen over to camp at Dalkey, in case any attempts were made to sneak up the coast. At the first hint of trouble from the hills, there'd be further squadrons coming out to Carrickmines—quite apart from the fact that the place was far too strong now for O'Byrne to break into. All the same, you could never tell. Was it possible that his little cousin was lurking by the rabbit warren for a more sinister purpose? Was she looking for troops? Was she noting the state of the walls and the castle gate? If so, she hadn't concealed herself very well. He would be sorry if his young kinswoman were careless about such things.

Or was there something else going on? His eyes searched the slopes. Were they up there already, waiting to sweep down as soon as the little girl ran back or gave a signal? He scanned the hills. He did not think so. The girl was moving away now. Which way would she go?

The falcon on his wrist was getting restless again. With a single sweep, he let her loose and watched her rise, magnificent and watchful, into the summer morning sky.

✢

Tom was on his way to church when he passed her. He usually went there in the afternoon, but today he was an hour later than usual because one of the fishermen had insisted on talking to him until long after the Angelus had sounded farther down the valley.

She was a pretty little thing. Long black hair. He had never seen her before. She had been loitering by the track that led across the common from the shore. As he had passed her, she had stared at him with the strangest green eyes.

Tom Tidy was a small man. His sandy moustache and pointed beard made a little triangle which the slope of his shoulders thrust forward. There was a quiet determination about him, yet also a hint of melancholy, as though God had required him to plough a furrow which, as it turned out, had no end. Tom Tidy might not be impressive, but you could always rely on him. Everybody said so. Why only the other day, when he had been paying his rent at the diocesan office, the archbishop himself had come in and said, "If there's one man I know I can trust, Master Tidy, then that man is you." Master Tidy, he had called him: a title of respect. That had made him blush with pride.

Tom Tidy had always gone to church every day when he still lived in the southern suburb of Dublin. After his children were married and he had lost his wife of thirty years, and wanted a change, the archbishop's bailiff, who was looking for reliable tenants, had offered him very good terms to move down to the fishing village of Dalkey.

And Dalkey was pleasant enough. Situated on a shelf of bare ground between the high hump of the bay's southern headland and the sea, it consisted of a single street with a little church and plots of land on which homesteads and gardens were laid out. Such a homestead was known as a messuage. Tom Tidy's plot was of average size—thirty yards of frontage, running back forty yards. But he also had the right to several strips in the communal field behind the plots and to pasture his livestock on the open common which lay on the seaward side. The town plot was known as a burgage, and the holder of such a property in a township—unlike the peasants and serfs who inhabited smaller cabins—was a freeman known as a burgess.

Though it looked and almost was a tiny town, Dalkey had no borough charter. It was a part of one of the archbishop's great manors. The archbishop was the feudal lord; his bailiff collected the ground rents, the feudal prise tax on the fishermen's catch, and certain other dues. For almost all offences, the inhabitants would be summoned to trial at the archbishop's court, for which his bailiff would select the juries. In short, the Irish settlement of Dalkey was organised in a typically English manner.

Tom Tidy paid three shillings a year for his holding, which totalled three acres. From this base he operated a small carrying business, taking goods from the little harbour into the local farmsteads or into Dublin. His homestead was one of the larger ones. The thatched dwelling house was modest; but behind it was a substantial yard with a long barn where he kept several vehicles: the cart for carrying fish, the big wagon for the great casks of wine and barrels of salt, and another for bales of cloth and furs. He also brewed some ale which he sold in the locality and for which he paid the bailiff a small tax on each brewing. Business was occasional. Some days he worked, some he did not. The slow pace of Dalkey suited Tom, the widower, very well.

There were thirty-nine burgages in Dalkey, though as some of them had been joined, the number of burgesses was actually less. Most of the burgesses, however, did not live in Dalkey. Landowners and Dublin merchants took the burgages and then sublet, often in smaller parcels to lesser folk. Tom Tidy, therefore, was one of the more important people in the place. Indeed, the position of head man, or reeve, being open at present, the bailiff had told him, "Although you haven't been in Dalkey long, Tom, we're thinking of appointing you."

It was the shoreline that had given Dalkey its name. Some way out from the beach, a small island and a line of rocks had suggested the Celtic name of Deilginis—which meant Thorn or Dagger Island—which Viking settlers had later converted to Dalkey. No great river from the interior came down there, so that for most of its life it had only been a fisherman's hamlet. More recently, however, Dalkey had acquired a new significance.

The sandbars and mudflats of the Liffey estuary had always been a hazard to ships, but since the days of the Vikings, the activities of the port had added to the silting up of the river, while the squat medieval cogs, with their broad beams and deeper drafts, found it harder to negotiate the Dublin shallows, even though they usually hired pilots to guide them in. Nearby were other havens with deeper waters. The little port at Howth on the bay's northern peninsula was one; down below the southern point of the bay, Dalkey was another. For the island acted as a natural harbour wall to protect any ships that came in, and the place had excellent deep water—eight fathoms even at low tide. Merchant ships with deep drafts would often unload there—sometimes all their cargo, sometimes just enough to lighten the vessel—so that they could then negotiate the Dublin shallows. Either way, it provided extra employment for the people of the settlement, including Tom Tidy.

After passing the girl, Tom went another fifty yards before he stopped. There was no vessel in the little harbour at present. The fishing boats, he happened to know, were all out. So why was that girl coming along the path from the water? There was nothing to see down there. What was she up to? He turned to take another look at her, but she had vanished.

The little stone church of Saint Begnet's stood on the northern side of the street. Beside it was a graveyard and the priest's house. The last priest had died that spring and a temporary curate had been coming over from another church to hold services on Sundays. In the meantime, Tom had been entrusted with the keys, both of the church, which he locked at night, and of the priest's house, which was being used at present by the officer of the visiting squadron, whose men were encamped in tents in the garden behind. Two of these men were always posted down by the shore to keep watch for the approach of the O'Byrnes or any vessels that might contain them.

Tom entered the church and, after genuflecting, made his way towards the altar. A little to one side there was a wooden screen behind which a prie-dieu afforded a private place to pray. Here Tom sank down on his knees, and for several minutes he was lost to the world in prayer—so that he hardly heard the church door open. Nor did he look up. If someone else had come to pray in the silence of the little church, he had no wish to disturb them. He remained where he was. A few moments passed as he heard the faint scuffling of soft leather shoes on the floor. It seemed to him that there were two people near the door, but because of the screen he could not see them and, presumably, they could not see him either. Then he heard a voice.

"I was trying to find you down by the shore."

"You saw the lookouts?"

"Of course." This voice, it seemed to him, was a girl's. The other belonged to a man. They were speaking in Irish, but he understood them well enough.

"You have a message for me from O'Byrne?"

"I have. He is not coming to Dalkey." The girl's voice again.

"I see. And if not Dalkey, where?"

"Carrickmines."

"When?"

"In a week, there will be no moon. It will be then. In the dark. Towards midnight."

"We'll be ready. Tell him that."

There was the sound of feet on the floor, and of the church door opening. Then the sound of its being closed.

Tom kept very still. As soon as he had heard the name O'Byrne
he had felt a stab of cold fear. You never knew what those people
might be plotting. And you didn't want to know. People who heard
too much, people who could turn into informers, had a way of disappearing. Ten years ago, he remembered, a fellow at Dalkey had
got word of some trouble brewing and informed the authorities.
One of the O'Byrnes had died as a result. A week later, they had
fished the informer's body out of the sea—without a head.

So as the rest of the conversation reached him, he wished he
could vanish into the floor. If they—whoever they were—moved
farther into the church and discovered him, what would they do?
He had felt a sense of panic running through him; a clamminess had
spread across his brow. Even after the door had closed and the
church returned to silence, he was still shivering. He remained for
some time, still on his knees, listening.

At last however, he looked cautiously round the screen. The
church was empty. He got up and went to the door. Slowly he
opened it. No one was in sight. He stepped out. His eyes searched
for a sign of the couple he had overheard. They seemed to have vanished. They were not in the churchyard, nor when he reached it did
he see them anywhere in the street. He went back and locked the
church door; then he started to make his way towards his house.
Still there was no sign of them.

He was halfway along the street when, glancing at the track that
led across the common towards the south, he caught sight of the
girl, her long dark hair streaming behind her, running like a deer.
That was her, the messenger, without a doubt, on her way back towards O'Byrne. He had a sudden, foolish instinct to rush after her,
but realised it was useless. He looked around for a sign of her companion, but there was none at all. He must certainly have been one
of the Dalkey men. But who? Was the man there, in one of the
homesteads, watching him at this very moment?

Slowly and thoughtfully Tom Tidy went along the street. When
he got home, he attended to his six cart horses. After they had been

fed and closed in their stalls for the night, he went into his house, took a meat pie from his larder, cut a large slice, and put it on a wooden platter on his table. He poured ale from a pitcher into a pottery mug; then he sat down to eat. And to think. He did not leave his house that evening.

The next morning, Tom Tidy was up with the dawn and working in the yard beside his barn. He was a tolerable carpenter and he had decided to make a new tailboard for the fish cart. He chose a plank and for more than two hours he worked quietly, shaping it to his satisfaction. Nobody came by to disturb him.

He had gone over the business carefully in his mind the night before; now he reviewed it calmly. Tom Tidy was a loyal fellow who knew where his duty lay. But he wasn't a fool. The dangerous information that had come into his hand had to be passed on; but if it was ever traced back to him, he wasn't sure he could answer for his life. How should it be passed on then? And to whom? The obvious answer might have been to inform the officer in charge of the squadron; but that was too close to home. Any sign from the soldiers that they suspected the true state of affairs would be noticed by the village, and whoever had been in the church with the girl would probably guess that Tom was the one who had given them away. There was the bailiff over at the archbishop's manor, but Tom had always thought the man was indiscreet. If he told the bailiff, it wouldn't be long before the whole area knew. The wisest course, he considered, would be to speak to someone in Dublin, but this would require some careful planning. Who was discreet as well as powerful? Who would protect him? Whom could he trust? He wasn't sure.

When he had finished the tailboard, Tom Tidy put his tools away, left his house, and walked up the street, glancing at the houses to the right and to the left as he did so. A breeze coming up from the harbour brought with it a sharp, salty tang that smelled good and invigorating. It was time to get some advice.

While the burgesses who owned the leases in Dalkey included

significant gentry and Dublin families like the Dawes and Stack-
pooles, the tenants who actually lived there were a mixed collection.
Several of the fishing families contained burly red-haired figures
who were obviously of both Irish and Viking descent. Others derived from the modest English townsmen and smallholders who had
come across in the decades that followed Strongbow's invasion—
men with names like Fox and White, Kendal and Crump. Most had
been there a generation or two and were scarcely distinguishable
from their Irish and Nordic neighbours. But in seeking advice, Tom
ignored them all.

The homestead into which he finally turned was quite unlike the
others. Indeed, it resembled nothing so much as a tiny castle. The
main house, though not much bigger than its thatched and gabled
neighbours, was three floors high, square, and made of stone.
This fortified house belonged to Doyle, a prominent merchant in
Dublin, who used it to store goods. And it was the man who lived
in the house and worked for Doyle—Tom's good friend and the one
man in Dalkey he could trust—that Tom had come to see.

Nobody would have been surprised at his going in there. Tom
and Michael MacGowan had been friends ever since Tom had
arrived in Dalkey. Despite their different ages they had much in
common. Both were Dublin men. MacGowan's brother was a well-
regarded craftsman in the city. He himself had been taken on by
Doyle as an apprentice, and now in his twenties, he had kept the
store for his master in Dalkey for nearly five years. The girl he was
courting in Dublin was quite content to move to Dalkey if they
married, so it was likely that he would be remaining there for a long
time. Tom Tidy had come to regard him as a steady young fellow,
with a wise head on his shoulders. He could trust him to be discreet.

He found MacGowan in the yard—a small, dark man with a
mop of black hair and a face that seemed to look out a little quizzi-
cally at the world. He greeted Tom and, when Tom indicated that
he wanted to talk, he led him to a pair of benches under an apple

tree. He listened attentively while Tom told him what had happened and explained his dilemma.

When Michael MacGowan was thinking, he performed a curious trick with his face. He would throw back his head, close one eye and open the other, under its raised eyebrow, very wide. As he did this now, staring up at the sky, it seemed to Tom that MacGowan's open eye had grown almost as big as one of the ripening apples on the tree. When Tom had finished, his friend was silent, but only for a short time.

"Are you asking my advice as to what you should do?"

"I am."

"I think you should do nothing. Tell nobody. Forget what you heard." He turned his single open eye upon the older man and stared at him disconcertingly. "There is danger here, Tom Tidy."

"I had thought perhaps that Doyle . . . I thought you would say we should tell him." The great merchant who owned the fortified house was not only one of the most prominent of the city fathers but was a man of awesome reputation, on close terms with the Justiciar himself.

One of the reasons why Dalkey had been especially popular as a landing place was that it had often been possible to avoid paying the customs which would have been due at the port of Dublin on all incoming goods. The customs tariffs were significant. A merchant who avoided them might easily increase his profits by a third. Taking the goods from Dalkey round the coast by lighter or overland by cart, it had not been too difficult to evade the customs inspectors. The problem had caused the government some irritation.

When the suggestion had been made to the royal servants in Dublin that they should give Doyle the appointment of water bailiff for Dalkey, it had seemed a good solution to this problem. And indeed, ever since he had held the position, a steady stream of revenue had come from the little harbour. No one down there would dare to do anything behind Doyle's back. His reach was long. It was not surprising, therefore, that Tom Tidy should have thought of the powerful merchant as a possible solution to his problem.

"They say he can keep secrets and that he is cunning as well as powerful," he ventured.

"You do not know him, Tom." MacGowan shook his head. "Doyle is a hard man. If we tell him, do you know what will happen? He will make sure that O'Byrne and his friends walk into a trap that will kill them all. And he will be proud of it. He'll tell everyone in Dublin that he was responsible. And where do you think that will leave me, out here in Dalkey? The O'Byrnes are a large clan, Tom. They will come and get me. And once they work out what happened, they'll kill you, too. You can count on it. Even Doyle could not prevent that if he tried—which he probably wouldn't," he added bleakly.

"You're saying that I should do nothing to save the Walshes and their people at Carrickmines?"

"Let their walls protect them."

Tom nodded sadly. It was a hard thing that MacGowan had said, but he understood. He got up to leave.

"Tom." MacGowan's voice was anxious. His eye was staring now like that of a creature caught in a trap and in pain.

"Well?"

"Whatever you're going to do, Tom, don't go to Doyle. Will you promise me that?"

Tidy nodded and left. But as MacGowan watched him go he thought to himself: if I know you, Tom Tidy, and your sense of duty, you are going to find somebody to tell.

✦

There was no doubting the fellow's good intentions. Harold had looked at Tom Tidy with some admiration when he turned up at his house with a wagonload of goods and demanded to speak with him. That had been an intelligent ruse to avoid suspicion, and he had

gladly bought a number of useful provisions to give Tidy his necessary cover.

"You have done the right thing," he assured the carrier, when he
learned the reason for Tidy's visit, "and you have come to the right
person."

Tidy was correct in thinking that Harold was a man who could
be trusted to act, as well as to be discreet. No one was a more
staunch upholder of English rule in Ireland than Robert Harold.
Two centuries had passed since his ancestor Harold had returned to
his father, Ailred the Palmer; in that time, the family had come to
be known as the Harolds, and as the Harolds they had prospered.
They had acquired a large tract of land, beginning south of Dublin
at a place called Harold's Cross and stretching south-westwards
down the borderland of the Dublin territory—the March, as the
English called it—beyond which the rule of the crown was shaky
nowadays. Marcher families like the Harolds, with their broad acres,
fortified houses, and armed men, were important in preserving the
established English order in this part of the island.

It was ten years since he had been elected as head of his family.
Several of the Marcher families, like the Celtic clans, had taken to
choosing the head of the family by election. Sometimes they would
even invite other families or an important figure like the archbishop
to help them choose. That the Harolds had done this was just another sign of their determination to ensure that they had strong
leadership in difficult times.

Robert Harold was only of medium height. Quite early in life his
hair had gone grey. His eyes, which were a startling, Nordic blue,
usually had a soft expression; but they could grow suddenly hard,
and when they did, whoever had crossed him discovered Harold's
ruthlessness. He had proved himself an effective leader, cautious but
tough.

As Tidy explained everything—from his sighting of the girl, to
her conversation with the unseen man in the church—Harold
watched him carefully. The fellow's nervousness was plain to see.

Again and again, Tom stressed that he had come to him, rather than the archbishop's bailiff or the Justiciar's officials, so that no one in Dublin would connect him with the business. "Please do not reveal where you got this information," he pleaded. Up to a point, Harold could reassure him. He couldn't see any reason why he should need to mention Tidy by name.

Sometimes Harold thought that he was almost the only person who really understood what was going on in Ireland. The Justiciar did, probably. The men who kept the accounts at the royal Exchequer surely must have. But some of his fellow gentry, men like Walsh at Carrickmines, failed to appreciate the seriousness of the case. Privately, he considered them weak.

The rot had really started when his father was a boy. Two things had set the downward course of events in motion. There had been several years of bad harvests and famines. That hadn't helped. Then there had been the English war with the Scots. King Edward I—Longshanks, the Hammer of the Scots—might have destroyed the Scottish hero Wallace; but after Wallace, the Scots had struck back. Robert the Bruce and his brother Edward had defeated the English army at Bannockburn and given the Scots new heart. It was hardly surprising, then, if the great Irish clans had started to wonder if they, too, might be able to take on the English power. A deal had been struck. The O'Connors and the O'Neills had allied themselves with Edward Bruce, who had brought over a big force of Scots to Ireland. "That way we give the English a war on two fronts," they judged, "and we may drive them out of Ireland as well as Scotland." If they succeeded, the Irish chiefs had promised Edward Bruce the position of High King.

Could it have succeeded? Possibly. Bruce and his allies had made a big show up in the north and then advanced almost to the walls of Dublin. But the Dubliners had shut them out and the rest of Ireland had failed to rise for them. It was the old Irish problem: there was no unity across the island. The mighty and ancient

O'Neills found they could only rally their friends. Before long, Bruce had been killed, and the Celtic military revival was over.

Yet something had changed. For a start, Ireland was poorer. English settlers were less inclined to come; some started leaving; the English government invested less. The Black Death had only made the existing trend worse. By the time Robert Harold came to manhood, England and France had become locked in that endless conflict known as the Hundred Years War, and the English king had little use for Ireland except to get what money he could from it— which was less and less as every decade went by. To Harold's knowledge, the King of England nowadays received only around two thousand pounds a year from Ireland; back in the days of Longshanks, it had been three times that amount. The king sent out his Justiciars, his royal servants, and even once his son; but the royal interest in the island was halfhearted.

Some years ago, in a fit of panic when they had supposed, quite wrongly, that Dublin wasn't safe, the royal Exchequer officials had decamped with all the accounts to a stronghold down in Carlow. It was the sort of feebleminded cowardice that Harold most despised. He had no great faith in the king's men.

"If the English in Ireland want to keep order, then they must do it themselves," Harold liked to say. They had their own parliaments, with considerable powers, which often met in Dublin. "But we haven't enough leaders," he would add. "That's the trouble."

It wasn't only the crown which had suffered. Many great lords with estates in England as well as Ireland had decided that the western island with its disaffected native population was not worth the trouble. They left their Irish estates in the hands of stewards and remained, absentees, across the water. Just as bad, some of the greatest feudal holdings, like the huge inheritance of Strongbow himself, had been subdivided amongst heiresses, and in later generations split up yet again. So the magnates who might have formed a bulwark against the forces of disorder were largely missing. Recognising this weakness, the English king had enacted one important measure: he had created three great earldoms which could only pass down, without subdivisions, in the male line. The earldom of Ormond he gave to the mighty Butler family; the earldoms of Kildare and of Desmond went to two branches of the Fitzgeralds, who had come over with Strongbow. These earldoms dominated regions that lay beyond the king's Dublin rule; but though they were certainly mighty enough to impose English order on large areas of the Irish hinterland, they were also more like independent Celtic kings than English noblemen and they were treated as such by the Irish chiefs. Their interests were all in Ireland. Privately, Harold suspected that if ever English rule collapsed in Ireland, the great earls would probably still be there, alongside the Irish kings.

No, it was up to the gentry, men like himself, to maintain English order, if not in all Ireland, at least in the broad arc of territory around the Dublin seaboard. Manor house, parish church, and village; market towns with their little town councils; English shires with their courts and royal justices. This was the settled order that Harold wanted to preserve, safe for himself and modest folk like Thomas Tidy. And it could be preserved, if only the English in Ireland themselves held firm.

But would they? Not long ago, down in the south, a descendant of bad old King Diarmait had proclaimed himself King of Leinster. Kavanagh, they called the fellow. It was an empty gesture, of course, just a native chief blowing his trumpet uselessly in the wind. But it was a reminder all the same. Show weakness now, and there would be other Kavanaghs. The O'Connors and the O'Neills could always rise again. This planned raid on Carrickmines might or might not be serious; but failure to deal with it would be seen as a token of the weakness of the English will, and be noted all over Ireland. It must be dealt with, and dealt with firmly.

Tidy was nearly finished.

"The essential thing," he pointed out, "is that we give no hint to the O'Byrnes or their friends that they are expected. If troops are moved up from Dublin, it will need to be at the last moment, under cover of darkness."

"I agree." Harold nodded.

"And the squadron in Dalkey," Tidy continued anxiously. "They'll need to remain where they are. So as not to give the game away," he explained.

And so as not to put yourself under suspicion, thought Harold grimly. Aloud he said, "Do not worry, Thomas Tidy. We shall be careful." And he gave Tom a reassuring smile.

Did the poor fellow really imagine that they could afford to leave an entire squadron sitting uselessly at Dalkey while Carrickmines was attacked? Well, that would be up to the Justiciar, anyway. But Tidy had better realise one thing. If he wanted to live in a secure Ireland, then he would have to take some risks, like the rest of them. Harold had no wish to sacrifice Tom Tidy. But if necessary, he would.

The conference was scheduled for noon. Doyle's dark eyes surveyed the quay with satisfaction. So far, things were working out very well.

If Ireland had suffered during the last century, you would not have known it from looking at Dublin quay. For a start, since the days of Strongbow, a steady process of land reclamation on both banks had altered the shape of the River Liffey so that, beside the town, it was only half its former width. A new stone wall now ran all the way along the waterfront from Wood Quay to the bridge, a hundred and fifty yards in front of the old rampart. Outside the city's wall, straggling suburbs had grown up, especially along the road to the south so that, if you included Oxmantown across the river, there were nearly three people living in the suburbs for every one inside the walls. Parish churches as well as monastic buildings graced the suburbs. And to ensure an adequate water supply, one of the southern rivers had been diverted to flow through channels and aqueducts into the growing city in a fresh and constant stream.

And few men in the new Dublin had done better than Doyle. Even the Black Death had worked to his advantage: for though the trade of the city had been hit, two of his business rivals had died, and he had been able to take over their trade as well as buy up all their property at very reasonable prices. Twenty years after the terrible plague, much of Dublin's trade had recovered. Wars no longer provided shiploads of captives and coastal raids were a thing of the past, so Dublin's old slave market had ceased to function. But Ireland had plenty of goods to export to Britain, France, and Spain.

The greatest export from the English realms, for many generations, had been wool. The trade was regulated through a limited number of ports, known as the Staple Ports, where customs duties were levied. Dublin was one of them. "We have never bred sheep with the finest fleeces, like the best of the English flocks," Doyle would readily admit. "But there's a market for coarse wool, too." Huge quantities of hides from the island's great cattle herds and furs from her forest animals went out from the Dublin quays. The fishing catch from the Irish Sea was enormous. Fish, fresh or salted, were constantly being carried across the seas. Timber also from Ireland's endless forest tracts was supplied to England. The roof timbers of some of England's greatest cathedrals, such as Salisbury, came from Irish oaks.

Doyle had a hand in all these shipments. But he found himself more interested in the import trade. The stout cogs with their single masts and deep bellies brought in all kinds of goods: iron from Spain, salt from France, pottery from Bristol, fine textiles from Flanders. Italian merchants would arrive with loads of oriental spices for the great summer fairs outside the western gate. But the trade that he liked the best was the shipping of wine from southwest France. Hogsheads of ruby red wine from Bordeaux: he loved the look, the texture, the scent of the great sixty-three gallon barrels as they were lowered off the ships; though the shipments were so huge that they were usually reckoned by the tun—two hundred and fifty-two gallons each. It was the wine trade that had made Doyle, with all his ships, such a rich man.

The Justiciar had summoned Doyle to the castle the day before, soon after Harold had been there. Indeed, the king's representative had called for the merchant even before he had informed the city's mayor. Like most of the larger cities in England, Dublin had a council of forty-eight who governed its roughly seven thousand inhabitants. The inner council, from which the mayor was chosen each year, consisted of only twenty-four of the city's most powerful men, and Doyle was one of these. It was because he was so impressed with Doyle that the Justiciar had let him collect the valuable prise on the imports through Dalkey and he knew that the merchant was extremely well-informed. "Doyle has eyes and ears everywhere," the Justiciar would say. "He is powerful, but he is also subtle. If he wishes something to happen, he will make it happen." The Justiciar had given him a full and private account of the news that Robert Harold had just brought, and Doyle had listened attentively.

"So if this information is correct," the Justiciar had summarised, "they will strike at Carrickmines in a few days' time. The question is, what should we do?"

If Doyle had not been entirely surprised, he did not say so. He considered carefully.

"Even if the information turns out to be wrong," Doyle had carefully replied, "I don't see how you can ignore it. I think you need to call in Walsh, and Harold, and some of the other men you can trust, as soon as possible for a council of war."

"Tomorrow, at noon," the Justiciar had said, decisively. "I shall want you, too," he had added, "of course."

As he made his way up from the quay towards the meeting, Doyle noted the scene around him with pleasure. Of the several streets leading down to the new river wall, the finest, which ran west of and parallel to the old Fish Shambles, was Winetavern Street,

where the greatest wine merchants, including Doyle himself, had
their houses. And some of these were truly splendid.

For the most striking change in the last two centuries in Dublin
lay not so much in the area covered as in its architecture. It was the
same across most of Europe. Instead of thatched-and-wattle dwellings behind wooden fences, the streets of Dublin were lined with
stout, timber-framed houses now, two or three storeys high, with
pointed gables and upper floors that jutted out to overhang the
street. Some of the roofs were thatched, but many were covered with
slates or tiles. The windows were mostly protected with shutters,
though those of rich men like Doyle had glass panes as well. As he
walked up Winetavern Street with an air of satisfaction, wearing his
rich red robe and soft blue hat, Doyle looked exactly what he was:
a wealthy city father in a prosperous medieval town. At the top of
the street he paused by a stall and bought a little mustard. He liked
the sharp taste of mustard with his meat. Yet though he looked well
contented, his long, saturnine face still seemed to bring a hint of
something dark to this clear and sunny morning.

He went through a gateway in the old wall, and thence up into
the precincts of Christ Church Cathedral. He did not go inside to
say a prayer, but skirted the great church, coming out at the crossroads above the Fish Shambles where the pillory stood. A short distance away to his right the city's great High Cross, twenty feet tall,
rose in the middle of the street opposite the big, many gabled town
hall, the Tholsel, where the city's greatest men would gather for a
guild meeting four times a year. Symbols of order; symbols of stability. Doyle stood for such things.

And was all this order threatened by the Carrickmines affair?
He knew that Harold would believe it was. The Justiciar, too.
Good men, both. And possibly right, in the long term. But as
Doyle stood in the centre of the high-gabled medieval city he alone
of them had further, secret information. Only he understood the
true nature of the danger to Walsh and to Harold, to Tom Tidy

and to MacGowan down at Dalkey, and even to himself. Whatever action was decided upon at the meeting today, there were hidden risks.

He was prepared to take them. Doyle liked taking risks. He turned left and continued towards the castle.

As Doyle was making his way up from the quay, John Walsh had already reached the city outskirts. The summons from the Justiciar had come the evening before but without any explanation. Neatly groomed and wearing his best tunic, Walsh had left Carrickmines early to be sure he was in good time. He passed the looming Gothic mass of Saint Patrick's Cathedral, and soon afterwards entered the city through one of its southern gates.

The castle sat in the city's south-eastern corner. Where the old royal hall had once been, there was now a large courtyard separated from the rest of the city by a high curtain wall and a ditch. The entrance, across a drawbridge, was through a big gateway with two round turrets. Inside stood the Great Hall, the mint where coins were issued, and the numerous offices and residences of the royal officials. There was also a small chapel, dedicated to the former English king and saint, Edward the Confessor.

On arrival, Walsh was taken to a large, richly furnished chamber where, standing before the great fireplace, he found half a dozen men he knew, including Doyle and Harold. The Justiciar opened the proceedings.

"Nothing that is said in this meeting must be repeated outside," he cautioned them. "Otherwise we could lose the essential element of surprise." He paused. "Today, gentlemen, we face a very serious threat." He outlined the expected attack on Carrickmines. "We have one week to prepare. That is all." He turned to Walsh. "Had you any hint of this?"

Walsh was about to say that he had not, but then he remembered the dark-haired little O'Byrne girl. He briefly described the way she had been lurking about near Carrickmines. "I didn't think it was significant," he confessed.

"It was," Harold interrupted. The others looked at him. "I'd prefer not to tell you how I know, but this girl is the message carrier. That is certain."

"Do we have any idea of the size of this supposed attack?" Walsh asked. "I'm not sure the O'Byrnes would be strong enough to take Carrickmines anyway."

He heard a grunt of impatience from Harold.

"We must take this threat seriously, Walsh," the Justiciar reproved him. "That is our responsibility. And yours," he added with a stern look.

"I can bring ten fully armed and mounted men," Harold volunteered. "No doubt Walsh can come up with as many."

Two of the other gentlemen indicated that they could bring small contingents. The Justiciar told them that he was awaiting news of what forces the city could produce. "But the important thing," he pointed out, "is to collect our forces without being seen. I don't want word getting out to the O'Byrnes that we're expecting them. That of course," he added, "may limit how many men we can pull together."

"What about the squadron down at Dalkey?" Walsh asked. "That's a valuable force of fully trained men."

But to his surprise, the Justiciar looked doubtful and Harold also pursed his lips.

"We can't be sure," Harold pointed out, "that O'Byrne won't strike Dalkey as well. We must also consider," he glanced at the Justiciar, "that if we move the squadron from Dalkey to Carrickmines before the attack, O'Byrne is sure to hear of it. We don't want to warn him off."

There was an awkward pause. Though Harold's point seemed reasonable enough, Walsh had the feeling that there was something he was not being told about the squadron at Dalkey. He also noticed that so far Doyle had listened, but said nothing. Now, however, the saturnine merchant spoke.

"It always seemed unlikely to me," he quietly observed, "that O'Byrne would strike at Dalkey. If he wants to plunder the land around Dublin, then he must take Carrickmines first, because he cannot afford to have the fort operating behind him. As for Dalkey, the only thing of value there is my own house where, as it happens, I have few goods stored at the moment. But I would gladly sacrifice my house and a ship's cargo, in any case, for a more important cause." He looked around them all grimly. "The Justiciar has said that we face a serious threat. I beg to differ. If this information is correct, then this is not so much a threat as a great opportunity. By attacking Carrickmines, O'Byrne would give us all the provocation that we need. Let him come. Let us be waiting for him. Let him fall into a terrible trap. Then we smash him." He pounded his fist into his hand. "We destroy him entirely. Kill his men. And let all Ireland hear of it."

Even Harold looked a little shaken. Walsh felt himself grow pale at the Dublin man's dark cruelty. But Doyle had not yet done.

"Fill Carrickmines with men the night before. Bring them up in darkness. Concentrate our strength. The Dalkey squadron should be brought back to Dublin straight away. This very day. Nobody will think anything of that. They've only been kicking their heels down there anyway. Then hide them in Carrickmines with the rest."

"If we put all the troops into Carrickmines, there's a risk that O'Byrne may spot them," Harold pointed out.

"Hide them wherever you like," said Doyle with an impatient shrug. "Hide them in Saint Patrick's Cathedral for all I care. But you must be ready to bring them up decisively when O'Byrne arrives. That is what matters."

"I agree," the Justiciar said. "This is a chance to break these people once and for all."

And despite his loyalty to the English crown, Walsh could not help feeling sorry for the O'Byrnes and their people.

✢

The following day the squadron left Dalkey. Tidy had made anxious enquiries as to where they were going, but the soldiers assured him that they had been told there was no further need for them to be there, and that they were to return to Dublin. Since there had been no sign of the O'Byrnes since their arrival, these orders did not seem to surprise them. A much relieved Tom Tidy and Michael MacGowan watched them go.

Tom had not told MacGowan about his meeting with Harold; nor had MacGowan ever asked him whether he had passed on the secret. Tom imagined that he must be curious, however. While the troops were leaving, neither man said anything; but after they had gone and the two of them were walking up the street together, MacGowan asked, "Do you think they'll be going to Carrickmines?"

"They say they're going to Dublin."

MacGowan didn't ask anything else.

The next day was quiet. In the morning, Tom walked up to the high headland above the village and gazed out. The great bay of Dublin was a serene blue. Eastwards the sky melted into the sea. Looking down the coastline to the south, where beyond a green carpet of coastal plain the gentle cones of the hills rose in hazy tranquillity, it was hard to believe that, somewhere behind those hills, the O'Byrnes were preparing a terrible attack on Walsh's castle.

That afternoon, a small ship came into the anchorage behind the island. It was a bright little vessel, broad in the beam; just below the top of its single mast, there was a wooden basket in which a lookout could stand. Many of the cogs had these crow's nests. Above the crow's nest a red-and-blue pennant fluttered jauntily in the breeze. The Dalkey men went out in their boats and unloaded five barrels of nails, five of salt, and ten hogsheads of wine. Thus lightened, the vessel continued on its way, while the goods were taken to Doyle's fortified house where MacGowan carefully made up the tallies. That evening he asked Tom if he would cart the salt into Dublin the next morning.

When Tom came to load up at dawn, MacGowan announced that he would accompany him. "I've got to give the tallies to Doyle," he explained, "and then I'm going to see my betrothed." The morning was fine; the journey passed without incident, and the stalls were opening when they reached the High Cross and started down towards Winetavern Street.

Tom spent the day rather pleasantly in Dublin. The weather was fine. He visited the Palmer's old hospital of Saint John; he walked across the bridge to Oxmantown; later on, he went out of the eastern gate, wandered over to Saint Stephen's, and followed the little stream that led down to the old Viking Long Stone that still stood by the estuary beyond the Thingmount. By late afternoon, when he picked MacGowan up to take him home, Tom was feeling rather cheerful.

MacGowan seemed contented, too, though perhaps a little thoughtful as the cart rolled out past Saint Patrick's.

The area around Saint Patrick's had a particular character. Several religious houses had manors there whose privileges made them almost independent of the royal courts and administrators. Such independent feudal holdings were known as "Liberties" and the Dubliners had come to refer to the area by that name. It was just after they had passed the Liberties and taken the track eastwards towards the sea that MacGowan turned to Tom and remarked, "Someone was asking questions about you."

"Oh, who was that? Someone in Dublin?"

"No." MacGowan hesitated. "In Dalkey." He paused again before continuing. "A fisherman. Never mind who. It doesn't matter anyway. He came up to me yesterday and he asked me, 'I saw Tom Tidy coming out of the church the other evening. Any idea why he went in there so late?' I told him I didn't know. Reckoned you'd been delayed. Then he said to me, 'He didn't say anything to you about it then? Nothing unusual?' So I just looked at him a bit puzzled and I said, 'Nothing at all. What would he have to say?' And he nodded and told me, 'Forget it. You're all right.' " MacGowan stared ahead, not wanting to look at Tom, it seemed. "I wasn't sure whether to tell you, yesterday. But this can only mean one thing, Tom. They're wondering if you heard anything. I don't know if you told anyone what you told me, but if anything goes wrong at Carrickmines, it's you they'll be coming after. I thought I ought to let you know."

For a little while the cart rolled on in silence. Tom said nothing. MacGowan supposed that, when he had finished digesting this information, Tom would say something. But he didn't. The cart took the lane that led southwards through a village called Donnybrook.

"Tom," MacGowan said at last, "you'd better go back into Dublin for a time. You can stay at my brother's house. He'll be glad to have you. I told him today you might be needing to stay with him awhile—though of course I didn't tell him why. He lives inside the wall. No one will trouble you there. I'll watch your house in Dalkey for you. Maybe in a month you can come back. I'll try to find out. But don't run the risk of staying, Tom. There's no need."

Tom didn't reply. Soon afterwards they went down the long track that led to the big strand of the bay, but even then, as they passed round the friendly headland at the bay's southern end and came in sight of Dalkey island, still Tom Tidy spoke not a word.

❖

If Doyle put a silver penny between two of his fingers, he could make it move across his knuckles from one finger to another with easy rapidity. This act of prestidigitation amused and relaxed him and he often did it when he was thinking. He was doing it now, as he sat in his countinghouse and thought about the situation in Dalkey.

Doyle's house on Winetavern Street consisted of three floors above a cellar. The main hall and kitchen were at ground level. On the floor above, which jutted out to overhang the street, there were three chambers, one of which served Doyle as his countinghouse. It had a window with glass panes looking down onto Winetavern Street, and beside the window an oak table on which were several stacks of silver pennies. Also on the table lay a scattering of pennies cut in two, or into four, to be used as halfpennies and farthings for smaller transactions.

If the penny had now made its progress back and forth across Doyle's knuckles a dozen times, it was because the question occupying his mind was by no means easy.

The arrangements for defending Carrickmines and dealing with the O'Byrnes had been carefully planned. Everything was working out very well. Their preparations had been so thorough that he did not think he could have improved on them had he made all the arrangements himself. There were only two days to wait.

There was just one problem: Tom Tidy. He knew that many people considered him a harsh man, but his secret discussion with MacGowan had left him in no doubt: Tidy must not remain in Dalkey. He had already served his purpose and done so very well; but if Tidy remained in Dalkey now, it seemed to Doyle inevitable that the carrier would be killed; he couldn't see any way round it. While Doyle was ready to run big risks himself—and to be ruthless when necessary—he had no wish to see Tom Tidy sacrificed. With luck, after MacGowan had given him the chilling piece of information, Tidy would return to Dublin of his own accord. Doyle certainly hoped so.

⁙

Two more nights. When Tom Tidy had parted from Michael MacGowan he had managed, at least outwardly, to appear unruffled. He had still made no mention of the danger he might be in, and bade MacGowan good night, he was pleased to note, in the calmest way imaginable. Then, just as deliberately, he saw to the horses, exactly as usual. After that, he went into his house, cut two large slices from yesterday's loaf of bread, two generous pieces of

cheese, and poured himself a tankard of ale. All as usual. Then he
sat down, very quietly, and began to consume them, staring straight
ahead as he did so. Afterwards, although there were still some hours
of summer daylight left, he decided to go to bed.

But he could not sleep. Try as he might, his tired brain would
not give itself up to unconsciousness.

What was he to do? Was MacGowan right? Should he return to
Dublin? The question in its various forms kept reasserting itself, a
voice in his head that would not be stilled. After a while he got up
and went out into the yard.

The sun was sinking behind the hill. Usually this was a time
when the rock-strewn common between the village and the shore
would be illumined by great gold-and-orange streaks and the fleeces
on the scattered sheep would glisten warmly; but this evening a
crowd of clouds had forgathered along the western horizon, blocking out the sunset. Past Tom Tidy's yard, under the harshly fading
light, the fields which were nearly ready for harvest seemed to have
turned a sullen bronze; and beyond, the common now looked
strangely desolate. The air was warm. Tom remained there, silently
watching as the common imperceptibly changed from deepening
green into grey.

The dusk was setting in when he noticed the first moving
shadow. He realised what it was, of course. He had been staring at
a small rock for so long that it had seemed to move. A trick of the
imagination. Nothing more. Sure enough, before long, other rocks
were seeming to move about in the twilight. He continued to gaze.
Were they rocks, though? Or sheep? Or other shapes? Could there
be ghosts, or even people, moving out there? Were they watching
him? Waiting to come to the house? Would there be a battering at
the door in the middle of the night, a forced entry? And then? He
found that his heart was beating fast. He took a deep breath and
told himself not to be foolish.

Still he remained there as the darkness grew deeper. Above him
and eastwards, over the sea, the glimmering night sky was clear.

Soon, the last sliver of the waning moon would hang like a silver sigh amongst the stars. One more night and then . . . Blackness. The night of the attack. The night of whatever terrible trap it was that Harold and the Justiciar had prepared. Doyle, too, no doubt. Darkness, now, was everywhere. The shadows on the common had all gone. There could be a hundred men out there, coming towards him, and he would not see them.

He knew he must sleep. Yet still he could not. A wave of fatigue would oppress his brain; but then his fear, like a pale dagger, would strike through the darkness at his heart. Dalkey was usually such a pleasant place. The high headland behind him with its views over the bay was like a friendly companion. But not anymore. The dark shape of the hill seemed like a huge, threatening mound from which, at any moment, the ghostly forces of vengeance might issue forth. The O'Byrnes were not far away. All around him in Dalkey, there were probably fishermen who were in league with them. Which of his neighbours could he trust? He had no idea. Their faces came before him one by one, in his mind, familiar faces suddenly transformed into masks of rage and hatred, until at last even his dear friend MacGowan seemed to be among them, gazing at him in his curious way, with one eye closed and the open eye growing larger and larger, terrible, cold, and malevolent.

Why was he staying here? Why wait? Let them burn his house and his carts if they wished, reduce him to poverty. Why should he await his own destruction?

In the end, however, fatigue overcame even his fear, and Tom Tidy wearily went back inside and got into bed. But before he did so, he did something which he had never done before: he barred the door.

The next morning Tom went straight to MacGowan and told him he was leaving for Dublin.

"You've no need to worry at all," MacGowan told him. "I'll be

round at your house every day. I'll keep an eye on the place." He'd
bring Tom's remaining horses to his own house, he promised.
"You're doing the right thing, Tom," he assured him. Tom could see
that his friend was quite relieved. Back at his house, he harnessed his
two best horses to the big cart and took one more horse on a lead
rein behind. Then he set out to Dublin.

He couldn't help feeling a welcome sense of relief as he came
down the long, straight line of Saint Francis's Street, where the high-
gabled houses pressed close together and came out onto the open
crossroads where he turned right to enter the city. A hundred yards
behind him stood Ailred the Palmer's old hospital; on his right, the
green where the big summer fairs were held; and in front of him, the
great western gate—more splendid than ever since it had been rebuilt with its two bulky towers and a little gaol. Through the western gate he went, therefore, with a shade more confidence than he
had felt before, and was soon at MacGowan's brother's house.

"How long will you be staying?" MacGowan's brother asked.
"Michael told me you might be coming," he added, without further
comment. No doubt he was glad to see his brother's friend, if not
overjoyed.

"Perhaps a week or two," Tom said, suddenly feeling that he was
imposing on the other's good nature too much.

The craftsman's house was quite spacious, with a big backyard.
His wife and children looked a little surprised to see Tom, but made
him welcome and insisted that he sleep in the house beside the
kitchen rather than in the loft over the stable as he had offered. A
good Irishman would have known how to sink comfortably down
on a bench and pass the time of day for a few hours without worrying himself; but although he had lived in Ireland all his life, Tom
Tidy's English nature would not allow him to rest so easy. True, he
did sit for an hour, and it was all as friendly as could be; but somehow after that, he felt he was in the way, and making an excuse he
went out for a walk.

The house was only a short step from the fine old church of

Saint Audoen, which lay just within the former riverside wall. Below the wall, the ground descended a short, steep slope, past some cookhouses and bakeries, to the level area of the land reclaimed from the river. There were views of the Liffey from the old wall by the church, and with the pleasant smell of the bakeries below it should have been considered a pleasant place. But to Tom Tidy in his present mood, its grey stones were gloomy, and even the tall shape of Saint Audoen's seemed oppressive. After walking about there for a while, he felt no more at ease and, not wishing to return to the house yet, he wandered off in the direction of the crown of the city's ridge and the precincts of Christ Church.

Perhaps it was sunnier up there than on the lower part of the ridge, but as he entered the precincts, Tom felt better. The thickset mass of Christ Church seemed solid and comforting. He went inside.

There was no doubt that Christ Church was the Christian heart of Dublin. Saint Patrick's, with its soaring Gothic vaults, was high and magnificent and seemed to have every intention of staring down old Christ Church or any other church that dared to raise its head. For a long time, indeed, the canons of Saint Patrick's and the monks of Christ Church had been frequently at loggerheads with each other. But that rivalry had finally worn itself out, and the two cathedrals were friendly enough now.

But it was in the quietness of Christ Church that one felt the presence of the ancient Celtic tradition of Patrick and Colum Cille. Its pillars and arches seemed to Tom to be as protective as a castle. The stained-glass windows, like pages from an antique Gospel book, gleamed softly with a mysterious light. From time to time, a monk would pass in the shadows.

Tom wandered there contentedly. He looked at the piece of the True Cross and the other holy relics. He walked amongst the tombs. The most impressive of these was the big raised slab and carved effigy of Strongbow. It was typical of the Plantagenets to have ensured that their vassal should have been given his final resting place and monument in one of the island's holiest places. Strongbow's tomb was the emblem of their rule over Ireland. But the greatest treasure of Christ Church, more venerated even than the True Cross, was the Staff of Saint Patrick himself.

It was nearly two centuries now since the monks of Christ Church, during the rule of Archbishop O'Toole, had secured this great treasure from its former sanctuary up in Ulster. It had been a triumph for their own prestige, of course. But the presence of the Staff in Dublin had a subtler significance also.

For if the English had failed to impose order on the whole of Ireland, the Church itself reflected a similar split. As far as the Pope was concerned, the King of England was the patron of the Irish Church and the Irish bishops owed him the allegiance proper to a feudal monarch. If the English king had increasingly insisted on having Englishmen as bishops in his Irish realm, the Pope might sometimes demur, but he mostly went along with it. In practice however, this English domination was only really effective in the areas under royal control. Most of the priests up in the north and west were Irish, preaching to Irish-speaking populations. Indeed, so great was the split that the English archbishop of Saint Patrick's own Ulster see of Armagh did not even reside in Armagh, where he was not very welcome, but in an English-speaking area to the south. It was ironic in a way, therefore, that the great Staff of the Irish patron saint should be in the heart of English-administered Dublin.

The Staff was magnificent. The great golden case which enclosed it was encrusted with gems. Tom knew that the saint had received it from the hand of Christ himself, and that it was often referred to as the Staff of Jesus, the Bachall Iosa. He gazed at it with awe.

"The staff of a hero." He had not noticed the priest come up beside him. He was a fair young man with an open, rather simple-minded face and he had addressed Tom in a local English dialect that suggested he had only recently arrived in Ireland.

"Indeed," said Tom politely.

"Nothing could frighten him," the young priest said. "Not the High King. Not the druids. He was fearless."

In the centuries since the beginnings of the Irish Church, the legends about its leaders had continued to grow. Like everyone else, Tom knew and believed in them all. He knew how Saint Patrick had confronted the High King and challenged his druids, in the manner of an Old Testament prophet, to see whose god could make an unquenchable fire; he knew how Saint Patrick had performed many miracles and even banished the snakes—a legend that would have come as a great surprise to the saint himself.

"Yes," he agreed, "he was fearless."

"Because he trusted in God," said the young priest, and Tom bowed his head in acknowledgement. The priest, however, had not finished his reflections. He gave Tom an engaging smile. "It is a fine thing for you and me that the tomb of Strongbow and the Staff of Saint Patrick should be there in this cathedral," he remarked.

"Indeed," said Tom again. And then, a little curiously, "Why is that?"

"They were both English," said the young man triumphantly. "That's us," he added. "Stout of heart," and having declared this great truth, he gave Tom Tidy a friendly nod and went upon his way.

Tom Tidy was aware of enough history to see the funny side of this. British Saint Patrick was, no doubt; but could one really call him English? As for Strongbow, did he think of the great Anglo-Norman lord as an Englishman like himself or like this simple priest? He scarcely knew. But there was one thing the young man had said that was not so funny. "Stout of heart." Strongbow and Saint Patrick, in their different ways, were certainly that. He gazed at the gleaming Bachall Iosa. Was he stout of heart? Not on his present performance, running in a panic from Dalkey to Dublin, forcing himself as a guest upon a family he hardly knew, and all on account of a threat that might not even be real. He shook his head sadly. He could not take much pride in himself today. Indeed, he began to think his behaviour was rather contemptible.

Half an hour later the Dublin MacGowans were surprised when Tom Tidy returned and informed them that he would not be staying after all. By late afternoon his wagon was trundling back past Harold's Cross. And there were still some hours of daylight left when, to his horror, Michael MacGowan saw Tom Tidy coming up the street and, running out towards him, received from his happy face the news.

"I've changed my mind. I'm staying here."

"You can't," MacGowan blurted out. But Tom had already driven past.

That evening, as the dusk was falling, Michael MacGowan did all he could to persuade his friend to leave again. "What is the necessity," he demanded, "of putting yourself in danger for no reason at all?" But he got nowhere. Tom was adamant. As a result, MacGowan spent a sleepless night. Before dawn, he went to his yard, mounted his horse, and rode out of Dalkey. As he rode through the grey predawn, the words of a secret conversation he had recently had were echoing, coldly, in his ear.

"He must leave, MacGowan. Or else . . ."

"I realise that," he had replied, "but I'm not going to kill him, you know."

"You will not be asked to do it, though the O'Byrnes might," the voice of the other had calmly replied. "Make him leave."

They came into Carrickmines during the night. It was cleverly done. They did not come in groups, but singly, leading their horses through the darkness with sacking on their hoofs, so that they should neither be seen nor heard. Nor were they, for even the stars were hidden behind a blanket of cloud. In this manner, at dead of night, the Dalkey squadron, Harold's men, and all the rest—a total of sixty horsemen and as many foot soldiers—passed through the gates of Carrickmines and vanished inside like so many ghostly warriors into a magic hill.

When dawn arose, Carrickmines looked exactly the same as before. The gate was shut, but that was not unusual. Corralled inside, the horses sometimes made a little noise, but the thick stone walls trapped these sounds within. In the middle of the morning, Walsh appeared on the walls with his falcon. He loosed it into the sky where it flew for some time before returning. That was the only movement seen that morning at the castle of Carrickmines.

It was in the afternoon, when he had gone up onto the wall alone, that Walsh thought he saw the girl concealed amongst some rocks a little way to the south. Unless she had been there the night before, he was sure she could not have any idea that Carrickmines was full of soldiers. After a short while he went down again. To make everything seem normal, he opened the gates and let a cart, driven by one of his men, leave the castle and creak across to a neighbouring farm, returning later with some provisions. In the meantime, the gate was left casually half open, and two of his children went out to play. They practised hurling until the cart came back, jumping on it as it went in through the gate, which was still left ajar for some time after it was inside. He knew that the dark-haired girl must have observed all this, because when he went up onto the wall as the children came in, he had seen her watching carefully from another vantage point some way farther up the slope.

In the early evening, however, when he went up again, he could not see her and concluded that she had gone.

"I am sure," he said to Harold when he had descended, "that they will attack tonight."

✤

There was something strange about Dalkey today. Tom felt it from the first moment when he went out into the street. Was it just his imagination? A case of nerves? He considered that, of course. But he didn't think so. Yet it had been a perfect Dalkey morning. The dawn

mist had given way to a light, salty haze. As the sky cleared to a soft
blue, little clouds came floating in, white as the spume from the sea.
Tom had even felt a sense of cheerfulness as he came out of his
house and began to walk down the street. Seeing one of his neighbours, he had wished him good morning, just as he would on any
other day. But though the man had answered something, it had
seemed to Tom that there was an awkwardness in his manner. A few
moments later, he had seen one of the fishermen mending nets in
front of his cottage give him a strange look; and as he went farther,
he had the distinct impression that he was being watched from both
sides of the street. It was an eerie sensation, as if he had suddenly become an unwelcome guest in his own village.

Then he had gone into MacGowan's house and found that
his friend had disappeared. He had looked around Dalkey and
asked several people, but no one seemed to have any idea where
MacGowan had gone. It was very strange. After a while Tom had returned to his home and stayed there for the rest of the morning. At
noon, he went round to MacGowan's again, but there was still no
sign of him. On his way back this time, he met a couple of men and
a woman in the street. Though they acknowledged his greeting, he
noticed the same awkwardness. One of the men tried to avert his
eyes, and the woman said, "I thought you were in Dublin," in a tone
of voice that suggested she thought that Dublin was where he belonged. By the time he reached his house again, he was in a sombre
mood.

There were only hours to go: a warm afternoon, a long summer
evening, the slowly gathering dusk, and then, at last, blackness. And
in the middle of that blackness, the terrible trap at Carrickmines.
The thought of it oppressed him. He wished he could put it out of
his mind. More than once, as he sat in his house alone, Tom wondered whether he had been wrong. MacGowan had vanished; was it
because he was afraid? His neighbours seemed to be no longer his
friends; did they know something he did not? Should he go back to
Dublin, after all? But two things prevented him. The first was

shame. If he turned up at MacGowan's brother's house again now, wouldn't he look like an idiot? The second might have been bravery, or it might have been obstinacy. But hadn't he taken a decision to stay here in Dalkey and face the danger, he reminded himself? He wasn't going to back down now.

The afternoon passed slowly. He tried to keep himself occupied. He washed down the horses and found chores to do indoors. Nobody came by. He paced about restlessly in the yard. By mid-afternoon he felt like going to the little church, but he forced himself to wait. He'd go at the usual time, not before. He went into the barn and cleaned out all the carts, not because it needed doing but to fill some more time, until, at last, he felt the hour approaching. And he was standing in the yard, gauging the light and just about to leave, when glancing out towards the common, he caught sight of something by one of the rocks. It was hard to tell what it was. A dark sheep, perhaps—many of the Dalkey sheep had dark fleeces. A trick of the light?

Or something else. A girl's black hair?

The dark-haired girl. Why should she have come into his mind? It was absurd. His imagination was playing games with him, and he knew it. He shook his head impatiently.

She would have a good view of his yard from out there. She'd have seen all his movements. Was there someone watching the other side of his house? Anybody in Dalkey could be doing that. He stared at the dark patch beside the rock, seeing if he could discern a face. He could not—and the reason he couldn't, he told himself firmly, was that there was no face there to be seen. He took a deep breath and turned away, refusing to let himself look at the spot anymore. He began to walk out of the yard. It was time to go to church. As he passed into the empty street, he looked back, and saw the dark-haired girl spring up and run swiftly from her hiding place towards the far end of the village.

The church was quiet. The shafts of afternoon sunshine falling from its small windows bathed the interior in a warm and gentle light. Nobody else was there. He went to his usual place behind the screen and, trembling, knelt down to pray. He said a paternoster, and several Ave Marias. Then another paternoster. The words seemed to coil themselves around him, soothing, healing. He accepted their protective power, gratefully.

He had been in quiet prayer for some time when he heard the church door opening.

There were two of them. One had a soft footfall; the other sounded heavier, as if he was wearing stout boots. There was no reason why two people shouldn't have entered the church, of course. But his mind raced back to the previous week. He couldn't help it. Was it the girl again? And her unknown companion? He felt himself go cold.

"You are sure he is here?" A deep voice. A voice he didn't know.

"I am sure." It was said softly, yet the voice sounded familiar. He froze.

"Where is he, then?"

If there was an answer, it was inaudible. But it made no difference. The footsteps were coming straight in his direction.

They were coming for him. There was nothing to be done. What a fool he'd been, when he could have stayed in Dublin. But now it was too late. He hadn't even a weapon with which to defend himself. They were going to kill him: he knew it for a certainty. Would they kill him there, in the church? No. This was Ireland. They wouldn't do that. They'd be taking him to a quiet place somewhere. Then he'd disappear. Perhaps he'd soon be out there, buried under Dalkey common. He hesitated whether to stay on his knees in prayer or get up and face them like a man; the footsteps were coming very close. They stopped. He turned and looked up.

It was MacGowan. And a tall, saturnine man, whom he recognised as Doyle. He frowned. His friend? And the Dublin merchant? Surely they could not be in league with O'Byrne? His mind reeled at the thought of such a betrayal. Then Doyle spoke.

"You must leave, Tidy. You must come with us now." And as

Tom stared uncomprehending, the merchant's dark face broke into a kindly smile. "MacGowan has told me everything. You're a brave man, Thomas Tidy. But we can't let you stay here." He reached out his long arm and took Tom gently but firmly by the elbow. "It's time to go."

Tom got up slowly. He frowned. "You mean . . . ?" he began.

"I mean that I'm taking you to Dublin," Doyle said quietly. "You'll be staying in my house for a little while, until this business is over."

"You think they know? They might suspect," Tom pointed out, "but they may not know."

"I'm sure they know." It was said with finality.

Tom considered.

"Harold must have talked," he said sadly. "There's no one else." He sighed. "Though even so," he added, "I don't know how it would have got to the O'Byrnes."

He saw Doyle and MacGowan exchange glances. He couldn't guess what they might know, but he realised that Doyle had informants everywhere.

"There are no secrets in Ireland, Tidy," the merchant said.

They led him out, and he didn't argue anymore. Doyle had a cart waiting with a servant holding the reins. "MacGowan will see to your house," the merchant said, as he manoeuvred Tom into the cart.

A dozen people had gathered outside to watch. Tom glanced at them. But though they were watching him, it was really Doyle they were looking at. As the merchant got into the cart after him, he stared round them all with a stern, dark scowl, and they bowed their heads. Tom couldn't help admiring the man: his power was palpable. As the cart rolled out of Dalkey and took the lane towards Dublin, he had to admit that he felt a secret sense of relief.

⁜

It was nearly midnight. Far above, high clouds obscured the stars; the black shadow of the moon hung, unseen, in another world.

To Harold, standing beside Walsh on the castle wall, the surrounding blackness was so silent, so intimate, that it seemed as if Carrickmines were enclosed within a huge oyster shell. In the castle yard below, the sixty horses were crowded together; their soft grunts and snorts, and the occasional scraping of hoofs pawing the ground, were the only sound within the walls.

Harold peered out towards the rock-strewn plain. Though his eyes were well accustomed to the dark, and he could sometimes make out vague shapes in the distance, he could not detect any sign of movement. He strained his ears, but heard nothing. It seemed almost unnatural, this smothered, black silence. He waited tensely.

Yet despite the tension, he could not help it if his mind strayed once or twice. He found himself thinking of his family. It was for them he was doing this, after all. Even if I am killed tonight, he thought, the sacrifice will have been necessary. It was worth it. He remembered the meetings with the Justiciar, and with Tom Tidy. The fellow from Dalkey had been brave enough, in his way. Harold was glad that the Justiciar had not made him disclose the source of his information, so that he'd been able to protect the Dalkey man. He'd been very discreet. He hadn't even mentioned Tidy to his wife. So unless Tidy had told his secret to someone else, he should be safe.

He felt a nudge at his elbow.

"Listen." Walsh's voice, very low, beside him.

Horses. Somewhere out there in front of the gate. Harold heard them now: a faint sound of hoofs, a snort. How many? Impossible to know. Not less than a dozen, he thought; but it could be a hundred. This was it, then. O'Byrne had come. "Get the men mounted," Walsh whispered. "I'll keep watch." Harold turned and hurried down from the wall. As he did so, he thought he heard the sound of footfalls coming towards the gate. Were they bringing ladders to scale the walls? A moment later he was running round the castle yard, hissing the order to mount, while one of his men called out softly, "Torches."

They were well prepared. Nobody spoke. Even the horses

seemed to know that they must be silent. The men on the gate had their orders. The foot soldiers had been waiting in Walsh's hall. Each carried two torches which they would now be lighting at the big brazier in there. On the order, they would rush out, handing a torch to each rider; then they would either race up to defend the walls or stream out of the gate after the cavalry. Walsh would make that call.

Harold waited as the moments passed. He was at the head of the mounted men, and he'd be the first man out of the gate. He felt his horse quiver, and patted its neck softly. He was still trying to hear what was happening outside, but the castle walls did not let through much sound. He looked up to where Walsh had been standing. He thought he could make out his shadowy form up there, but he wasn't sure.

Bang! The sudden crash at the gate took everyone by surprise. Harold's horse reared and he almost came off.

"Battering ram." Walsh's voice, quiet but distinct, from the wall. "Get ready."

"Bring torches," Harold called quietly. A moment later the lights appeared on his right and came streaming towards the riders.

A second crash. The gate shuddered, and there was a sound of splintering wood.

"One more," called Walsh, and Harold signalled to the men on the gate. All the riders had torches now, including himself. "Walls are clear," called Walsh. There was a brief pause.

And then came a third, shuddering crash at the gate.

"Now!" cried Harold.

The attackers outside did not have a proper battering ram, which would have been suspended on rope slings. All they had was a large, thick pole with which they had been taking cumbersome runs at the gate. And they had just started back to make a fourth run when, instead of remaining barricaded, the gates suddenly opened and a stream of cavalry with blazing torches came charging out and bore down upon them. It was a terrifying sight. Dropping the battering ram, they scattered into the darkness.

Harold rode forward. The torches were everywhere, swooping in the air, darting hither and thither on the ground. The attackers were like fleeting shadows in the flashing and flickering light. Swords were slashing; there was the sound of metal meeting metal. Somewhere ahead he heard a voice cry out, "We are destroyed."

They'd caught them by surprise all right; but the business wasn't going to be so easy. The terrain was uneven. His horse had already nearly stumbled. The torch he carried gave light, but it also used his free hand. After a few moments, Harold pulled up and looked around. He heard Walsh's voice approaching from behind. He could see the running forms of the men on foot, but where were the horsemen? While the torch illuminated everything that was close, it was hard to see far beyond its bright light. A little way ahead, though, he thought he could make out the vague shapes of mounted men. With a single, sweeping motion of his arm, he hurled the torch into the air, in a high arc towards the shapes ahead.

⁘

The first flicker had come just before midnight. A tiny pinpoint, a glimmer across the water. A candle in a glass-fronted box—modest but effective. The light came from the tip of Dalkey island. Almost at once, an answering light came from the first of the three ships. Another light shone out now, from the boat anchored just past the last of the rocks. They were useful, these glass-fronted lamps. Nobody in Dalkey possessed such a thing; they'd been supplied from Dublin. Two more lights appeared now, from the other ships. So deep was the night that, had it not been for these little intimations across the water, their silent shapes would scarcely have been seen in the blackness. There was just enough breeze to bring the ships into the anchorage under sail. As they came in, the boats from the shore came swiftly to their sides. Ropes were thrown; more lamps appeared. Voices called out softly. On the shore, carts were waiting. The whole town of Dalkey was up and busy that night; for the hours of darkness were brief and there was much work to be done.

✥

Walsh rode beside Harold. The riders all kept close together. Their torches had gone out, but the sky overhead had cleared and the stars gave enough light to see the track.

In the first dash out of Carrickmines, O'Byrne had managed to pull away from them; but he had not been able to increase his lead. As they followed the track up towards the Wicklow Mountains, he was occasionally out of sight, but never for long. Sometimes Walsh would hear the sound of the hoofbeats ahead, sometimes not. At first he had supposed that the Irish riders would scatter in order to lose them; but they had kept to the track instead, and it soon became clear that they intended to use the bridges over the two rivers they had to cross before they could reach the wild high ground beyond.

And that was what had happened. Nearly an hour had passed since they had clattered over the second bridge, and here they were riding amongst the hilltops, under the gleaming stars, on the great plateau that stretched all the way to Glendalough. The stars were making a faint sheen on the dark heath as the two parties of ghostly horsemen passed across it. For the most part they rode in silence, but after they had been riding across the plateau for some time Walsh remarked, "There are woods farther on. They'll probably scatter and try to lose us there."

"We'll run them down first," Harold replied.

Walsh was not so sure. There was an implacable force in Harold that he could not help admiring; but that didn't mean that he was going to catch the clever Irishman. He had already noticed that whenever they increased their pace, O'Byrne did the same, and when they had to walk to rest their horses, the Irishman did likewise. If O'Byrne let them keep in sight, he never let them get close. He might have been caught by surprise down at Carrickmines, but ever since, he had been coolly calculating. Indeed, Walsh thought uneasily, it was almost as if O'Byrne was playing a game with them.

This uncomfortable idea had been with him for some time, and he had considered carefully, before he spoke again.

"I think he's leading us a dance," he finally remarked.

"What do you mean?"

"O'Byrne. He wants us to follow him."

Harold received this news in silence. They rode on for another quarter mile.

"We'll hunt him down," he growled.

They continued their progress as before. O'Byrne kept his distance; they never got any closer. Ahead, the dark shape of the wood came into sight and slowly grew more definite. They drew closer. The men ahead entered the wood and were instantly swallowed up. They were nearly at the wood themselves now. Another moment and they'd be in. Walsh was still beside Harold, and Harold was pressing forward strongly.

"Stop!" Walsh called out. He couldn't help it. An overwhelming instinct, a certainty born of years living on the frontier made him do it. He pulled up his horse. "It's a trap," he cried.

The other riders brushed past him. He heard Harold curse. But they did not pause. A moment later they were swallowed up in the darkness ahead, pressing on regardless.

It was a trap. He knew it in his bones. In this deserted wood up on the high ground, miles from any kind of help, they made a perfect target for an ambush. O'Byrne undoubtedly knew every yard of this woodland; he could probably ride through it with his eyes shut. It would be easy for him to double round in the blackness and slaughter them all. They were doing exactly what he wanted. Walsh listened. At any moment he expected to hear the cries of anguish ahead as his friends were ambushed. He heard nothing; but it was only a matter of time.

He sighed. So what was he doing, waiting out here? Was he going to turn back? Leave the others to their fate? Of course not. He couldn't do that. However foolish, and whatever the consequences, he had to go in after them. He drew his sword, and walked his horse forward, into the darkness of the wood.

The track was like a tunnel. The branches overhead closed out the stars. The trees on each side were tall presences, felt rather than seen in the blackness. He strained to hear the sound of hoofbeats ahead or of any movement in the surrounding woods, but there was nothing. Only silence. The track made a turn. Still nothing. His horse almost stumbled, but he caught him. He wondered how far ahead the others could be and whether to call out.

The movement from his right was so sudden that he hadn't even time to think; a crash from the undergrowth as a horse and rider sprang forward onto the track and almost collided with him. Automatically, he slashed with his sword towards where the rider seemed to be, but his blade met nothing. He wheeled to strike again. But how do you fight in the pitch dark, when you might as well be blind? You fight by instinct, he realised, because there is nothing else to do. He raised his sword and struck again. This time the blow was met. There was a ringing bang of metal on metal, and a wrenching shock down his arm. He winced; there was a red-hot pain in his wrist. The sword in his hand felt suddenly heavy, but he started to swing it up to strike again.

A crash. The blow smashed into the base of the blade so hard that it drove the sword clean out of his hand. He gave a gasp of pain. His wrist was bent over at a crazy angle and he did not seem to be able to move it. He heard his sword strike the ground. He had just time to wonder where his assailant was and if he could somehow see in the dark when, to his horror, he felt a hand seize his foot and heave it up, toppling him from his saddle and sending him down to fall with a heavy thud on the ground. Half winded, his wrist now sending hot daggers of pain up his arm, he groped with his free hand for his sword, which had to be lying near, but couldn't find it. Then a voice spoke, above him.

"You're beaten, John Walsh." The words were spoken in Irish.

He tried to look up, and answered in kind. "You know my name. But who are you?"

"Not a name that will do you any good."

Walsh didn't need any further telling. It was O'Byrne himself. He couldn't see his face, but he knew it all the same. His left hand was still trying to locate his sword.

"You're done for, John Walsh."

It was true enough. Walsh took a deep breath.

"If you're going to kill me," he said, "you'd better get on with it."

He awaited the blow, but none came. Instead he thought he heard a quiet chuckle.

"I'll be taking your horse. It's a fine horse you have. You can walk home." Walsh heard his horse move as O'Byrne took the bridle. "What's his name?"

"Finbarr."

"A good Irish name. Are you hurt?"

"I think I broke my wrist."

"Ah." O'Byrne was already starting to move away. Walsh got up painfully. He'd have some bruises in the morning. He could make out the shadows of the two horses moving down the track. He stared after them. Then he called out.

"What's the game?"

But the only reply he thought he could discern was a soft laugh.

⁓✥⁓

Dawn would soon be breaking over the sea. The sky was still dark, but a faint hint of lightness was just perceptible along the eastern horizon, and soon Dalkey island would turn from a shadow into a shape.

Michael MacGowan gazed across the water. The last of the three ships was already well out to sea. The business had been accomplished.

The organisation had been brilliant—there was no question about the fact and he was proud of it. The whole town of Dalkey had been busily employed that night in what was probably the biggest single unloading of cargo that the little harbour had ever seen. Hogsheads of wine, bales of fine cloth, barrels of spices. And not a single load dropped in the water. A miracle, really.

Everything had been stored away by dawn. Some of the goods were in Doyle's fortified house; but there were other, secret hiding places that MacGowan had prepared. Every cart and barrow in the town had been brought into service. Tom Tidy's transport had come in useful there; indeed, his unexpected return from Dublin the day before had meant that there was another large wagon available that MacGowan had not originally been counting on. All in all, things could hardly have gone better. But it had been a nerve-racking business dealing with Tidy, all the same. His presence there could have spoiled everything. For needless to say, though he had been living in Dalkey some time now, Tom Tidy knew nothing about Doyle's business.

When Doyle had contrived to get himself appointed as water bailiff, there had been little doubt in anybody's mind what the true nature of the arrangement would be. Indeed, the feudal world was largely constructed upon such accommodations. True, the obligations which a feudal king and his officials could exact from the lords and landholders were a good deal more thoroughgoing than the rough-and-ready tribute payments of old Celtic Ireland, but especially in the great feudal Liberties, where the lord was almost like a petty king, and in the Marcher borderlands, where law and order only existed if the local lord could impose it, the feudal landholder essentially paid the crown a ground rent after which he was free to make what he could of the place. In a similar fashion, collectors of royal taxes were often in practice and sometimes in name, tax farmers. The royal officials in Dublin, with modest manpower and falling revenues, were glad enough to get in what taxes they could. So if Doyle could bring them a reasonable stream of revenue from the customs due at Dalkey, they were unlikely to trouble him too much over the details of his accounting. If certain discrepancies and irregularities may have existed, if a certain percentage of the shipments was imperfectly accounted for, well, that was the merchant's profit from his office. It might not be quite legal, it might not be quite moral, but given the circumstances on the island at the time, it was surely the most intelligent way to proceed. Entrepreneurial talent, in government as in trade, thrives on profit.

This was what Doyle had done. The accounts he submitted were always thorough, and seemed to be complete. And they were, nearly. But the tallies which MacGowan kept differed from Doyle's official records by about ten percent. The goods which left Doyle's strong house all bore his official stamp stating that customs dues had been paid. And so they had: but one shilling in ten had gone to him instead of to the Exchequer. An interesting variation on a theme, and even harder to check, was to stamp the goods and send them on at cost price to Bristol, where they could be landed duty free. The procedure was a little cumbersome, but he had used it once or twice as a favour to kinsmen or friends with whom he did business at the English port.

Perhaps it was inevitable that one day he would be tempted to go further. The thought had occurred to him in the past, of course, but he probably would not have attempted it if MacGowan had not shown himself so skilled at managing the people at Dalkey. By the time that the opportunity—a truly splendid opportunity—had presented itself, MacGowan had convinced him that he could pull the business off successfully and safely. Yet even so, the powerful merchant had hesitated. The risks were large. Had he been caught in his usual skimming of the customs dues—and proving this would have been difficult anyway—he risked little more than a reprimand and a payment to the authorities. He might not even have lost his office. But this wholesale smuggling was another matter entirely. For a start, it meant involving not just his own man, but the whole of Dalkey. Discovery would have serious consequences: loss of office, a hefty fine, perhaps worse. The profit, the customs due on three entire shiploads of valuable goods, would be huge, but he was a rich man anyway and had no need of the money. So why did he do it?

He'd asked the question of himself, and he thought he knew the answer. It was the risk. The difficulty and the danger of the thing were what really appealed to him. No doubt his distant Viking ancestors would have felt the same way. It was a long time since the powerful, saturnine merchant and city father had had any real excitement. This was an adventure on the high seas.

The planning and logistics had been formidable. The three ships had to come from different ports, meet off the southern coast of Ireland, and proceed together. The goods had to be unloaded with incredible speed, in the dark; and then they had to be hidden and later on distributed for sale in several markets, without arousing suspicion. It was only after all these complex problems had been provided for that the huge difficulty had arisen—the sudden appearance of the squadron in Dalkey, to keep watch on the coast. As soon as he had reported this, MacGowan had assumed that the plans would have to be aborted.

"I suppose it's over," he had said to Doyle sadly, and had been surprised when the merchant had calmly responded, "Not at all."

In fact, Doyle had rather enjoyed the extra challenge. How could he persuade the squadron to leave Dalkey? By convincing them that the enemy they were seeking was actually going to strike somewhere else. The castle of Carrickmines had been the obvious choice. But the merchant's genius lay in the way it was done. It had been MacGowan who had put Tom Tidy into his mind originally, when he had warned him that the carter was the one person in Dalkey who would not be a party to the smuggling. "If he even guesses what's going on, he'll go straight to the authorities," he had warned Doyle. "I've got to get him out of Dalkey for a while."

"Let us use Tidy to do our work for us then," Doyle had told the astonished young fellow. It had been Doyle's idea that Tidy should be followed when he went into the church to pray, and that he should overhear the conspirators planning the attack on Carrick-mines. "You must pretend to dissuade him from telling anyone, if he comes to you for advice, as he probably will," Doyle had in-structed MacGowan. "That way, he'll never dream that you've set him up. And if what you tell me about his character is correct, then our friend will go to the authorities anyway."

So it had proved. Both MacGowan and Doyle himself, when he had been called by the Justiciar, had played their parts to perfection. The plan to raid Carrickmines had been believed; the squadron had been withdrawn; the coast was clear again for the landing. But Doyle had not stopped there. In order for the thing to look con-vincing, he explained to MacGowan, "We'll need a raid upon Carrickmines."

Only a man with the long reach of Doyle could have arranged such a thing—even MacGowan was not told how it was done—but word was carried to O'Byrne and a deal was struck. The Irish chief would lead a convincing-looking raid upon the castle in the middle of the night and make sure that his men drew the defenders well away from Dalkey. It seemed the plan had amused O'Byrne, and he had been well paid. Indeed, a fair amount of the profit of the oper-ation had had to be sacrificed, but Doyle was too far in now to pull back. The Irishman had been warned of the danger from Harold and the squadron, but the risk of the operation had only added to its appeal. "In any case," he had remarked, "my boys will melt into the night." It was he himself who had sent the dark-haired girl to hang around at the castle and the harbour. "I've told her," he prom-ised Doyle, "to make sure that she is seen."

And so it had all been arranged. Doyle, of course, would never be seen. From Dublin, he could even deny any knowledge of the business at all; as for MacGowan, he knew very well that should things go wrong, Doyle would have him safely into hiding, and if necessary across the sea, before the Justiciar's men ever got their hands on him.

There had been only one problem. He had not realised how difficult it would be to get Tom out of Dalkey. He had done everything to frighten him back into Dublin, exactly as Doyle had suggested, with invented stories of danger and the calculated hostility of the Dalkey people; but when Tom had turned up again on the very eve of the landing, MacGowan had been in despair. In the end, Doyle himself had come to pull him out. The merchant had not been too pleased about that.

However, MacGowan thought now, as he surveyed the successful completion of the night's work, Doyle would probably forgive him before long for that one error in his calculations.

⁘

It was three weeks later that John Walsh, riding up into the foothills, encountered the girl.

Life had been relatively quiet at the castle of Carrickmines since the night of the raid. The plan to inflict a massive defeat upon O'Byrne had not succeeded. Several of his men, undoubtedly, had been wounded. But somehow, in the darkness, every one of them had managed to get away, although the search in the foothills had gone on well into the day. As for Harold and his party, they had finished up wandering around in the dawn, empty-handed, in the woods above Glendalough. The business had been a failure. Yet it was not long—less than a week—before it was accounted a success. "We gave them a fright. We sent them flying. That was a lesson they won't forget in a hurry." These were the verdicts that were soon on the Dublin people's lips, such is the history of warfare.

Walsh said nothing. He knew it had been a trick, a scam of some sort; but he hadn't quite worked out of what kind. Obviously, O'Byrne had known what was going to happen. If he knew the troops would be waiting for him, then he must have wanted them to be there. As he considered the business further, however, it seemed to him that if O'Byrne, or whomever he was working with, wanted all the available military forces at Carrickmines, it could only mean that they did not want them to be somewhere else. So where had the troops come from? Dublin, Harold's Cross, and Dalkey. Nothing that he knew of had happened at any of those places, but the more he thought about it, the more his suspicions centred on Dalkey. Perhaps he would never know, but he would remember and watch with interest in the future. Life on the frontier, he reflected with satisfaction, was never dull.

She was lying on a rock in the sun. She must have fallen asleep; he'd never have come upon her like this otherwise. Her long, dark hair had cascaded down the side of the stone. She sprang up and flashed an angry glance at him, at which he only smiled. It amused him to remember that this fleet little figure was actually his cousin. She turned to run away, but he called after her.

"I've a message for you."

"You've nothing to say to me," she cried back defiantly.

"You'll take a message to O'Byrne," he answered. "Tell him," he thought quickly, "tell him that my wrist is healing, but that I've nothing to show for my trouble." He hadn't planned any such message—he'd thought of it on the spur of the moment—but he was pleased with it. Then, before the girl could make any further response, he turned his horse's head and rode away.

It was a week later that, coming out of the castle soon after dawn, he found half a dozen kegs of wine had been left during the night just outside the gate.

He smiled to himself. So that was the game. Dalkey was only just down the road from Carrickmines. Perhaps it was time, he thought, that the Walsh family started to take more of an interest in the place.

EIGHT

The pale

I

IF HISTORIANS WISH to designate a date to mark the ending of the Middle Ages and the beginning of the modern era, the voyage of Christopher Columbus to the New World in 1492 would seem a reasonable choice. In British history, convention has usually selected 1485; for in that year, the long feud now known as the Wars of the Roses between the York and Lancaster branches of the royal Plantagenet house was brought to an end when Richard III, the last Plantagenet king, was killed in battle by Henry Tudor. Under the new Tudor dynasty, England entered the world of the Renaissance, the Reformation, and the age of exploration.

But in the western island of Ireland, a better date must surely be just two years later, in the year 1487. For on May 24 of that year, the city of Dublin witnessed an event unique in Ireland's history, and whose long-term repercussions were to be profound: the Irish set out to conquer England.

✛

The crowd outside Christ Church Cathedral was large. The great men of Ireland were all inside, as were most of the local gentry.

"I wish we could go in, Father," said the red-haired girl. "Weren't we invited?"

"Of course we were. But we got here too late," he replied with a smile. "We'll never get through the crowd now. Besides," he added, "this is better. We shall see the procession as they come out."

Margaret Rivers looked at Christ Church eagerly. Her freckled face was pale with excitement, her blue eyes shining. She knew her family was important. She wasn't sure exactly why, but she knew it must be true, because her father had told her. "And you, Margaret, are going to be a great success," he would tell her.

"How do you know, Father?" she would ask him.

"Because you're my special girl," he'd reply, as she knew he was going to, and she would feel a little rush of happiness. She had three brothers, but she was the only girl, and she was the youngest. Of course she was his special girl. She wasn't quite sure what she had to do to be a great success, but earlier that year, on her eighth birthday, her father had announced to the whole family: "Margaret will make a brilliant marriage. To a man of wealth and importance." So she had supposed that success must be something to do with this.

She knew her father was a wonderful man. Sometimes she had seen her mother cast her eyes up to heaven when he was speaking; she didn't know quite what it meant, since her mother never said; but then her mother was subject, sometimes, to strange moods.

The nuns always treated her father with the greatest respect when he visited the old convent. There were only seven of them, and one of these was deaf, but it seemed their lives were entirely in his hands. "Where would we be without you?" they used to say. Her father looked after all their affairs, managed their extensive lands, and advised them so that they never had to worry that their abbey's large endowments would fail to support their few and modest needs. "We know we can always trust your dear father," one of the faithful nuns remarked to little Margaret one day. "Your father is a gentleman."

A gentleman. Their house in the suburb of Oxmantown might be no different from those of the local merchants, but all over Fingal and beyond, Margaret knew, the landowners were, in one way or another, her kinsfolk. "We are related," her father liked to say, "to every family of consequence in the Pale."

The Pale: that was what they called the counties around Dublin now—a name that suggested an invisible palisade enclosing the region. Conditions there were pretty much as they had been the century before. Within the Pale, as in England, lay a pattern of parishes and counties, where sheriffs collected royal taxes and the justices decided cases by English common law. Around the edge of the Pale, the Marcher lords still led their frontier existence; and beyond the Pale, whether ruled over by Irish chiefs or the great magnates like the Butlers and Fitzgeralds, lay the world of Gaelic Ireland. Beyond the Pale, as far as Margaret's father was concerned, civilization ended. But within the Pale, order was assured by the English in Ireland, the Irish of English blood, men like himself: not, perhaps, all that he might have liked to be, but in his own eyes at least and those of the nuns, an English gentleman.

Yet today, in Dublin's Christ Church Cathedral, gentlemen like himself were preparing to invade the English kingdom.

"Look, Father." The cathedral doors were swinging open. Men-at-arms were coming out, pushing back the crowd. A broad pathway was being cleared. Figures were appearing, in glittering robes, in the doorway. Her father lifted her up and Margaret could see them clearly: three bishops with mitres on their heads led the procession; then came the abbots and priors. Next, in their robes of office, red and blue and gold, came the mayor and the aldermen of the city; behind them walked the Archbishop of Dublin with the Lord Deputy, the Earl of Kildare, head of the mighty Fitzgerald clan and the most powerful man in all Ireland. Next came the Lord

Chancellor, and the Treasurer, followed by the major officeholders and nobility. And then came the boy.

He was only a little fellow, hardly older than herself. For a crown, they had taken a circlet of gold, which had formed the halo over a statue of the Blessed Virgin, and placed it upon his head. And to make sure that this new boy king should be clearly seen, they had selected a gentleman from Fingal, one Darcy by name, a giant of a man who stood six and a half feet tall, and put the boy king to ride upon his shoulders.

Bringing up the rear of the procession came two hundred German mercenary landknechts, sent from the Low Countries by the Duchess of Burgundy, carrying fearsome pikes and accompanied by fife and drum.

For the boy, Edmund, Earl of Warwick, had just been crowned King of England, and was about to set forth to claim his rightful kingdom. But how had it come to pass that he should be crowned in Dublin?

A generation ago, during a period when the royal house of York was in the ascendant over that of Lancaster, one of the princes of York had governed Ireland for a number of years and, uncommon for an Englishman, had made himself popular. Ever since, in many parts of the Irish community, and especially in Dublin, there had been a loyalty towards the Yorkist cause. But now the House of York had been defeated. Henry Tudor, who held the crown by right of conquest, had based his claim to royalty on the fact that his forebears, though only an upstart gentry family from Wales, had married into the House of Lancaster. As royalty goes, this was quite a shaky claim; and although the new Tudor king cleverly married a Yorkist princess to strengthen his royal position, he could not really sleep easy if there were other, more legitimate Plantagenet heirs still at large.

And suddenly, some months ago, an heir had appeared, with a far more legitimate claim to the throne than Henry Tudor. He was Edmund, Earl of Warwick, a royal prince of the house of York. His appearance under the care of a priest had caused consternation at the Tudor court. King Henry had immediately called him an impostor. "His real name is Lambert Simnel," he declared, the son of an organ maker in Oxford—though the craftsman in question was conveniently dead. Then Henry produced another boy, whom he kept in the Tower of London, and announced that he was the real Edmund of Warwick. The trouble was that two of Edmund's Plantagenet relations—one of them was the Duchess of Burgundy, a Yorkist princess—having interviewed the two boys, both declared that the priest's boy was indeed Edmund, and that Henry's boy was a fake. For the boy's own safety, the priest had brought him across to Ireland. And today he was being crowned.

Yet however much they preferred the House of York, why would the great men of the English community of Ireland choose to defy the Tudor king? Seen from a later century it may seem strange, yet in the year 1487, after decades of power shifting back and forth between York and Lancaster, there was no particular reason to suppose that the only half-royal Henry Tudor would be able to keep his crown. If many of the great nobles believed they would be better off under a Yorkist prince than a Lancastrian conqueror, the bishops, abbots, and royal officials would hardly have crowned the boy if they weren't honestly convinced that he was, indeed, the rightful heir.

The procession had just started down the street when Margaret and her father were joined by a young man to whom her father remarked pleasantly, "Well, John, have you decided?"

Her eldest brother, John. Like Margaret, he had inherited red hair from their mother's family, for she had been a Harold. But where Margaret's was dark, almost auburn, John's was light and rose like a carrot-coloured flame from his head. Twenty years old, tall, athletic, to Margaret he had always been a hero. And never more so than today. For the last week he and his father had been discussing whether he should join the coming expedition. Now he announced: "I have, Father. I'm going with them."

"Very well." Her father nodded. "I've been talking to a man who knows Thomas Fitzgerald. That's the brother of Kildare himself, you know," he explained to Margaret. "We'll not have you going as a common foot soldier. I should hope that my son," he added rather grandly, "would be shown some consideration."

"Thank you, Father." Her brother smiled affectionately. He had a beautiful smile.

"You are going to England?" Margaret asked him excitedly. "To fight for the boy?"

He nodded.

"You're right to go, John," her father said. "Do well, and there could be rewards."

"Let's follow the procession," her brother cried, and scooping Margaret up, he placed her on his shoulders and started to stride along the street with his father walking in a dignified manner beside him. And how happy and proud Margaret felt, to be riding on her brother's shoulders, just like the boy king ahead of them, on that sunny morning in May.

They went down the street between the high-gabled houses, with the fifes and drums sounding cheerfully in front; out through the eastern gateway known as Dame's Gate, and across to Hoggen Green and the ancient Thingmount. Having made the circuit of that, the procession, still followed by a large crowd, made its way back to the city before finally disappearing through the gateway into Dublin Castle where there was to be a banquet given in the boy king's honour.

"Are you going to the banquet, Father," Margaret asked, as her brother put her down.

"No," he replied, then smiled confidently. "But many of the great lords in there would be your kinsmen. Always remember this day, Margaret," he went on firmly, "for it will go down in history. Remember you were here, with your brave brother and your father."

It was not only her father who was so confident. Within days, the Parliament of Ireland had met and the English gentlemen and

Church representatives had enthusiastically ratified the crowning. They had issued a proclamation of his kingship. They had even caused new coins—groats and half-groats—to be struck with the boy's head depicted on them. As well as the German landknechts, Thomas Fitzgerald had collected Irish mercenaries and young enthusiasts like John so that before the end of May he could tell his brother, Lord Kildare, "We're ready to go. And we should strike at once." Indeed, only one discordant note was sounded in those heady days.

It might have been expected. If the two mighty earldoms of the Fitzgerald clan—Kildare stretching out from the centre of the Pale, and Desmond to the south—were the most powerful lordships in the land, the third great lordship, the Butler family's earldom of Ormond, was still an impressive power to be reckoned with. Sometimes the Butlers and the Fitzgeralds were on good terms, but more often they were not; and it was hardly surprising if the Butlers were jealous of the Fitzgerald domination. So when Henry Tudor had taken the throne from the House of York, to which the Fitzgeralds were known to be so friendly, the Butlers had been quick to let Henry know that they were glad to support his Lancastrian cause.

And now, just after the Parliament in Dublin had declared for him, a messenger came from the Earl of Ormond, the head of the Butlers. "Lord Ormond refuses to do homage to this boy pretender," he announced, "and declares all these proceedings to be illegal."

The Fitzgerald reaction was swift. Lord Kildare had the messenger taken straight down to the Thingmount on Hoggen Green, and hanged.

"That is harsh," Margaret's father declared with a shake of his head. "He was only the messenger." But Margaret could hear the tone of sneaking admiration in his voice. Two days after that, Kildare's brother Thomas and his little army set sail for England, taking her brother John with them.

÷

The boy king's expedition landed in England on the fourth day of June. Making their way towards York, they were joined by some of the Yorkist lords and their retinues; soon their numbers had swelled to six and a half thousand men. Then they turned south.

And Henry Tudor, caught by surprise, might even have lost his kingdom if several of the English magnates, who owed him loyalty and who reckoned that he offered the best chance of order, hadn't rallied to him at once with unexpectedly large contingents of troops. On the morning of June 16, near a village called East Stoke in the Midlands, the boy king's army found itself confronted by fifteen thousand well-equipped and trained fighting men. Though the Germans had deadly crossbows, Henry Tudor's Welsh and English longbowmen could loose continuous volleys of arrows that fell like a hailstorm. Against the half-trained and mostly unarmoured contingents from Ireland, Henry had trained pikemen and armoured knights.

The Irish army was smashed. The boy king was captured; and having secured him, Henry Tudor gave no quarter. At the place where they fought, there was a ditch which from that day onwards was to be known as Red Gutter since, it was said, by the end of the morning it was filled with blood. For they hacked the Germans and Irish to pieces, almost every one.

Fortunately, Margaret only ever knew that her brother had been slain.

But Henry Tudor was more than ruthless; he was also clever. Having got the boy Edmund alive, he did not kill him or even put him in prison. Still insisting that he was only an impostor called Lambert Simnel, he set him to work in the royal kitchens from which he would cheerfully summon him sometimes to serve the guests at feasts. During Henry's reign, and for centuries to come, hardly anybody believed the boy to be the royal prince that, quite possibly, he really was.

Yet the lessons which Margaret learned from these events had little to do with the boy king himself.

In the immediate aftermath of the tragedy, she knew only a numbing sense of grief. And though she had been brought up proud that she was English, the unconscious thought formed in her mind that England itself was somehow an alien and threatening place. How was it, she asked herself, if there was a God in heaven, that the English king could take her brother from her like this? But as she grew older and pondered the events that had led to his death, a new and more perceptive question occurred to her.

"How was it, Father, that John was killed, but that the Fitzgeralds were not punished?" It was a question that went to the root of Ireland's political situation.

For when the boy king was crowned in Dublin, it was Kildare himself, head of the Fitzgeralds and, as Lord Deputy, King Henry Tudor's own representative and governor on the island, who had led the treasonable business. The Butlers, on the other hand, had stayed loyal. Yet Henry had forgiven Kildare, while the Butlers had received no great reward for their pains.

"The Fitzgeralds have the most territory. They're intermarried with so many gentry families, and with the greatest Irish princes as well, that they can call on more men and more favours than any other clan," her father told her. "Moreover," he explained, "though the Butlers' power is huge as well, their territory lies between the two Fitzgerald earldoms—Kildare on their northern flank and Desmond in the south. If the Fitzgeralds want to, they can squeeze the Butlers," he made a gesture with his two hands, "like a pincer. So you see, Margaret, of the two great English lordships, Fitzgerald is the natural one to govern. And if the English king tries to ignore them both and send his own man to govern, they would soon make life so difficult for him that he gives up."

And during the rest of her childhood, this was exactly the political pattern that Margaret was to see. Even when Henry sent over his trusted deputy Poynings—who bluntly told the Irish Parliament they could no longer pass any laws without the Tudor king's approval, and even arrested Kildare, who was sent to London—the Fitzgeralds made it so difficult for him to govern that before long even Poynings gave up. And back in England, when he was told, "All Ireland cannot govern Kildare and his Fitzgeralds," Henry Tudor, that supreme realist, calmly observed, "If all Ireland cannot govern Kildare, then Kildare had better govern Ireland," and sent the head of the Fitzgeralds back as his Lord Deputy again.

"It's Kildare who rules in Ireland, Margaret," her father told her, "and always will be."

⁜

Margaret was thirteen when she learned that her father had been cheated. It happened quite by chance.

It had promised to be an uneventful morning at Oxmantown. Her father had been at the house with no particular business to do that day, when a neighbour had come by to ask if he was going across the river to watch the fun. "Did you not hear," he explained, "that a group of Butler's and Fitzgerald's men are having a fight over by Saint Patrick's?"

"What about?" her father asked.

"Who knows? Because they're Butlers and Fitzgeralds."

"I suppose I may as well," said her father. And he certainly would have gone without Margaret if she had not begged him to let her come. "If there's any danger," he told her firmly, "you'll have to go straight home."

When they got to Saint Patrick's, they found a crowd gathered outside. They seemed in a cheerful mood, and their neighbour, who went ahead to find out what was happening, soon reported that the fight was now over and the rival groups, both in the cathedral, had agreed to a truce.

"There's only one problem," he explained. "The Butler men are on one side of a big door and the Fitzgerald men on the other; but the door is locked and no one has the key. And until they've shaken hands neither side intends to move from the place where they are, on account of their mistrust."

"Do they mean to stay there forever, then?" asked her father.

"Not at all. They will cut a hole in the door. But it's a mighty door, so it will take some time."

It was just then that Margaret saw the little girl.

She was standing with her mother, not far off. She might be five years old, Margaret guessed, but she was tiny. She was dressed in a bright patterned dress; her eyes were dark, her olive-coloured features finely drawn and delicate. She was the neatest little person that Margaret had ever seen. One glance at her mother, a small, elegant Mediterranean woman, explained the child's looks at once. She must be Spanish.

"Oh, Father," she cried, "can I go and play with her?"

It was unusual but not unexpected to encounter Spanish features in Ireland. The Black Irish, people often called them. Notwithstanding the legend that some of the island's earliest inhabitants had come from the Iberian peninsula, the reason for the Black Irish was very simple. Centuries of trade between Spain and the Irish ports had probably resulted in a few intermarriages, but the greatest sources of the Black Irish were the regular visits of the great Spanish fishing fleets which for generations had come for the rich catch off the island's southern coast, especially off the lands of the O'Sullivans and the O'Driscolls down in West Cork. Ships from these fleets would often put into the creeks to process their catch with salt, paying the O'Sullivan and O'Driscoll lords a levy for the privilege. Sometimes a sailor would find a local sweetheart and settle there, or leave a child.

The mother had no objection to Margaret amusing her tiny daughter. Her name was Joan. For some time Margaret played with the doll-like child who was obviously fascinated by the older, red-haired girl and never took her large, brown eyes off her. Finally, however, her father called Margaret back and told her that it was time to be going. And he had just smiled in a friendly way at the

Spanish woman and her daughter, and started to turn away, when a cheer from the crowd announced that the men from the cathedral were coming out, and so they stayed to watch.

The Fitzgerald men came first, about a score of them. They moved off swiftly towards the city gate. A few moments later, the Butler group emerged. Most of them started to leave in the direction of Saint Stephen's hospital; but a few split away, and one of these came through the crowd towards them. He was a handsome, well-set man with thinning brown hair and a broad, English-looking face. As he came out of the throng, the little Spanish girl caught sight of him, cried out, "Papa!" and in an instant had thrown herself into his arms. Margaret smiled. It was a charming scene. So she was surprised when she glanced at her father to see him scowling with fury.

"We're going," Rivers said suddenly, and taking her by the arm, he almost dragged her away.

"What has happened?" she asked. "Is it Joan's father?"

"I never guessed she was his child," he muttered.

"Who is he, Father?"

"Henry Butler," he said, but the anger in his voice warned her not to ask him any more.

They had reached the bridge across the river before he broke his silence.

"Many years ago, Margaret, there was an inheritance—not huge, but large enough—that fell between two cousins of my mother's family. My mother was cheated of her rightful share. With the connivance of Ormond, it all went to the mother of that man you saw back there. His name is Henry Butler. He's from a junior branch of the Butlers, but still a distant kinsman of the earl. And he has been living on the fruits of that fine estate which should have been mine. So it hurts me and angers me to see him." He paused. "I never told you this before because I don't like to speak of it."

A disputed inheritance: Margaret had often heard of such things.

Disputes between heiresses, in particular, were common enough in Ireland.

"Does Henry Butler know he has your inheritance?"

"Most certainly he does," her father replied. "I met the man once. As soon as he heard my name, he turned his back and walked away."

"Joan is sweet," Margaret said. It made her sad that the pretty little child should be the daughter of her father's enemy.

"She has your money," he answered grimly.

They did not speak about it anymore, but that night, when her mother supposed she was asleep, Margaret heard her parents talking.

"It was so long ago," she heard her mother pleading, in a low voice. "Do not think of it."

"But that is why I am forced to live like this, a miserable agent working for others, instead of a gentleman on my own estate."

"We manage well enough. Can you not be happy with what you have? A wife and children who love you?"

"You know I love my family more than anything in the world." His voice descended so that she could not hear it, then rose again. "But how can I provide for them? Henry Butler has it all. Where is Margaret's dowry, tell me? The little Spanish girl has it." There was a pause. Then her father's voice again, almost in tears. "Oh the pain of it. The pain."

After that, Margaret stopped her ears, and lay there shaking for a long time until at last she fell asleep.

⁙

Margaret was eighteen when her father started the quest to find her a husband.

"We shall look," he told her confidently, "in Fingal. Fingal's the place," he said firmly, "for an English girl like you." She knew what he meant. It was not only that Fingal was the area of English farms,

where landlords looked out on huge orderly fields of wheat and barley; Fingal was a family network. There were the Fagans and the
Conrans and the Cusacks; the Finglas family, the Usshers, the
Bealings, the Balls, the Taylors up at Swords. All English gentry
families who married amongst each other and with the greatest merchant families in Dublin. The marriage network spread outwards
also, to the Dillons in Meath, the Bellews, the Sarsfields, and the
Plunketts—some of the best of the English in Ireland. At the apex
of the Fingal families were three, whose lands lay along the coast.
The family of St. Lawrence held the headland of Howth; just to the
north, by the next inlet, were the Irish branch of the great aristocratic family of Talbot, and nearby the Barnewalls. These were the
people her father meant when he referred to Fingal.

She knew a good many of them—not well, but enough to talk
to. Sometimes her father would take her with him if he rode over to
some fine estate on business. Occasionally the family would be invited to an entertainment in one of the houses; or one of her brothers might come by in the company of a friend who belonged to a
Fingal family. Two years ago she had chanced to strike up a friendship with a younger daughter of the St. Lawrence family. For about
a year they had been almost inseparable. Margaret would go across
and stay with her friend for days at a time. They would walk along
the strand above the Liffey estuary to where the Tolka stream came
down at Clontarf; or on sunny days they would spend hours up on
the headland gazing southwards across the bay and down the coast
to where the volcanic hills rose magically through the haze. It was a
happy friendship. The St. Lawrence family were always kind to her.
But then they found a husband for her friend, who left Fingal; and
there was no reason for Margaret to go to Howth after that.

"Margaret's hair," her father said, "is her greatest asset." And no
one disagreed.

Some might have said that her face was a little plain, but thanks
to her hair, she had only to enter any gathering for all heads to turn.
Rich, dark red—if she did not put it up it fell like a gleaming cur-

tain down her back. She hoped that she also had other attractions: good skin, a handsome figure, a lively personality. But she wasn't a fool. "They will notice you for your hair, Margaret," her mother told her. "The rest is up to you."

The opportunity for all Fingal to see her came the summer when she was eighteen.

It was a day in mid-June when her father came into the house one afternoon looking pleased with himself and announced, "Did you hear that one of the Talbot boys has just returned from England? Edward Talbot. He's been there three years, you know. He visited the royal court. A fine young gentleman by all accounts. There's to be a great entertainment out at Malahide," he continued, "to welcome him back. All Fingal will be going." He paused, so that they should think this was the end of the information. "We're going, too, of course," he added with a straight face that only gradually broke into a triumphant grin.

How had her father managed to procure an invitation to such a grand event? Margaret didn't know. But the next week was spent helping her mother make her a fine new gown and in all the other preparations necessary for such an occasion. As it happened, both her brothers were away at the time, and the day before her mother fell and sprained her ankle and so decided to remain at home, but Margaret and her father set off upon the afternoon in question in high spirits. Margaret's gown, of green-and-black silk brocade, was a triumph. "It sets off your hair perfectly," her mother assured her. And though he did not say much, she could see that her father was excited. When he said admiringly, "You'll be the best-looking young lady there, Margaret," she was quite as pleased that she had made him happy as she was by the thought of any good looks she might possess.

The castle of Malahide lay on the far side of the ancient Plain of Bird Flocks, on land that adjoined the rolling fields upon which, centuries before, Harold the Norseman had gazed out from his farmstead. On the northern edge of the estate, where a small river flowed to the sea past some fine oyster beds, stood the busy little village of Malahide. Down its eastern flank lay the open sea. The estates of the gentry in Fingal were not large—most ran to hundreds rather than thousands of acres—but the Malahide land was good and the estate was valuable. The castle was set in pleasant parkland sprinkled with fine old oaks and ash trees which gave the place a stately air. For a long time it had been only a bleak defensive tower; but two decades ago, the Talbots had added several features, including a great hall, so that it had become a more impressive and domestic building. In front of the main entrance stretched an expanse of open grass. To one side was a walled garden. As they approached, the light on the stone gave the castle a pleasing look of softness in the afternoon sun.

A large company had already gathered. It was warm and they had set up trestle tables outside heaped with sweetmeats and other delicacies. Servants in livery were serving wine. As she looked around, Margaret could see numerous faces she recognised—aldermen and royal officials from Dublin, gentry from various parts of the region. "The flower of Fingal," her father murmured, before adding, as if they had all come there for her benefit, "take your pick."

If she had felt a little daunted by such a crowd of important people, she was glad to see several young people she knew, including her former friend the St. Lawrence girl; so that in no time she found herself engaged in easy conversation. She was conscious also that she had attracted some attention. When she moved, several male heads turned. Her mother had been right: the combination of the green silk with her red hair was working well. A distinguished old gentleman even came over to compliment her—one of the notable Plunkett family, her friend told her.

The banquet in the castle hall was a splendid affair. The hall was packed. Her father was seated some distance away from her, but she had cheerful young people for company. Three fish courses were served. There was roast beef turning on a spit, venison, pork, and even swan. She knew only a little of wines, but she could tell that the French wines being served were of the best. She had never been to such a sumptuous affair before, but she took care to remember her father's advice, "Taste everything that is offered, but take only a tiny portion of each. That is the way to enjoy a great feast." There were so many guests that there was not room for dancing, but there were pipers and a harpist playing. When the sweet courses were being served, Edward Talbot, in whose honour all this was done, stood up and made a charming speech of welcome. He was in his early twenties, with an oval face and finely drawn features. Margaret thought he looked pleasant and intelligent. His hair was brown with a trace of ginger in it and was already thinning; but she decided that the fine, domed forehead it revealed would make him, if anything, more attractive as he grew older. Once he sat down, however, he was hidden from her view, and she did not catch sight of him again.

At the end of the banquet, she was reunited with her father. It was still light outside, and entertainments were to be provided by a troupe of dancers. Some of the company gathered in front of the castle to watch, others split into groups and walked about. When her father asked her if she had seen the walled garden and she said she had not, he took her round the side of the castle to a gate in a wall and led her in.

If monasteries had their cloisters for gentle exercise and contemplation, the medieval manor house had its walled garden. The garden before Margaret now was laid out rather geometrically, with low, clipped hedges and, here and there, leafy arbours where gentlemen and ladies might sit and enjoy the enclosed quiet and read, and talk, and flirt. As they entered, Margaret smelled the sweet scents of lavender and honeysuckle. At one end of the enclosure was a herb garden. At the other end, the whole wall was covered in climbing roses. There were paths between the clipped hedges. In the centre was a little lawn strewn with wild strawberries and a single pear tree whose unripe fruit hung from its branches like pale green gemstones. There were several other people there who, respecting the garden's peace, spoke in low tones. Turning towards the herb garden, they walked quietly down a path.

"You are a great success, Margaret," her father murmured, with satisfaction. "People have been asking who you are. Indeed, one gentleman already has asked if he may talk to you, and that is why I brought you in here." He smiled. "He's a little older than I should have liked, but there's no harm in your talking to him. Make a good impression and he will speak well of you. You would do that for me wouldn't you?"

"I will do as you please, Father," she said pleasantly, for she wanted, at the least, to make him happy.

"Stay here, and I shall go and find him," he said, and made his way out of the gate.

Margaret was quite content. She went down to the herb garden and began to inspect it. She started to see how many different kinds she could count, and was sufficiently engrossed not to notice that anyone was coming up behind her until she heard a soft cough. Turning round and expecting to see her father, she instead found herself facing a young man whom she recognised at once as Edward Talbot.

"You like our herbs?"

"I was counting them."

"Ah." He smiled. "How many can you name?"

"There is thyme, parsley, of course, mint, basil, nutmeg . . ." she named a dozen or so.

"And what about that one?" He pointed, but she shook her head. "It came," he explained, "from Persia." It was extraordinary what he knew. He went along the bed, showing her herbs from France, from Africa, from the Holy Land and far beyond. Herbs she had never heard of, herbs whose history he knew. But he showed his knowledge with such humour, intelligence, and enthusiasm that, rather than being overwhelmed, she found herself smiling with pleasure.

He asked her who she was, and Margaret was able to give him enough information about her family and her kinsfolk in Fingal for him to discover that she was related to several people he knew. "Perhaps we are kinsfolk, too," he suggested.

"Oh no, my family can't make any such claims. We're not grand at all," she was careful to say. "As for myself," she smiled, "my parents tell me that my only asset is my hair."

He laughed and answered, "I'm sure you must have many others." Then, gazing at her hair with the same careful observation that he had applied to the herbs, he thoughtfully remarked, "It is very fine. Quite wonderful." And almost forgetting what he was doing, he raised his hand as if to run it through her hair, before checking himself and laughing. She wondered where else this conversation might be going when, at that moment, her father reappeared at the gate and came towards them.

He was alone. Evidently he had not found the man he was looking for, but he was smiling as he came up and she explained to Talbot, "This is my father."

She was pleased to see how politely Talbot greeted her father and how well-informed, in turn, her father seemed to be as he asked the young man some questions about his time in England, which Talbot seemed delighted to answer. The two men had just started an interesting discussion when Margaret observed that a fine-looking lady, who had entered the garden while she and Edward Talbot had been discussing the herbs, was now coming rapidly towards them. She was wearing a white-and-gold damask gown which, with each step she took, made a little hiss upon the path.

"Ah, Mother," said Edward Talbot. And he was about to introduce Margaret when the lady turned to Margaret's father, and coolly demanded, "This is your daughter?"

The lady Talbot was tall. Her face was strong. Her grey eyes seemed to look at the world from a great height.

"Yes, my lady. This is Margaret."

Margaret now found herself the object of an aristocratic stare: that is to say, the lady Talbot looked at her in exactly the same, dispassionate way as she would have observed an item of furniture.

"You have very fine hair." Though technically this was a compliment, her tone suggested that she might have added: there is nothing more to say about you. She turned to her son. "Your father is looking for you, Edward. There are guests from Dublin Castle you should attend to."

With a polite bow to her father and a smile at Margaret, Edward Talbot left them. The lady Talbot, however, did not move. She waited until Edward had left the garden and then, turning to her father as though Margaret was not even there, she addressed him with the greatest coldness.

"How many of your kinsmen did you use to secure an invitation here today?"

"I believe several of my kinsmen are known to you, my lady."

"You came here to show off your daughter to the world."

"I am her father, my lady. What else should a father do?"

"I agreed to your being invited, though by rights you should not be here." She paused. "I agreed to let your daughter and her hair be seen." She paused again. "And I did not agree that you should come here so that your daughter could try to insinuate herself with my son. You have abused my trust."

This was so breathtaking that, for a moment, neither father nor daughter said anything. But it was so unfair that Margaret could not help bursting out: "I never spoke a word to your son, until he came up to me."

The stony grey eyes were upon her again. Was there a faint hint of recognition there now?

"That may be true," the lady conceded. She turned back to Margaret's father. "But perhaps you know more than your daughter."

Margaret glanced at her father. Was it possible that he had somehow arranged the meeting? Had he gone out, not to find an older suitor but to send in Edward Talbot? Faced with the lady Talbot's cold accusation, Margaret was so glad that he did not blush or bluster, but remained very calm.

"I did not bring my daughter here in order that either of us should be insulted," he replied quietly.

"Do not bring her here again, then," the lady Talbot answered curtly. She turned to Margaret. "Find yourself a merchant in Dublin, Miss Red Hair. You do not belong in the castle of Malahide." Then she swept away.

Neither Margaret nor her father felt much like talking as they returned home. The evening sun was still casting long shadows on the Plain of Bird Flocks as their cart rolled across its empty greenness. If Margaret wondered whether the lady Talbot's accusation could be true, it was not something she wanted to ask her father. It was he, in the end, who broke the silence.

"It's not our family that made her speak like that. I am a gentleman you know."

"I know."

"It's because I am poor, Margaret, that she treated you like that." He spoke bitterly, but he hung his head in shame. She put her arm round him.

"Thank you for what you tried to do for me, Father," she said gently. "You're a wonderful father."

"If only I were." He shook his head. "I had not meant you to discover the harshness of the world," he said miserably. "Not like this. I had hoped . . ." He trailed off. Feeling his body sob, she was not sure whether to keep her arm round him or not, but she left it where it was.

"It's not important," she said after a while. "Not really."

"It is to me," he murmured, then fell silent again for a little while, until his shoulders had ceased to heave. "Those Talbots are not so fine," he muttered finally. "They say they're mixed up with the Butlers. They'll probably come to grief. We'd do better to look at the Barnewalls." He seemed to brighten a little. "They, you know, are your distant kin."

"Oh, Father," she cried in frustration, "for God's sake find me a boy in Dublin who will love me as I am."

And truly at that moment, and when she went to bed in secret tears that night, this was all that Margaret wanted. But when she awoke, refreshed, the next morning, she felt a new sense of rebellion. The proud Talbots might not want her, but she'd show them.

II

⊨ 1518 ⊨

It was an unusual sight. Women—about a hundred of them, waiting down by the crane house on the waterfront. Not just ordinary women: many of these were fine ladies, richly dressed, laughing and chattering on a bright September morning.

The crane house was a solid, unlovely, two-storey building that served as a customhouse, from which there projected a massive timber structure whose grinding cogs and squealing pulleys allowed heavy cargoes to be lifted from dockside vessels and weighed. It stood roughly halfway along the extended waterfront. To the east, having advanced with continued rebuilding many yards into the river now, lay the old Wood Quay. To the west, on the reclaimed land that ran towards the bridge, the riverside was known as Merchants Quay. And though the crane was a surly-looking thing, and a chilly breeze had now begun to blow along the waterfront, the women were cheerfully ignoring the cold. For after all, this was a special occasion.

The Riding of the Franchises only took place once in three years. At dawn that morning, the mayor of Dublin, resplendent in his robes of office and preceded by a man carrying the city's ceremonial sword, had left Dame's Gate in the east, and riding out past the Thingmount and the old Viking Long Stone, made his way along the Liffey estuary towards the sea. Riding behind him came the twenty-four aldermen, the members of the common council, and a large party of local gentlemen—almost a hundred riders in all. At the seashore, the water bailiff had hurled a spear into the water, to symbolise the city's rights over the Dublin coastline. Then they had set out to ride round the city boundaries.

This was a huge circuit. For the city's authority—excepting the big Liberties, mostly belonging to the Church—stretched far out beyond the city walls, and in places was marked now by gateways and tollbooths on the approach roads. Their course took them firstly down the coast, almost halfway to Dalkey; then they turned inland, across to the village of Donnybrook, on past the environs of Saint Stephen's and the Liberties by Saint Patrick's, and after that still farther westwards to the hamlet of Kilmainham, some two miles upstream from the city, where the mayor could take the horse ferry across the Liffey. North of the Liffey, the boundary followed a huge arc which passed a mile north of Oxmantown, crossed the Tolka stream, and continued up the coast by the old battlefield of Brian Boru at Clontarf and even a mile beyond that.

It was past noon. The procession, having ridden a total distance of over thirty miles, was returning through Oxmantown and would shortly cross the bridge back into the city. The wives were starting to catch sight of their husbands now. Silk handkerchiefs were being waved. There was laughter. And nowhere did the company seem gayer than in the group around a small, Spanish-looking woman, dressed in a gown of rich brocade with a fur collar to guard her from the wind.

Margaret was waiting at some distance from this group. She knew few of the city women more than slightly. She did not often come into Dublin; there was always so much to be done on the farm. She was dressed in good cloth, of which she had no reason to be ashamed; and with a growing family to think of, she wouldn't have let her husband give her an expensive, fur-trimmed gown even if he had offered. She turned to a woman standing nearby.

"That Spanish-looking lady over there: who is she married to?"

"Oh," the woman's voice dropped respectfully, "that is the wife of Alderman Doyle. She's very rich, they say." She looked at

Margaret with some surprise. "Do you not know Alderman Doyle? He's a powerful man in Dublin."

Dublin people were proud of their wealth and power. That, after all, was exactly what the ceremony today was about. In the Riding of the Franchises, the mayor and his company were inspecting and confirming the outer boundaries of the city's extensive land. It was a ceremonial, but also a legal event. And if any other landholder, even the Holy Church, disputed the extent or boundary line of the city's holdings, they could be sure the mayor would make good his claim, either with a lawsuit or by physical force. Dublin might be only a tenth of the size of mighty London, but it was a major city by any standard and was the key to holding Ireland. For a long time now, the rich aldermen of Dublin had become used to kings of England courting their favour and feeding their pride. The great sword carried before the mayor had been given to the city a century ago by a grateful king after a former mayor had led a successful campaign into the Wicklow Mountains against the troublesome O'Byrnes. The mayor nowadays held the office of Admiral, too, which gave him the right to the royal customs dues from the harbours on the Dublin coast, all the way down to Dalkey and beyond—though the royal officials may have been ready enough to grant these taxes away since they had always had such difficulty collecting the dues themselves.

Even the involvement of the Dublin men in the business of Lambert Simnel the boy king had done them no harm. Indeed, it had only made Henry Tudor more anxious to cultivate good relations with them; and for the last nine years his son, Henry VIII, had continued the same policy. The message from the royal court to Dublin's leading citizens was clear: "The King of England wants you for his friends." It was no small thing, therefore, to be the wife of Alderman Doyle.

It was not the first time that Margaret had seen the Doyle woman. She had caught sight of her only two weeks ago.

One of the few Dublin events that Margaret always attended was the Donnybrook Fair. It took place late in August, at the village just a mile south of Saint Stephen's. Sometimes her husband came to buy or sell cattle there; all kinds of cloth were on sale, with traders from all over Europe; she would usually pick up some delicacies and spices for the larder at home. Then there were the eating booths and entertainments—singers and jugglers, music makers and magicians. "Donnybrook's my outing for the year," she would say.

It had been during the fair. She had noticed the woman at once because of her Spanish looks, but she had not thought much about her. Not at first. Only as she was inspecting a stall of medicinal herbs a short time later did she realise that the woman's face was familiar. But why?

Twenty-five years had passed since her father and she had seen the family of Henry Butler, and if it hadn't been for the terrible thing her father had told her about them, and the pain it had caused him, she would certainly have forgotten what they looked like long ago. But because of that, all three faces—Butler, his wife, and the little girl—had remained stamped upon her mind. And now, she was suddenly aware, this woman at Donnybrook Fair looked exactly like the Butler woman all those years ago. Was it possible that this could be the little girl? With a shock, Margaret realised that she would be the right age.

She had turned to study her, and noticed that the woman, meanwhile, had been observing her—with what, it seemed to Margaret, was a look of recognition. So, she thought, she knows who I am. And she was just wondering what she should feel about the Butler girl now and whether she should speak to her or not, when she saw something that first made her freeze, then sickened her. The woman had smirked. There was no mistaking it, she thought—a little smirk of triumph and contempt. Then, while Margaret stared in sudden fury, she had turned away. Soon after that, Margaret saw her leave the fair.

Margaret had done nothing about it. What could she do? She did not even try to find out anything more about the woman. When her husband had asked her that evening why she seemed upset, she had made up some excuse. She wanted to put the incident out of her mind.

But now, standing on the waterfront, she had discovered who the woman was. The wife of a rich alderman, with a big house no doubt, and all the luxuries that money could buy. Not, she reminded herself, that she had anything to be ashamed of. Doyle might be rich, but he was still a merchant. Her own husband was a gentleman, a grandson of Walsh of Carrickmines, no less, and significant enough to be invited to take part in the Riding of the Franchises today. Their estate might be down in the southern borderlands rather than in Fingal, as she would have liked, and it might yield only a modest income, but her husband had been educated in England, and his earnings as a lawyer made up for the shortcomings of the estate. She had no reason, she told herself, to feel at any disadvantage if she encountered this woman whose family had stolen from hers. But when she remembered that ugly little smirk, she still found herself tensing with anger. It would be better to avoid her entirely. Stay away, and not think about her.

So what spirit of self-destruction was it that caused her, a few moments later, to edge forward in the Doyle woman's direction?

⁘

"There he is. There's my man." Joan Doyle waved a silk handkerchief. "He still doesn't see me," she said laughing. "One thing we know," she announced cheerfully. "They'll be hungry."

Joan Doyle had known sorrow; but it seemed to her nowadays that she was the luckiest person alive. At eighteen she had been married, very happily, to a gentleman near Waterford. Six years later, having lost two children to fever, she lost her third child and her husband in a shipping accident. At twenty-four she was a widow, and for many months she entered a place of silent sadness from which she did not see any escape.

But then she met John Doyle who, with great patience, coaxed her out of her misery and, after more than a year, into marriage. That had been six years ago and now, with a home and two children, Joan Doyle knew more happiness than she had ever dreamed to be possible. And being in any case a warm and affectionate soul, and having known what it was to suffer great pain, she made a point never, if possible, to give pain to others. She was always doing little kindnesses; and it would amuse her rich and genial husband that hardly a week went by without her coming to him with a new scheme to help someone in trouble.

"It must be your Spanish blood that makes you so warm," he would laugh. Having no malice herself, she could never imagine it in others. This, too, her husband loved: it made him feel protective.

Joan became aware of Margaret when she was still a dozen yards away. She didn't turn to look at her, at first, because the woman beside her had just started to engage her in conversation; but even out of the corner of her eye, she could see that it was the woman she had noticed the other week at Donnybrook Fair. For there couldn't, surely, be two women in the Dublin area with such wonderful dark-red hair. Not a trace of grey in it, either, though she guessed that the woman might be a little older than herself. Joan's own hair had a few strands of grey, which she skilfully disguised; indeed, she had been smiling with rueful amusement at the thought that this red-headed woman clearly had no need of such artifice, when Margaret had seen her and taken that expression for a contemptuous smirk.

For Margaret's assessment of Joan Doyle was based upon a misapprehension. Of the quarrel between their two families, Joan knew nothing at all. The dispute over the inheritance had been so ancient that Henry Butler had never bothered to tell his daughter about it. As for the present, Joan hadn't the least idea who Margaret was.

So it was unfortunate that by chance, as Margaret came within earshot, the woman beside Joan had been talking about a recent case of a disputed inheritance in Dublin. The family who lost, she had just remarked, were very bitter.

"My husband says that the time to secure an inheritance is before someone dies, not after," Joan had replied. "He's a terrible man," she continued with a laugh. "Do you know what he says?" And now, to imitate the alderman's voice, she spoke more loudly. "The disinherited have only themselves to blame."

It was these last words that Margaret heard, as Joan laughed and turned to look at her.

If people usually hear what they expect to hear, then every expectation Margaret might have had was now fulfilled. There was no doubt in her mind: she had heard what she had heard. This rich little Dublin woman, whose family had stolen her own poor father's inheritance, was mocking her to this group of women, insulting her in public. Well then, she thought, let her mock me to my face.

"Tell me," she calmly intruded on the conversation, "how would you feel if you were disinherited yourself?" And with that she gave her a cold, unyielding stare.

Joan Doyle did not return this gaze, though she certainly looked at Margaret. She thought it perhaps a little rude of this stranger to butt in as she had, and she seemed to be wearing rather a long face for such a festive occasion. But it wasn't in Joan's nature to criticise. And there really was no question, she thought, that this severe-looking woman had the most wonderful hair.

"I don't know," she answered simply. And then, thinking to lighten the other's apparently solemn mood with a cheerful compliment, she went on with a laugh: "I'm sure I could bear it if I had your hair." She had no sooner said it than she was distracted by one of the other women pointing out that the riders were on the bridge and that her husband was waving to her. By the time she turned back again, the red-haired woman was gone. She asked her companions who she was, but none of them knew.

⁘

She was to learn, however, the following month.

If there was one thing the English of the Pale were proud of, it was their religion. They had their language, laws, and customs, of course, and these were important; but after three centuries of living side by side with the Irish on the island, what could the English point to as the one important thing which held them together as a community and proved their superiority to even the best of the natives? What gave them the moral high ground? The answer was simple.

The English knew they were superior because they were Roman Catholic.

The native Irish were Catholic, too, of course. But outside the Pale, in the great native hinterland, everybody knew that the Celtic Church was much as it had always been. Divorce was allowed, priests married, monasteries were run by local chiefs—in short, the native church was still tolerating those degenerate practices which the Pope had asked the English to clean up when they first invaded the island. To the English in Ireland, the thing was clear as day: true Catholicism, Roman Catholicism, was only to be found within the English Pale.

Indeed, of all the kingdoms in Christendom, none was more loyal to the Pope in Rome than the kingdom of England. In Germany, or in the Low Countries, the heretical Protestants, those followers of Luther and others who threatened good Catholic order, might be tolerated. But not in England. Young Henry VIII and his loyal wife, Catherine, the princess from Spain, would see to that. The King of England detested Protestants; he was ready and willing to execute them. The English in Ireland, therefore, could truly claim, "We are the guardians of the Roman faith."

But one thing, in Ireland, had for a long time been missing. The Church was the repository of culture and learning; the higher priesthood were nearly always educated men. But Ireland had no university. Ambitious young men thinking of the priesthood had to travel to Paris or Italy—or, more usually, to Oxford or Cambridge. And in 1518, a first step was taken to correct that situation.

They were a lively party. There was Doyle, tall and handsome, and sporting a splendid fur hat into which he'd pinned a circular

badge encrusted with jewels. Joan, in rich brown velvet laced with
pearls, was sitting happily beside him. The wagon was handsome—
padded seats, silk curtains. Inside the wagon also rode James
MacGowan and his wife. They were more quietly dressed, as befit-
ted their less exalted station. For though MacGowan could probably have afforded clothes as fine as Doyle's, he was far too clever to
wear them. Perched up in front, beside the coachman, was Tidy, a
glover just finishing his apprenticeship, whom MacGowan had
brought along with him. The October day was overcast, but there
were bright gashes in the clouds, and no sign of rain, as they rolled
westwards. They were going to Maynooth.

The castle of Maynooth lay about a dozen miles west of Dublin.
Far larger than the fortified manors of the gentry like Malahide, it
was one of several impressive centres where the mighty Earl of
Kildare held court. And no doubt it was because of Maynooth's
proximity to Dublin and the heart of the Pale that the earl had chosen it for his new religious foundation.

For if the English of the Pale were proud of their faith, they invested in it, too. In Dublin especially, rich men like Doyle might be
reluctant to contribute to civic buildings, but in the churches their
memorials and the chantries where the priests sung masses for their
souls were more splendidly endowed than ever. What then should
the Fitzgeralds do, if not something on a grander scale?

The new College of Maynooth was housed close to the castle. It
had a hall, a chapel, and a dormitory. Its stated purpose was to be a
small community for religious study and instruction. "But if I know
anything about the ambition of the Fitzgeralds," Doyle had remarked, "this will only be a beginning." For everyone knew that it
was in just such small colleges that the universities of Oxford and
Cambridge had first begun.

And with the building completed, the earl had invited people
from far and wide to witness the service of consecration.

Joan looked at her companions with affection. Her husband:
tall, dark, capable; some people, she knew, were afraid of him, but

to her he was strong as a lion, yet gentle as a lamb. MacGowan, younger than her husband, strangely ageless, with his thinning hair, drooping lip, and his eye always so sharp. He traded all over the Pale and far beyond. "I know a lot," her husband had once remarked, "but our friend MacGowan knows everything." And on several occasions he had returned home shaking his head with wonderment and told her, "That fellow is more cunning than the devil himself." But MacGowan and his homely wife had always seemed a warm and kindly couple to Joan. Perhaps, she considered, both assessments might be true. As for young Tidy, his case was simple enough. "The Tidy family are good people," her husband had informed her. "One of the best of the craftsmen families, and very devout." Henry Tidy was going to be a glover. A good trade. In a few years, she supposed, young Tidy would be looking for a wife. Perhaps, she thought contentedly, she could help him find a good one.

Late in the morning the Doyle party arrived at the castle of Maynooth in a happy mood. And this was appropriate for it was immediately clear that, on this day at least, all quarrels were to be forgotten.

Everyone was there. Fitzgeralds and Butlers, Talbots and Barnewalls, royal officials from Dublin and some of the greatest Irish chiefs from beyond the Pale. For though the new college was clearly a triumph for the Fitzgeralds, and situated within the English Pale, it was still, in its way, a foundation that did honour to the whole island.

No sooner had the Doyles arrived than a host of people came up to greet them. Even the Talbots of Malahide came over to say a few friendly words. For all his riches, it wasn't every day that the proud Talbots would walk across to talk to Alderman Doyle. "It's because they know you were born a Butler," he said with a smile to Joan. But what Joan was really hoping for was a chance to see, at close quarters, the Earl of Kildare himself.

Of course, she had seen him from time to time in Dublin, com-

ing or going at the castle or the great Kildare town house. But he
had always been a distant presence, protected by retainers. Even at
his town house, there were sentries on duty at the gates, armed with
German muskets. The last time she had seen him in the street, he
had been surrounded by a phalanx of gallowglasses, as they called
the fearsome Scottish mercenaries with their terrible battle axes,
which some of the island's chiefs had taken to using as bodyguards
and shock troops nowadays.

If twenty years earlier, Henry Tudor had cynically decided it was
easier to leave the old earl alone than it was to break him, the relationship of the new generation was closer. The present earl and King
Henry VIII were friends, and in the last few years, the English king
had let his friend rule Ireland almost as he pleased. Kildare was allowed all the crown revenues, and so long as he kept order, he didn't
even have to render accounts.

"The truth is," Doyle had remarked to Joan one day, "Kildare is
practically the High King of Ireland now." And the analogy was
valid. For after generations of intermarriage with the greatest Irish
princely families, the head of the Fitzgeralds not only had a huge
political network amongst the native Irish princes but the blood of
Irish kings flowed in his veins, too. In his strongholds beyond the
Pale, Irish bards at the banquets sang songs about his Irish ancestors,
and he dispensed law according to the old Irish brehon laws just as
easily as he would use English law elsewhere. "He uses whichever
law suits him best," some litigants grumbled. To the English king he
would say, "Sire, without you I am nothing." To the mighty
O'Neills, his kinsmen, who acknowledged him as their overlord,
he'd point out, "We're doing very well out of this." As for keeping
order, just as the High Kings had done in the centuries before, he
would raid the territories of any chiefs who gave him trouble and
carry off their cattle. The only difference between the old days and
now was that Kildare had Tudor artillery.

As it happened, Joan got her wish sooner than she expected. It
was after the Talbots had moved on that she became aware of an-

other party coming in their direction. They were being escorted by the mayor of Dublin, but they seemed to be foreigners. There was a priest whom, by the look of him, she judged to be Italian; an aristocratic gentleman dressed in black who was undoubtedly from Spain; and two ladies, whose bodices and gowns flashing with jewels were altogether richer than anything to be seen in Dublin. But what struck her most was the handsome figure who accompanied them. He was dressed in hose with padded feet. His tight-fitting doublet, sewn with golden thread and studded with pearls, had huge slashed puffs at the shoulders. She had not seen anyone dressed quite like this before, but she knew enough to guess that this must be the aristocratic fashion at the English court. He came forward with the graceful pad of a great cat; she heard him say a few words in French to the ladies, who laughed, and she wondered who this gorgeous, courtly creature might be. Then suddenly she recognised him, with a little start. It was the Earl of Kildare.

A moment later, the mayor was introducing them. Kildare, his eyes twinkling pleasantly, said a few appropriate words, and the group moved on, leaving Joan to watch them, fascinated.

She had known that the earl had been sent for many years to the English court by his father. That was where he had formed his friendship with the present king, Henry VIII. And she had known that the English court was nowadays a centre of learning, where courtiers would be expected to be familiar with classical literature and the arts as well as be able to dance, and play the lute, and compose a verse. But this was the first time that she had glimpsed the gilded face of the Renaissance, and she sensed that new world even if she did not know exactly what it was.

"Impressed?" Her husband was looking at her with amusement.

"He seems like a man who lives in another world." She smiled. "With the angels in paradise."

"He does indeed," Doyle nodded thoughtfully as Kildare and his party moved farther away. "And some say," he went on softly, "at our expense. He billets his troops on people whenever he likes. He taxes high and keeps all the money. That's how he can so easily endow this new college of his. Some people would welcome reform."

Joan had heard people muttering about reform in Ireland for most of her life, but she had learned not to take it too seriously. "My Butler relations used to complain about the Fitzgeralds," she remarked with a laugh, "but given the chance I'm sure they'd behave just the same." She looked at Doyle more seriously. "He has the friendship of the king," she pointed out. "Now more than ever, they say."

Doyle nodded thoughtfully. She saw his eyes following Kildare as he continued his progress round the guests.

"I'll tell you a story," he said. "Years ago, the king's father had two councillors. They had served him very faithfully for many years, and thanks to them, when Henry Tudor died, there was more money in the royal treasury than ever before in England's history. Our present king had known the two men all his life. They were like uncles to him. But by serving his father so well, they had made many enemies. So when the old king died, the English Parliament wanted to impeach them." He paused. "So you know what young Henry did? Executed both men. Without a second thought. Because it suited him." He paused. "The friendship of King Henry VIII is a dangerous thing. For he loves only himself."

And now Joan found herself gazing after the golden figure of Kildare and the grey October light upon his back seemed more sombre, even melancholy.

Then she saw the woman with the red hair.

This time she discovered who she was quite easily. MacGowan was still standing close by and he knew at once. "She's the wife of William Walsh. I've done business out at their place. She hardly ever comes to Dublin."

"William Walsh the lawyer?" asked Doyle. "They say he's a good man. Will you bring them over?" he said to MacGowan.

÷

William Walsh looked at his wife in surprise.

"It will look very strange," he said, "if you don't." He was a tall, rangy man with long arms, long legs, close-cropped grey hair, and a nervous energy in his kindly face; but his square jaw still gave a hint of his military forebears. He couldn't imagine why his wife was so reluctant to come and speak to the Doyles, especially on such a happy occasion; and though he was used to Margaret's occasional moods, he felt he must be firm. "They're not people I'd wish to offend," he admonished her gently as she unwillingly accompanied him.

Doyle greeted them courteously. He seemed to Margaret to be straightforward enough. Joan Doyle smiled her pretty smile. "I know who you are," she said to William Walsh, and continued, as she turned her smile towards Margaret: "I know everything about you." It was one of those bright little phrases that could mean anything or nothing. Margaret did not reply, but remained watchful.

Doyle did most of the talking, but it was clear that he wanted to hear William Walsh's views on various subjects. Margaret's impression was that the alderman prided himself on knowing everyone who mattered in the Pale, and that, being acquainted with William Walsh the lawyer, he had decided to know him better. As far as she could judge, William had impressed him.

During this time, neither of the wives was called upon to speak. But then the conversation turned to families.

"You're a kinsman of Walsh, at Carrickmines, I believe," Doyle remarked. It was a signal, a polite acknowledgement of the lawyer's status amongst the gentry.

"A kinsman, yes," William answered pleasantly.

"We were speaking to the Talbots of Malahide just now," Doyle continued, with evident pleasure. "My wife knows them well," he exaggerated just a little, "being a Butler herself. You know them perhaps?"

"Slightly," said William Walsh, with perfect truth. Then with a quiet smile, he added: "Malahide's a long way from where we live."

And now, with her ready little smile, Joan Doyle turned to Margaret.

"You wouldn't want to go out there, I'm sure." She turned back to the rest of them. "All that way up in Fingal."

It sounded so harmless. No one but herself, Margaret realised, could know what the Doyle woman really meant. "I know all about you," she had said. And how slyly, now, she was humiliating her with this knowledge. She clearly knew that Margaret's family came from Fingal. The Talbots must have told her how they'd sent Margaret packing when she was a young woman. The bitter memory of it still cut deep after all these years. And now the alderman's wife had decided to taunt her with it under the guise of friendly conversation. The viciousness of the dark little woman almost took her breath away.

But nobody else had noticed anything, and a moment later the conversation moved on to the new college, and then to Kildare himself.

"I have to say," Walsh told the alderman, "that the earl has been very good to me." Indeed, it was partly as an expression of loyalty and gratitude that he had made a point of coming to Maynooth with his wife that day. "For it's thanks to him," he explained, "that I've just got to farm some good Church land."

If the English of the Pale were proud supporters of the Church, the Church in turn was good to them. As a lawyer, William Walsh looked after the business of several religious houses, including the house of nuns whose affairs Margaret's father had turned over to him some years before his death. Another way that the Church could reward the local gentry was to lease Church lands to them at very modest rents. The Walsh family—solid gentry who had supplied several distinguished churchmen down the generations, too—were good candidates for such treatment; but it had been a friendly word from Kildare that had recently ensured William Walsh the lease of a monastic farm at a rent that was almost laughable.

Margaret well understood that by informing Doyle of this, her husband was skilfully letting the alderman know two things: first, that he had the favour of Kildare and was loyal to him; and second, that he was actively engaged in acquiring wealth. Doyle seemed impressed.

"Do you think of standing for Parliament?" the alderman enquired.

Though the Irish Parliament was supposed to represent the whole island, in practice nearly all of its thirty or forty members came from Dublin and the nearby Pale. Parliament's power might be limited by the English king, but there was prestige in membership.

"I think of it," said Walsh. "And you?" There were several rich merchants in the Parliament.

"I, too," Doyle agreed, and gave Walsh a look which said: we'll talk further.

During this exchange, Margaret had watched in silence. She knew how hard her husband had worked for his family—it was one of the many things she loved about him—and she was glad to see him having some success. She had nothing in particular against Doyle. If only his wife had been someone else.

The conversation moved on. The two men were discussing the king. She was not paying close attention but she heard the Doyle woman say to her husband, "You should tell him the story you just told me." And the alderman started to relate the tale about the two councillors that the king had executed. "These Tudors are quite as ruthless, perhaps more so, than the Plantagenets ever were," she heard him say. As he said it, she found her mind carried back to that fatal expedition in her childhood, when the Irish gentlemen had so unwisely invaded England and Henry Tudor had killed them all. And suddenly, for the first time in years, the youthful face of her brother John rose up before her—that happy, excited face, before he had gone to his death—and she felt a wave of sadness pass over her.

She hadn't been listening. The Doyle woman was talking.

"My husband's very cautious," she was saying, "especially about the English. He says"—and now it seemed to Margaret that the Doyle woman glanced sideways to make sure she was listening—"he says that if people get into trouble with the Tudors, they have only themselves to blame."

That same little phrase: the identical words she had used before about the inheritance. Was it possible that the woman could be so vicious, so low as to make a cruel reference to the loss of her brother? Margaret looked at the two men. Neither of them had noticed anything, but then they wouldn't. Wasn't this exactly the trick that this dark little woman had played before? She was smiling, too, as if butter wouldn't melt in her mouth, and turning to her.

"You really do have wonderful hair."

"Thank you." Margaret smiled back. I see through you, she thought, but this time you've gone too far. If it was war the Doyle woman wanted, she would get it.

As she and her husband moved away a few minutes later, Margaret murmured, "I hate that woman."

"Really? Why?" Walsh asked.

"It doesn't matter. I have my reasons."

"I thought," he unwisely remarked, "that she was pretty."

III

⊰ 1525 ⊱

Sean O'Byrne's face remained very calm. That was his way. But he wasn't pleased. A damp March breeze ruffled his hair. He glanced up at the pale blue sky, then stared at their accusing faces: how superior they thought themselves.

As it happened, the accusation was true. He'd slept with the girl. But they couldn't possibly know. That was what annoyed him. They were accusing him on the basis of suspicion and of his reputation. And as far as he was concerned, that made it unfair. In fact, it was intolerable. In the curious mind of Sean O'Byrne, that made them more at fault than he was.

Not that he could really blame his wife. God knows, he'd given her enough to complain about, down the years. And he probably shouldn't resent the friar, since the friar was a good and holy man who, so far at least, hadn't said a word. The priest, however, was another matter. In a little place like this, people needed to stick together.

Sean O'Byrne never forgot that he was of princely blood. Four generations ago his forebear, the younger son of the chief of the O'Byrnes, had been given some desirable lands on the eastern side of the Wicklow Mountains. Much of that inheritance had gone by now; the portion which remained was called Rathconan; and Sean, who was known as O'Byrne of Rathconan, loved it.

He loved the small, square stone tower—four storeys high, one room per floor—that had once been the fortified centre of his family's local rule and was now, in truth, no more than a modest farm. He loved the tufts of grass that grew everywhere from its crumbling masonry. He loved to look out from its roof at the great, green sweep down towards the coast. He loved the gaggle of farm buildings where his untidy children were playing at this moment, and the tiny stone chapel where Father Donal administered the sacraments. He loved his few fields, the little orchard, the pasture where he kept the cattle, which were his main occupation, in winter; and above all, he loved the open ridges of the hills behind where, in summer, he drove his herds and where he could wander, free as a bird, day after day.

He loved his children. The girls had grown up strong and were turning into beauties. The eldest was dark, her younger sister fair. Both had their mother's blue eyes. He'd already had a few offers for the dark one. "You'll hardly have to give more than a token dowry to see them well married," a neighbour had said to him recently. He was pleased to hear that and hoped that it was true. His only concern was his eldest son, Seamus. The boy was a good worker, and he

knew his cattle. But he was sixteen now and Sean could sense that
he was restless. He had the idea that he should give him some responsibility, but he didn't yet know what. His little son Fintan was
only five. There was no need to worry about him yet.

Sean also loved his wife. He'd chosen her well. She was an
O'Farrell, from the island's Midlands, out past Kildare. Cattle country. A fine, upstanding, fair-haired woman. He'd wooed her and
won her in the old-fashioned way; and treated her in the old-fashioned way ever since. And that was the trouble.

"It is pride that is causing you to behave as you do," Father
Donal was saying to him now. "The terrible sin of pride."

He was not only a princely O'Byrne; his ancestor who had been
given Rathconan had noticed the dark-haired, green-eyed little girl
who used to run errands for his father down to the harbour at
Dalkey or the fort at Carrickmines. He'd fallen in love and married
her. Sean knew that the blood of Walsh of Carrickmines had flowed
in her veins, and even the blood of the half-remembered Ui Fergusa
of Dublin, too. For as part of her meagre dowry, she had brought
into his family an ancient drinking skull with a gold rim—a strange
and fearsome memento of that clan's princely past. Was he proud of
his descent from all these rulers of the land? Certainly. And did this
make him think he had the right to every woman he could find? No,
the priest was wrong about that.

It had been greed, when he was younger, that made him chase
after women. Simple greed. He knew it very well. Wasn't every
woman proof that life was being lived to the full? If he had sometimes gone from one to another, two in a day, he was like a man at
the banquet of life, seeing how many of the dishes he could taste. It
was greed. And vanity. He had a reputation to keep up. "Sean
O'Byrne of Rathconan. Ah, he's a devil with the women." That's
what they all said about him. He was proud of his reputation, and
he wasn't going to give it up—not as long as he could still get the
women. And then, of course, there was one thing more. Perhaps it
came as you grew older, but it seemed to Sean that it had been there

from the beginning. Fear of death. Wasn't every woman proof that he was still young, still alive—not wasting a single one of the precious moments of life remaining? Yes, that was it. Live to the full before you die, before it's too late.

As for the girl, she wasn't bad. Brennan's wife. Brennan had been a tenant for five years now, farming a part of Sean O'Byrne's land. His little house—it was hardly more than a hut, really—lay on the other side of a small wood about half a mile away down the slope. Brennan was a reliable sort of man, paid his rents on time, was a good worker. Like many such tenants, he had no security; under Irish law, O'Byrne could turn him out any time he wanted to; but good tenants weren't so easy to find, and Sean had been glad enough to have him, even if he was a dull, ungainly sort of fellow. Strangely enough, Sean had never taken much notice of Brennan's wife until the previous year. He supposed Brennan must have kept her out of sight down in the hut. But then one evening at harvest time, he had noticed her alone in a field and gone to talk to her.

She was a pretty little thing. Broad faced. Freckled. She smelled of farm, of course, but there was another, subtle scent about her, something in the quality of her skin. By the autumn, that scent, and everything else about her, had become an obsession with him. Before winter began, she was his. But he'd been careful. He'd never had a woman quite so close to home before. He was sure that his wife had never seen them. Whether Brennan had any idea about the affair, he wasn't sure. The girl said he didn't know. If he did, he was certainly giving no sign of it. Afraid of losing his tenancy, probably. As for the girl, she seemed willing enough; he supposed she must be bored with Brennan. Of course, it might be that she was only keeping him happy because he had power over them, but he preferred not to think of that. She and her husband would be down at their hut now, unaware of the shameful interrogation taking place at the entrance to the tower house.

"It isn't true," he said to his wife, ignoring Father Donal entirely. "There's nothing more to say."

He wondered why his wife should have chosen to attack him now. The Brennan girl was too close to home, he supposed: that would be it. His wife's eyes had a steady, fixed look, as though she'd made up her mind about something. But what? Was there pain concealed in the cold stare of those eyes? He knew very well there was. She was just hiding it. He had no doubt that he would bring her round again, as he always had before; though he supposed he might have to give up the girl. Well, if it came to that, so be it.

"You deny it?" Father Donal cut in. "Do you seriously mean us to believe that?"

There had been one or two times when his own absences had been unexplained, and when Brennan had come looking for the girl. Once, just once, his wife had seen him with his arm round the girl, but he had explained that away. There was nothing they could prove. Nothing. So why should the tall, bare-boned priest be giving him the accusing eye in the doorway of his own house?

He'd been good to Father Donal. In a way, they were lucky to have him there. Unlike many of the priests in the smaller parishes, he was a man of some education, something of a poet even. And he had taken proper orders: he was able to administer the sacraments. But also, like many priests in the poorer Irish parishes, he was forced to work for his living as well. From time to time, he would go out with the fishermen at Dalkey, or one of the other harbours in the region, to earn some extra money. "Saint Peter himself was a fisherman," he would growl. And like many priests in the Irish Church, he had a wife and several children. "Down in the English Pale, you couldn't do it," Sean O'Byrne had remarked to him on more than one occasion. "It has always been the custom in the Irish Church," Father Donal had replied with a shrug. And indeed, it was said that the Holy Father himself was aware of the custom and did not choose to make an issue of it. Sean did not know whether a marriage ceremony had ever been performed between the two, and had never asked. All he did know was that he was good to Father Donal's children, gave them little errands to do, and helped to keep them fed.

So it hardly seemed right that the priest should be taking this stern moral tone with him about his own shortcomings now.

"Are you ready to swear to it?" Father Donal's eye was piercing him from under his iron brow. It was disconcerting. And then suddenly Sean thought he understood. Was the priest offering him a way out? Perhaps that was the game. He glanced at his wife, silently watching. He must answer, now, to his watching wife.

"I am indeed," he said without a blush. "I swear it on the Blessed Virgin."

"Your husband has sworn," the priest declared to Eva O'Byrne. "Will that satisfy you?"

But she had turned her face away.

She couldn't look at him. Not just then. It was too painful.

Sometimes, when she looked back, Eva blamed the trial marriage for the problems in her life. It was not uncommon, outside the English Pale, for couples to live together for a time before committing to formal marriage. Her father hadn't approved, but Eva had been headstrong in those days; she had gone to live with Sean O'Byrne. And they had been the happiest and most exciting months of her life. If only, she thought, I'd paid more attention to studying his character and less to the joys of our love life. Yet how could she have felt otherwise, when she thought of his splendid, athletic body, and his skilful caresses? Even now, after all these years, his magnificent physique had hardly changed. She still wanted him. But the years of pain had taken their toll as well.

When had he first started to stray to other women? At the time their first child was born. She knew such things were not uncommon. A man had needs. But she had been terribly hurt at the time. Was it her fault that he had continued to stray ever since? For a while she had supposed that it might be, but as the years went by she had decided that it really wasn't. She had taken good care of her appearance. She was still attractive, and her husband clearly found her so. Their married life together was entirely satisfactory: she supposed she should thank God for that. And above all, she had been a good wife. The land they had left at Rathconan was only just enough to keep them. The chief of the O'Byrnes might be their kinsman, but like most of the Irish local rulers, he exacted heavy payments for his rule and protection, just as he, in turn, had to pay heavy taxes to the Earl of Kildare. The system might be English in name, but for all practical purposes, Kildare's rule over the O'Byrnes was that of a traditional Irish king. It was she, as much as her straying husband, who made sure these obligations could always be fulfilled each year; she who made sure the harvest was brought in when he was wandering, often as not, with the cattle on the ridges above; she who kept an eye on the Brennans and the other dependents of the place. That was why it particularly angered her that he should have started a relationship with the Brennan woman. "How can you be so stupid?" she had stormed. "You have a good tenant, so you go and play the fool with his wife."

But above all, how could he humiliate her like this, practically in her own house? Nearly two decades of marriage, a loving wife, children—didn't that mean anything to him? Had he no respect for her? It wasn't just the woman she objected to so much. It was the lie that hurt. He knew she knew, yet he could lie to her face. Didn't he even realise the profound contempt for her that he was showing? That was why she had persuaded the priest to make him swear: in the hope that, for once, she could force him to tell the truth. She just wanted to break through to him, to make something change.

She had thought he would hesitate to lie to the priest. Especially when there happened to be a friar there as well. For whatever his behaviour might be, she knew that her husband had a respect for his religion. She had seen him giving extra money to the travelling friars when he thought she wasn't looking. And she had loved him for that. Like most people, even those who were cynical about the worldly priests, or the sedentary monks, he liked to give alms to the poor friars who preached and tended the sick, and led a simple life.

And he wasn't without reverance, either. Once, when they had gone into the Cathedral of Christ Church to see the Bachall Iosa and the other sacred relics there, she had seen him gaze at them with awe and fear in his eye. Sean O'Byrne might like to give out that he was a bold fellow, but he was still afraid of the sacred relics, like anybody else.

Yet he'd just lied again. He'd sworn a sacred oath as casually as he had seduced the girl. It had probably been a mistake to choose Father Donal for the task, she decided. The priest was too familiar to him. He somehow thought he could lie to Father Donal, and that it did not matter. As for the friar, he was just a bystander who could hardly be involved. And so after this embarrassing scene, she was no better off than she had been before. She knew very well that he was looking at her, even now, with a smile of triumph on his face. It was too painful. She had failed to get anywhere at all. No wonder she had turned away.

The friar, who had been brought to the house by Father Donal, was on his way to visit a hermit who lived over at Glendalough. Her husband was turning to the friar now, inviting him in. Of course, the good friar should be fed. She took a deep breath and prepared to do her duty. But even in defeat, she secretly vowed that she was not done with Sean O'Byrne yet.

Cecily was just walking through the Dame's Gate that same morning when they seized her. Two men grabbed at her arms; the third marched in front, looking pleased with himself. For a moment when it happened, she had been so taken by surprise that she could only give a little scream. By the time she had understood what they were doing, they were triumphantly marching her up the slope.

"You can't arrest me," she protested, "I've done nothing wrong."

"We'll see about that," the man in front replied, "at the Tholsel."

The ramshackle old town hall with its heavy gables was not a building the Dublin corporation could be very proud of. Every year someone among the aldermen would declare that the place must be refurbished, and everyone would agree; but somehow the funds were never available. "We'll get to it next year," they always said. Nevertheless, as its battered old face gazed sleepily towards Christ Church, the Tholsel had a kind of shabby dignity. And today, from their confabulations therein, a group of city officials had decided to send out parties of men to sweep the city streets in search of offenders—and useful fines. They were waiting for Cecily in an upper chamber.

Her offence—and it was a minor crime—was that she was wearing a saffron-coloured scarf over her head.

"Your name?"

She gave it. Cecily Baker. A straightforward English name, misleading only to the small extent that, like plenty of other people with English names in Dublin, she had an Irish mother—an O'Casey, as it happened. She was English officially though, resident in Dublin, and therefore not allowed to wear the saffron-coloured scarf that was popular amongst the native Irish.

It wasn't only the long-prohibited Irish dress that the guardians of the law had been looking for that day. In Dublin, as in London and other cities, there were plenty of ancient laws regulating what people could wear. Craftsmen weren't to dress themselves up like aldermen, who were their betters; nuns were forbidden to wear fine furs. It was all part of the business of maintaining social order and morals. Some of these laws were more observed than others, but they were there to be remembered whenever the authorities decided to assert themselves or needed to collect some money. In answer to their questions, she told them that she was unmarried, though betrothed, a seamstress, and that she lived a short distance outside the city's southern gate.

"Can I go now?" she asked. If they wanted to prosecute, they knew where to find her. But to her irritation, they still wouldn't let her go. Someone had to come and answer for her, they insisted. So she gave them the name of the young man she was to marry: Henry

Tidy, the glover. And they sent a man off to fetch him. Then they told her she could sit on a wooden bench while she waited.

Cecily Baker was a serious young woman. She had a round face, red cheeks, a pointed nose, and a sweet smile. She was a very nice young woman. She also had some very strong opinions.

It was Cecily's opinion that Holy Church was sacred; others might criticise the shortcomings of some of the religious orders, but it was the faith that was important, and the faith should be firmly defended. Those people in other countries—she had heard of Luther and the so-called Protestant reformers on the Continent— who wanted to upset the order sanctified by the centuries were wreckers and criminals as far as she was concerned; and if sound Catholic monarchs like King Henry VIII of England wanted to burn them, she had no objection. She thought it was probably for the best. She went to mass regularly, and confessed her sins to her priest; and when once he forgot how many Ave Marias he had given her as a penance for a small offence the previous month and allotted her too few the next time, she gently but firmly reminded him of his mistake. She also had very clear ideas about what a young couple, like herself and Tidy, once they were betrothed and soon to be married, should do together. And these ideas were physical and unrestrained—so much so that young Tidy had been quite startled. The fact that these sins of the flesh should then be confessed to her priest was, as far as she was concerned, a very proper part of the process.

And perhaps it was the confidence of knowing she'd fulfilled all her religious obligations that gave Cecily an equal conviction that the secular authorities had no right to impose on her unjustly. She knew perfectly well that her arrest—just for wearing an old scarf of her mother's—was an absurdity. She knew about the rule, but she could see that the men at the Tholsel were simply trying to collect a few fines. She wasn't impressed, and she certainly wasn't afraid. But she did wish that Henry Tidy would turn up. After a while, she began to feel quite lonely, sitting on the hard bench.

She had to wait nearly an hour. When he finally appeared, he wasn't alone. And he was looking worried.

She rose to greet him. The young man she loved. She smiled. She took a step towards him, expecting at least a kiss. But to her surprise, he made no move towards her at all. He stood where he was, his face strained, and his blue eyes gazing at her reproachfully.

"You gave my name."

Of course she had. Weren't they getting married? Wasn't he supposed to protect her?

"They said they needed someone to answer for me."

"I brought MacGowan."

"So I see." She nodded politely to the merchant. Why did he make her feel uncomfortable? Was it his searching eye? Or was it just the fact that he had the reputation of being clever, and she could never make out what he was thinking? Yet she knew that many people trusted MacGowan and went to him for advice.

"He has the freedom," Tidy explained. Having the freedom of the city was an important matter of status in Dublin. Being a freeman of the city entitled you to vote for the city council, to trade freely without paying tolls, and even to trade with merchants from overseas. Henry Tidy, ready to set up on his own as a master craftsman, was due to be considered for the freedom quite soon; a committee of aldermen would decide whether it was granted or not. The fact that he had brought a freeman of the city with him now showed that, in his mind at least, this foolish arrest was a serious matter. MacGowan had already moved over to talk to the men who were sitting comfortably behind a trestle table. They seemed to treat him with more respect than they had used towards her. She heard them murmuring.

Meanwhile, Henry Tidy wasn't being very nice. He was gazing at her as if there was something about the business that he couldn't believe.

"How could you do it, Cecily? You know the law." Of course she knew the law. But the arrest was absurd. Couldn't he see that? "You know the law, Cecily." He'd said it again. His attitude was starting to hurt her. Did he have to be so timid?

The men at the table had finished their conversation. She saw MacGowan nod. A moment later he came across and told her that she could leave. But when Tidy glanced at him questionably, MacGowan shook his head; and as soon as they were outside, he announced, "They won't drop it."

"What shall we do?" asked Tidy.

"My advice? We should go and see Doyle."

"Doyle." Tidy looked thoughtful. She knew that he had known the alderman slightly for many years, because he had told her about the fact with some pride. She also knew that Henry was in some awe of him. He turned to her. "I suppose," he said doubtfully, "that you'd better come, too."

She stared at him. That was all he had to say? Still not a word of sympathy? Did he really think this was all her fault?

His shoulders stooped forward slightly. She had never noticed it much before, except to think that it made him look determined. A sign of strength. Now she suddenly wondered: did it make him look like a hunchback? His little, pointed yellow beard jutted forward. It irritated her, though she couldn't exactly say why.

"There's no need," she said abruptly. "I'm going home." She turned and started to walk away.

And he didn't even try to stop her.

❖

The alderman's house was close by. Doyle was out, but his wife was at home. So MacGowan left Tidy with her while he went to find the alderman.

Sitting in the alderman's big house in the company of his attractive, Spanish-looking wife, Henry Tidy felt a little awkward at first. He had known Dame Doyle, as he respectfully referred to her, ever since he was an apprentice, and secretly he had always admired her; but he had never kept company in her house like this before. She was in her parlour, sitting quietly at her spinning wheel with one of her daughters; they did not talk much, but from time to time she would ask him a question, to which he would shyly reply. After a while, she sent her daughter out on an errand, so that he was alone with her. Then she gave him a kindly smile.

"You're worried, aren't you?"

It didn't take long for him to confide in her. The trouble wasn't just the arrest, he explained; he knew Cecily had been roughly treated, and he wanted to defend her. But it wasn't as simple as that. Word travelled fast in Dublin. He knew what people would be saying: "Young Tidy's got himself a foolish girl. A troublemaker." Didn't Dame Doyle feel Cecily should have thought about that? He didn't want to be angry, but shouldn't Cecily have shown him more consideration? It worried him also that she hadn't displayed much wisdom. During all this complaint, Joan Doyle watched him carefully.

"You're betrothed, aren't you?" she asked. He nodded. "And you're having doubts? It's not unusual, you know."

"It's not that," he confessed. "But you see," he went on awkwardly, "I'm up for the franchise soon."

And now Dame Doyle understood entirely.

"Oh dear," she said. "That is a problem."

In Dublin, as in most cities, there were several ways to become a freeman of the city. One was through guild membership; the other, just as frequently used, was by a direct grant from the city fathers. What made Dublin unusual, however, was the role it allowed to women. Perhaps it reflected the traditionally high status of women on the island, but they certainly had more opportunity in Dublin than they had in any English city. Not only did a widow take over her husband's freedom if he died; women in Dublin, married or single, could be granted the freedom in their own right. More remarkable still, a man who married a woman who had the freedom was then given it as well. Doyle had already promised his wife that he would obtain the freedom for each of their daughters. In addition to the dowries he could afford, this would make them highly desirable brides.

But if a man's widow would succeed him in the freedom of the city, then it seemed to Tidy that the city fathers might reasonably consider what sort of woman a man was marrying when that man was applying for the franchise. And judging by today's performance, he wasn't too sure what they'd think of Cecily. Indeed, he could hardly blame them if they thought she was unsuitable. What could have possessed her to behave like that?

"I'm wondering if I should be marrying her," he confessed miserably, "after what she did to me today."

"I'm sure she didn't mean to hurt you," the alderman's kindly wife assured him. She observed him carefully. "Do you love her?"

"Yes. Oh yes." He did.

"Good." She smiled. "Ah," she cried, "here comes my husband."

The alderman entered briskly, kissed his wife, and gave Tidy a friendly nod.

"You're not to worry about this stupid business," he said to the glover firmly. "MacGowan's told me what they did. I can get the charges dropped, though she'll be given a warning, of course. She must expect that." He looked at Tidy a little more severely now. "If you have influence over this young woman, you should persuade her to be more careful in future." The alderman's dark hair was grey at the temples nowadays. It added to his authority.

The interview now being over, as far as Doyle was concerned, he smiled pleasantly to indicate that Tidy was free to leave.

"They're getting married," his wife gently intervened. "He's going to apply for the franchise. And now he's afraid . . ."

Doyle paused and pursed his lips. He turned to Tidy and asked him a few questions about his position in the glovers' guild, about the girl and her family. Then he shook his head. He had long ago learned that if there was bad news to impart, the kindest thing was to do it quickly.

"I think they'll turn you down," he said frankly. "They'll say your wife is Irish."

If the old prohibitions against Irish dress were still enforced in the Pale, the franchise of Dublin itself was certainly supposed to be reserved for the English, and the city fathers were rather strict about keeping the Irish out. More subtle was the question: who's English and who's Irish? MacGowan, for instance, was Irish by name and Irish by ancestry. But the MacGowans had been important crafts-men in the city since the days of Brian Boru. Respectable Dubliners for centuries, they counted as English, and MacGowan had the freedom. Amongst the city councillors, you wouldn't expect even to find any Irish names at all; yet a rich Irish merchant named Malone had reached such wealth and prominence that he had even become an alderman. His Irishness had simply been ignored. Conversely, the Harolds had sternly upheld English rule against the Irish in the Marches for generations; but in the opinion of the Dublin alder-men, some of the Harolds had recently become a bit too wild and Celtic in their ways, and one of them had just been refused the free-dom. Perhaps the reality was best expressed by Doyle himself when he trenchantly observed in committee one day, "People are English if I say they are."

Cecily Baker might have an Irish mother, but nobody would have bothered to question her Englishness if it hadn't been for to-day's event. Doyle could quash the charge, but she had drawn at-tention to herself; people would talk, and when Tidy came up for consideration in the committee, some busybody would be sure to know and to raise the matter. It would not be liked. Tidy was only a modest fellow from one of the lesser craft guilds and had no pow-erful backers; his betrothed was running around making a nuisance of herself in Irish dress. He'd never pass. Doyle didn't know Cecily, but it seemed to him she couldn't have much sense, and he privately wondered if young Tidy mightn't do better. His bleak glance at his wife said as much.

"He loves her," she said gently. "Couldn't we do something?"

Do something? Do what? Tell the aldermen of grey old Dublin that Henry Tidy loved Cecily Baker and should be given the freedom of the city? He gazed at his wife affectionately. That's probably just what she would do, he thought. And get away with it, too. But it wasn't so easy. If he really put his mind to it, he could probably manage to get young Tidy the franchise. But even a powerful man like himself had only so much goodwill he could call upon. He still had to obtain the freedom for his own daughters. Should he really be squandering his precious goodwill on account of a girl young Tidy would probably be better off without?

"They might be as happy as we are," said his wife sweetly, as if answering his thoughts.

Would Tidy really find the warmth, the tenderness, the generosity of spirit that he had known? Children, relations, friends, and now even this glum young fellow and his silly girl—his wife drew them all into the circle of kindness that she had made of their home. He shook his head and laughed.

"You are involved in this, too, you know." He gave his wife's shoulder a little squeeze. "Cecily Baker must be made to understand that she may never repeat her behaviour. She must be a model citizen. If she transgresses again," he gave his wife a hard look, "it would hurt my reputation and my ability to help my own family. So please be certain that she means to reform." He turned to Tidy. "I can't promise you anything, but I'll speak for you." And now he gave the young man an even sterner look. "If you marry this girl, be sure you can keep her in order. Or I shall cease to be your friend."

Tidy promised gratefully that he would do so; and kindly Dame Doyle went in person to see Cecily the very next day.

⁂

Spring passed uneventfully for the Walsh family. It was during the summer that Margaret noticed that her husband was worried.

One reason for this was obvious. The spring weather had been fine enough, but the summer had turned into a disaster. Cloudy days, cold winds, drizzle; she couldn't remember a worse summer; and it was already clear that the harvest would be ruined. Everyone looked gloomy. It would be a poor year for the Walsh estate.

It was during July that she guessed there was something else on his mind. She could always tell when he was worried: he had a little trick of locking his fingers together and staring down at them. But she knew it was best to wait for him to tell her about it, and about a week before the festival of Lughnasa, he did so.

"I've to go down into Munster shortly," he announced.

The request that he would undertake the legal affairs of a monastery down in Munster had come as a welcome surprise a few months earlier. The fees would cover the shortfall from the bad harvest, and Walsh had been busy with the monastery's affairs in Dublin in recent weeks. He had reached the point now, he explained, where he needed to spend a little time down at the monastery itself.

"You think I won't be able to manage while you're away?" she asked, teasingly.

"Not at all." He smiled ruefully. "I expect you'll be glad to have me out of the house for a while." He paused. "But I don't want you to say where I'm going."

"I'm not to say you're down in Munster?"

"It might be misunderstood."

"And why," she asked, "is that?"

✣

William Walsh was a careful observer of the political scene. He was still hoping to get a seat in Parliament; but the last seven years had not been an easy time to become involved in politics.

Superficially, the situation in Ireland looked the same as usual. The king was far away; the Butlers and the Fitzgeralds were still rivals for power, and the Fitzgeralds, as always, were the stronger. But there was one subtle difference.

Walsh had remembered the story Doyle had told about King

Henry when they met at Maynooth, and the warning it contained. It had been only a year afterwards that something of Henry's character had been exhibited when Kildare and his royal friend had had a falling out. The cause had been a complex legal matter concerning the Butler inheritance: Henry had taken one view; Kildare, in Ireland, had flatly contradicted him. And soon afterwards, Kildare had been called by Henry to England, and a great English nobleman was sent to govern Ireland in his place. Walsh had been quietly cultivating his relationship with Doyle ever since their friendly exchange at Maynooth, and it was during one of their conversations in Dublin that the alderman had enlarged on the theme he had discussed before.

"You have to understand," he remarked, "that underneath all the royal splendour, Henry is like a spoilt child. No one has ever told him: *no*. If he wants something, he thinks he should have it. Thanks to the huge fortune his father's loyal councillors left him, he's been able to build new palaces and engage in some foolish expeditions on the Continent. All in search of glory. He'll soon empty his treasury. His father had to bend with the wind—he forgave Kildare over the Simnel business, and let him govern Ireland because nobody else could. The father was pragmatic; the son is vain. And if Kildare contradicts him or makes a fool of him, he can't stand it. His friendship, as I've already told you, is worth nothing."

Yet while Walsh suspected that the alderman was probably right, he also believed that the Fitzgeralds would continue to get their way; and events seemed to bear this out. After little more than a year, the great English nobleman had begged to be recalled. "You'd need a huge army and a ten-year campaign to bring English order to this island," he told the king. "You're better off leaving it to Kildare." Henry didn't give up so easily. He put Butler in charge. But as usual, the Fitzgeralds soon made it impossible for the Butlers to govern. There were numerous incidents. One of the Talbots, a good friend to the Butlers, was even murdered by Kildare's own brother. There was nothing for it: last year Kildare had been sent back to govern Ireland—on condition that he cooperate with the Butlers in the administration. Of course, it was all done in the best face-saving manner. Henry clasped him to his chest; the two men swore eternal loyalty and friendship. Henry even gave his friend one of his own cousins as an English bride. But his eyes were not smiling. And for their part, the Fitzgeralds were not deceived. "He'd like to destroy us, but he can't," they concluded. They weren't alarmed. They'd been surviving English kings for generations.

To William Walsh, it seemed that his loyalty to the house of Kildare was likely to work to his benefit now. Indeed, the chance of a parliamentary vacancy had recently arisen and he had hopes that, with Fitzgerald support and the goodwill of a number of important men in Dublin, including Doyle, he might well find himself in Parliament shortly. But one still had to be careful. Very careful. And never more so than at present. For the latest rumours he had heard in Dublin frightened him, and with good reason. They concerned Munster.

When reports from spies, that the Fitzgeralds were sending envoys to his enemies, had begun to filter through to the royal council in England, King Henry at first could scarcely believe it. "What the devil," he wanted to know, "are these damnable Fitzgeralds up to now? It looks to me," he added ominously, "like treason."

In fact it was the other great Fitzgerald lord, Kildare's kinsman the Earl of Desmond, down in Munster, who had sent the envoys to the King of France; and it was not quite so strange as it seemed. With its ancient trading links to France and Spain, the province of Munster had always looked after its own interests overseas, and the earls of Desmond had been known to send representatives to France and the court of Burgundy since Plantagenet times. In this case, however, King Henry was right to be suspicious: for what Desmond had actually agreed, in a secret treaty, was that if Tudor rule in Ireland became too unpleasant, he would transfer his allegiance to France and seek her king's protection. To Desmond, accustomed to generations of old Irish independence down in his Munster lordship, this might be cheeky, but it was still business as usual. To Henry, Desmond was a subject, and his embassy looked like treason. When Henry challenged Kildare about the reports, the Irish magnate laughed it off. "Desmond's a strange fellow," he told him. "I can't answer for everything he gets up to in Munster." "You'd better," the king let him know, "because I'm holding you responsible." That had been some months ago, and in Dublin, at least, the matter seemed to be dormant.

But recently Walsh had heard another and even more disturbing rumour. There were still members of the Plantagenet dynasty at large. Most preferred to stay out of trouble, and out of England. But it was always possible that one of them could be used by a foreign power to mount an expedition against King Henry, like the invasion of Lambert Simnel against his father. It was something Henry dreaded. So when Walsh heard the rumour that the King of France was now planning such a challenge with one of the Plantagenets, he could be sure of two things: that the Tudor king would be suspicious of anyone who went to see the French-loving Desmond; and that he would be sure to have spies in Dublin and the other ports watching out for people travelling to Munster.

"The trouble is," he now explained to Margaret, "not only do I, a lawyer who's had favours from the Fitzgeralds, have to go down into Munster but part of my business there is to see the Earl of Desmond himself."

"Must you go?"

"I really have to. I've been putting it off, but the business can't wait."

"What can I do to help you?"

"I shall go straight to the monastery. With luck I may even be able to see Desmond there. But I shan't say I'm going into Munster, and I don't want you to say so either. If anyone asks, which they won't, just say I'm up in Fingal. On no account say I'm to see Desmond."

"I won't," she promised.

✛

By the second week in August, it should have been harvest time. But there was no harvest. The stalks in the fields were brown and sodden. Summer had collapsed. Recently, however, a strange, damp heat seemed to have been building up in the atmosphere, and even in the ground. Out in Dublin Bay, under the grey sky, the sea looked whitish and sullen, like milk in a pan before it swells and froths over. As the groom had remarked to Joan Doyle that morning, "It isn't this time of year at all."

Joan and her husband had gone down to Dalkey three days earlier. The village had not changed its overall shape much in the last century and a half, but the Doyle's fortified house had been joined by half a dozen similar merchant forts belonging to important traders and gentry, including the Walshes of Carrickmines, who wanted to take advantage of the deep-water harbour. Doyle would go down there from time to time to check the storehouse or supervise the unloading of a cargo, and Joan would usually accompany him. She enjoyed the intimate quiet of the fishing hamlet below the hill. They had been there two days when Doyle was called back into Dublin on business, and she had decided to ride in with the groom the following day at her leisure.

It was a mistake. She should have gone in the morning. The oppressive atmosphere and the darkening sky in the south should have told her. But she had been slow getting out of the house, finishing little chores that really could have been done some other time. By early afternoon, when they finally left, it was obvious that a storm was coming. "We can still be in Dublin before it reaches us," she said. As they passed Carrickmines and heard the distant rumble of thunder over the Wicklow Mountains, she remarked ruefully to the groom that they might get a bit wet; and a little later, as the sky grew black and the first gusts of wind suddenly came through the trees, she laughed. "We'll be drowned." But when the storm finally swept down from the hills and broke over them, it was beyond anything she could have imagined.

There was a huge bang and a flash of lightning. Her horse reared and almost threw her; and the heavens opened. Moments later the rain was falling so hard that they could scarcely see the road in front of them. They edged forward, looking for shelter. At first they saw nothing, but after a short distance, round a curve in the road, they became aware of a squat, grey mass just ahead to their left. They pressed towards it.

⁜

It had been an uneventful day so far. Walsh was now away. Margaret had only one of her daughters and her youngest son, Richard, in the house with her. The boy was making a new chair in the barn; he was good with his hands. Her daughter was busy with the servants in the kitchen. Margaret had just been glancing out at the storm through one of the greenish windowpanes—she was rather proud of the glass windows that had recently been installed in the house's big hall— when she was called to the door. Finding two bedraggled figures seeking shelter, she naturally took them inside at once.

"Dear Lord," she cried, "we'd better get you some dry clothes."

So she was quite astonished when one of the two pulled off the scarf she'd put over her head and remarked cheerfully, "Why, it's the woman with the wonderful hair."

It was the cursed Doyle woman. For just a moment, she wondered whether, for some obscure reason, the alderman's wife had come there deliberately to annoy her; but a huge crash of thunder from outside made her admit the absurdity of the idea.

Seven years had passed since they had met at Maynooth. Occasionally her husband had mentioned seeing the woman in Dublin, and once or twice she had caught sight of her herself, on her rare visits into the city—though she had always turned aside to avoid her. And now here the creature was in her own house, her soft brown eyes lighting up with pleasure and her pretty face, as far as Margaret could see, looking even younger than her thirty-seven years.

"The woman with the red hair," she cried again, though there were one or two streaks of grey in it now.

"You'd best come to the fire," said Margaret. With luck, she thought, the storm would soon pass and the unwelcome visitor would be gone.

But the storm did not pass. It seemed on the contrary that, having crossed over the Wicklow Mountains, the storm had come to a halt beside the great curve of Dublin Bay and that it meant to release all its noise, and livid flashes, and its great deluge of water upon Dalkey, Carrickmines, and environs.

While the groom was taken to the kitchen, Margaret sent her daughter to fetch the alderman's wife some dry clothes, while Joan Doyle cheerfully removed her wet ones by the fire, and gladly accepted the proffered glass of wine. Then, having put on one of Margaret's robes, remarking that she might be there for some time, she sat on a big oak bench, comfortably tucked her feet under her, and settled down, as she put it, to have a good talk.

Perhaps it was just her cheerfulness that Margaret found irritating. The harvest was ruined, William Walsh was away taking risks with his reputation; yet while the thunder crashed outside, this rich little Dublin woman chatted away as though there was nothing wrong in the world. She talked of events in the city and her life there, suddenly remarking, for no reason Margaret could see, "But you're so lucky to live down here." She ran on about the delights of Dalkey. She described a visit she'd paid to Fingal. But it was when, as an aside, she expressed her sorrow about the Talbot murder at the turn of the previous year that Margaret lost patience and almost before she realised what she was saying, sourly remarked, "One less Talbot never did any harm."

It was quite unforgivable really. It would have been cruel even if she hadn't known that Joan's Butler family were close to the Talbots.

And however much the Doyle woman might have taunted her in the past, it was worse than bad manners to insult her like this when she was a guest in her own house. The words were scarcely out of her mouth before she felt ashamed. The insult found its mark. She saw the Doyle woman give a little gasp and flush. And she hardly knew where the conversation might have gone next if her fifteen-year-old son, Richard, had not just then come into the house from the barn.

"This is your son?" The Dublin woman turned and smiled; and Margaret secretly gave a sigh of relief.

There was no denying it, her youngest child was a very handsome boy. Slim, with red hair, not quite as dark as hers, a few freckles, an easy temper. If, like most boys of his age, he was sometimes moody, with strangers like the alderman's wife he was always engaging. Margaret could see that he had charmed the Dublin woman in no time. Thank God, she thought ruefully, that he has his father's good manners. He was soon answering all their guest's questions about himself and describing his simple country life with such artless enthusiasm that Joan Doyle was quite delighted; and if she had not forgotten Margaret's insult, she chose to believe as if she had, so that Margaret was only too glad to let the two of them talk. Only once did she interrupt. The Doyle woman had been asking Richard about his brothers and sisters when she enquired, "And your father, where is he?"

"He's up in Fingal," Margaret answered sharply, before her son could speak. He glanced at her with a hint of annoyance as though to say: do you think I'm so stupid that I'll blurt out the wrong thing? The Doyle woman saw it, but all she said was, "My husband has a very high regard for your father."

By late afternoon the storm had not abated. The thunder had rolled out into the bay, but the rain was still pounding down with the same monotonous hiss. "You won't be going anywhere this evening," Margaret heard herself say. When she went into the kitchen to supervise the preparation of the evening meal, Joan

Doyle accompanied her; but she waited and didn't get in the way until, seeing there were some peas to be shelled, she quietly made herself useful. Whatever her feelings about the woman might be, Margaret couldn't really complain of her.

It was early evening when they began to eat. Normally it would still have been bright outside, but so black were the storm clouds that Margaret had to light candles on the big oak table. As well as a fish stew, beef, and sweetmeats—her guest was, after all, the wife of a Dublin alderman—Margaret provided a flagon of their best red wine. I'll need it myself, she had thought, to get through this evening. Yet during the meal, at which, in the Irish manner, the whole household ate together, the Dublin woman was so easy with everybody, laughing and joking with her children and the groom, the men from the farm and the women who worked in the house, that Margaret had grudgingly to acknowledge that she was, after all, a wife and mother not so unlike herself. And perhaps it was the wine she was drinking—for when she had wine, it usually softened her mood—but Margaret even found herself laughing at Joan Doyle's jokes and telling a few herself. The whole party stayed at the table late, and after they were done and the table cleared, the two of them still sat and drank a little more. When it was finally time to retire to sleep, Joan Doyle remarked that she'd be well enough there on the broad bench in the hall. "Just give me a blanket," she suggested.

For a moment, Margaret hesitated. While the groom had gone to the kitchen, it was normal enough in an old-fashioned house like this for a guest to sleep in the big hall. But upstairs in the one formal bedchamber, Margaret and her husband had a large and handsome canopied bed. It was the most valuable item in the house and Margaret was proud of it.

"Not at all," she said. "You'll come upstairs and sleep in the bed."

It was a well-appointed chamber. Last year, William had received a fine tapestry hanging in lieu of payment for some work he had done, and this graced one of the walls. As Margaret put the candle on a table, the great oak bed gleamed softly and Joan Doyle re-

marked what a fine bed it was. As she always did, Margaret let down
her hair and brushed it, while the Dublin woman sat on the bed and
watched her. "You've wonderful hair," she said. As Margaret got into
one side of the bed, Joan Doyle undressed, and Margaret again
noted with admiration that she had still kept her figure only a little
plumper than it must have been when she was a young woman.
Then she got into bed beside Margaret and laid her head down. It
was strange, Margaret thought, to have this pretty woman lying so
close. "You've excellent pillows," Joan said, and closed her eyes. The
sound of the falling rain came softly from the window, as Margaret
closed her eyes, too.

The huge bang of the thunderclap in the middle of the night was
so sudden and so loud that they both sat bolt upright together.
Then Joan Doyle laughed.

"I wasn't asleep. Were you?"

"Not really."

"It was the wine. I drank too much wine. Will you listen to that
storm?" The rain was falling in torrents now, in a steady roar. There
was a blinding flash from outside; a crash of thunder seemed to
shake the room. "I shan't be able to sleep now," sighed Joan Doyle.

They started to talk again. Perhaps it was the strange intimacy of
the darkness, as the rain poured down and the thunder continued
to crackle and rumble round the sky, but the conversation became
quite personal. Joan spoke about her children and her hopes for
them. She also described how she had been trying to help young
Tidy and Cecily. "I tell you," she declared, "I had to give that girl
such a talking-to." And so evident were her kindness and her good
intentions, that Margaret wondered: was it possible that she had
misjudged her in the past? Their quiet conversation continued almost another hour, and the Dublin woman became quite confiden-
tial. It seemed she was worried about her husband. She hated all the
politics of the city, she told Margaret. "I don't so much mind that
the Fitzgeralds want to rule all our lives," she said, "but why do they
have to be so brutal?" The Talbot they had killed the previous year

had been a good man of whom she was fond, she explained. Whether this was a gentle reproach for her earlier remark, Margaret wasn't sure, but Joan went on. "Stay out of it all, I'm always begging my husband. You can't imagine the hateful, ridiculous rumours. And they're spread by busybodies who don't know the harm they cause, or spies of the English king. Do you know the royal councillors suspect any man who visits Munster for any reason? All because Lord Desmond is suspected at present on account of some foolish business he had with the French. Can you believe it? My husband had to vouch for an innocent man only the other day."

She paused and then patted Margaret's arm. "You're better off not to be involved in such things out here," she said.

And it was then, perhaps because she decided that she could trust this Doyle woman after all, perhaps also she thought that, if need be, the alderman might provide her own husband with a similar protection, and perhaps even because that last remark suggested that Doyle's wife supposed she wasn't worldly enough to know about such things, that Margaret now confided, "Oh, but we are involved." And she told her about William Walsh's visit to Munster. "Only you must promise not to tell a soul," she begged her, "as William would be furious if he knew I'd told you."

"He's very wise," Joan assured her. "I shan't even tell my own husband. What a foolish world it is," she sighed, "that we should have to keep these secrets." She was silent for a while after that. "I think," she murmured, "that I could go to sleep now."

The sun was up when they awoke. The storm had passed; the day was clear. Joan Doyle was smiling contentedly when, thanking Margaret warmly and embracing her, she took her leave. As she rode out of the yard she turned to Margaret one last time.

"I'm sorry you don't like the Talbots," she said with a smile.

⁜

It was ten more days before William Walsh returned from Munster. Margaret was glad to see that he was looking pleased with himself.

The business had gone well. He had met the Earl of Desmond at the monastery without incident. "Unless I was followed," he remarked, "I shouldn't think anyone knows I saw him at all."

She told him of Joan Doyle's visit, leaving out any mention of their conversation about Munster, and he was amused. "Doyle's wife is a good woman," he said, "and Doyle himself is more powerful than ever. I'm glad that you should be friendly with her."

He remained for several days at the house before going into Dublin one morning.

He returned late that evening. As soon as he entered the house, she knew something was wrong. He ate his meal with her alone, looking thoughtful but saying little. But at the end of the meal, he asked her quietly, "You didn't tell anyone I was down in Munster, did you?"

"Munster?" She felt herself go pale. "Why would I do that? What has happened?"

"It's very strange," he answered. "You know there was a chance I might be offered a seat in the Parliament. I was talking to one of the fellows in the office of the royal council about it today, and he as good as told me not to bother to apply. I'd hoped for quite wide support, you know. Men like Doyle as well as the Fitzgeralds. But according to this fellow, Kildare has commitments to other people now—which is a way of saying that he doesn't want to support me. I asked around and I got the impression that something has been said against me." He shook his head. "Even Doyle, whom I do trust, looked awkward and said he didn't know anything. But just as I was leaving, he gave me a strange look and he said, 'Dublin's so full of rumours at the moment, none of us is safe.' Those were his very words. And the only thing I can think of that could be held against me is if someone heard about this Munster visit and started a rumour. Are you sure there's no one you can think of?"

Margaret stared at the window. There was still a little light outside. The glass panes formed a faint, greenish rectangle.

It was Joan Doyle. It had to be. She must have told her husband.

Had she done so innocently, in confidence? Or had she done it with malice? Margaret remembered her parting words: "I'm sorry you don't like the Talbots." Yes, that was it. She had got the information with which to damage the Walsh family, and she was letting Margaret know she remembered the insult and that she was her enemy. And suddenly now the thought came to Margaret with a cold, sinking feeling. The story the Doyle woman had told about the man going to Munster. Might she have made it up? After the little awkwardness with Richard about his father's whereabouts, had Joan Doyle guessed it was William's journey down into Munster that the family was hiding? With all her sweet words during the night, had the Dublin woman just been fishing for information?

"No," she said. "There isn't." She was ashamed of the lie. But how could she tell him it was she herself who was the cause of the rumour? How would he ever forgive her? She supposed the Doyle woman had probably foreseen that, too.

"I shall never find out," Walsh said sadly. "When these people decide not to talk, you could be asking questions of a grave." He sighed. "Silence."

"Perhaps," she said, without much hope, "they'll change their minds about the Parliament."

"Perhaps," he said. She knew he didn't believe it.

And so all Margaret could do was to think of Joan Doyle and wonder when, and in what form, she could have her revenge.

⁜

Eva O'Byrne didn't say a word when her husband came home. She had prepared everything with the greatest care.

Tomorrow would be Michaelmas, the twenty-ninth of September, one of the main days of the Church calendar for the settling of accounts. She couldn't help smiling to herself at that coincidence. It was so appropriate.

During the morning, she had walked down to the Brennans' place. Brennan was out in the field with his cattle, and she saw him glance curiously in her direction. His wife was standing by the door of their hut. She had a broad face, freckled skin; her eyes, Eva considered, looked dishonest. She was a pretty little slut, she thought, hardly worth her attention. There was a three-year-old boy playing in the dirt at the girl's feet. The thought suddenly crossed her mind that the child could be her husband's. She looked at the little boy sharply but couldn't see any likeness. Then she shrugged. What did it matter? She said a few words of no consequence to the girl. More important, she wondered what the hut was like inside. It had been bare enough when she had last been in there some years ago, but she couldn't really see from outside. She let her eye wander over the field that ran down the slope. It was good land. After a few moments, she nodded to the girl and walked back towards the house. The Brennans must have wondered why she had come. Let them wonder.

The rest of the morning she had spent with her children. Seamus, her eldest son, had gone out with his father. There were five others, a boy and four girls. She loved them all. But if she had a favourite child—which she would never admit—it would be Fintan. Five years old, he looked very much like her: the same fair hair; the same blue eyes. But above all, it seemed to her, he thought the same way as she did. Straightforward, honest. Trustworthy. She had spent an hour telling him stories about her own family in the Midlands. He loved to hear about her side of the family, and she always reminded him, "They are your people, too, as well as the O'Byrnes." He had told her the day before that he'd like to visit her family. "I promise I'll take you there one day," she had said; and then added: "Maybe soon."

The friar from Dublin had arrived early in the afternoon. She had seen him approaching and gone out to meet him.

"You have brought it?"

He had nodded. "It is here." He had tapped a small bulge under his habit.

Like most people on the island, whether in the English Pale or the Irish heartlands, Eva revered the friars. Father Donal was a good man, and she respected him. When she received the sacrament from his hands, she had no doubt that the miracle of the Mass was accomplished; when he heard her confession, gave her penance and absolution, the fact that he was himself a husband in all but name, and a father of children, did not trouble her in the least. He was a fatherly man, he was learned, he carried the authority of the Church within him, which by itself was fearsome. His rebuke, also, had that same, unanswerable moral authority. But the friar was something special. He was a holy man. His thin, ascetic face was not unkindly, but it contained an inner fire. He was like a hermit, a desert dweller, a man who had walked alone in the terrible presence of God Himself. His eyes, when they fixed upon you, seemed to cut through to the truth like a knife.

It had been back in the spring, when he was leaving in the morning on his way to Glendalough, that she had first sought his advice. His words then had been kindly, but not encouraging. It was while he was away in the mountains that she had conceived her inspired idea, however, and when he had passed through again, on his return, she had come to him in private and made her request. Even then, it was only after much pleading that he had finally agreed to help her.

The friar had spent the afternoon with Father Donal, while Eva, helped by her children, had made preparations for the evening.

She was proud of her home. In most respects, the tower house of O'Byrne was not unlike that of Walsh. The modest stone stronghold had a hall in which most of the activities of the household took place. Though there were separate larders and storerooms, Eva cooked over the fire in the centre of the floor, in the traditional manner, rather than in a kitchen; but she and Sean O'Byrne had their own bedchamber—a concession to the modern fashion which Sean's father would not have troubled with. The O'Byrnes spoke Irish. The Walshes spoke English, and because Walsh was a lawyer, educated in London at the Inns of Court, that English was of a high standard. But the Walshes would have been perfectly comfortable speaking Irish in the O'Byrne's house. Walsh wore an English tunic and hose; O'Byrne wore his shirt and cloak and usually preferred his legs bare. Walsh played the lute badly; O'Byrne played the harp well. Walsh had a small collection of printed books; O'Byrne possessed a hand-sized illuminated Psalter and could recite poetry with the visiting bards for hours. Walsh's eyes, through reading by candlelight, were a little weak; O'Byrne's were keen. But the meal that Eva now prepared for her visitor, the fresh rushes she spread on the floor, and the big platters and beakers her daughters placed upon the table were no different to those that Margaret Walsh would have used. As she looked round this domestic scene, with her children and the two servants all so fruitfully engaged, she hoped very much that the evening would be successful. She would be sorry, indeed, to leave all this.

When Sean O'Byrne came home, he was rather surprised to find the friar and Father Donal at his house. But naturally, they must be given hospitality; and the household gathered for the evening meal in a good humour. The harvest might have been ruined, but Eva had provided delicious oatcakes, a watercress salad, blood pudding, and a meat stew in the visitors' honour. The friar blessed the food, and though he ate sparingly, he tasted everything out of courtesy to his hosts and accepted a little of the wine that Sean offered. He took a particular interest in the children, especially Seamus, the eldest boy. "You are becoming a man," he told him seriously, "and you must take on the responsibilities of manhood." Only when the meal was over did the friar indicate that he would like to have a private conversation with the two O'Byrne parents.

Eva watched her husband. If he looked slightly surprised, she could tell that he had no idea what was coming. Perhaps he'd forgotten how he swore his innocence before the two men that spring. Knowing him, even that was possible, she thought wryly. When the children had left them and the four of them were alone, the friar began to speak.

He spoke very softly. They must both understand, he told them, that the sacrament of marriage was not just a matter of convenience for the better ordering of society. "Here in Ireland," he remarked, "the inviolate nature of marriage and the importance of chastity have not traditionally been regarded as absolute requirements. Yet that is a pity. For if we follow the teachings of Our Lord, they should be. Above all, even if we fail to achieve these high standards, there must between two married people be an understanding and a respect for each other's feelings. We may have to ask forgiveness of each other, but husbands must not scorn their wives, nor wives their husbands." He looked at Sean severely. "To humiliate the one we should love is a greater crime than to be unfaithful." He spoke with such quiet authority that even Sean could hardly complain.

Yet the friar himself had originally counselled her not to pursue the matter, when they had discussed it in the summer. "Your husband has sworn an oath," he had told her, "and you would be wise to accept it."

"Even when I know it is a lie?" she had asked.

"Perhaps, yes," he had answered frankly, and given her a little lecture on her duty humbly to submit to these trials. "God may be testing you," he explained. But she had been unable to accept this counsel, even from the saintly friar.

"It's the humiliation," she had burst out, "the scorn of his lie that allows him to continue sleeping with that girl almost in my own house. It's too much," she had cried, "I can't bear it anymore. He does nothing but lie to me, and if I try to pin him down, he just slips away, leaving me with nothing. Something has to change." She had looked at the friar desperately. "If he goes on, I won't answer for what I might do. Perhaps," she added with a wild menace, "I'll put a knife in his heart while he's asleep." And as he looked at her in horror, she had repeated the threat. "Even if I go to Hell for it," she swore. Only then had he reluctantly agreed to consider her request for help. "There is one thing I could do," he had suggested.

As she looked at her husband now, it was hard to tell what he was thinking. He must have some idea, by this time, what was coming, and no doubt he was already preparing his usual defence. But there was one thing he didn't know.

"Your tenant Brennan," the friar began, giving Sean a hard look, "has a wife, with whom you . . ."

"I have already sworn as to that," Sean cut in, quick as a flash.

"I know you have." The friar raised his hand. "But you may wish to reconsider. It would be a terrible thing, Sean O'Byrne, to have the sin of a false oath upon your conscience, when all you need to do is ask forgiveness of this woman," he indicated Eva, "who loves you and is ready to let bygones be bygones. Can you not see," he went on urgently, "that your cruelty is hurting her?"

But if Sean did see, he wasn't admitting it. His face was set stubbornly.

"I have sworn," he said, "to Father Donal here."

"So you wouldn't object to swearing again, to me?" asked the friar.

Did her husband hesitate now, just for a moment? It seemed to Eva that he did. But he was cornered.

"I'd swear to the bishop himself," he declared angrily.

"Very well." Reaching into his habit now, the friar drew out the small parcel.

"What's that?" asked Sean suspiciously.

Slowly and carefully, the friar unwrapped the cloth that had been wound around the small wooden box, blackened with age, which he placed upon the table. Reverently, he took the lid off the box to reveal, contained within it, another box, this one made of silver, its top encrusted with gems.

"This comes from the Church of Saint Kevin in Dublin," he said quietly. "It contains the finger bone of Saint Kevin of Glendalough himself."

And this time, Eva heard her husband give a little intake of breath as they all gazed at the jewelled box with awe.

The most splendid of the holy relics, like the Bachall Iosa of

Saint Patrick, were to be found in the Cathedral of Christ Church;
but several of the lesser churches had treasures of great sanctity
which, everybody knew, had awesome powers. When you touched
the relic before them now, you were in the presence of the Saint of
Glendalough himself.

"Will you place your hand, Sean O'Byrne, over the body of Saint
Kevin and swear that you have never had carnal knowledge of the
Brennan woman?" the friar invited quietly. "Will you do it?"

There was silence. The three of them watched him. Sean stared
first at the friar, then at the little box. For a moment it really seemed
that he might stretch forth his hand.

But whatever his faults, Sean O'Byrne still had a healthy fear of
God and of the power of His saints. After an agonising hesitation,
he scowled at the three of them and drew his hand back.

"You cannot do it," said the friar. "And you should be glad you
could not; for if you had, Sean O'Byrne, it would have been a sin so
terrible that nothing could have kept you from the eternal fire of
Hell. Thank God that you did not."

But if Sean O'Byrne was thanking God, he did not show it. As
the friar put the lid back on the dark little box, he sat sullenly staring at the table, saying not a word. In the end, it was Eva who spoke.

"The Brennans go. Seamus can take over their place."

Sean turned towards her and gazed, fixedly, at her face.

"I will decide about that," he said.

"You can decide what you like," she answered. "But if the
Brennans stay, then it's me who'll be leaving, tomorrow." She meant
it, and he could see it. She'd thought it all out. She'd take little
Fintan and the youngest girl with her; the older ones could stay.
There wasn't much Sean could do about it. Anything was better
than staying here with Sean and the Brennan girl mocking her
every day.

The silence that followed was broken by Father Donal.

"It would be good for Seamus to have that land," he remarked.

There was a pause.

"I should lose the Brennans' rent."

"The land might still be worth more to you," the priest observed.

"The Brennans will have to go," O'Byrne said finally, as if by saying it he was recovering control of the situation. "They're tenants-at-will, you know. They can be told to go at any time." He glanced at Eva, who quietly nodded. "They'll be told we need the farm for Seamus."

⁂

The next day, the Brennans were sent away. The explanation given was that their place was required for young Seamus. Whether Brennan believed this or not was unclear.

He might have done. For just as O'Byrne himself occupied a small portion of the wide territories of his princely ancestors, so, all over Ireland, as one generation succeeded another, these smaller holdings were being subdivided amongst the descendants until even their humblest tenants might find themselves turned out to make way for one of the family's many heirs. O'Tooles, O'Byrnes, even the mighty O'Neills—it was always the same. "Every damned Irish cottager seems to think he's the descendant of princes," the English would sometimes complain. The reason was that many of them were.

So the Brennans left in search of another place, and young Seamus O'Byrne made himself a home in their hut, and Eva repaired her dignity.

Before he had left, the friar had given the couple some good advice. "It's the right thing that you've done," he told Sean. "You've a fine wife and I hope you've the wisdom to see it. And you," he turned to Eva, "have a fine husband. Remember that now and honour him."

In the weeks and months that followed, she had done her best to take his advice, and to make herself agreeable and attractive to her husband in every way she knew. It seemed to work. He became quite amorous, if not exactly affectionate. And God knows, she thought, one might as well be grateful for that. During that winter and far beyond she had no cause, she thought, to regret what she had done.

It did not occur to her that in the mind of Sean O'Byrne, only one thing had happened on the day that the friar brought the relic. He, Sean O'Byrne of Rathconan, a prince among men, had been tricked and humiliated by her in front of the priest. He had had his position usurped. He wasn't the master in his own house. That was all that he knew; but he said nothing.

silken thomas

T HE YEARS that followed her marriage should have been happy for Cecily; and in a way they were. She loved her husband. She had two pretty little girls. Tidy's business was thriving: he made some of the best gloves in Dublin; MacGowan and Dame Doyle recommended him to all their friends; he already had a boy apprentice in the workshop. He had also become a busy and rising member of his craft guild; on feast days, Cecily would watch him go off dressed in the guild's bright livery, so pleased with himself that it was touching to see. And, of course, he had the freedom of the city.

"Your husband is making quite a name for himself," Dame Doyle remarked to her with a smile when they met in the street one day. "You must feel very proud of him."

Did she? She knew she should. Wasn't he everything a good Dublin craftsman should be? Hardworking, reliable. When she saw him sitting in his chair in the evening, with a little girl on each knee, she felt a deep sense of joy and contentment; and she would go to him and kiss him, and he would smile happily up at her, and she would secretly pray for more children, and hope that she might also give him the son for whom—though he denied it—she knew he longed. Yes, her husband was a good man, and she loved him. She could go to her confessor with a clear conscience, secure in the knowledge that she was never cold towards her husband, never denied him her body, scarcely ever showed anger, and always made amends if she did. What could she possibly confess except that, from time to time—perhaps quite frequently—she wished he were different?

Yet the occasion for their first serious disagreement had nothing to do with their own lives at all. It had to do with events in faraway England.

✦

To most people in Dublin, the last eight years had seemed like business as usual. The rivalry between the Butlers and the Fitzgeralds had continued. Building on King Henry's suspicions of the Fitzgerald family's foreign intrigues, the Butlers had persuaded him to give them the office of Lord Deputy for a while, but the great pincer of Fitzgerald power had soon squeezed them out again. Dublin itself had been quiet enough, but out in the hinterland, the Irish allies of the Fitzgeralds had been extorting protection money from the weaker chiefs and landowners—Black Rent, they called it—and on one occasion they had kidnapped one of the Butler commanders and held him for ransom for several months. Even in Dublin, these shenanigans were viewed with some wry amusement. "The cheek of those fellows," people said. For in Ireland, there was always an element of sport in these skirmishes. Hadn't brave young Celtic warriors been raiding their enemies since time immemorial?

But blunt King Henry in London and his order-loving officials never saw the joke. "I have told you before that if you will not govern yourselves, we'll rule you from England," he declared. And so, in 1528, an English official arrived to take over the ordering of the island. Nobody wanted him, of course; but he also came with one enormous handicap.

As far as King Henry was concerned, if he sent a royal servant to govern in his name, then that servant was invested with his kingly authority, and should be obeyed, no matter who you were. But that wasn't how things were seen in Ireland at all. The genealogies of Irish chiefs, whether real or imagined, stretched back into the mists of Celtic time. Even the English magnates like the Butlers and Fitzgeralds had been aristocrats when they first came to the island more than three centuries ago. Irish society was and always had been aristocratic and hierarchical. Irish servants in traditional Irish houses might eat and sleep beside their masters, but the family of the chief was treated with reverence. The thing was mystical.

The new Lord Deputy was the king's Master of Artillery. A bluff soldier, whose blood was fiery red but not blue. "I have come to bring English order," he let the Irish know. "Has he indeed," they responded. "Princes of Ireland bow the knee to this lowborn fellow?" they protested. "Never." The Gunner, they contemptuously called him. And though he did his best, and though Kildare himself, on King Henry's orders gave him a grudging support, it wasn't long before they undermined him.

King Henry was furious. And had there not been other larger problems to deal with in his realm, he might have taken sterner measures. But as he had neither money nor energy to involve himself more deeply with Ireland just then, he impatiently gave the island back to Kildare. "Let him rule there for the time being," he declared grumpily, "until we can think of something better." To the Irish it seemed that, once again, they had proved that the English king could never impose himself upon them. For better or worse, Kildare was back. It was business as usual.

But in England, greater changes were now beginning.

When, around the time the Gunner came to Ireland, King Henry had let it be known that he wished to annul his long-

standing marriage to his Spanish queen, Catherine of Aragon, there
were riots in London, where the pious queen was popular. But few
people in Ireland had been much concerned. In the territories outside the Pale, divorce had never been viewed as such a shocking
business. Even in the stricter English Pale, most people knew that
annulments were commonly granted to aristocrats and princes; and
the king believed he had valid grounds for an annulment anyway.
This was a matter between the English king and the Holy Father.
Besides, everyone in Dublin was too busy trying to get rid of the
Gunner to worry about Queen Catherine very much.

⁖

Why then should King Henry's business have been the cause of a
quarrel between Cecily and her husband? The truth was that she
hardly knew herself. It had begun so innocently, too, with a chance
remark from her one day that it hardly seemed right that the king
should be putting away his loyal wife after all these years.

"Ah," he had looked at her with a trace of condescension, "but
you must consider his difficulty. He only has a daughter, and he
needs a son."

"So if I only give you daughters," she demanded, "will you be
putting me away?"

"Don't be foolish, Cecily," he said. "I am not a king."

Why was it that his manner irritated her? Was it the trace of
smugness in his voice? Since he had been making a name for himself in the guild, he had become a little bit self-important sometimes, in her view.

"His daughter could be queen. There have been reigning queens
in their own right before now," she pointed out correctly.

"You don't understand the situation in England," he replied, dis-
missively. There was no doubt of it now. He was talking to her as if
she were a fool. She stared at him furiously. Who did he think he
was? But then hadn't there always been a trace of contempt in his attitude towards her, ever since that foolish incident with the saffron

scarf, before they were even married? However, she had no wish to quarrel with her husband, and so she did not reply.

As time went by, the events in England became more shocking. Every kind of pressure was put on the poor queen to make her give up her position, but her Spanish pride and her piety made her declare, quite rightly, that she was King Henry's loyal wife until the Holy Father told her otherwise. Meanwhile the king, it was said, was bewitched by a young lady called Anne Boleyn, and wanted to marry her as soon as possible. But though the Pope agreed to look into the matter, he still had not granted King Henry his annulment even though the king had begun to hint that he might go ahead anyway. Cecily had been shocked.

"How can the king even think of marrying his whore"—this was how many people referred to Boleyn, despite Anne's well-known refusal to give her body to the king without a wedding ring—"until the Holy Father has issued his ruling?" she asked.

"You have not considered the Pope's position," Tidy replied, in a somewhat pompous tone. And he explained how the new King of Spain, who was Queen Catherine's nephew, had also inherited the huge Hapsburg family dominions in other parts of Europe, together with the title of Holy Roman Emperor. Hapsburg family pride was too strong. The Emperor would never allow his aunt to be cast aside by the upstart Tudor king of little England. "The Pope dare not offend the Emperor, so he can't give Henry his annulment," Tidy explained. "Everyone knows that," he added, unnecessarily.

But to Cecily, this wasn't the point. King Henry was defying the Pope. And when King Henry declared that he was Supreme Head of the English Church instead of the Pope, and told the Holy Father that if he excommunicated him "I care not a fig," her outrage and contempt for the king were complete. The English Chancellor, Sir Thomas More, resigned at once. "More at least is a true Catholic," she declared. But what of the rest of Henry's subjects? What of the English Catholics of Dublin and the Pale?

"It was you and your friends," she pointed out to her husband, "who told me I was too Irish. Wasn't it to defend the true Church that the English came to Ireland with a papal blessing in the first place? Yet it's I who protest at this infamy, while I don't hear a word from any of you." And seeing that he had no answer to this she continued, "They say the Boleyn whore is a Lutheran heretic as well."

"That doesn't make it true," Tidy snapped. But she knew he'd heard the stories, too. And when a rumour came to the port that the Emperor might invade the English kingdom and seek help in Ireland, she irritably remarked, "Let him come, I say."

"Dear God don't even think such things," he cried in horror. "That would be treason. How can you say such wickedness?"

"Wickedness?" she retorted. "And is it wicked of poor Queen Catherine to refuse to deny her wedding vows and the Holy Father, and to make herself a heretic like King Henry's whore?"

For it seemed to Cecily that she saw the matter very clearly. She imagined the poor queen's pain. Didn't Tidy think of that? She saw the cruelty of the English king. Did such things count for nothing? Not in the harsh world of politics. The unhappy queen in England was being put upon, just as, in her insignificant way, she had been put upon that day years ago when she'd been so stupidly arrested. It was all the same thing, the tyranny of men who would never be happy until they forced every woman to submit to their foolishness. She admired the queen for standing up for the truth and for her rights; and she admired, certainly, the few like Thomas More who had the courage of their convictions. But as for the rest of the men, whether in England or in Dublin, who thought they knew everything, she saw now that behind their pompous bluster, there lay only cowardice. And it was painful to think that her husband was no better than the rest of them. As the years of these stormy events in England went by, therefore, in her heart—though she never admitted it to her confessor and scarcely even to herself—she loved her husband less.

It was soon after this last conversation that Cecily began to want a new house.

Their lodgings lay outside the city walls in the Liberty of Saint Patrick and consisted of a workshop and two rooms. They had been happy enough there, but the rooms were not large and were overlooked by everyone else in the little courtyard; the children were growing, and so it was not unreasonable that Cecily should one day tell her husband, "We need more space." During the last two years, Tidy had become aware of Cecily's occasional irritation and dissatisfaction, but he had never quite known what to do about it; so he was only too glad of the chance to do something that would apparently make her happy. He started to look for something at once. But after a month, he had still not found anything that seemed satisfactory, and he was wondering what to do, when one day as he and Cecily were walking into the old walled city, she suddenly remarked, "I wish we could live in one of the towers."

There were numerous towers nowadays in Dublin's city wall; each century seemed to have added a few. There were gate towers at the five big entrances in the outer wall, not counting the various river gates along the waterfront. Besides these, there were numerous small towers at intervals between the gates, some of which were habitable. A number of these gates provided lodgings, mostly for city functionaries of some kind, but some were let to craftsmen.

"It would be nice to look out on something, instead of being overlooked," she sighed.

"If you had one of those towers, do you think you would be happy?" he had asked.

"Yes," she said, "I believe I should."

"I shouldn't think there's much chance," he said; but secretly he set to work to secure one if he could, applying to Doyle himself for help. It would be a wonderful way to surprise and delight her.

The months that followed had been particularly trying. Several times he heard that there might be a tower becoming available, but each time it proved to be a false report. He was so determined to surprise her that he never told her about his efforts, with the result that she would often badger him to find lodgings, and several times went out to look for something herself. In the meantime, events in England were going from bad to worse. Not only had King Henry made all the clergy submit to him, but he had appointed his own archbishop, who declared his marriage void and obligingly married him to Anne Boleyn who, whatever her earlier scruples, was now visibly pregnant. The final shocking event came in May of that year, when, with every pomp and ceremony, Anne was formally crowned queen. Cecily was beside herself with disgust.

"If I don't find her a tower soon," Tidy confessed to Alderman Doyle one day in June, "my life won't be worth living."

"As it happens," the alderman replied, "I have news for you. There is a tenancy coming free and I can secure it for you. You could have it quite soon. On the Feast of Corpus Christi."

If Margaret Walsh looked back over the last eight years, she could feel reasonably pleased with herself. The worst years had been the first, when Butler had been in charge. It had come as no surprise that Doyle should have become a member of the Irish Parliament at that time while her own husband had not; but it had hurt all the same. On the rare occasions when she encountered Joan Doyle, the Dublin woman would always greet her warmly, as if they were friends, but Margaret had perfected a technique of smiling enigmatically and as soon as she politely could, moving away.

But two years later, when the Gunner was made Lord Deputy and Kildare was allowed to return to the island on condition that he supported the artilleryman, Walsh's hopes of a seat in the Parliament had revived. Whatever suspicions had been raised about Walsh at the time of his visit to Munster, the passage of a few years and the changes in administration had been enough to erase them. "I've been told that the Gunner has nothing against me," he reported to Margaret, "and Kildare's on my side. I think it's time for another try." The opportunity to help him came one day in spring.

"I need you," Walsh announced, "to come to Dublin Castle and be nice to the Gunner."

The entertainment took place the following week. Though the grey old castle was normally dark and rather shabby, Margaret could see that an effort had been made to smarten up the big courtyard, and the great hall, decked with hangings and lit by a thousand candles, looked quite festive. She had gone to endless trouble over her appearance. She had taken out her best gown, hardly worn for many a year, and made some cunning alterations, adding a panel of fresh silk brocade down the centre so that it looked like new. Thanks to the judicious use of dye, carefully applied by her eldest daughter, she entered the hall with hair that was restored to almost the same shade of red that it had been a decade ago. She had even put on scent, from a little phial of oriental perfume which she had guiltily bought some years before at Donnybrook Fair. And when her handsome, distinguished husband turned to her and said with admiration, "Margaret, you're the most beautiful woman in the castle," she actually blushed with pleasure.

"All you need to do is make a good impression on the Gunner," he had explained. "Most of the nobles make it clear that they despise him, so he's glad enough if anybody's civil. You can even flirt with him, if you like," he added with a grin.

As it happened, she had rather liked the Gunner. He was a short, sharp-eyed, bristling man; she could imagine him directing his cannon with great effect. For a moment, as they approached and saw that the group around him included the Doyles, she had felt her heart sink. Nor had it helped when Joan Doyle, seeing her, had smiled and declared, "It's my friend with the wonderful red hair. It looks better than ever," she had added, while Margaret smiled back and thought: if that's your way of saying I dyed it, you won't succeed in embarrassing me. But when she was presented to the little Lord Deputy, he made her a very handsome bow. And a few moments later, when a visiting English nobleman joined the group, he introduced the alderman's wife as "Dame Doyle," whereas Margaret, as the wife of a gentleman landowner, he introduced as "The lady Walsh"—a distinction which pleased her considerably.

She must have made a good impression anyway, for some time later, when she happened to be standing alone, she saw the Gunner coming briskly in her direction to engage her in conversation. The military man certainly made himself very pleasant. He asked her questions about her house and her family, and she took good care to stress her origins amongst the loyal English gentry of Fingal. This seemed to reassure him, and soon he was telling her very frankly of the difficulties of his position.

"We must have order," he declared. "If only all Ireland were like Fingal. But look at the troubles we suffer from. It's not only the Irish chiefs who raid and plunder. Look at the killing of poor Talbot, or the kidnap of one of our own commanders not a year ago." As Margaret had applauded the first, and knew very well that the Fitzgeralds had been behind the second, she contented herself with murmuring tactfully that something must be done. "Money's the problem, Lady Walsh," he confessed. "The king gave me cannon and soldiers but no money. As for the Irish Parliament . . ."

Margaret knew how the Parliament, like all legislatures, hated paying taxes. Even when the former Butler deputy had got his own men like Doyle into Parliament, they had still kept him short of funds.

"I'm sure my husband understands your needs," she said firmly. This seemed to please the little Englishman, and he soon turned to the political situation.

"You know," he explained, "with this business of the king's divorce, we truly fear that the Emperor might try to use Ireland as a place to foment trouble for His Majesty. The Earl of Desmond, for a start, can never be trusted not to intrigue with foreign powers."

He was giving her a hard look. Had he heard about her husband's trouble over Munster? Was this a warning?

"My husband always says," she answered carefully, "that the Earl

of Desmond seems to live in another world from the rest of us."
This seemed to satisfy him, because he nodded briskly.

"Your husband is a wise man. But privately, I can tell you, we are
watching all the merchants, in case any of them are in contact with
the Emperor."

And now Margaret saw her chance.

"That must be difficult," she said. "There are so many merchants
in Dublin trading with Spain and other ports where the Emperor
has agents. Look at Doyle, for instance. Yet you surely wouldn't
imagine that the Doyles would be involved in anything like that."

"True," he conceded; but she saw him look thoughtful, and she
felt a little thrill of excitement at what she had done. For hadn't she
just put the idea into his mind in the same breath as she assured him
that the Doyles were innocent? She had never done such a thing before and it seemed to her to be a masterpiece of diplomacy. She
could play Joan Doyle at her own game. Soon after this, the Gunner
moved on, but not without giving her hand a tiny squeeze.

Two months later, William Walsh had heard that he would have
a seat in the next Parliament, and she felt justified in taking some of
the credit. Though whether the Gunner ever investigated the Doyles
during his remaining time in office, she never discovered.

Another success for the family had been her son Richard. It had
been his father's idea that he should go away to Oxford. At first she
had opposed the plan—partly because she hated to part with him,
but also because, charming though he was, he had never shown
much interest in study. "He has a good brain, all the same," his father had insisted, "and since he'll have no inheritance to speak of,
he'll have to make his way in the world. He must get an education.
And that means going to England." For although there had been
high hopes for the Fitzgeralds' new college at Maynooth, it had
never developed into anything approaching a university. It was still
necessary to go overseas for that.

Walsh had prepared the boy himself, teaching him every day that
he could spare and driving him on firmly. And Richard had applied

himself manfully and made such progress that after a year his father had told Margaret, "He's ready." And hiding her tears behind a smile, Margaret had watched him sail away to England. He had not returned. From Oxford, he had proceeded to the Inns of Court in London, to train as a lawyer like his father. "If he can make his way in London, so much the better," William told Margaret. "And if not, he'll return with excellent prospects here." Margaret hoped he would return. It was hard, never to see him.

But these successes brought one problem. As William rose to a higher position in society, he spent more time in Dublin, and it was sometimes necessary for Margaret to accompany him. He dressed more expensively; he bought Margaret new clothes—things that were necessary, but did not come cheap. Richard in England was also a greater drain upon the family resources than Margaret had expected. As a poor scholar at Oxford, he spent a lot; but once he went to the Inns of Court, his letters requesting money had become frequent. To Margaret, who sometimes worried that her husband was working too hard, it had seemed strange that he should need so much, but William would shake his head with wry amusement and tell her, "I remember how it was when I was there. Living with those young bloods . . ." When she had wondered if her favourite child couldn't lead a quieter, less fashionable life, her husband would only say, "No, let him live as a gentleman. I wouldn't wish it otherwise." There were hints in his letters that he was popular with the ladies, and Margaret remembered how, even as a boy, he had so quickly charmed Joan Doyle. But such things involved expense. Shouldn't he be paying for himself now, she asked? "It'll be a while before he earns much," William explained. "Meanwhile he must have decent lodgings and be seen in the world."

How like her own dear father he sounded when he said that. She could almost hear her father declaring that her brother John should not go to England as a common foot soldier. Poor John, who never returned; poor father, with his desire to be a gentleman. And looking at her husband now, she understood that Richard in London was an extension of himself, and she felt a wave of affection for them both. "He could live as a gentleman and be a credit to you in Dublin, too," she pointed out, "for less expense."

So great was the flow of money out that, although Walsh was doing well, she knew that their income could not possibly be meeting their expenses. Once or twice she raised this with William, but he assured her that he had matters under control; and since he had always been a careful manager, she supposed it must be true. Yet it seemed to her that her husband was more preoccupied than usual. One hope for increasing their income would have been to acquire another Church estate on easy terms. Walsh was well placed to do this, and he had already let it be known that he was looking for something. But here a new difficulty had arisen. It came from no less a person than the Archbishop of Dublin.

Now that King Henry had made himself Supreme Head of the English Church, his eye had soon fallen on its huge, underused wealth. The Church needed reform, he declared, by which he did not mean a move towards Protestant doctrines—for King Henry still considered himself a better Catholic than the Pope—but that it should be better organised and yield more revenues. The rumour was that the royal servants were also casting hungry eyes at some of the rich old monasteries whose huge revenues were used to support only a handful of monks. So it was not surprising if Archbishop Alen, an English royal servant who also held the post of Chancellor, and who was naturally eager to please his royal master, should have announced, "No more of these easy leases. Whoever they are, Irish tenants must start paying the Church the proper rents for their land."

"Of course," Walsh conceded to his wife, "he has a point. But it's the way things have always been done in Ireland. This won't be liked by the gentry." He made a face. "I can't say I like it much myself."

"Will we manage?" she asked a little anxiously. But though he assured her that they would, she could see, by the spring of 1533, that William was worried.

It was sometime around midsummer that she detected an alteration in her husband's mood. He appeared to walk more lightly. The worry lines on his face were not so deep. Had he word of a Church estate, she asked? No, he told her, but his business affairs were looking better. Yet it seemed to Margaret that there was a new happiness, almost an excitement in his manner. He had been a distinguished, grey-haired man for many a year now, but in some strange way, as she remarked, "You look younger." Nearly three weeks after midsummer, they received a long letter from Richard describing the entertainments at the house of a gentleman in the country, where he had evidently been staying, promising to come to see them in Dublin soon, and asking for a substantial sum of money. It frightened her, but William seemed to view it with perfect equanimity— so much so that she honestly wondered if his mind might be elsewhere. And then a week after the letter, MacGowan came to call.

Margaret liked MacGowan. His position in the merchant society of Dublin was special. Most of the Dublin merchants bought and sold their goods within the Dublin markets; yet they also needed to buy commodities like timber, grain, and cattle from the huge hinterland beyond the Pale. There were a number of merchants, therefore, who traded freely across these borderlands, acting as go-betweens for the English and Irish communities. They were known as grey merchants, and MacGowan was one of the most successful. His specialty was in purchasing timber from the O'Byrnes and O'Tooles in the Wicklow Mountains, but he carried out all kinds of business, and frequently carried out commissions for Doyle. As a result of his travels, MacGowan not only made an excellent living but he was also a mine of information about what was going on in the country. William, who happened to be at home on the day he called, was also delighted to see him.

He arrived in the middle of the day. He had just spent the night, he said, at the house of Sean O'Byrne of Rathconan, farther to the south. Margaret had heard of Sean O'Byrne as a man for the ladies, but did not know him. She tried to persuade MacGowan to stay with them, too, but after taking some light refreshment he said that he must be on his way to Dublin, and William had gone outside with him to see him off. It was completely by chance that she should have gone up into the big bedchamber and happened to hear the two men talking below the casement.

"Your business with Doyle goes well?" she heard William enquire.

"It does. And yours—your private business, I mean, with his wife?" This was said in a low tone. "She thinks you very handsome, you know. She told me herself," the traveller added with a chuckle.

William's private business with Joan Doyle? What could that possibly be?

"You know everybody's secrets," Walsh murmured. "That makes you a dangerous man."

"If I know secrets," MacGowan answered, "I assure you it's because I am very discreet. But you did not answer my question about the lady."

"All is well, I think."

"Does Doyle know?"

"He doesn't."

"And your wife?"

"No. God forbid."

"Well your secret is safe with me. And have you brought matters to a conclusion?"

"On Corpus Christi day it shall be consummated. She has promised me."

"Farewell."

She heard the sound of MacGowan moving off.

She stood there, transfixed. Her husband and the Doyle woman. They might both be quite long in years, but she knew her husband was physically capable of consummating an affair. Entirely so. But that he would ever do such a thing to her: that was what stunned

her. For a moment or two she could hardly believe what she had
heard. They seemed like voices from another world.

Then she remembered: the Doyle woman thought him handsome. So he was. But what had he said about her, all those years ago
when they had met at Maynooth? That he thought she was pretty.
They were attracted. It made sense. The voices had not come from
another world. They had come from her own. And her own world,
it seemed, had just collapsed in ruins.

Corpus Christi. That was in two days. What was she going
to do?

⁕

When Eva O'Byrne considered the last eight years, one thing was
clear to her. She had done the right thing when she had called in the
friar. For the years that followed had been some of the best in her
life.

If Sean O'Byrne had other women, he kept them out of sight.
When he was at home, he was an attentive husband. A year after the
Brennans left, she had another baby girl, who kept her busily occupied. The baby seemed to delight Sean as well; watching him play
with her on the grass in front of the old tower, she experienced moments of pure joy. Meanwhile Seamus had made a great success of
the Brennans' place. He'd practically rebuilt it with his own hands;
and two years ago he'd found a wife as well—not a great catch, perhaps, the daughter of one of the lesser O'Tooles, but a sensible girl
whom Eva liked.

As for Fintan, the boy became her special companion. It was almost funny, she knew, to see her with her youngest son; for it was
clear by now to everyone that he both looked and thought like her.
They would go for walks together, and she would teach him all the
plants and flowers that she knew; as for the cattle and livestock, he
was a born farmer. He often reminded her of her own father. And
he gave her affection, constantly. Every winter he would make
something for her—a wooden comb, a butter press—and these lit-

tle gifts became like treasures, bringing a smile to her face when she used them every day. She and the boy were so close that she had almost feared that her husband might become jealous. But Sean O'Byrne seemed more amused than anything and glad that the boy should bring her such happiness. As for his own relationship with Fintan, it was very simple. "Thank you," he would say, "for giving me a son who's such a good cattleman."

And he, in his turn, had brought his wife one other wonderful gift in return. Their baby girl was two years old when Sean arrived back from a journey into Munster one day and casually asked her, "How would you like an addition to our family?" And she was wondering what he meant when he explained: "A foster son. A boy of Fintan's age."

Though the practice of fostering went back into the depths of Celtic history, it was still very much alive amongst the noble families, English or Irish, on the island. When the son of one family went to live with another, it formed a bond of loyalty between them almost like a marriage. To send one's child into the house of a great chief was to give him a step up in the world; and for an important family to confide their son to your keeping was a huge compliment. Assuming that her husband was doing a favour to some poorer family, Eva did not look overjoyed; but seeing this Sean only grinned.

"It's one of the Fitzgeralds," he calmly informed her. "A kinsman of Desmond."

A Fitzgerald, related to the mighty Earl of Desmond. Quite a distant kinsman, from a modest branch of the southern Fitzgeralds. But still a Fitzgerald.

"How did you manage that?" she asked in frank admiration.

"It must be my charm." He smiled. "He's a nice boy. You've no objection?"

"It would be a fine thing for Fintan to have such a friend," she answered. "Let him come as soon as he likes."

He came the following month. His name was Maurice. He was the same age as Fintan, but dark where Fintan was fair, slimmer, a little taller, with finely drawn Celtic features that served to remind you that the Fitzgeralds were as much Irish princes as English nobles, and beautiful eyes, that she found strangely compelling. He was very polite, and declared that her house was exactly like that of his parents—"Except," he added, "that ours is beside a river." Though slim, he was athletic, knew his cattle, and seemed to slip easily into Fintan's life as an unassuming friend. But you could tell, she observed, that he came from an aristocratic household. His manners, though very quiet, were courtly. He always referred to her as "the lady O'Byrne"; he obeyed her husband with instant respect, and said "please" and "thank you" more than they were used to. He could also read and write considerably better than Fintan, and played the harp. But beyond all this, there was a fineness about him that she couldn't quite describe, but which marked him out, and privately she confessed to her husband, "I hope that Fintan will learn from him."

Certainly the two boys became good friends. After a year, they seemed as close as brothers, and Eva came to think of Maurice as an extra son. Sean was a good foster father. Not only did he ensure that the boy came to know all that there was to know about the farming and the local affairs of the Wicklow Mountains and the Liffey Plain, but he would send him out with MacGowan sometimes, to visit the farms and houses of people like the Walshes, or to go down to Dalkey or even to Dublin itself with the grey merchant.

Eva had supposed that perhaps the boy would wish to meet his Kildare kinsmen also on these occasions. But Sean had explained to her that with the suspicions attaching to the Earl of Desmond recently, this might not be wise. "His parents will make those arrangements when they see fit," he said. "It's not for us to introduce him to his relations." And Maurice seemed perfectly content with his quiet life in the O'Byrnes' household.

Yet, in some strange way, he was also a being apart. It was not only his love of music—for sometimes, when he played his harp, he seemed to drift away into a sort of dream. It was not only his apti-

tude for the things of the intellect—for Father Donal, who taught
the two boys, would sometimes wistfully remark, "It's a pity he is
not destined to become a priest." It was his melancholy moods.
They were rare, but when they fell upon him, he would wander up
into the hills alone and be gone for perhaps a day, not striding vigorously over the mountains like Sean, but walking alone as if in a
trance. Even Fintan knew better than to offer to accompany him at
such times, but left him alone until the mood had passed. And
when it had he would emerge, it seemed, refreshed. "You're a strange
fellow," Fintan would say affectionately. And it surprised no one
that, when the friar had passed once or twice on his way to visit the
hermit at Glendalough, he had sat for hours with the boy and upon
departing given him his blessing.

Yet none of this seemed to affect the Fitzgerald boy's friendship
with Fintan. They worked together, went hunting, and played practical jokes exactly as other healthy boys of their age would do; and
once, when she had asked Fintan who his greatest friend was, he had
looked at her in astonishment and said, "Why Maurice, of course."

As for Maurice's relationship with her, it was like that of a son to
a mother except that, with the faint reserve of a priest, he always
held himself just a little distant from her—a fact which after a year
or two had almost grieved her until she had realised that he was doing so to ensure that he did not encroach upon her relationship with
Fintan; and she admired his fineness.

Though no one could say quite when or why, the atmosphere in
the house of O'Byrne of Rathconan subtly changed with the coming of Maurice Fitzgerald. Even Sean seemed gradually to become
more thoughtful towards her. And what better proof could there be
than the fact that, as the day of her birthday approached in the summer of 1533, he invited all the neighbours to a feast at the house.
There was a fiddler, and dancing, and a travelling bard recited tales
of Cuchulainn, and Finn mac Cumaill, and other heroes of legend
in the old way, while Sean and Fintan sat beside her; and Maurice
also played his harp for all the company. And then Sean made her a

present of a pair of Henry Tidy's finest embroidered gloves together with a length of silk brocade, which pleased her no less because she guessed that they had been chosen by Maurice on one of his journeys to Dublin with MacGowan.

So they feasted and sang and danced late into that night, which was the eve of Corpus Christi.

❖

There were several great days of pageant in the Dublin calendar. Some years there was the Riding of the Franchises; there were always parades upon Saint Patrick's Day and Saint George's, the patron saints of Ireland and of England. But the greatest pageant of all came in July, four Fridays after midsummer, at the Feast of Corpus Christi.

Corpus Christi, the Body of Christ, the celebration of the miracle of the Mass. What better day for the city's corporate bodies, religious fraternities, and the guilds to celebrate themselves. For if the mayor, aldermen, and freemen of the city were the rulers of Dublin, nearly all of them were members of one or another of these. There were the great religious fraternities, like the mighty Holy Trinity to which Doyle belonged, which had its chapel in the Christ Church and concerned itself with charity and good works; and there were the numerous guilds—merchants, tailors, goldsmiths, butchers, weavers, glovers, and many more—which regulated their own trades and most of which had modest chapels in the lesser city churches. And on Corpus Christi day, they had their great pageant.

It had followed a set pattern for generations. Each guild had its carnival float, with painted scenery like a little stage. Eight feet wide, so that they could just pass through the Dame's Gate, drawn by six or eight horses, they were proudly maintained to make a splendid show. Each one depicted a famous scene from the Bible or from popular legend. The order of procession was laid down in the Chain Book of city regulations kept in the Tholsel. First came the glovers, depicting Adam and Eve; then the shoemakers; then the mariners, who represented Noah and his Ark; then the weavers, followed by the smiths—nearly twenty pageants in all, including a splendid tableau of King Arthur and his Knights of the Round Table performed by the city auditors. Finally, making its way like a two-man pantomime horse, and nodding in a stately manner to the crowd, came the great dragon of Saint George, the emblem of Dublin corporation.

Congregating in the early morning on open ground near Ailred the Palmer's old hospital outside the western gate, the procession would make its way through the gate, up the High Street to the High Cross by the Tholsel, past Christ Church and the castle, and then down through the Dame's Gate, finishing by the archery practice grounds on the edge of Hoggen Green, where some of the guilds would perform short plays from their floats.

Tidy was excited. This year he had been selected by his fellow glovers to play the part of Adam. During the procession he would be standing on the float in a white hose and vest, wearing a huge fig leaf of vaguely indecent design; but afterwards he had a spoken part to learn, and for weeks Cecily had listened to him solemnly rehearsing such lines as, "Oh foolish woman, what have you done?"

The sun was already bright when Tidy set off, looking pleased but determined. An hour later, Cecily left the children with a neighbour and went into the city to watch him.

It seemed to Margaret as if the entire region had converged upon Dublin that day. So thick were the crowds that she was obliged to leave her horse at a tavern near Saint Patrick's, for an outrageous charge, and to join the throng making its way on foot through the southern gate. This had the advantage of making her inconspicuous, but she wondered if she would ever catch sight of her husband.

Walsh had left at dawn. She had waited an hour, then telling the groom that she'd be back that evening, she had ridden after him without a word of explanation. She had wondered if she might catch sight of him ahead, but he had been too quick for her and she had failed to do so. As for how she would explain her absence from home on her return, that would depend upon what happened today.

She had wondered whether to confront him with his affair with the Doyle woman, but decided against it. She had no proof. If he denied it, where would that leave her? In a state of perpetual uncertainty. Some women, she knew, would have ignored it, and no doubt that made life easier. But she didn't think she could. Nor did she have any other woman she could confide in: faced with this unexpected crisis in her life, she found herself alone. So she had decided to follow him into Dublin. She knew it was foolish. She knew she might not catch sight of him. And if she did, if she saw him with the Doyle woman, what was she going to do? She didn't know that either.

How cheerful everyone was. The colourful crowd flowed through the gateway laughing and chattering while Margaret, her hair pushed under a black velvet hat, her face looking solemn and gaunt, was carried along in its flow like a stick in a stream. Up Saint Nicholas Street they went, past Shoemaker Lane, and thence to the big intersection with the High Street where the tall gables of the old Tholsel could be seen. The crowd at the crossing was too thick to get through but fortunately the stewards let a group, including Margaret, surge across the street into the precincts of Christ Church where there was more room for the crowd to stand. Moments later the street was cleared again. The procession was coming.

A party of horsemen, sergeants of the city, and other officials led the way. Then came a band with pipes and drums. And, lumbering slowly behind, came the first of the floats.

The glovers certainly got the carnival off to a good start. In the middle of the float stood a tree made of board painted with green leaves and golden apples. Adam and Eve, both men, were wearing the appropriate fig leaves; Eve sported a pair of huge breasts, held a golden apple the size of a pumpkin, and made lascivious movements to the cheers of the crowd, while Adam looked solemn and cried out from time to time, "Oh foolish woman, what have you done?" The serpent—a tall, thin man—wore an ingenious headpiece which, with the aid of a string, he caused to writhe from side to side or dart its head in a frightening manner towards the crowd.

Margaret watched it pass with a grim smile. She started to inch her way eastwards through the crowd. Another float rumbled by: Cain and Abel. Soon after this she reached the place she wanted, and finding a spot on a low wall where some children were standing, she was able to enjoy a good view, over the heads of the spectators, of the doorways of the houses on the other side.

The section of the High Street opposite the cathedral was known as Skinners Row. The big gabled houses there were the Dublin residences of some of the nobility and gentry, including the Butlers. Others belonged to the greatest merchants. Alderman Doyle had moved there from Winetavern Street on his marriage. Their timber-framed upper floors overhanging the street provided perfect galleries for viewing the pageant and all the windows were crowded. The place Margaret had chosen was opposite Doyle's house.

It was certainly impressive; four storeys high, built of stone at street level, timber and plaster above, with two gables and a slate roof—it was a permanent pageant of the alderman's wealth. Margaret stared up at its windows, full of faces: servants, children, friends at every one. At the biggest she could see Doyle and his wife. Was her husband in there, too? She couldn't see him.

The floats went by: Noah and his Ark, the Pharaoh of Egypt and his army, several Nativity stories; Pontius Pilate accompanied by his wife. Just after this, Doyle's face disappeared from the window, and as King Arthur and his Knights came by, she saw the alderman, in his scarlet robes of office, emerge from the street door and walk towards the Tholsel. She continued to watch until the splendid green-and-red dragon of Saint George, which also had silver wings, brought up the rear of the pageant, together with another band of pipes and drums.

As the end of the procession passed, many of the crowd were falling in behind. Realising that she might become conspicuous, Margaret retreated a little to a small tree in the precincts from which she could still watch the Doyle house. The faces had already left the windows and people were starting to come out of the street door, presumably to follow the pageant to Hoggen Green and see the plays. It looked as if the entire household might be leaving, servants and all, but though she watched carefully, she didn't see Doyle's wife. By the time the door closed, the big house appeared to be empty. She waited while the people following the procession reduced to a trickle. Had Joan Doyle left after all? Had she missed her? She wondered what to do.

And then, walking jauntily along the street, she saw her husband. He paused in front of Doyle's door, glanced about, and seemed about to knock on it when the door opened and there, smiling in the entrance, stood Joan Doyle. He stepped in and the door closed behind him.

Margaret stared. Her heart missed a beat. It was true then: her husband and the Doyle woman. She felt an icy coldness strike her in the chest. She was suddenly breathless.

What should she do now? Were they really alone? Surely there would be a servant, at least, in the house. Unless the Doyle woman had deliberately sent them all away. That might be it: the Corpus Christi pageant was the perfect excuse. They would go to watch the plays while her husband slipped into the empty house. She looked along the street in the direction in which the procession had gone. The ebbing tide of people was just drawing away from the pillory which stood alone at the end of Skinners Row. She heard the distant blast of someone blowing a trumpet down by the Dame's Gate, a haunting warning like a tocsin sound.

She must go in and confront them. It was now or never. But what excuse could she use? That she happened to have raced into Dublin that day? That she had just caught sight of him entering the house? What if his visit had some other purpose, purely innocent?

It would be, to say the least, embarrassing. And as she tried to formulate what she should say, she realised the uselessness of it. For if they were in fact making love, the door would certainly be bolted so that they wouldn't risk being caught in the act. If she hammered on the door, William would either vanish through a back window or, more likely, be found there fully dressed with a plausible excuse. She'd be left looking a fool and perhaps none the wiser. She wondered whether to go across to the house and try to peer in through the windows.

She decided to wait a little and see what happened. Time passed. But she was so distressed that, after a while, she realised that she had no idea how long she had been watching. A quarter of an hour? Half an hour? It seemed like an eternity. She was just trying to work out how long it might have been when the door opened and William came out. He turned and walked swiftly towards the pillory as the door closed behind him. Margaret stayed where she was. More time passed. The door did not open again.

⁘

The pageant floats had come to rest near the edge of Hoggen Green where there was a small chapel dedicated to Saint George. While their horses grazed on the green, a group of five floats had been arranged in a large semicircle on the grass; and these were to give a succession of short plays, starting with the glovers' Adam and Eve.

Cecily smiled. It was a charming scene, in sight of the old Thingmount. A few booths had been set up selling ale and other refreshments. The sky was clear blue, the sun hot. There was a smell of horse and human sweat and barley ale that was not unpleasant.

Though it was brief, the glovers' play was well performed. Tidy's cry, "Oh foolish woman, what have you done?" was taken up by the crowd who, all together, had bellowed it back with great good humour. Adam, Eve, and the Serpent were duly banished from Paradise to general applause. Shortly it would be the turn of the next group to perform Cain and Abel.

Cecily's attention had already been drawn to the group of young men standing nearby during the glovers' play. It was obvious from their bright silk shirts and tunics that these were rich young aristocrats, and some of them sounded like visitors from London. They had also clearly been drinking; but they seemed harmless. And it didn't shock her that, seeing her watching them, they began to banter with her.

What was a pretty woman like herself doing alone? Where was her husband? On the stage, she told them. Who was he? Adam. This was greeted uproariously. Then she must be Eve. Was she a temptress? Which one of them would she tempt? All this she could take in good part. But as the next play began, and they started to make lewder remarks, she decided she had to put them in their place.

"Attend to the play, Sirs," she cried, "not to me. Remember," she added, "that this is still the Feast of Corpus Christi."

Yet if she supposed that this reproof would quieten them, it had quite the opposite effect. They started making vulgar puns, asking her if she would be "corporal" on Corpus Christi day, until finally she had had enough.

"Do not mock the miracle of the Mass," she called out sharply, expecting this to silence them once and for all. So she was utterly astonished when one of the young bloods, who was clearly English, made a disparaging remark about the Mass. It wasn't said very loudly, but it was audible; and even more amazing, some of his companions laughed.

She even forgot the play. She stared at them in disgust. Who did these English fops think they were? And why were their Irish companions letting them get away with it? They might be the sons of great lords—she didn't know and she didn't care—but they shouldn't be allowed to come and utter profanities in Dublin. She stepped towards them.

"You may be Protestants and heretics in London," she called out firmly, "but you need not bring your blasphemy to Dublin." Some of them, she thought, looked awkward, but not all.

"Oh, Tom," called the impudent one, "you have some fiery women in Ireland." She could hear that he was a little drunk, but that was no excuse. And when he made her a mocking and insolent bow, that only infuriated her more. Why should the foreign fop think he could be condescending to her just because this was Ireland and she was only a woman? "Are we heretics, then, in England, Madam?" he taunted her.

"Since your new queen," she emphasised the last word with contempt, "is a heretic, you may all be so," she snapped.

"A hit, Tom, a hit," the young lordling cried. He clasped his hand to his heart. "I am hit." He staggered to one side as though wounded. The people around, instead of watching the play, were turning to look at him. But now, switching abruptly from this comedy, he gave her a dangerous stare. "Have a care, Madam, before you accuse the queen of heresy. The king is Supreme Head of our Church."

"Not of my Church, Sir," she answered bitterly. "The Holy Father is Head of my Church, thank God," she added with fervour.

Technically, this was still true. As the matter of King Henry's supremacy had not been brought before the Irish Parliament, it was not yet the law in Ireland, and Cecily could correctly say that she answered to the Pope. She stared at him angrily. Was there something effeminate about this fashionable young man with his sudden changes of mood? Her look became contemptuous. He saw it.

"Why, Madam," he called out so that all around should hear, "I believe you do speak treason." He almost sang the last word. It hung, horribly, in the air. Even Cain and Abel on their stage paused for a moment to glance towards her nervously. But Cecily was by now so angry that she did not notice.

"I would rather be guilty of treason than deny the true faith and the Holy Father," she cried out. "As for you," she shouted, "you'll rot in Hell beside King Henry!"

The play stopped. Everyone turned to look at her, the woman who had just condemned the king to Hell. Outraged though she was, Cecily knew that she had gone too far. This was dangerous territory, the borderland of treason. But even worse than the stares of the crowd was the look on the face of the man who was now striding towards her.

Tidy's face was as pale as his costume. But his eyes were blazing. He had MacGowan at his side. He came bursting through the crowd. He was still dressed as Adam with the preposterous fig leaf bumping round his midriff. He seized her by the arm.

"Are you mad?" he hissed.

For the young aristocrats, it was all too much. For them, at least, the dangerous tension of the moment was broken.

"Adam!" they called out. "Oh Adam! Look to your wife!" And then, catching the idea from each other, all together, "Oh foolish woman, what have you done?"

⁜

Tidy did not say anything. Taking his wife by one arm while MacGowan took the other, he led her away, while the youths called out, in mock solemnity, "Treason. Off with her head. Treason." He didn't pause until they had reached the city gate.

So this was the special day. He had planned it all so carefully. After the plays were over, he'd been going to lead her into the city and, on a pretext, take her to the western gate tower where Alderman Doyle was to meet them and deliver them the keys to their new abode. And then he was going to watch her face as she looked round her spacious and airy new lodgings. How joyful she would be. What a perfect surprise. A perfect day. All planned.

"You cursed the king, Cecily," he said miserably. "People will say we are traitors. Don't you see what you've done?"

"He denied the Mass," she said bitterly.

"Oh Cecily." His eyes were full of reproach.

"You know who they were?" MacGowan spoke now, in a quiet

voice. "They were English friends of young Lord Thomas. He was with them." He paused, and seeing Cecily had not yet understood, "Lord Thomas Fitzgerald, the heir of the Earl of Kildare."

"Kildare's son?" Tidy cried in dismay.

"Then they shouldn't have spoken as they did," said Cecily defensively.

"That may be so," MacGowan allowed. "But they are young bloods who'd been drinking. It was all in jest."

Tidy shook his head.

"Now Kildare and the royal councillors will hear that my wife has cursed the king," he said miserably. And though he said nothing more, at that moment he was frankly thinking: I wish I had married someone else.

It was with a heavy heart, and without any smile of pleasure, that late in the afternoon, he took Cecily to the tower apartment and, showing her the splendid accommodation asked her, "Do you think that you could be more contented now?"

"I believe I could," she answered. "Yes, I do."

But he wondered if it was true.

✤

By the time that the Tidys were inspecting their tower, Margaret had arrived home. She had waited over an hour outside Doyle's house, seen Joan Doyle finally go out, followed her down towards the Dame's Gate, and then lost sight of her. In the end she had given up and returned home.

William did not arrive until late in the evening. He looked pleased with himself. He said he had dined in the city, and he seemed to have drunk a good deal. Saying he was tired, he went up to the chamber and fell asleep.

The next day he spent quietly at the house. The day after, he had business in Dublin, but was back by early evening. And so for two weeks life continued in the usual way. Was he having illicit meetings with Joan Doyle in Dublin? She couldn't be sure. At least once, after spending the day in Dublin, he returned and made love to her in the usual way. So what did it all mean? Had something happened on Corpus Christi day in Dublin? Assuming it had, was it being repeated? Margaret found it hard to believe that it wouldn't be. Yet what was she to do? Share her husband with Joan Doyle until their affair ended? Confront him with something she couldn't prove? Wait? Watch? She had not known that uncertainty could bring such pain.

Two weeks later he went into Dublin early and returned very late at night. A week after that he was away in Fingal for a few days. There was nothing unusual in these absences, but now all his movements had taken on a new significance. And Margaret hardly knew what she might have done next if, during the month of August, he hadn't come in looking concerned one day and told her, "The monastery needs me to go down into Munster again; but I hardly know if it's wise."

"You should go," she said, "at once."

⁜

He was gone for three weeks. When he got back, he was so busy that she hardly thought he could find time for an affair.

And besides, during his absence she had made one change in her own lifestyle. She had started going into Dublin.

She did not follow any set pattern. Some weeks she mightn't go at all. But from the end of that summer, she would ride in to visit the markets and return later in the day. In the city, walking past the Doyle house in Skinners Row, or picking up a casual conversation at a market stall, it was easy to find out the whereabouts of the Doyles; so that when in October William had to spend several days in Fingal, she was able to ascertain that Joan Doyle was safely in her own house and nowhere near William. It was an imperfect check, but it was something. In November, the Doyles both went to Bristol and remained there almost four weeks. Nor, she thought, did William and the Doyle woman meet in December. As Christmas

approached, it seemed possible that the affair, if indeed it had begun, might have been abandoned. She could even suppose that the
whole business might have been a figment of her imagination.

So it was in quite a cheerful mood that, just a few days before
Christmas, she accompanied William into Dublin to attend a winter banquet given by the Trinity Guild.

It was the usual, good-humoured city celebration. A splendid
company attended, city fathers in their robes and liveries, gentlemen
from the Pale, many of them members of the Trinity Guild or
freemen of the city. But the particular interest of the banquet was
whether the head of the Fitzgeralds would attend.

It had not been a surprise to anyone when, during the autumn,
King Henry had yet again summoned the Earl of Kildare to
London. Everyone knew that the king was still smarting from the
way that the Fitzgeralds had forced him to give them back the Lord
Deputy's post, and you could be sure that the Butlers were supply-
ing the English court with information to use against him. While
Kildare had sent polite excuses to the king, he had muttered to his
friends that he would take his own good time before he went to
England again; and to remind the English monarch that the
Fitzgeralds were not to be trifled with, he had coolly removed the
king's cannons from Dublin castle and put them in his own strong-
holds. For the last few months Kildare had remained calmly in
Ireland while Henry was left fuming.

But recently Walsh had heard that Kildare was unwell. Injuries
he had received on campaign had returned to trouble him. He was
said to be in great pain, then seriously unwell. "I wondered if it was
a pretended sickness, an excuse for not going to England," Walsh
told Margaret, "but the word is that the earl has suffered a real decline." And indeed, instead of coming to the banquet, Kildare was
sending his son Thomas to represent him instead. The Kildare family was large: the earl had no less than five brothers. "But if anything
should happen to the earl," Walsh pointed out, "it's Thomas and
not his uncles who will succeed to the title and the lordship. Few

people in Dublin knew very much about the young man, except that he was a fashionable fellow who had appeared with some English fops who got drunk at the last Feast of Corpus Christi. "Silken Thomas, his friends call him," the lawyer said with some disapproval. But like the rest of the gentlemen of Dublin, he was quite curious to take a look at him.

In fact, young Lord Thomas made quite a favourable impression. He had the aristocratic good looks of his family; he was certainly dressed in the finest silk tunic and belt that would have been the height of fashion in the court of England or France, but his clothes were not gaudy; as he made his tour of the company before the meal began, he treated everyone with the greatest courtesy, and after being called across to speak to him, Walsh returned and reported, "He's young, but well informed. He's no fool."

The banquet was excellent. After they had eaten, the company mingled once more. And it was while she was accompanying her husband round the hall that Margaret suddenly found herself confronted with Joan Doyle. The alderman had just stepped over to talk to Silken Thomas and his wife was standing alone. Seeing the Walshes, Dame Doyle's face lit up.

There was no way of escaping her. In response to her greeting, Margaret put on her best masklike smile. The three of them exchanged the usual, meaningless courtesies; then Joan Doyle turned to Margaret.

"You really should come into Dublin more often," she said.

"I come in to the markets sometimes," Margaret replied quietly.

"Don't you think she should?" Joan said to Walsh.

"Oh, I do," he answered politely.

Margaret considered the two of them. The conversation sounded so innocent. But if they were fencing round her, they did not realise how closely she was observing them.

"Perhaps you're right," she said. "I should at least come in for the festivals." She nodded, as though to herself. "Like Corpus Christi."

Did they, just for an instant, glance at each other? Yes, she was sure they did. Then the Doyle woman laughed. "Corpus Christi was a wonderful day," she said with a smile to Walsh, who also smiled and nodded.

They were mocking her. They thought she didn't know it.

"As a matter of fact," Margaret said brightly, "I came in for Corpus Christi this year."

There was no mistaking it. Her husband blanched. "You did?"

"I never told you, did I? Just a sudden impulse. I saw the pageants going along Skinners Row." She gave them both a smile. "I saw all sorts of things."

It was a perfect moment. The two of them seemed stunned into silence. Joan Doyle recovered first.

"You should have come into the house," she cried. "We were all up at the window. You'd have had a better view."

"Oh, the view I had was fine," said Margaret.

She had them. She felt a wonderful sense of power. It was almost worth the pain. She could see them trying to work out how much she knew, whether her remarks were ironic or not. They couldn't tell. She had them on the run.

She smiled and took her husband by the arm. "We should pay our respects," she murmured, indicating a gentleman from Fingal standing nearby, and moved away, leaving the Doyle woman standing alone.

Yet it was a hollow triumph. For if they were left in uncertainty, their awkwardness had told her all she needed to know about their complicity. They had deceived her before; so they probably meant to do it again. That night she turned to him in bed.

"So how attractive is Joan Doyle?"

"You think I find her attractive?" he responded cleverly. He paused, as though considering. "She's a good woman," he answered easily, "but I prefer redheads."

Over Christmas he was especially loving and attentive, and she was grateful for that. Knowing Joan Doyle's devious nature, she didn't even blame her husband so much. She had never thought he would do such a thing to her, but now that he had, her main concern was to bring it to an end. She made no reference to their affair, but she did take care to warn him. "You can't trust that Doyle woman. She's two-faced and dangerous."

Her feelings for Joan Doyle, however, hardened into a secret, ice-cold rage. She's been mocking me and cheating me all my life, she thought, and now she's busy stealing my husband. She wasn't yet sure what form her defence was going to take, but if Joan Doyle thought she would get away with it, she promised herself, she would discover the meaning of revenge.

⁜

Perhaps it was this state of flux in her own life, but sometimes in the spring of 1534, it seemed to Margaret as if everything around her was changing. There was a sense of instability in the air.

Soon after Christmas there was a heavy fall of snow and the winter weather kept Walsh at home for most of January. In February he made several journeys into Dublin, returning each evening. The situation there, he reported, was uncertain.

"Kildare is undoubtedly sick. He's finally going to London, but the word is that he's only going because he wants to persuade King Henry to confirm his son Thomas as Lord Deputy in his place."

The week after Kildare's departure, Walsh stayed in Dublin for three days, and Margaret wondered if he was seeing Joan Doyle; but when he returned he was looking grave, and the news he brought put all other considerations out of her mind.

"It's the lease on our Church land," he told her. "You know it's up for renewal this year. I've just had Archbishop Alen's terms." He shook his head. "It seems," he added grimly, "that he won't even negotiate." The terms were crushing. The rent was more than doubled. "And the trouble," explained Walsh, "is that as a lawyer and steward myself, I'd do the same in the archbishop's place. The land is worth what he asks." He sighed. "But he's taken away most of my profit."

For two days he considered the problem from every angle. Then, finally, he announced, "I shall have to go to London to see Richard." He left at the start of March.

They were not the only ones affected in this way. During the coming weeks Margaret heard of several families who were being forced off their Church estates, some of them even kinsmen of Kildare himself. Under normal circumstances, even the Archbishop of Dublin would hesitate to offend the Fitzgeralds, and she wondered what this meant. Meanwhile, the news from England suggested that events there had reached a crisis.

"The Pope's excommunicated Henry." London was secure, but there were fears that there could be risings in the outer regions, especially the north and west, where the traditional loyalties were very strong. It was rumoured, even, that the Hapsburg Emperor might send an invasion from Spain. For all his arrogant bluster, the Tudor king could lose his throne if this came to pass. And then, at the end of the month, William Walsh returned. She would never forget the evening he arrived, standing in the doorway, and announced, "I have brought someone with me."

Richard. Her Richard. The same Richard, with his red hair, merry eyes, and smiling face, but taller, stronger, even more handsome than when he had left. Richard, the strapping young man, who enfolded her in his arms. If he had felt bitter disappointment at being forced to leave London and return home, he concealed it for her sake. For this, Walsh told her that night, was the conclusion he and Richard had come to when they discussed the business together in London. "We can't afford to keep him in London anymore. He'll come and live with us for a while. I can certainly help him get a start in Dublin." So he was home at last, to stay. Every cloud, she thought privately to herself, has a silver lining. And what, she wondered, was to be done with the Church estate? "I shall give it up," said Walsh. "In the meantime," he grimaced, "there'll be no new gowns for you or cloaks for me for a while."

The month of April was mainly devoted to Richard. His father did not leave him at home to be idle. For several days he took him up into Fingal. Then they went down into Munster for ten days. He also took him into Dublin where, his father was glad to report, "He charmed all he met." Margaret had to admire her husband's activity. By early May, Richard seemed to know everybody.

"And who in Dublin has impressed you most?" she asked her son one evening, as they were sitting by the fire together.

"I think," he replied after a moment's thought, "perhaps the merchant, Doyle. I've never met a man who knew his business better. And of course his wife," he added cheerfully, "is lovely."

If Walsh was pleased with his son, however, the news he was hearing in Dublin caused him more concern. When the Earl of Kildare arrived in London, he had been courteously received. But in mid-May, a number of his household arrived back in Dublin with the news that his health was failing and that King Henry had abruptly deprived him of his governorship and refused to give it to his son. Even worse: "Can you believe it," they protested, "he's sending the Gunner again." Word also came that several of the Butler clan were to have key appointments in the new administration. But perhaps the most ominous rumour was that the Butlers had given a guarantee to King Henry that they would not support any claims made in Ireland by the Pope. "That can mean only one thing," Walsh declared. "Henry believes the Spanish will invade."

What would the Fitzgeralds do? Everyone was watching young Silken Thomas and his five uncles. There had already been one furious quarrel with Archbishop Alen over the Church estates. Before May was out, the young Fitzgerald heir had been up in Ulster talking to the O'Neills, and down in Munster, too. There was no sign of the Gunner yet. Would the Fitzgeralds bide their time or start stirring up the provinces right away? The measure of the danger, for Margaret, was the day late in May when her husband arrived at the house carrying an arquebus, gunpowder, and shot. "I bought the gun off a ship's captain," he explained. "Just in case."

So how was it, in the middle of all this uncertainty, that William Walsh found time and energy to pursue his affair with Joan Doyle?

Margaret could hardly believe it, yet this was what he seemed to be doing.

There had been several occasions, since his return with Richard, when she had guessed that her husband might be seeing the alderman's wife. In early May, he had gone into Dublin with Richard and then—she only discovered later—sent Richard on an errand into Fingal for two days. The same thing had happened the following week, when he had dispatched Richard to Maynooth and a nearby monastery. How could he use their own son to provide his cover, she wondered? But it was no doubt the Doyle woman who'd suggested it, she thought in disgust. If there was any doubt in her mind about what was going on, however, it was dispelled in early June.

A ship had arrived in Dublin with news that the invalid Earl of Kildare had been executed in London. The Fitzgeralds were beside themselves. "It may not be true," Walsh pointed out. He went into Dublin anyway, to find out more, taking Richard with him. Two days later, Richard appeared back at the house.

"Silken Thomas has just been summoned to London. We still don't know what's happened to Kildare," he told Margaret. "Father says you should hide anything valuable and prepare for trouble. We may even need the arquebus." Nobody in Dublin knew what was going to happen. Even the king's men in Dublin Castle seemed in the dark, he reported. "I told Father he should discuss the situation with Doyle," Richard went on confidently. "He's got the best judgement. But we can't," he said regretfully, "because he's away in Waterford all this week."

"Away all week?" Without meaning to, she allowed her voice to rise almost to a shriek. He looked at her, surprised.

"Yes. What of it?"

"Nothing," she said quickly. "Nothing." So that was it. She saw their game. It had all been arranged. The Doyle woman had known her husband would be away. Joan Doyle had made a fool of her yet again, and sent her own unsuspecting son to her with the message. What was she supposed to do? Send Richard back? Risk his discovering the truth? The woman's evil cunning passed belief. But still nothing had prepared her for what came next.

"I'll tell you a strange coincidence, by the way," Richard said. "Father and I found out this morning." He smiled a little sadly. "Do you know who just took up the lease on that Church land we surrendered? Alderman Doyle. Still," he added philosophically, "I suppose he can afford it."

Doyle? It took a moment for the full implication to sink in. But then, gradually, it seemed to Margaret that she understood. Wasn't this exactly what Joan Doyle had done before? First she had lulled her into a false security, the night of the thunderstorm, and then used the information she had so foolishly provided to strike at the family. Now she had deliberately set out to seduce William while her own husband, who was no doubt close to Archbishop Alen, stole away the Walshes' land. Was there no limit to what she'd do to destroy them? Poor William. She even felt sorry for her husband now. What was any man, after all, in the hands of a really determined and unscrupulous woman? Joan Doyle had seduced and duped him just as viciously as she'd duped Margaret herself before. At that moment, she hated Joan Doyle more completely than she had ever hated any human being in her life.

She saw it all. Even now William, clever though he was, probably didn't realise that he had been betrayed. The Doyle woman would have had an explanation for everything: you could be sure of that. He was probably making love to her at that very moment, the poor fool.

That was when Margaret knew she was going to kill her.

⁘

MacGowan was standing with Walsh and Doyle in front of the Tholsel when the business began. It was the day after Walsh had sent his son back home; Doyle had arrived from Waterford that morning. They had just been discussing the political situation when the commotion started.

It happened so fast. That was what astonished him. The first shouts from the gate that a body of men was approaching had scarcely died away before the clattering and jingling and drumming of hoofs began; and as the three men pulled back into the doorway of the Tholsel, the huge cavalcade of riders, three abreast, came past—there were so many that it took several minutes—followed by three columns of marching men-at-arms and gallowglasses. MacGowan estimated more than a thousand men. In the centre, accompanied by twelve dozen cavalry in coats of mail, rode the young Lord Thomas—not in armour but wearing a gorgeous green-and-gold silk tunic and a hat with a plume. He looked as blithe as if he were partaking in a pageant. Such was the style, the confidence, and the arrogance of the Fitzgeralds.

Arrogant it might be, yet carefully calculated, too. Having ridden through the city and then clattered over the bridge to the hall where the royal council was meeting, Silken Thomas calmly handed them the ceremonial sword of state which his father, as Lord Deputy, had in his keeping, and renounced his allegiance to King Henry. The gesture was medieval: a magnate was withdrawing his oath of loyalty to his feudal overlord. Not only was the English king losing his vassal but the Fitzgeralds were now declaring themselves free to give their allegiance to another king instead—the Holy Roman Emperor in Spain, for instance, or even the Pope. There had been nothing like it since Lord Thomas's grandfather had crowned young Lambert Simnel and sent an army to invade England nearly fifty years ago.

It only took an hour before all Dublin knew.

MacGowan spent the rest of that day with Walsh and Doyle. Though well-informed, both men had been taken by surprise at Silken Thomas's radical move, and they looked shaken. Seeing them together, MacGowan could not escape a sense of irony. The grey-haired, distinguished-looking lawyer and the dark, powerful merchant—one tied to the Fitzgeralds, the other to the Butlers—were opposites in politics; Doyle had just taken over Walsh's best land; as for Walsh's dealings with Doyle's wife, MacGowan still wasn't sure what Doyle knew about that business. Yet whatever reasons these two men might have had to fall out during all these years, here they both were, still courteous and even cordial towards each other. Until today, when young Silken Thomas, whom they hardly knew, had provoked a crisis so serious that it would probably lead to civil war. Would they now be forced into deadly opposition? Perhaps it was this same thought which caused Doyle to sigh, as they parted: "God knows what will become of us now."

Yet the remarkable feature of the next two months was how little seemed to happen. Having made this point, Silken Thomas and his troops didn't linger in Dublin. First he withdrew across the river, then sent out detachments all over the Pale. Within ten days they reported that no one was offering any resistance. The countryside was secure.

But not Dublin.

"I can't think why Fitzgerald let us do it," Doyle confessed to MacGowan. "Perhaps he just assumed that we wouldn't dare." But while the Fitzgerald troops were busy securing the countryside, the city fathers quietly closed all the Dublin gates. "It's a gamble," Doyle confessed, "but we're betting on the English king."

Were they right? It wasn't long before news came back that the Earl of Kildare was still alive. He hadn't been executed, although as soon as King Henry had heard of the revolt he had put the earl in the Tower. MacGowan suspected the earl probably approved of his son's actions. Kildare was a dying man, but King Henry was clearly rattled. His officials at court were denying that there was any trouble in Ireland at all. As for the Gunner, who should have been rushing to Ireland with troops and artillery, he was showing no sign of wanting to take up his post at all. Meanwhile, a Spanish envoy had arrived, given Lord Thomas supplies of gunpowder and shot, and told him that Spanish troops would follow. This was exciting news indeed. If people had suspected his declaration in Dublin had just been a bluff, the usual Fitzgerald troublemaking to force King

Henry to restore them to office again, the news from Spain put matters in a different light.

"With Spanish troops," young Lord Thomas told his friends, "I can remove Ireland from King Henry by force." And soon afterwards he issued a startling proclamation. "The English are no longer wanted in Ireland. They must get out." Who was English? "Anyone not born here," Fitzgerald declared. That meant King Henry's men. Everyone could agree about that. Archbishop Alen of Dublin and the other royal servants hastily locked themselves up in Dublin Castle. In a fine gesture, Silken Thomas even turned out his young English wife and sent her back to England, too.

And if many people had been sympathetic to Lord Thomas's cause, during the summer their feelings were strengthened by events in England. All Christendom knew that King Henry had been excommunicated. Spain was talking of invasion; even the cynical King of France thought Henry a fool. But now, in the summer of 1534, the Tudor king went further. Brave men like Thomas More had refused to support his claims to make himself, in effect, the English pope; now, when the English order of friars likewise refused, Henry closed their houses and started throwing them into prison. The holy friars: the men most loved and revered in Ireland, inside and outside the Pale. It was an outrage. No wonder then that Silken Thomas now declared to the Irish people that his revolt was in defence of the true Church as well. Envoys were sent with this message to the Hapsburg Emperor and to the Holy Father. "My ancestors came to Ireland to defend the true faith," Fitzgerald declared, "in the service of an English king. Now we must fight against an English king to preserve it."

At the end of July, Archbishop Alen made a run for it and tried to jump on a ship leaving Ireland. Some of Fitzgerald's men caught him, there was a skirmish, and the archbishop was killed. But nobody was shocked. He was only a royal servant wearing a bishop's mitre. The friars were holy men.

As August began, it seemed to MacGowan that young Silken

Thomas might get away with it. The city was in a curious mood. The gates were closed by the council's orders, but since Fitzgerald was out at Maynooth and his troops widely scattered, the small doors in the gates were open for people to pass in and out, and life was proceeding almost as normal. MacGowan had just been on his way to visit Tidy in his gatehouse when he chanced to meet Alderman Doyle in the street, and pausing to talk, expressed the opinion that Dublin would soon be forced to welcome Lord Thomas with his Spanish troops as its new ruler. But Doyle shook his head.

"The Spanish troops will be promised, but they will never arrive. The Emperor will gladly embarrass Henry Tudor, but open war with England would cost him too much. Lord Thomas will have to manage alone. He'll be weakened also by the fact that the Butlers are already using this opportunity to get favours from Henry. Fitzgerald may be stronger than the Butlers, but they can undermine him."

"Yet King Henry has difficulties of his own," MacGowan pointed out. "Perhaps he can't afford to subdue Lord Thomas. He's done nothing so far, after all."

"It may take time," Doyle replied, "but in the end Henry will crush him. There's no doubt in my mind. He'll fight, and he will never give up. For two reasons. The first is that Lord Thomas has made a fool of him in the eyes of all the world. And Henry is deeply vain. He will never rest until he has destroyed him. The second is more profound. Henry Tudor now faces the same challenge that Henry Plantagenet faced nearly four centuries ago when Strongbow came to Ireland. One of his vassals is threatening to set up a kingdom of his own just across the western sea. Worse, it would become the platform for any power like France or Spain which wishes to oppose him. He cannot allow that to happen."

⁜

It was clear to Eva that Silken Thomas had given her husband a new lease on life. Sean O'Byrne had been slowing up a bit in the last year or two. But since the revolt began, he'd been looking ten years younger. Almost like a boy. The chance of action, a fight, excitement, and even danger—she supposed that the need for these things was as deeply ingrained in her husband's nature as the need to have children was in hers. It was the thrill of the chase. Most men were the same, in her opinion—at least, the best ones were.

Sean O'Byrne wasn't alone. The excitement had spread throughout the communities in the Wicklow Mountains—a sense that something was going to change. No one could quite say what. The rule of the Fitzgeralds wasn't so light. The O'Byrnes and other clans like them had no illusions that they would be allowed to sweep down into the Pale and kick the Walshes and the rest of the gentry off their ancient lands. But once the English king was removed from the scene, a new freedom of some kind would inevitably be born. If the Fitzgeralds and the Walshes had been English Irish up to now, henceforth they would be Irish, and so would Ireland.

Sean had thrown himself into the business with gusto. There was plenty to do. He'd been out on several patrols down into the southern Pale, ensuring that the country was solid for the Fitzgeralds. As an O'Byrne, with a Fitzgerald for a foster son, no less, Sean was highly trusted, and this gave him pleasure. He'd taken his sons and young Maurice with him. Eva had been a little nervous seeing them go, but there hadn't been any trouble. Soon, Sean believed, there would be a big raid down into Butler territory. "Just to make sure they keep quiet," he told her cheerfully. She wasn't certain what she felt about that. Would he be taking the boys?

Her boys: she didn't count Seamus as a boy anymore. He was a family man with his own children now. He'd enlarged the house where the Brennans had lived and built up a cattle herd nearly half the size of his father's. But Fintan and Maurice were still her boys.

Some children will look like one parent for a few years, and then come to resemble the other. But not Fintan. He still looked so like her it was absurd. "Could you not have let him take after me in some respect?" Sean had jokingly chided her once. "He is like you.

He's wonderful with the cattle," she replied. "But so are you," he had pointed out, with a laugh. Fintan's hair was as fair as it had been when he was a child, his broad face still broke easily into an innocent smile. He had the same sweet nature. And Maurice, too, was still the same boy, handsome and thoughtful, his fine eyes looking distant and melancholy sometimes. "A poetic spirit," as Father Donal would say. There had been moments when she had felt almost guilty, half afraid that she loved him as much as her own son; but then a glance into Fintan's blue eyes would remind her, with a little rush of warmth, that however dear Maurice was to her, it was Fintan who was her own flesh and blood, to whom she had given birth, who was her true son.

It made her smile to watch the two boys together. They were getting so manly—bursting with energy, still a little shy, yet so proud of themselves. She would see the two of them walking together, Maurice slim and dark, somewhat taller, and fair Fintan, as squarely built as a young ox now, sharing their private jokes together; in the evenings, sometimes, Maurice would play the harp, her husband would join him on the fiddle, and Fintan, who had a pleasant voice, would sing. Those were the best times of all.

The patrol in early August was routine. The previous patrols had toured the areas where some trouble might have been anticipated; now it had been decided to go to the houses of even the Fitzgerald supporters. For Lord Thomas wanted to try out a new oath of loyalty; and Sean O'Byrne had been given quite a broad area to cover. Eva couldn't say why she should have had a sense of unease about this patrol. There was no reason to expect any trouble. All the men were going: Seamus had come up from his house, Maurice and Fintan were ready to go. But just before they set off, she called out to Sean, "Are you taking all my men away?" And giving him a little look, "Am I to be left alone?"

He glanced at her and seemed to guess her feelings. He decided to be kind.

"Which one will you keep?"

"Fintan," she said, after a moment's hesitation, and regretted it immediately. She saw his face fall.

"But Father . . ." he began.

"Don't argue," said Sean. "You'll stay with your mother."

And I shall be blamed, Eva thought sadly; but she didn't change her mind, though her heart went out to her son as he came and stood by her side, doing his best to smile at her affectionately. As the party drew away, she put her arm round him.

"Thank you for staying with me," she said.

⁜

Margaret Walsh was already standing outside her door with her husband when the patrol arrived. There were a dozen riders. The Walsh estate was the third that O'Byrne and his men had come to.

So this was Sean O'Byrne who was such a devil with the women. She took a good look at him. He was a dark, handsome fellow certainly. She could see that. There was some grey in his hair now, but he looked lean and fit. She saw his vanity and did not dislike it, though she didn't think she was attracted to him as he greeted William and herself with cool politeness.

To Walsh's offer that they should all come in for refreshment, he answered that it was only himself and two of the other men who need detain him inside for a few moments and so, without more ado, Walsh was obliged to go in with them to the big oak table in the hall where, with an official air, Sean O'Byrne took out a little book of the Gospels in Latin, and laying it on the table asked William to kindly place his hand upon it.

"Is it an oath you're wanting?" Walsh enquired.

"It is," O'Byrne replied easily.

"And what kind of an oath should that be?" asked Walsh.

"Of loyalty to Lord Thomas."

"Of loyalty?" Walsh's face clouded. "I hardly think," he said with some feeling, and drawing himself up to his full height, "that Lord Thomas would wish to compel an oath from me who has so freely given his loyalty to his father the earl all these years." He gave O'Byrne a look of gentle rebuke. "You offend me," he said with quiet dignity.

"There is no compulsion."

"You come here with armed men."

"I will tell the Lord Thomas that you gave the oath freely," O'Byrne answered smoothly, "if that will satisfy you."

It did not seem to satisfy Walsh, for he looked seriously displeased. Going to the door, he asked his wife to call all the men into the hall at once, and stood by the door until they were assembled. Then with a glare at O'Byrne, he went swiftly to the table, slammed down his hand upon the Gospels and declared: "I swear on the Gospel the same love, respect, and loyalty to the Lord Thomas Fitzgerald that I have always given, and still give, to his father the Earl of Kildare." He picked up the Gospels and handed them back to O'Byrne with finality. "I have sworn, which given my known affections I should never have been asked to do. But I swear gladly all the same. And now," he added with some coldness, "I bid you good day." He indicated with a brief bow that he wished O'Byrne to leave.

"It's not enough," said Sean O'Byrne.

"Not enough?" It was not often that William Walsh became angry, but it seemed that this was about to happen. Some of O'Byrne's men were looking awkward. "Have you come here to insult me?" he cried. "I have sworn. I will swear no more. If the Lord Thomas doubts my loyalty—which he does not—then let him come here and say it to my face. I have done." And with a furious expression he started to stalk out of the hall.

But O'Byrne placed himself before the door.

"The oath requires that you swear loyalty to Lord Thomas," he said evenly, "and also to the Holy Father, and also to the Holy Roman Emperor Charles of Spain."

This triad had been carefully devised. Once you had sworn to it, there could be no going back to the English king. As far as King

Henry VIII was concerned, once you had given that oath you had sworn to treason, for which the fearful penalty was to be hung, drawn, and quartered. For those who understood its implications, the oath was awesome in its finality.

But Walsh was so heated now that he was scarcely listening.

"I'll swear no more," he shouted. "Let the Lord Thomas come here with a thousand men and I'll offer him my own head to cut off if he doubts me. But I'll not be treated like a villain by you, O'Byrne." He gave the man from the Wicklow Mountains a look of contempt, while he himself had gone red in the face. "To you I'll swear nothing. Now leave my house," he shouted in fury.

But Sean O'Byrne did not move. He drew his sword.

"I have already killed men better than you, Walsh," he stated dangerously, "and burned down houses bigger than this," he added, with a glance towards Margaret. "So," he concluded softly, "you have your choice."

There was a pause. Walsh stood very still. Margaret watched him anxiously. Nobody said a word.

"I do it," Walsh said, with infinite disgust, "at sword point. You are witnesses," he looked round the men gathered there, "at how I have been treated by this man."

Moments later, at the table, O'Byrne administered the oath, and Walsh, looking dignified and contemptuous, with his hand on the Gospels, repeated the words tonelessly. Then the patrol left. It was not until they were safely out of sight that Walsh spoke.

"I'm glad Richard was down in Dublin today," he remarked. "I hope he won't have to take that oath."

"I was afraid for a moment that you wouldn't," said Margaret.

"I was trying not to," her husband explained. "The oath I swore voluntarily, to support Lord Thomas as I had his father, was harmless enough. Kildare, after all, was the king's deputy in Ireland. But I'd already heard about this new oath of theirs, and I knew what a terrible thing it was. The reference to the Emperor is the worst part. It's treason pure and simple." He shook his head. "If he wasn't going to let me get out of it, then I had to have witnesses that it was extracted from me under compulsion. That's why I called everybody in. It's not a complete defence, but if things go badly for Lord Thomas, it might save my neck."

Margaret looked at her husband with admiration.

"I didn't realise that was what you were doing," she said. "You act very well."

"Don't forget," he said with a smile, "that I'm a lawyer."

"But do you really think that Lord Thomas will fail?" she asked.

"When the Fitzgeralds fight the Butlers it's one thing," he replied. "But when they make war on the King of England it's another. We'll have to see how it turns out."

That night, as she fell asleep, Margaret found two sets of images coming into her mind. The first was of Sean O'Byrne with his sword, threatening her husband who, she realised, was the finer and cleverer man. The second was of her brother as she imagined he might have looked, sword in hand, as he went into battle against the Tudor King of England. She slept badly after that.

⁂

If Tidy had supposed that finding the new accommodation in the tower might bring greater harmony to his family, by that August he decided that it was the worst thing he had ever done in his life.

In early August, Silken Thomas returned to Dublin, to find the gates closed. He demanded admittance. The mayor and aldermen refused. He told them he would attack, but they weren't impressed. So Silken Thomas had to sit outside the walls.

The siege of Dublin that followed was a desultory affair. Fitzgerald hadn't enough troops to rush the walls. He burned some houses in the suburbs, but it did no good. And even if he had been able to cut off all the supplies to the city, the aldermen had already seen to it that there were enough provisions within the walls to last for months. Young Lord Thomas could only make a show of force from time to time and hope to frighten the Dubliners into changing their minds. And this was what he was doing one morning in August when Alderman Doyle came across to inspect the defences at the western gate.

The instructions to the guards at the western gate were simple. The gate itself was double barred. They were not to provoke Fitzgerald and his men, but if attacked, they were to respond with arquebus and bows from the battlements. Just before Doyle arrived, Tidy had seen from one of the tower windows that Lord Thomas and about a hundred horsemen were approaching the gate, and he had gone down to make sure the sentries were aware. As a result, he found himself standing beside the alderman on one side of the gate as Lord Thomas reached the other, and heard quite clearly as the young lord called out to anyone on the battlements or behind the gate who could hear, that if they did not soon open the city to him, he would be forced to bring up his cannon. "Even with what the Spanish envoy gave him, and his own supplies," Doyle calmly pointed out to the men standing round, "I know for a fact that he hasn't enough powder and shot to take the city. It's an empty threat." And it seemed that Fitzgerald was to get no reply at all, when suddenly another voice was heard. It came from a window somewhere up in the tower.

"Is that the Lord Thomas himself?" A woman's voice, calling down. It was followed by a pause, and the sound of horses wheeling about. Perhaps Fitzgerald's men thought someone was going to take aim at him. But Tidy knew better. He froze. The voice belonged to Cecily. A moment later, to his even greater astonishment, the aristocrat replied, "It is."

Was it true, Cecily called down, that he would defend the Holy Church against the heretic Henry? It was. He didn't deny the Mass? Certainly not. But now Tidy thought he could hear a trace of humour in Fitzgerald's voice when he asked if she was the woman who had cursed King Henry at Corpus Christi last. She was, she replied, and she'd curse Lord Thomas and his friends, too, if they denied the Mass.

"No friends of mine, I promise," he cried. And why was he being kept out of Dublin, he demanded genially. Was he not welcome?

"You'll be welcomed by all except a few heretic aldermen," she called down, "who need to learn a lesson."

Until this moment, Tidy had been so surprised that he hadn't moved. He'd known how Cecily felt, of course. As the events of that spring had unfolded, she had told him just what she thought of the excommunicated English king. But he had begged her to keep her thoughts private within the home, and though she had seemed rather moody of late it had never occurred to him that she would do anything like this. He glanced at Doyle, his best patron, who had just been called a heretic. The alderman's face was growing dark.

He raced into the tower and up the spiral stairs. Breathless, he burst into the upper room from which Cecily was calling down to Lord Thomas's men that they'd find a warm welcome if they broke down the gate, and dragged her away from the window. She struggled, and he struck her, once in anger and the second time in fear—because he thought she might start again—much harder, so that she fell, bleeding, to the floor. Hardly caring, he dragged her to the door and down the stairs to the lower chamber where there was no window that looked out from the wall. Then he locked her in there and went down to the gate again to apologise to Doyle. But the alderman had gone.

⊹

Cecily did not speak to her husband very much in the days that followed. They both understood what had happened; there was nothing to say. In front of their children and the apprentice they were quietly civil; when alone, silent. If either was waiting for the other to apologise, the wait seemed to be in vain. Nor did matters improve.

A little later in the month of August, Silken Thomas decided to send a party to raid the farms in Fingal. For the task he chose a contingent of Wicklow men led by the O'Tooles. When the Irish cat-

tlemen got out of hand, burning down and plundering the rich
Fingal farms, a large column of Dubliners, many of whom had
property up there, broke out of the city and raced northwards to the
Fingal farmers' aid.

Cecily saw them returning from the tower. They were streaming
across the bridge. She could tell from the way they rode that they
were fleeing, and as they crossed the bridge she could see that many
were wounded. It was an hour later that Tidy came back to the
house with the awful news.

"There were eighty men killed." His face was pale as he stared at
her solemnly. "Eighty."

She watched him quietly. She knew this was the moment for her
to say something, to express the sympathy that might break the barrier between them. She knew it, but found that she could not.

"I'm not sorry," she said. And she let the ensuing silence fall and
remain like an invisible sea, until it had frozen into finality.

During the days that followed, the city was in shock. There was
hardly a family that hadn't lost a relation or a friend. A growing
party in the town was beginning to ask what would happen next.
Would Fitzgerald's troops start killing the people in Oxmantown?
Would the O'Byrnes come down and raid the southern farmlands?
Doyle and his friends were all for holding out, but even some of the
aldermen were wondering whether a compromise with Fitzgerald
wouldn't be wiser. "Let us at least negotiate," they said. And once
they were allowed to do so, an agreement was soon reached. The
gates of Dublin would be opened. Lord Thomas and his troops
might occupy the city in return for a promise not to harm the inhabitants. Everything would be available to him with the exception
of the castle stronghold itself. The royal servants and a section of the
aldermen would retire to the castle and take their chances on the
outcome of events. It wasn't what Lord Thomas wanted, but it was
an improvement on what he had. So he took the deal.

"I'm going into the castle with Doyle. He's taking his whole family with him." It was eleven o'clock in the morning when Tidy came

to give Cecily this news. "So I think we should all go," he added. "We need to get ready at once."

"I'm staying here," she said simply.

"And the children?"

"They'll be safer with me. Fitzgerald will do no harm to me and the children. It's you who'll be in danger if he attacks the castle."

"The walls are too thick. They've already stocked it with provisions. We could hold out safely in there for years."

She gazed at him bleakly.

"You are afraid to offend Doyle. I'm afraid to offend God. I suppose that's the difference between us."

"If you say so," he answered. By noon he had left the house.

And whether her religion had caused her to split from her husband or whether it had only provided an excuse for her to maintain a separation she now desired, Cecily herself could not with certainty have said.

⁕

The siege of Dublin Castle continued through September without success. But as the month progressed, news from England made the business more urgent.

The English were finally coming. Troops were actually assembling, cannon being taken towards the port, a ship been found. Even the Gunner himself had made an appearance. It seemed that they might really be going to put up a fight at last.

As MacGowan stood in Castle Street and stared at the grey old castle walls, he felt discouraged. The day was fine; the mossy slates and stones of Dublin returned a greenish glow to the blue September sky. A few yards in front of him, a group of Fitzgerald's men were shooting arrows over the wall in a gesture that was probably futile—unless anyone inside the castle was stupid enough to stand in their path. But none of this concerned him. What worried MacGowan was how he was going to help the wife of Alderman Doyle. He didn't want to let her down.

The previous month, he'd been able to do the alderman a good turn. Doyle had needed a new tenant on the estate he had taken over from the Walshes and the grey merchant had thought of the Brennan family who had once been on Sean O'Byrne's land and had recently become unhappy with their subsequent tenancy. "You always know everything," Doyle had said to him admiringly. That had given MacGowan great pleasure. The transfer of the Brennans had taken place just in time for them to get the harvest in—and since they had several strong children now, they had been the greatest help to Doyle. With his present commission, however, MacGowan had been having less success.

The siege of Dublin Castle had been a lacklustre affair. The feeble efforts in the street in front of him now were quite typical. But even on the better days, when they had brought cannon, troops, and ladders up, the task had been too difficult. For the castle was a formidable obstacle. From the outer wall there was a high, sheer drop down to the old pool, now almost silted up, of Dubh Linn. Its other walls, though they lay within the city, were tall and stout and easy to defend. If Fitzgerald had more ammunition he might have been able to destroy the gates or knock down a section of wall; but as he was still short of cannonballs, he couldn't achieve this. Nor had he enough troops for a mass assault. Though he had sent a large force down into Butler territory to raid them and frighten them into submission, the Butlers were still ready to attack, and so he had forces dispersed in numerous different places. As for the people of Dublin, they obeyed his orders, but when it came to storming the castle, they did it without much conviction since many of them had friends inside.

It had been easy enough for MacGowan to send a message to Alderman Doyle. He had just wrapped it round a blunted arrow which he had fired over the wall. The message had asked if there was anything the alderman wanted. It was the sort of communication between the city and the castle that was happening every day. The reply had come attached to a stone dropped at his feet in front of

the gate the day before. Doyle was concerned, he told the grey merchant, on two counts. Firstly, with the English probably on the way,
he thought it possible that Lord Thomas might mount a more
determined assault to try to secure the stronghold for himself.
Secondly, his wife was unwell. He wanted to secure her a safe-
conduct out of the castle so that MacGowan could escort her to the
greater security of the house at Dalkey. And he was prepared to
pay the besiegers handsomely for this privilege. This was what
MacGowan had just been trying to arrange.

The trouble was, Doyle wasn't the first person to enter a private
negotiation of this kind. Rather to his surprise, the grey merchant
had been taken into the presence of Silken Thomas himself, where
the young aristocrat politely informed him: "I have given enough
safe-conducts already. Unless, of course, the alderman cares to pay
me with some of the cannonballs which earlier this summer I so
unwisely left in the castle."

And MacGowan was just wondering what to do next when he
saw William Walsh and his wife approaching, and realised that this
might be a stroke of singular good fortune. Moments later he had
taken the lawyer to one side.

Fortunately, Walsh was quick to see his point of view. The lawyer
and his wife had come into Dublin that day precisely to see for
themselves how the siege was progressing. As a Fitzgerald adherent
who had nonetheless disliked the treasonable oath, Walsh was anxiously watching events now that the English might be coming. If the
Gunner were to prove too strong for Silken Thomas, it would do
him no harm, MacGowan pointed out, to have helped Alderman
Doyle. "And I should think," the grey merchant tactfully added,
"that you might be glad to do a good turn to Dame Doyle as well."
As a longtime adherent of the Fitzgeralds, he suggested, Walsh
might have more luck persuading young Lord Thomas than he had
himself. To all this the lawyer readily agreed.

"Indeed, I'll go and see if he will speak with me," he suggested, "straightaway." And asking MacGowan to look after his wife, he hurried off.

MacGowan spent nearly an hour with Margaret Walsh. The men had stopped shooting over the walls, so they walked round the outside of the castle. They discussed the political situation and she gave him a detailed account of how Sean O'Byrne had forced her husband to take the oath. It was clear to MacGowan that she shared her husband's caution. "We were always loyal to Kildare," she remarked, "but that foolish oath was going too far." It was when she asked what business her husband was engaged upon now, that he paused. Walsh and the alderman were civil, but he wasn't sure what Margaret's feelings about the Doyles were, nor how much of Joan Doyle's dealings with her husband she might have discovered. So he contented himself with saying, "He's doing me a favour, trying to help some people in there." He indicated the castle. "You'll have to ask him." She looked thoughtful, but seemed quite contented. After a little while, however, she looked up brightly and remarked, "I expect that'll be Alderman Doyle. My husband likes him, you know, and his wife is quite a friend of mine."

"She is?" It wasn't often that MacGowan was taken in, but on this occasion he was. And supposing that it might look strange if he withheld the information, he briefly told her what the errand was. She seemed delighted.

Shortly after noon, Walsh reappeared looking pleased.

"I told your wife what you were doing," MacGowan told him quickly. "So you've no need to explain."

"Ah." Did Walsh look awkward just for an instant? If so, he recovered at once. "I was able to persuade him," he announced with a smile.

"How did you do it?" asked MacGowan with frank admiration.

"My husband is not a lawyer for nothing," said Margaret, linking her arm affectionately through his. "When is she to leave the castle?" she asked.

"Tomorrow evening at dusk. Not before. You're to conduct her quietly out of the city through the Dame's Gate," Walsh informed MacGowan.

The lawyer and his wife had left after that to return to their estate; and MacGowan, having sent in a message to the alderman telling him of the arrangements, had gone gratefully back to his house. It was a piece of providential good fortune, he considered, that the gentleman lawyer should have chanced to come by when he did.

So the grey merchant could find no explanation for the strange feeling that came over him that evening when he thought about Dame Doyle. There was something about the arrangements he didn't like. He didn't know why. An instinct. A sense of unease. These were dangerous times.

Well, he told himself, he must escort her to Dalkey, whatever the danger, since he had given Doyle his word and Doyle, as well as being a friend, was a powerful man. But he resolved to take extra precautions.

··:··

At dawn the next morning, leaving word for her sleeping husband that she had gone into Dublin and would return that afternoon, Margaret Walsh set out from her house. But she had only gone a short distance out of sight when she wheeled her horse round and, instead of going towards the city, headed south towards the Wicklow Mountains.

··:··

The threat of the Gunner and his English troops might concern the people in Dublin, but to Eva O'Byrne it hardly seemed to matter. To those who dwelt in the hills, the slow rhythm of cattle raising in the high and silent places was hardly impinged upon by the ebb and flow of the rival ruling clans down the generations—except when these provided the occasional excitement of a cattle raid. The government of the Pale would change from time to time, but it seemed to her that this underlying pattern of Irish life would always remain the same.

And wasn't this exactly the case now? The quarrel between Silken Thomas and King Henry might be about profound issues across the sea; but for the O'Byrnes it had meant some patrols and a big raid down into Butler territory. Rather to his disappointment, Sean O'Byrne had not been called upon to go to raid the Butlers; but now, while Dublin awaited the Gunner, Fitzgerald's friends in the Wicklow Mountains were preparing for the Butlers to return the compliment. Any day now, parties of men might be expected to appear on the slopes to raid the cattle and even burn down the farms. The O'Byrnes were ready to deal with them, and Sean had made extensive preparations at Rathconan. Secretly, Eva was well aware, her husband was hoping the Butlers' men would come, and was looking forward to it. "They'll get more than they bargained for," he told her cheerfully, "when they start a fight with the O'Byrnes."

The stranger came quite early in the morning, a single rider from the north. Having hissed at a man in the yard to fetch Sean O'Byrne, the rider remained outside, still mounted, wrapped in a cloak and with a covered face. When O'Byrne came out, the stranger insisted on moving a short distance away from the house so that their conversation should be private. They were together a quarter of an hour; then the stranger rode away.

When Sean came back inside, Eva thought he looked somewhat amused, but also excited. He'd be leaving in an hour, he told her, and not returning until the following morning.

"I'll be taking the boys and some of the men," he announced. He sent the stable boy to fetch Seamus. "Tell him to bring his weapons," he instructed. Fintan was to ride over to two of the neighbouring farmsteads and ask each to gather as many armed men as possible. "I'll pick you up," his father told him, "along the way." But even this, he indicated, would not be enough. "I need at least a dozen, maybe twenty men."

What was this all about, Eva asked? Was it a party of Butler men that he had to fight? No, he said, something else. He'd explain it all tomorrow. In the meantime, he said, she mustn't say a word to anybody. Just that he'd gone out on a patrol. Could he at least, she demanded, tell her where he was going? No, he could not.

"And what," she asked, "if a Butler raiding party comes here while you and the men are away? What am I to do then?"

This made him pause.

"There's been no sign of them yet," he said. "And we'll be gone less than a day." He considered. Then he turned to Maurice. "You're to stay here," he ordered quietly. "If there's danger you are all to ride up into the mountains. Do you understand?"

For an instant, just an instant, she saw the look of dismay in the boy's handsome eyes. She knew very well how he must be longing to go with Fintan and her husband on this adventure—whatever it was. But in another instant it was gone. He bowed his head gracefully, acknowledging the order, and then turned to her with a smile.

"It will be my pleasure." You had to admire his aristocratic style. Sean O'Byrne gave him an appreciative nod.

"Fintan had to stay at home last time. It's your turn now." Soon afterwards he left.

⁘

It was one of those warm September days when a huge blue sky stretched cloudless, over the hills, and the great sweep down to the plain spread out until it turned into a haze. There was a hint of smoke in the air.

Eva spent the rest of the morning quietly. After she had completed her household chores, she went into the little orchard and picked up the apples that had fallen, taking them back to the storeroom where she laid them out on a long wooden table. Later they would be boiled and preserved. Maurice attended to the cattle. The herd was all down from the hill, grazing now. He had an old cattleman to help him; also Seamus's wife and young children. In her care also were a stable boy and three women who worked in the house, Father Donal and his family, and the old bard. These were the only people at Rathconan that day.

The hours passed slowly. In the early afternoon, Eva sat in the orchard. It was very quiet. Apart from the occasional lowing of the cattle on the pasture above and the soft scraping of the breeze on the crisp apple leaves, all was silence. She wondered where Sean was and what he was doing, but she had no idea. Whatever it was, he had seemed cheerful and confident enough. After sitting for an hour, she got up to return to the house. Perhaps, she thought, she would start boiling those apples now.

But before she reached the door, she heard a shout. It came from Maurice. He was running towards her. She saw Father Donal just behind him with the old bard.

"Troops!" Maurice called. "Butler's men. Coming up the valley."

She saw them herself just a moment later: a party of men, some on horse and some on foot coming towards Rathconan. They were not two miles away.

"You think they are Butler men?" she asked Father Donal.

"Who else?" he replied.

"I'll have horses ready in a moment," Maurice told her. "Then we must go up into the hills."

"They'll take the cattle," she pointed out.

"I know." The young fellow didn't look happy about it. "But those were your husband's instructions." He paused. "Perhaps," he suggested, "if we can get you and the women to a place of safety, Father Donal could stay with you and I and the men . . ."

She smiled. There looked to be twenty armed men approaching. Was this brave and handsome boy really proposing to tackle them with the aid of the old cattleman, the stable boy, and the bard? "No," she told him. "We'll stay together." Yet it was a terrible thing, to abandon the house and the herd to the raiders. The cattle were their wealth, their livelihood, their status. Deep within her, genera-tions of her forefathers, cattlemen all, rose up in anger. Sean might have foolishly left the herd at risk, but if she could possibly do so, she meant to save it, or part of it, anyway. Could the herd be split and some of the cattle hidden? Was there time? And it was then, re-membering something she had once seen in her childhood, that Eva had an idea. It was daring and dangerous. And it would also take skill. She looked at Maurice Fitzgerald.

"Would you like to try something with me?" she asked. "It's a risk, and if it doesn't work, they'll maybe kill us." Then she ex-plained what would have to be done.

How strange it was, she thought, as she watched his face. Moments before, torn between his desire to do something and his duty to follow Sean's instructions, the handsome, dark-haired boy had looked so anxious. Yet as he listened to her proposal, which might cost them all their lives, his face seemed to relax. A light came into his eye. An expression she had seen once or twice on her hus-band's face in his youth suddenly appeared on Maurice's—a look of fine, devil-may-care excitement. Yes, she thought to herself, these Fitzgeralds were Irish, right enough.

"Listen then," she said, "and I will tell you what it is we need to do."

＋

At the time when the Butler raiding party was approaching Rathconan, Sean O'Byrne and his men were high in the mountains and far to the south. The party now consisted of eleven riders. All of them, including young Fintan, were armed.

Not that Sean expected a fight—a brief scuffle was more likely. They'd be attacking in the dark, with the advantage of surprise; there was a limited and clearly defined objective; and it was quite probable that their quarry would only be accompanied by two or three men. The main thing was to find the right place for the am-bush before dark, and to rest the horses. He thought he knew the place. A quiet spot with some trees for cover on the road that led to Dalkey.

It had certainly surprised him when the Walsh woman had turned up like that. He'd remembered her from the time he'd gone to take the oath from her husband, the lawyer; but he hadn't paid much attention to her then. Her proposal that he should kidnap the alderman's wife had surprised him even more.

Why was she doing this? he had asked. She had her reasons, she told him. That was all she would say. But she must hate the Doyle woman considerably, he thought, to take such a step. Why do women feud? Over a man, usually. You'd have thought she'd have been a bit old for that, really, he mused; but perhaps a woman was never too old to be jealous. Anyway, whatever her reasons, the rewards of this business could be huge. That was what attracted Sean O'Byrne.

The deal that he and Margaret Walsh had struck was simple enough. He was to capture Dame Doyle and hold her for ransom. It wouldn't be the first kidnap of this kind in recent years; but normally there would have been serious repercussions if a relatively obscure figure like Sean O'Byrne had dared to abduct the wife of a man as important as Doyle. The present circumstances, however, with Doyle in armed conflict with the Fitzgeralds, presented a wonderful opportunity; and though Silken Thomas had granted Joan Doyle a safe-conduct out of the city, that would hardly extend beyond the suburbs. On the open road down at Dalkey, she was on her own, and Lord Thomas Fitzgerald probably couldn't care less what happened to her there. Once O'Byrne had obtained the ransom money from the alderman, he was secretly to pass half of it to Margaret. Very secretly. No one—neither his own family nor Margaret's husband—was to know that she had any part in the business; but her claim to a half share was clearly reasonable. She had brought him the idea, and was telling him when and where Dame Doyle would be travelling. O'Byrne had agreed to the bargain at once.

There was only one thing he hadn't worked out. How much money should he ask for? He realised that it would be a substantial amount—probably more money than he had ever seen in his life. Though he knew exactly the worth of any cattle inside or outside the Pale, O'Byrne had no idea of the price of a Dublin alderman's wife.

"When you have her," the Walsh woman had promised, "I will tell you what to ask." And O'Byrne was ready to acknowledge that the lawyer's wife would know best. "But what if we can't get the asking price?" he had enquired. "What if they won't pay?"

The Walsh woman had given him a grim smile.

"Kill her," she said.

✛

They were coming slowly up the slope, taking their time. There were twenty of them: ten mounted, ten on foot. Six of the foot soldiers were simple kerne—men drawn from the land to fight for pay. But four were the terrifying gallowglasses with their long-handled axes and two-handed swords: they would make mincemeat of all but the most highly trained men-at-arms.

They had already been to Seamus's house and found it deserted. Eva had wondered if they would set fire to it, but they hadn't bothered. They were gradually approaching her house.

She had taken good care. If the raiding party thought the house was defended, they might spread out so they could take cover. But even from a distance, it was evident that the house had been hastily abandoned. The door was wide open; one of the window shutters was flapping in the wind, creaking and banging. Still packed close together, they advanced.

The open ground below the house was flanked on one side by a stand of trees; on the other was a low wall. The ground sloped very gently. The riders were still about a hundred yards from the house when Father Donal, who was standing concealed by the trees, gave the signal.

The thunder of hoofs began quite suddenly. It seemed to be coming from two places at the same time, so that the raiding party paused for a moment in confusion, looking from one side to the other. Then, gazing in horror, they saw what it was.

The two herds of cattle came round the tower house from both sides. They were already running hard, and as the two bodies came round the tower and converged, they became a single mass of horned heads, the riders behind them whooping, shouting, and cracking whips so that they broke into a stampede. One, two, three hundred cattle were pounding and thundering down the shallow slope, a great wall of horns, a huge weight, ten, a dozen beasts deep, bearing down upon the raiders unstoppably. The men looked for an escape. There was nowhere to go. The great herd filled the whole space between the trees and the wall, and in any case, there was no time to reach either of these. They turned to flee, but the cattle were already upon them. There was a crack, a crash, a terrible roar.

From where she was riding, by the line of trees, Eva saw the moving wall of cattle smash into the men. She saw a sword fly up into the air, heard a shout and a horse scream; and then, only the flowing banks of the cattle, like a river in spate. Behind her, also mounted, she could hear the old bard, whooping and laughing, as excited as a boy; across on the other side near the wall, his face tensely concentrated, his cheeks lightly flushed, she could see Maurice riding in amongst the herd. How handsome he looked, how fearless. Just for an instant she realised that she was half in love with him. Perhaps in all the heat and excitement she had become a young woman again herself, but in the magnificent illusion of the moment, it seemed to her that the young aristocrat was what her own husband might have been, in the years of their youth, if he'd been finer.

The cattle had passed over the attackers now, and were spilling down the slope below. Maurice was working his way round, skilfully turning them. Behind, where the raiding party had been, was a scene of carnage.

If the horsemen had been quicker, if they had not hesitated, they might have survived by wheeling round and running with the herd.

Several had tried, but too late, and had collided either with each other or the foot soldiers. Three had started to run, but not fast enough. The great engine of the herd had either smashed into the horses or overtaken them from behind, borne them down and then trampled them into the earth. The destruction of the men on foot had been even more complete. It made no difference whether they were horsemen, kerne, or the mighty gallowglasses: the herd had passed over them all. Arms, legs, skulls, and breastbones had been cracked and crushed; their bodies mangled or pulped. The great axes of the gallowglasses lay with cracked shafts, their heads useless.

For this was the ancient stampeding of the cattle, an Irish battle tactic as old as the hills. Though Eva had only seen it done once, when she was a child, it was not something you could ever forget; and as every person at Rathconan, from herself down to Seamus's youngest child, was adept at driving cattle, it had not been too difficult for them, few though they were, to stampede and drive a herd of three hundred.

Seamus's wife was coming across now. She'd been driving them from behind. The women from the house arrived, too. They surveyed the wreckage. A number of the men were already dead. Others lay groaning. One of the big mercenaries was even trying to get up. The women knew what to do. At a nod from Eva they took out their knives and went from one man to another, slitting their throats. Eva dismounted and did the same for the unfortunate horses. It was a bloody business, but she felt triumphant; she had saved them all. And as Maurice came back, just as she was finishing, he too gave her a look of triumph, love, and joy.

‹‡›

Sean O'Byrne took his time. They had rested for some hours once they had got back into the safety of the hills. They had not been followed. There was no reason to hurry. It was a little before dawn when they set out to cross the mountains with their burden.

The ambush had been well prepared. Before dusk he had found

the place he was looking for. The men had been carefully placed. He and Fintan were to go in and make straight for the Doyle woman while the rest of the party, led by Seamus, drove off her escorts. Though all his men were armed, he had told them to use the flats of their swords unless they encountered serious opposition. With luck they could accomplish the business without having to kill anybody. In particular he was concerned about MacGowan. Walsh's wife had been certain that the grey merchant would be escorting Dame Doyle to Dalkey, and O'Byrne couldn't imagine him giving her up without a fight. He liked MacGowan and would be sorry to harm him, but there wasn't much he could do about it. The game had to be played; the rest was up to fate.

The only other problem might be in seeing her. There was a half-moon, however. That should give enough light. He had waited, therefore, in reasonable confidence with Fintan close beside him.

Darkness had fallen. The moon gave a soft light on the road as it wound between the trees. If she had left the castle at nightfall, assuming the party rode at a reasonable speed, he had estimated when they should get there; but the time passed and there was still no sign of them. He waited patiently all the same. The Walsh woman had seemed clear enough. They might have been delayed. An hour passed, and he was beginning to have doubts, when he heard something. Footfalls. Quite a number of them. That was strange. He'd assumed the party would be on horseback. He hissed to his men to be ready. He could hear them mounting. He felt his own body tense in expectancy. Then in the moonlight he saw the party coming round the bend.

There were only two riders: MacGowan and the woman rode in front. Behind them, however, marched twenty men on foot. They were a mixed collection: armed townsmen, regular soldiers; even Brennan, armed with a long pike, had been brought in from Doyle's new estate. But it was the eight men marching at the front who caught O'Byrne's attention. He stared in disbelief. Gallowglasses. Their huge axes and swords were carried sloped over their shoulders.

MacGowan must have hired them. He cursed under his breath and hesitated.

Should they still attack? Their numbers might be roughly even, but the gallowglasses were each worth two or three of his own untrained men. He didn't like the risk.

He felt a nudge at his side. Fintan.

"Aren't we going?" the boy whispered.

"Gallowglasses," he hissed back.

"But they're on foot. We can ride in and out and they'll never catch us." It sounded so reasonable. He saw exactly what his son was thinking. But Fintan didn't understand. He shook his head.

"No."

"But, Father . . ." There was a hint not just of disappointment but even of reproach. How could his father be such a coward? "Watch."

Sean couldn't believe it. Fintan was kicking his horse forward, breaking out of their cover, racing towards the soldiers in the moonlight. Thinking the signal had been given, Seamus and the rest of his men were racing out, too. MacGowan and the woman had stopped. The gallowglasses were moving swiftly round them in a protective ring. It was too late now. There was nothing he could do but go forward himself. He dashed towards the gallowglasses to help his son. Perhaps, after all, the boy was right.

⁜

It had only been hours ago, yet already, such is the strangeness of battle, their fight with the gallowglasses seemed an age away, as if it had taken place in another world. It was not even the fight that he remembered but, just after he had knocked MacGowan off his horse, the sight of Fintan reaching out his arms to try and grasp the Doyle woman, and then the feel of the boy brushing close beside him as they all raced away. They'd left four men on the road with the gallowglasses, but that couldn't be helped. Even in the moonlight he could see from their wounds that they were dead or dying already. He remembered the dash up the slope with the voices of the gallowglasses hurling curses from far behind, and then Seamus coming beside him and laughing in a friendly way at Fintan for the boy's wild bravery. Then Fintan fainting.

The stars were beginning to fade as they left the dark outlines of the mountaintops behind them and began the slow descent towards Rathconan.

And the sun was already rising over the eastern sea, its fierce light flashing up the slopes and into the crevices of the Wicklow Mountains, when Sean O'Byrne and his party came in sight of the house. Long before they reached it, Eva and Maurice and old Father Donal were coming out to meet them, their faces smiling broadly until they saw that they brought with them no trophy, no captive, but only their burden, wrapped tightly in a blanket and tied to his horse: Fintan, who had bled to death on the mountainside from the huge wound, which Sean had failed to see, made as it happened, not by the great two-handed sword of a gallowglass, but by Brennan's long spear which, like a dark spike, had pierced Fintan's ribs as he reached for Joan Doyle.

Late that morning, Margaret rode out to the meeting place up in the hills, where Sean O'Byrne had told her he would come to give her news of the previous night's expedition. She waited there half the afternoon, but he never came. She was almost tempted to ride down to Rathconan, but decided it would be too great a risk. By evening she was glad that she had not.

Richard Walsh had gone into Dublin alone that morning. He returned in the evening with a report that Dame Doyle had been attacked near Dalkey. "But luckily," he added, "she escaped." Four of the assailants had been killed. "It seems they came from up near Rathconan. They say Sean O'Byrne was involved." MacGowan had been knocked off his horse, but was not much hurt.

"You say Dame Doyle is safe in Dalkey now?" asked Margaret.

"She is, thank God."

"What will they do about O'Byrne?" she enquired.

"Nothing, I should say. Doyle's shut up in the castle. Lord Thomas doesn't care. And O'Byrne's boys had the worst of it anyway."

There hadn't seemed much point in going to see O'Byrne after that.

It was a few days later that MacGowan arrived at the house. As always, the lawyer was glad to see him, remarking cheerfully that the grey merchant looked none the worse for his recent encounter. And MacGowan seemed grateful to rest inside and take a little wine. He appeared tired as they sat down in the hall.

"It's on account of the other night that I've just come from Sean O'Byrne's," he said wearily. "For I was at the wake for his son."

"His son?" Margaret looked up in surprise. "He lost a son?"

"He did. Fintan. The other night. A sad wake it was. A terrible thing."

"But . . ." she gazed at him in astonishment as she considered the implications of this news. "It must have been the men you hired that killed him."

"There is not a doubt of it."

"I'm surprised you went to the wake," she said.

"I went to his wake out of my respect for his father," MacGowan quietly replied. "His death was no fault of mine, and the O'Byrnes know that. What's done is done."

She was silent. MacGowan closed his eyes.

"Did he tell you how it was he came to know of Dame Doyle's going to Dalkey?" asked Walsh. "That is the thing that puzzles me."

"He did not." MacGowan's eyes were still closed.

"Nothing's a secret in Dublin, I know," the lawyer remarked. "I had to conclude that when I asked for the safe-conduct, one of the men around Lord Thomas must have set up the ambush."

"They would know Sean O'Byrne," agreed MacGowan, apparently still seeking sleep; and neither man spoke for a moment of two. "Whoever carried the information," he continued quietly, "has the death of young Fintan O'Byrne on their conscience." And now he opened one eye. And with it he stared straight at Margaret.

Margaret gazed back. His eye remained fixed upon her. It seemed so large, so accusing, so all-knowing.

What did he know? How much had the clever merchant guessed? Had O'Byrne said something? If he did know, did he mean to tell her husband, or the Doyles? She tried to keep calm, to give nothing away. But she felt only a cold, awful dread. Her gaze fell. She could not, any longer, look at that terrible eye.

Slowly MacGowan rose.

"I must be on my way," he announced. "I thank you," he said to Walsh, "for your hospitality." To Margaret he said not another word. She wasn't sorry to see him go.

But if she thought that her tribulation was at an end with his departure, she was wrong.

It was about an hour later, after attending to some business, that her husband came into the hall to find her sitting alone. As she had been brooding about the uncomfortable interview with MacGowan, she was grateful to have someone to distract her thoughts and turned to him with a hopeful smile as he sat down in the heavy oak chair by the table. He seemed to have something on his mind also, since he paused thoughtfully before he began.

"It's as well, you know, that no harm came to Joan Doyle the other night. For us as a family, I mean."

"Oh?" She felt a little catch in her breath, to hear him bring the subject of Joan Doyle up like that. "Why?"

"Because . . ." he hesitated a moment, "there is something I never told you."

So, it was coming at last. She felt a coldness, a sinking sensation. Did she want to hear it? Half of her wanted to stop him. Her throat was dry.

"What?"

"On Corpus Christi day, last year, I borrowed a large sum of money from her."

"On Corpus Christi?" She stared at him.

"Yes. You may recall," he went on quickly, "that Richard had caused us great expense in London. I was embarrassed for money, worried. More worried than I wanted you to know. It was our friend MacGowan, seeing me looking rather glum in Dublin one day, who suggested she might be able to help me. So I went to see her for a loan."

"She makes loans herself? Without her husband?"

"She does. You know our Dublin women have more freedom than even the London women do. I discovered she makes quite a few. She usually consults the alderman but not always. In my case, because I felt embarrassed, she lent me the money privately. There's a written agreement, of course, properly drawn up, but so far as I know it's private between myself and Dame Doyle." He paused. Then he gave a small laugh. "Do you know why she made the loan? She remembered Richard. That time she took shelter at this house. 'He's a sweet boy,' she said. 'He must be helped.' And she gave me the money. On very easy terms as well."

"On Corpus Christi day?"

"I went to see her. She was quite alone, apart from an old servant. The rest of the house had gone to see the plays. And she gave me the money there and then."

"When will it have to be repaid?"

"It was due after a year. I thought I could manage it. But after we lost the Church estate . . . She's given me another three years. Generous terms."

"But it's her husband who got our land."

"I know. 'Your loss has been our gain,' she said to me. 'I can hardly refuse to extend your loan after that, can I?' " He shook his head. "She has treated us—me, if you like—uncommonly well. My crime, Margaret, is that because I was ashamed, I concealed it from you. If she had been killed the other night, the loan document would have been found in her papers, and Doyle might have come after the money. I don't know." He sighed. "Anyway, it was time I told you. Can you forgive me?"

Margaret gazed at him. Was this the whole truth? She had no doubt about the loan. If her husband said there was a loan, then there was one. The story about Corpus Christi was probably true, also. But was there more to it than her kindness and her liking for Richard? Wasn't there still something between this woman, who had always despised her, and her husband?

For if there was not, then she had sent Sean O'Byrne to attack her, and caused the death of his boy for nothing. Nothing at all.

"Dear God," she said, in sudden doubt. "Oh dear God."

For Cecily, the month of September brought a new and awkward decision. Two days after MacGowan's return from Fintan O'Byrne's wake, the city changed its mind. Perhaps it was the increasingly urgent news that an English army was about to arrive, or that the citizens were tired of billeting Fitzgerald's troops, or a perception amongst the council members that Silken Thomas's rule lacked conviction; but whatever the reasons, the city turned.

The first Cecily knew was when one of the children ran up the tower stairs looking frightened. Then she heard bangs and shouts in the street. Looking out, she saw a party of Fitzgerald's gallowglasses beating a hasty retreat through the western gateway. And close behind them followed a huge angry tide of people armed with spears, swords, axes, staves—whatever they could get their hands on— flooding out through the gate. They caught and killed dozens of Fitzgerald's men. If Silken Thomas was offering to save Ireland for the one true Church, they didn't seem to care. "Heretics," she called them furiously. But Silken Thomas was back outside Dublin now, and though he put the city under siege again, he couldn't get back in. Within days, Silken Thomas and the aldermen agreed to a six-week truce. "He won't fight us," the Dubliners said, "he'll wait and fight the English."

This return to stalemate had one other result. Dublin Castle opened its gate, and Henry Tidy came home.

It was a pity that one of the children had upset a pitcher of milk just before he came, and Cecily was not in a good temper. She had been waiting for this day for so long. Time and again, while her husband was in the castle, she had thought about the moment of his return. What was it she wanted? As she looked at her children and remembered the early days of their marriage, she knew very well. She longed to return to the warmth of their married life. She couldn't change her religious views. That was impossible. And she didn't suppose that her husband could change his attitude, either. But surely they could manage to live in peace.

If only he would be kind. When he had struck her that awful day, it had not been the blow itself that hurt—although she had been shocked—but the coldness she had sensed behind it. And something within her had died. Could it be revived?

She needed to know that he loved her. Whatever her views about King Henry, however much she embarrassed him in front of Doyle and the city authorities, she needed to know that he truly loved her. That was what she would be watching for, upon his return. How would he act? What would it mean? Could she trust him?

It was a pity therefore that, in a moment of irritation, she should have turned when he appeared at the door and greeted him coldly.

"You don't seem very pleased to see me."

She stared at him. She wanted to smile. She had meant to. But now that the moment she had waited for had come, and had started all wrong, she felt strangely paralyzed. She felt something inside her shrink back.

"You left your family," she answered bleakly.

Would he apologise? Would he make the first move? Would he give her some reassurance?

"You refused to come with me, Cecily."

No. Not a word. Nothing had changed.

"It is not my fault that King Henry is excommunicated."

"I am still your husband."

She gave a tiny shrug. "And the Holy Father is still the Holy Father."

"I have returned, anyway." He tried a smile. "You could make me welcome."

"Why?" She could not help the bitterness in her voice. "Do you wish to be here?"

He stared at her. What was he thinking? He's thinking what a cold and cruel woman I am, she thought. This is partly my fault.

"No."

So that was it. He'd spoken the truth. Was it the truth, though, or was he just hitting back? She waited for him to add something else. He didn't.

"We've nothing to say to each other," she said, feeling strangely helpless, and stood there waiting as the coldness descended, falling quietly between them.

By the next day, the Tidy household had evolved a new way of life. The workshop was at the street level. There Tidy and the apprentice worked and slept. On the floor above was the main room, where the family ate together. Above that, in the tower, Cecily and the children slept. From her window up there, Cecily overlooked some potteries where they made crockery.

It became a refuge for her, that window in the tower. Sometimes during the day she would go up there to be alone and watch the crockers, or even catch sight of Fitzgerald's men in the distance. In the evenings, cut off from her husband, after the children had gone to sleep, she would sit there for hours watching the sunset or the stars, and thinking of what was passing in the world.

Soon after she began her vigils came the news that the Earl of Kildare had died of his sickness in England. Sad though this was, it also meant that Silken Thomas was now the new earl, with all the authority and prestige that name evoked. It could not be long now, she hoped, before the cause was won. In mid-October, the English ships at last arrived. Doyle and the other aldermen welcomed the Gunner and his men into Dublin. The English troops were numerous and seemed to be trained; they also brought artillery. She had hoped to see them destroyed in an open battle with Silken Thomas, and felt some disgust when, from her window, she saw parties of Thomas's troops quietly withdrawing. But she took comfort from the prevailing view amongst Kildare's supporters.

"He'll wait at Maynooth. The Fitzgeralds still have all their strongholds. He'll wear the Gunner down, and when the Spanish troops arrive, they'll kick the English out of Ireland forever."

Within a month, the Gunner set out. Word came that he had taken back one of the castles Fitzgerald had seized, at Trim. Still more ominous came the news that two of Thomas's five Fitzgerald uncles were cooperating with the Gunner. As she looked out of her window after hearing that, it was hard not to feel a sense of dismay. How was it possible, she wondered, that there could be such treachery? But when she prayed, she knew she must keep faith, and so she told herself to have patience.

And indeed, in the winter months, there was reason to hope. The winter was cold and wet. The Gunner retired to Dublin and stayed there, and soon complained that he was unwell. Cecily would see him occasionally, riding through the streets with his escort. Instead of the brisk military man he had been, he now looked pale and haggard. His troops were suffering, too. There were desertions. Better yet, Silken Thomas was back in the strongholds the Gunner had taken earlier. Most important of all, around Christmas Cecily heard that the Spanish were sending ten thousand armed men. Once they arrived, the Gunner would be gone.

January came, cold and dreary. The English troops were being sent out now to key garrisons around the Pale; but there was no action. Still Silken Thomas waited for the Spanish soldiers, but no word of them came. One day, in February, at their meal in the main room, Tidy quietly remarked, "You know what people are saying now. The King of Spain has other things to think about. He's going to leave Silken Thomas twisting in the breeze."

"So you say," she answered dully. It wasn't often they even spoke, nowadays.

"A ship came into port yesterday," he continued calmly. "From Spain. There's no sign and no word of any soldiers to be sent over here."

"The enemies of the Fitzgeralds will say what they will say," she countered.

"You don't understand." He gazed at her evenly. "It's not their enemies saying so. It's their friends."

That night there was a fall of snow. When she looked out of her window in the morning, gazing towards the interior of Ireland, she saw only a dismal, white silence.

But the real blow came in March. The Gunner had finally bestirred himself to launch a proper campaign. Boldly, he had gone to Maynooth, the mighty Fitzgerald stronghold. Even with his artillery, Cecily imagined, he'd be held up by that huge fortress for weeks. Then, after no time at all, the news came.

"Maynooth has fallen." It was her husband who came all the way up to her tower refuge to tell her.

"The Gunner took it?"

He shook his head.

"He'll claim he took it, of course," he said. "But it was some of Fitzgerald's own men who betrayed him and let the English in." Then he went back down the stairs again.

That night, after watching the sunset, she could not sleep, and sat staring out at the gleaming stars until, at last, they faded before the cold, harsh dawn from the east.

It was in April, when Silken Thomas was already a fugitive, moving down into the marshes, that Cecily went to see Dame Doyle. It had not been easy to approach the house of the alderman who had sided so gladly with the heretic King Henry; but his wife was different, and she trusted her.

"I can't go on like this," she told the older woman. "I don't know what to do." And she explained all that had passed between her and Henry Tidy. But if she expected sympathy, or that Dame Doyle would offer to mediate, she was disappointed.

"You must go back to living with your husband," Dame Doyle told her bluntly. "It's as simple as that. Even," she added quite severely, "if you don't love him." She gazed at Cecily thoughtfully. "Could you bring yourself to love him," she asked her frankly, "enough?"

It was what Cecily had been wondering herself.

"The trouble is," she confessed, "I think he doesn't love me."

"Are you sure of that?"

"It's what I believe."

"Perhaps," Dame Doyle said more kindly, "you should give your husband the benefit of the doubt. Marriage is like religion, in a way," she gently suggested. "It requires an act of faith."

"But that's not the same at all," Cecily protested. "For about the true faith I haven't any doubt."

"Well at least you could hope," Dame Doyle remarked with a smile. And seeing Cecily still looking uncertain, "My child, you'll have to rely upon charity then. Be kind to him. Things may get better. Besides," she added shrewdly, "you've said yourself things can't continue as they are. The plain fact is, you've nothing to lose."

So that night, after putting the children to sleep in the main room, Cecily went down to the workshop and suggested that Tidy should join her in her refuge above.

⁘

The old man arrived at Rathconan on a fine day at the end of August. He was a brehon, he informed Eva, a man skilled in the old Irish laws and an adviser to the Fitzgeralds down in Munster. He had come from Maurice's parents with a message that must be delivered only to the boy himself and to Sean. As they were away with the cattle up on the mountain pastures, she sent one of the men to fetch them while, with the proper show of respect to the old man, she set out a flagon of ale and some refreshments for him in the hall where he said he would like to rest. Until Sean and Maurice arrived, she could only guess as to what the nature of the brehon's business might be.

One possibility, clearly, concerned the Fitzgerald family. When his garrison had betrayed him at Maynooth, Silken Thomas had escaped and gone to rally the Irish chiefs who were loyal to his family. The Gunner might hold some strongholds and possess most of the artillery, but he only had a few hundred troops and he wasn't well himself. The English force could be worn down and destroyed.

But the Gunner had the power of England behind him. The Irish chiefs were cautious. Silken Thomas was still saying that the Spanish would come; but weeks passed and there was no sign of them. Silken Thomas was learning the bitter lesson of power: friends are the people who think you will win. "At least people up here are loyal to the Fitzgeralds," Eva had remarked to Sean one day; but he had only given her a wry look. "Some of the O'Tooles and our own O'Byrne kinsmen are talking to the Gunner now," he told her. "He's offering good money." By midsummer, Silken Thomas was hiding out in the forests and bogs like a warrior chief from times gone by.

But he wasn't an ancient Irish chief; he was rich young Silken Thomas. If the Gunner was sluggish, the Fitzgerald heir was starting to lose heart. And a week ago, when one of his aristocratic English kinsmen, a royal commander, had found him miserably encamped down in the Bog of Allen and promised him his life and a pardon if he gave himself up, he had agreed to do so. The news had reached Rathconan three days ago.

So now, though it was hard for Eva to believe, it seemed that the power of the mighty house of Kildare was fading away like the sound of pipers disappearing over the hill. And if Kildare's power had collapsed, what would that mean for the Desmond Fitzgeralds in the south? Uncertainty at best. Perhaps the southern Fitzgeralds would want their son Maurice safely back with them?

She hoped not. Since the death of Fintan, young Maurice had been such a tower of strength, helping Sean and giving her his quiet affection. You couldn't keep a foster son forever, of course, but she couldn't bear to part with him just now. Not yet.

Sean and Maurice arrived at the house early in the evening. Sean greeted the brehon respectfully and having sipped a little ale, sat in the big oak chair in the hall, looking rather impressive. Maurice sat quietly on a stool, gazing at the old man curiously. Eva sat on a bench. Then Sean politely requested the brehon to state his business.

"I am Kieran, son of Art, hereditary brehon, and I come on behalf of the lady Fitzgerald, mother of Maurice Fitzgerald, foster son of Sean O'Byrne," he began in a formal manner that signalled the seriousness of his business. "Would you confirm to me," he turned to Maurice, "that you are that Maurice Fitzgerald?" Maurice nodded. "And that you are that same Sean O'Byrne?"

"I am," said Sean. "And what is your message?"

"For some years, Sean O'Byrne, this Maurice has lived in your house as your foster son." He paused, eyeing Sean, it seemed to Eva, a little severely. "But as you also know, this young man has a greater claim upon you."

Sean acknowledged this odd statement with a gracious inclination of his handsome head.

"And under the ancient usages of Ireland," the brehon continued, "I'm to tell you, Sean O'Byrne, that his mother the lady Fitzgerald is now calling upon you to admit your responsibility in this matter and to make the proper provisions."

"She names me?"

"She does."

Maurice was listening to this dialogue with utter astonishment. Eva was staring at the old man with a look of horror on her pale face. Only Sean seemed quite at ease, sitting in his big chair and nodding quietly in recognition of what the brehon was saying.

"What responsibility?" Eva broke in. "What provision?" A sudden panic added a sharpness to her voice. "What is it you're saying?"

The brehon turned towards her. It was hard to tell what expression was in his face, which seemed as old as the hills.

"That your husband, Sean O'Byrne, is the father of this boy." He indicated Maurice. "The lady Fitzgerald has named him. You did not know?"

She did not reply. Her face was entirely white; her mouth formed into a small O, from which no sound emerged. The old man turned to Sean.

"You do not deny it?"

And now Sean was smiling. "I do not. She has the right."

It was the law and custom in Ireland that if a woman named a man as the father of her child and it was acknowledged, then the child was entitled to make claims upon the father, including a share of the father's estate when he died.

"When?" Eva found her voice at last. "When was this known?"

Sean did not seem in any hurry to reply, so the old man answered. "It was admitted privately between the parties when Sean O'Byrne came down to ask for Maurice as a foster son."

"When Maurice first came here. He brought Maurice here because he was his son?"

"That would be it," said the brehon. "The lady Fitzgerald's husband did not wish to embarrass himself or his wife at that time, so once he had been informed of the matter, he agreed that Maurice should go with his father as a foster son. But as he's not wanting to provide for him now, Sean O'Byrne is named."

"You are my father?" It was Maurice who spoke now. He was very pale. He had been watching Eva; now he turned to Sean.

"I am." Sean smiled. He seemed delighted.

"But why?" Eva's voice was a cry of pain. She couldn't help it. "Why in God's name would you have your own son by another woman to live in my house all these years, under my very nose, and never a word to me about who he was? You watched me look after him and love him like my own. And it was all a lie! A lie to make a fool of me. Was it for that you did it, Sean? For my humiliation? In the name of God, when I think of the good wife I've been to you, why would you do such a thing?" She paused, staring at him. "You were planning this for years."

And now, as he looked at her with the blandest of smiles on his handsome face, she saw, also, a little gleam of angry triumph in his eye.

"It was you who brought the friar here and made me swear upon the Saint Kevin." He paused and she saw his fingers close upon the arms of the oak chair as his body leaned forward in the seat. "It was you that humiliated me, Eva, in front of the friar and the priest," his voice was rising in suppressed fury, "in my own house." He threw himself back in his seat. Then he smiled. "You've done a good job looking after my son. I'll say that."

And in a terrible, searing flash, Eva understood as she had never understood before the vanity of a man, and the long, cold reach of his vengeance.

Just then, Maurice ran out of the hall.

⁂

Sean and Eva ate in silence that night. The brehon, having gone to visit Father Donal, had sent word that he would remain with the priest and his family until his departure early in the morning. Maurice had gone to the barn to be alone. Though Eva had asked him to come back in, he had requested, politely as always, that he might be allowed to remain alone with his thoughts; and so, after giving his arm an awkward but affectionate squeeze, Eva had left him there.

Sean had already announced that he would be going up to the high pasture again in the morning. The two of them sat—he apparently satisfied, she in stony silence—until at last, when the meal was done, she remarked to him: "I shall never get over this, you know."

"You will in time." He had an apple in his hand. He cut it into four pieces with his knife, leaving the seeds in, and ate one of the quarters, swallowing the seeds. "What's done is done," he observed. "You love him anyway. He's a fine boy."

"Oh, he is fine," she acknowledged. "It is amazing to me only," she added bitterly, "that someone so fine could be your son."

"Do you think so?" He nodded thoughtfully. "Well, it would seem that with his mother I could make a finer son than I could with you." And he picked up another piece of the quartered apple.

Her head went forward. The pain of the cruel words was so great, it was like a dagger stabbed into her stomach. She thought of Fintan.

"Do you love anybody?" she asked at last. "Other than yourself?"

"I do." He let the words dangle like a bait before a fish in the stream, but she had wisdom enough to turn away.

They remained in silence for as long as it took him, at his calculated leisure, to eat the other two quarters of the apple.

"He must go," she said.

"You're a great one for throwing people out of my house," he remarked. "Is it my own son you're wanting to be rid of now?"

"He must go, Sean. You say that I love him, and it's true. But I can't stand it. He must go."

"My son will stay in his father's house," he replied with finality; and with that he got up and went to bed, leaving her sitting in the hall, wondering what she should do. She sat there all night.

Did she really want him gone? She thought of all that Maurice had meant to her. Certainly none of this was the boy's fault. How must he be feeling now, out there in the barn, thinking about the deception that everyone had practised upon himself all these years. Was she re-enacting the business with the Brennan girl, insisting that he go? Wasn't it just the same battle with her husband's will? Wasn't it the same, all over again, except that now he had increased the pain and the humiliation? Now he had even made her love the boy, the cause of her pain, and then poisoned that love. Oh, he had been clever. You had to give him that. He'd made her drain a bitter cup.

And that was why she couldn't bear to have Maurice there anymore. It seemed to her, as the dawn broke, that she had no way out.

But a few hours later the decision was taken out of their hands by Maurice himself who, for the first time in the years he had been with them, quietly but firmly refused to obey the man that he now knew was his father. He told them he wanted to leave.

"I will visit you often, Father," he said, "and you, too, if I may," he added to Eva, with a gentle look of sadness in those wonderful eyes of his, so strange and emerald green.

"You needn't go, Maurice," she cried. "You don't have to go."

But his determination was absolute. "It's for the best," he said.

"Where will you go?" Sean asked him, a little heavily. "To Munster?"

"To see the mother who betrayed me and her husband who doesn't want me?" He shook his head sadly. "If I see my mother I might curse her."

"Where, then?"

"I have decided, Father," he said, "to go to Dublin."

MacGowan was most surprised when Maurice arrived at his house. And he was even more astonished when Maurice told him his story. It wasn't often that the grey merchant discovered a long-standing secret, however intimate, that he didn't already know.

"And you're asking me to take you on as an apprentice?" he confirmed.

"I am. I'm sure that my father—Sean O'Byrne, that is—will pay the apprenticeship fee."

"No doubt."

"If you would consider me."

MacGowan did consider, but he had no need to do so for long. It was clear to him that with his knowledge of life with the O'Byrnes and his courtly education and manners, the young man would be the ideal grey merchant, welcomed beyond the Pale and in the best Dublin circles, too. He could go far, MacGowan thought, farther even than I.

"There is a problem," he said.

"What is that?"

"Your name."

Maurice Fitzgerald. What a name to possess. There would be a splendid dash, even effrontery in a young grey merchant owning such an aristocratic name; but given the present political climate in Dublin, it might be unwise.

"The name of Fitzgerald might put you in some danger now," he said.

"It's not my name anymore," Maurice answered with a wry smile. "You forget that I'm an O'Byrne."

"So you are." MacGowan nodded thoughtfully. "So you are." He paused. "That also, in Dublin, could be a problem." He smiled sadly. "It's too Irish."

Given the young man's character and manners, he would probably overcome any prejudice in time. But nonetheless, to advertise oneself as the son of Sean O'Byrne—the Irish friend of Fitzgerald, who had tried to kidnap the wife of Alderman Doyle—was not, he gently pointed out to Maurice, the best way to begin. "And you'll want the freedom one day," he predicted. "Be sure of that."

"In that case, since to be truthful with you, I feel more like an orphan than any man's son, and I mean to make a life of my own, I'd be glad enough to take another name. I really don't care." The young man stared at MacGowan for a few moments and then smiled. "Your own name, for instance. MacGowan in English would be Smith."

"It would. Near enough."

"Well then, if you'll have me as an apprentice, let me be Maurice Smith. Would that do?"

"It would do very well," said MacGowan with a laugh. "You shall be Maurice Smith."

And so it was, early in the autumn of 1535, while Silken Thomas was on the perilous sea to London, that a descendant of the princely O'Byrnes and the noble Walshes, and, though he did not know it, of Deirdre and of Conall and of old Fergus himself, came down to live in Dublin under the English name of Maurice Smith.

One week later, to his great surprise, Maurice received a visitor. It was his father.

It had taken Sean a little while to find his son. He had supposed that Maurice might have gone to MacGowan, but when he first approached the merchant's house and asked if there was a young man named O'Byrne living there, he had been told by the neighbours that there was not. He did not seem particularly put out by Maurice's decision not to use his proper name.

"You've been living under another name for so many years, that I expect it has become a habit," Sean told him with a smile.

He did not stay long, but with him he had brought a square box.

"You may not choose to live at Rathconan," he said, "but you may as well have something to remember your family by."

Then he left.

After his father had gone, Maurice opened the box. To his surprise and delight, he found that it contained the drinking skull of old Fergus.

᛭

In the Irish Parliament that met from May of 1536 until December of the following year, no member was more assiduous in his efforts to please the king than William Walsh the lawyer.

Acting under the direction of the king's council in London, the Irish Parliament passed measures to centralise the rule of Ireland in

England, to raise taxes, and, of course, to recognise King Henry, and not the Pope, as Supreme Head of the Irish Church, while allowing his divorce and remarriage to be valid. And whether William Walsh and his fellow Members of Parliament liked all these measures or not, they passed them because they had to.

The fall of the Fitzgeralds was terrifying. Silken Thomas, having first been politely received at the English court as promised, had been suddenly transferred to the Tower. Then his five uncles, including the two who had actually been on the English side, were taken to London and sent to the Tower, too. "We are to accuse them all of treason," Walsh told his wife grimly when he returned from the Parliament one day. In the depths of that winter, the six Fitzgeralds were taken to London's public gallows at Tyburn and brutally executed. It was vicious, it broke assurances given, it had been legalised by Parliament: it was pure Henry.

Meanwhile, seventy-five of the principal men in Ireland who had acted with Silken Thomas were sentenced to execution. It sent a shudder through the community. And the lesser gentry, like William Walsh, who had gone along with the Fitzgeralds, were told that, depending upon the royal will, they might be able to get a pardon in return for a fine. "Thank God," Walsh remarked, "that I had witnesses to prove that I took that damned oath under duress. But what the fine will be I don't yet know, and half the men in Parliament are in a similar position." Henry was keeping them waiting until they had passed all his legislation. "He has us," Walsh confessed, "exactly where he wants us."

Some opposition there was, from gentlemen not under threat. When Henry demanded a harsh new tax on income, these loyal men were able to persuade him to be more lenient. "By the grace of God," Walsh reported back to his family, "the tax will only be paid by the clergy." But this was one of the few concessions that Henry made; and so that no one should doubt his determination to be Ireland's lord and master, his lieutenants continued the forays around the edge of the Pale to subdue the territories and implacably hunted down any remaining members of the Kildare family who could give any trouble.

Even so, it rather surprised Margaret that there was not more protest about Henry's taking over the Church and his attack on the Pope. "Some of the clerical members have protested," William told her. "But some of the strongest voices were so involved with Silken Thomas that they've either been deprived of their benefices or fled abroad. The fact is," he added, "that although Henry has put himself in place of the Pope—which is an outrage, of course—there's little sign that he means to make any changes to the forms and doctrines of the faith." A new archbishop named Browne appeared in Dublin, who was said to have Protestant leanings, but so far he hadn't said or done anything offensive. "The real question is what Henry means to do about the monasteries."

In England, the great process had already begun. Under the guise of a religious reform, the Tudor king, who always spent money faster than he got it, was planning to take all the rich lands and possessions of England's medieval monasteries into his own hands and to sell them. Would he do the same in Ireland?

"One effect of the business in England," Walsh told his son Richard at the family meal one day, "is that it's creating a huge amount of work for lawyers. Every monastery wants to be legally represented and to argue its case." Working closely with his father, Richard had already made himself well liked by a number of the monastic houses. "For lawyers like ourselves, Richard," his father continued, "the fees could be lucrative."

Though she said nothing, Margaret was secretly a little shocked by this attitude. Whatever their faults, surely the ancient monasteries of Ireland merited better treatment than this? When a measure to close just thirteen of the Irish monasteries was set before the Parliament, she was glad to hear that there had finally been some opposition. And when William, who had been away at the debates for several days, returned to the house one afternoon, she questioned him quite eagerly.

"I was sure, in the end, our people wouldn't stand for it," she said.

But William only chuckled.

"That isn't it at all," he let her know. "The problem is who gets the land. The fear is that it will go to the king's men and the Butlers. Some of your friends, the Fingal gentry, are going to Henry to demand their share. Doyle and his fellow aldermen have already been promised one of the monasteries to reward the city for opposing Silken Thomas."

"You make it sound as if it's all about money," she objected.

"I'm afraid," the lawyer sighed, "that it usually is."

The subject of money could never be far from Walsh's mind at this time. Not only was the question of his royal pardon and fine an unresolved issue for many months but there was also the debt to Joan Doyle which remained unpaid. "And yet," he remarked upon several occasions to Margaret, "these difficulties have also been a kind of blessing." This was because of the effect they had on young Richard.

For if Richard Walsh had cost his family more than they could afford while he lived as a young gentleman in London, he was only too painfully conscious of the fact now. If he had lost none of his boyhood charm, if with his mother's dark red hair he possessed the most striking good looks, he was also a tolerably good lawyer and as determined as any young man could be to repay to his family what he believed he owed them, and then to make for himself a fortune in the world. Side by side with his father, he worked assiduously. He himself made any journey that he thought might tire his father; if William at day's end needed to pore over ancient documents, he'd sit up all night with them so that his father would awake to find the job already done. He sought out new business, covered for William when he was busy in Parliament, learned everything he could about Ireland's law.

"I have to tell him, sometimes, to stop," his father said proudly. "But he's young and strong, these efforts will do him no harm."

Despite all these efforts, however, the Walshes were so far only able to pay the interest on Dame Doyle's loan and put a little aside towards the coming royal fine.

If he hadn't been aware of the transaction before, the alderman himself was clearly aware of his wife's loan now. Walsh knew this for a certainty one morning when he encountered Doyle on his way to a parliamentary session. He had heard the day before that the alderman's daughter Mary had just been granted the freedom of the city and so he politely congratulated him on this event, which Doyle received with affability. Then, falling in beside Walsh, the alderman genially murmured, "Here's the fellow that's borrowed a fortune from my wife." Seeing Walsh wince, he grinned. "She told me all about it. I haven't the least objection, you know."

It was easy enough for Doyle to be sanguine, Walsh thought a little enviously. As a loyal alderman who'd opposed Silken Thomas, with a wife connected to the Butlers and who'd even been attacked by O'Byrne, the rich merchant was high in royal favour and likely to profit from any monastic property or royal offices that might be going.

"I can pay the interest," William had answered, "but repaying the principal is going to take a time. I've the royal fine to consider, too."

"They say your son Richard is helping you."

"He is," Walsh added with a little flush of pride, and told him of the young man's efforts.

"As to your loan," Doyle said when Walsh had finished, "I'd just as soon she lent to you as any other borrower. You're sounder than most." He paused. "As to the fine, I'll be glad to speak to the royal officials on your behalf. I have some credit there at present." And a week later, encountering him again, Doyle had told him, "Your fine will be a token payment only. They know you're not to blame."

When William related these conversations back to Margaret, she greeted the good news with a smile. But she still trembled inwardly. No word of her involvement in the kidnap attempt had ever been heard, so that she supposed that O'Byrne had kept silent or that, if he had told MacGowan, the grey merchant had for his own reasons decided to say nothing. But he could change his mind, or O'Byrne could talk. And hardly a day went by when, in her imagination, she didn't find herself confronted by the memory of MacGowan's terrible, cold, accusing eye, or the echo of the last words she had spoken to O'Byrne when he asked her what to do with Joan Doyle if he couldn't complete the kidnap. "Kill her."

It was in the autumn of 1537, with the Parliament still in full deliberation, that Richard Walsh called at the house of Alderman Doyle to deliver a payment to his wife. He had only meant to remain there for as long as it took her to check the amount, and as he had been busy investigating some records in Christ Church that morning, he was in a rather dusty state. He was a little disconcerted, therefore, on being ushered into the parlour to find several of the Doyle family there. Besides Dame Doyle, there was the alderman, looking resplendent in a tunic of red and gold, one of his sons, his daughter Mary, and a younger sister. They might, he thought, have been taken for the family of a rich merchant or courtier in fashionable London whereas he, now, looked like a dusty clerk. It was a little humiliating, but it couldn't be helped. They eyed him curiously.

"I didn't mean to intrude upon your family," he said to Dame Doyle politely. "I only came to leave with you what was owed," and he passed to her a small bag of coins. "I can return another time."

"Not at all." Joan Doyle took it with a kindly smile. "I shan't need to check it," she remarked.

"I hear you're holding everything together while your father and I get through this session of Parliament," Doyle remarked with a friendly nod; and Richard was grateful for this implication that the rich alderman and his father were on collegial terms. "He speaks well of you," he added.

It seemed to Richard that the alderman's son, despite these encouraging words, was looking at him without much respect; the daughter Mary was watching him also, but he couldn't tell what she was thinking. It was the youngest girl—she might have been thirteen, he supposed—who giggled. He looked at her enquiringly.

"You're all dirty." And she pointed.

He hadn't seen the great dirt mark he had collected down one side of his sleeve. He also noticed that the cuff was frayed. He might have blushed. But fortunately the years in London as a fashionable fellow now came to his aid. He burst out laughing.

"So I am. I hadn't noticed." He glanced at Doyle. "This is what comes of working in the Christ Church records. I hope," he turned to Joan Doyle, "that I haven't been dropping dust all over your house."

"I don't expect you have."

"It has to be said, Richard," Doyle's tone might have been used to a member of his own family, "that you need some new clothes."

"I know," Richard answered him frankly. "It's true. I suppose that until our affairs are in a better state, I'm putting it off as long as I can." He turned to the girl who had giggled and gave her a charming smile. "And when I get a nice new tunic, you may be sure I'll come straight and show it to you."

Doyle nodded, but apparently bored by the subject of clothes, now cut in.

"You mean to make your fortune, Richard?"

"I do. If I can."

"A lawyer like yourself can do well enough in Dublin," Doyle remarked, "but there's more money in trade. A legal training can be useful in trade."

"I know, and I considered it; but I've no means of starting in that line. I must work with the assets I have."

Doyle nodded briefly, and the interview was over. Richard bowed politely to them all and turned to go. Just as he reached the door, he heard Joan Doyle.

"You've wonderful hair," she said.

He was already out in Skinners Row when Mary Doyle spoke.

She was quite a handsome girl, with her mother's Spanish looks and her father's hard, intelligent eyes.

"He was at the Inns of Court?" She addressed her father.

"He was."

"Is he a Walsh of Carrickmines?"

"A branch of them, yes." He gazed at her. "Why?"

She looked back at him, with the same eyes.

"Just wondering."

It was early in the year 1538 that MacGowan, chatting to Alderman Doyle one afternoon, was rather surprised when the rich merchant turned to him and asked him what he thought of young Richard Walsh.

"It seems," he confessed, "that my daughter Mary's interested in him."

MacGowan considered. He thought of all that he knew of the parties concerned. He thought of the O'Byrne business, and of the strange figure who had come to Rathconan. O'Byrne had refused to tell him who it was. If O'Byrne wouldn't tell him, MacGowan reckoned, he wouldn't be telling anybody. But then he already knew. The idea had occurred to him as soon as the attack had begun. Apart from a few people around Silken Thomas, no one else could have known of Joan Doyle's journey. And when, on the way back from poor Fintan's wake, he had learned that Margaret had ridden out early that fatal day, he had been certain. He wasn't sure why she'd done such a thing, but it had to be the Walsh woman. And hadn't he seen it all in her face when he had stared at her: fear, guilt, terror?

Could he prove it? Would any purpose be served if he could? Would it do his friend Doyle any good to know such a thing? No, he did not think it would. There were some secrets that were so dark they were better left at rest, under the hills. Let Margaret Walsh fear him and be grateful for his silence. That had always been his power: to know secrets.

"I've heard nothing against young Richard Walsh at all," he answered with perfect truth. "Everyone seems to like him." He looked at Doyle curiously. "I'd have thought that you might be looking for a rich young gentleman. A girl like Mary—why, she's even got the freedom of the city—would be a fine match for any family in Fingal."

Doyle grunted. "I thought of that, too. The trouble is," and here the merchant sighed with a lifetime of experience, "rich young gentlemen don't usually want to work."

"Ah," MacGowan acknowledged quietly, "this is true."

⁂

When, in the summer of 1538, her son Richard asked her to call upon Joan Doyle, Margaret experienced a moment of panic. To enter the big Dublin house, to find herself face-to-face with the woman whose daughter Richard was about to marry—and she still *has no idea*, she thought, *that I tried to kill her. How could she sit there and look the woman in the eye?*

"She keeps asking when you're coming to see her," Richard reported. "She'll think it very rude if you don't."

And so, inwardly quaking, on a warm summer day, Margaret Walsh found herself entering through the heavy street door whose lineaments she remembered so well, to find herself moments later sitting comfortably in the parlour, alone with the wealthy little woman who thought she was her friend—and who disconcerted her even more, after embracing her warmly, by declaring with the happiest smile: "I'll tell you a secret. I always thought that this would happen."

"You did?" Margaret could only stare at her in confusion.

"Do you remember the time I came to you for shelter in the storm and he talked to us? I thought then: that's just the boy for Mary. And look how well he's turned out."

"I hope so. Thank you," poor Margaret stammered.

There was a pause, and hardly knowing how to fill the little silence, Margaret offered, "You were very good to us with the loan." She thanked God that at least the royal fine had all been paid off recently so that, William had told her, he would soon be able to start the repayments to the Doyle woman. At the mention of the loan, Joan positively beamed.

"It was my pleasure. As I said to your husband, 'If it will help that lovely boy, that's all I need to know.' " She sighed. "He has your wonderful hair."

"Ah," Margaret nodded weakly. "He does."

"And our husbands being in this Parliament together—my husband has such a high regard for yours, as you know—it has brought our two families quite close together."

For a moment Margaret wondered whether to say it was a pity they'd been on opposite sides in Silken Thomas's revolt, and then thought better of it. But one question did come into her mind.

"There was a time," she was watching the Doyle woman carefully, "when my husband had hoped to enter Parliament and was denied."

"Ah." Joan Doyle looked thoughtful. "My husband told me." She paused for only a moment. "He told me I mustn't speak of it, but that was long ago. Did you know what happened? Some busybody down in Munster, a royal spy, put your husband under suspicion. My husband spoke up for him, you know. He was furious. He said the whole business was absurd and he'd vouch for your husband. But there was nothing he could do." She sighed. "These men and their endless suspicions. Affairs of state are mostly foolishness. That's what I think."

Margaret was learning so much, however uncomfortable it might be to her own former understandings, that she could not help raising one other matter.

"I'm surprised all the same that you allowed your daughter to marry my son, and not a boy from one of the important families." She paused. "Like the Talbots, at Malahide."

Joan Doyle looked at her curiously.

"Now why do you mention them?" She thought for a moment. "You told me you didn't like them, didn't you? But I never knew why."

"They weren't very kind to me when I went there," she said. "At least, the mother wasn't. I was just a girl."

"The old lady Talbot that would have been." Joan Doyle gazed at the wall behind Margaret for a few moments. "I never saw her myself. She died just before I first went to Malahide. I didn't know you'd met her. The rest of them were all very kind." Then she smiled. "You know, my daughter Mary is quite in love with your son. Were you in love when you married?"

"Yes," said Margaret. "I think so."

"It's better to be in love," sighed Joan Doyle. "I know plenty of couples who aren't." And then she smiled a contented smile. "I've been very fortunate myself. I came to love John Doyle quite slowly, but I was in love when I married, and I've been in love with him every day of my life since." She gave Margaret a look of great sweetness. "Think of that. In love every day for more than twenty years." And there could be no doubt, Margaret realised, no possible shadow of a doubt, that every word that Joan Doyle had spoken since they sat down together had been the truth. The Doyles had never informed against Walsh, she knew nothing about her humiliation by the Talbots, she had never been unfaithful to her husband. There was only one thing left to discover.

"Tell me," Margaret said, "did you know that your family and mine had had a falling out, a long time ago?" And she told her the story of the disputed inheritance.

There was no question—Joan Doyle was not an actress—her look of astonishment and of horror was not, could not have been dissembled. She had never heard of the inheritance in her life.

"This is terrible," she cried. "You mean we had your father's money?"

"Well, my father certainly believed the Butlers had it unjustly,"

Margaret corrected. "He may," she felt she had to add, "have been wrong."

"But it must have caused him terrible pain." Joan looked thoughtful again, then had an idea. "At least," she suggested, "we can cancel the loan."

"Dear God," said Margaret, in utter confusion now. "I don't know what I should say."

But Joan Doyle appeared hardly to hear her. She seemed lost in a contemplation of her own. Finally she stretched out her hand and touched Margaret's arm.

"You might have disliked me," she said with a smile. "It was very good of you not to dislike me."

"Oh," said Margaret helplessly, "I could never do that."

✠

On a raw, cold day in the middle of that winter the city of Dublin witnessed a most extraordinary scene, which drew the curious from all over the area.

When Cecily Tidy heard what was going on, she ran quickly from the western gate up toward Skinners Row. For there, in the broad precinct of the Cathedral of Christ Church, and observed by a crowd that included Alderman Doyle, a bonfire was burning. It was not to warm the poor folk of that area, to whom the monks gave food and shelter every day. Nor was it part of any midwinter celebration. It had been gathered and lit on the orders of no less a person than George Browne, the Archbishop of Dublin who, only minutes before Cecily's arrival, had been outside to make sure that its flames were bright.

The purpose of the archbishop's fire was to burn some of the greatest treasures in Ireland.

When Cecily arrived, two small carts, accompanied by half a dozen gallowglasses, had just pulled up beside the fire. The two clerks who now began to unload them had just returned from a tour of some of the suburban churches. One of them carried a hammer and chisel. His colleague, at that moment, with the help of one of the soldiers, was manhandling a small but somewhat heavy wooden statue of the Blessed Virgin onto the fire. The statue's crime, to merit such punishment, was that it had been prayed to.

"Dear God," murmured Cecily, "are we all to be made Protestants?"

⁂

The views of Archbishop Browne of Dublin had not always been easy to follow. Appointed by King Henry, during his first year in Dublin he had done nothing. His main contribution in the last eighteen months had been to insist that his clergy should lead prayers for King Henry as Supreme Head of the Church. Browne was, after all, the king's appointed man, and the Irish Parliament had passed the necessary legislation.

"Yet the fact that legislation has been passed," Alderman Doyle gently informed the English bishop one day, "does not necessarily mean that anything is going to happen."

"I assure you, Sir, that when the king's will is known and his Parliament has proclaimed it, there can be no resistance of any kind," Browne had retorted. "Orders must be obeyed."

"That may be so in England," the alderman had answered courteously, "but in Ireland you will find that matters are arranged differently. Above all," he cautioned, "do not forget that the English gentry of the Pale are very devoted to the ancient forms and customs of their faith."

And so the new archbishop had discovered. The gentry might, under the threat of fines, have passed the legislation; the clergy might even have taken a cursory oath to the king. But in practice, most of the time, nobody bothered with the royal prayer. When he protested, "My orders are not obeyed," even a fellow bishop, who knew the territory better, counselled him wisely: "I wouldn't worry about that too much, Archbishop, if I were you." But Archbishop Browne did worry. He preached the supremacy in every church he visited. And merchants like Alderman Doyle, or gentlemen like William Walsh, listened but were not impressed. He thought them sluggish or disreputable. It did not as yet occur to him that they, who were neither, thought he was rather stupid. And perhaps it was because of his growing frustration that the reforming archbishop had turned his attention that winter to a new campaign.

If there was one aspect of the Catholic faith which angered Protestants, it was the practice, as they saw it, of paganism in the ancient Church. Saints days were celebrated, they said, like pagan festivals; relics of the saints, genuine or fake, were treated like magic charms; and the statues of saints were prayed to like heathen idols. These criticisms were not new: they had been made within the body of the Catholic Church before; but the weight of tradition was heavy, and even thoughtful, reforming Catholics might conclude that by such celebrations and venerations, properly guided, the faith could be made strong.

That King Henry VIII of England was a perfect Catholic could not be in doubt: for he said so himself. But since his Church had broken away from the Holy Father's, then it must show itself to be better in some way. The English Church, it was claimed, was Catholicism purified and reformed. And what was the nature of this reform? The truth was that nobody, least of all Henry himself, had much idea. The ordinary laity were told to be more devout, and Bibles for them to read were placed in churches. Few good Catholics found this objectionable. The practice of indulgences—time off purgatory for a payment to the Church—was clearly an abuse and was to be stopped. And then there was the question of pagan rites, idols, and relics. Were they acceptable or not? Churchmen whose reformist views had a Protestant flavour were sure these were abuses. The king, whose mind seemed to change like the wind, hadn't told them they were wrong; and so Archbishop Browne could believe that he was doing not only God's but, more importantly, the king's will when he announced, "We must cleanse the Church of all these popish superstitions."

✜

There was quite a collection of relics in the carts. Some, like the fragments of the cross to be found all over Christendom, might not be genuine. An object belonging to one of the Irish saints, however, was quite likely to have been preserved down the centuries for pious veneration. Having got the statue on the fire, the two clerks were turning their attention to these. On the cart next to the pyre, amidst the reliquaries and jewelled boxes, lay a skull with a gold rim, a vessel of some kind. An English soldier had taken it from the home of an insolent apprentice with blazing green eyes. The soldier didn't know exactly what it was, but his orders were to burn anything that stank of the pagan, idolatrous past, so he'd thrown it in with the rest of the swag. The gold could be worth something, anyway. The green-eyed apprentice protested vehemently that the skull was a family heirloom and had tried to fight him for it before the soldier had drawn his sword and the young fellow reluctantly let him past.

Cecily stared in horror. If anything was needed to prove the true nature of the heretic king and his servants, surely this was it. She felt a wave of fury at their impiety and of despair at the thought of such terrible loss. She gazed at the crowd. Wasn't anyone going to do anything? She had long ago given up hope for most of the Dubliners, but it was hard to believe that no one was even saying a word.

Yet what was she doing herself?

Three years ago, she would, at the least, have shouted at the clerks and called them heretics. She'd gladly have let them arrest her. But since the failure of Silken Thomas's revolt, and her husband's return to his family in the tower, something had changed in Cecily Tidy. Perhaps it was that she was older, or her children were, or that she now had another on the way; perhaps it was that she did not want to upset her hardworking husband or that she simply could not face the stress of a quarrel with him anymore. Whatever the cause, though her religious convictions had not changed in the least, something had died in Cecily Tidy. Even faced with the destruction of all that was holy, she wasn't going to make a scene. Not today.

Then she caught sight of Alderman Doyle. He was standing in the crowd with his son-in-law Richard Walsh, watching the proceedings with the greatest disgust. They might have had their differences in the past, but at least he was a figure of authority. And he could not approve of what was happening now. She went over.

"Oh Alderman Doyle," she said. "This is a terrible sacrilege. Cannot anything be done?"

She hardly knew what she expected him to say; but then, to her great surprise, as he looked down at her, it seemed to Cecily that in his eyes she saw a look of shame.

"Come," he said quietly, and taking her by the arm he led her towards the two clerks with Richard a few steps behind them. The gallowglasses looked as if they might intervene, but one of the clerks, recognising Doyle, said, "Good morning, Alderman," and the soldiers fell back.

"What have you here?" Doyle asked.

"Relics," one of the clerks said blandly. His colleague at that moment was chipping at a small gold reliquary encrusted with gems. "Some of them are tough to open," he remarked as the other, having successfully prized the lid off, threw a lock of saintly hair into the fire where it instantly flared up.

"The casket?" Doyle enquired, pointing to the gold reliquary that had just been so rudely opened. "It's gold for the king." Even as he said so, Cecily observed that the fellow with the chisel had just detached one of the gems from the lid and calmly dropped it into a leather pouch that hung from his belt.

"The Church must be purified," the clerk remarked to the alderman. And if Cecily was astonished by the coolness of his effrontery, she need not have been. For it was thus in parishes all over England, too. While the desire of many honest Protestants may have been to purify their religion and come into a closer communion with God, the Reformation was turning into one of the greatest campaigns of public and private looting that had been seen in many centuries.

"They desecrate the shrines, Cecily," Doyle quietly remarked, "but it's the gold they want, you see."

And white-faced Cecily for the first time had a new and more accurate insight into the true nature of King Henry VIII and his followers—not so much as heretics, however that might be, but as vulgar thieves.

"The king has come to rob Ireland," she burst out at the clerk. But he only laughed.

"Not at all." He grinned. "He'll rob anyone."

At just this moment, his friend had started to open another little silver box. This one had opened easily, since it contained a smaller, blackened box inside.

"What's that?" asked Doyle.

"Finger of Saint Kevin. Of Glendalough," said the clerk.

"Give it to me," said Doyle, pointing to the black box.

"There's a gemstone on it," the second clerk objected, reaching for his chisel.

"Enough," said Doyle in a voice of such authority that the clerk handed it to him quickly.

"I can't do more for you, Alderman," he said a little nervously.

Doyle held the little relic in his hand, gazing at it reverently.

"The Saint Kevin," he remarked quietly. "They say it has great power, you know."

"You'll keep it safe?" Cecily asked anxiously.

Doyle paused before replying. His dark face seemed to be contemplating something strangely distant. Then, to her great astonishment, he turned and, gazing down at her, placed the little relic in her hands.

"No," he said. "You will. I can't think of anyone in Dublin who will look after it better. Go quickly, now," he told her, "and hide it."

Cecily had just crossed the street, and had paused to gaze one final time at the great fire, when she saw MacGowan arriving.

Doyle and Richard Walsh were greeting him. She saw MacGowan stare at the flames. Then he gestured towards the cathedral. She saw Doyle and Richard leaning towards him. MacGowan seemed to be saying something to them, urgently.

Just then, a soldier casually tossed a yellowed old skull, stripped of its gold rim, into the flames.

·:·

It was two hours later that the news began to spread through Dublin. At first, the thing was so shocking that people hardly believed it, but by evening there seemed to be no doubt.

The Bachall Iosa, one of the holiest, the most awesome relics in all Ireland—the great, gem-encrusted reliquary of the Staff of Saint Patrick himself—had gone.

Some said that it had been thrown on the fire in front of Christ Church. Others said that the ancient staff had been burned on another fire elsewhere. The archbishop, faced with a chorus of horror, denied that the sacred staff had been selected for destruction at all; but when people, English or Irish, inside or outside the Pale, considered the archbishop's contempt for what was cherished, and the gold and gems with which the Bachall Iosa was furnished, there seemed not the slightest reason to believe him.

Nor, in all the years that followed, was the Staff of Saint Patrick ever seen again.

Some, it is true, hinted that along with other relics, it might have been spirited away to a place of safekeeping—and it is to be hoped that it was. But nobody seemed to know. None of the clergy ever admitted to it. None of the Dublin aldermen, not even John Doyle, had any idea. And if, which is most unlikely, MacGowan knew anything, he remained, as always, silent as the grave.

AFTERWORD

FAMILY NAMES

THE FAMILIES whose fortunes this novel follows down the centuries are fictional. MacGowan and Doyle are both common names, and their probable derivations are given in the narrative. The O'Byrnes, of whom there are many branches, were prominent in the region, and their activities are correctly reflected. But the individual O'Byrnes in the narrative and the O'Byrnes of Rathconan are invented. The Norse family of Harold was also prominent and the name is still found in the region. Ailred the Palmer and his wife are historical, and founded the Hospital of Saint John the Baptist at approximately the date given in the story, though they are believed to have been childless. I have therefore allowed myself to invent a Viking ancestor for the Harolds, and to trace the line through Ailred the Palmer. Walsh is a common name, and the Walshes of Carrickmines were real. John Walsh of Carrickmines, his ancestor Peter FitzDavid, and all other Walshes in the story are fictional, however. The Ui Fergusa did exist, and are presumed to have been chiefs at Dublin until the coming of the

Vikings, but their identity is shadowy. Their distant ancestor Fergus, his daughter, Deirdre, and her lover, Conall are all inventions. Tidy is an English name, but so far as I know, there was never a Tidy family settled in Ireland, and the Tidy family of Dalkey and Dublin is fictional.

In the spelling of personal and dynastic names, I have made use of the following convention. Where an ancient name has passed into modern use, it is given in the modern and easily recognizable form. Thus Deirdre is used even in the time of Saint Patrick, rather than Deirdriu, and the Norse name of Harald is given as Harold. But where a name is only known in its ancient form—Goibniu, for example—then that ancient form is used. Similarly, the archaic Ui Neill and Ua Tuathail are given as the more familiar O'Neill and O'Toole; but the name Ui Fergusa is left, as it is always found in histories, in the ancient form.

Readers familiar with Ireland will know that the ancient family and tribal groupings are usually referred to as septs. However, there is scholarly doubt at present about what the most appropriate terminology should be for the various social groupings in historical Ireland. Occasionally I have referred to an extended ruling family by the general and nonspecific term of clan.

pLaces

Except in the case of Dublin itself, I have chosen not to burden the reader with archaic place names and I have not hesitated to use familiar place names—Wicklow, Waterford, Munster, and so forth—at a much earlier date than they would have been in use.

Places are generally as described. The rath of Fergus is sited at Dublin Castle, and it is quite possible that there was a rath there, just as it is possible that the Viking Thingmount was raised over a preexisting burial mound. The walled garden at Malahide Castle has been added for narrative convenience. Harold's farmstead and Rathconan are inventions.

bistoric events

Wherever possible, I have tried to give the reader some account of the historical context, which has often been reevaluated by modern scholars, within the body of the text.

In particular, readers will have noticed a great degree of uncertainty surrounding the mission of Saint Patrick. I have not given the High King a name, for instance, because we are not sure who it would have been. Indeed, the dates given in the chapter headings for these first three chapters can only be taken as general guides to aid the reader. As to whether Saint Patrick ever came to Dublin, we do not know. But he could have done. The familiar legend of Cuchulainn may in fact have been formulated at a later period, but I have chosen to believe that it already existed then. As to the question of the sacrifice of Conall, there is clear evidence that human sacrifice was practiced, as described, by the druid priests of Celtic Europe. Whether such a ceremony might have taken place as late as this upon the pagan western island of Ireland is simply not known, but it is not impossible.

Readers familiar with the history of Brian Boru will be aware that the names of the various kings of Leinster and of the O'Neill kings can become highly confusing. For this reason, I have decided to avoid their names as far as possible, and to refer to the O'Neill King Mael Sechnaill, quite properly, as the King of Tara.

The account of the siege of Dublin at the time of Strongbow is well documented. Some believe that the O'Connor king's men may have been surprised while bathing in the Tolka stream, rather than the River Liffey, but I have chosen the latter as more likely. As for the delightful idea that, while his men bathed in the stream, the king himself may have been sitting in a bathtub, I am indebted to Mr. Charles Doherty for sharing with me his note: "Ruaidhri Ua Conchobair's Bath."

The fourteenth-century story of the smuggling at Dalkey and the raid of the O'Byrnes at Carrickmines are a novelist's invention. But the activities of the O'Byrnes at this time are accurately given; there was undoubtedly an organized evasion of customs dues through Dalkey at this period, and a generation later, a Walsh of Carrickmines was accused by the Dublin authorities of withholding the customs dues he had collected at Dalkey for his own personal use.

I have allowed myself some very minor simplifications of the often complex chain of events during the years of tension between the Fitzgeralds and the Tudor kings of England. It may surprise readers that I suggest that the pretender Lambert Simnel, in the time of Henry VII, may in fact have been the royal Earl of Warwick, as his supporters claimed. We shall never know for certain, but I have followed the arguments of the late Professor F. X. Martin, which show strong circumstantial evidence for this possibility. The version of the curious dispute between the Fitzgeralds and the Butlers at Saint Patrick's Cathedral is my own. And I am grateful to Dr. Raymond Gillespie for pointing out to me that despite the usual version of Archbishop Browne's burning of the relics in 1538, some of the relics, including the great Staff of Saint Patrick, may in fact have survived.

PRONUNCIATION GUIDE

THE GUIDE that follows is designed to be helpful to the general reader. It in no sense represents a definitive, correct version of how to pronounce every word, and indeed, in many cases, no such correct rendering exists. For in modern Irish, there are often two different, regional pronunciations for a single word, and the spelling and pronunciation in Old Irish may be different yet again. Thus the May festival known to modern Irish as Bealtaine, and described during the ancient period in the novel, is in fact Beltaine in Old Irish, and would be pronounced *Bell-ti-ne*. But since the modern form is widely familiar, it is that form which is given here. The following list, therefore, represents, it is hoped, a sensible compromise.

A *-ch* indicates a soft sound, like that at the end of the Scottish word *loch*. A final *-h* indicates a similar sound, but much softer, hardly sounded at all.

Each syllable is usually pronounced separately in Irish words, and this is clearly shown. The stressed syllable is in capital letters.

Amairgen	AV-irr-gen
Armagh	Arm-AAH
Ath Cliath	Aw KLEE-ah
Bachall Iosa	BO-chal EE-o-sa
Bealtaine	Be-AL-ti-ne
brehon	BRE-hon
Brian Boru	Brian Bo-ROO
Brigid	BRIG-id
Brodar	BRU-dar
Caoilinn	KAY-lin
Carmun	KOR-mun
Cessair	KE-sar
Chi-Rho	Kiy-Row
Clontarf	Klon-TARF
Colum-Cille	KUL-um-KIH-le
Conall	KON-al
Connacht	KON-aht
Cormac	KOR-mak
Cuailnge	KOOL-ne
Cuchulainn	Koo-HU-lang
currach	KUR-ah
curragh	KUR-ah
Dagda	DAG-tha
Dal Cais	Dal Gash
Deirdre	DARE-dra
derbfine	De-re-VI-ne
Diarmait	DEER-mat
Dubh Linn	Doov Lin
Dyflin	DIF-lin
Eriu	E-ri-oo
Eva	EE-fa
feis	Fesh
fili	FEE-lee
filidh	FEE-leeh

Fingal	Fin-GAWL
Finn mac Cumaill	Fiong mok KOOL
Fionnuala	Fin-OO-la
Fir Bolg	Fir BOL-ug
Gaedhil and Gaill	Gay-ill and Guy-ill
geissi	GESH-ee
Glendalough	Glen-da-loch
Glen Mama	Glen MAA-ma
Goibniu	GOV-ni-oo
Imbolc	IM-bolg
Lagin	LIE-in
Larine	LA-ri-ne
Leth Cuinn	Leh KING
Leth Moga	Leh MOW-a
Lir	Lirr
Lugh	Loo
Lughnasa	LOO-na-sa
Manannan mac Lir	MAN-an-awn mok Lirr
Moher	MO -her
Morann	MO-ran
Morrigain	MUR-ig-an
Nemed	NEV-ed
Nuadu	NOO-ad-oo
Ogham	Owm
Padraic	PAA-drig
Partholon	PART-o-loan
rath	Raah or Rath
Rathmines	Rath-MINES
Rian	REE-an
Ronan	ROO-naan
Ruairi	ROO-a-ree
Samhain	SOW-wan
Sid	Shee
Slieve Bloom	Shleev Bloom

Slige Mhor	Shlee voor
Tanaiste	TAWN-ish-te
Tuatha De Danaan	Two-a-ha day DAN-an
Ui Fergusa	Ee FER-gu-sa
Uisnech	ISH-nah
Ulaid	UL-ad

ACKNOWLEDGEMENTS

O URING THE COURSE of the research for this novel I
have consulted over a hundred books, but in addition to
the works of authors mentioned below, I should like in particular
to draw readers' attention to the works of the following authors
whose writings would be especially helpful to anyone wishing to
know more of Ireland's history. These are: Sean Duffy, Alan J.
Fletcher, R. F. Foster, Emmett O'Byrne, Liam de Paor, and Alwyn
and Brinley Rees.

I am grateful to the following, whose kind cooperation and pro-
fessionalism were at all times of the greatest assistance: the director
and staff of the National Library of Ireland; the director and cura-
torial staff of the National Museum of Ireland; the librarian and
staff of Trinity College Library; the director and staff of Dublinia at
Christ Church; the management and staff of the Office of Public
Works at Dublin Castle.

Special thanks are due to Sarah Gearty, of the Royal Irish
Academy, for kindly preparing maps, and to Mrs. Jenny Wood,

without whose patience and astounding proficiency in the typing and revising of the manuscript, this book could never have been completed.

I owe a large debt of gratitude to the following, whose help, guidance, and technical advice were invaluable during this project: Dr. Declan Downey, lecturer at the School of History, University College, Dublin; Dr. Raymond Gillespie, senior lecturer in the Department of Modern History, National University of Ireland, Maynooth; James McGuire, editor of the Royal Irish Academy's *Dictionary of Irish Biography*; and Mary Moloney Lynch.

But above all, I am indebted to three scholars without whose guidance, patience, encouragement, and extraordinary efforts this project could not have been undertaken and would certainly never have been successfully brought to completion. Between them they have read, and helped me revise, the whole of this manuscript—a time-consuming and complex task. Any errors that remain are mine alone. I am privileged to thank Professor Howard Clarke, lecturer in Medieval History at University College, Dublin; Charles Doherty, lecturer in Early Irish History at University College, Dublin; and Professor Colm Lennon, Department of Modern History, National University of Ireland, Maynooth.

Finally, as always, I thank my agent, Gill Coleridge, without whom I should be entirely lost, and I thank my wonderful editors, Oliver Johnson at Century and William Thomas at Doubleday, whose exemplary thoroughness and creative responses to problems have so hugely improved this manuscript.